DON QUIXOTE

The Ingenious Gentleman

DON QUIXOTE

DE LA MANCHA

Miguel de Cervantes

COMPLETE IN TWO PARTS

*A new translation from the Spanish, with a Critical Text
Based upon the First Editions of 1605 and 1615, and with Variant
Readings, Variorum Notes, and an Introduction by*

SAMUEL PUTNAM

THE MODERN LIBRARY · NEW YORK

THE MODERN LIBRARY

is published by

RANDOM HOUSE, INC.

BENNETT CERF   DONALD S. KLOPFER

CONTENTS

". . . *el que lee mucho y anda mucho, vee mucho y sabe mucho.*"

DON QUIXOTE (Part Two, Chapter xxv)

TRANSLATOR'S INTRODUCTION

Toda afectación es mala.

CERVANTES

I

THE four-hundredth anniversary of the birth of Miguel de Cervantes Saavedra, one of the world's best-beloved writers, whose masterpiece has been translated into more languages than any other work with the exception of the Bible, came near to passing wholly unobserved in this country in 1947. There were, it is true, a certain number of academic tributes, but our men of letters, who should have been especially concerned, and the more literate reading public were for the most part unaware of the occasion, or would have been if the timely appearance of Aubrey F. G. Bell's fine study, *Cervantes,* had not served to remind them of it.[1]

Mr. Bell is a scholar who has devoted a long and useful life to the task of making the English-speaking peoples better acquainted with the treasure house of Iberian culture, and as he looks out over the present scene he is inclined to be rather pessimistic with regard to the fate of the Ingenious Gentleman of La Mancha in this modern age. "The question arises," he says, "whether *Don Quixote* as a universal classic has not now joined Dante and Milton, Shakespeare and the Bible, in being universally praised but comparatively seldom read." He then goes on to speak of an inquiry he had made "among a dozen persons of keen intelligence and wide reading and culture" which "elicited some disconcerting results."[2] To begin with, "six of the twelve persons consulted had not read *Don Quixote,* and not one of the twelve (they were not Spanish scholars) spoke of it with unqualified admiration." Mr. Bell's parenthesis is significant, for the individuals whom he interviewed were naturally dependent upon English-language translations, "none of which do justice to the Spanish original," and hence it is not surprising if they found this great classic, which for more than three centuries has enjoyed so tremendous a popularity, to be dull and all but unreadable.

It is not, however, in our country alone that Cervantes' readers would seem to be falling away. Nearly forty years ago, in the charming introduction that he wrote for his popular edition of *Don Quixote*, the late Francisco Rodríguez Marín, to whom all students in this field owe so much, is to be heard complaining that the work is little read in the Spain of today, being absent from many cultured homes, while certain schoolmasters regard it as "antiquated"; and he adds the biting comment that more people pretend to have read it than have actually done so. With this Mr. Bell would agree. "Even in Spain today," he notes, "it cannot be said that *Don Quixote* is really popular. New editions appear at moderate prices, but they have only a faint appeal to the millions, who confine their reading to the cheaper newspapers." [3]

There are some—Mr. Bell is one of them—who would explain all this by what they see as the degeneration of our times. They tell us that, having abandoned a primitive, close-to-the-soil simplicity, we have lost our hold upon life's deepest meaning, the "eternal verities," and that as a consequence genius is threatened with banishment and the classics with a living death. In the case of the English-language reader at least, we have already witnessed the practical interment of more than one work that once was the mirror of an age: the *Orlando Furioso*, the *Faerie Queene*, and (if we are to be honest with ourselves) even the *Divine Comedy*, in spite of such excellent renderings of the Dante poem as those by Laurence Binyon and Professor Fletcher. How many others are there that might be mentioned?

With the term "classic" we commonly associate the idea of immortality; but can it be that, in place of being deathless, these masterpieces in the end must inevitably lose their vital appeal and be nicely bound, embalmed, and laid upon the shelf? "Nothing that is human is eternal but is ever declining from its beginning to its close"—these are the words of Don Quixote's creator. [4] Would he have applied them to his own work and similar manifestations of the human spirit? It is a kind of heresy to believe so. Homer's age or that of Dante or of Cervantes is far removed from ours, but a basic faith in that humanity of which the *Iliad* and the *Odyssey*, the *Divine Comedy* and *Don Quixote*, afford us a supreme artistic expression forbids us to doubt the enduring germ of life that is in them and compels us to look for other causes of the neglect into which they have undeservedly fallen.

The truth of the matter is that the modern reader and his civilization are not altogether to blame. It is characteristic of great works of art that they have something new to say to each succeeding age that discovers them, whether it be a period in the life of the individual or of the world; [5] and it well may be that a particular work will speak more clearly to one era than to another, but at no time can it fail to have a message for those whose ears are attuned to it and whose minds are properly receptive. Certainly, the profound faith of a Cervantes, his cheerful acceptance of life in its simplest and sublimest terms, with all its tragedy and all its enveloping mystery, is not an easy one for us to attain today, and there are many who will spurn it; yet on the other hand there are many also who would welcome it if—and this is the point—they could but come to grips with the author's mind, with what he thought and what he really wrote, shorn of irrelevancies and presented with the greatest possible fidelity, clarity, and simplicity.

The problem, then, is how to overcome those obstacles that have unavoidably been erected by time and distance and that tend to bar the way to a full and satisfying comprehension of the classics, and here is where the task of the scholar and translator begins. In a sense it may be said that such works, especially where the medium of translation is involved, need to be brought back to their original luster, as precious antiques from time to time need to be refurbished; but this must be done with the utmost care and reverence, with no attempt at "improvement" or a modernization that would represent a betrayal of the original. This is far more readily accomplished in the case of prose than of poetry, the adequate rendering (re-creation) of a poem being a miracle that rarely occurs, for which reason it is that some of the most satisfactory versions of poetical masterpieces have been done in prose and not in verse. [6] What an all but insuperable stumbling block *terza rima* has proved to be for the translator of Dante!

There can be no doubt that the life view which a classic embodies may limit its audience in another and remote era. The spirit of the age of chivalry as reflected in Ariosto is one that is foreign to all but a handful of present-day readers; and what of Dante, who stands like a magnificent Janus-headed statue on the threshold between the late Middle Ages and the early Renaissance? The *Divine Comedy* and the *Iliad* are perhaps the two works in all literature that may be said really to sum up and embody an age, but time has laid its hand upon both of them, rendering popular comprehension and appreciation increasingly difficult. As a result they are coming more and more to be relegated to the famous Five-Foot Shelf or some pedagogic list of the world's great books. [7]

With *Don Quixote* the case is different. It is a work essentially popu-

lar in inspiration,[8] which the peoples of the earth at once claimed as
their own, making of it for centuries a phenomenal and world-wide
best-seller. While no book could be more thoroughly, unmistakably
Spanish and of its age, it still, by reason of the fascinating story it tells,
its rich vein of humor, and the wealth of wisdom that it contains, has
an appeal for readers of every land that is in reality timeless. And this
is not to speak of its importance, the interest it should hold for writers,
critics, and students of literature, as the prototype of the modern novel.[9]
If, then, it shows signs of losing today the enormous popularity that it
once enjoyed, other explanations must be found.

Even in Spain, as Rodríguez Marín observes, the modern reader of
Don Quixote encounters certain difficulties. For the very reason that
it is so immersed in its period, so filled with topical allusions, a classic
not infrequently grows more and more obscure in the course of the
centuries. This is true of Dante, Rabelais, and, to a lesser degree, Cervantes. And so it is not strange that the ordinary cultured twentieth-century
Spaniard should stand in need of the services of an annotator, a specialist,
if the text of *Don Quixote* is to be perfectly clear to him. Nor is it
merely a question of the numerous references to contemporary personages and events; the author's language as well often calls for clari-
fication. Like Rabelais, Cervantes drew upon the rich and racy idiom
of the people and, in particular, the speech of the Andalusian countryside, making use often of expressions that have not been preserved in
the lexicons and must be run down to their sources.[10]

As for the foreign reader who is unfamiliar with Spanish, he has the
additional handicap of being forced to rely upon the linguistic knowledge, textual fidelity, literary ability, and faithfulness to the spirit of
the work that may or may not be possessed by the one who has undertaken to translate it. In this regard the English-speaking public has had
on the whole an unfortunate experience, especially here in America
where "the odious Motteux translation," as Bertram D. Wolfe has
termed it, has been the medium through which most of us, including
most American writers, have formed our impression of this "father of
all novels, and the novel most nearly coextensive with humanity." [11]
In discussing what he sees as "the underestimation of one of the world's
greatest works," Mr. Wolfe says:

> . . . most of all, it is due to the wretched but time-hallowed transla-
> tion of Motteux, who was traducer more than translator, who was
> too lazy and swift of pen to stop for rhythms and subtle meanings
> where they eluded his first dip into the inkpot, and who, miscon-

ceiving Cervantes as another Rabelais, did not hesitate to change the tenor and mood of the whole work into a gross caricature of itself by keying his extravagant slapstick English to a different conception of the characters. Since he thereby substitutes two rather ridiculous fools of low comedy for Cervantes' two lovable ones of high humor and deep humanity, it is not surprising that so many readers have failed to reach the richer Part II or go much beyond the windmills and the blanket-tossing in Part I. Appalled by the surfeiting prospect of a thousand pages of belly laughs, how many have abandoned the work without suspecting that Sancho and Don Quixote grow steadily in character and significance, grow together in oneness until they are the two inseparable poles of a single human archetype, insinuate themselves into our hearts until we begin to resent the pranks that are played upon them and to consider the players of the pranks more foolish than the ever-more-admirable butts of their jokes? Still less can the too-soon-wearied reader sense the wealth of sanity, philosophy, wisdom and essential humanity that is embodied in their peculiar madness.

This is stern censure, but there are few competent critics who would not concur in it. *Traduttori traditori*, the old proverb has it. By thus betraying the entire character and animating spirit of a great work, a translator may condemn his author to something like oblivion for a huge body of readers to whom the original is inaccessible. It is enough to inspire fear and trembling in one who practices the trade, if indeed it does not lead him to abandon his calling once and for all, when he thinks of the harm he conceivably may do.

But Motteux was not the only offender by any means. It is worth our while to glance for a moment at the rather curious history of the English versions of *Don Quixote*.

II

The popularity of the tale was instantaneous. The ink was scarcely dry on the first printing in 1605 before pirated editions were under way,[12] and within seven years after the publication of Part II in 1615 the book had been translated into French, German, Italian, and English.[13] The first of the foreign-language renderings was Thomas Shelton's version of Part I, which was published at London in 1612 but was probably made about 1608, Part II appearing in 1620.[14] Shelton had the advantage of being a contemporary of the author and his "fine old crusted English," as the scholarly nineteenth-century translator John

Ormsby describes it,[15] is that of Shakespeare's day. For this reason his *Don Quixote*, like Urquhart's Rabelais, remains a cherished item on many a library shelf even though it is far from satisfactory as a carrying-over of Cervantes' text. For one thing, it was done with extreme haste —the First Part, he informs us, was completed in forty days! What is more, it is often, to quote Ormsby once again, "barbarously literal," with no regard to the variety of fine shadings of certain Spanish words as employed by the author.

But Shelton at least does not undertake to improve or expand upon the original or to turn those two superb creations, Don Quixote and Sancho Panza, into a pair of English clowns in the manner of Motteux. His language is pleasingly colloquial and of his time; he avoids the affectation of an archaic style that, save in passages where the romances of chivalry are definitely being parodied, is wholly uncalled for in the case of Cervantes.

It was well toward the end of the seventeenth century, in 1687, that the second and by all odds the worst English version—it cannot be called a translation—appeared from the pen of John Phillips, nephew of the poet Milton. This is truly a disgraceful performance, coarse and clowning, based not upon the Spanish original but upon Shelton and the French work by Filleau de Saint-Martin with its gross distortions of Cervantes' text.[16] The less said of Phillips the better. In 1700 Captain John Stevens published his revision of Shelton, and in that same year what is commonly known as the Motteux version ("translated from the original by several hands and published by Peter Motteux") took its place upon the bookstalls.

Peter Anthony Motteux was a tea merchant who dabbled in literature, and it might have been better if he had confined himself to the China trade. How much of the *Don Quixote* is by him and how much by the other "hands," it is impossible to say.[17] In any event it seems certain that, in place of having been done "from the original," it is rather a pastiche of Shelton, Phillips, and Filleau de Saint-Martin. A fifth edition in 1725 was revised by J. Ozell, and this is the one that is best known in America today. In 1822 the five-volume edition of Motteux by John Gibson Lockhart was published at Edinburgh, the notes of the Spanish commentator Juan Antonio Pellicer being taken over without credit to their author.[18]

As to the general character of the Motteux "translation," the opinion we have heard expressed by Bertram D. Wolfe is identical with that of leading specialists in the field of Hispanic studies. "Worse than worthless" is Ormsby's verdict; "the very worst," says Richard Ford.[19] The prevailing slapstick quality of the work, especially where Sancho is involved; the obtrusion of the obscene where it is not to be found in Cervantes; the slurring over of difficulties through omissions or by expanding upon the text; [20] the substitution of English for Spanish proverbs where there is often no close correspondence—these and other grave faults fully support the judgment that has been pronounced by Motteux's critics.

From all of this it may be seen that Cervantes was very badly handled by his early English-language translators, and the reason for it may be found in the fact that *Don Quixote* was looked upon as being in essence a farcical production designed solely to provoke side-splitting laughter of the more ribald sort. True, there is plenty of humor in its pages, which accounts for the favor with which it has been received by the simple and wise of heart all over the earth, but Cervantes' humor is of that higher kind that consists in a perception of the incongruous and, as Mr. Bell has pointed out, in the ability to see both sides of a question. This is a humor and a wisdom—the two are one—that is of the people and is incomprehensible to men like John Phillips, Peter Motteux and his collaborators, Ned Ward, and Edmund Gayton. Because *Don Quixote* was a popular work, they assumed that it must be low comedy; and, possessing little or no acquaintance with Spanish or with Spain and its inhabitants, they thought that the way to translate a Spanish peasant was to make of him at best a Shakespearean buffoon. Accordingly, Gayton from his Oxford study gives us his smut-filled *Festivous Notes*, and Ward a *Don Quixote* "translated into Hudibrastick verse." [21]

It is to a reaction against this betrayal of the text and spirit of Cervantes' masterpiece, particularly as represented by Motteux, that we owe our first truly faithful English version of it: that by Charles Jervas, who was a portrait painter by profession and who, owing to a printer's error, has come to be known to posterity as Charles Jarvis. Jarvis [22] was a contemporary of Pope; [23] his translation appeared in 1742, three years after his death. It has since run through nearly a hundred printings (ninety-nine to be exact, down to 1933), which shows that it has met with widespread approval on the part of the reading public; yet for one reason or another critics in the past have been especially harsh toward it, and some have even had the bad taste to prefer Motteux.[24] The worst that may be said about Jarvis is that he is inclined to be ponderous and dull, but there are many who will prefer this dullness to a pumped-up vitality and out-of-place clowning that are in reality a desecration.[25]

The version published by T. G. Smollett in 1755 merits little consideration as it is merely a working over of Jarvis. In 1769 George Kelly brought out what purports to be a translation but is actually a twofold theft: that of Motteux's text and Jarvis's notes.[26] Charles Henry Wilmot's abridgment (1774) was not made from the Spanish, and Mary Smirke's *History of Don Quixote* (1818) and the work of the same title by J. W. Clarke (1867) are no more than revisions.[27]

Such were the unfortunate adventures, down to the latter half of the nineteenth century, of the Knight of the Mournful Countenance as he fared forth in English garb. As should be evident by now, he had with one or two exceptions been made the victim of literary hacks and impostors, without a knowledge of Spanish and with no respect for their author, who were simply out to turn an easy penny. It was not until the 1880's that a new, scholarly, and conscientious type of Cervantes translator began to appear. The version by Alexander J. Duffield (1881) and those by John Ormsby (1885) and Henry Edward Watts (1888) may be said to mark the turning point. Here were men who knew and loved Spain, its language, its people, and its literature, and from now on, during the turn-of-the-century decades, many of these Hispanic students and Cervantes specialists, like Ormsby, James Fitzmaurice-Kelly, Robinson Smith, Aubrey F. G. Bell, and others, were to tramp, faithfully and enthusiastically, those same monotonous plains of La Mancha over which Don Quixote and Sancho had ridden in the pages of their chronicler. They would stop at the same roadside inns, little changed by the centuries, encountering there the same stone watering troughs and "starry" garrets and the same human types, as they listened to more than one proverb that had dropped from Sancho Panza's lips.

It is scholars such as these who are to be credited with having restored *Don Quixote* to its rightful place among the classics as a serious work that not only is important from the point of view of the history of the novel, but that holds a deeper meaning for those that would seek it, while at the same time losing nothing of its appeal as a masterpiece of humor. If none of those who tried their hand at turning the book into English wholly succeeded in the formidable task—and we have heard what Mr. Aubrey Bell has to say as to this—their failure is not to be ascribed to any lack of background, of good will and integrity, or even of literary ability, but rather is to be explained by other factors. Both Duffield and Watts, for example, believed that an archaic style was the only one suited for an English rendering, while Ormsby, in his striving for a minute verbal accuracy (not to be confused with literalness) and a strict adherence to the Spanish text, is seemingly willing to sacrifice all thought of style and sentence clarity.

But despite what has just been said, Ormsby remains a translator whom present-day Cervantists respect most highly.[28] On the linguistic side his contribution is outstanding. He was the first to insist that Cervantes wrote an essentially modern Spanish [29] and that there was no excuse for employing an antiquated idiom in rendering an author who had declared that "all affectation is bad." [30] He was the first also to make a close study of the nuances of certain key words as they occur in different parts of the work, in which respect he anticipated the labors of the semantics investigator.[31] One often becomes impatient with his long, tangled sentences and obscure pronoun antecedents, but one is none the less grateful to him for his painstaking honesty and the light he has thrown on Cervantes' vocabulary. He is, indeed, so likely to use the inevitable word or expression that a subsequent translator will be hard put to it to find a better one.

The latest English version is by Robinson Smith. First published in 1908, it has been reprinted four times, a fifth and new edition having been brought out on this side of the Atlantic by the Hispanic Society of America in 1932.[32] Smith is of that new race of *cervantistas* that began with Duffield, Ormsby, Watts, Fitzmaurice-Kelly, and others at the end of the last century. Like Duffield and Watts, he is concerned with patiently carving out a flavorous and somewhat mannered prose which he believes will do justice to the original, and, like Ormsby, he is extremely meticulous in his choice of words. Perhaps the chief criticism to be made of his translation, although this is largely a matter of one's personal taste and feeling for the author, is that it is a bit too mannered, a little stiff, with somewhat of the rigidity of a carving, and hence is lacking in the freedom and ease, the vitality, and the fluency combined with terseness that is so characteristic of Cervantes' own prose. The verse is omitted entirely (which, it must be confessed, is no great loss), and the copious notes follow the pattern set by the older commentators who concentrated their attention upon the literature of chivalry.

III

What, then, it may be asked, can be the excuse for yet another attempt to bring over into English the adventures of the inimitable Knight? Is the task really one that is impossible to accomplish? Mr. Bell asserts

as an "undeniable fact" that "the best of Cervantes is untranslatable,"
and he and others would advise the reader to master Spanish and turn
to the original. It would, of course, be an ideal state of affairs if the
great body of readers were able to do so, but unfortunately, in connection with this and other classics, it remains an ideal. Are the classics for that reason to go unread? Or must the translator rather keep
hammering away at what he knows can only be wrought by a kind of
miracle? Cervantes himself has some harsh things to say about the craft:
see his remarks on the translation of poetry in Part I, Chapter vi, and
on translations in general in Part II, Chapter lxii:

> But for all of that, it appears to me that translating from one lan-
> guage into another, unless it be from one of those two queenly
> tongues, Greek and Latin, is like gazing at a Flemish tapestry with
> the wrong side out: even though the figures are visible, they are full
> of threads that obscure the view and are not bright and smooth as
> when seen from the other side.

"And yet," says Ormsby, "of all great writers there is not one that
is under such obligations to translation as Cervantes. The influence of
Homer and Virgil would be scarcely less if they had never been translated; Shakespeare and Milton wrote in a language destined to become
the most widely read on the face of the globe, and no reader of any
culture needs an interpreter for Molière or Le Sage. But how would
Cervantes have fared in the world if, according to his own principles,
he had been confined to his native Castilian?" [33]

The fact of the matter is that Cervantes was very much gratified that
his book, during the few years of life that remained to him, had found
so large an audience in foreign countries: "In short, I feel certain that
there will soon not be a nation that does not know it or a language
into which it has not been translated." [34]

For one thing, in connection with the English rendering of *Don Quixote*, there would appear to be reason for believing that the translator's
two basic problems have not as yet been solved: that of attaining a
style which, like the original, shall be free of affectation—colloquial
and modern without being flagrantly "modernized"; and that of com-
bining textual and linguistic fidelity with a readable prose. But an even
more urgent consideration is the need of a version which shall take
full advantage of the great strides in Cervantes scholarship that have
been made since the beginning of the century, as regards the critical
reconstruction of a text based upon the first Spanish editions of 1605

and 1615, and in the field of specialized lexicography and literary-historical research.

It is the year 1905, marking the three-hundredth anniversary of the first publication of *Don Quixote*, that seems to have provided the impetus for a whole series of important studies by inspiring the Cervantist with a fresh enthusiasm for his subject. In that year Don Clemente Cortejón y Lucas began the publication of his critical edition with variants and notes, a work that was completed in 1913,[35] and it was during this period that the Hispanic Society of America brought out its reprint of the first and fourth La Cuesta editions (1605, 1615). In 1905, also, Don Julio Cejador y Frauca made an extremely valuable contribution with his treatise on Cervantes' vocabulary and syntax,[36] and Rodríguez Marín about this time entered upon his lifelong and monumental task of editing and annotating *Don Quixote*, his first and more popular edition of 1911–13 being followed in 1927–28 by his new critical edition, which constitutes a veritable landmark. In 1914 the late Rudolph Schevill, an American scholar,[37] and Don Adolfo Bonilla y San Martín published the first two volumes in their *Obras Completas* series, culminating with a *Don Quixote* edited by Schevill, the four volumes of which appeared during the years 1928–41.[38]

It is obvious that this wealth of new scholarship came too late for Duffield, Ormsby, and Watts to be able to avail themselves of it, and Smith's original version was completed some time before Rodríguez Marín's edition and that by Schevill had seen the light of day.

One of the most important accomplishments of the modern specialist has been a reconstruction of the text of the first editions, such as that achieved by Professor Schevill. In the past the best of the English-language translators of *Don Quixote* have had a very unsatisfactory text from which to work and too often have relied upon later printings and the "emendations" to be found in them;[39] whereas the principle followed by textual critics of today, as in the case of this work, is the one laid down by Schevill, to the effect that the first editions are to be treated with the same reverence as if they were the original manuscript itself and must accordingly be employed as the scientific base for any edition—and this applies to any translation as well—that aims at being definitive.[40]

There is a valid reason for such an attitude. The latest authorities appear to be agreed that Cervantes never read over his manuscript before sending it to the printer; had he done so he would have avoided more than one minor inconsistency and the confusion over the theft of Sancho's ass in Part I.[41] And it is equally apparent that he did not make any corrections either in the proofs or when a new edition was put out by his own publisher.[42] This is understandable if we remember his uncertain health and failing eyesight—let us not forget that he was on the verge of sixty when he wrote Part I, and that Part II was composed in the seventh decade of his life. There would seem, then, to be nothing to do but rely upon the first editions in the absence of a manuscript; nor should their text be departed from by editor or translator save for very good reason. This is the opinion of such scholars as Schevill and Rodríguez Marín. As Fitzmaurice-Kelly has put it, no attempt should be made to correct or improve upon the author, but one should rather strive, in cases of doubt and where possible, to determine *what he wrote*.

It is Schevill's reconstructed text that has been used as a base for this translation; where another reading has been adopted the fact has been noted and the explanation given. Other important variants that have a bearing upon the English version will also be found.

As to the general character of my rendering, I would once more stress the point that I have striven to avoid on the one hand an antiquated style and vocabulary, and on the other hand any modernism that would be out of place and savor of flippancy. Cervantes, it may be repeated, wrote the language of his day or he would never have been so popular, and there is therefore no excuse for making him out to be archaic save where he is deliberately seeking such an effect with humorous intent. There is, of course, the argument that in dealing with any work that is removed by centuries from our own era there should be some stylistic indication of its period; but in the present instance this is hardly necessary, the subject matter in itself providing about all that is needed in the way of a chronological differentiation. In this regard the translator should confine himself at most to the delicate nuance and turn of phrase rather than endeavor to maintain a painfully wrought manner and idiom which after all do not reflect his author.

Cervantes, when all is said, is one of the most modern of Spanish writers, and hence stands in no need of modernizing. Aside from certain changes in the shadings of words and a few locutions that have since been dropped from general usage, and apart from the semantics of his highly personal vocabulary, his Spanish is in essence the Spanish of today;[43] in this respect he differs radically from a writer like Rabelais whose language is still middle, not modern, French. And so the thing to do would seem to be, simply, to leave him alone, let him speak for himself, while his translator strives for perfect naturalness and shuns all affectation.

One cannot, however, lay down any hard-and-fast rule in drawing the line between that which is affectedly quaint and that which is honestly modern. This question comes up in connection with the title of the work: *The Ingenious Gentleman, Don Quixote de la Mancha.* "Ingenious," needless to say, is not, or was not originally, a proper translation of *ingenioso*. In his first edition Robinson Smith substitutes "imaginative" for "ingenious," and in his fifth and revised edition of 1932 he employs "visionary." Now, either "visionary" or "imaginative" is unquestionably closer to the original if one does not take into account the semantic associations; but it seems to me that by this time the word "ingenious" in the sense that the literal-minded Shelton gave it has so embedded itself in our consciousness as we think of Don Quixote that it would be a mistake to change it on the title-page. And similarly with the spelling of the Knight's name: Smith later adopts the modern form, *Quijote*, which to most American readers would be as disturbing —and distracting—as it is to see Mexico spelled Méjico. Has not the adjective quixotic long been a part of our language? [44]

On the other hand I cannot, as Ormsby does, feel a pang at parting with such an expression as "Curious Impertinent," which is one of the worst linguistic barbarisms ever coined. Ormsby's substitute, "Tale of the Ill-Advised Curiosity," would have been all right if he had omitted the definite article (the phrase "ill-advised curiosity" occurs a time or two in the course of the narrative); but inasmuch as the original here cannot be translated concisely or with any degree of literalness, I have felt free to expand upon it and try to give what I take to be the meaning of the episode "Story of the One Who Was Too Curious for His Own Good."

In the present version names of persons other than monarchs have been retained in their original form; thus, Luscinda, Dorotea, Grisóstomo (in place of Chrysostom), Lotario, Ambrosio, Anselmo, etc. This has been done not only as a matter of principle, but for the sake of consistency as well. Why should a translator in one and the same chapter Anglicize Grisóstomo and let Ambrosio stand? [45] I have likewise preferred the Italian Orlando to the Spanish Roldán or the French Roland. But in the case of geographical names the form current in English has been used: Andalusia in place of Andalucía, Cordova in place of Córdoba, Saragossa in place of Zaragoza, etc.

Something should be said as to the rendering of certain other words. I have not followed Ormsby's example by leaving such terms as *alforjas* and *bota* in the original, a procedure that inevitably tends to slow up the average reader. In the case of *alforjas*, "saddlebags" would appear to be a near enough equivalent, one approved by the Spanish-English lexicographer, while in the latter case "wine flask," or even "flask," may serve, providing it is made clear—by a note rather than by an obtrusive circumlocution in the text—that *bota* is not our "bottle." And the same would apply to *cura*, which previous translators, including Ormsby, have rendered as "curate." As for *rucio*, the common term for Sancho's ass, it raises another point. I have rejected "Dapple" as being, by now at least and here in America, too quaint, as laying too much stress upon a mere adjective that as a noun has come to mean simply a donkey. *Rucio* originally means a light silver-gray color as applied to a horse, and I have accordingly translated it, as best suited the context, sometimes as "gray" (a noun) and sometimes as "ass" or "donkey." "Dapple," I must confess, is for me a little too unpleasantly reminiscent of the old light-and-merry school.

One of the most noticeable innovations that I have made, and to my mind one of the most important so far as modern readability is concerned, lies in the substitution of "you" for "thou" in Don Quixote's speeches addressed to Sancho and in other passages where an archaic effect is not sought; "thou" has been used in the more high-flown apostrophes of the Knight to his ladylove, some of the verse, and places of that sort. After all, the second person singular as a form of address in speaking to intimates and social inferiors still persists in Spanish and other languages, yet we would not employ "thou" in translating a contemporary novel. Why, then, should we make Cervantes out to be more archaic or mannered than he is? I have never been able to understand why Ormsby, who stresses the modern character of his author's prose, should have seen fit to retain this antiquated form.

On the other hand there is a very definite old-fashioned flavor to *vuessa merced* [46] that is not to be sacrificed, as it accords admirably with the gentle humor of the tale and with the portrait of the eldering country gentleman of La Mancha in the opening chapter of the book. As a translation I have preferred "your Grace" to "your Worship," [47] though there are objections that may be raised to the use of either one.

Properly speaking, I think I may say that I have in reality "modernized," that is, taken some liberties with, only the punctuation, paragraphing,[48] the dialogue transitions now and then, and to a certain degree the sentence structure. This is something the modern translator is compelled to do if he is not to betray the spirit by too faithful an adherence to the letter. The Spanish language in general, and the Spanish of Cervantes in particular, have a terseness which, one may as well admit it, cannot be carried over into English; but with Cervantes this is a terseness that is achieved *within* a long and sprawling sentence marked by an intricate interweaving of clauses loosely connected by a series of *que's* and relative pronouns. Any attempt to preserve this sentence structure—and Ormsby does attempt it—can lead only to obscurity in English, as it sometimes does in Spanish,[49] conveying an impression of dullness which is decidedly unfair to the author.

Something also has to be done with regard to pronoun antecedents or the result is confusion, as in this sentence fragment from the passage describing Camacho's wedding in Part II, Chapter xxi, in the Ormsby version (I have here indicated within brackets the person to whom the pronoun refers): "Camacho was listening to all this, perplexed and bewildered and not knowing what to say or do; but so urgent were the entreaties of Basilio's friends, imploring him [Camacho] to allow Quiteria to give him [Basilio] her hand so that his [Basilio's] soul, quitting this life in despair, should not be lost . . ." In order to avoid such an effect as this it is often necessary to introduce a word or two not found in the text, but they should always be words that are in consonance with it, such as the author himself employed.[50] And the same principle should be observed where extra words are (sparingly) introduced for the sake of cadence or rhythm.

Among the most modern and surprising aspects of Cervantes' art as a novelist is the freedom and fluency of his dialogue. Here I have merely endeavored to vary the transitions a little, as the author does at times, through the employment of some locution other than the constant "said" or "replied" that will not be out of context.

Cervantes' greatness as a writer, like that of Shakespeare in a way, lies in the sweep of the whole rather than in minute particulars or the details of polished craftsmanship. "Careless" and "slovenly" are adjectives that have been used by his most devoted admirers in speaking of his method of composition; and that there is a basis for the charge must be evident to any reader who observes the rather numerous contradictions and inconsistencies. If I, like other translators, editors, and commentators, have called attention to some of these in my notes, the reader may be assured that this has not been done out of any desire to pick flaws in a masterpiece, but simply in order to present as true a picture as possible of the writer and his work.

One evidence of the carelessness and undoubted haste with which the author of *Don Quixote* wrote is to be seen in his frequent word repetitions. He will sometimes use the same verb three times within a couple of lines; [51] he is fond of piling up synonyms or near-synonyms, whether verbs, adjectives, or nouns, for the pleasure of doing so; [52] and he is also inclined to overwork the superlative; in all of which it may be there is to be discerned a trace of the Góngora influence. This poses yet another problem for the translator, one which he must solve with only his literary conscience to guide him as he strives to convey the feeling of the original without undue offense to modern canons of taste.

Regarding Cervantes' verse there is not a great deal that need be said. His was the misfortune of being a poet by temperament, in his attitude toward and feeling for life, but unsuccessful in the practice of his art. He is at his best in certain passages of the *Journey to Parnassus*,[53] an occasional ballad, a stray sonnet or two. Perhaps the only pieces in the *Don Quixote* that merit serious consideration are Antonio's Ballad in Part I, Chapter xi, and Grisóstomo's Song in Part I, Chapter xiv, and they are chiefly remarkable for their intricate use of assonant and medial rhymes, as experiments in versification, rather than as poems in the true sense of the word. Between the verse in Part I and that in Part II there is a difference to be noted: in the former instance Cervantes is taking himself seriously as a poet and upon occasion introduces into the text a sonnet he had composed years before and which he obviously thinks is worthy of being preserved; whereas in the latter part of the work he is for the most part frankly writing doggerel. But in either case the verse is not of a high order, and the problem of how to treat it in another language becomes a somewhat embarrassing one for any translator.

Smith, as has been stated, employs the simple expedient of omitting the verse entirely. Duffield makes use of the version of James Y. Gibson.[54] Ormsby, who possesses a metrical gift, will sometimes abandon the original form for one in which he can move about more freely, and again he will seek to achieve the impossible by imitating the Spanish assonance, the result being a surprising and not unpleasing, even if not wholly satisfying, *tour de force*. As for the renderings in the Motteux version, especially after they have gone through the hands of subsequent editors and revisers, it may merely be said that they bear little if any resemblance to the original. For my part I have not felt that it was desirable, assuming it could be done, to make Cervantes' work as a versifier appear better than it is, and in the case of the metrically more interesting pieces, I have made no effort to reproduce the assonance and similar intricacies, but I have preserved the rhyme schemes.

IV

So much for translation and the problems involved; and now a final word as to the notes.

It seems to be the fate of writers of the stature of Cervantes, Rabelais, Dante, and Shakespeare to attract about them a swarm of that frequently terrible species known as commentator. Running off on innumerable tangents and becoming the victims of some interpretative *idée fixe* or other, many of them impress one as being far madder than the windmill-tilting Don Quixote ever was and almost as amusing at times,[55] and are capable of all but burying their author under a host of impertinences and irrelevancies that are annoying in the extreme. Fitzmaurice-Kelly, Duffield, Rodríguez Marín, and others have had their say as to this tribe, and in the Prologue to Part I Cervantes himself pokes fun at their pomposity and mock-erudition.

This, of course, is not to imply that all commentators are of this sort. From an early date two types are to be distinguished. The venerable dean of one school is that English clergyman, the Reverend John Bowle, who in 1781 published a six-volume Spanish edition, three volumes of which were filled with notes;[56] Bowle, to whom all his successors will freely acknowledge a considerable debt, was a man of wide reading in the literature of chivalry, which with him becomes an obsession,[57] and in this respect he has had all too many followers. The other school was founded by Don Juan Antonio Pellicer with his edition of 1797–98, where in his distinguished commentary he turns his attention to Spanish folklore rather than the old romances, and in this sets a precedent for the editor of today.

Then, in 1833–39, came Don Diego Clemencín's six quarto volumes with extensive notes devoted to clearing up linguistic difficulties and obscure allusions. His contribution is well summarized by Ormsby, who states that "Clemencín . . . has done more toward the elucidation of *Don Quixote* than all the rest of the commentators and annotators together."[58] In the past he has been unpopular in certain quarters by reason of his critical temper, his impatience with Cervantes' careless writing, an attitude which to those who insist upon a blind, unreasoning adulation is an unforgivable sin.

The modern Cervantist realizes that criticism is not incompatible with reverence, a reverence that is best shown on the part of editor and translator by adhering as strictly as possible to the most satisfactory text that can be established, and on the part of the annotator by confining oneself on the whole to making that text clear and intelligible to the present-day reader. This type of commentator will look upon the life of Cervantes' century, of sixteenth-century Spain, as being of greater importance than all the minutiae of chivalry already so well explored, and will deem a cooking or cosmetic recipe—for *manjar blanco* or "angel water"—to be of far more interest than an obscure and long-forgotten incident in the *Orlando Furioso* or the *Amadis of Gaul*. He will not neglect allusions of the latter sort, but his stress will be on the aspects of daily life, on Sancho's proverbs, on folk customs, popular traditions, and the like.[59]

The notes to this translation, it may be remarked, are not intended for scholars or special students but for the general reading public; like Rodríguez Marín in his popular edition, I have had in mind those who know little about Cervantes rather than those who know much.[60] For this reason they have been held down to a minimum, and I have endeavored to keep them as concise as possible. I not only have made no attempt to trace all the references and parallels to the literature of chivalry, but have avoided going into the subject of the influence of *Don Quixote* upon our own and other modern literatures, as that would open up too vast a field. My guide always has been intelligibility for the modern reader.

In connection with the textual variants I have naturally limited myself to those more important ones that affect the English version. Where I have quoted the Spanish text I have retained the orthography of the first editions. In cases where I have wished to compare my translation with the work of my predecessors, I have usually cited Motteux, Ormsby, Jarvis, or Shelton, occasionally Duffield, as being the ones best known and most accessible in America. Like Ormsby I have paid particular attention to the proverbs, since they represent that wealth of popular wisdom that is one of the outstanding traits of the Spanish people.[61]

For the material in the variorum notes I am under a special debt to Rodríguez Marín, Schevill, Ormsby, and such older commentators as Pellicer, Clemencín, Hartzenbusch, and Don Juan Calderón, and I must also express my obligation to Cortejón, Cejador, Covarrubias, and Correas.[62] Professor Raymond L. Grismer's *Cervantes: A Bibliography* has been an invaluable aid.[63]

V

With this I bring to a close a task that was begun in Europe some sixteen years ago, the result of an impulse deriving from a sojourn in Spain in the late 1920's. In the course of those years I have read Cervantes' own works, his commentators, translators, critics, and imitators, only to realize how he in the end inevitably eludes them all. In the meanwhile, as time and the exigencies of a troubled world permitted, I have labored over this version, which I had vainly hoped to complete by 1947. I can only say that it has not been done carelessly or in haste, but with that love and reverence that are due so great and lovable a writer. I now present it simply for what it is: the result of one man's— a translator's—prolonged communings with one of the fine, rare spirits of our "usable past."

SAMUEL PUTNAM

Philadelphia, 1948

A NOTE ON THE AUTHOR OF

DON QUIXOTE

THE life of Miguel de Cervantes Saavedra like that of Shakespeare is largely shrouded in darkness, a darkness that modern scholarship has not succeeded in dispelling to any considerable extent.[1] We do not even know the exact date on which he was born, but we do know that his birth occurred in the little town of Alcalá de Henares near Madrid and that he was christened there, in the church of Santa Maria, on October 9, 1547. The son of a wandering ne'er-do-well apothecary-surgeon, he came of an old family of Northern Spain that had seen better days but was now harassed by debt and poverty. Cervantes was to be accustomed as long as he lived to the condition of penniless gentleman.

For the first twenty-one years his biography is a blank, there being no definite evidence as to the whereabouts of his family or the nature of his schooling. It is believed that he may have attended the Jesuit college in Seville, but there is nothing to show that he had any university education. The first dependable date that we have following his christening is 1568, at which time he was a student in the City School of Madrid. Meanwhile, it is possible that he had left his studies for a period of service with the army in Flanders. In December 1569 he is to be found in Rome, serving as chamberlain to Cardinal Acquaviva, and from there he writes home for a certificate of legitimacy, setting forth that he is of "old Christian" stock, in order that he may be able to enter his Majesty's armed forces. He then enlisted in the Spanish legion stationed in Italy and in 1571 took part in the campaign under John of Austria that culminated on October 7 in the naval battle of Lepanto and a decisive victory over the Turks.

Lepanto from that time forth was to be a magic word in Cervantes' vocabulary, marking what obviously was for him the high point of his career; for he remained to the end of his days the old soldier reliving the past and priding himself on his honorable scars.[2] And he had good reason to remember that famous battle, for a maimed left hand was ever there to remind him of the heroism he had displayed. Though ill with malarial fever, he had insisted that his comrades carry him on deck that he might join in the fight, and even after he had been wounded, he fought on. Two of the wounds were in the chest, and a third shattered his hand, rendering it useless for the rest of his life.

Cervantes also participated in the Tunis campaign in the fall of 1573, and in November of the following year his military service ended with letters of commendation to the King given him by John of Austria and by the Duke of Sessa, Spanish viceroy in Naples. He was a model soldier, and this fact—which must have resulted in his close confinement to camp and barracks—may go to explain the rather superficial impressions that he seems to have derived from contact with the culture of the Italian Renaissance.[3] In September 1575 he and his brother Rodrigo, who was also serving on the peninsula, embarked for Spain and on the way were captured by Algerian pirates, an experience that is reflected in the captive's tale in Part I of *Don Quixote*.[4] After five years' imprisonment by the Moors he was finally ransomed by his family and friends and by December 1580 was back in Madrid.

Miguel was now thirty-four years of age, and it was about this time, in the early 1580's, that he turned to writing and, in particular, to the theater, while eking out a livelihood by any means that was afforded him.[5] He may even have returned to the colors in the campaign of the Azores, but this is not likely. It was during this period that he became the father of a bastard daughter, Isabel, whose mother was perhaps an actress; for he was now in contact with the world of actors and managers and is said to have written between twenty and thirty plays in the course of three years, although none of them was produced and only two have come down to us.[6]

He did not confine his efforts to the theater, however, but also tried his hand at the pastoral romance, then at the height of its popularity. His first published work, *La Galatea* (1585), was in this genre and revealed the influence of such writers as Montemayor, Gil Polo, and Montalvo. Even as he was struggling for a foothold in the literary world, he was married, in 1584, to the daughter of a well-to-do peasant of Esquivias. She brought him little dowry, and, while they had no children, Cervantes was saddled for the rest of his life with a houseful of womenfolk to support, including his two sisters, his illegitimate daughter, his niece, and a maidservant, in addition to his wife. He must, accordingly, have rejoiced when in 1588 he was appointed deputy purveyor to the fleet, with the task of requisitioning supplies for the Invincible Armada. He did not know all the trouble that was in store for him in connection with this post.

The territory assigned to him was Andalusia, and it was while roaming the countryside as a government commissary that he became familiar with the colorful folk speech and folklore of that province, of which he has given us a vivid reflection in more than one passage of *Don Quixote*. This for him was doubtless the more agreeable side of his new employment, but it was not so pleasant when he found himself temporarily excommunicated for having confiscated supplies belonging to the dean of the cathedral of Seville; and the worst was yet to come. The peasants made it hard for him, and Cervantes was no bookkeeper; he soon came up with a shortage in his accounts. As a result, he was thrown into jail on two occasions (1592 and 1597) and possibly a third time, in 1602. This gave rise to the legend, for there is no evidence to support it, that Part I of *Don Quixote* was composed in a prison cell. One thing that the author did gain from the experience was a first-hand acquaintance with underworld types and their jargon, as is clearly to be seen from from his *Exemplary Novels* [7] and his plays.

All this took place while Cervantes was engaged in a losing battle with poverty and an ill luck that seemed constantly to pursue him. Dissatisfied with his lot, he had applied to the King, in May 1590, for an overseas appointment but had been told to "look for something nearer home." In literature he fared little better than in practical life. In 1595 he won a first prize, consisting of three silver spoons, in a poetry contest at Saragossa, and three years later (1598) his sonnet "At the Bier of King Philip II in Seville" attracted some attention, but that was about all he had to show. In the meantime, as his poems and stories went unpublished, he would appear to have moved his burdensome household from one city to another. In November 1598 he was in Seville, but from then until 1603, when he was summoned to Valladolid [8] in connection with the money that he owed the Crown, we have no knowledge as to his whereabouts.[9] Wherever he was in the early years of the seventeenth century, he must have been at work on his masterpiece.

It was, then, not in the glow of youth nor in the mature vigor of middle age, but in his later fifties, as an old and ailing man ground down by poverty and hardship and sadly in need of funds, that Miguel de Cervantes sat down to write a book that was to prove to be the first modern novel and one of the greatest—many would say the greatest— of all time.[10] He was in his fifty-eighth year when Part I was put on sale by the Madrid bookseller Francisco de Robles, in 1605, and sixty-eight when the superb Part II came off the press of Juan de la Cuesta.

How did *Don Quixote* come to be written? What was the inspiring purpose in the author's mind? There is every reason to believe that, spurred on by want, Cervantes began the work with the object of making a little money and that he laid aside his poems, plays, and pastoral novels, which he looked upon as more serious productions, in order to compose a tale that would have a widely popular appeal, one designed, as he put it, "for the universal entertainment of the peoples." [11] And so, what could be more natural than that he should have conceived the idea of a parody or satire, not on the institution of chivalry, as has wrongly been assumed in the past, but on those romances dealing with knights-errant and their fantastic adventures that, having enjoyed so tremendous a vogue in the sixteenth century, had some while since begun to fall into disrepute with discerning readers? The theme was there, ready at hand, and offered unlimited possibilities.[12]

This may be said to have been Cervantes' original intention; it was a task similar to the one that Richardson was to undertake in his *Pamela* during the following century. The pretense, the fiction (for it is scarcely more than that) of an attack on the books of chivalry is kept up throughout; but as the story develops and deepens beyond the author's expectations as well as those of the reader, *Don Quixote* becomes nothing less than a novelistic treatment of the essential nature of human life and man's greatest metaphysical problem: that of illusion and reality. It is a problem as old as Plato—and a good deal older—and as new as Jean-Paul Sartre.[13] It is one that, as Lionel Trilling has rightly observed, has always been the serious novelist's chief concern. In this light, there can no longer be any question as to Don Quixote's "madness" in the ordinary acceptation of that term. In Waldo Frank's finely expressive phrase, he is "a man possessed, not a madman." [14]

This aspect of the work, however, could not have been apparent to Francisco de Robles when Cervantes presented his manuscript for publication. Indeed, it does not become fully evident until Part II is reached; for the author was to grow with the book, and there is an appreciable gulf between the first and second parts. What Robles must have seen was a story that was sufficiently amusing, with enough good laughs in it, to justify his taking a chance on it. The aging author, on the other hand, amid all the luminaries of Spain's Golden Age, was practically unknown and might well have been described as a literary failure. Cervantes, it appears, had given readings from the manuscript before the book was published, and the great Lope de Vega had declared that "there is none so foolish as to praise *Don Quixote*." The result was that Robles did not take the trouble to protect his own and the author's rights outside of Castile.

Then the miracle occurred. The work was pirated almost at once, and there were five printings within a year, including a second authorized one, the publisher meanwhile having secured the rights not only for Castile but for Aragon and Portugal as well. All Spain was now laughing over Don Quixote's "adventures" and Sancho's drolleries, and foreign editions and translations were not long in coming. Cervantes had lived to see himself famous, almost overnight, but his material burdens were not lightened to any extent [15] and misfortune continued to dog his steps. In 1605, even as Part I was appearing upon the stalls, he became involved in an investigation concerning the death of a nobleman slain in a duel, which may have led him to go into hiding, since we do not know where he was from 1605 to 1608.

From 1608 until his death in 1616, Cervantes' chief residence was at Madrid, where he labored upon Part II of the *Don Quixote*, his

Exemplary Novels and his plays, his long poem, the *Journey to Parnassus*, and, assuming it was written at this time, his *Persiles and Sigismunda*.[16] And all this, it is to be remembered, between the ages of fifty-eight and sixty-nine! In 1610 he was deeply disappointed when left out of a group of literary men who were accompanying his patron, the Count of Lemos, to Rome. The *Exemplary Novels* were published in 1613 and the *Journey to Parnassus* the following year. It was in 1614, also, that the spurious and vicious "sequel" to *Don Quixote*, signed by one Alonso Fernández de Avellaneda, fell into his hands, and this induced him to hurry the completion of Part II, which appeared in 1615, together with his *Eight Comedies and Eight Interludes*. The *Persiles and Sigismunda* was not published until 1617, a year after his death.

In his last days Cervantes turned to the Church for comfort, joining the Tertiary Order of St. Francis, and it was the Franciscans who carried him to his grave. His death, due to dropsy, occurred on April 23 (New Style),[17] but the place of his burial remains unknown.

PART ONE

The Ingenious Gentleman

DON QUIXOTE

DE LA MANCHA

woman. My Teresa is one of those that won't deprive themselves of anything though their heirs may have to pay for it."

"Well, all I have to say," observed Don Quixote, "is that he who reads much and travels far, sees much and learns a great deal. For what could ever have led me to believe that there are apes in this world that can divine things as I have seen this one do with my own eyes? I am that same Don Quixote de la Mancha this animal has mentioned, though he has gone a bit too far in his praise of me. But whatever sort of man I may be, I thank Heaven that it has endowed me with a tender and compassionate heart, always inclined to do good to all and evil to none."

"If I had money," said the page, "I would ask Señor Ape what is going to happen to me in the course of my wanderings."

Master Pedro by this time had risen from his position at Don Quixote's feet. "I have told you," he said to the page, "that this little beast does not answer questions about the future; if he did, it would make no difference whether you had money or not. In order to be of service to Don Quixote here present, I am willing to sacrifice all profits; and now, because I have promised to do so [15] and in order to afford him pleasure, I should like to set up my show and provide amusement for all those that are in the house, at no cost whatsoever."

Delighted at this, the landlord pointed out a place where the puppet theater might be erected, and Master Pedro at once began his preparations. Don Quixote, meanwhile, was not wholly satisfied with the performance that had just been given; for it did not seem to him quite proper that an ape should be able to divine either past or present things. And so, while the puppet master was getting his show ready, the knight retired with Sancho to a corner of the stable where no one could hear them.

"Look, Sancho," he said, "I have given considerable thought to the extraordinary ability this ape displays, and it is my personal opinion that Master Pedro, his owner, must have a pact with the devil, either tacit or express."

"If the pack is express [16] and from the devil," said Sancho, "then it must undoubtedly be a dirty one; but of what use are such packs as that to Master Pedro?"

"You don't understand me, Sancho. What I mean to say is, he must have made some bargain with the devil for Satan to put this power into the ape so that he, Master Pedro, can earn a living by it; and then, when he is rich, he will give the devil his soul, which is the thing that this enemy of mankind is after. I was led to believe this when I learned that the animal answers only questions about the past or the present, for that is as far as the devil's knowledge extends; he does not know what is to be, but can only guess at it and not always rightly, since it is for God alone to know all times and seasons, and for Him there is no past or future but only the present.

"This being true, and true it is," the knight continued, "I wonder that they have not denounced him to the Holy Office so that he might be questioned and forced to confess from whom it is he derives that power of divination. For it is certain that this ape is no astrologer; neither he nor his master set up, nor do they know how to set up, those figures that are known as judiciary,[17] now so popular in Spain that there is not a wench or a page or a cobbler that does not presume to try his or her hand at them just as readily as one would pick up from the ground a knave from a deck of cards, thus bringing to nought with their lies and ignorance the marvelous truths of science. I know a lady who asked one of these figure-makers if a little lap dog she had was going to have pups and how many of them and what color they would be; to which Sir Astrologer, after he had made his calculations, replied that the bitch would have a litter of three, one green, one flesh-colored, and one striped, provided she was covered between ten and eleven o'clock, in the morning or at night, and on a Monday or a Saturday. But what happened was, the bitch died of overeating two days later, and as a result, Sir Horoscope-caster, like most of his kind, continued to be looked upon as being most expert in the matter of planetary science."

"But, nevertheless," said Sancho, "I wish you would have Master Pedro ask his ape if what happened to your Grace in the Cave of Montesinos is true or not; for, begging your Grace's pardon, it is my opinion that it was all humbug and lies, or else it was something that you dreamed."

"That may be," admitted Don Quixote. "In any event, I will act upon your advice, though I have my scruples about doing so."

Master Pedro now came up to look for Don Quixote and tell him that everything was in order for the show and that his Grace should come see it as it was worth his while. The knight thereupon told the puppet master what was on his mind and requested him to ask the ape if certain things that had taken place in the Cave of Montesinos were true or if they were but dreams, as it seemed to him they were partly true and partly imaginary. Without a word in reply, Master Pedro went back and got his ape and put it down in front of Don Quixote and Sancho.

"Look, Sir Ape," he said, "this gentleman would like to know if certain things that happened in a cave known as the Cave of Montesinos are true or false." He then gave the accustomed signal, and the animal jumped up on his left shoulder and to all appearances began speaking in his ear.

"The ape," announced Master Pedro, "says that the things your Grace saw or experienced down there are in part false and in part credible, and that is all he can tell you. He says that if your Grace wishes to know more, he will answer any questions you have to ask him next Friday, as his power has left him for the present and will not return until then."

"Didn't I tell you, my master," said Sancho, "that I couldn't believe all those happenings in the cave that your Grace told us about were true, or even the half of them?"

"Time will tell, Sancho," was Don Quixote's reply; "for time, the discoverer of all things, never fails to bring them to the light of the sun even though they be hidden in the bosom of the earth. But enough of this. Let us go see the good Master Pedro's show, for I fancy there is going to be something novel about it."

"What do you mean, something?" said the puppet master. "This spectacle of mine has sixty thousand novelties to offer. I assure you, Señor Don Quixote, it is one of the things best worth seeing that are to be found in the world today; but *operibus credite, et non verbis*,[18] and now, fall to! for it is growing late and we have much to do and say and show."

Don Quixote and Sancho did as they had been requested and went to the place where the puppet theater had been set up. It was uncovered and surrounded on all sides by lighted wax tapers, which made it look very bright and gay. Since he was the one who had to manipulate the puppets, Master Pedro took his place in the rear, while out in front, to act as interpreter, stood a lad who was his servant. It was the interpreter's business to explain the mysteries of the performance, and he had a rod with which he pointed to the figures as they came out. When all those in the house had taken their places in front of the stage, some of them standing, and with Don Quixote, Sancho, the page, and the cousin in the best seats, the interpreter began speaking. As to what he had to say, that will be heard and seen by the one who reads or listens to the chapter that is to follow.

CHAPTER XXVI. *Wherein is continued the droll adventure of the puppet master, with other things that are truly quite good.*

The Tyrians and Trojans were silent all,[1]
by which I mean to say that all those watching the show were hanging on the lips of the one who announced its marvels, when of a sudden, from behind the scene, there came the sound of drums and trumpets with much artillery firing. This lasted but a short while, and then the lad raised his voice and spoke.

"This true story,"[2] he said, "which your Worships are about to witness, is taken word for word from the French chronicles and Spanish ballads that you hear in the mouths of people everywhere, even the young ones in the street. It tells how Señor Don Gaiferos freed his wife, Melisendra, who was held captive by the Moors in Spain, in the city of Sansueña, for that was the name then given to what is now known as Saragossa. Here your Worships may see Don Gaiferos playing at backgammon, as in the song:

> *At backgammon playing is Don Gaiferos,*
> *Melisendra's already forgotten now.*[3]

And that personage whom you see there, with a crown on his head and a scepter in his hand, is the Emperor Charlemagne, Melisendra's supposed father, who, angered by his son-in-law's idleness and unconcern, comes to chide him. Observe how vehemently and earnestly he does it. You would think he was going to give him half a dozen raps with his scepter, and there are some authors who say that he did let him have it, and properly.

"After making a long speech on how his son-in-law is imperiling his honor by not endeavoring to procure his wife's release, Charlemagne, according to the ballad, addresses these words to him:

> *Enough I have said; see to it.*[4]

Your Worships will observe how the emperor turns his back on Don Gaiferos and leaves him fretting and fuming. Impatiently and in a towering rage, Gaiferos flings the draughtboard far from him; he hastily asks for his armor and begs his cousin, Don Orlando, to lend him his sword, Durindana.[5] Orlando refuses to do this but offers his company in the difficult undertaking. The valiant Gaiferos, however, in his anger will not accept it, saying that he is well able to save his wife single-handed though she were hidden away at the center of the earth. He then goes to don his armor and set out on his journey.

"Notice, your Worships, the eyes on the bull you see there, which is supposed to be one of those of the palace at Saragossa, today known as the Aljafería. That lady who appears upon the balcony, dressed in the Moorish fashion, is the peerless Melisendra, who from that vantage point often gazes out upon the road that leads from France, for this is the way she consoles herself in her captivity, by thinking of Paris and of her husband. Note, also, the strange thing that is about to happen now, the like of which has never been seen before, it may be. Behold that Moor who silently and stealthily, a finger on his mouth, creeps up behind her. Next, he gives her a kiss full on the lips, and she cannot wait to spit it out as she wipes her mouth with the white sleeve of her smock. Hear her moans; watch her as she tears her hair, as if it were to blame for the wrong that has been done her.

"That stately looking Moor you see in that corridor is King Marsilio of Sansueña.[6] He has witnessed the other Moor's insolence, and although the man is a kinsman and a great favorite of his, he has him arrested at once and orders that he be given two hundred lashes as he is borne through the streets in accordance with the custom of the city,

> *with criers in front*
> *and rods of justice behind.*[7]

You will note how quickly they carry out the sentence, though the offense has barely been committed; for with the Moors there are no indictments, warrants, and similar processes as there are with us."

"Child, child," said Don Quixote in a loud voice at this point, "keep to the straight line of your story and do not go off on curves and tangents; for a great deal of proof is required in such cases."

From behind the scenes Master Pedro also spoke up. "Boy," he said, "don't try any flourishes but do as this gentleman says, that is the safest way. Stick to your plain song and don't try any counterpoint melodies, for they are likely to break down from being overfine."

"I will do so," replied the lad; and then he went on, "This figure on horseback, wearing a Gascon cloak, is Don Gaiferos himself, and this is his wife, who has now been avenged for the enamored Moor's bold affront. With calmer mien she has taken her place on the balcony of the tower, from which she speaks to her husband, believing him to be some traveler, and holds a long conversation with him:

> *If to France you go, Sir Knight,*
> *Ask for Gaiferos,*[8]

as the ballad has it. I will not repeat it all, since prolixity begets disgust. It is enough for you to observe how Don Gaiferos makes himself known, and how Melisendra by her happy manner shows that she has recognized him. We now see her lowering herself from the balcony to take her place upon the crupper of her worthy consort's steed—but ah! the unfortunate one! The edge of her petticoat has caught on one of the iron railings and she is left hanging in the air, unable to reach the ground.

"But see how merciful Heaven sends aid when it is needed most. Don Gaiferos now comes up and, without minding whether or not he tears the rich petticoat, he brings her down by main force and then in a trice lifts her onto his horse, seating her astride like a man and bidding her put her arms around him so that she will not fall, for the Señora Melisendra is not used to riding in that manner.[9] See, too, how the steed neighs, as a sign that he is proud to bear such a burden of valor and beauty in the persons of his master and mistress. See how they wheel and leave the city behind them and joyfully take the road for Paris. Go in peace, O true and peerless lovers; may you find safety in your beloved fatherland, and may fortune place no obstacle in the way of your happy journey. May the eyes of your friends and kinsfolk rest upon you as you spend in peace and tranquillity the remaining days of your life—and let them be as many as those of Nestor!"

Here, once again, Master Pedro raised his voice. "Speak plainly, lad, and don't indulge in any flights. All affectation is bad."

The interpreter made no reply to this, but continued as follows:

"There was no want of idle eyes of the kind that see everything; and, seeing Melisendra descend from the balcony and mount her husband's horse, these persons notified King Marsilio, who at once ordered the call to arms to be sounded. Observe with what haste they go about it. The entire city is now drowned in the sound of bells, pealing from the towers of all the mosques."

At this point Don Quixote interrupted him. "No," he said, "that won't do. In this matter of the bells Master Pedro is far from accurate, for bells are not in use among the Moors; instead, they employ kettledrums and a kind of flute somewhat like our flageolet. So, you can see that this business of bells ringing in Sansueña is beyond a doubt a great piece of nonsense."

Hearing this, Master Pedro stopped ringing the bells. "Don't be looking for trifles, Señor Don Quixote," he said, "or expect things to be impossibly perfect. Are not a thousand comedies performed almost every day that are full of inaccuracies and absurdities, yet they run their course and are received not only with applause but with admiration and all the rest? Go on, boy, and let him talk; for so long as I fill my wallet, it makes no difference if there are as many inaccuracies in my show as there are motes in the sun." [10]

"You have spoken the truth," was Don Quixote's reply.

With this, the lad resumed his commentary. "And now, just see the glittering cavalcade that is leaving the city in pursuit of the Catholic lovers; [11] listen to all the trumpets and flutes, the drums and tabors. I fear me they are going to overtake them and bring them back tied to the tail of their own horse, which would be a dreadful sight to behold."

Upon seeing such a lot of Moors and hearing such a din, Don Quixote thought that it would be a good thing for him to aid the fugitives; and, rising to his feet, he cried out, "Never as long as I live and in my presence will I permit such violence to be done to so famous a knight and so bold a lover as Don Gaiferos. Halt, lowborn rabble; cease your pursuit and persecution, or otherwise ye shall do battle with me!"

With these words he drew his sword, and in one bound was beside the stage; and then with accelerated and unheard-of fury he began slashing at the Moorish puppets, knocking some of them over, beheading others, crippling this one, mangling that one. Among the many blows he dealt was one downward stroke that, if Master Pedro had not ducked and crouched, would have sliced off his head more easily than if it had been made of almond paste.

"Stop, Señor Don Quixote!" cried Master Pedro. "Those are not real Moors that your Grace is knocking over, maiming, and killing, but pasteboard figures. Sinner that I am, if you haven't destroyed and ruined all the property I own!"

But this was not sufficient to halt the rain of cuts and slashes, downstrokes, back-strokes, and doublehanded blows that Don Quixote was dealing. The short of the matter is, in less time than it takes to say two Credos he had knocked the entire theater to the ground and had slashed to bits all its fixtures and its puppets, King Marsilio being badly wounded while the Emperor Charlemagne had both his head and his crown split in two. The audience, meanwhile, had been thrown into confusion; the ape fled over the roof of the inn, the cousin was frightened, the page was intimidated, and even Sancho Panza was terrified, for, as he swore upon his word when the tempest was over, he had never seen his master in such a towering passion.

When the destruction of the theater had been completed, Don Quixote calmed down a bit. "I only wish," he said, "that I had here before me right now those who do not or will not see how useful knights-errant are to the world. Just think, if I had not been present, what would have become of the worthy Don Gaiferos and the beauteous Melisendra? You may be sure that those dogs would have overtaken them by this time and would have committed some outrage upon them. And so I say to you: Long live knight-errantry over all living things on the face of this earth!"

"Let it live, and welcome," said Master Pedro in a sickly voice, "and let me die, since I am so unfortunate that I can say with the king, Don Rodrigo:

> *Yesterday I was lord of Spain,*
> *And today I do not have a tower left*
> *That I can call my own.*[12]

Not half an hour ago, nay, not half a minute ago, I was lord of kings and emperors; my stables were filled with countless horses and my trunks and bags with any number of gala costumes; and now I am but a poor beggar, ruined and destitute. Above all, I have lost my ape; for I give you my word, my teeth will sweat before I get him back, and all owing to the ill-advised wrath of this Sir Knight. I have heard it said of him that he protects orphans, sets wrongs to right, and performs other acts of charity; but in my case alone he has failed to manifest his generous intentions, blessed be the highest heavens! I can well believe that he is the Knight of the Mournful Countenance, seeing he has so disfigured mine!"

Sancho Panza was quite touched by the puppet master's words. "Don't cry, Master Pedro," he begged him; "don't carry on like that, you break my heart. For I can tell you that my master, Don Quixote, is so Catholic and scrupulous a Christian that if he can be brought to see he has done you any wrong, he will own up to it, and what's more, he will want to pay you for all the damage he has caused you and a good deal over and above it."

"If Señor Don Quixote," replied the puppet master, "will but pay me for some small part of my fixtures which he has destroyed, I will be satisfied and his Grace will have a clear conscience; for one cannot be saved who holds the property of another against its owner's will without making restitution."

"That is true enough," said Don Quixote, "but up to now I am not aware that I hold anything of yours, Master Pedro."

"How is that?" replied the showman. "Those remains lying there on the hard and barren ground, what was it scattered and annihilated them if not the invincible strength of that mighty arm? Whose puppets were those if not mine? And how else did I make my living?"

"I am now coming to believe," said Don Quixote, "that I was right in thinking, as I often have, that the enchanters who persecute me merely place figures like these in front of my eyes and then change and transform them as they like. In all earnestness, gentlemen, I can assure you that everything that took place here seemed to me very real indeed, and Melisendra, Don Gaiferos, Marsilio, and Charlemagne were all their flesh-and-blood selves. That was why I became so angry. In order to fulfill the duties of my profession as knight-errant, I wished to aid and favor the fugitives, and with this in mind I did what you saw me do. If it came out wrong, it is not my fault but that of my wicked persecutors; but, nevertheless, I willingly sentence myself to pay the costs of my error, even though it did not proceed from malice. Reckon up what I owe you, Master Pedro, for those figures I have destroyed, and I will reimburse you in good Castilian currency."

Master Pedro bowed. "I expected no less," he said, "of so rare a Christian as the valiant Don Quixote de la Mancha, the true friend and protector of all needy vagabonds. Mine host here and the great Sancho shall act as arbiters between your Grace and me and they shall appraise the value, or likely value, of the properties destroyed."

Both the landlord and Sancho agreed to act in this capacity, and Master Pedro then picked up off the ground King Marsilio of Saragossa, minus his head.

"You can see," he said, "how impossible it is to restore this king to his former state; and so, it seems to me, saving your better judgment, that for his death, demise, and final end I should have four and a half reales."

"Proceed," said Don Quixote.

"As for this one who is split open from top to bottom," Master Pedro went on, taking in his hands the late Emperor Charlemagne, "it would not be too much if I were to ask five reales and a quarter."

"That's no small sum," said Sancho.

"Nor is it very much," replied the innkeeper.

"Give him the whole five and a quarter," said Don Quixote. "The sum total of this memorable disaster does not hang on a quarter more or less. And please be quick about it, Master Pedro, for it is suppertime and I feel the stirrings of hunger."

"This figure," continued Master Pedro, "without a nose and with one eye missing, is that of the beauteous Melisendra; and for it I ask, and I think I am right in doing so, two reales and twelve maravedis."

"The devil," said Don Quixote, "must have a hand in it if Melisendra and her husband have not reached the French border, at the very least, by this time, for the horse they rode on seemed to me to fly rather than gallop; and so there is no need to try to sell me the cat for the hare [13] by showing me here a Melisendra without any nose when she is now, if things went right, stretched out at her ease and enjoying herself with her husband in France. God help everyone to his own, Master Pedro. Let us deal plainly and with honest intent. You may continue."

Master Pedro perceived that Don Quixote's wits were wandering and that he was beginning to harp on the old chord again, but he was not disposed to let him off so easily.

"This cannot be Melisendra after all," he said; "it must be one of the damsels that waited upon her; and if you will give me sixty maravedis for her, I will consider myself well paid."

In this manner he went on putting a price on each of the puppets that had been destroyed, and after these estimates had been adjusted by the two arbiters to the satisfacion of both parties, it was found that the total came to forty reales and three quarters, and Sancho promptly handed over this sum; whereupon Master Pedro asked for two reales more for the trouble of catching the ape.

"Give them to him, Sancho," said Don Quixote, "not for catching the ape, but for getting the she-ape by the tail.[14] And I would further give two hundred right now to anyone who could assure me that Melisendra and Don Gaiferos are safe in France with their own people."

"No one can tell you that better than my ape," said Master Pedro, "but there's no devil that could catch him now, although I fancy lonesomeness and hunger will force him to come looking for me to-night, and God will bring another day, and we shall see what we shall see."

The storm centering around the puppet theater having finally subsided, they all sat down to eat their supper in peace and good companionship, and all at Don Quixote's expense, for he was extremely generous. Before daybreak the one who was conveying the lances and halberds took his departure, and shortly after sunup the cousin and the page came to bid Don Quixote good-by, as the former was returning home, while the latter wished to be upon his way; and to help the soldier out the knight made him a present of twelve reales. Not caring to engage in any further arguments with the one of the Mournful Countenance, whom he knew very well, Master Pedro was up before the sun, and, having caught his ape and gathered up what was left of his show, he too was off to seek adventures.

As for the innkeeper, to whom Don Quixote was a stranger, he was equally astonished at his guest's madness and his liberality. Sancho, upon his master's orders, paid very generously for their lodgings, and, having said farewell, they left the inn around eight in the morning and took to the road once more. Here we shall leave them, as it is necessary to do so in order to clear up certain other matters that are pertinent to this famous history.

CHAPTER XXVII. *Wherein is set forth who Master Pedro and his ape were, with the misfortune that befell Don Quixote in the braying adventure, which did not end as he had hoped and expected it would.*

CID HAMETE, the chronicler of this great history, begins the present chapter with these words: "I swear as a Catholic Christian"; which leads his translator to remark that, being a Moor as he undoubtedly was, the author merely meant that, just as a Catholic Christian when he takes an oath swears, or is supposed to swear, to tell the truth in all that he says, so in what he himself has to set down about Don Quixote he will adhere to the truth just as if he were taking such a Christian oath, especially when it comes to explaining who Master Pedro was, as well as that ape of his whose divinations had astonished all the towns and villages in those parts.

He then goes on to say that whoever has read the first part of this story will very well remember Ginés de Pasamonte, who was one of the galley slaves that Don Quixote freed in the Sierra Morena,[1] a favor for which he received poor thanks and worse payment at the hands of that vicious, low-life crew. This Ginés de Pasamonte, whom Don Quixote insisted upon calling Ginesillo de Parapilla, was the one who stole Sancho's ass, although, through a fault of the printers, there was no explanation as to how or when the theft was committed,[2] a circumstance which has led many to attribute a typographical blunder to bad memory on the part of the author. But the short of the matter is, Ginés did steal the gray by creeping up on the sleeping Sancho Panza and making use of the stratagem that Brunello employed when he stole the horse from between Sacripante's legs at Albraca,[3] and Sancho afterward recovered his beast as has been related.[4]

This fellow Ginés, then, fearful of being brought to justice for his innumerable crimes and villainies, which were so many and so great that he himself composed a big book about them, had made up his mind to go over into the kingdom of Aragon;[5] and there, covering his left eye with a patch, he had taken to the trade of puppet master, for he was exceedingly skillful at this, and at the art of juggling as well. He accordingly had purchased the ape of some freed Christians coming from Barbary and had taught it to jump on his shoulder when he made a certain sign, and whisper, or pretend to whisper, in his ear. Before entering a village with his show he would make inquiries in the neighboring one, or of the person who could best give him the information, as to what special events had occurred there and which individuals were involved, and he would then commit to memory the facts he had thus gathered.

Upon arrival, he would first put on his puppet show, which now had to do with one story and now with another, but all of them lively, merry, and familiar to his audience. When the performance was over, he would introduce his ape and extol the cleverness of the animal, which was able to divine anything past or present but which possessed no skill so far as the future was concerned. For each question answered he charged two reales, but he would sometimes make a reduction, depending upon the attitude which he sensed in his listeners. Occasionally he would come to a house where people lived that he knew something about, and even though they asked him nothing, not caring to pay for it, he would signal to his ape and assert that the beast had told him such and such things that fitted in perfectly with the facts of the case. By this means he acquired an extraordinary reputation and everyone ran after him. At other times he would give so crafty an answer that it was bound to suit the question; and inasmuch as no one pressed him to explain how his ape did it, he made monkeys of them all and filled his pouch.

Thus, the moment he entered the inn he recognized Don Quixote and Sancho, and so it was easy to astonish them both and all those present. But it would have cost him dearly had the knight dropped his hand a little more that time he cut off King Marsilio's head and destroyed all his cavalry, as told in the preceding chapter.

So much for Master Pedro and his ape. Returning now to Don Quixote de la Mancha, I may state that after having sallied forth from the inn, he resolved to take a look at the banks of the Ebro and the surrounding region before entering the city of Saragossa, for there was still plenty of time to spare between then and the day of the tournament. With this purpose in mind he continued his journey for a couple of days without anything happening to him that is worthy of being set down in writing. On the third day, as he was ascending a hill, he heard a great din of drums, trumpets, and musket fire. At first he thought it must be some regiment of soldiers that was passing that way, and in order to have a sight of them he spurred Rocinante and hastened to the top of the hill, at the foot of which on the other side he could see what appeared to be more than two hundred men armed with various kinds of weapons, such as lances, crossbows, truncheons, halberds, pikes, a few muskets, and many bucklers.

Coming down the slope, he drew near enough to see their banners plainly and make out their colors and devices. He noted in particular one of white satin, mounted upon a standard, upon which was painted a very lifelike ass, resembling a Sardinian pony,[6] with its head reared, its mouth open, and its tongue out, in the posture and seeming act of braying, while round about it in large letters were these verses:

> They did not bray in vain,
> Those judges twain.

From which Don Quixote surmised that these must be the people from the braying town, and he remarked as much to Sancho, informing him at the same time what was inscribed on the banner. He further observed that the one who had told them of this affair in the first place had been wrong in stating that it was a couple of aldermen who had done the braying, since according to those verses they were officers of justice.[7]

"Sir," said Sancho Panza in reply, "you need not let that trouble you, for it may be that the aldermen who did the braying in the course of time have come to be justices of the peace of their village, and so it is all right to call them by either title, especially since it makes no difference so far as the truth of the story is concerned whether the brayers were one or the other, so long as bray they did, and a judge can bray just as well as an alderman."

In short, they perceived that one town had come out to do battle with the other which had jeered at it more than was right or neighborly. Don Quixote now went up to them, not without some misgivings on the part of Sancho, who never liked to get mixed up in such affrays. Those who were drawn up in squadron formation opened ranks to receive him, for they thought he was someone on their side, and with considerable dash and self-composure the knight rode up to where the standard was. There, all the leaders of the army gathered around to stare at him, for they were as astonished as everyone was when they beheld him for the first time. Seeing them gazing at him so attentively, before anyone had spoken or asked him a single question, he chose to be the first to break the silence by raising his voice and addressing them in this manner:

"Good sirs, I would beg you as earnestly as I can not to interrupt what I am about to say to you unless you disagree with it or find that it wearies you. If that should happen, you have but to raise a hand and I will put a seal upon my mouth and a gag upon my tongue."

They all thereupon informed him that he might say whatever he liked and they would be very glad to listen to it; and with this permission, he continued.

"I, my dear sirs, am a knight-errant, whose profession is that of arms and whose business it is to lend aid and favor to all those that stand in need of it. Some days ago I learned of your unfortunate plight and am aware of the reason that has led you to take up arms and avenge yourselves upon your enemies. Having thought the matter over a great many times, I find that according to the rules of honor you are mistaken in thinking that you have been insulted, for no one individual can insult an entire community unless, not knowing who is guilty of some act of treason, he defies it as a body. Of this we have an example in Don Diego Ordoñez de Lara, who, ignorant of the fact that Vellido Dolfos alone was guilty of slaying his king, challenged them all, laying upon them all the burden of answering for the crime and exacting vengeance accordingly.[8] It is true that Don Diego went a little too far, indeed he went very much beyond the rules governing a challenge; it was not proper for him to defy the dead, nor the waters, nor the loaves of bread,[9] nor those as yet unborn, with all the other details that he set forth. But let that pass; for when anger is spawned, the tongue has no father, governor, or bridle to control it.

"This being true, that no single person can insult a kingdom, province, city, state, or entire town, it plainly follows that there is no excuse for seeking to avenge such an insult since it really is not one. A fine thing it would be if the inhabitants of the Clocktown [10] were to be constantly falling out with everyone who called them by that name; and the same goes for those known as the Scullions, Eggplant-growers, Whalers, and Soapmen,[11] and those to whom other appellations are applied such as are prevalent in the mouths of children and the common people! It would be a pretty state of affairs, surely, if these distinguished communities were all the time to go about seeking vengeance and making sackbuts of their swords over every misunderstanding however slight a one it might be!

"No, no, God forbid! There are four conditions under which prudent men and well-ordered states may take up arms, draw their swords, and risk their persons, lives, and fortunes.[12] The first is in order to defend the Catholic faith; the second, to defend their lives, which is in accordance with natural and divine law; the third, to defend their family honor and possessions; the fourth, to serve their king in a just war; and if we care to add a fifth, which may be included under the second, to defend their native land.[13]

"To these five justifications for war, which may be looked upon as the principal ones, other causes may be added that are right and reasonable and that make it a duty to resort to arms. But to go to war over trifles and things that, in place of constituting an insult, are in reality laughable and amusing, would appear to be the act of one who is lacking in sound sense. Moreover, to take an unjust revenge—and there can be no just vengeance—runs directly counter to the holy law that we observe, which teaches us to do good to our enemies and love those that hate us,[14] a commandment which may seem to be rather a difficult one to keep but which is so only for those that think less of God than they do of the world and more of the flesh than of the spirit. For Jesus Christ, who is God and true man and our legislator, who neither lies nor could lie, has said that His yoke is easy and His burden light,[15] and

He would not lay upon us any commandment that was impossible to fulfill. And so, my dear sirs, your Worships are bound by human and divine laws to desist."

"May the devil take me," said Sancho to himself, "if my master's not a tologian, and if not, he's as like one as one egg is like another."

Don Quixote took a breath and, seeing that they were all keeping silent, was about to continue with his sermon, and would have done so had not Sancho taken advantage of the pause to display his own wit.

"My master, Don Quixote de la Mancha," he began, "who formerly was known as the Knight of the Mournful Countenance and who now is called the Knight of the Lions, is a very learned gentleman who knows both Latin and his mother tongue like a bachelor and in everything that he does and advises others to do acts like the best kind of soldier. He has all the laws and ordinances of what they call combat at his fingertips; and so there is nothing to do but be guided by what he says, and let it be on my head if you make any mistake in doing that. He has told you that it is foolish to lose your temper just because you hear someone braying. Why, I can remember that when I was a lad I brayed every time I happened to feel like it without anyone's trying to stop me, and I did it so nicely and properly that all the asses in the village answered me; yet I did not for that reason cease to be the son of my parents, who were most respectable folks. And though I was envied for this accomplishment by a number of the gentry, I didn't give two cents for it myself.[16] And so that you can see that it's the truth I'm telling you, just wait and listen. It's like swimming, once you learn it you never forget it."

And, with this, putting his hands to his nose, he began braying so lustily that all the neighboring valleys echoed with the sound. One of those who was standing near him, thinking that he was making sport of them, raised a staff that he held in his hand and brought it down with such force that Sancho dropped helplessly to the ground. Seeing his squire thus mishandled, Don Quixote, lance in hand, then attacked the one who had dealt the blow; but so many thrust themselves in his way that he was unable to chastise the aggressor, and since a rain of stones was falling upon him and innumerable crossbows and muskets were aimed at him, he turned Rocinante's head and at the best gallop he could manage fled from their midst, meanwhile praying to God with all his heart to deliver him from this peril. He feared at every step that some arrow might pierce his back and come out through his bosom, and he was constantly drawing in his breath to make sure it had not failed him.

The members of the squadron, however, were satisfied to see him take flight like this and did not fire upon him. As for Sancho, as soon as he had somewhat recovered his senses, they placed him upon his mount and permitted him to follow his master. He was in no condition to guide the beast, but the gray went along in Rocinante's foot-tracks as he could not bear to be separated from his companion for a single moment. When he was a good distance away, Don Quixote turned his head and, perceiving that Sancho was coming and that no one was in pursuit, stopped to wait for him. The squadron from the braying town remained there until nightfall, and then, since their enemies had not come out to join battle with them, they returned to their village in very high spirits; and had they been familiar with the custom of the ancient Greeks, they would have erected a monument upon that spot.

CHAPTER XXVIII. *Of things that, Benengeli says, the reader will come to know if he reads attentively.*

WHEN the brave man flees, it means that treachery has been uncovered, and it is the part of the wise to save themselves for better occasions.

This truth was brought out in the case of Don Quixote, who, having aroused the fury of the townspeople and the ill will and indignation of the squadron, showed his heels and, without thought of Sancho or the danger in which he was leaving him, put as much distance between himself and the enemy as he deemed necessary in order to assure his own safety. Sancho followed, slung across his ass in the manner that has been described. He finally came up, in full possession of his wits by this time, and as he did so he slid from the gray's back to Rocinante's feet, all battered and bruised and in a sorrowful plight. Don Quixote then dismounted to examine his squire's wounds and, finding him sound from head to foot, addressed him angrily enough.

"An evil hour it was, Sancho," he said, "when you learned how to bray! Where did you ever hear that it was a good thing to mention the rope in the house of the hanged man? [1] What counterpoint can braying music have except that of cudgels? You may give thanks to God, Sancho, that they made the sign of the cross on you just now with a club and not with a cutlass."

"I'm in no condition to answer," replied Sancho, "for it seems to me that I'm talking through my shoulders. Let's mount and get away from here. I'll not bray any more, but I can't help remarking [2] that knights-errant appear to run away and leave their faithful squires in the hands of the enemy to be pounded like privet or like wheat in the hopper."

"He who retires," said Don Quixote, "does not flee. I would have you know, Sancho, that valor not based upon prudence can only be termed temerity, and the triumphs of the foolhardy are to be attributed to good luck rather than to courage. I admit that I retired, but not that I fled; and in this I have merely followed the example of many brave men who have saved themselves for a more propitious time. The histories are full of such instances, but as it would do you no good to refer you to them, I shall spare myself the trouble for the present."

Sancho by now was once more on his gray's back, having been helped up by Don Quixote, who then mounted Rocinante; and, riding slowly along, they made for a grove that was visible about a quarter of a league away. Every so often Sancho would heave a deep sigh or moan as if in pain, and when his master asked him what the cause of it was, he replied that he ached all over, from the base of his spine to the nape of his neck, and it was nearly driving him crazy.

"The reason for that," remarked Don Quixote, "is undoubtedly the fact that the club they used was a long one and caught you all the way down your back where those aching parts are located; and if it had gone any farther down, you would ache still more."

"By God," exclaimed Sancho, "your Grace has taken a great load off my mind and made everything as clear as can be! Body of me! Is the cause of my pain such a mystery that it is necessary to explain to me that I ache wherever the club reached me? If it was my ankles hurting me, there might be some sense in trying to find out what caused it, but to tell me that I'm sore because they beat me is not much in the way of a discovery. On my word, master of mine, the misfortune of another hangs by a hair, [3] and I am every day discovering how little I have to hope for from keeping company with your Grace. This time you have let them club me. Another time, or a hundred times more, it will be the old story of the blanketings and other foolish pranks all over again; and if up to now I've had it only across the shoulders, I'll be getting it later straight in the eyes.

"I'd do a lot better," he went on, "if I wasn't a numbskull who will never do anything well as long as he lives—I'd do a lot better, I say, by going home to my wife and young ones, to support and bring them up on whatever God may see fit to give me, instead of trailing after your Grace along roads that lead nowhere and highways and byways that don't deserve the name, with little to drink and less to eat. And as for sleeping! Pace off seven feet of earth, brother squire, and if you want any more than that, take another seven; the dish is in your hands,[4] help yourself; so stretch out to your heart's content, and welcome. I'd like to see the one who started this knight-errantry business burned to ashes, or at least the first man who was willing to be a squire to such fools as all the knights-errant of times past must have been. As to those of the present day, I say nothing, for since your Grace is one of them, I must respect them; and what's more, your Grace knows a little more than the devil when it comes to talking and thinking."

"I would like to lay a good wager with you, Sancho," said Don Quixote, "that since you have been running on like this with no one to stop you, you don't feel an ache in your entire body. Talk on, my son; say anything that comes to your mind or to the tip of your tongue; for if it will relieve your pain, I will gladly put up with the annoyance which your impudence causes me. If you are so anxious to go home to your wife and children, God forbid that I should stop you. You have my money; reckon up how long it has been since we left our village this third time[5] and what your wages should be each month, and then pay yourself out of hand."

"When I worked for Tomé Carrasco,"[6] replied Sancho, "father of the bachelor Sansón Carrasco, your Grace's acquaintance, I earned two ducats a month and my board; but with your Grace, I can't say what it should be, for your Grace knows that the squire to a knight-errant does more work than a farmer's helper. The work in the fields may be hard, but at the worst, when night comes we have our *olla* and a bed to sleep in—and that's something I haven't had since I've been serving your Grace, except for the brief time we spent at Don Diego de Miranda's house, and the feast I had on the skimmings that I took from Camacho's pots, and the bed and what I had to drink at Basilio's.

All the rest of the time I've slept on the hard earth, under the open sky, in what they call the inclemencies of the weather. I've kept myself alive on scraps of cheese and crusts of bread; and as for drinking, it has been water from the brooks or springs in the bypaths that we traveled."

"I admit," said Don Quixote, "that everything you say, Sancho, is the truth. How much more do you think I should give you than what you had from Tomé Carrasco?"

"As I see it," said Sancho, "if your Grace would give me a couple of reales more for each month, I could consider myself well paid. That is to say, so far as my wages go, for the work I've done. But seeing that you gave me your word and solemn promise to make me the governor of an island, it would only be fair for your Grace to add another six reales, making thirty altogether."

"Very well," Don Quixote agreed, "it is now twenty-five days since we left our village; so reckon it up, Sancho, on the basis of the wage you think you ought to have, and see how much it is I owe you; and then, as I have said, you can pay yourself by your own hand."

"O body of me!" cried Sancho, "your Grace is very wrong in this reckoning; for so far as the island is concerned, we have to count from the day your Grace promised it to me down to the present hour."

"Well," said Don Quixote, "and how long has it been since I made you the promise?"

"If I'm not mistaken," replied Sancho, "it must be more than twenty years and three days, more or less."

At this Don Quixote slapped his forehead with his hand and burst into a hearty laugh.

"Why," he said, "with my wanderings in the Sierra and all the rest barely two months have gone by. And are you trying to tell me, Sancho, that it was twenty years ago I promised you that island? I am convinced now that you would take all the money I have as your wages; and if such is the case and that is what you want, I hereby give it to you; it is yours from now on, and much good may it do you. In order to be rid of so faithless a squire, I shall be content to remain a pauper, without a penny to my name. But tell me, you perverter of the laws of chivalry and the rules that govern squires, where have you ever heard of a squire who made such terms with his lord: 'You must give me so much a month for serving you?' Plunge, O rogue, scoundrel, monster—plunge, I say, into the *mare magnum* of their histories; and if you find one single squire who ever said or thought of saying such a thing as you have just said, I would have you nail it to my forehead and in addition give me four resounding slaps in the face.

"Turn, then, the reins, or better, the halter of your ass, and go back to your home; for you are not going one step farther with me. O bread ungratefully received! O promises ill bestowed! O man who has more of the beast in him than of the human! So you are leaving me now, are you, just when I was about to elevate you to a position in life where, no matter what your wife might say, people would address you as your Lordship? So you are leaving me just when I had firmly resolved to make you governor of the best island in the world? In short, as you have said before, honey is not for the ass's mouth.[7] An ass you are and an ass you will be to your dying day, for I think that day will come before you ever realize that you are a stupid beast."

Sancho stared hard at Don Quixote as the knight heaped these insults upon him and was so smitten with remorse that the tears came to his eyes.

"Master," he said in a weak and sorrowing voice, "I will grant you that all I lack is a tail and I would be an ass; and if your Grace wants to put one on me, I'll look upon it as well placed and will serve you as a beast of burden all the days of my life that are left me. Forgive me, your Grace; have mercy on my foolishness. Remember that I know little, and if I talk much, that is due to weakness rather than to malice. But he who sins and mends his ways, commends himself to God."[8]

"I should have been surprised, Sancho," said his master, "if in the course of your speech you had not rung in some proverb. Very well, I forgive you, on condition that you do mend your ways and that from now on you do not think so much of your own interests. Rather, you should take heart, be of good cheer, pluck up courage, and trust me to fulfill my promises. Fulfillment may be late in coming, but that does not mean that it is impossible."

Sancho assured him that he would do so, contriving somehow to draw strength from weakness. By this time they had reached the grove, and Don Quixote now sat down at the foot of an elm and Sancho at the foot of a beech (for trees of this sort and others like them always have feet but no hands). Sancho spent an uncomfortable night, his aches returning with the evening dew. Don Quixote as always was deep in reveries; but, in spite of everything, the two of them had some sleep and at sunup resumed their journey toward the banks of the famous Ebro, where they had an experience that is related in the chapter to follow.

CHAPTER XXIX. *Of the famous adventure of the enchanted bark.*

BY the stages described or undescribed, two days [1] after leaving the grove Don Quixote and Sancho reached the River Ebro, the sight of which afforded the knight great pleasure as he beheld the charm of its banks and gazed upon its clear and abundant, gently flowing waters, which had the appearance of liquid crystal. It was a sight that brought back a thousand fond memories, reminding him in particular of the things he had viewed in the Cave of Montesinos; for although Master Pedro's ape had said that a part of those things were true and the rest were lies, he was inclined to regard them all as true rather than false, whereas for Sancho they were all lies from beginning to end.

As they were going along the bank in this manner, they came upon a small boat without oars or rigging of any kind that was lying at the water's edge, being moored to the trunk of a tree. Don Quixote looked around in all directions, and, seeing no one, he without more ado dismounted from Rocinante and ordered Sancho to get down off the ass and tie both animals very securely to an elm or a willow that stood near by. When Sancho wanted to know the reason for all this, his master answered him as follows:

"I may tell you, Sancho, that the bark you see there is plainly and unmistakably calling and inviting me to enter it and proceed in it to give succor to some knight or other highborn personage who stands in need of my assistance and who must be in dire straits indeed; for that is the way it is in the books of chivalry, in the stories where enchanters figure and speak. When one knight is in some difficulty from which he can be freed only by the hand of another knight, though they be two or three thousand leagues distant from each other, or even more, the enchanters will either snatch him up in a cloud or provide a bark for him, and in less than the wink of an eye they will carry him through the air or over the sea, wherever it is they wish to take him and where his aid is needed. And this bark, O Sancho! is placed here for the same purpose. I am as certain of that as I am that it is now day, and so, before this day passes, tie Rocinante and the gray together, and then let it be in

God's hand to guide us, for I would not refrain from embarking though barefooted friars should beg me to do so."

"If that is the way it is," replied Sancho, "and your Grace must be getting into this kind of foolishness (if I may call it that) at every turn, there's nothing for me to do but bow my head and obey; for, as the old saying goes, 'Do what your master bids you and sit with him at table.' [2] But, for all that, just to get it off my conscience, I want to warn your Grace that this boat doesn't look to me as if it belonged to any enchanters but to some fishermen; for you catch the best shad in the world in this river."

Sancho said this as he was tying the beasts. It grieved him deeply to have to leave them to the tender mercies of the enchanters, but Don Quixote assured him that he need not worry about their going uncared for, as the one who was taking them on so long a journey, into such far longitudes, would see to it that they were fed.

"I don't know anything about logitudes," [3] said Sancho, "nor did I ever hear such a word in all my born days."

"*Longitude*," Don Quixote explained, "is an expression that is used in referring to distance. But it is no wonder that you do not understand, seeing you are not obliged to know Latin, like some who think they know it but are in reality ignorant of it."

"I have them tied," Sancho informed him. "What do we do now?"

"What do we do?" replied Don Quixote. "We cross ourselves and weigh anchor; by which I mean, we climb aboard and cut the moorings by which this bark is fastened."

With this, he leaped into the boat, followed by Sancho, and severed the rope that held it. The bark then began drifting slowly away from the bank, and when Sancho found himself some two yards out in the river, he started trembling all over, fearing that he was lost. What pained him most of all was the braying of the ass and the sight of Rocinante struggling to get loose.

"The gray," he said to his master, "is heartbroken because we are leaving him, and Rocinante wants to get free so he can plunge in after us. Peace be with you, O dearly beloved creatures! May the madness that takes us from you be turned into sound sense and bring us back to you once more!"

As he said this, he began weeping so bitterly that Don Quixote became angry.

"What are you afraid of, cowardly one? Why those tears, you butter-heart? Who is pursuing or attacking you, O man with the soul of a tame mouse? What do you lack, O beggar in the very midst of plenty? Are you perchance tramping barefoot over the Riphaean Mountains [4] in place of being seated like an archduke on a bench as you drift with the gentle current of this pleasant river, from which we shall soon come out upon the broad expanse of the ocean? But we must surely be on the sea by now; indeed, we must have gone seven or eight hundred leagues, and if I but had an astrolabe with which to take the latitude of the pole, I should be able to tell you exactly how far we have traveled. Either I know little about it or we already have passed, or soon shall pass, the equinoctial line which lies between the two opposite poles at an equal distance from each."

"And when we get to that lane [5] your Grace is speaking of," said Sancho, "how far shall we have gone?"

"Very far," said Don Quixote, "for of the three hundred and sixty degrees on the terraqueous globe, according to the computation of Ptolemy, the greatest known cosmographer, we shall have traversed half that number in arriving at the line I have mentioned."

"By God," exclaimed Sancho, "if it isn't a nice sort of person your Grace produces to witness what you say—a tall hoggifer [6] with a *me* or something or other on the end of his name!"

Don Quixote had to laugh at what his squire had contrived to make out of Ptolemy the cosmographer.

"I may inform you, Sancho," he continued, "that one of the ways the Spaniards who embark at Cadiz for the East Indies have of telling when they have passed that equinoctial line is this: if the lice die upon every man aboard so that not a one is to be found anywhere even though they offer its weight in gold for it, then they know they are past the line; and so, Sancho, just run your hand over your thigh and if you come on anything that's alive, it will remove all doubt, but if you find nothing, then we have made the crossing." [7]

"I don't believe a word of it," declared Sancho, "but, nevertheless, I will do as your Grace bids me, although I must say I don't know why we have to make all these experiments, for I can see with my own eyes that we're not five yards away from the bank, nor have we dropped two yards below the spot where the animals stand; for Rocinante and the ass are still there where we left them, and if you take a fixed point as I am doing now, then, I swear, we're not moving any faster than an ant's pace."

"Make the test that I asked you to, Sancho," said Don Quixote, "and do not be bothering your head with anything else; for you know nothing of colures, lines, parallels, zodiacs, ecliptics, poles, solstices, equinoxes, planets, signs, and points of the compass, these being the units of which the celestial and terrestrial spheres are composed. If you knew all these things, or even a part of them, you would clearly perceive what parallels we have crossed, what zodiacal signs we have seen, and what constellations we have left, and are now leaving, behind us. But I tell you again: feel and hunt, for I am certain that you are cleaner than a smooth white sheet of paper."

Sancho did so and, having run his hand gently all the way down to the inside of his left knee, he looked up at his master and said, "Either the test is a false one or we're not within many leagues of where your Grace says we are."

"How is that?" said Don Quixote. "Did you find something?"

"Yes, a number of somethings," [8] said Sancho. And, shaking his fingers, he dipped his entire hand in the river, down which the bark was gently drifting without being moved by any occult intelligence or invisible enchanter but merely by the current itself, which was there flowing along very smoothly.

At that moment they descried some big watermills moored in the middle of the river, and no sooner did Don Quixote catch sight of them than he called out to Sancho in a loud voice, "Do you see that, my friend? There is the city, castle, or fortress where they must be holding some knight in captivity, or some sorely wronged queen, infanta, or princess, to rescue whom I am being brought there."

"What the devil city, fortress, or castle is your Grace talking about?" said Sancho. "Can't you see, master, that those are nothing but watermills on the river, where they grind corn?"

"Be quiet, Sancho," Don Quixote admonished him, "for though they may appear to be watermills, they are not. I have already explained to you how enchanters change and transform things from their natural shape. I do not mean that they actually change them from one shape to another, but they appear to do so, as experience has taught us in connection with the transformation of Dulcinea, sole refuge of my hopes."

By this time the bark was in midstream and was not moving as gently as it had been up to then. The millers, seeing this boat coming down the river and perceiving that it was about to be sucked in by the millwheels, came running out in all haste to stop it. Many of them carried poles, and, as their faces and their clothes were covered with flour, they presented a sinister appearance.

"Devils of men!" they cried out, "where are you going? Do you come in desperation to drown yourselves or be battered to pieces by those wheels?"

"Did I not tell you, Sancho," said Don Quixote, "that we had come to a place where I would have to display the might of my arm? Look at those rogues and scoundrels who have sallied forth to meet me! Look at those monsters who would oppose me! Behold the hideous countenances with which they think to frighten us! You shall soon see, you villains!" And then, standing up in the boat and shouting at the top of his voice, he began hurling threats at the millers: "Lowborn and ill-advised rabble, set free and restore to liberty the person whom you hold in durance vile in that fortress or prison, whether that person be of high or low degree, whatever his station or walk in life; for I am Don Quixote de la Mancha, otherwise known as the Knight of the Lions, for whom it is reserved, by order of the highest heavens, to bring this adventure to a fortunate conclusion!"

Saying this, he drew his sword and began brandishing it in the air by way of intimidating the millers, who, hearing but not understanding these nonsensical remarks, now fell to with their poles to prevent the bark from entering the millrace, as it was on the verge of doing. Sancho, meanwhile, had dropped to his knees and was devoutly praying to Heaven to deliver him from so manifest a peril; and thanks to the quick work of the millers, his prayer was granted. By the aid of their poles they succeeded in stopping the boat, but not without upsetting it and throwing Don Quixote and Sancho into the water. Luckily for the former, he could swim like a duck, but the weight of his armor twice dragged him under, and if it had not been for the millers who dived in and hauled them both out, it would have been the fall of Troy for the two of them.

As soon as they had been brought to land, drenched to the skin but hardly suffering from thirst, Sancho again fell on his knees, clasped his hands, turned his eyes heavenward, and made a long and fervent prayer in which he besought God to deliver him, from that day forth, from his master's rash designs and undertakings. While he was thus engaged, the fishermen who owned the boat, which had been hacked to pieces by the millwheels, came up and, seeing what had been done to their property, fell upon Sancho and stripped him of his clothing, demanding at the same time that Don Quixote make good their loss. The knight was not in the least perturbed by this, but with a calm manner, as if nothing whatever had happened, informed the millers and the fishermen that he would be very glad to pay for the boat on condition that they would deliver up to him, free and unharmed, the person or persons whom they were holding in durance in that castle.

"What persons and what castle are you talking about, you fool?" one of the millers answered him. "Do you by any chance, want to carry off those who come to grind corn in these mills?"

"That will do," said Don Quixote to himself. "It would be preaching in the desert to attempt by entreaties to induce this rabble to perform any worthy deed. In the course of this adventure two powerful enchanters must have clashed, and one has undone what the other proposed to do. God help us all, this world is nothing but schemes and plots, all working at cross-purposes. I can do no more."

Raising his voice, he continued speaking as he gazed at the mills. "Friends," he said, "whoever ye may be who are locked within these prison walls, forgive me. It is my misfortune and yours that I am unable to rescue you from your dire peril. This emprise must doubtless be reserved for some other knight." [9]

Having said this, he came to an understanding with the fishermen and paid them fifty reales for their boat, which Sancho handed over with a very ill grace. "A couple of more boat rides [10] like this," he said, "and we'll have sunk our entire capital."

Both fishermen and millers were filled with wonder at beholding these two figures, so different to all appearances from the common run of men. Unable to make out what Don Quixote was driving at with his speeches and his questions, they decided that the pair were crazy and went back to their tasks, the millers to their mills and the fishermen to their shacks. Don Quixote and Sancho then returned to their beasts and the life of beasts that they led, and thus ended the adventure of the enchanted bark.

CHAPTER XXX. *Of what befell Don Quixote upon meeting with a beautiful huntress.*

THE knight and his squire were in a bad humor and more than a little downcast as they returned to their beasts. This was especially true of Sancho, for anything that touched their supply of money touched his heart, and when any of it was taken from him it was as if he were being deprived of the apple of his eye. And so, without saying a word, they mounted and rode away from the banks of the famous river. While Don Quixote was immersed in thoughts of love, Sancho was thinking of the worldly advancement that had been promised him. It all seemed to him very far away now; for while he may have been a simpleton, he could not help perceiving that all or most of his master's actions were quite mad, and he began casting about in his mind for some occasion that one day would afford him an opportunity to slip away and return home without getting into any arguments or so much as saying good-by. Fortune, however, had something better in store for him.

The next day, as they emerged from a wood at sunset, Don Quixote looked out over a green meadow, at the far end of which he could see a group of people. Drawing closer, he saw that it was a hawking party, and upon coming nearer still he perceived among the company a fine lady seated upon a gleaming white palfrey or hackney caparisoned in green and with a silver sidesaddle.[1] The lady was in green also, and so richly clad that she appeared to be elegance itself. On her left hand she bore a hawk, which to Don Quixote signified that she must be some great dame and the mistress of the party, which proved to be the case.

"Run, Sancho, my lad," he said, "and inform that lady of the palfrey and the hawk that I, the Knight of the Lions, humbly salute her great beauty,[2] and if her Highness will grant me permission, I will come and kiss her hands in person and serve her as my strength may enable me and her Highness may command. Take care how you address her, Sancho, and see that you do not mingle any of your proverbs with the message."

"Why say that to me?" replied Sancho. "I'm no mingler! This is not the first time in my life that I've carried messages to high and mighty ladies!"

"With the exception of the one you carried to the lady Dulcinea," said Don Quixote, "I do not know of any other, at least not since you have been in my service."

"That is the truth," Sancho admitted, "but he who can pay doesn't worry about pledges,[3] and in the house where there's plenty supper is soon on the table.[4] By that I mean to say, you don't need to tell me or warn me of anything, for I'm equal to anything and know a little of everything."

"I believe that, Sancho," his master assured him, "and so good luck and Godspeed."

Forcing his mount out of its usual pace, Sancho hastened to where the beautiful huntress sat, and there, slipping down off his gray and kneeling before her, he spoke as follows:

"Beautiful lady, the knight you see there, known as the Knight of the Lions, is my master and I am a squire of his, Sancho Panza by name. This same Knight of the Lions, who not long ago was called the Knight of the Mournful Countenance, has sent me to beg your Highness to be pleased to grant him permission, with your full approval and consent, to come and fulfill his desire, which I believe to be none other than that of serving your Highness's exalted beauty.[5] If your Ladyship sees fit to bestow this permission, it will be to her advantage, and he will be most happy to receive so distinguished a favor."[6]

"Most certainly, good squire," replied the lady, "you have conveyed the message with all the formalities that are required in such a case. Rise from the ground; for it is not fitting that the squire to so great a Knight as is he of the Mournful Countenance (of whom we have already heard a great deal) should remain on his knees. Rise, friend, and say to your master that he is welcome to my own services, and those of my husband the duke, in a country house that we have not far from here."

As Sancho rose, he was as much impressed by the good lady's beauty as by her high breeding and her courtesy, and he was particularly surprised that she should have heard of his master, the Knight of the Mournful Countenance—if she had not referred to him as the Knight of the Lions, that must be due to the fact that he had but recently assumed the appellation. The duchess (whose full title he did not know) now went on speaking to him.

"Tell me, brother squire," she said, "is not your master the one concerning whom they have printed a story called *The Ingenious Gentleman, Don Quixote de la Mancha*, and who has as lady of his heart a certain Dulcinea del Toboso?"

"He is the same, my lady," replied Sancho, "and I am that squire of his that figures, or is supposed to figure, in the story, the one named Sancho Panza—that is to say, unless they changed me in the cradle—I mean, in the press."

"I am very happy to hear all this," said the duchess. "Go, brother Sancho, and tell your master that he will be most welcome at my estate, as I can think of nothing that would give me greater pleasure."

With so gracious an answer as this to convey, Sancho hastened back in high spirits to his master, to whom he repeated everything that the great lady had said to him, extolling her beauty to the heavens in his own rustic way and dwelling upon her gentle demeanor and her courtesy. Don Quixote at once drew himself up in the saddle, settled himself firmly in the stirrups, adjusted his visor, put spurs to Rocinante, and with a graceful ease of manner rode forward to kiss the duchess's hands. In the meantime, as Don Quixote was approaching, the duchess had summoned her husband and told him of the message, and inasmuch as they had read the first part of this story and were familiar with the knight's nonsensical whims, they were both delighted and extremely eager to make his acquaintance. As they waited for him, they decided that they would humor him in every way and fall in with everything he said, and that as long as he stayed with them they would treat him as a knight-errant, with all the customary ceremonies as described in the books of chivalry; for they had read those books and were very fond of them.[7]

Don Quixote then rode up with his visor raised, and as he went to dismount, Sancho came alongside to hold his stirrup for him; but unfortunately, as he descended from his gray, the squire caught his foot in one of the ropes of his packsaddle in such a manner that he could not get it loose and was left hanging there with his face and bosom on the ground. Now, Don Quixote was not used to dismounting without his stirrup being held, and, thinking that Sancho was already there to see to it, he threw himself off with a lurch, bringing with him Rocinante's saddle, which must have been poorly fastened, and, as a result, both he and the saddle came tumbling to the earth. Needless to say, he was very much ashamed and could only mutter curses between his teeth at the unfortunate Sancho, who still had his feet in the stocks.

The duke thereupon ordered his huntsmen to assist the knight and squire, and they proceeded to lift Don Quixote, who was greatly shaken by his fall but who nonetheless, limping along as best he could, now came forward to kneel before the noble pair. The duke, however, would by no means consent to this, but, dismounting from his own steed, advanced to meet and embrace his guest.

"Sir Knight of the Mournful Countenance," he said, "I deeply regret that the first time you set foot in my domains you should have met with so unfortunate an accident, but the carelessness of squires is often the cause of worse ones."

"Whatever might have happened to me, valorous prince," was Don Quixote's reply, "could not possibly have been evil, even though I had fallen all the way to the depths of the bottomless pit; for the great honor of meeting you would have raised me up and delivered me. My squire, God curse him, is better at loosening his impudent tongue than he is at tightening a saddle girth so that it will stay. But in whatever state I may be, fallen or erect, on foot or on horseback, I shall always be at your service and that of my lady the duchess, your worthy consort, beauty's deserving queen and sovereign princess of courtesy."

"Be careful what you say, Señor Don Quixote de la Mancha," the duke advised him, "for where my lady Doña Dulcinea del Toboso is, other beauties are not to be praised."

Sancho Panza, who by this time had been freed of the noose, was standing close by, and before his master could answer, he spoke up. "It cannot be denied," he said; "indeed, it is to be maintained, that my lady Dulcinea del Toboso is very beautiful; but the hare jumps where you least expect it,[8] and I have heard folks say that what is called nature is like a potter who makes vessels out of clay: he who makes one beautiful jar can make two, three, or a hundred. I say that because, on my word, my lady the duchess is not one whit behind my mistress."

At this, Don Quixote turned to the duchess. "Your Highness," he said to her, "can well imagine that no knight-errant in the world ever had a more talkative or droller squire than I have, and he will prove to you that I speak the truth if your exalted Highness be pleased to accept my services for a few days."

"If the worthy Sancho is droll," replied the duchess, "that is a very good thing, for it shows that he is possessed of sound sense. As your Grace is aware, Señor Don Quixote, drollery and wit do not go with a dull mind and so, since Sancho is both droll and witty, I shall regard him from now on as a shrewd fellow."

"And a talkative one," added Don Quixote.

"So much the better," said the duke; "for many drolleries cannot be expressed in a few words. But come, great Knight of the Mournful Countenance, let us not waste our time talking."

"Knight of the Lions, your Highness should say," Sancho reminded him. "There is no Knight of the Mournful Countenance any more, nor of any kind of Countenance." [9]

"Of the Lions let it be," the duke went on. "What I started to say was that Sir Knight of the Lions should come to a castle of mine that is hard by, where he will be accorded the reception that is justly due to so exalted a personage, such a reception as the duchess and I are accustomed to give to all knights-errant who arrive there."

Sancho lost no time in saddling Rocinante, seeing to it this time that the girths were properly fastened, and they then set out for the castle, with the duke mounted upon a handsome steed and the duchess in between them, the lady having requested Sancho to ride with her, as she took a great delight in listening to his witticisms. Sancho required no urging, and, riding in the center of the group, he made a fourth in the conversation, all to the vast enjoyment of the titled pair, who were only too happy to receive in their castle such a knight-errant and his arrant squire. [10]

CHAPTER XXXI. *Which treats of many and great things.*

SANCHO was supremely happy at finding himself, as he thought, in the good graces of the duchess, for he expected the same kind of treatment in her castle that he had received in Don Diego's house and at Basilio's place. Fond of good living always, he never failed to take opportunity by the forelock and enjoy a feast whenever he could.

The history then goes on to relate that before they reached the country house or castle the duke went on ahead and gave orders to all his servants as to how they were to treat Don Quixote. Accordingly, the moment the knight arrived at the castle gates in the company of the duchess, two lackeys or equerries came out clad from head to foot in what are known as morning robes of finest crimson satin, and, taking the guest in their arms before he had seen or heard them, they said to him, "Your Highness should go and help the duchess to dismount." He started to do as they had suggested, and there followed an elaborate exchange of courtesies regarding the matter, with the duchess insisting that she would descend only in the arms of the duke, since she did not deem it proper to impose so useless a burden on so distinguished a knight; and in the end she had her way and the duke came out to help her down.

They then entered a large patio, and as they did so two beautiful maidens threw over Don Quixote's shoulders a great cloak of sumptuous scarlet cloth, and upon the instant all the galleries of the courtyard were filled with male and female servants of the noble pair, crying loudly, "Welcome, O flower and cream of knight-errantry." And all or most of them spilled vials of scented water upon the knight and the duke and duchess. All of which greatly astonished Don Quixote; indeed, it may be said that this was the first time that he really and wholly believed himself to be a true knight-errant and not a fanciful one, for here he was being treated in the very same manner as knights-errant in ages past, according to the storybooks he had read.

Dismounting from his gray, Sancho contrived to keep close to the duchess and entered the castle with her, although it hurt his conscience a bit to leave the ass alone like that. There he encountered a dignified duenna who with the other womenfolk had come out to receive their mistress, and he took occasion to say to her in a low voice, "Señora González, or whatever your name may be—"

"Doña Rodríguez de Grijalba is my name," the duenna replied. "What is your pleasure, brother?"

"I would have your Grace do me the favor," said Sancho, "of going out to the castle gate, where you will find a gray ass of mine. Will your Grace be pleased to have them put him in the stable, or else put him there yourself, for the poor beast is a little timid and simply can't bear being alone."

"If the master is as wise as the man," replied the duenna, "we're in for it. Be off with you, brother! You and the one who brought you here can go to blazes! As for your ass, the ladies of this household are not used to work of that sort."

"Well," said Sancho, "the truth is, I've heard my master, who is a wizard when it comes to stories—I've heard him say of Lancelot:

> *When from Britain he came,*
> *ladies took care of him,*
> *duennas looked after his hack.*[1]

And so far as that ass of mine is concerned, I wouldn't exchange him for that hack of Sir Lancelot's."

"Brother," said the duenna, "if you are a jester [2] save your jokes for those that appreciate them and will pay you for them, for you'll get nothing out of me but a fig." [3]

"It will be a ripe one at least," was Sancho's answer, "for if years are trumps, you won't lose the game for want of a point." [4]

"Son of a whore!" cried the duenna, who was now very angry. "How old I am is a matter between me and God and no business of yours, you garlic-stuffed rascal!"

She had raised her voice to such a pitch that the duchess heard her; and the lady of the castle, upon turning her head and seeing her waiting woman so excited, with her eyes all aflame, thereupon wished to know who it was with whom she was quarreling.

"This fine fellow here," replied the duenna. "He has been urging me to go out and stable an ass of his that is standing at the castle gate; and he tells me by way of precedent that somewhere or other some ladies took care of a certain Lancelot in that fashion and some duennas looked after his horse. What's more, for good measure, he called me an old woman."

"I should consider that the greatest insult that anyone could offer me," said the duchess and, turning to the squire, she went on, "I must advise you, friend Sancho, that Doña Rodríguez is very young, and if she wears a hood, it is merely to lend her dignity and because it is the custom and not on account of her years."

"May all the years that are left to me be bad ones," said Sancho, "if I meant it that way. What I was trying to say was that I am very fond of my beast and I thought I could not entrust him to a more kind-hearted person than Doña Rodríguez."

Don Quixote, who had been listening all the while, now put in a word. "Is this the place, Sancho," he asked, "for such talk as that?"

"Sir," replied Sancho, "everyone must say what he has to say wherever he may be. I happened to think of my gray, and so I spoke of him. If it had been in the stable that I thought of him, I'd have spoken of him there."

"Sancho," said the duke, "is quite right about that and is not to be blamed for anything. The gray shall have all he wants to eat and Sancho need not worry; the ass will receive the same good treatment as his owner."

Following this conversation, which was very amusing to all of them except Don Quixote, they ascended the stairs to the floor above, and there they took the knight into a chamber richly adorned with cloth of gold and brocade, where six damsels, acting as his pages, proceeded to disarm him. They had all been well instructed by the duke and duchess as to what they were to say and do and how they were to behave toward Don Quixote so that he would have reason to believe he was being treated as a knight-errant. With his armor off, their guest stood there in his tight-fitting breeches and chamois-skin doublet, tall, lean, lanky, with cheeks that appeared to be kissing each other on the inside of his mouth. In short, he presented such an appearance that, if the damsels waiting on him had not done their best to restrain themselves —this being one of the definite orders their master and mistress had given them—they would have burst with laughing.

They then wanted to strip him so that they could put a shirt on him, but he refused to consent to this, saying that modesty was as becoming as valor in knights-errant. Instead, he directed them to give the shirt to Sancho, and shutting himself up in a room where there was a sumptuous bed, he undressed himself and put on the garment.

"Tell me, you old simpleton turned buffoon," he said upon finding himself alone with Sancho, "do you think it was right to insult so venerable a duenna and one so worthy of respect as that one? Was that any time to be thinking of your gray? Are these the kind of people to let beasts suffer when they treat their owners so royally? For God's sake, Sancho, restrain yourself and do not be showing your fiber so that they can see of what coarse, clownish stuff you are made. Bear in mind, sinner that you are, that the more respectable and well bred his servants are, the more is the master honored, and one of the great advantages that princes have over other men is that they are waited upon by those who are as good as themselves.

"Do you not know," he continued, "small-minded creature that you are and unfortunate man that I am, that if they perceive you to be a boor and a clown they will take me for an impostor, for some swindler or other? No, no, friend Sancho, that is a stumbling block you should avoid; for whoever falls into the way of being a prattler for the amusement of others, the first time he trips will end as a wretched buffoon. Put a bridle on your tongue, then; think over and ruminate on your words before they leave your mouth, remembering that we have now reached the point where, by God's help and the might of my arm, we shall come forth greatly bettered in fame and fortune."

Sancho earnestly promised to do as his master had commanded and keep his mouth closed, vowing that he would bite his tongue out before he uttered a word that was not in place and well considered. The knight could set his mind at ease on one point: no one would ever know through him, Sancho, who they were. Don Quixote then put on his clothes, strapped on his baldric and his sword, threw a scarlet cloak over his shoulders, and donned a cloth cap [5] which the damsels had given him; and dressed in this manner he descended to the great hall, where he found the maidens drawn up in two equal rows to present him with what was needed for washing his hands, all of which was done with many curtsies and great ceremony.

Twelve pages,[6] accompanied by the seneschal, next made their appearance to bring him to the dinner, as his hosts were awaiting him. Placing him in their midst, they conducted him with truly regal pomp into another room where a rich table was laid with four places only. The duke and duchess came to the door to receive him, and with them was a solemn-faced ecclesiastic, one of those who rule over noble households and who, not having been born to the nobility themselves, are unable to instruct their charges in the proper behavior. He was one of those who would measure the greatness of great men by their own narrow minds, one of those who, desirous of inculcating economy, merely succeed in making misers.[7] Such a one, I repeat, must have been the grave-appearing churchman who now came forward with the lord and lady of the castle to greet Don Quixote. There were innumerable compliments on either side, after which, the knight walking between his host and hostess, they went to take their places at the table.

The duke invited Don Quixote to take the head of the table and insisted upon it so strongly that, although the knight at first declined, there was nothing to do but yield. The ecclesiastic took the seat opposite, while the duke and duchess sat at the sides. Sancho, meanwhile, was watching all this in open-mouthed amazement, unable to believe his eyes as he saw the honor that was being shown his master by these noble personages; and as he observed the ceremonies that marked the dinner and heard the duke begging Don Quixote to take the place of honor, he could not refrain from speaking up.

"If your Worships will grant me permission," he said, "I will tell you a story concerning something that happened in my village. It has to do with this matter of seats."

No sooner did he hear these words than Don Quixote began trembling, for he thought that undoubtedly his squire was going to give utterance to some absurdity. Sancho saw the look on his face and understood it.

"You needn't fear, master," he assured him, "I'm not going to disobey you or say anything that's not to the point. I haven't forgotten the advice your Grace gave me a while ago about speaking much or little, well or ill."

"I remember nothing about it," replied Don Quixote. "Say what you like, so long as you say it quickly."

"What I am about to tell you," Sancho went on, "is the truth, and my master here present will not let me lie."

"So far as I am concerned, Sancho," said Don Quixote, "you can lie all you want to and I shan't stop you; but watch your words, that's all."

"I've considered and reconsidered them," was the answer, "and the bell-ringer's in a safe place,[8] as you will see."

"It would be a good thing," remarked Don Quixote, "if your Highnesses would have them throw this fool out, for he will talk all kinds of nonsense."

"By the life of the duke," exclaimed the duchess, "I am not going to part with Sancho for a moment. I am extremely fond of him, for I know him to be very discreet."

"And may your days be discreet, your Holiness," [9] said Sancho, "in return for the good opinion you have of me, even if I don't deserve it. But the story I want to tell you is this. There was a gentleman of my village, a very rich and important one, seeing that he came of the Alamos of Medina del Campo and was married to Doña Mencia de Quiñones, who was the daughter of Don Alonso de Marañon, a knight of the Order of Santiago who was drowned at Herradura, the same one who was the cause of that quarrel in our town some years ago in which my master, Don Quixote, was mixed up, so I've heard them say, and Tomasillo the scapegrace, son of Balbastro the blacksmith, who was wounded—isn't all that the truth, my master? Speak up, on your life, so that these good people will not take me for a lying prattler."

"Up to now," said the ecclesiastic, "I have taken you for a prattler rather than a liar, but I cannot say what I shall take you for later on."

"You cite so many witnesses, Sancho," said Don Quixote, "and go into so much circumstantial detail that I am forced to admit you must be telling the truth; but get on with your story and cut it short, for at the rate you are going you will not be finished in a couple of days."

"He is not to cut it short on my account," said the duchess. "Rather, let him tell it in his own way, even if it takes him six days, for they would be the best I ever spent in my life."

"Well, then, as I was saying, good people," continued Sancho, "this certain gentleman—I know him as well as I do my own hands, for from my house to his it is not a crossbow shot—this gentleman invited a farmer, who was poor but respected—"

"Get on, brother," said the churchman at this point, "or otherwise you will not be through with your story until you get to the other world."

"I'll stop a little this side of halfway, please God," replied Sancho. "And so, as I was saying, this farmer, coming to the house of this gentleman I was telling you of who had invited him—God rest his soul, for he is dead now, and what's more, they say he died the death of an angel—I wasn't there, having gone down to Tembleque for the harvest at that time—"

"On your life, son," said the churchman, "hurry back from Tembleque [10] and finish your story without stopping to bury the gentleman, unless you want more funerals on your hands."

"Well, then," Sancho went on, "it so happened that as the two of them sat down at the table—it seems to me I can see them now plainer than ever—"

The duke and duchess were delighted at the churchman's annoyance, occasioned by Sancho's prolixity and digressions in the telling of his story, but Don Quixote was consumed with rage.

"As I was saying," Sancho rambled on, "just as the two of them were about to sit down to eat, the farmer began insisting that the gentleman should take the head of the table and the gentleman insisted that the farmer should take it, saying that in his house his orders had to be obeyed; but the farmer, who had been well brought up and was proud of his manners, would not hear of it until the gentleman, becoming quite angry, laid both hands on the farmer's shoulders and forced him into the place, saying, 'Sit down, you stupid ass, for wherever I sit will be the head of the table to you.' That is my story, and to tell the truth, I don't think it's out of place here." [11]

Don Quixote turned a thousand colors that mottled his brown face until it took on the appearance of jasper. The duke and duchess had to conceal their laughter so as not to add to his embarrassment, for they had seen through Sancho's maliciousness; and in order to change the subject and prevent his squire from running on in this manner, the duchess now inquired of the knight what news he had had of the lady Dulcinea and asked if he had made her a present lately of any more giants or evildoers, as he must surely have vanquished a great many of them.

"Lady," he replied, "my misfortunes, though they had a beginning, will never have an end. Giants I have conquered and rascals and scoundrels I have sent her, but where are they to find her if she is under a magic spell and has been turned into the homeliest peasant lass that could be imagined?"

"I don't know about that," said Sancho Panza. "To me she seemed the most beautiful creature in the world. At least, when it comes to nimbleness and frisking, she won't give in to a tumbler. My word, Duchess, she leaps from the ground onto the back of a she-ass as if she were a cat."

"Have you seen her, Sancho, since she has been enchanted?" the duke asked.

"Have I seen her!" exclaimed Sancho. "Who in the devil was it but me that first thought up this enchantment business! She's as much enchanted as my father."

The ecclesiastic, upon hearing this talk of giants, rogues, and enchanters, decided that their guest must be none other than Don Quixote de la Mancha whose story the duke was always reading—he had reproved him for it many times, telling him it was nonsensical to waste his time on such nonsense—and now, becoming convinced that his suspicions were correct, he turned to the duke and addressed him angrily.

"Your Excellency, *Señor mio*," he said, "will have to give an account to the Lord for what this good man does. This Don Quixote, or Don Simpleton, or whatever his name is, surely cannot be such a dunce as your Excellency would make him out to be by thus lending encouragement to his foolish carryings-on." Addressing himself, then, to Don Quixote, he continued, "And as for you, addlepate, who ever put it into your head that you are a knight-errant who conquers giants and captures malefactors? I say to you: go your way and Heaven be with you; return to your home, see to bringing up your children if you have any, look after your property, and stop wandering about the world like a gaping ninny, making a laughingstock of yourself in the eyes of all, whether they know you or not. Where in the name of goodness [12] did you ever come upon any knights-errant living or dead? Where are there giants in Spain, or bandits in La Mancha, or enchanted Dulcineas, or any of the other silly things they tell about in connection with you?"

Don Quixote listened very attentively to what the reverend gentleman had to say, and when he saw that the speaker had finished, disregarding the presence of the duke and duchess he sprang to his feet with an angry and excited look on his face, and said— But his answer deserves a chapter to itself.

CHAPTER XXXII. *Concerning the answer which Don Quixote gave to his reprover, with other incidents, some serious and some amusing.*

As Don Quixote rose from his seat, he was trembling from head to foot like a man with an overdose of mercury, and he spoke in a hurried, agitated voice.

"The place and presence in which I stand," he began, "and the respect I have always had for your Reverence's profession, tie and bind the hands of my just wrath. For this reason, and because I am aware that the weapons of men in gowns [1] are the same as those of a woman— namely, the tongue—I shall employ that same weapon in doing battle with your Reverence, from whom one might have looked for good counsel rather than infamous abuse. Reprehension that is righteous and well meant should be administered in a different way and calls for other arguments. By reproving me in public and so rudely, you have exceeded all proper bounds; for Christian reprehension should be based upon mildness not upon asperity, nor is it right, knowing nothing of the sin you are censuring, to call the sinner straightaway a simpleton and a fool.

"Otherwise," he went on, "tell me, your Reverence, what manifestation of foolishness have you discerned in me that leads you thus to vituperate and condemn me and order me to return home, look after the management of my affairs, and care for my wife and children, when you do not even know whether or not I have a house or family? Is nothing more required than to make your way by hook or crook into other people's houses to rule over their masters, and that, perhaps, after having been brought up in some poverty-stricken seminary [2] and having seen no more of the world than was to be found within a radius of twenty or thirty leagues? Is such a one suddenly to take it upon himself to lay down the law for chivalry and pass judgment on knights-errant? Is it, perchance, a vain occupation or a waste of time to wander over the earth, seeking not the pleasures of this life but those hardships by which the virtuous may mount to the seat of immortality? [3] If true gentlemen or great lords of high and noble station were to call me a fool I should take it as an irreparable insult, but for the opinion of mere bookworms who have never entered upon or trod the paths of chivalry I would not give a penny. A knight I am and a knight I shall die, if it be pleasing to Almighty God.

"Some men," the knight concluded, "take the broad field of ambition,[4] others the road of low and servile adulation; some choose the way of hypocrisy and deception, and others still that of religion; but, as for me, led on by my star, I follow the narrow path of knight-errantry, and in the exercise of that profession I despise wealth but not honor. I have undone wrongs, righted grievances, chastised the insolent, overcome giants, and trampled monsters under foot. I am enamored, for the very good reason that knights-errant must be. I am not, however, one of those vicious lovers, but, rather, chaste and platonic. My intention is always a worthy one: that of doing good to all and harm to none. As to whether a man with such a purpose and who puts it into execution deserves to be called a simpleton, that is for your Highnesses to say, O excellent Duke and Duchess."

"By God," exclaimed Sancho, "that's good! Say no more, master mine, in your own behalf, for there's nothing more in the world to be said, thought, or insisted upon.[5] So far as that goes, seeing that this gentleman denies, as he has denied, that there are or have been knights-errant in the world, is it any wonder if he doesn't know what he's talking about?"

"Brother," said the ecclesiastic, "are you by any chance that Sancho Panza to whom, so they tell me, his master has promised an island?"

"I am," replied Sancho, "and I am one who deserves it as well as any other. I am one of those of whom it is said, 'Keep good company and you'll be one of them,' [6] and, 'Not with whom you are bred but with whom you are fed,' [7] and, 'Who leans against a good tree is covered by a goodly shade.' [8] I've leaned against a good master, it's many months now that I've been going about with him, and, God willing, I'll be just such another as he is. Long life to him and long life to me, and may he never lack empires to rule and may I always have islands to govern."

"Have them you certainly shall, friend Sancho," said the duke at this point; "for in the name of Señor Don Quixote, I hereby confer upon you the government of an island that I happen to possess, and one of no small importance."

"Get down on your knees, Sancho," said Don Quixote, "and kiss his Excellency's feet for the favor he has done you."

Sancho did as he was bidden and when he saw this, the ecclesiastic rose from the table in a temper.

"By the habit that I wear," he said, "I feel like saying that your Excellency is as much of a crackbrain as these sinners. It is not surprising that they are mad when those who are sane applaud their madness. Let your Excellency stay with them if you like, but as long as they are in this house I shall remain in mine and shall ask to be excused from reproving that which I cannot remedy."

And without uttering another word or eating another bite, he left the room, despite the entreaties of the duke and duchess. The duke, in fact, did not say much, as he was laughing too hard at the churchman's uncalled-for anger.

"Sir Knight of the Lions," he said to Don Quixote when he had finally stopped laughing. "Your Grace has answered him so well that there is no further satisfaction to be sought. While this may appear to be an affront, it is not so in reality; for, as your Grace knows, ecclesiastics, like women, can give no offense."

"That is true," agreed Don Quixote, "and the reason for it is that he who is not to be offended cannot offend another. Women, children, and churchmen, since they cannot protect themselves, even though they may be wronged cannot be insulted; for between an offense and an insult there is this difference, as your Excellency is aware: the insult comes from one who can and does sustain it; an offense may come from any quarter, with no insult attached to it. Let us take an example. A man is standing unsuspectingly in the street when ten armed ruffians come up and start beating him. He draws his sword and does his duty, but his opponents are too many for him and he cannot carry out his intention, which is that of avenging himself. This man is offended but not insulted. Or let us take another case. A man is standing with his back turned when another comes up and strikes him and then flees. He pursues his assailant but is unable to overtake him; and so we may say that the one who was struck received an offense but no insult, since the insult has to be sustained.

"On the other hand," continued the knight, "if the one who struck him, even though he did it by stealth, should lay hand to his sword and face it out with his enemy, the latter would then be both offended and insulted at one and the same time; he would be insulted for the reason that the one who dealt the blow did not turn tail but stood and backed it up. And so, in accordance with the laws of the accursed duel, I may have been offended but not insulted; for neither women nor children can maintain an affront, nor can they flee or stand their ground, and the same is true of those who are in the Church, since these three classes of people lack both offensive and defensive arms and, though they are naturally obliged to defend themselves, should offend no one.

"I said a moment ago," Don Quixote went on, "that I might have been offended, but now I say no, by no manner of means; for he who cannot receive an insult is still less capable of giving one; and for this reason I ought not to resent, nor do I resent, what this good man said to me. My only regret is that he did not wait a while so that I might have shown him how wrong he is in thinking and saying that there are not and never have been any knights-errant in this world. Had Amadis heard him, or any one of that knight's innumerable progeny, it would not have been well for his Reverence."

"That I can surely swear to," said Sancho. "He would have given him a slash that would have laid him open from top to bottom like a pomegranate or an overripe melon. They were not the fellows to put up with jokes like that! Faith, and if Rinaldo de Montalbán [9] had heard the little man he'd have rapped him over the mouth so hard his Reverence wouldn't have had anything more to say for three whole years. He'd better not get mixed up with them or he'll see how he comes out!"

The duchess nearly died laughing as she listened to Sancho. In her opinion he was even droller and more insane than his master, and there were many at that time who would have agreed with her. Finally, Don Quixote quieted down and the meal was finished; and as they removed the cloth, four damsels appeared, one with a silver basin, one with a jug likewise of silver, a third with the finest of white towels over her shoulder, while the fourth, whose arms were bare to the elbow, carried in her white hands (for white they assuredly were) a rounded cake of Neapolitan soap.[10] The one with the basin then came up with a graceful, free, and easy manner and held the vessel under Don Quixote's beard. The knight did not say a word, being quite astonished at such a ceremony, but thinking it must be the custom of that region to wash the beard in place of the hands, he stretched his whiskers out as far as he could, and at that very moment the damsel with the jug began to pour and the one with soap started scrubbing most energetically, raising snowflakes out of the lather that covered not only the beard of the obedient knight but his entire face, compelling him to keep his eyes closed.

The duke and duchess, who were wholly unprepared for all this, waited to see what the outcome of these extraordinary ablutions would be. The barber damsel, when she had her victim a palm's breadth deep in lather, pretended that the water had run out and ordered the maid with the jug to go fetch some more while Don Quixote remained like that, the weirdest and most laughable-looking figure that could be imagined. All those present, and there were many of them, stared at him, at his neck half a yard long and uncommonly brown, his closed eyes, and his beard full of soap, and it was all they could do to keep from laughing outright. As for the damsels who had thought up the joke, they kept their gaze lowered, not daring to look up at their master and mistress, who were torn between laughter and anger and did not know what to do, whether to punish the girls for their boldness or reward them for the pleasure of seeing Don Quixote in this plight.

At last the girl with the jug came back and they finished bathing the knight, after which they brought in towels and cleaned and dried him very matter-of-factly. Having done this, all four of them made deep bows, and curtsied and were about to withdraw when the duke, who did not wish Don Quixote to discover the jest, called to them and said, "Come and wash me too, and be sure there is plenty of water."

The girl, being sharp-witted, promptly placed the basin in front of the duke as she had done with Don Quixote, and with the same energy and thoroughness they proceeded to bathe and lather him. Then, with more curtsies, they all went away and it was afterward learned that the duke had sworn that if they had not bathed him in the same manner as they had the knight, he would have punished them for their impudence, but, as it was, they had cleverly made amends.

"So help me God!" muttered Sancho to himself as he watched this ceremonious bathing. "Could it be the custom in this country to wash squires' beards as well as knights'? For, by God and 'pon my soul, I have need of it. And if they gave me a shave as well, I'd take it as an extra favor."

"What are you mumbling about, Sancho?" the duchess inquired.

"I was just saying to myself that in the courts of other princes, so I've heard tell, when they take the cloth away they bring water for the hands but not lye for the beard. For that reason, it's good to live a long time so that you'll see a lot of things.[11] They also say that he who has a long life has to go through much trouble,[12] though I'd call it pleasure, not trouble, to have a bath like that."

"Do not let it worry you, friend Sancho," said the duchess, "for I will have my damsels bathe you and they will even put you in the tub if necessary."

"I'll be satisfied with the beard," replied Sancho, "for the present at least. As for the future, God knows what is to be."

"Seneschal," called the duchess, "see that the good Sancho has whatever he asks for, and carry out his wishes in every respect."

The seneschal replied that he was wholly at Señor Sancho's service, and with this he went off to eat, taking the squire with him, while the duke and duchess and Don Quixote were left at the table talking of many and various things, but all of them having to do with the profession of arms and the calling of knight-errantry. The duchess then requested her guest, since he appeared to have so good a memory, to describe for her the features of the beautiful Dulcinea del Toboso, who, if what fame had trumpeted abroad concerning her loveliness was true, must surely be the fairest creature in the world and even in all La Mancha. Upon hearing this, Don Quixote heaved a sigh.

"If," he said, "I could but take my heart out and lay it before your Highness's eyes, upon a plate here on this table, I should be able to spare my tongue the trouble of telling what is scarcely to be conceived; for in my heart your Excellency would see her fully portrayed. After all, why should I undertake to describe and depict, point by point and feature by feature, the beauty of the peerless Dulcinea? That is a task that should be laid upon other shoulders than mine, being one worthy of the brushes of Parrhasius, Timanthes, and Apelles and of the chisel of Lysippus;[13] artists such as they should preserve that beauty in pictures, in marble, and in bronze, and a Ciceronian and Demosthene eloquence are called for to eulogize it."

"What does Demosthene mean, Señor Don Quixote?"[14] asked the duchess. "That is a word I never heard in all my life."

"Demosthene eloquence," Don Quixote explained, "is equivalent to saying the eloquence of Demosthenes, just as Ciceronian means of Cicero, for they were the two greatest orators in the world."

"That is right," said the duke. "Your mind must have been wandering," he added, speaking to the duchess, "or you would not have asked such a question. But, for all of that, it would give us a very great pleasure if Señor Don Quixote would portray her for us; for I am sure that, even though it be the merest outline or sketch, she will emerge in such a manner as to arouse envy in the fairest of ladies."

"I should most certainly do so," said Don Quixote, "if it were not that the misfortune that befell her a short while ago, of a kind to be wept over rather than described, had blurred my mental image of her. For I must inform your Highnesses that, some days past, when I went to kiss her hand and to receive her blessing, her approval, and her permission for this third sally of mine, I found her quite a different being from the one I sought. I found her under a magic spell, converted from a princess into a peasant girl, from a beautiful creature into an ugly one, from an angel into a devil, from a fragrant-scented being into a foul-smelling wench, from a fine-garbed, dignified lady into a rustic clown, leaping in the air—in short, from Dulcinea del Toboso into a Sayago country woman." [15]

"God save us!" cried the duke in a loud voice at this juncture. "Who is it could have done such a wrong to the world? Who could have deprived it of that beauty that rendered it joyful, that grace that charmed it, and that modesty that so redounded to its credit?"

"Who?" Don Quixote repeated. "Who could it have been except some malign enchanter of the many envious ones who persecute me? That cursed race of beings was born into the world to darken it, to frustrate the achievements of the virtuous and exalt those of the wicked. These enchanters have persecuted, are persecuting, and will continue to persecute me until they shall have sunk me and my high deeds of chivalry into the deep pit of oblivion. They seek to harm and wound me where they know I am most vulnerable, for to take away his lady from a knight-errant is to rob him of the eyes with which he sees, the sun that lights him, and the sustenance that is his life. I have said many times before and I will say it again, that the knight-errant without a lady is like the tree without leaves, a building without a foundation, or a shadow without the body that casts it."

"There is no more to be said on the subject," observed the duchess; "but, nevertheless, if we are to believe the tale about Señor Don Quixote that was recently published in these parts and that won the praise of all—we are to gather from this tale, if I remember rightly, that your Grace has never seen the lady Dulcinea, that there is, in fact, no such lady in existence, or, rather, that she is a purely fanciful one, created in your Grace's own mind, whom you have endowed with all the charms and perfections that you chose to give her."

"That," replied Don Quixote, "is a long story. God knows whether or not there is a Dulcinea in this world or if she is a fanciful creation. This is not one of those cases where you can prove a thing conclusively. I have not begotten or given birth to my lady, although I contemplate her as she needs must be, seeing that she is a damsel who possesses all those qualities that may render her famous in all parts of the world, such as: a flawless beauty; dignity without haughtiness; a tenderness that is never immodest; a graciousness due to courtesy and a courtesy that comes from good breeding; and, finally, a highborn lineage, for beauty is more resplendent and more nearly perfect in those of lofty extraction than in creatures of a humbler origin."

"True enough," said the duke, "but if Señor Don Quixote will permit me, after having read the story of his exploits I am compelled to remind him that it is stated there that, granted there is a Dulcinea in or out of El Toboso, and granted that she is as supremely beautiful as your Grace has depicted her, she still cannot compare in the matter of ancestry with the Orianas, the Alastrajareas, the Madásimas,[16] or others of that sort with whose names the histories that your Grace knows so well are filled."

"As to that," Don Quixote answered, "I can say only that Dulcinea is the daughter of her works,[17] that virtues shed luster upon the bloodstream, and that a person of low degree who is possessed of them is more to be esteemed than the vicious one who has risen to high station.[18] Moreover, Dulcinea has qualities that well may bring her to a crown and scepter; for a woman who is at once beautiful and virtuous may by her merits come to work miracles, and has locked within her, potentially if not actually, a higher fortune than the one she knows."

"I must remark," said the duchess, "that in everything your Grace tells us you proceed with leaden foot and plummet in hand, as the saying is.[19] As for myself, I shall continue to believe and shall see to it that all in my household do the same—even my lord the duke if necessary —that there is a Dulcinea now living in El Toboso, and that she is beautiful and highborn, a lady worthy of being served by such a knight as Señor Don Quixote, which is the highest praise I can bestow upon her. But, for all of that, there is still some small doubt in my mind, and here I hold a grudge against Sancho Panza; for the story that I have mentioned states that when Sancho brought the lady Dulcinea a message from your Grace, he found her winnowing a bag of wheat, and red wheat at that, a circumstance that leads me to question her exalted lineage." [20]

"My lady," replied Don Quixote, "your Highness should know that all or most of the things that happen to me are beyond the common experience of other knights-errant, being brought about either through the inscrutable will of the fates or through the malice of some envious enchanter. For it is a known fact that all or most of the famous knights-errant either had a special gift that was proof against enchantment or else had flesh that was impenetrable so that they could not be wounded. There was, for example, Orlando, one of the Twelve Peers of France, of whom it is related that he could be wounded only in the sole of his left foot, and with no other weapon whatever than a large pin; and so when Bernardo del Carpio slew him at Roncesvalles,[21] upon perceiving that he could not reach him with his sword, he was compelled to lift him from the ground and strangle him, thus recalling the manner in which Hercules disposed of Antaeus, the ferocious giant who, they say, was Earth's own son.

"By this," he went on, "I mean to infer that I may possibly possess some gift of this sort. Not the gift of invulnerability, however, since experience has frequently taught me that my flesh is tender and by no means impenetrable; nor am I proof against enchantment, having, before now, found myself thrust into a cage,[22] a thing which all the world combined could never have accomplished except through the power of magic. But inasmuch as I succeeded in freeing myself from that spell, I am of the opinion that no one will henceforth be able to hurt me. Accordingly, those enchanters, seeing they can no longer lay their evil hands upon my person, are avenging themselves upon the object that I most love and would deprive me of life by mistreating Dulcinea, in whom I have my being.

"What I think is that when my squire brought her my message, those same enchanters transformed her into a country wench and set her at so low a task as is that of winnowing wheat. But I have already said that the wheat in question was not red, nor was it wheat, but oriental pearls; and, in proof of this, I may inform your Highnesses that when I came to El Toboso not long ago, I was able to find Dulcinea's palace; and the very next day Sancho, my squire, beheld her in her proper form, which is the most beautiful of any on earth, while to me she appeared as a coarse and ugly peasant girl and very rude in her speech, though she herself is the soul of propriety. And seeing that I am not enchanted and, it stands to reason, cannot be, she must be the one who has suffered this injury and has been thus altered, changed, and transformed. That is to say, my enemies through her have had their revenge on me, and it is on account of her that I live amid ceaseless tears until I shall once more have beheld her in her pristine state.

"All this," continued Don Quixote, "I have told you in order that no one may believe what Sancho says about Dulcinea's winnowing or sifting grain; for if they altered her in my sight, it is no wonder if they transformed her for him. Dulcinea is illustrious and wellborn and comes from one of those noble lines such as are to be met with in El Toboso,[23] where they are numerous, ancient, and respected; and, without a doubt, much of the credit for the esteem in which these houses are held must go to her, on account of whom her town will be as famous and renowned as Troy was on account of Helen or Spain by reason of Cava,[24] and with an even better title to fame.

"On the other hand, I would have your Highnesses know that Sancho Panza is one of the drollest squires that ever served a knight-errant. He is so sharp in his simple-mindedness that one may derive no little amusement from trying to determine whether he is in reality simple or sharp-witted. He has in him a certain malicious streak that seems to indicate he is a rogue, and from his blundering you would take him for a dunce. He doubts everything and believes everything, and just as I think he is about to tumble headlong, owing to some stupidity, he will come up with some witticism or other that sends him skyward in my estimation. The short of the matter is, I would not exchange him for another squire even though they threw in a city to boot.

"And so I am in some doubt as to whether it would be a good thing to entrust him with that governorship that your Highness has done him the favor of bestowing on him; although it is true that I discern in him a certain aptitude for governing, and with a little brushing-up of his wits he might make out as well with any government whatsoever as a king with his taxes.[25] Especially since we know from long experience that neither much ability nor much learning is necessary in order to be a governor; for there are a hundred hereabouts who are barely able to read and who yet acquit themselves of their task like so many ger-falcons.[26] The main thing is for them to be possessed of good intentions and a desire to do the right thing always, for they will never lack those who can advise and direct them in what they have to do, just as those who are knights and not scholars pass judgment with the aid of an assessor. My advice to him would be to take no bribe and surrender no right,[27] and there are a few other little points I have in mind that I can bring up when the time comes and that will be useful to Sancho and of benefit to the island he is to govern."

The duke, the duchess, and Don Quixote had reached this point in their conversation when they heard the sound of many voices and a great uproar in the palace, and of a sudden Sancho burst into the room in a rage, with a straining cloth under his chin for a bib, followed by a large number of lads, or, more precisely, scullions and other kitchen help. One of the pursuers carried a small trough filled with a liquid that, from its color and unclean appearance, was clearly seen to be dish-water, and he kept insisting on placing the receptacle under Sancho's beard while one of his companions sought to give the squire a bath.

"What is this, brothers?" the duchess demanded. "What is this? What are you trying to do to this good man? Do you not know that he has just been appointed a governor?"

"The gentleman does not want to let us bathe him," replied the barber-scullion, "as is the custom and as we bathed my lord the duke, and his own master."

"Yes," said Sancho wrathfully, "I do want to be bathed, but with cleaner towels, clearer suds,[28] and hands that are not so dirty. There is not so much difference between my master and me that they should bathe him with angel water [29] and me with these damnable suds! The customs of countries and of princely palaces are good so long as they do not cause hardship, but the custom of bathing as in use here is worse than the rule of the flagellants. My beard is clean and does not need to be freshened up in that way, and I will say, with all due respect, that if anyone tries to wash me or touches a hair of my head, I mean, of my beard, I'll give him a punch that will leave my fist buried in his skull; for, in my opinion, cirimonies [30] and soapings such as these are more of a joke than they are the kind of treatment that should be shown to a guest."

The duchess nearly died with laughter as she saw how very angry Sancho was and listened to his words; but Don Quixote was not greatly amused at seeing his squire in such a plight, with the dirty towel about him and surrounded by the pranksters from the kitchen. And so, making a profound obeisance to the duke and duchess, as if begging their permission to speak, the knight turned and addressed the rowdies in these words:

"I say there, you gentlemen,[31] leave this young man alone and go back where you came from, or anywhere else that you please. My squire is as clean as any other, and he likes those troughs of yours no better than he does slim, narrow-mouthed wine jars; [32] so take my advice and leave him alone, for neither he nor I is fond of jests."

At this point Sancho took the words out of his mouth.

"Let them come on," he said, "and try their jokes on this bumpkin. It's as likely I'll stand for them as it is that it is now night.[33] Let them bring a comb or whatever they like and curry this beard of mine, and if they bring out of it anything that's not clean, I'll let them give me a fool's haircut."[34]

"Sancho Panza," said the duchess, laughing still, "is right in everything he has said or will say. He is clean and, as he has told us, has no need of a bath; so, if our custom is not pleasing to him, let him do as he likes. What is more, you ministers of cleanliness have been entirely too careless and remiss, perhaps I should say audacious, in bringing such a person as this, with such a beard, a wooden trough and dishclouts in place of a basin and jugs of purest gold and towels of Holland linen. In short, you are ill behaved and ill bred and, knaves that you are, cannot refrain from showing the grudge you harbor against the squires of knights-errant."

The impudent servants and even the seneschal who had come with them believed that the duchess was speaking in earnest. They now removed the straining cloth from around Sancho's neck and, more than a little embarrassed and out of countenance, went away and left him there; whereupon, seeing himself delivered from what he looked upon as a supreme peril, the squire ran over and fell on his knees in front of the duchess.

"From great ladies great favors are to be expected," he said, "but in order to repay the one your Highness has shown me, I can only wish that I could be dubbed a knight-errant so that I could spend all the days of my life in serving your exalted Ladyship. I am a peasant, Sancho Panza by name, I am married and the father of a family, and I serve as a squire. If in any of these respects I can be of service to your Highness, I shall hesitate less in obeying than your Ladyship in commanding."

"It is quite apparent, Sancho," replied the duchess, "that you have studied in the school of courtesy itself; by that I mean to say, that you have been nourished at the bosom of Señor Don Quixote, who is the very cream of courtesy and flower of ceremony—or cirimony, as you yourself would say.[35] Well may such a master and man fare, the one being the north pole of knight-errantry while the other is the star of squirely fidelity! Arise, friend Sancho, that I may repay your courtesy by having my lord the duke fulfill as soon as possible the promise of a governorship that he has made you."

This ended their conversation. Don Quixote now went off to take his siesta, and the duchess requested Sancho, in case he was not too sleepy, to spend the afternoon with her and her damsels in a very cool apartment that they had. He replied that, although it was true that he liked to take a nap of four or five hours in the summertime, in order to be of service to her Excellency he would strive with all his might to go without sleep that day and in obedience to her command would come to her chambers. The duke, meanwhile, gave fresh orders to the effect that Don Quixote was to be treated as a knight-errant in every way, without departing one jot from the formalities that, according to the storybooks, were observed in the case of knights of old.

CHAPTER XXXIII.   *Of the delightful conversation which the duchess and her waiting women had with Sancho Panza, worth reading and worth noting.*

THE history goes on to relate that Sancho did not take his siesta but, by way of keeping his word, came in to see the duchess before he had scarcely done eating. As she was very fond of listening to him, she insisted on his sitting down beside her on a low chair. Merely out of good breeding, Sancho declined at first, but the duchess made matters right by telling him that he should sit as a governor and talk as a squire, since in either capacity he deserved nothing less than the seat of Cid Ruy Díaz, the Campeador himself.[1] Shrugging his shoulders, Sancho obeyed and sat down, and all the damsels and duennas then gathered around him and, preserving a deep silence, waited to hear what he might have to say. It was the duchess, however, who was the first to speak.

"Now that we are alone," she said, "with no one to hear us, I should like the Señor Governor to resolve certain doubts that I have, growing out of the story of the great Don Quixote that has already been printed. For one thing, inasmuch as the worthy Sancho never saw Dulcinea, I mean the lady Dulcinea del Toboso, and never brought her Don Quixote's letter, which was left in the memorandum book on the Sierra Morena,[2] how did he dare make up the answer and that tale about her winnowing wheat, a hoax and a falsehood so detrimental to the reputation of the peerless Dulcinea, and so unbecoming to the character of a good and faithful squire?"

Sancho listened to these words without making any reply whatsoever. Instead, he rose from his chair and, with his back bent and a finger on his lips, went all around the room lifting the draperies. Having done this, he came back and sat down again. It was only then that he broke his silence.

"My lady," he began, "now that I have seen that there are no eavesdroppers but only the bystanders to hear what is said, I will answer your question and any other that you may wish to ask me. In the first place, I must tell you that I look upon my master Don Quixote as stark mad, even though at times he says things that to me and all those who listen to him seem so wise and directed in such a straight rut that Satan himself could not do any better. But, for all of that, there is not the slightest doubt in my mind that he's cracked. Well, then, having this in my noddle, I can venture to make him believe things that don't make head nor tail, like that business of the answer to his letter, and that other that only happened six or eight days ago and so is not in the story yet, by which I mean, the enchantment of my lady, Doña Dulcinea; for though I gave him to understand that she was under a spell, there's no more truth in it than over the hills of Ubeda." [3]

The duchess then asked him to tell her about the hoax having to do with the enchantment, and he narrated the incident just as it had happened, at which his audience was not a little amused. The duchess then resumed the conversation.

"As a result of what the worthy Sancho has told me," she said, "there arises a question in my mind, a certain whispering in my ear which says: if Don Quixote is crazy, weak-minded, crackbrained, and Sancho his squire knows it and still continues to serve him and to cling to the empty promises his master has made him, he must undoubtedly be the more foolish and the more insane of the two; and if this is the case, my lady the Duchess, as I am sure it is, you are bound to be reproached for having given him an island to govern; for if he cannot govern himself, how can he govern others?"

"By God, lady," said Sancho, "you've spoken straight to the point; but go ahead, your Highness, and say whatever you like, as plain as you like, for I know it to be the truth. I know that if I had good sense I'd have left my master long ago. But this is my luck, my misfortune, and I can't help following him. We're from the same village, I've eaten his bread, I like him very much, he's generous to me,[4] he gave me his ass-colts, and, above all, I'm loyal; and so it's impossible for anything to separate us except the pick and spade.[5] And if your Highness doesn't want to give me that island that you promised me, well, I didn't have it when God made me, and it may be that your not giving it to me will be all the better for my conscience.

"I may be a fool," he went on, "but I know what is meant by the saying, 'To her harm the ant grew wings.'[6] It may be that Sancho the squire will go to Heaven sooner than Sancho the governor. They make as good bread here as in France, and at night all cats are gray. He is hard up who hasn't broken his fast by two in the afternoon, and there's no stomach that's bigger than another by the breadth of your palm, and you can fill it with straw or hay, as the saying goes. The little birds of the field have God for their provider, and four yards of Cuenca frieze keep you warmer than four of Segovia broadcloth.[7] Once we have left this world and gone down under the earth, the prince travels by as narrow a path as the day laborer, and the pope's body takes up no more feet of earth than does the sacristan's, [8] even though one is higher than the other; for, when we go to the grave, we all make ourselves as small as we can, or they do it for us whether we like it or not, and then it's good night all.

"And so I will say once again that if your Ladyship doesn't care to give me that island because I'm a fool, then like a wise man I'll not let it worry me. I've heard it said that behind the cross stands the devil, and all is not gold that glitters.[9] The peasant Wamba[10] was taken from behind the oxen, the plows, and the yokes to be king of Spain, and Rodrigo [11] was taken from among his brocades, pastimes, and riches to be devoured by serpents, if the old ballads do not lie."

"Of course they do not lie!" exclaimed the duenna Doña Rodríguez, who was one of the listeners. "Why, there is a ballad that tells how they put King Rodrigo while he was still alive into a tomb full of toads, snakes, and lizards, and two days later he cried out from inside the tomb in a low, pain-stricken voice:

> 'They are eating me now, they are eating me now,
> There where I most have sinned.' [12]

And according to that, this gentleman is quite right in saying he would rather be a peasant than a king if he is to be eaten by reptiles in the end."

The duchess could not help laughing at the simplicity of her duenna, nor could she get over her astonishment as she listened to Sancho and his proverbs. She now addressed herself to him.

"The worthy Sancho well knows," she said, "that once a knight makes a promise he strives to fulfill it though it cost him his life. The duke, my lord and husband, though not of the errant variety, is nonetheless a knight, and he accordingly will keep his word with regard to that island he promised despite the envy and malice of others. Let Sancho be of good courage, for when he least expects it he will find himself on some island throne, in the seat of authority, and he will then take over the government, that he may exchange it for another of triple brocade.[13] The charge that I would lay upon him is this: that he look well to the manner in which he governs his vassals, in view of the fact that they all are loyal and wellborn."

"As to this business of governing them well," said Sancho, "there's no need of charging me to do that, for I am by nature kindhearted and charitable toward the poor. You don't steal the bread from one who kneads and bakes,[14] and, faith, they'd better not throw false dice with me. I'm an old dog and know all about *tus, tus*.[15] I can get the dust out of my eyes when the time comes, and there are no specks in front of them, either. I know where the shoe pinches me.[16] I say this by way of letting you know that the good will find in me a support and a refuge and the bad will not get a foothold. As I see it, in this matter of governments, everything depends on the kind of start you make; and it may be that after I've been governor for a couple of weeks, I'll have my hand in and will be better at the job than at work in the fields, which I was brought up to do."

"You are right, Sancho," the duchess assured him, "for no one is born educated, and bishops are made out of men, not out of stones. But to return to the subject of which we were speaking a short while ago, the lady Dulcinea's enchantment. I hold it to be certain and thoroughly established that Sancho's idea of hoaxing his master and making him think that the peasant girl was Dulcinea, and of leading him to believe that if he did not recognize her it must be because she was under a magic spell—I maintain that all this was indeed the invention of one of those enchanters that persecute Don Quixote; for, in all seriousness, I know from good authority that the country maid who leaped upon the she-ass was Dulcinea del Toboso, and that the worthy Sancho, thinking he is the deceiver, is in reality the deceived.

"There is no more reason to doubt the truth of this than there is to doubt anything simply because we have not seen it with our own eyes. I would inform Señor Sancho Panza that we also have enchanters here, friendly ones, who tell us what goes on in the world, plainly and simply, without any plotting or scheming; and, believe me, Sancho, that sportive lass was and is Dulcinea del Toboso, who is as much enchanted as the mother that bore her,[17] and when we are least expecting it we shall behold her in her proper form, and then Sancho will be freed of the misapprehension under which he is laboring."

"That may all very well be," said Sancho Panza, "and now I am ready to believe what my master told me he saw in the Cave of Montesinos. He says that when he saw the lady Dulcinea del Toboso there, she was wearing the same clothes that I told him I had seen her wearing when I enchanted her for my own pleasure. But it must be just the other way around, as you say, my lady; for it is not to be, and cannot be, supposed that one who is no brighter than I am should have been able to concoct so clever a trick in a moment's time, nor do I think my master is so mad that my weak and feeble persuasion could bring him to believe a thing that is so beyond the bounds of reason. But your Ladyship must not on this account look upon me as a mischief-maker, since a stupid fellow like me cannot be expected to see through the evil designs of those wicked enchanters. I made all that up simply in order to escape a scolding from my master, Señor Don Quixote, and not with any intention of harming him, and if it has come out just the opposite way from what I intended, God's in his Heaven and He judges our hearts."

"That is true," said the duchess, "but tell me, Sancho, what is all this about the Cave of Montesinos? I should like to hear it."

Sancho then related the adventure point by point as it has been set down here.

"From this episode," remarked the duchess when he had finished, "one may infer that, since the great Don Quixote says he saw down there the same peasant girl that Sancho encountered on the El Toboso road, she must undoubtedly be Dulcinea, and that means that there are some very clever and meddlesome enchanters at work around here."

"That is what I say," replied Sancho Panza, "and if my lady Dulcinea del Toboso is enchanted, so much the worse for her; I'm not going to pick a quarrel with my master's enemies, who must be many and wicked. The truth is that the one I saw was a peasant lass and that was what I took her to be and set her down for; and if Dulcinea it was, that is not to be held against me, nor should I take the consequences. But they have to be after me at every step with Sancho said this and Sancho did that, Sancho here and Sancho there—just as if Sancho was nobody at all, instead of being that same Sancho Panza that is now going about the world in books, according to what Sansón Carrasco told me, and he at least is a bachelor of Salamanca, and people like him can't lie, unless the fancy happens to take them or they find it very convenient to do so. There's no reason for anybody's falling out with me, for I have a fine reputation, and I've heard my master say that a good name is worth more than great riches; [18] so, stick me into this governorship and you'll see marvels. He who has been a good squire will make a good governor."

"All that the worthy Sancho has just said," remarked the duchess, "is out of Cato's maxims [19] or, at the least, drawn from the very entrails of Miguel Verino himself, who *florentibus occidit annis*.[20] In short, speaking after his own manner, under a bad cloak you commonly find a good drinker." [21]

"Well, to tell you the truth, lady," replied Sancho, "I never in my life have drunk from malice, though it well may be that I have from thirst, for there's nothing of the hypocrite in me. I drink when I feel like it, and even when I don't feel like it, if they offer it to me, so as not to appear strait-laced or ill bred. If a friend drinks to your health, you'd have to have a heart of marble, wouldn't you, not to raise your glass with his? But though I put on my shoes I never get them dirty.[22] And, anyhow, the squires of knights-errant commonly drink water, for they are always going through forests, woods, and meadows, and over mountains and cliffs, without finding a paltry drop of wine, though they'd be willing to give one of their eyes for it."

"I believe all that," the duchess answered him, "but, for now, let Sancho go and take his rest and later we will talk of all these things at greater length and will make arrangements to stick Sancho into that governorship, as he himself would put it, as soon as possible."

Sancho once more kissed the duchess's hand and begged her to do him the favor of seeing that his gray was well cared for, as it was the light of his eye.

"What gray is that?" inquired the duchess.

"That ass of mine," replied Sancho. "So that I won't have to mention him by that name, I'm in the habit of calling him 'the gray.' When I first came into the castle, I asked this lady duenna to look after him, and she was as angry about it as if I had said she was old or ugly, though it ought to be more fitting and proper for duennas to feed the beasts in the stable than to pose in halls of state. There was a certain gentleman in my village—Heaven help me, how he had it in for those ladies!"

"He must have been some clown or other," said Doña Rodríguez. "If he had been a gentleman and wellborn, he would have placed them in his estimation higher than the horns of the moon."

"Come now," said the duchess, "that will do for the present. Be quiet, Doña Rodríguez, and let Señor Panza rest easy and leave the care of his gray to me. Seeing that the ass is his precious jewel, I will put it on the apple of my eye."

"He will do well enough in the stable," said Sancho, "since neither he nor I is worthy of being on the apple of your Highness's eye for a single moment, and I would as soon stab myself as consent to it; for although my master says that in the matter of courtesies it is better to lose by a card too many than a card too few,[23] when it comes to beastly and asinine civilities,[24] we must be careful to steer a middle course."

"Take him along with you to your government, Sancho," said the duchess. "There you'll be able to feast him as much as you like, and you can even pension him off so that he will not have to work any more."

"Do not think, my lady the Duchess," replied Sancho, "that there would be anything so strange in that. I have seen more than one ass go up to a government, and so it would be nothing new if I took mine with me."

The duchess was more delighted than ever with Sancho's amusing conversation, and, having packed him off to bed, she went to tell the duke of what had happened. Between the two of them they arranged to play a famous joke upon Don Quixote, in true knightly style; and, in fact, they carried out a number of jests of that sort which are the best adventures to be met with in this great history.

CHAPTER XXXIV. *Which relates how they found the way of disenchanting the peerless Dulcinea del Toboso, one of the most famous adventures in this book.*

GREAT was the pleasure which the duke and duchess found in the conversation of Don Quixote and Sancho Panza, and being more anxious than ever to play a few jokes upon them that would have all the appearance of adventures, they decided to take what the knight had told them concerning the Cave of Montesinos [1] as their starting point in perpetrating a hoax that should be truly out of the ordinary. What astonished the duchess most of all was Sancho's vast simplicity; for he had come to believe it to be the gospel truth that Dulcinea had been enchanted, though he himself had plotted the whole business.

And so, a week later, having instructed the servants in everything that was expected of them, they proceeded to take Don Quixote on a hunting expedition with as large a retinue of huntsmen and beaters as might have accompanied a crowned monarch. They presented their guest with a hunting suit, and Sancho with another of the finest green cloth, but the knight declined the garment, saying that he would soon be returning to the arduous life of a man of arms and did not wish to carry with him a wardrobe or luggage of any sort. Sancho, however, accepted the gift, meaning to sell it at the first opportunity.

When the appointed day arrived, Don Quixote donned his armor and Sancho trigged himself out; and, mounted on his gray, from which he was unwilling to part despite the fact that they had provided him with a horse, the squire took his place among the troop of beaters. The duchess rode forth in splendid attire, and out of pure courtesy the knight held her palfrey's rein though the duke protested that he should not do so. At length they came to a wood between two very high mountains, and here they took up their various posts and hiding places and spread out along the paths; and then, when all was in readiness, the hunt began, accompanied by such a din of shouting voices, barking dogs, and blaring horns that they could not hear one another speak.

With a sharp-pointed javelin in her hands, the duchess dismounted and posted herself where she knew the boars were in the habit of passing. The duke and Don Quixote did the same, stationing themselves at her side, but Sancho remained behind, seated upon his gray, which he did not care to leave unprotected lest some misfortune should befall it. No sooner were they in position, with the many servants drawn up in a line, than they saw coming toward them, hotly pursued by the hounds and followed by the hunters, a huge boar, gnashing his teeth, grinding his tusks, and scattering foam from his mouth; and immediately upon catching sight of the beast, Don Quixote braced his shield, drew his sword, and went forward to meet it. The duke, armed with a spear, followed the knight's example; and as for the duchess, she would have left them all behind had not her husband restrained her; but Sancho, frightened by the animal's fierce mien, left his gray to shift for itself and ran as fast as his legs would carry him.

Trying in vain to scramble up a tall oak, the unfortunate squire was caught on a branch midway, and as he was struggling to reach the top the bough broke and he fell, only to be hooked by another snag and left hanging there, unable to reach the ground. Finding himself in this plight and perceiving that his green hunting coat was ripping, and, moreover, being afraid that if the boar came that way it might succeed in getting at him, he began screaming so loudly and calling for help so earnestly that all those who heard him without being able to see him thought he must surely be in the teeth of some wild beast.

Finally the boar fell, pierced by the many spears that were thrust in his way; and it was then that Don Quixote, who had heard and recognized Sancho's cries, turned his head and beheld his squire hanging head downward from the oak, with the gray standing close by, for it had been unwilling to forsake its owner in his calamity. (And here Cid Hamete goes on to observe that he seldom saw Sancho Panza without the ass or the ass without Sancho Panza, such was the friendship and loyalty that existed between them.) The knight came up and freed the captive, who, as soon as he was safe on the ground once more, looked at the rent in his hunting coat. It pained him deeply, for that garment was like an ancestral estate to him.

In the meantime, they had slung the mighty boar across the back of a mule and, covering it with branches of rosemary and myrtle, they brought it as the spoils of victory to some large field tents that had been set up in the middle of the wood. Here they found the tables laid and a meal prepared, so sumptuous and so plentiful that it was easy to see the rank and magnificence of the one who had provided it.

"If we had been hunting hares or small birds," remarked Sancho to the duchess as he showed her the rents in his hunting suit, "my coat would never have been in this state. I'm sure I don't know what pleasure there is in waiting for an animal that will be the death of you if he reaches you with one of his tusks. I remember hearing an old song that goes like this:

> *By the bears be thou eaten*
> *as was Favila the famed.*"

"He was a Gothic king," said Don Quixote, "who went out hunting and was eaten by a bear." [2]

"That is what I was saying," replied Sancho, "and I would not have kings and princes put themselves in such danger in exchange for a pleasure which, as I see it, ought not to be one, since it consists in killing an animal that has done no harm whatever."

"That is where you are wrong, Sancho," said the duke, "for the hunting of big game is an exercise that is more becoming in kings and princes, and more necessary to them, than any other. It is an image of war; [3] in it will be found stratagems, wiles, and ambuscades for the purpose of overcoming the enemy in safety; the hunter must endure the greatest cold and the most intolerable heat and must forego ease and sleep, while at the same time his bodily strength is increased, his limbs rendered supple. In short, it is an exercise that harms no one and gives pleasure to many. And the best thing about it is that it is not a diversion for everyone as are other field sports, with the exception of hawking, which also is only for kings and great lords. And so, Sancho, you would do well to change your mind and take up hunting when you become a governor. You will see how worth-while it is." [4]

"Not I," said Sancho. "The worthy governor has broken his leg and cannot leave the house. [5] It would be a fine thing, wouldn't it, if when people went to the trouble of coming to see him on business he was always out in the woods having a good time? That way, the government would go to pot. My word, sir, hunting and such like amusements are for loafers rather than for governors. I mean to amuse myself by playing a game of brag [6] at Eastertime and bowling a little on Sundays and feast days, but hunting doesn't agree with either my constitution or my conscience."

"Please God it may be so, Sancho, for it is a long way from saying to doing." [7]

"Be that as it may," replied Sancho, "pledges don't bother a good paymaster,[8] God's help is worth more than getting up early,[9] and it's the tripes that carry the feet, not feet the tripes.[10] What I mean to say is, that if God helps me and I do what I ought to do with the right intentions, I'll undoubtedly make out better at governing than a gerfalcon. Otherwise, let them put a finger in my mouth and see whether I bite or not."

"May God and all his saints curse you, accursed Sancho!" exclaimed Don Quixote. "As I have said many times before, will the day ever come when I shall hear you talk plainly and coherently without all those proverbs of yours? My lord and lady, your Highnesses had best leave this fool alone, for he will grind your souls between, not two, but a thousand old saws, which he will drag in with as much rhyme and reason as I hope God gives him health—or me, for that matter, if I am foolish enough to listen to them."

"Sancho's proverbs," observed the duchess, "granting that they exceed in number those of the Greek Commander,[11] are not for that reason to be less esteemed on account of their brevity. For my own part, I can say that they give me greater pleasure than others, even when those others are more timely and to the point."

Conversing on such subjects as these, they left the tent and returned to the wood to visit some of the hiding places that had been set up, and thus the day quickly passed and night came, but a night not as bright and tranquil as was to have been expected at that season, for it was midsummer. There was a kind of haze in the air that was a great help to the duke and duchess in carrying out what they had in mind. A little after twilight, just as night was falling, it seemed of a sudden as if the entire wood was on fire; and a moment later, here, there, and everywhere, a countless number of trumpets and other martial instruments were heard, as if many troops of cavalry were passing by, and the light of the fire and those warlike sounds all but blinded and deafened the eyes and ears of the onlookers, and, indeed, of all those that were in the wood.

Then were heard innumerable cries of the kind the Moors give when joining battle,[12] mingled with the blare of trumpets and bugles, the roll of drums, the sound of fifes, all at one and the same time, creating so furious and continuous a din that he could have had no senses who would not have lost them as a result of all this uproar. The duke was astounded, the duchess was amazed, Don Quixote was astonished, Sancho Panza was trembling all over, and even they who knew what the cause of it was were frightened. In the midst of their fear, silence fell upon them as a postilion dressed like a demon passed in front of them, playing upon a huge hollow horn that served him as a bugle and that gave forth a hoarse and terrifying sound.

"Ho, there, brother courier!" cried the duke. "Who are you, where are you going, and what army is that which appears to be passing through this wood?"

"I am the devil," replied the courier in a horrendous voice. "I come to seek Don Quixote de la Mancha. Those whom you see here are six troops of enchanters who are bringing with them in a triumphal car the peerless Dulcinea del Toboso. She is under a magic spell and is accompanied by the gallant Frenchman, Montesinos. They come to inform Don Quixote as to how she, the said lady, may be disenchanted."

"If you are a devil as you say and as your appearance shows you to be, you would have recognized Don Quixote de la Mancha, for he stands here before you."

"In God's name and upon my conscience," said the devil, "I did not take a good look at him. I have so much on my mind that I am forgetting the chief thing for which I came."

"There is no doubt about it," said Sancho, "this demon must be a good man and a good Christian, for if he wasn't, he wouldn't swear by God and his conscience. For my part, I'm convinced now that there are good people even in Hell."

Then, without dismounting, the demon fastened his gaze upon Don Quixote. "O Knight of the Lions," he said, "for I can see you between their claws at this very moment, it is that ill-starred but valiant knight, Montesinos, who has sent me to you to inform you that you should wait for him in whatever place you chance to be, as he is bringing with him the one who is known as Dulcinea del Toboso in order that he may show you what you must do to disenchant her. And since I came for no more than that, I need tarry no longer. May demons like me be with you, and good angels with these gentle folk."

Saying this, he blew upon that monstrous horn of his and turned his back and went away without waiting for an answer from anyone.

They were more astonished than ever now, especially Sancho and Don Quixote: Sancho at seeing how, in spite of the truth, they would have it that Dulcinea was enchanted; [13] while Don Quixote was unable to make up his mind as to whether what had happened to him in the Cave of Montesinos was real or not. He was immersed in these thoughts when the duke spoke to him.

"Does your Grace intend to wait, Señor Don Quixote?"

"Why not?" was the reply. "I will wait here, strong and intrepid, though all Hell should come to attack me."

"If I see another devil or hear another horn like that last one," said Sancho, "I will wait here about as much as I would in Flanders."

Night had closed in by now, and many lights could be seen darting through the wood, just as those fiery exhalations of the earth that appear to us to be shooting stars are to be descried flitting across the sky. At the same time there came a frightening rumble, like that caused by the solid wheels of ox-carts, the strident and constant creaking of which is said to put the wolves and bears to flight if there happen to be any along the way.[14] And this tempest of sound was still further increased when it was discovered that on all four sides of the wood were what really seemed to be four encounters or battles, going on simultaneously: on one side, the dread thunder of artillery; on another, a heavy musket fire. The shouts of the combatants apparently came from close at hand as the battle cry of the Moors rose again in the distance.

In short, the bugles, horns, clarions, trumpets, drums, artillery, muskets, and, above all, that terrifying rumble of wagon wheels created so horrible a tumult that Don Quixote had to summon all his courage in order to endure it. Sancho fell in a faint on the duchess's skirt and she, letting him lie there, ordered them to throw water on his face. This was done, and he came to himself again just as one of the carts with the creaking wheels reached the spot. It was drawn by four sluggish oxen, all of them covered with black trappings. On each of the oxen's horns was a lighted wax taper, and on the bed of the cart was an elevated seat on which sat a venerable old man with a beard that was whiter than snow itself and so long that it fell below his waist. He was clad in a robe of black buckram; for, as the cart was brilliantly lighted, it was easy to see and make out everything that was in it. The oxen were led by two demons, also dressed in buckram, whose faces were so ugly that, once having had a glimpse of them, Sancho shut his eyes that he might not have to look at them a second time.

As the cart came up the old man rose from his seat and cried in a loud voice, "I am Lirgandeo the magician."

And the cart passed on, without his saying another word. It was followed by another of the same sort, and here, too, there was an old man seated upon a throne, who, ordering them to halt the vehicle, cried in a voice that was no less portentous than that of the one who had gone before, "I am the sage Alquife, great friend of Urganda the Unknown." [15] And he, like the other, went his way.

A third cart now passed; but in this case the one who was seated on the throne was not an old man but a large robust fellow with an evil-looking countenance, who, as he reached the spot, rose as the others had done.

"I," he announced in a voice that was hoarser and more devilish than those of his predecessors, "I am Archelaus, mortal enemy of Amadis of Gaul and all his kin." And with these words he was gone.

When they were a short distance away the three carts came to a stop and the monotonous rumble of their wheels was heard no more. Then there came another sound, not a noise this time, but a soothing melody, at which Sancho was greatly relieved, since he took it to be a good sign. He remarked as much to the duchess, from whose side he had not stirred one step.

"Lady," he said, "where there is music there cannot be anything evil."

"Or where there is light and brightness," replied the duchess.

"Fire gives light," said Sancho, "and brightness may come from bonfires, as we see from those all around us, which yet may burn us; but music is always a sign of feasting and merrymaking."

"That remains to be seen," said Don Quixote, who had been listening to all that was said. And he spoke truly, as will be clear from the following chapter.

CHAPTER XXXV. *Wherein is continued the information that Don Quixote received concerning Dulcinea's disenchantment, with other astonishing incidents.*

To THE sound of the pleasing strains they saw coming toward them a cart, one of the kind known as triumphal chariots, drawn by six gray mules with white linen trappings, and on each of them rode a penitent, likewise clad in white, with a lighted wax taper in his hand. This car or chariot was twice, and even three times, as big as those that had gone before, and on top and along the sides of it stood twelve other penitents, in snow-white garb and with their tapers. It was an astonishing and at the same time an awe-inspiring sight. Seated upon an elevated throne was a nymph who wore countless cloth-of-silver veils, all of them glittering with a countless number of embroidered gold spangles, which gave her, if not a sumptuous, at least a showy appearance. Her face was covered with a fine, transparent sendal, the warp of which did not prevent the features of a most beautiful maiden from being discovered. In the light of the many tapers her comeliness was revealed, and her age as well; she was apparently not older than twenty nor younger than seventeen.

Beside the maiden was a figure wearing what is known as a robe of state, which fell all the way down to its feet, while its head was covered with a black veil. When the cart was directly opposite Don Quixote and the ducal pair, the music of the flageolets ceased, and then that of the flutes and harps on the car; whereupon the figure rose up, parted her robe, and, removing the veil from her face, disclosed for all to see the ugly, fleshless form of Death itself, which startled Don Quixote, filled Sancho with terror, and even made the duke and duchess a little afraid. Having risen to its feet, this living Death, in a somewhat sleepy voice and with a tongue that was not quite awake, began reciting the following verses :

> "Merlin am I, who, so the histories say,
> had the devil for a sire (it is a lie
> that with the course of time hath stronger grown).
> The prince of magic, monarch and archivist
> of Zoroastric science, with unfriendly gaze
> I view the ages and the centuries
> that would conceal the deeds of high emprise
> of brave and errant knights, toward whom I bear
> a great affection, always, and esteem.
> For granted that enchanters and their kind—
> sages, magicians, call them what you will—
> are mostly hard of heart, of temper stern,
> my own heart's soft and tender, loving-kind,
> and fond of doing good to one and all.
>
> In Pluto's murky pit I was absorbed
> in contemplation of the mystic shape
> of geometric figures, when there came a voice,
> the grief-filled voice of the ever beauteous

Dulcinea del Toboso without peer.
'Twas then I learned of her enchantment foul
and heard how she had been vilely transformed
from highbred lady into rustic wench.
My pity was aroused, I turned the leaves
of a hundred thousand books of demonic art,
then wrapped my spirit in the frightful shell
of this grisly skeleton and hied me here
to announce the remedy that must be had
for such a sorrow, such a dreadful wrong.

O thou, the pride and glory of all that wear
the knightly coat of adamantine steel,
O beacon-light, north star, pathfinder, guide
of all that would forsake the downy couch
and numbing sleep for the unbearable toil
of bloody combat and a warrior's life!
Be thou forever praised, O valiant one,
O Don Quixote, wise as thou art brave,
La Mancha's splendor and of Spain the star!
To thee I say that if the peerless maid,
Dulcinea del Toboso, is to be restored
to the state that once was hers, it needs must be
that thy squire Sancho on his bared behind,
those sturdy buttocks, must consent to take
three thousand lashes and three hundred more,
and well laid on, that they may sting and smart;
for those that are the authors of her woe
have thus resolved, and that is why I've come.
This, gentles, is the word I bring to you."

"For Heaven's sake!" cried Sancho, "I'd just as soon give myself three stabs as three thousand lashes. To the devil with that kind of disenchanting! I don't see what my backside has to do with it. By God, if Señor Merlin hasn't found any other way of taking the spell off the lady Dulcinea del Toboso, she can go to her grave that way!"

"What!" exclaimed Don Quixote. "I myself will take you, Don Clown stuffed with garlic, and bind you to a tree, naked as when your mother bore you, and I will give you not three thousand three hundred but six thousand six hundred, and so well laid on that you will not be rid of them though you rub yourself as many times as you have been sentenced to have lashes. And say not a word in reply or I will snatch your heart out."

"No," said Merlin when he heard this, "it cannot be that way; for the lashes that the worthy Sancho is to receive must be inflicted of his own free will and not by force. It may be done at any time he chooses, there is no time limit set; but should he wish to spare himself half the pain of this flogging, he may do so by permitting the strokes to be given by the hand of another, even though it be a somewhat weighty hand."

"Neither the hand of another nor my own hand nor weighty nor weighable,"[2] replied Sancho. "No one is going to lay a hand on me. Am I, by any chance, the one that bore the lady Dulcinea del Toboso that my backside should pay for the sins of her eyes? My master, yes, seeing that he's a part of her—for he is always calling her 'my life, my soul,' his 'sustenance and support'—he may, and ought, to flog himself on her account and do everything that is necessary to disenchant her, but as for me, *abernuncio!*"[3]

No sooner had Sancho finished saying this than the silver-clad nymph who accompanied Merlin's ghost stood up and, casting aside her thin veil, disclosed what seemed to all of them a most beautiful face. With a masculine assurance and a voice that was not precisely feminine, she then began speaking directly to Sancho Panza.

"O wretched squire," she cried, "soul of a pitcher,[4] heart of a cork tree, with entrails of flint and pebbles! If, brazen thief, they ordered you to hurl yourself down from a tall tower to the earth below; if they asked you, enemy of the human race, to swallow a dozen toads, two lizards, and three snakes; if they wished you to slay your wife and young ones with a deadly, keen-bladed scimitar—if any of these things were required of you, it would be no wonder if you were squeamish and loath to comply with such commands. But to make so much of three thousand three hundred lashes, when every charity schoolboy,[5] poor lad, receives as many every month, is enough to amaze and confound the bowels of compassion in all those who hear of such a thing or who may come to know of it in the course of time.

"O miserable, hardhearted animal!" she went on, "turn those red-owl's eyes of yours—turn them, I say, upon mine, which have been compared to gleaming stars, and you will behold the tears flowing in rivulets, making furrows, tracks, and bypaths in the fair fields of my cheeks. Does it not move you, O crafty, ill-intentioned monster, that the flower of my youth (for I am still in my teens, being a little under twenty) should thus be consumed and wither away beneath the rude bark of a country wench? If I do not appear in such a shape at this moment, that is owing to the special favor which Señor Merlin, here present, has done me, with the sole thought that my beauty might soften your heart. For the tears of a lovely woman in affliction have power to turn stony cliffs into cotton and tigers into ewe lambs. Lay on, then, lay on, O untamed beast! Flay that coarse hide of yours; rouse that energy that you possess but that inclines you only to eat and eat again; and set at liberty my own smooth flesh, my loving disposition, my beautiful face. If for my sake you will not relent or come to reason, do so for that poor knight at your side—I mean, your master. I can see his heart right now, it is stuck in his throat not ten fingers from his lips and only awaits your yielding or unyielding reply to leap forth from his mouth or go back to his stomach."

At this point, Don Quixote felt his throat and turned to the duke. "By God, sir," he said, "Dulcinea has spoken the truth. My heart *is* stuck in my throat, like a crossbow nut."

"What do you say to that, Sancho?" asked the duchess.

"I say, my lady," he answered her, "just what I have said: so far as lashes are concerned, *abernuncio!*"

"*Abrenuncio,* you mean to say, Sancho," the duke corrected him.

"Let me alone, your Highness," replied the squire. "I'm in no humor for fine points just now and can't be bothered by a letter more or less. Those lashes that they are to give me or that I have to give myself have got me so upset that I don't know what I'm saying or doing. But what I'd like the lady to tell me—my lady Dulcinea del Toboso—is where she learned that way of asking for a favor. She comes to ask me to lay my flesh open, and she calls me a soul of a pitcher and an untamed beast and a string of other foul names that the devil himself wouldn't stand for. Am I made of brass, do you think? What difference is it to me whether she's disenchanted or not? Does she come bringing me a hamper of fine linen, shirts, handkerchiefs, socks—even if I don't wear 'em—in order to soften me? No, nothing but abuse heaped upon abuse, although she knows that old saying in these parts, 'An ass laden with gold goes lightly up the mountain,' and, 'Gifts break rocks,' and, 'Pray to God and ply the hammer,' [6] and, 'One "take" is better than two "I'll give you's." ' [7]

"And now," continued Sancho, "my master, who ought to stroke my neck and pet me until I turn to wool and carded cotton, says that if he gets hold of me he'll tie me naked to a tree and give me double the number of lashes. You kindhearted people ought to bear in mind that it's not merely a squire but a governor that you're asking to have flogged, just as if it was 'Have a drink with your cherries.' [8] Let them learn, plague take it! Let them learn, I say, how to ask for something in the right way and show they had some bringing-up. They should know that there is a time for everything,[9] and people are not always in a good humor. Here I am, feeling so bad I'm fit to burst at seeing my green coat torn, and they come around asking me to flog myself of my own free will, when I feel as much like doing that as I do like becoming an Indian chief." [10]

"Well, the fact is, friend Sancho," said the duke, "that unless you become softer than a ripe fig, you are not going to have that governorship. It would be a fine thing for me to send to my islanders a cruel governor, with bowels of stone, who would not yield to the tears of damsels in distress or the entreaties of ancient, wise, and powerful enchanters and magicians. The short of it is, Sancho, either you whip yourself, let them whip you, or give up all idea of being governor."

"Sir," replied Sancho, "can't they give me a couple of days to think it over and decide what is best for me to do?"

"By no manner of means," said Merlin. "This matter must be settled here, on the instant, and on this very spot: either Dulcinea goes back to the Cave of Montesinos and her former peasant-girl state, or else she will be conveyed as she is to the Elysian fields, there to wait until the requisite number of lash strokes has been administered."

"Come, good Sancho," said the duchess, "pluck up your courage and show a proper appreciation of your master Don Quixote's bread that you have eaten; for we are all obligated to serve him and gratify his wishes, by reason of his generous nature and high deeds of chivalry. And so, my son, consent to this flogging, let the devil go to the devil, and leave fear to little minds; for, as you well know, a stout heart breaks bad luck." [11]

To this Sancho replied with the following foolish question, addressed to Merlin. "Señor Merlin, will your Grace tell me this: after the devil came running up here to hand my master a message from Señor Montesinos, requesting him to wait here as he, Montesinos, was coming to arrange for Señora Dulcinea del Toboso's disenchantment, what happened, anyway? Up to now we've seen nothing of Montesinos or any of his likes."

To which Merlin's answer was, "The devil, friend Sancho, is an ignorant wretch and a great scoundrel. I sent him to your master with a message, not from Montesinos, but from me; for Montesinos is still in his cave, expecting, or better, waiting for, his disenchantment, for there is still the tail to be skinned.[12] If he owes you anything or you have any business with him, I'll fetch him for you and set him down wherever you say; but for the present the thing to do is for you to consent to this penance, which, I can assure you, will be very good for your soul as well as your body: for your soul on account of the charitable impulse that leads you to submit to it; and for your body because, as I happen to know, you are of a sanguine disposition and a little blood-letting will do you no harm."

"There are a lot of doctors in this world," remarked Sancho. "Even the enchanters are doctors now. But since you all urge me to do it, though I can't see it myself, I am willing to give myself those three thousand three hundred lashes, on condition that I can lay them on whenever I feel like it, without any limit on the days or the time. I'll try to get out of debt as soon as possible, however, so that the world may enjoy the beauty of my lady, Doña Dulcinea del Toboso; for it appears that, contrary to what I thought, she really is beautiful after all. Another condition must be that I am not to be obliged to draw blood with that penance, and if some of the strokes happen to be fly-swatters,[13] they are to be counted just the same. And here's another item: if I should make a miscount, Señor Merlin, who knows everything, is to keep track of them and tell me if I'm giving myself too few or too many."

"It will not be necessary for me to stop you from giving yourself too many," said Merlin, "for when you have reached the proper number, the lady Dulcinea will be immediately disenchanted, and she will be so grateful that she will come to seek out the worthy Sancho and thank and reward him for his good work. So you do not need to worry about too many or too few, since Heaven will not permit me to cheat anyone out of so much as a hair of his head."

"Well, then," said Sancho, "it's in God's hands. I accept my hard luck—I mean, I consent to the penance with the conditions that have been laid down."

No sooner had he said this than the clarions struck up once more, accompanied by a great firing of muskets, and Don Quixote threw his arms about Sancho's neck, giving him a thousand kisses on the forehead and on the cheeks. The duke and duchess and all the bystanders showed that they were very pleased, and as the cart got under way once more the beauteous Dulcinea bowed to the ducal pair and dropped a low curtsy to Sancho.

With this, the merry-smiling dawn hastened her coming, the little flowers in the fields lifted their heads, and the liquid crystal of the brooks, murmuring over their white and gray pebbles, went to pay tribute to the waiting rivers. The earth was joyous, the sky unclouded, the air limpid, the light serene, and each of these things in itself and all of them together showed that the day which was treading on the skirts of morning was to be bright and clear. Satisfied with the results of the chase and with having carried out their intention so cleverly and successfully, the duke and duchess now returned to their castle with the object of following up the jest which had thus been begun, as there was no serious occupation that gave them greater pleasure than this.

CHAPTER XXXVI. *Wherein is related the weird and never-before-imagined adventure of the Distressed Duenna, otherwise known as the Countess Trifaldi, together with a letter that Sancho Panza wrote to his wife, Teresa Panza.*

THE duke had a major-domo who was of a very jovial and playful disposition, and he it was who had impersonated Merlin and made all the arrangements for the adventure that has just been described; he had also composed the verses and had seen to having a page take the part of Dulcinea. And so he now, with the assistance of his lord and lady, proceeded to contrive an episode of the strangest and drollest sort that could be imagined.

The duchess inquired of Sancho the next day if he had as yet begun his penitential task which had to be performed in order to obtain Dulcinea's disenchantment, and he replied in the affirmative, saying that the night before he had given himself five lashes. When she wished to know what he had given them with, he informed her that he had made use of his hand.

"That," she said, "is slapping rather than flogging yourself, and it is my belief that the wise Merlin will not be satisfied with such soft measures. It will be necessary for the worthy Sancho to make himself a scourge with prickles or employ a cat-o'-nine-tails—something that can be felt—for learning enters with blood,[1] and the liberty of so great a lady as is Dulcinea is not to be granted for so small a price. Mark you, Sancho, works of charity that are performed lukewarmly and halfheartedly are of no merit but are, indeed, worthless." [2]

"If your Ladyship," replied Sancho, "will give me some proper kind of strap or scourge, I will lay on with it, so long as it doesn't hurt too much; for I would have you know that, though I am a countryman, my flesh is more like cotton than it is like matweed, and it would not be a good thing for me to ruin myself for another's gain."

"So be it," said the duchess. "I will give you tomorrow a scourge that will suit you nicely, one that will accommodate itself to your tender flesh like a sister."

"Lady of my soul," Sancho said to her at this point, "I would have your Highness know that I have a letter written to my wife, Teresa Panza, giving her an account of everything that has happened since I left her. I have it here in my bosom; all it lacks is an address. I would have your learned Highness read it, for it seems to me to be in true governor style, I mean, the way governors ought to write."

"And who composed it for you?" inquired the duchess.

"I composed it myself, sinner that I am," replied Sancho.

"And did you write it out yourself?"

"That I did not, for I can neither read nor write, though I can sign my name."

"Let us have a look at it," said the duchess. "I am certain that it shows the quantity and quality of your wit."

Sancho drew out an unsealed letter and handed it to her. It read as follows:

SANCHO PANZA'S LETTER
TO TERESA PANZA, HIS WIFE

Though they gave me many good lashes, I went mounted like a fine gentleman;[3] if I have got a good government, it is costing me a good flogging. You will not understand this for the present, my Teresa, but later you will hear all about it. I want you to know, Teresa, that I have made up my mind you are to go in a coach; that is how you ought to go, for any other way of traveling is but creeping on all fours. You are a governor's wife now; see that no one treads on your heels! [4] I am sending you here a green hunting suit that my lady the duchess gave me; you can alter it so that it will make a petticoat and bodice for our daughter.

Don Quixote, my master, according to what I hear in these parts, is a madman with good sense, and a crackbrain who amuses people, and I don't lag behind him. We have been in the cave of Montesinos, and Merlin the magician has laid hold of me for the disenchantment of Dulcinea del Toboso, who down our way is known as Aldonza Lorenzo. With three thousand three hundred lashes minus five that I have to give myself, she will be as much disenchanted as the mother that bore her. Do not say anything about this to anyone; for if you show your privates to other people, some will say they are white and others will make them out to be black. [5]

In a few days from now I will be setting out for my government, where I go with a great desire to make money, which they tell me is the case with all new governors. I will see how things are and will let you know whether you are to come and be with me or not. The gray is well and sends you his warm regards. I don't mean to part with him even though they take me away to be Grand Turk. My lady the duchess kisses your hand a thousand times, so you must return it with two thousand; for, as my master says, there is nothing that costs less or comes cheaper than good manners. God has not seen fit to provide me with another valise containing eight hundred crowns as He did some time ago, but don't let that worry you, Teresa mine, for the bell-ringer's in a safe place, [6] and so far as the government is concerned, it will all come out in the wash. [7] The only thing is, I am told that after I once try it I'll be eating my hands off for it, [8] and if that is the case, it will not come so cheap after all, though, to be sure, the maimed and the crippled have their benefice [9] in the alms that they beg. And so, one way or another, you are going to be a rich woman and a lucky one. God give you luck the best way He can and keep me to serve you. From this castle, the twentieth of July 1614.

Your husband, the governor,

SANCHO PANZA

"In a couple of respects," said the duchess, when she had finished reading the letter, "the worthy governor goes a little astray. In the first place, he states that this governorship was bestowed upon him in return for the strokes that he is to give himself, when he knows very well—and he cannot deny it—that my lord the duke had promised it to him before that flogging was ever thought of. And in the second place, he shows himself to be too covetous; I would not have him be a gold-seeker,[10] for avarice bursts the bag,[11] and where there is an avaricious governor there is ungoverned justice."

"I don't mean it that way," said Sancho, "but if your Highness thinks that the letter is not what it should be, there is nothing to do but tear it up and write another, which may be an even worse one if it's left to my gumption."

"No, no," protested the duchess, "this one is very good, and I wish the duke to see it."

With this, they repaired to a garden where they were to dine that day, and the duchess showed Sancho's letter to the duke, who was exceedingly amused by it. When they had finished their repast and the cloth had been removed, they found entertainment for a while in listening to the squire's delightful conversation; and then, of a sudden, the melancholy notes of a fife and the hoarse, discordant roll of a drum fell upon their ears. They were all startled by this martial air which was at the same time so dull and mournful-sounding, especially Don Quixote, who was so excited he could not remain seated. As for Sancho, there is nothing to be said except that fear took him to his accustomed refuge, at the duchess's side or on the edge of her skirts; for, without any exaggeration, that sound was a most depressing one.

As they waited in suspense, they saw coming toward them through the garden two men clad in mourning robes so long and flowing that they trailed upon the ground; and these two were beating large drums, which were likewise covered in black. At their side came the fife player, a pitch-black figure like the others, and the three of them were followed by an individual of gigantic size, wrapped rather than clad in a gown that was the blackest of all, with a skirt of enormous dimensions. Over his gown this personage wore a wide baldric of the same hue, from which dangled a huge scimitar, with black scabbard and trimmings. His face was covered with a dark veil through which could be glimpsed a very long snow-white beard. He strode forward to the sound of the drums with the utmost dignity and composure; and the effect of it all—his size, his bearing, his somber appearance, and his retinue— was to fill with amazement those who beheld him without knowing who he was.

Clad in this manner and with the slow and measured pace that has been described, the figure in black came up and knelt before the duke, who with the others was standing to receive him. The duke, however, would not permit him to speak until he had risen. The monstrous scarecrow did so, and as he rose he cast aside the veil from his face, revealing the most terrifyingly long, white, and bushy beard that human eyes had ever seen. He then brought forth from the depths of his broad, capacious chest a grave and sonorous voice, and, fixing his eyes upon the duke, he began speaking:

"All-highest and mighty lord, I am called Trifaldín [12] of the White Beard, squire to the Countess Trifaldi, otherwise known as the Distressed Duenna, on whose behalf I bring your Highness a message. She beseeches your Magnificence to be pleased to grant her authority and permission to come in person and tell you of her plight, which is one of the strangest, most astonishing cases that could be conceived, even by those who are most familiar with the afflictions of this world. To begin with, she would know if that valiant and never-conquered knight, Don Quixote de la Mancha, is in this castle; for she has come on foot to seek him, without once breaking her fast, all the way from the kingdom of Candaya [13] to this your realm, a thing which may and deserves to be looked upon as a miracle, or else as something due to the power of magic. She is now at the gate of this fortress or country-seat and only awaits your pleasure that she may enter. I have spoken." [14]

The speaker coughed and stroked his beard from top to bottom with both hands as he calmly waited for the duke's reply.

"Squire Trifaldín of the White Beard," said the duke, "it is now many days since we heard of the plight of my lady, the Countess Trifaldi, whom the enchanters have caused to be known as the Distressed Duenna. You may bid her enter, O marvelous squire, and you may inform her that the valiant knight, Don Quixote de la Mancha, is indeed here, in view of whose generous disposition you may safely promise her all aid and protection; and you may further say to her that if my own assistance should be needed, it will not be lacking, for that is no more than my duty as a knight requires of me, a knight being bound to show favor to all women, and especially to widowed dames who have been wronged and are in distress as her Ladyship appears to be."

Hearing these words, Trifaldín bent one knee to the ground; and then, making a sign for the fife player and the drummers to strike up, he left the garden at the same slow and solemn pace with which he had entered it.

They all wondered at his presence and composure, and, turning to Don Quixote, the duke said, "O famous knight, when all is done the shades of malice and of ignorance cannot cover over or obscure the light of valor or of virtue. What leads me to say this is the fact that it is barely a week that your Excellency has been in this castle, yet already the unhappy and the afflicted are coming from far and out-of-the-way lands to seek you; and they come not in coaches of state or upon drome-daries, but on foot and fasting, being confident that they will find in that exceeding brave arm of yours the remedy for all their woes and troubles, thanks to your great exploits which are famed throughout the known world."

"I only wish, Señor Duke," replied Don Quixote, "that it were pos-sible for that blessed priest I had at my table not long ago to be here now, the one who was so ill-humored toward knights-errant and held such a grudge against them. I should like him to see with his own eyes whether or not knights-errant are needed in this world. He would at least be able to perceive, and at first hand, that those who are suffering extraordinary afflictions, those who are prey to some tremendous sor-row, do not come for a remedy to the houses of the learned, nor to the village sacristan, nor to the gentleman who never has set foot beyond the bounds of his village, nor to the idling courtier who is more inter-ested in news that he may talk about and pass on to others than he is in performing deeds and exploits which others may relate and set down in writing. It is, rather, in the persons of knights-errant that relief for the afflicted, succor for those in need, protection for damsels, and con-solation for widows are to be found. I thank Heaven with all my heart that such a knight am I, and any hardship or misfortune that may come to me in the exercise of so honorable a profession I look upon as well worth while. Let this dame come and ask what she may; I will set her at liberty through the strength that lies in my arm and in the undaunted resolution of my stout heart."

CHAPTER XXXVII. *In which is continued the famous adventure of the Distressed Duenna.*

THE duke and duchess were greatly pleased to see how Don Quixote had fallen in with their plan; and then Sancho spoke up.

"I hope," he said, "that this lady duenna will not put anything in the

way of my getting that government that has been promised me; for I
have heard a Toledo apothecary, who talked like a linnet, say that
whenever duennas were mixed up in something, nothing good could
come of it. God help me, but how he did have it in for them, that
apothecary! From which my conclusion is that, since all duennas, no
matter what their station or walk in life, are busybodies and nuisances,
what must they be like when they are distressed, as they say this
Countess Three Skirts,[1] or Three Tails, is? For in my country skirts and
tails, tails and skirts, it's all one and the same thing."

"Be quiet, friend Sancho," said Don Quixote; "for, seeing that this
lady, the duenna, comes from distant lands to seek me, she cannot be
one of those that the apothecary had in mind; especially since she is a
countess, for when countesses serve as duennas, that means that they
wait upon queens and empresses, but in their own houses they are great
ladies themselves with other duennas to act as their servants."

Doña Rodríguez, who was among those present, now put in her
word. "My lady the Duchess," she said, "has in her service duennas
who might well have been countesses, if fate had so willed it. However,
laws go as kings like,[2] and let no one speak ill of duennas, particularly
those elderly maiden ones; for although I am not one myself, I can see
the advantage which a maiden duenna has over a widow, but he who
clipped us kept the scissors." [3]

"For all of that," said Sancho, "when it comes to duennas, there's
so much to be clipped, according to what my barber [4] tells me, that it
would be better not to stir the rice even though it sticks." [5]

"Squires," observed Doña Rodríguez, "are enemies of ours; and since
they haunt the antechambers and keep an eye on us every minute when
they're not saying their prayers, which is often enough, they spend
their time whispering about us, digging up our bones, and burying our
reputations. But I can inform these walking logs that we mean to go
on living in spite of them, and in great houses at that, even though we
die of hunger and cover our flesh, whether delicate or not, with a black
mourning robe, just as one covers over and conceals a dunghill with a
carpet on procession day. Faith, and if it were permitted me and time
allowed, I would prove not only to those present but to all the world
that there is no virtue that is not to be found embodied in a duenna."

"I think," said the duchess, "that my good Doña Rodríguez is quite
right; but she will have to wait for another time to fight her battle and
that of the other duennas, to refute the ill opinion that is held of them

by that wicked apothecary, and to root out the prejudice against them in the great Sancho Panza's breast."

But Sancho had an answer for her. "Ever since I had a whiff of that governorship," he said, "I'm through with the notions of a squire and don't give a wild fig for all the duennas that there are."

And so the duenna dispute would have continued had they not heard the sound of the fife and drums once more, which told them that the Distressed Duenna was entering the garden. The duchess thereupon inquired of the duke if it would be the proper thing to go out to meet her, seeing that she was a countess and an important personage.

"So far as her being a countess is concerned," remarked Sancho before the duke had a chance to reply, "I am all for your Highnesses going out to meet her, but regarding her as a duenna, I'm of the opinion that you should not stir a step."

"Who asked you to meddle in this, Sancho?" Don Quixote wanted to know.

"Who, sir?" answered Sancho. "I meddle of my own accord, and well I may, as a squire who has learned the forms of courtesy in your Grace's own school, you being the most courteous and best-bred knight that there is in all the world of courtliness. And in these matters, as I've heard your Grace say, as much is lost by a card too many as a card too few,[6] and to the good listener few words."[7]

"Sancho is right," said the duke. "We will see what this countess is like, and we shall then be able to measure out to her the courtesy that is her due."

At this point the fife and drums entered as they had before. And it is here that the author ended this brief chapter to begin another continuing the same adventure, which is one of the most notable to be found in the history.

FOLLOWING the musicians who produced those mournful strains, as many as a dozen duennas began filing into the garden. There were two rows of them, and they were all clad in wide-flowing widow's weeds, apparently made of milled serge.[1] They also wore white hoods of the thinnest cotton cloth,[2] and so long that only the hems of their robes could be seen. Behind these ladies came the Countess Trifaldi with her squire, Trifaldín of the White Beard, leading her by the hand. Her garment was of unnapped baize; and had it been napped, each tuft would have stood out like one of those big Martos chickpeas.[3] The tail or skirt, or whatever you choose to call it, was a three-pointed one and was borne by three pages, likewise in mourning, who with their mistress formed a beautiful mathematical figure with three acute angles.

This led all the beholders to the conclusion that it must be on account of those three points that she was known as the Countess Trifaldi, as one might say: the Countess of the Three Skirts, an opinion that is supported by Benengeli, who asserts that the lady's right name was the Countess Lobuna and that she was so called on account of the many wolves [4] in her country. If they had been foxes instead of wolves, she would have been called the Countess Zorruna,[5] it being the custom in those parts for the nobility to derive their names from the thing or things that were most abundant in their domains. And so this particular countess, in honor of the new fashion in skirts that she had adopted, ceased to be Lobuna and became Trifaldi.

The twelve duennas and the lady came on at processional pace, their faces covered with black veils which were not transparent like Trifaldín's but so heavy as to afford no glimpse of anything beneath them. As soon as the little band had made its entrance, the duke and duchess and Don Quixote rose to their feet, and all the others did the same as they watched the slowly moving procession. The duennas then halted and opened ranks, and the Distressed One advanced, still without letting go of Trifaldín's hand. Seeing this, the ducal pair and the knight stepped forward a dozen paces or so to receive their guest and she, dropping to her knees, thereupon addressed them in a voice that was hoarse and rough rather than fine and delicate.

"May your Highnesses be pleased not to show such courtesy to their manservant—I mean, their handmaiden [6]—for I am too stricken with grief to be able to make a fitting reply, owing to the strange, unheard-of misfortune that has borne away my wits—I know not whither, but it must be very far indeed, seeing that the longer I look for them the farther I am from finding them."

"He would truly be a witless one, Lady Countess," replied the duke, "who from a sight of your person did not at once discern your great worth, which merits the cream of courtesy and the flower of well-bred ceremony." And, taking her by the hand, he conducted her to a seat beside the duchess, who received her with the utmost graciousness.

Don Quixote, meanwhile, was silent, but Sancho was dying to glimpse Trifaldi's face and those of some of her duennas. This, however, was out of the question until the ladies themselves, of their own free will, should choose to disclose their features. A silence having fallen upon all of them, they waited to see who would be the first to break it. It proved to be the Distressed Duenna, with these words:

"O most powerful lord, most beautiful lady, and most discreet bystanders, I am confident that my indescribable woe will meet with a reception no less dispassionate than generous and sympathetic in your valiant breasts; for it is such as to melt marble, soften diamonds, and mollify the most steel-hardened hearts this world can show. But ere it is made public in your hearing,[7] I would have you inform me if there be present in your midst, your group, or company, that knight immaculatissimus, Don Quixote de la Manchissima, and Panza, his squirissimus." [8]

At this point Sancho spoke up before anyone else had a chance to reply. "Panza," he said, "is here, and Don Quixotissimus as well; and so, Distressedissima Duennissima, you may say whatever you pleasissimus, for we are all readissimus and preparedissimus to be of servissimus to you."

Don Quixote then arose and, addressing the Distressed Duenna, spoke as follows:

"If your woe, O grief-stricken lady, admits of any hope of remedy through the valor and strength of arm of any knight-errant, here are my arm and my courage which, though weak and insufficient, are wholly at your service. I am Don Quixote de la Mancha, whose business it is to succor all those who need my aid; and this being the case, as indeed it is, my lady, there is no need of your appealing to our benevolence or seeking to compose preambles; rather, you should tell us your troubles plainly and without any circumlocution, for you have here listeners who, if they cannot give you any help, will lend you at least a sympathetic ear."

Hearing these words, the Distressed Duenna threw herself at Don Quixote's feet and sought to embrace them. "O invincible knight," she cried, "I cast myself down before these feet and legs as before the very bases and pillars of knight-errantry. If I would kiss thy feet, it is because all the remedy for my misfortune hangs and depends upon the steps that they may take, O valiant and errant one whose true exploits leave far behind and eclipse the fabled ones of the Amadises, the Esplandians, and the Belianises!"

Turning then to Sancho Panza, she took his hands and continued, "O thou most loyal squire that ever served a knight-errant, either in the present age or in times past, thou whose goodness is longer than the beard of Trifaldín, my companion, here present! Well mayest thou pride thyself upon the fact that in serving Don Quixote thou art figuratively serving all that host of knights who have borne arms in this world. I conjure thee, by all that thou owest to thine own goodness and loyalty, kindly to intercede for me with thy master that he may show favor to this humblest and most unfortunate of countesses."

"So far as my goodness is concerned, your Ladyship," replied Sancho, "it makes little difference to me whether or not it is as long as your squire's beard; what matters is that my soul should have a good beard and mustache when it comes to leave this world; for whiskers here below I don't give a rap.[9] But without all this flattery and all this begging on your part, I will ask my master to favor and help your Grace in any way he can—he likes me, and, what's more, he has need of me just now in connection with a certain matter. So your Grace may go ahead and unpack your troubles and tell us all about them, leaving the rest of it to us, for we understand one another very well."

The duke and duchess were bursting with laughter at all this, for it was they who had planned the adventure; and they congratulated themselves upon the clever acting of La Trifaldi, who, as she resumed her seat, continued speaking.

"The famous kingdom of Candaya,"[10] she said, "which lies between great Trapobana[11] and the Southern Sea, two leagues beyond Cape

Cómorin,[12] had for its sovereign Queen Doña Maguncia, widow of King Archipiela, her lord and husband, and from their union sprang the Infanta Antonomasia,[13] heiress to the realm. The said Infanta Antonomasia grew up and was reared under my tutelage and direction, for I was her mother's oldest and ranking duenna. By the time she had reached the age of fourteen, her beauty was so perfect that nature's self could not have improved upon it in any particular, nor is it to be supposed that her mind was that of a child. She was, in fact, as intelligent as she was lovely, and with her loveliness there was nothing in this world to compare; and this is still true, unless it be that those envious sisters, the hardhearted Parcae, have severed her life thread; but that I cannot believe, for Heaven would never permit so great a wrong to be done to earth as would be the case if this unripe cluster from the fairest of vineyards were to be plucked before its season.

"Endowed with such beauty as this, which my halting tongue cannot fittingly praise, she was loved by princes, both native and foreign; and in addition to these, there was a certain private gentleman at the court who, trusting in his youth and elegance, his many graces and accomplishments, and his ready and pleasing wit, dared to raise his eyes to this heaven of pulchritude. For—if I am not boring you—I would have your Highnesses know that he played the guitar in such a way as to make it talk, and he was also a poet and a great dancer and could make a birdcage so well that, if worst came to worst, he might have earned his living in that fashion;[14] and these are accomplishments sufficient to lay low a mountain, not to speak of a tender maid.

"However, all his cleverness and grace of manner would have been of little or no avail when it came to reducing the fortress of my young mistress's heart had not the impudent rascal first taken the precaution of subduing me, her guardian. Scoundrel and heartless vagabond that he was, he strove to win my good will and induce me to comply with his wishes, so that I, faithless warden, would hand him over the keys to the castle which it was my duty to guard. The short of the matter is, he flattered me and won me over with the gift of this or that little trinket; but what really brought about my downfall was some verses that I heard him singing one night through a street railing. If I remember rightly, they went like this:

> *From that sweet enemy of mine*
> *is born a woe that wounds my heart,*
> *and what adds torment to its smart:*
> *I must keep silent, make no sign.*[15]

The words of the song were as pearls to me, and the singer's voice sweet as sugar sirup; and ever since then, in view of the evil into which I have fallen through these and other similar verses, I have been led to reflect that poets ought to be banished from well-ordered states, as Plato advised,[16] at least those that write amorous poetry, not couplets after the manner of 'The Marquis of Mantua,'[17] which are the delight of women and children and bring tears to their eyes, but poems containing sharp-pointed conceits[18] that pierce the heart like soft thorns and, like the lightning, wound it while leaving the body sound and clothed.

"Another time he sang:

> Come, Death, so well disguised that I
> thy nearing presence may not feel,
> lest Life should once more on me steal,
> when I find how sweet it is to die.[19]

There were other stanzas and refrains of the same sort, which cast a spell over you when they are sung and hold you fascinated as you read them. And when they condescend to compose a poem of the kind that was once very popular in Candaya and that went by the name of *seguidilla*[20]—ah! then it is that hearts frolic and laughter bursts forth, while the body grows restless and all the senses finally turn to quicksilver. And so I say, my lord and lady, that such troubadours as these should rightfully be banished to the Lizard Islands.[21]

"Yet they, after all, are not to blame, but rather those simple-minded ones that praise them and the foolish girls who believe them. And had I been the good duenna that I ought to have been, I should not have allowed myself to be moved by such labored conceits, nor should I have believed that the poet was speaking the truth when he declared, 'I live dying, burn in ice, tremble in the fire, hope without hope, go and stay,' along with other contradictory conceptions of this sort with which their writings are filled. And when they come to promise the Phoenix of Arabia, the crown of Ariadne, the horses of the Sun, the pearls of the South, the gold of Tibar, and the balsam of Panchaia[22]—it is then that they really let their pens go, seeing that it costs them little to make a promise they never dream of fulfilling.

"But I am permitting myself to wander. Poor me! What folly, what madness, is it that leads me to dwell on the faults of others when there is so much to be said regarding my own? Ah, I was luckless once again! It was not the verses that overcame me but my own simplicity; it was not the music that softened me but my own levity. It was my great ignorance and want of caution that opened the road and cleared the path that Don Clavijo was to tread—for that is the name of the gentleman in question. With me as go-between, he made his way not once but many times into the apartment of my deceived Antonomasia (deceived not by him, but by me). He did this as her true husband; for, though I am a sinner, I otherwise would never have consented even to his touching the edge of her shoe soles. No, no, nothing like that; marriage comes before anything else whenever I have such a business in hand! The only trouble in the present instance was that they were so unequal in rank, Don Clavijo being a mere private gentleman while the Infanta Antonomasia was, as I have said, the heiress to the kingdom.

"For some time this entanglement remained a secret, carefully concealed by the precautions that I took, until I perceived that a certain swelling of Antonomasia's belly was bound to reveal it shortly. Frightened by this, we held a consultation and decided that, before the affair came to light, Don Calvijo should appear before the Vicar and ask for Antonomasia's hand in marriage, by virtue of a written promise to marry him which she had made under my dictation and which was so bindingly worded that not even Samson with all his strength would ever have been able to break it. The proper steps were accordingly taken; the Vicar was shown the agreement and, after hearing her confession, committed her to the house and custody of a highly respectable bailiff."

At this point Sancho put in a word. "So," he said, "in Candaya, too, they have court bailiffs, poets, and *seguidillas*. I swear, the world is the same all over! But hurry up, Señora Trifaldi, for it's getting late and I'm dying to hear the end of this long story."

"I will do so," replied the countess.

CHAPTER **XXXIX** . *In which La Trifaldi goes on with her wondrous and memorable story.*

EVERY word that Sancho uttered delighted the duchess and drove Don Quixote to despair. The latter now ordered his squire to hold his tongue, and the Distressed One then resumed her tale.

"After many questions and answers, with the infanta always standing her ground, never varying from her original declaration, the Vicar finally decided in favor of Don Clavijo and gave the princess to him as his lawful wife, at which the queen, Doña Maguncia, the infanta's mother, was so grieved that within three days' time we had buried her."

"She died, no doubt," put in Sancho.

"Obviously," replied Trifaldín. "In Candaya we do not bury people alive, only the dead ones."

"I, Sir Squire," Sancho answered him, "have seen them, before now, bury a person who had no more than fainted, in the belief that he was dead; and it seems to me that Queen Maguncia ought to have fainted rather than died, for in this life there are so many things that come out all right in the end that she ought not to have felt so bad over the foolish thing the infanta did. If the young lady had married some page or other household servant as many others have done, or so I've heard tell, there'd have been no repairing the damage; but for her to have married such a fine gentleman as you say this one is—well, while it may have been a piece of foolishness, it was not so big a one as you seem to think. For, according to the rules laid down by my master, who is here present and will not let me lie, just as they make bishops out of men of learning, so may knights, especially if they be errant ones, become kings and emperors."

"Right you are, Sancho," said Don Quixote. "A knight-errant, if he has two fingers' worth of luck, has it in his power to become the greatest lord on earth. But let the Distressed Lady go on with her story; for I have an idea that she has yet to tell us the bitter part of this tale that up to now has been a pleasing one."

"What is to come is indeed bitter," replied the countess; "so bitter that by comparison the colocynth is sweet and the oleander savory. The queen, then, died—she did not faint—and we buried her; and no sooner had we covered her with earth and said the last farewell when, *quis talia fando temperet a lacrimis?* [1] over the queen's grave there appeared, mounted upon a wooden horse, Malambruno, Maguncia's first cousin, who is not merely a cruel being but an enchanter as well. In order to punish Don Clavijo for his rashness and avenge his cousin's death, and also out of spite over Antonomasia's stubbornness, Malambruno thereupon, by the exercise of his magic arts, proceeded to cast a spell upon the two of them and left them there upon the grave itself, the infanta having been transformed into a female ape while her lover had become a crocodile made of some unknown metal, with a pillar, also of metal, standing between them, bearing an inscription in Syriac characters that, translated into the Candayan, and now into the Castilian, read as follows:

" 'These two rash lovers shall not regain their former shape until the valiant Manchegan shall come to meet me in singlehanded encounter, since it is for his great valor alone that the fates have reserved this unheard-of adventure.' [2]

"Saying this, he drew forth from its scabbard an enormous broad-bladed scimitar and, seizing me by the hair, pretended that he was going to slash my throat and cut off my head. I was so frightened and distressed that my voice stuck in my throat, but, nevertheless, I forced myself to exert what strength I had, and in a trembling, sorrow-filled voice I pleaded with him so long and in such a way as to lead him to suspend execution of so rigorous a sentence. Finally he had them bring before him all the palace duennas, who are the ladies that you see here; and, after having spoken in exaggerated terms of our offense, holding them all guilty where I alone was to blame, and railing against duennas in general and their evil schemes and plottings, he went on to say that he did not choose to inflict a capital punishment upon us but preferred a more long-drawn-out penalty such as would leave us in a perpetual state of civil [3] death.

"At the very moment, the very instant, that he said this, we felt the pores of our faces opening, as if our countenances were being pricked all over with needle points, and when we put our hands up to see what the trouble was, we found ourselves in the condition in which you see us now."

With this, the Distressed One and all the other duennas raised their veils, revealing faces covered with heavy beards, some red, some black, some white, and some grizzled, at sight of which the duke and duchess feigned astonishment, while Don Quixote and Sancho were truly astounded and all the others present were filled with wonder.

"Such was the punishment," continued La Trifaldi, "which that malign scoundrel, Malambruno, meted out to us, by covering our soft white faces with these coarse bristles. Oh, would to Heaven that he had cut off our heads with that monstrous scimitar of his in place of dimming the light of our countenances with these wool-combings that cover them! For, gentle folk, if we stop to consider the matter—and I wish my eyes could weep like fountains as an accompaniment to what I am about to say; but, alas, I have brooded so long upon our woes and have already wept so many oceans of brine that these orbs are now as dry as beards of wheat, and so I must tell it without tears—as I was saying, then, where is a bearded duenna to go, what father or mother will take pity on her, who will aid her? For even if she have a smooth face, one that has been martyred by a countless variety of cosmetics, it is hard enough to find someone to care for her; and what will happen when she discloses a visage that is like a wood or a thicket? O ye duennas, companions of mine, it was indeed an unlucky moment, an unfortunate hour, when our parents did beget us!"

As she said this, she seemed about to swoon away.

CHAPTER XL. *Of things relating and pertaining to this adventure and this memorable history.*

REALLY and truly, all those who enjoy such histories as this one ought to be grateful to Cid Hamete, its original author, for the pains he has taken in setting forth every detail of it, leaving out nothing, however slight, but making everything very clear and plain. He describes thoughts, reveals fancies, answers unasked questions,[1] clears up doubts, and settles arguments. In short, he satisfies on every minutest point the curiosity of the most curious. O author celebrated above all others! O fortunate Don Quixote! O famous Dulcinea! O droll Sancho Panza! May all of you together and each of you separately live for unnumbered centuries, for the delight and general pastime of your fellowmen!

The history then goes on to inform us that as soon as he saw the Distressed One in a swoon, Sancho Panza spoke up. "By the faith of an honest man," he exclaimed, "and the souls of all the Panzas that have gone before me, I swear that I have never seen nor heard of such an adventure as this, nor has my master ever thought up such a one or told me of anything like it. A thousand devils take you, Malambruno—not that I mean to curse you—for the enchanter and the giant that you are! Couldn't you have found any other kind of punishment for these lady sinners that you had to put beards on them? Wouldn't it have been better for them if you had slit their noses down the middle, even if, as a result of it, they did sniffle when they talked? And I'll bet they do not even have the price of a shave!" [2]

"That is the truth, sir," replied one of the twelve, "we have not the money for that purpose, and some of us accordingly have resorted to the use of sticking plasters; by applying them to our faces and pulling them off with a jerk, we are left as smooth and bare as the bottom of a stone mortar.[3] It is true that we have in Candaya women who go from house to house, removing hair, trimming eyebrows, and making cosmetics,[4] but we, my lady's duennas, never would admit them to our presence, as they have about them the third-rate odor of women who have come down in the world.[5] And so, if Señor Don Quixote does not lend us help, we shall carry these beards to our graves."

"I will pluck out my own beard," said Don Quixote, "in the land of the Moors, if I do not do something about those that you wear."

At this juncture La Trifaldi recovered from her swoon. "The echo of that promise, O valiant knight," she said, "has reached my ears even as I lay in a faint; it is, indeed, the thing that has enabled me to recover my senses. And so I beg you once more, O renowned errant and indomitable lord, let your gracious promise be converted into deeds."

"It will be no fault of mine if there is any delay," was Don Quixote's answer. "Tell me, lady, what it is I have to do, for my stout heart is ready and at your service."

"As it happens," said the Distressed One, "the distance from here to the kingdom of Candaya, if one goes by land, is five thousand leagues, a couple more or less, but if one goes by air and in a straight line, it is three thousand two hundred twenty-seven. I must further inform you of what Malambruno told me: that whenever fate should provide me with a knight who would seek to free me, he himself would send a mount much better and less skittish than those that are to be had for hire;[6] for the mount in question is none other than that same wooden horse upon which the valiant Pierres carried off the beauteous Magalona.[7] This steed is guided by means of a peg that he has in his forehead, which serves as a bridle, and he goes through the air at such a speed that it seems as if the very devils themselves must be carrying him.

"This horse," she went on, "according to ancient tradition, was created by Merlin the Sage. He lent him to his friend, Pierres, who upon his back made long journeys and, as I have said, bore off the fair Magalona, leaving all those that beheld them from the earth gaping with astonishment. He never permitted anyone to make use of the steed unless it was someone he dearly loved or who paid him dearly, and no mortal that we know of, save the great Pierres, has mounted him from that day to this. Malambruno, through his arts, contrived to get possession of him and employs him in the journeys which he is all the time making here and there throughout the world. He is here today and tomorrow in France, and the next day in Potosí and the best of it is, this horse neither eats nor sleeps nor does he have to be shod. Without wings, he ambles through the air so smoothly that his rider can carry a cup full of water in his hand without spilling a single drop; for which reason it was, the fair Magalona was very fond of riding him."

"When it comes to smooth ambling," said Sancho at this point, "give me my gray. He doesn't go through the air, but on the ground I'll back him against all comers."

They all had a good laugh, and then the Distressed One continued, "And this horse that I am telling you of, if Malambruno is of a mind to put an end to our sufferings, will be here in our presence within half an hour after night has fallen; for such, he told me, was to be the sign by which I should know that I had found the champion I was seeking. As soon as I had found him, the mount was to be sent to me with all speed."

"And how many can ride him?" Sancho inquired.

"Two persons," was the reply, "one on the saddle and the other on the crupper. Usually those two persons are a knight and his squire, unless some maiden is being carried off."

"And what is this horse's name?"

"His name," said the Distressed One, "is not that of Bellerophon's horse, which was called Pegasus; nor is it Bucephalus, like that of Alexander the Great's steed; nor Brigliador, as Orlando's mount was known; nor Bayard, after that of Rinaldo of Montalbán; nor Frontino, after that of Ruggiero; nor Bootes or Peritoa, which, they say, were the names of the horses of the Sun; nor is he called Orelia, after the horse on which the unfortunate Rodrigo, last king of the Goths, rode into battle where he lost his life and kingdom."

"I will bet you," said Sancho, "seeing they haven't given him any of the famous names of well-known horses, they never thought of naming him after my master's Rocinante either, though when it comes to an all-around mount, he has it over all those that you have mentioned."

"That is true enough," replied the bearded countess, "but the name that he does have fits him very well; for he is called Clavileño the Swift, due to his being made of wood with a peg in his forehead [8] and the speed at which he travels. And thus, so far as his name goes, he may very well compete with the famous Rocinante."

"I don't mind the name," said Sancho, "but what kind of bridle or halter do you use to control him?"

"I have told you," said La Trifaldi, "that the knight who rides him directs him this way or that by turning the peg. It may be through the air or skimming, one might say sweeping, the earth, or else he may take that middle course that is to be sought out and adhered to in all well-regulated actions." [9]

"That I should like to see," said Sancho, "but to think for one minute that I'm going to mount him, either in the saddle or on the crupper, is to ask pears of the elm tree. [10] A fine thing that would be! Why, it is all I can do to hold on to my gray, seated on a packsaddle that is softer than silk itself; and now they'd have me straddle a wooden crupper without a pad or cushion of any kind! By Heaven, I don't intend to bruise myself to get rid of anyone's beard; let each one shave himself the best way he can, I don't mean to accompany my master on any long journey like that. And, anyhow, I can't help as much with the shaving of those beards as I can with the disenchanting of my lady Dulcinea."

"Yes, you can, my friend," said La Trifaldi. "Indeed, without your presence I do not think we shall be able to accomplish anything."

"In the king's name," cried Sancho, "what have squires to do with the adventures of their masters? Are they to get all the fame for what they accomplish while we do all the work? Body of me! If the historians would only say, 'Such and such a knight brought such and such an adventure to a successful conclusion, with the aid of So-and-So, his squire, without whom it would have been impossible—' But no, they simply write down, 'Don Paralipomenon of the Three Stars accomplished the adventure of the six monsters,' without so much as mentioning the squire, who was present all the time, just as if he didn't exist! And so, ladies and gentlemen, I tell you once more: my master may go alone if he likes, and much good may it do him, but I am going to stay right here, in the company of my lady the duchess; and it may be that when he comes back he will find the lady Dulcinea's affair greatly advanced, for in my leisure moments I mean to give myself a batch of lashes without a hair to cover me." [11]

"Nevertheless," said the duchess, "you will have to go along if necessary, my worthy Sancho; for these are good people that ask it of you, and besides, the faces of these ladies must not remain in such a condition and all on account of your foolish fears. It would indeed be a pity if that were to happen."

"In the king's name again!" exclaimed Sancho. "If he was asked to do this for some modest, retiring damsels or charity girls, a man might venture to put himself to a little trouble; but to ask him to suffer in order to rid duennas of their beards—devil take it, no! I'd rather see them all with beards, from the highest to the lowest and from the most prudish to the most simpering of the lot."

"You certainly have it in for duennas, Sancho, my friend," remarked the duchess. "You seem to be very much of the same opinion as that Toledo apothecary, but, upon my word, you are wrong. There are in my household some most excellent ladies of this sort, and here is Doña Rodríguez, who will not permit me to say anything else."

"Your Excellency may say what you like," replied Rodríguez, "for God knows the truth of every matter, and good or bad, bearded or smooth-faced, we are our mothers' daughters just like other women, and it was God who sent us into this world. He knows why He did so, and I cling to His mercy and not to anybody's beard."

"Well, Señora Rodríguez," said Don Quixote, "and Señora Trifaldi and company, I trust to Heaven to look with favoring eye upon your woes. As for Sancho, he will do as I bid him. Let Clavileño come that I may meet Malambruno face to face; for I can assure you that no razors would shave you ladies as easily as my sword will shave Malambruno's head from his shoulders. God may suffer the wicked for a time but not forever."

"Ah," exclaimed the Distressed One, "may all the stars of the celestial regions gaze down upon you, O valiant knight; may they infuse your heart with courage and prosper your undertaking, that you may be the shield and protector of the downtrodden and much maligned race of duennas, which is abominated by apothecaries, slandered by squires, and made sport of by pages. Woe to the wench who in the flower of her youth would not sooner become a nun than one of us! Ah, how unfortunate we are! Even though we be descended in direct male line from Trojan Hector himself, our mistresses never fail to address us with a *vos* if they think that will make them queens! [12] O giant Malambruno, you may be an enchanter but you keep your promises most faithfully. Send us now the unequaled Clavileño, that our misfortunes may come to an end; for if the hot weather sets in and our beards are with us still, we shall be in a very bad way."

This was said with such feeling as to bring tears from the eyes of all the bystanders, and even from Sancho, who resolved in his heart that he would accompany his master to the end of the world, if it had to be done in order to remove the wool from those venerable countenances.

CHAPTER XLI. *Of the coming of Clavileño, with the conclusion of this long-drawn-out adventure.*

NIGHT came on, and with it the appointed moment at which the famous steed, Clavileño, was to arrive. Don Quixote was uneasy over the animal's delay in making an appearance; for it seemed to him that, if Malambruno was slow in sending the mount, it must mean either that the adventure was reserved for some other knight, or that the enchanter did not dare come forth to engage in single combat. These thoughts were running through his mind, when, lo and behold! four wild men clad in green ivy [1] entered the garden, bearing upon their shoulders a great wooden horse. Having deposited it upon the ground, one of the savages addressed the company.

"Let him who has the courage," he said, "mount this contrivance."

"I am not going to mount," said Sancho, "for I have not the courage, nor am I a knight."

"And let his squire, if he has one," the wild man went on, "seat himself upon the crupper, putting his trust in the valiant Malambruno, for he need fear no other sword or wile of any sort.[2] There is nothing to do but give a twist to this peg on the horse's neck [3] and he will carry them through the air to where Malambruno waits. But lest the great altitude should cause them dizziness, they must cover their eyes until they hear him neigh, which will be the sign that they have reached the end of their journey."

Saying this, they gracefully retired the way they had come, leaving Clavileño behind them. The moment she caught sight of the horse, the Distressed One turned to Don Quixote and, on the verge of tears, said to him, "O valiant knight, the promises of Malambruno are to be depended upon, the steed is here, our beards are growing; and each one of us, by every hair in those same beards, herewith beseeches you to shave and shear us, to accomplish which you have but to mount this horse, along with your squire, and make a happy beginning of your new journey."

"That I will do, Señora Countess Trifaldi," said Don Quixote, "and with right good will. I will not even lose time by looking for a cushion or putting on my spurs, so great is my desire to see you, my lady, and all the other duennas clean-shaven as you should be."

"That I will not do," declared Sancho, "good will or ill will, it makes no difference. If this shaving business can be accomplished only by my getting up on the crupper, my master can very well look for another squire to go with him, and these ladies can find some other way of making their faces smooth again. I am no wizard to go flying through the air like that. What will my islanders say when they hear that their governor is going out for a stroll on the winds? And there's something else: seeing that it is three thousand odd leagues from here to Candaya, if the horse should tire or the giant become vexed, it would take us half a dozen years to get back again, and there won't be isle or islander [4] in the world that will know who I am. It's a common saying that there's danger in delay, and when they offer you a heifer, run with the halter.[5] Begging the pardon of these ladies' beards, St. Peter is very well off in Rome.[6] By which I mean to say, I'm very well off in this house where everyone treats me so well, and whose master, I hope, is going to be so good as to make me a governor."

"Friend Sancho," said the duke, "the island that I promised you is not a movable one, nor is it likely to fly away; it has roots so deeply sunken in the bowels of the earth that it is not to be torn up or so much as budged by a few stout pulls. What is more, you know as well as I do that there is no office of any importance that is not obtained through some sort of bribe, great or small; and what I ask in exchange for this governorship is that you accompany your master, Don Quixote, so that he may be able to bring this memorable adventure to a conclusion. And whether you come back mounted on Clavileño, with all the speed that is to be expected of him, or whether contrary fortune brings you back as a pilgrim, on foot, going from inn to inn, whenever you do return you will find your island where you left it and your islanders with the same desire of having you for their governor that they always had, nor will I have changed my mind on the subject. And so, Señor Sancho, do not doubt the truth of what I tell you, for that would be to do me a grievous wrong when I am so eager to be of service to you."

"Sir," replied Sancho, "you need say no more. I am but a poor squire and do not know how to return such courtesy in the proper way. Let my master mount, then, cover my eyes, pray God for my soul, and tell me if, when we are away up there on high, it is all right for me to call upon Our Lord and ask the angels to protect me."

"You may pray to God or anyone you like, Sancho," said Trifaldi; "for although Malambruno is an enchanter, he is a Christian and very sagacious and circumspect in the practice of his art, taking care not to meddle with other people's concerns."

"Well, then," said Sancho, "God help me, and the Holy Trinity of Gaeta!" [7]

"Since the memorable adventure of the fulling mills," observed Don Quixote, "I have never seen Sancho so frightened as he is now; and if I were as much given to omens as others are, his pusillanimity would shake my own courage a bit. However— Come here, Sancho; with the permission of these ladies and gentlemen I should like to have a couple of words with you."

With this, he led the squire to one side, among some of the garden trees, and there, taking both of his hands, spoke to him as follows:

"You are aware, brother Sancho, of the long journey that awaits us. God knows when we shall return or how much leisure it will allow us; and so I wish you would retire to your room as if you were seeking something that is needed for the road, and there in a twinkling pay something on account toward those three thousand three hundred lashes that you are supposed to give yourself, even if it be no more than five hundred for the present. It will be just so many of them out of the way, and a thing well begun is half done." [8]

"By God," exclaimed Sancho, "your Grace must be out of your mind! As the saying has it, you see me pregnant and you want me a virgin. Here, I'm supposed to go seated on a bare board and you'd have me skin my backside before I start! No, no, your Grace is all wrong. Let us go now and see to shaving those duennas, and when we come back, I give you my word, I'll make such haste to fulfill my obligation that your Grace will be more than satisfied. That is all I have to say."

"Well, my good Sancho," replied Don Quixote, "I shall console myself with that promise; and I believe you will keep it, too, for while you may be a simpleton, you are really a trusty fellow."

"I'm not rusty," said Sancho, "only sunburned; [9] but even if I was a little of each, I'd still keep my word."

With this, they came back to mount Clavileño; and as they did so Don

Quixote said, "Cover your eyes, Sancho, and take your place; for he who is sending us to such far lands cannot be doing it merely to deceive us, inasmuch as there would be little glory for him in thus tricking those who had put their trust in him. And even though everything should go contrary to what I expect, the honor of having undertaken such an exploit is such as no malice could dim."

"Let us go, sir," Sancho answered him, "for the beards and tears of these ladies are more than my heart can bear, and I shall not eat a bite that agrees with me until I have seen them smooth-faced as they were before. Mount, then, your Grace, but be sure to blindfold yourself. If I am to ride the crupper, it is plain that the one in the saddle must be the first to mount."

"That is true enough," Don Quixote agreed. And, taking a handkerchief from his pocket, he asked the Distressed One to cover his eyes very carefully; but no sooner had this been done than he uncovered them.

"If I remember rightly," he said, "I have read something in Vergil about that Trojan Palladium,[10] which was a wooden horse that the Greeks offered to the goddess Pallas, and which, being pregnant with armed knights, was later the ruination of Troy. For this reason, I think it would be a good thing to see what Clavileño has in his belly."

"There is no need of that," said the Distressed One. "I will vouch for him. I know that Malambruno is in no wise treacherous or malicious; and, accordingly, Señor Don Quixote, your Grace may mount without any hesitancy whatsoever, and may it be on my head if anything happens to you."

The knight felt that anything he might say regarding his safety would but cast doubt upon his valor; and so, without any further argument, he mounted Clavileño. Trying the peg, he discovered that it turned very easily; and as he sat there, with no stirrups and his legs hanging down, he looked like nothing so much as a figure in some Roman triumph, painted or woven upon a Flemish tapestry. Against his will and little by little, Sancho climbed up and made himself as comfortable as he could on the crupper, which he found to be quite hard; whereupon he asked the duke if it would not be possible to provide him with a pillow or cushion, even though they had to take one from the couch of my lady the duchess or from some page's bed; for the flanks of this horse seemed to him more like marble than they did like wood.

At this point Trifaldi spoke up, saying that Clavileño would not endure any kind of trappings and that the best thing for the squire to do was to sit sideways so that he would not feel the hardness so much. Sancho did as she advised, and, bidding them farewell, he let his eyes be bandaged. He promptly removed the cloth, however, and, gazing tenderly and tearfully at all those in the garden, begged them to aid him in his present trouble with plenty of Hail Marys and Our Fathers,[11] so that God might provide someone to do the same for them when they should find themselves in such straits.

"Thief," exclaimed Don Quixote, "are you by any chance on the gallows or at death's door that you resort to such entreaties? Are you not, soulless and cowardly creature, in the very spot that the beauteous Magalona occupied and from which she descended, not to her grave, but to become queen of France,[12] unless the histories lie? And I here at your side, am I not on a par with the brave Pierres, who sat in this same saddle where I now sit? Cover your eyes, you spiritless animal, cover them I say, and do not give voice to your fears, at least not in my presence."

"Let them go ahead and blindfold me," said Sancho; "but since you won't allow me to commend myself or be commended to God, is it any wonder if I'm afraid we may be going to some region of devils [13] who will make off with us to Peralvillo?" [14]

When their eyes had been covered and Don Quixote had settled himself to his satisfaction, the knight tried the peg, and no sooner had he laid hands upon it than the duennas and all the others there present began calling out to them, "God guide you, valiant knight! God be with you, intrepid squire! Now, now, you are going through the air, swifter than a dart! Already those below are gazing up at you in astonishment! Try not to sway so much, brave Sancho; see to it that you do not fall, for your fall would be worse than that of the rash youth who sought to drive the chariot of his father, the Sun!"

Sancho, meanwhile, was clinging tightly to his master, with his arms about him. "Señor," he asked, "what do they mean by saying that we are riding so high when their voices can reach us just as plainly as if they were right alongside us?"

"Think nothing of that, Sancho," said the knight, "for such flights as these are out of the ordinary course of events, and at a distance of a thousand leagues you can still see and hear anything you like. And do not squeeze me so much or you will throw me off. There is really no reason for you to be disturbed or frightened, for I can swear that in all the days of my life I never had an easier-going mount. It is as if we never stirred from one spot. Banish all fear, my friend, for the truth is, everything is going as it should and we have the wind to our poop."

"So we do," replied Sancho. "On this side it's as strong as if they were blowing on me with a thousand pairs of bellows."

This was the truth, for a number of large bellows were producing the breeze in question. The whole adventure had been so thoroughly planned by the duke and duchess and their major-domo that not a single essential detail was lacking to make it perfect.

"Without any doubt, Sancho," remarked Don Quixote as he felt the puff, "we must have reached the second aerial region, where the snow and hail are produced; it is in the third region that the thunder and lightning are engendered, and if we keep on ascending at this rate, we shall soon be in the region of fire. I do not know how to control the peg to keep us from mounting so high that the flames will scorch us."

Even as he said this they felt a warmth upon their faces, which came from pieces of tow, easy to ignite and to extinguish, suspended from the end of a reed held at some distance from them.

"May they slay me," said Sancho, "if we're not already in that fiery place, or somewhere very near it, for a good part of my beard is singed already. I've a mind, master, to take a peep and see where we are."

"Don't do that," Don Quixote advised him. "Remember that true story they tell about the licentiate Torralba,[15] whom the devils carried through the air upon a reed, with his eyes shut; in twelve hours' time he arrived in Rome and dismounted at Torre di Nona, which is a street in that city,[16] where he witnessed the rioting, the assault, and the death of Bourbon;[17] and by the next morning he was back in Madrid to give an account of all he had seen. He himself stated that as he was sailing through the air the devil ordered him to open his eyes, which he did, only to discover he was so near the body of the moon that, as it seemed to him, he could put out his hand and take hold of it, and he did not dare look down at the earth or it would have made him dizzy.

"And so, Sancho," the knight concluded, "there is no good reason why we should uncover our eyes, since he who has us in charge will take care of us. It may be that we are merely gaining altitude in order to swoop down upon the kingdom of Candaya as the saker or the falcon does upon the heron, that he may be able to seize the bird no matter how high it may soar.[18] And although it seems to us that it has not been a half hour since we left the garden, believe me, we must have gone a very long way."

"I do not know as to that," said Sancho. "All I can say is that if that Señora Magallanes[19] or Magalona found any pleasure in riding this crupper, she couldn't have had very tender flesh."

The entire conversation of the two brave horsemen was heard by the duke and duchess, who were extremely amused by it; and, wishing to put a finishing touch to this extraordinary and well-planned adventure, they now set fire to Clavileño's tail with some bits of tow, whereupon the horse, which was filled with detonating rockets, at once blew up with a loud noise, hurling Don Quixote and Sancho Panza to the ground half scorched.

By this time the entire band of bearded ladies, La Trifaldi and all the others, had disappeared from the garden, and those that remained lay stretched out on the ground as if unconscious. The knight and his squire rose, rather the worse for wear, and, glancing about them in all directions, were very much astonished to find themselves back in the same garden from which they had started, with all those people prostrate on the earth. And their wonder grew as, at one side of the garden, they caught sight of a long lance that had been thrust into the ground, with a smooth white parchment hanging from it by two silken cords. Upon the parchment, written in large gilt letters, was the following inscription:

The renowned knight, Don Quixote de la Mancha, merely by undertaking it, has finished and concluded the adventure of the Countess Trifaldi, otherwise known as the Distressed Duenna. Malambruno is satisfied in every way,[20] *the faces of the duennas are once more smooth and clean, King Clavijo and Queen Antonomasia have been restored to their former state, and as soon as the squirely flogging shall have been completed, the white dove shall be free of the annoying gerfalcons that persecute it and shall return to the arms of its beloved mate. For it is so ordered by Merlin the Sage, proto-enchanter of enchanters.*

Having read the inscription, Don Quixote understood clearly that it had reference to the disenchantment of Dulcinea; and, giving thanks to Heaven with all his heart that he had been able to achieve so great a deed at so little peril, thus restoring to the venerable but no longer visible duennas their former countenances, he went over to where the duke and duchess lay, still in a state of unconsciousness.

"Ah, my worthy lord," he said, taking the duke's hand, "be of good cheer—be of good cheer, for it is all over now! The adventure is finished and no harm done, as the inscription on that post yonder plainly shows."

Little by little, like one coming out of a deep slumber, the duke recovered his senses, and the same was true of the duchess and all the others there in the garden who had fallen to the ground; and they all gave such evidence of wonder and astonishment as almost to convince anyone who saw them that the thing they pretended so cleverly by way of jest had actually happened to them. The duke read the inscription with half-closed eyes and then threw open his arms to embrace Don Quixote, assuring him that he was the best knight ever seen in any age.

Sancho in the meantime was gazing about in search of the Distressed One, for he wished to see what she looked like without her beard and whether or not she was as beautiful as her gallant exterior appeared to indicate; but they told him that as soon as Clavileño had dropped to the earth in flames, the entire band of duennas, and Trifaldi with them, had disappeared, but that they were already clean-shaven, without a sign of hair on their faces. The duchess then inquired of him how he had made out on the long journey.

"Señora," replied Sancho, "as we were flying through the region of fire, or so my master told me, I wanted to uncover my eyes a little, but when I asked him if I might do so, he would not let me. However, I have a little bit of curiosity in my make-up and always want to know anything that is forbidden me; and so, very quietly and without anyone's seeing me, I lifted the handkerchief ever so little, close to my nose, and looked down at the earth. It seemed as if the whole earth was no bigger than a grain of mustard and the people walking about on it were a little larger than hazelnuts. You can see from that how high up we must have been."

"Friend Sancho," said the duchess, "you had better mind what you are saying. From what you tell me, you did not see the earth at all, but only the people on it; for if the earth itself was like a grain of mustard and each person on it like a hazelnut, then, obviously, one man would have covered the entire earth."

"That is true," Sancho admitted, "but I had a peep at it from one side and saw it all."

"Look here, Sancho," said the duchess, "with a side peep like that you don't see the whole of anything you are looking at."

"I don't know anything about that way of looking at things," the squire answered her, "but I do think your Ladyship ought to bear in mind that we were flying by enchantment, and it was by enchantment that I was able to see the whole earth and all the people on it, no matter which way I looked. And if your Highness doesn't believe me, neither will you believe me when I tell you that, having uncovered my face all the way to the eyebrows, I found myself so close to the sky that there was not a palm-and-a-half's distance between it and me; and a mighty big place it is, my lady, I can tell you that! Then we went through the region where the seven little she-goats [21] are, and, seeing that as a lad I had been a goatherd in my country, the minute I laid eyes on them I felt like getting down and playing with them a bit, and if I hadn't done so I think I would have burst. And so, what do I do? Without saying anything to my master or anybody else, I slip down off Clavileño as quietly as you please and for three-quarters of an hour I have a good time with those goats, which are like gillyflowers,[22] and all the time Clavileño doesn't stir from the spot."

"And while the worthy Sancho was playing with the goats," said the duke, "how did Señor Don Quixote amuse himself?"

It was the knight himself who answered this question. "Since all these things," he said, "all these happenings, are outside the natural order, it is not surprising that Sancho should say what he does. As for myself, I can only state that I looked neither upward nor downward, nor did I behold either the sky or the earth or the sea or the sandy shore. It is true, I was aware that I was passing through the aerial region and was close upon the region of fire; but that we went any farther than that I cannot believe; and inasmuch as the fiery region lies between the heaven where the moon is and the outmost portion of the aerial one, we could not have come to the heaven where the seven young she-goats are, of which Sancho speaks, without being burned, and since we were not burned, either Sancho is lying or Sancho is dreaming."

"I am neither lying nor dreaming," replied Sancho. "If you don't believe me, ask me to describe those goats for you, and you will see whether I'm telling the truth or not."

"Do describe them for us, Sancho," said the duchess.

"Two of them are green, two are flesh-colored, two are blue, and one is a mixture."

"That," said the duke, "is a new kind of goat. Here in our earthly region we do not have such shades—I mean, goats of such hues."

"Naturally," said Sancho, "there is a difference between heavenly goats and earthly ones."

"Tell me, Sancho," continued the duke, "did you see any he-goat among them?"

"No, sir," was the answer, "and I've heard tell that none ever passed the horns of the moon."

They did not care to question him any further regarding his journey, for they perceived that he was in a mood to go rambling all over the heavens, giving them news of everything that went on there without ever having stirred from the garden. In brief, this was the end of the adventure of the Distressed Duenna, one that provided amusement for the duke and duchess all the rest of their lives. As for Sancho, he had something to talk about for ages, if he lived so long.

Don Quixote now came up to him, to whisper in his ear. "Sancho," he said, "if you want us to believe what you saw in Heaven, then you must believe me when I tell you what I saw in the Cave of Montesinos. I need say no more."

CHAPTER XLII. *Of the advice which Don Quixote gave Sancho Panza before the latter set out to govern his island, with other well-considered matters.*

THE duke and duchess were so well pleased with the successful and amusing outcome of the adventure of the Distressed One that they made up their minds to continue with the jest, seeing what a suitable subject they had when it came to accepting the imaginary for the real. Accordingly, having instructed their servants and vassals as to how to behave toward Sancho in the governorship of his promised island, they informed the squire the next day (which was the one following Clavileño's flight) that he was to make ready to go and assume his gubernatorial duties, as his islanders were waiting for him as for the showers of May. Sancho made a low bow.

"Ever since I dropped down from Heaven," he said, "ever since I looked at the earth from up there and saw how little it is, I am not as anxious to be a governor as I was once upon a time. What greatness is there in ruling over a grain of mustard, or imperial dignity and power in governing half a dozen human beings the size of hazelnuts? For there did not seem to me to be any more than that. If your Lordship would be pleased to give me a little bit of Heaven, even if it was no more than half a league, I'd rather have it than the biggest island in the world."

"See here, friend Sancho," replied the duke, "I cannot give anyone a bit of Heaven, even if it were a piece no bigger than your fingernail.

It is reserved for God alone to grant such grace and favors as that. What I can give, I do give you; and that is an island, perfect in every respect, tight and well proportioned and exceedingly fertile, where, if you know how to make use of your opportunities, you may contrive to gain Heaven's riches along with those of earth."

"Very well, then," said Sancho, "let the island come, and I'll do my best to be such a governor that, in spite of all the rascals, I'll go straight to Heaven. It's not out of greed that I want to quit my humble station or better myself; it is because I wish to see what it's like to be a governor." [1]

"Once you try it, Sancho," the duke warned him, "you will be eating your hands off after it,[2] so sweet a thing it is to give orders and be obeyed. You may be sure that when your master gets to be an emperor —as he undoubtedly will, the way things are going for him now— no one will be able to take that office away from him without a struggle, and he will be sick at heart over all the time he lost in not being one."

"Sir," said Sancho, "in my opinion, it is a good thing to be the one to give the orders, if only to a herd of cattle."

"Let them bury me with you, Sancho," said the duke, "if you do not know everything, and I only hope you will be such a governor as your wit seems to promise. But let us leave the matter there. Remember, it is tomorrow that you go to assume the governorship of your island, and this afternoon they will fit you out with the proper apparel and all the other things needed for your departure."

"Let them clothe me any way they like," replied the squire, "for however I go dressed, I'll still be Sancho Panza."

"That is true enough," agreed the duke, "but clothes must be suited to one's rank or dignity. It would not be well, for example, for a jurisconsult to wear the garb of a soldier, or a soldier that of a priest. You, Sancho, will go clad partly as a man of learning and partly as a captain, for in the island that I am bestowing on you arms and letters are equally necessary."

"I don't know much about letters," said Sancho; "in fact, I don't even know my ABC's; but to be a good governor, it's enough for me to be able to remember the Christus.[3] As to arms, I'll handle those that they give me till I drop, and God help me from then on."

"With so good a memory as that," observed the duke, "Sancho cannot go wrong."

At this point Don Quixote came up and, upon hearing that Sancho was to leave so soon for his government, with the duke's permission, took him by the hand and led him to his room, with the intention of advising him as to how he was to conduct himself in office. Having entered the room and closed the door, he almost forced Sancho to sit down beside him, and then, very calmly, he began speaking as follows:

"Sancho, my friend, I thank Heaven with all my heart that good Fortune should have come your way before I have met with her. I had counted upon my luck to enable me to pay you for your services, but here am I at the beginning of my adventures while you, ahead of time and contrary to all reasonable expectation, are seeing your desires fulfilled. Some there be that count upon bribery, importunity, begging, early rising, entreaties, and pertinacity, and still do not attain what they seek; and then some other will come along and, without knowing the why or wherefore of it all, will find himself in the place and office that so many covet. Here it is that the common saying fits in well, to the effect that there is good luck and bad luck in all the strivings of men. You to my mind are beyond any doubt a blockhead, you neither rise with the sun nor keep nightly vigil, you are not industrious, and yet, as a result of the mere breath of knight-errantry that has been breathed upon you, you find yourself without more ado the governor of an island, as if it were nothing at all.

"I say all this, Sancho, in order that you may not attribute to your own merits the favor you have received. Rather, you should give thanks to Heaven for its beneficence, and, after that, to the great profession of knight-errantry for the potentialities inherent in it. Having, then, disposed your heart to believe what I have said to you, be attentive, my son, to this your Cato,[4] who would counsel you and be the guiding star that leads you to a safe harbor as you set forth upon the storm-tossed sea[5] that is now about to engulf you; for office and high trusts are nothing other than a deep abyss of trouble and confusion.

"First of all, my son, you are to fear God; for therein lies wisdom,[6] and, being wise, you cannot go astray in anything. And in the second place, you are to bear in mind who you are and seek to know yourself, which is the most difficult knowledge to acquire that can be imagined. Knowing yourself, you will not be puffed up, like the frog that sought to make himself as big as the ox.[7] Do this, and the memory of the fact that you once herded pigs in your own country will come to serve as the ugly feet to the tail of your folly."[8]

"That is true," said Sancho, "but it was when I was a lad. Afterward, as a young fellow, it was geese, not pigs, that I guarded. But I

can't see what all this has to do with the case. Not all those that govern come from the race of kings."

"You are right," replied Don Quixote, "and for that very reason those
who are not of noble origin should be suave and mild in fulfilling the
grave duties of their office. In this way they will be able to free themselves of that malicious gossiping to which no station in life is immune.
Look to humility for your lineage, Sancho, and do not be ashamed to
say that you come of peasant stock, for when it is seen that you do
not blush for it, no one will try to make you do so. Pride yourself more
on being a good man and humble than on being a haughty sinner. The
number of persons of lowly birth who have gone up to the highest
pontifical and imperial posts is beyond counting; by way of proving
the truth of this, I could give you so many examples that it would tire
you to listen to them.

"Remember, Sancho, that if you employ virtue as your means and
pride yourself on virtuous deeds, you will have no cause to envy the
means possessed by princes and noble lords; [9] for blood is inherited but
virtue is acquired,[10] and virtue by itself alone has a worth that blood
does not have. This being the case, as indeed it is, if perchance one of
your relatives should come to your island to visit you, do not neglect or
offend him, but rather receive, welcome, and entertain him. By so
doing, you will be pleasing Heaven, which does not like anyone to
despise what it hath wrought, and at the same time you will be acting
in accordance with the laws of your own better nature.

"Should you bring your wife to be with you—and it is not well for
those in government to be long without their womenfolk—teach and
instruct her and smooth down her native roughness; for all that a wise
governor may acquire, a foolish and boorish wife may well squander
and lose for him. In case you become a widower (a thing that may
happen), by virtue of your office look for a better consort. Do not take
one to serve you merely as a hook and fishing rod or as a friar's hood for
the receiving of alms; [11] for, of a truth I tell you, all that the judge's
wife receives her husband will have to account for on Judgment Day,
when he will have to make in death a fourfold payment for things that
in life meant nothing to him.

"Never be guided by arbitrary law, which finds favor only with the
ignorant who plume themselves on their cleverness. Let the tears of the
poor find more compassion in you, but not more justice, than the testi-
mony of the rich. Seek to uncover the truth amid the promises and gifts

of the man of wealth as amid the sobs and pleadings of the poverty-stricken. When it is a question of equity, do not bring all the rigor of the law to bear upon the delinquent, for the fame of the stern judge is no greater than that of the merciful one. If the rod of justice is to be bent, let it not be by the weight of a gift but by that of mercy. When you come to judge the case of someone who is your enemy, put aside all thought of the wrong he has done you and think only of the truth. Let not passion blind you where another's rights are concerned, for the mistakes you make will be irremediable, or only to be remedied at the expense of your good name and fortune.

"If some beautiful woman come to you seeking justice, take your eyes from her tears, listen not to her moans, but consider slowly and deliberately the substance of her petition, unless you would have your reason drowned in her weeping and your integrity swept away by her sighs. Abuse not by words the one upon whom punishment must be inflicted; for the pain of the punishment itself is enough without the addition of insults. When a guilty man comes under your jurisdiction, remember that he is but a wretched creature, subject to the inclinations of our depraved human nature, and insofar as you may be able to do so without wrong to the other side, show yourself clement and merciful; for while the attributes of God are all equal, that of mercy shines brighter in our eyes than does that of justice.

"If you observe these rules and precepts, Sancho, your days will be long, your fame will be eternal, rewards will be heaped upon you, indescribable happiness shall be yours, you will be able to marry off your children as you like, your children and your grandchildren will have titles to their names, you will live in peace with all men, and in your last days death will come to you amid a ripe and tranquil old age, and the gentle, loving hands of your great-grandchildren will tenderly close your eyes.

"What I have said to you thus far has been in the nature of instructions for the adornment of your soul. Listen now to those that will serve you where your body is concerned."

CHAPTER XLIII. *Of the further advice which Don Quixote gave to Sancho Panza.*

WHO, upon listening to the foregoing speech of Don Quixote's, would not have taken him for a very wise person, one whose wisdom was exceeded only by his integrity? It has frequently been remarked in the course of this great history that it was only when he came to touch upon the subject of chivalry that the knight talked nonsense and that when any other topic was under discussion he showed himself to be possessed of a clear-seeing, unfettered mind, the result being that his deeds were all the time contradicting his own best judgment and his judgment his deeds. And so, in the course of these further instructions that he gave Sancho, marked by a lively play of fancy, he carried to a high pitch both his good sense and his folly.

Sancho listened to it all most attentively, seeking to commit to memory the counsels thus given him, as if to preserve them for future use that he might make a success of his governorship.

"As to your own person, Sancho, and the mode of ruling your household," Don Quixote continued, "the first thing to bear in mind is that you must be neat-appearing. Remember to trim your nails, and do not let them grow as some do who in their ignorance have been led to believe that long fingernails make the hands look beautiful, just as if that growth, that excrescence, that they neglect to cut were really a nail and not rather the claw of a lizard-catching kestrel.[1] This, I may tell you, is a filthy and unnatural abuse. Another thing, Sancho: do not go with your girdle loosened and your garments slack; for slovenly attire is the sign of a disorderly mind, unless such carelessness is deliberate, as is believed to have been the case with Julius Caesar.[2]

"Be sure to ascertain very carefully just what the revenues of your office are, and, if they suffice for the purpose, provide your servants with respectable and serviceable, rather than showy and brilliant, liveries. And what is more, divide the liveries between your servants and the poor; by which I mean to say: if you have three pages to clothe, see that you clothe three of the poor also, and in that way you will have pages both in Heaven and on earth. This is a new mode of bestowing liveries and one that is beyond the conception of the vainglorious.

"Eat neither garlic nor onions that your breath may not betray your rustic origin.[3] Walk slowly and speak with deliberation, but not in such a manner as to give the impression that you are listening to yourself; for all affectation is bad.[4] Eat sparingly during the day and have a light supper,[5] for it is in the workshop of the stomach that the health of the entire body is forged. Be temperate in your drinking, remembering that he who imbibes too much wine keeps neither secret nor promise. And take care, Sancho, not to roll your food from one cheek to the other or to eruct in front of anyone."

"I don't know what you mean by *eruct*," said the squire.

"To *eruct*, Sancho, is the same as to belch, which is one of the most unpleasant words in our Castilian tongue, although an expressive one.[6] For this reason, those that are careful of their choice of language, in place of 'belch' and 'belchings,' say 'eruct' and 'eructations.' If someone fails to understand these terms, it makes little difference; in the course of time they will come to be readily understood and thus the language will be enriched, for it is determined by popular usage." [7]

"In truth, sir," said Sancho, "that is one bit of advice that I mean to remember: not to belch; for I do it very often."

"Eruct, Sancho, not belch," Don Quixote corrected him.

"Eruct I will say from now on," replied Sancho; "I give you my word, I won't forget."

"Also, Sancho, you must not introduce such a host of proverbs into your conversation; for although proverbs are concise maxims, you very often drag them in by the hair of the head, with the result that they sound more like nonsense than wisdom."

"That is something only God can remedy," said Sancho; "for I know more old sayings than would fill a book, and when I start to speak they all come rushing into my mouth at once, fighting with one another to get out, and so, what happens is, my tongue throws out the first ones it gets hold of, whether or not they are to the point. But I'll remember after this to use the ones that are suited to the dignity of my office; for in the house where there is plenty supper is soon on the table,[8] and he who binds does not wrangle,[9] and the bell-ringer's in a safe place,[10] and keeping and giving call for brains." [11]

"That's it, Sancho!" cried Don Quixote. "Go on threading and stringing and coupling your proverbs, there is no one to stop you! My mother whips me and I keep right on.[12] I have just done telling you that you should avoid proverbs, and here in a moment you have let go with a

whole litany of them that, so far as what we are talking about is concerned, are over the hills of Ubeda.[13] Mind you, Sancho, I do not say that
a proverb aptly brought in is not all right, but when you overload your
speech with them and string them together helter-skelter, it makes your
conversation dull and vulgar.

"But to continue: When you mount your horse, do not throw the
weight of your body against the back of the saddle nor ride with your
legs held stiffly, straight out in front of you or away from the horse's
belly; and, on the other hand, do not sit so limply that it will seem as if
you were astride your gray. The way they ride makes gentlemen of
some and grooms of others.

"Observe moderation in the matter of sleep, for he who is not up with
the sun does not make the most of the day. Bear in mind, Sancho, that
diligence is the mother of good fortune,[14] and sloth, its contrary, never
yet achieved anything worth while.

"There is one more piece of advice which I should like to give you,
and—although it does not have to do with the care of your person—I
wish you would be sure to remember it, as I think it will be no less useful
to you than the counsels I have already imparted to you. It is this: that
you never become involved in a discussion of family trees, at least not
when it is a matter of comparing one with another; for, of necessity, one
of the two will have to be better than the other, and you will be hated
by those whose lineage you have disparaged, while those whose ancestry
you have exalted will in no wise reward you.

"As for your dress, you should wear full-length hose, a long jacket,
and a cloak that is a little longer still; and by all means eschew Grecian
wide-breeches, for they are becoming neither to gentlemen nor to governors.

"For the present, that is all that I think of, Sancho, in the way of advice. As time goes on and the occasion arises, I will send you further
instructions if you will take care to keep me informed of the state of
your affairs."

"Sir," replied Sancho, "I can see very plainly that all the things your
Grace has said to me are good, holy, and profitable, but of what use
are they going to be if I do not remember a single one of them? True,
what you told me about not letting my nails grow and about marrying
again if I have a chance will not slip out of my noddle; but as for all
that other mess of hash, I don't remember, nor will I remember, any
more of it than I do of last year's clouds. And so you will have to put
it down in writing for me. While I may not be able to read or write, I

will give it to my confessor so that he can run over it with me and hammer it into my head whenever necessary."

"Ah, sinner that I am!" exclaimed Don Quixote. "How bad it looks for governors not to be able to read and write! For I would have you know, Sancho, that when a man cannot read or is left-handed, it points to one of two things: either he comes of exceedingly mean parentage, or else he himself is of so wayward a disposition that good companionship and good training are wasted upon him. That is a grave shortcoming on your part, and for that reason I would have you at least learn to sign your name."

"I can sign my name well enough," said Sancho. "When I was steward of the confraternity in my village I learned to make certain letters such as they use in marking bundles and which, so they told me, spelled out my name. And, anyway, I can always pretend that my right hand is crippled and have someone else sign for me; for there's a remedy for everything except death,[15] and, seeing that I'm in command and hold the rod, I can do anything I like. 'He whose father is a judge—' you know.[16] And I'll be a governor, which is higher than a judge; so come on and see! Let them make fun of me and slander me; let them come for wool and go back shorn.[17] For whom God loves, his house knows it,[18] and the silly sayings of the rich pass for maxims in this world.[19] Being a governor, I'll be rich, and I mean to be generous at the same time; and that way no one will find any fault with me. Only make yourself some honey and the flies will come to suck you, as much as you have so much are you worth,[20] as my grandmother used to say, and there's no way of getting even with a man of means."[21]

"May God curse you, Sancho!" cried Don Quixote at this point. "May sixty thousand devils carry you off, and your proverbs with you! For an hour now you have been stringing them, and every one is a torture to me. I can assure you that these sayings of yours will one day bring you to the gallows; on account of them your vassals will take the government away from you, or else there will be conspiracies among them. Tell me, where do you find them all, you ignorant lout, or how do you manage to apply them? If I utter one and apply it properly, I have to sweat and labor as if I were digging a ditch."

"In God's name, master," replied Sancho, "you are complaining over very little. Why should you be vexed if I make use of my own property, seeing that I have no other—no other wealth except sayings and more sayings? Here are four that have just popped into my head, as pat to the purpose as could be, or like pears in a basket; but I'm not going to repeat them, for to keep silence well is called *Sancho*." [22]

"That Sancho is not you," said Don Quixote, "for not only do you not know how to keep silent, but you are a mischievous prattler in the bargain. Nevertheless, I am curious to know what the four sayings are that you have just remembered and that fit in so aptly here; for I have been ransacking my own memory—and it is a good one—and none of the sort have occurred to me."

"What better could you ask for," said Sancho, "than these: 'Never put your thumbs between two of your back grinders'; [23] and 'To "Get out of my house" and "What do you want with my wife?" there is no answer'; and 'Whether the pitcher hits the stone or the stone the pitcher, it will be bad for the pitcher,' [24] all of which fit to a hair? Let no one fall out with his governor or with the one who is in command or he will be sorry for it in the end, like him who puts his thumb between his grinders, whether they be back teeth or not, so long as they are grinders that's all that matters. And to whatever the governor may say there's no answer to be made, any more than there is to 'Get out of my house' or 'What do you want with my wife?' As for the stone and the pitcher, a blind man could see that. And so it is that he who sees the mote in another's eye should see the beam in his own, [25] that it may not be said of him, 'The dead woman was frightened at the one with her throat cut'; [26] for your Grace is well aware that the fool knows more in his own house than the wise man in the house of another." [27]

"That is not true, Sancho," said Don Quixote, "for the fool knows nothing, in his own house or in the house of another, for the reason that upon a foundation of folly no edifice of wisdom can be reared. But let us leave the matter there. If you make a bad governor, the fault will be yours and mine will be the shame, but I find consolation in the thought that I have done my duty in thus earnestly advising you, with all the wisdom at my command; in this way am I released from my obligation and my promise. May God guide you, Sancho, and govern you in your government, and may He deliver me from the fear I have that you are going to turn the whole island upside down, a thing that I might prevent by revealing to the duke what you are, telling him that your fat little person is nothing other than a bag stuffed with proverbs and mischief."

"Sir," replied Sancho, "if your Grace is of the opinion that I am not fitted for this governorship, I give it up here and now; for I am more concerned for the black-of-the-nail of my soul than for my entire body. As plain Sancho, I can make out just as well on bread and onions as I can as governor on partridges and capons. When it comes to that, all are equal when they are asleep, the great and the small, the poor and the rich; and if your Grace will stop to think, you will remember that you alone were the one who put me up to being a governor, for I know no more about governing islands than a buzzard does, and if I thought for a minute that in order to be a governor the devil would have to carry me off, then I would rather go to Heaven as Sancho than go to Hell as a governor."

"So help me God, Sancho," said Don Quixote, "if only by reason of these last words that you have spoken, I hold you fit to be the governor of a thousand islands. You have by nature a good disposition without which no knowledge is worth anything. Commend yourself to God, then, and try not to lose sight of your main purpose; by which I mean, that you should make it your unswerving aim to do the right thing in all matters that come up for your judgment, for Heaven always favors good intentions. And now, let us go to dinner, for I think our hosts are waiting for us."

CHAPTER XLIV. *How Sancho Panza was taken away to be governor, and the strange adventure that befell Don Quixote in the castle.*

THEY say that in the original version of the history it is stated that the interpreter did not translate the present chapter as Cid Hamete had written it,[1] owing to a kind of grudge that the Moor had against himself for having undertaken a story so dry and limited in scope as is this one of Don Quixote. For it seemed to him he was always having to speak of the knight and of Sancho, without being able to indulge in digressions of a more serious and entertaining nature. He remarked that to go on like this, pen in hand, with his mind fixed upon a single subject and having to speak through the mouths of a few persons only, was for him an intolerable and unprofitable drudgery.

By way of relieving the monotony, in the first part of the work he had employed the artifice of introducing a few *novelas,* such as the *Story of the One Who Was Too Curious for His Own Good* and *The Captive's Story,*[2] tales that, so to speak, had nothing to do with the narrative proper, the other portions being concerned with things that had happened to Don Quixote himself, such as could not be omitted.[3] He also felt, he tells us, that many readers, carried away by the interest attaching to the knight's exploits, would be inclined to pass over these novelettes either hastily or with boredom, thereby failing to note the fine craftsmanship they exhibited, which, however, would be plainly evident when they should be published by themselves instead of appearing as mere adjuncts to Don Quixote's madness and Sancho's foolishness.

Accordingly, in this second part it was not his intention to insert any more tales of that kind, whether separate or interwoven with the narrative as a whole, but rather only a few episodes that resembled them, arising naturally out of the course of events; and even with these he meant to be sparing, employing as few words as possible in the telling. He goes on to say that, while thus confining himself closely within the narrow limits of the plot, he wishes it understood that he has sufficient ability and intelligence to take the entire universe for his theme if he so desired and he asks that his labors be not looked down upon, but that he be given credit not for what he writes, but for what he has refrained from writing.

He then goes on with the story by saying that, on the afternoon of the day on which he had given the oral advice to Sancho,[4] Don Quixote presented him with a written copy of what he had said to him, that the squire might look for someone to read it to him. Scarcely had he done so when Sancho lost the document and it found its way into the hands of the duke, who communicated its contents to the duchess, whereupon they both marveled once again at the knight's folly and good sense. And with the object of carrying on the jest, they sent Sancho that same afternoon, with a large retinue, to the place that for him was to be his island.[5]

Now, it happened that the one who was in charge of Sancho and his train was a major-domo of the duke's, a fellow with a keen sense of humor who was at the same time very discreet (for there can be no humor where there is not discretion). He it was who had played the part of the Countess Trifaldi so amusingly, as has been related, and so was well suited for his present role. In addition, he had been thoroughly instructed by his lord and lady as to how he was to behave toward the squire, and as a result everything went off marvelously well.

The moment Sancho laid eyes upon the major-domo, he had a vision of La Trifaldi. "Sir," he said, turning to his master, "may the devil take me right here and now, as a righteous man and a believer,[6] if your Grace is going to have to admit that the face on that steward is the Distressed One's very own."

Don Quixote gazed at the man attentively. "There is no reason why the devil should take you, Sancho," he replied, "either as a righteous man or as a believer—I don't know what you mean by that—for, while the Distressed One's face is that of the major-domo, the major-domo's countenance is not that of the Distressed One, for if such were the case it would imply too great a contradiction. However, this is not the time for going into all that, as it would involve us in an endless labyrinth. Believe me, friend, we must pray Our Lord most earnestly to deliver us from the wiles of wizards and enchanters."

"It is no joke, master," said Sancho, "for a while ago I heard him speak, and it was like La Trifaldi's voice sounding in my ears. Very well, I'll keep silent; but from now on I intend to be on my guard to see if I can discover any other sign that will tell me whether I am right or wrong in what I suspect."

"That you should do, Sancho," agreed Don Quixote, "and you must keep me advised of all that you discover in regard to this matter and of everything that happens to you in connection with your government."

Finally Sancho and his train set out. He was dressed like a man of the law, and over all wore a tawny-hued, wide-flaring greatcoat of watered camlet, with a cap of the same material.[7] He was mounted upon a mule, his saddle being of the high-backed short-stirrup variety,[8] and behind him, by order of the duke, came the gray, decked out in brilliant[9] silken trappings and such ornaments as are suited to an ass. Sancho every now and then would turn his head to look back at the beast, being so glad of the animal's company that he would not have changed places with the emperor of Germany.

Upon taking his leave of the duke and duchess, he kissed their hands and received the blessing which his master bestowed upon him. Don Quixote was in tears, and he himself was blubbering.

And now, gentle reader, let the worthy Sancho go in peace and good luck go with him. You may expect two bushels[10] of laughter when you hear how he deported himself in office. Meanwhile, listen to what happened to his master that same night, and if it does not make you laugh, it will at least cause you to part your lips in an apelike grin; for Don Quixote's adventures are to be greeted either with astonishment or with mirth.

As soon as Sancho had gone, the story continues, Don Quixote felt his loneliness [11] so keenly that, if it had been possible for him to have done so, he would have revoked his squire's commission and had his government taken away from him. Seeing how melancholy the knight was, the duchess inquired the cause of his sadness, observing that if it was Sancho's absence, there were squires, duennas, and damsels a-plenty in her household who would serve the guest to his entire satisfaction.

"It is true, my lady," replied Don Quixote, "that I miss Sancho, but that is not the chief reason that I seem so sad. Of the many offers that your Excellency has made me, I choose and accept but one: the good will with which they are made. As for the rest, I beg your Excellency to consent to my waiting upon myself, in my own chamber."

"Really, Señor Don Quixote," said the duchess, "I could not think of that. Four of my damsels, lovely as flowers, shall be at your service."

"For me," said Don Quixote, "they will not be as flowers, but rather as thorns that pierce my soul, and neither they nor any like them shall enter my chamber any more than they would fly.[12] If your Highness would do me yet another favor, though I deserve none, permit me to serve myself as I prefer behind closed doors; for I would place a wall between my desires and my virtue. It is a habit of mine, and I do not wish to abandon it by reason of the generosity that your Highness would show me. The short of the matter is, I will sleep with my clothes on before I will consent to anyone's undressing me."

"Say no more, say no more, Señor Don Quixote," the duchess begged him. "I promise you I will give orders that not so much as a fly, not to speak of a maiden, shall enter your room. I am not the one to impair the decency of Don Quixote de la Mancha; for it appears to me that of his many virtues the one that shines forth most clearly is that of modesty. Let your Grace dress and undress alone, as and when you like; there will be no one to hinder you. Within this chamber you will find those vessels that are necessary for one who sleeps behind locked doors, and you will not have to open the door to satisfy any call of nature. May the great Dulcinea del Toboso live a thousand ages, and may her fame be extended all over the surface of the globe, seeing that she has merited the love of so valiant and so chaste a knight; and may a kind Heaven put it into the heart of Sancho Panza, our governor, to have done soon with his penance, that the world may once more enjoy the beauty of so exalted a lady."

"Your Highness," replied Don Quixote, "has spoken as befits the person that she is; for worthy ladies never take upon their lips the name of any who is bad,[13] and Dulcinea will be more fortunate and better known throughout the world by reason of your Highness's praise than she would be as a result of the eulogies of the most eloquent tongues on earth."

"Very well, then, Señor Don Quixote," said the duchess, "the supper hour has come and the duke must be waiting for us. Let us go to supper, your Grace, after which you may retire early; for the journey from Candaya yesterday was not a short one and must have tired you somewhat."

"I do not feel in the least tired, my lady," Don Quixote assured her. "I will venture to give your Excellency my oath that never in my life have I mounted a beast that was easier riding or better paced than Clavileño, and I do not understand what could have induced Malambruno to do away with so swift and gentle a steed by burning it the way he did, as if it were nothing at all."

"I fancy," said the duchess, "that he must have repented of the harm he had done to La Trifaldi and her companions, and to other persons as well, and of the misdeeds which, as a wizard and enchanter, he must have committed, and, as a consequence, he wished to have done with all the instruments of his art, chief among which was Clavileño, the one that bore him, a restless wanderer, from land to land. And so he burned it, and by its ashes and the inscription that was set up in the form of a trophy the valor of the great Don Quixote de la Mancha remains established for all time to come."

Once more Don Quixote thanked the duchess; and, after he had supped, he retired to his room alone, declining to permit any servant to enter with him, so greatly did he fear an occasion that might move or compel him to part with that decency and modesty that he preserved in honor of his lady Dulcinea; for he had ever in mind the virtue displayed by Amadis, flower and mirror of knight-errantry. Having locked his door, he proceeded to undress by the light of two wax candles; and as he went to take off his stockings—O disaster that never should have befallen such a person as this!—there burst from him, not sighs or anything of an indelicate nature, but up to two dozen stitches in one of his stockings, which now had the appearance of a piece of lattice work.

The worthy gentleman was deeply grieved over it and would have given an ounce of silver then and there for half a dram of green silk—since the hose that he wore were green.

Here Benengeli, as he goes on writing, exclaims:

"O poverty! poverty! I know not what could have led that great Cordovan poet to call thee a 'holy, unappreciated gift.' [14] I, though a Moor, know well, through the intercourse I have had with Christians, that holiness consists in charity, humility, faith, obedience, and poverty; but, for all of that, I assert that he must indeed be possessed of much godliness who can be content with being poor, unless it be that kind of poverty of which one of their greatest saints was speaking when he said, 'Possess all things as though ye possessed them not.' [15] That is what is known as poverty of spirit. But there is another kind of poverty, and it is of thee I speak. Why dost thou love to dog the steps of gentlemen and the wellborn rather than those of other folk? Why dost thou oblige them to go with patched shoes,[16] while some of the buttons on their doublets are of silk, others of hair, and others still of glass? Why must their ruffs be all wrinkled instead of being properly crimped with an iron?" (From this may be seen how ancient is the use of starch and of crimped ruffs as well.)

"How wretched," continues Benengeli, "is he who comes of good family who must all the time be pampering his honor! Eating badly behind closed doors, he plays the hypocrite when he steps out into the street with a toothpick in his mouth although he has had no cause to clean his teeth.[17] Poor wretch, I say, so worried about his honor that he fancies the patch on his shoe can be seen a league away and who is concerned over the sweat stains on his hat, his threadbare cloak, and his empty stomach, imagining that they must all be equally visible!"

Don Quixote was led to reflect on all this as he surveyed the burst threads in his stockings; but he was relieved to notice that Sancho had left behind him a pair of traveling boots, and he resolved to wear these the next day. He finally went to bed, moody and heavyhearted, owing as much to Sancho's absence as to the irreparable damage done to his hose, which he would even have been willing to patch with thread of another color, one of the greatest signs of poverty that a gentleman can exhibit in the course of his long-drawn-out and threadbare existence. He put out the candles, but it was warm and he could not sleep. Rising from his bed, he partly opened a grated window that looked out on a beautiful garden, and as he did so he became aware of people walking and talking down below. He listened attentively, and as the speakers raised their voices somewhat, he overheard the following conversation:

"Do not urge me to sing, Emerencia, for you know that ever since that stranger entered this castle and my eyes beheld him, I cannot sing but only weep. Moreover, my lady sleeps rather lightly, and I would not have her find us here for all the wealth in the world. And even if she did not awake but slept on, my song would be in vain if this new Aeneas who has come here only to scorn me should likewise be deep in slumber and fail to lend a listening ear."

"Give no heed to that, my dear Altisidora," a voice replied. "There is no doubt that the duchess and all those in the house are sleeping now, all save the lord of your heart and the awakener of your soul; for I heard him opening the window of his room a moment ago, and that must mean that he is awake. Sing, my poor dear, low and softly, to the sound of your harp, and if the duchess should hear us, we will blame it on the heat of the night."

"That is not the point, Emerencia," said Altisidora. "I do not wish that my song should lay bare my soul and that I should be taken for a light and frivolous maid by those who know nothing of the mighty power of love. But, come what will, shame on the cheek is better than an ache in the heart." [18]

There came then the sound of an instrument very gently touched, hearing which Don Quixote was deeply moved; for at that moment all the innumerable adventures of a like sort, at windows, gratings, and in gardens, to the accompaniment of serenades, love-making, and fainting fits, that he had read of in those vapid books of chivalry of his, came back to mind. He at once fancied that one of the duchess's waiting women must be enamored of him but was compelled by her modesty to conceal her passion. He feared that he would yield to temptation, but took a firm resolve not to permit himself to be overcome; and, commending himself with all his heart and soul to his lady Dulcinea del Toboso, he decided that he would listen to the music, giving as a token of his presence a feigned sneeze, which pleased the maidens very much, since their one desire was for him to hear them. And then, having tuned her harp and run her fingers over it, Altisidora began the following ballad: [19]

> O thou above who in thy bed,
> 'Tween sheets of linen fine,
> With outstretched legs dost sleep all night,
> Ah, 'tis for thee I pine!

O thou, La Mancha's bravest knight,
The purest, when all is told,
Thy virtue and thy noble worth
Outweigh Arabia's gold!

Then, hear the plaint of gentle maid
Aweary with desire,
Who in the light of thy twin orbs
Doth feel her heart catch fire.

Seeking adventures, thou dost roam,
To others bringing woe;
Wounds thou dost deal, deniest balm:
No mercy wouldst thou show.

Tell me, O valiant-hearted youth—
God prosper thine emprise!—
Wast born 'mid Jaca's barren crags
Or 'neath the Libyan skies? [20]

And was it serpents suckled thee?
Thy nurses, who were they,
In forest wild, dark mountain cave,
Amongst the beasts of prey?

Ah, well may Dulcinea boast,
The plump and sturdy lass,
That she a tiger fierce hath tamed
And doth all maids surpass.

For this, her fame shall spread abroad
From Jarama to Henares,
From Pisuerga to Arlanza,
From the Tagus to Manzanares. [21]

How gladly would I change with her,
Give a petticoat to boot,
My gayest one with golden fringe,
To win my hapless suit.

Oh, to be clasped within thine arms
Or sit beside thy bed,
Fondly caress thee with my hand,
And scratch thy scurvy head!

But I am asking far too much,
Ah, no, it is not meet;

Most humbly I should be content
Playing with thy feet.

What coifs I'd bring thee, wert thou mine,
And silver slippers, too,
And damask breeches, Holland capes:
With gifts like these I'd woo! [22]

What finest pearls of gallnut size;
Unrivaled they would be
Thus, each "La Sola" [23] *would be called*
For want of company.

Then, gaze not from Tarpeian rock
Upon this kindling blaze.
Manchegan Nero, spare thy wrath
Ere it my heart doth raze.

I'm but a child, a virgin young,
Just three months past fourteen;
By God and on my soul I swear,
'Tis all of life I've seen.

I am not lame, I do not limp,
I'm whole of limb and sound;
My lily locks [24] *thou may'st perceive,*
Go trailing on the ground.

My mouth is wide, my nose is flat,
These faults I'll not deny,
But topaz teeth my beauty save,
Exalt it to the sky.

My voice thou knowest to be sweet,
If thou dost hear me now;
My build is middling, a little less,
It is not bad, I vow.

And these and all my other charms
Thy quiver hath won for thee.
Altisidora is my name;
This house is home to me.

Here the sorely wounded Altisidora brought her song to a close, and it was then that Don Quixote, object of her wooing, began to be perturbed. Heaving a deep sigh, he exclaimed to himself, "Oh, why must

I be so unfortunate a knight that no damsel who looks upon me can help falling in love with me! Why must it be the misfortune of the peerless Dulcinea del Toboso not to be left in peace to enjoy my incomparable fidelity! What would you of her, O queens! Empresses, why do you persecute her! Why do you pursue her, O maids of fourteen and fifteen years of age! Leave, oh, leave the wretched one to rejoice in her triumph and to glory in the lot that Love has bestowed upon her by rendering her my heart and delivering to her my very soul! Listen, enamored ones: to Dulcinea alone I am a doughy paste, but to all other females I am made of flint. To her I am honey, aloes to you. For me, Dulcinea alone is beautiful, prudent, modest, elegant, and wellborn, and all the rest are ugly, stupid, frivolous, and of ignoble lineage. Nature sent me into the world to belong to her and none other. Then, weep or sing, Altisidora; let that Madam [25] on whose account they belabored me in the castle of the enchanted Moor [26] continue to despair; I still must be Dulcinea's, boiled or roasted,[27] and I shall remain clean, well bred, and chaste in spite of all the witching powers on the face of the earth."

With this, he banged the window shut and, gloomy and out of sorts as if some dire misfortune had befallen him, went to bed. There we shall leave him for the present; for the great Sancho Panza, now about to enter upon his famous governorship, is beckoning to us.

CHAPTER XLV. *Of how the great Sancho took possession of his island and of the way in which he began to govern.*

O PERPETUAL discoverer of the antipodes, great taper of the world, eye of the heavens, sweet shaker of the water-coolers,[1] Thymbraeus [2] here, Phoebus there, archer in one place, in another a physician, father of poetry, inventor of music, thou who dost ever rise and, though appearing to do so, dost never set! [3] 'Tis thee, O Sun, by whose aid man doth beget man,[4] 'tis thee whom I beseech to favor and enlighten my darkened intellect that I may be able to give an absolutely exact account of the government of the great Sancho Panza; for without thee I feel lukewarm, fainthearted, and confused.

To continue, then: Sancho with all his train arrived at a village of around a thousand inhabitants, one of the best in the duke's domains.[5] They informed him that it was called Barataria Island, either because the real name of the village was Baratario, or by reason of the *barato* [6] which had led to the government being bestowed upon him. As they reached the town, which had a wall around it, the officers of the municipality came out to meet them, the bells rang, and all the townspeople evidenced their satisfaction. With much pomp they conducted him to the cathedral to give thanks to God, and then, with a few mock ceremonies, they handed over to him the keys of the city, acknowledging him to be the island's perpetual governor.

The new governor's apparel, his beard, and his little fat figure astonished all those who were not in on the joke, and even those who were, and they were many. Finally, upon leaving the church, they took him to the judge's chair and seated him in it, and the duke's major-domo then addressed him.

"Sir Governor," he said, "it is an ancient and obligatory custom in this famous island for the one who comes to take possession of it to answer a question that is put to him, one that shall be somewhat difficult and intricate, so that from his answer the people may be able to form an idea of their ruler's intelligence and judge for themselves as to whether they should hail his coming with joy or look upon it with sorrow."

All the time the major-domo was saying this, Sancho was gazing steadily at some large letters inscribed upon the wall facing him, and inasmuch as he did not know how to read, he asked what they were.

"Sir," was the reply, "that inscription is a notation of the day upon which your Lordship took possession of this island. It reads: 'On this day—such and such a day of such and such a year—Don Sancho Panza took over the government of this island and many years may he enjoy it.'"

"And who is it that they call 'Don Sancho Panza'?" asked Sancho.

"Your Lordship," the major-domo answered, "for no other Panza has set foot here except the one who is seated in that chair."

"Well, then, brother," said Sancho, "I will let you know that there has never been any 'Don' in my family. Plain Sancho Panza they call me, and Sancho was my father's name before me, and my grandfather's before him; they all were Panzas, without any 'Dons' or 'Doñas' tacked on.[7] In this island, I imagine, there must be more 'Dons' than there are stones. But enough of that; God knows what I mean. It may be, if my government lasts four days, I'll weed them all out; for there are so many of them they must be as troublesome as gnats.[8] Go ahead with your question, Señor Major-domo, and I'll reply the best way I can, whether the people are sorry or not."

At this moment there came into the court two men, one dressed like a peasant, the other like a tailor, for this latter held in his hands a pair of shears.

"Sir Governor," said the tailor, "I and this peasant have come before your Grace to have you settle a difference between us. Yesterday this good man entered my shop—for, begging the pardon of those present,[9] I am a licensed tailor, God be praised—and, putting a piece of cloth in my hands, he asked me, 'Señor, is there enough here to make me a cap?' Feeling the cloth, I told him there was. He must have supposed—as I supposed, and I supposed right—that I undoubtedly meant to make away with a part of the material, being led to think so by his own maliciousness and the bad opinion that people have of tailors. He then asked me to look and see if there would be enough for two. Guessing what was in his mind, I said yes; whereupon he, persisting in his damnable first intention, went on adding cap after cap, with me saying, yes, yes, until we were up to five caps in all. Just a while ago he came to call for them and I gave them to him, but he doesn't want to pay me for my labor but insists I should pay *him* or give him back his cloth."

"Is all this true, brother?" inquired Sancho.

"Yes, sir," replied the man, "but will your Grace please have him show the five caps that he made for me?"

"I'll be glad to," said the tailor. And, with this, he at once brought his hand out from under his cloak, displaying the five caps upon his four fingers and thumb. "There they are, and I swear by God and my conscience there's not a scrap of cloth left; I am willing to submit my work to the inspectors of the trade."

All those present had a laugh over the number of caps and the novel character of this lawsuit. As for Sancho, he considered the matter for a while and then said, "It appears to me that in this case there is no need of lengthy arguments; all that is called for is the judgment of an honest man. And so my decision is that the tailor shall lose his work and the peasant his cloth, and the caps shall go to the prisoners in the jail,[10] and let us hear no more about it."

If the decision in the case of the cattle-driver's purse [11] had aroused the admiration of the bystanders, this one provoked them to laughter; but the governor's orders were nonetheless carried out. Two old men were the next to present themselves before him, one of whom carried a reed by way of staff. It was the one without a staff who was the first to speak.

"My lord," he began, "some days ago I lent this good man ten gold crowns by way of service duly rendered,[12] on condition that he should repay me upon demand. A long time went by without my demanding payment, for the reason that I did not wish to cause him an even greater hardship than that which he was suffering when he sought the loan. However, when I saw that he was making no effort to pay me, I asked him for the money, not once but many times, and he not only failed to reimburse me, he even refused to do so, saying I had never let him take the ten crowns in question. I have no witnesses of the loan, and naturally there are none of the payment since no payment was made. Accordingly, I would have your Grace put him under oath, and if he swears that he did pay me, then I will cancel the debt, here and before God." [13]

"What do you say to that, old man with the staff?" Sancho asked.

"My lord," replied the old man, "I admit that he lent them to me; but your Grace may lower that rod,[14] for, seeing that he has had me put under oath, I will also swear that I paid him back, really and truly."

The governor lowered the rod that he held, and in the meanwhile the old man who had spoken handed his staff over to the other one while he took the oath, as if he found it in his way. Then, placing his hand upon the cross of the rod, he once more affirmed that it was true that he had borrowed the ten crowns that were being demanded of him but that he had paid them back into the other's hand, the only thing being that the other old man did not appear to realize it but was all the time asking for his money. In view of this, the great governor then asked the creditor what he had to say in reply to his adversary's statement; whereupon the old fellow who now held the staff replied that his debtor must undoubtedly be speaking the truth, as he knew him to be a worthy man and a good Christian. The one who had lent the crowns added that he must surely have forgotten how and when they had been repaid and that from that time forth he would never ask his adversary for anything.

The debtor thereupon took back his staff and, with bowed head, left the court. When he saw the defendant leaving in this manner, without saying another word, and when he perceived how resigned the plaintiff was, Sancho dropped his chin to his bosom and, placing the forefinger of his right hand in turn upon his eyebrows and his nose, remained lost in thought for a short while. Then he raised his head and ordered them to call back the old man with the staff who had already left.

They did so, and as soon as Sancho saw him, he said, "Good man, give me that staff. I have need of it."

"Gladly," replied the old man. "Here it is, my lord." And he placed it in the governor's hand.

Sancho took it and handed it to the other old man, remarking, "Go in peace, for you are now repaid."

"Repaid, my lord? And is this reed worth ten gold crowns?"

"Yes," said the governor, "it is; or if it is not, then I am the biggest blockhead in the world. We will see right now whether or not I have it in me to govern an entire kingdom."

With this, he ordered that the reed be broken and laid open there in the sight of all, and in the heart of it they found the ten gold crowns. They were all greatly astonished at this, looking upon their governor as another Solomon. When they inquired of him how he knew that the crowns were there, he replied that it had come to him when he saw the old man hand the staff to his adversary while he was taking an oath to the effect that he had really and truly paid his creditor, and then, when he was through, had heard him ask for it back again. From which it was to be deduced that, even when those who governed were simpletons, God sometimes guided them in their judgments. Moreover, he had heard the curate of his village tell of another case like this one,[15] and if it was a question of not forgetting what he had need to remember, there was not another memory like his own in all the island.

The short of the matter is, one old man went off crestfallen, the other with his money in hand, while those present continued to marvel at the thing. As for him whose duty it was to record Sancho's words, deeds, and movements, he could not make up his mind as to whether he should take the new governor for a fool or set him down as a wise man.

When this case had been concluded, there came into the court a woman holding on tightly to a man who was dressed like a rich drover.

"Justice, Señor Governor! Justice!" she cried, "and if I don't find it on earth, I'll go look for it in Heaven! Beloved Governor, this evil man caught me in the middle of a field and made use of my body as if it had been some filthy rag. Ah, poor me! he has taken from me that which I had guarded more than twenty-three years, defending it alike against Moors and Christians, foreigners and native-born. I was always hard as corkwood, keeping myself as pure as a salamander in the flames or wool among the brambles, and now this fine fellow comes along and handles me with clean hands!"

"It remains to be seen," said Sancho, "whether this gallant has clean hands or not." And, turning to the man, he ordered him to reply to the complaint which the woman had made against him.

The defendant was in a state of confusion. "Good sirs," he answered, "I am but a poor dealer in hogs. This morning I left the village to sell— begging your pardon [16]—four pigs, and what with taxes and cheating they took away from me practically all that they came to. As I was returning home, I fell in with this good dame, and the devil, who likes to jumble everything, saw to it that we were yoked together. I paid her quite enough, but she, dissatisfied, laid hold of me and would not let me go until she had dragged me here. She says that I forced her, but she lies by the oath that I am taking or am ready to take. And that is the whole truth, every particle of it."

The governor asked the man if he had any silver coins with him, and the drover replied that he had some twenty ducats in a purse that was hidden in his bosom. Sancho then directed him to take the purse out and hand it over to the plaintiff, which the drover did, trembling all the while. The woman took it and, with many curtsies to all present, offered a prayer to God for the life and health of the Señor Governor who thus looked after damsels and orphans in distress. With this, she left the court, grasping the purse with both hands, but not until she first had looked to see if the coins in it were of silver. No sooner was she gone than Sancho turned to the drover, who, with eyes and heart following the purse, was on the verge of tears.

"My good man," he said, "go after that woman, take the purse away from her whether she is willing to give it up or not, and come back here with it."

He was not talking to a fool or a deaf man, for the drover was off at once like a streak of lightning, to carry out the order that had been given him. The bystanders, meanwhile, waited eagerly to see what the outcome of this case would be. Within a short while the pair returned, engaged in more of a struggle than before; she had her petticoat up with the purse in the lap of it while he strove to take it from her. This was not possible, however, so stoutly did she defend herself.

"Justice!" she was crying, "God's justice and the world's justice, too! Behold, Señor Governor, how bold and shameless this ruffian is. In the center of the town and middle of the street he tried to take away from me the purse which your Grace had ordered him to give me!"

"And did he take it?" asked the governor.

"Take it?" replied the woman. "I'd give up my life sooner than I would the purse. A fine young thing I'd be! They'll have to throw other rats in my face! [17] Hammers and pincers, mallets and chisels, would not be enough to get it out of my clutches, nor even a lion's claws. They'd take the soul from out my body before they'd do that!"

"She's right," said the man. "I give up. I admit I haven't the strength to take it away from her." And he let go his hold.

Sancho then addressed the woman. "Let us have a look at that purse, my respectable and valiant one," he said. She gave it to him and he then handed it back to the man, saying, as he did so, to the one who had been forced and who had not been forced, "Sister, if you had shown the same or even half the courage and valor in defending your body that you have in protecting the purse, the might of Hercules would not have been sufficient to overcome you. Be on your way, in God's name, and bad luck to you, and do not show yourself again in this entire island or for six leagues around, under pain of two hundred lashes. Go, then, I say, you shameless, cheating hussy! Be off with you!" [18]

Frightened by this, the woman left with her head down, very much disgruntled.

"My good man," said Sancho to the defendant, "return to your village with your money and may God go with you; and hereafter, if you do not want to lose your purse, see to it that you do not take it into your head to yoke with anyone."

Mumbling his thanks, the man departed, and the spectators once again expressed their astonishment at the wise decisions made by their new governor. All of which the chronicler duly noted down, to be forwarded to the duke who was eagerly awaiting his report. And here, let us leave the worthy Sancho; for his master, greatly excited by Altisidora's music, urgently claims our attention.

CHAPTER XLVI. *Of Don Quixote's bell-and-cat fright in the course of the enamored Altisidora's wooing.*

WE LEFT the great Don Quixote lost in revery as a result of the enamored damsel Altisidora's serenade. Upon going to bed, he found that his thoughts were like fleas: they would not let him sleep nor give him a moment's rest, and mingled with his amorous fancies were the torn stitches in his stockings. But Time, which is swift-footed and knows no obstacle, came riding on the hours, and very soon it was morning. As soon as he saw that it was daylight, being by no means slothful, the knight quitted his downy couch and proceeded to dress himself, donning his chamois-skin suit and drawing on his traveling boots to hide the rents in his hose. Over all he threw his scarlet cloak and, placing upon his head a cap of green velvet trimmed in silver, he strapped on his baldric and his good keen-bladed sword and then picked up a large rosary that he always carried and with a solemn strut set out for the anteroom where the duke and duchess, already dressed, appeared to be expecting him.

As he made his way down a corridor he came upon Altisidora and the other maiden who was her friend, and the moment the enamored one laid eyes upon him, she promptly fainted. Her companion caught her and at once began undoing her bosom, and when Don Quixote saw this, he went over to them.

"I know," he said, "what causes such attacks as that."

"I do not understand it," replied the friend, "for Altisidora is the healthiest damsel in this household. I have never heard her so much as utter an *Ay!* in all the time that I have known her. Bad luck to all the knights-errants in this world if they are all of them so ungrateful! Go away, Señor Don Quixote, for this poor girl will not come to herself as long as your Grace stands there."

"Lady," said Don Quixote, "I wish you would have them put a lute in my chamber this evening, and I will console the unfortunate lass as best I can; for when love is in its first stages, a prompt disillusionment is recognized as the most efficacious remedy."

With this, he went his way in order that his presence might not be noted by any passers-by; and he was no sooner out of sight than the swooning Altisidora recovered her senses.

"We shall have to place that lute there for him," she said, "for if Don Quixote means to give us a serenade, it ought not to be bad, coming from him."

They then went to inform the duchess of what had happened, telling her that the knight wished a lute. Their mistress was delighted with the idea and at once arranged with the duke and her waiting women to play a joke upon their guest, one that should be more amusing than harmful. With this in mind, they looked forward eagerly to the night, which was as quick in coming as the day, a day spent by the ducal pair in pleasing conversation with Don Quixote.

It was on this day that the duchess really and truly dispatched one of her pages—the one who in the wood had impersonated the enchanted figure of Dulcinea—to Teresa Panza with the letter that her husband had written her, and also with the bundle of clothes that Sancho had left to be sent to her, the servant being duly charged to bring back a full account of all that happened.[1]

The arrangements having been made, when Don Quixote retired to his room at eleven o'clock he found there a guitar.[2] He first tried it out, then opened the window, and, perceiving that there was someone in the garden, once more ran his hands over the frets, tuning the instrument as well as he could. Having done this, he spat and cleared his throat and in a voice that was a little hoarse but well modulated began singing the following ballad, which he had composed that very day:[3]

> *Love is mighty, love is powerful,*
> *Wrecks the heart without redress,*
> *And with maids the tool he uses*
> *Commonly is idleness.*
>
> *Let them sew, do household labor,*
> *Busied always they should be:*
> *Such the antidote most certain*
> *'Gainst Love's envenomed malady.*
>
> *Damsels modest and retiring,*
> *Who to marriage do aspire,*
> *Have their virtue for their dowry,*
> *Highest praise they could desire.*

Courtiers and knightly errants
With the wanton take their ease,
But to the good their troth is plighted,
For modesty doth ever please.

There are loves that start with morning,
As between guests at an inn,
But they quickly end at sunset—
Ended ere they scarce begin.

Here today and gone tomorrow,
Love of that kind doth impart
Little lasting joy or pleasure,
Leaves no imprint on the heart.

Painting laid upon a painting
Makes a very sorry show;
Where one beauty holds the canvas,
None other can subdue its glow.

On my own heart is engraven
Dulcinea's image fair,
And there's naught that can erase it,
'Twill be always printed there.

Loyalty's the thing most valued
In the one who loves and sighs;
It is this that doth work wonders,
Raising him up to the skies.

Don Quixote had come to this point in his song, with the duke and duchess, Altisidora, and nearly all the household listening, when suddenly from a gallery directly above his window they let down a rope to which were attached more than a hundred bells, and then they emptied a large bag filled with cats that had bells of a smaller size fastened to their tails. And so great was the din of the bells and so loud the squalling of the felines that even though the duke and duchess were the ones who had thought up the joke, they still were startled by it all. As for Don Quixote, he was quaking with fear. As luck would have it, two or three of the cats came in through the window of his room, darting from side to side, and it was as though a legion [4] of devils had been let loose there. As they ran about seeking a means of escape, they put out the candles that were burning in the chamber. In the meantime, those above kept hauling up and letting down the rope, while the majority of the castle inmates, being unaware of what was going on, were left gasping with astonishment.

Getting to his feet, Don Quixote drew his sword and started slashing at the window grating as he shouted, "Away with you, malign enchanters! Out with you, witching rabble! Know that I am Don Quixote de la Mancha, against whom your evil intentions are of no avail!"

Turning on the cats that were rushing around the room, he made many thrusts at them, but they dashed for the window and leaped out —all except one, which, upon finding itself thus belabored by Don Quixote's sword, sprang at his face and seized his nose with its claws and teeth, causing him to cry out with pain at the top of his voice. When they heard this, the duke and duchess, who suspected what the trouble was, ran to his room and opened the door with their master key, only to behold the poor knight struggling with all the strength that he had to pull the cat away from his face.

As they entered the chamber with lights in their hands, they had a full view of the unequal combat; but when the duke came forward to part the two, Don Quixote called to him, "Let no one take him away from me! Leave me to fight this demon, this wizard, this enchanter hand to hand. I will show him who Don Quixote de la Mancha is!"

The cat, however, only growled and held on; but the duke finally pulled it off and tossed it out the window. Don Quixote's face was perforated like a sieve and his nose was not in very good shape; yet for all of that, he was very much displeased that they had not permitted him to finish the hard-fought battle with that scoundrelly enchanter. They then sent for some oil of Hypericum,[5] and Altisidora herself, with her fair white hands, applied bandages to all his wounds.

As she did so, she said to him in a low voice, "All these misfortunes have befallen you, hardhearted knight, as a punishment for your stubborn cruelty. I hope to God that Sancho, your squire, forgets to flog himself so that your beloved Dulcinea may never be released from her spell and you may never enjoy her or go with her to the marriage bed, at least not so long as I, who adore you, am still among the living."

To all this Don Quixote replied not a word. He merely heaved a deep sigh and stretched out on his bed, after which he thanked his hosts for their kindness, not because he had been afraid of that witching bell-decked feline rabble, but because he was grateful to them for their good intentions in coming to his aid. Leaving him to calm himself, the duke and duchess thereupon took their departure, worried not a little over the unfortunate outcome of the jest; for they had not thought that this adventure would prove so painful and costly a one to the knight. It did cost him five days in bed, where he had yet another, more pleasant than the one just described, which the historian does not care to relate at this time since he wishes to hurry back to Sancho Panza, who all the while was going ahead with his government most diligently and in a way that was very amusing.

CHAPTER XLVII. *Wherein is continued the account of how Sancho Panza deported himself in his government.*

THE history goes on to relate how they conducted Sancho from the court to a sumptuous palace, where, in a great hall, a royal and truly magnificent board was spread. He entered to the sound of flageolets, and four pages came forward to present him with water that he might wash his hands, which he did in a most dignified manner. As the music ceased, he took the seat at the head of the table, that being the only one there was, since no other place had been laid. An individual with a whalebone wand in his hand, who later turned out to be a physician, then stationed himself at Sancho's side, after which they lifted up a fine white cloth, revealing an assortment of fruit and many other edibles of various sorts.

One who appeared to be a student said grace as a page put a lace bib under the governor's chin and another who performed the functions of a butler set a dish of fruit in front of him. No sooner had he taken a bite, however, than the personage at his side touched the plate with the wand and it was instantly removed. The butler thereupon presented a dish containing other food, but before Sancho had had a chance to taste it—indeed, before it had so much as come within his reach—the wand had been laid upon it and a page had withdrawn it as swiftly as the other attendant had borne away the fruit. Astonished at this, the governor looked around at all the others present and demanded to know if this meal was supposed to be eaten by sleight of hand.[1]

"Señor Governor," replied the man with the wand, "one may eat here only in accordance with the usage and custom in other islands where there are governors. I, sir, am a physician and am paid to serve the rulers of this particular island. I am far more attentive to their health than I am to my own, and study night and day to become acquainted with my patient's constitution in order to be able to cure him when he falls sick. My chief duty is to be present at his dinners and suppers and permit him to eat only what is good for him while depriving him of anything that may do harm or injury to his stomach.[2] Thus I had them remove that dish of fruit for the reason that it contained too much moisture, and I had them do the same with the other dish because it was too hot and filled with spices that tend to increase the thirst. For he who drinks much slays and consumes that radical moisture wherein life consists." [3]

"Well, then," said Sancho, "that dish of roast partridges over there, which appears to be very properly seasoned, surely will not hurt me."

"Ah," was the physician's answer, "so long as I live my lord the governor shall not partake of those."

"And why not?" asked Sancho.

"For the reason that our master, Hippocrates, lodestar and luminary of the science of medicine, in one of his aphorisms has stated: '*Omnis saturatio mala, perdicis autem pessima,*' which is to say, 'All surfeit is bad, but a surfeit of partridges is the worst of all.'" [4]

"If that be true," said Sancho, "will the Señor Doctor kindly see what dishes there are on this table that will do me the most good and the least harm and then let me eat them without any more tapping; for by the life of the governor, and may God let me enjoy it, I'm dying of hunger, and in spite of the Señor Doctor and all that he may say, to deny me food is to take my life and not to prolong it."

"Your Grace is right, my Lord Governor," replied the physician. "And so, I may tell you that in my opinion you should not eat of those stewed rabbits, for it is a furry kind of food.[5] And that veal—if it were not roasted and pickled, you might try it, but as it is, there can be no question of your doing so."

"Take that big dish," said Sancho, "that I see smoking down there —it looks to me like an olla-podrida; [6] and, considering all the different things that go to make it up, I can't fail to hit upon something that will be tasty and at the same time good for me."

"*Absit*," declared the doctor. "Let us put far from us any such evil thought as that. There is nothing in the world that affords less nourishment than an olla-podrida. Save them for canons, university rectors, or peasant weddings. Its presence is out of place on the tables of governors, where all should be delicacy and refinement. The reason for this is that always, everywhere and by everybody, simple medicines are more esteemed than are the compounded ones, since in the case of the former it is impossible to make a mistake whereas with the others one may readily do so by altering the proportion of the ingredients. In my opinion, what my Lord Governor should eat at the present time is a hundred wafers [7] and a few thin slices of quince marmalade, which will be good for the stomach and an aid to digestion."

Upon hearing this, Sancho leaned back in his chair and, staring hard at the doctor, asked him what his name was and where he had studied.

"I, my Lord Governor, am Doctor Pedro Recio de Agüero, native of the village of Tirteafuera,[8] which is on the right-hand side going from Caracuel to Almodóvar del Campo, and I hold the degree of doctor from the University of Osuna." [9]

Sancho was greatly incensed by now. "Very well, let the Señor Doctor Pedro Recio de Mal-Agüero, graduate of Osuna and native of Tirteafuera, a village which is on the right-hand side as we come from Caracuel to Almodóvar del Campo—let him get out of here at once; for, if he does not, I swear by the sun that I will take a club and by making use of it, starting with him, will see to it that there is not a doctor left in this whole island, or, at any rate, none of those that I look upon as being ignorant. As for the wise, prudent, and learned ones, I will honor them as divine beings.[10] And so I say once more, let Pedro Recio be gone or I will take this chair in which I am sitting and break it over his head; and if I am called into court for it, I will clear myself by saying that I did God a service by slaying a bad physician and a public executioner. Either give me something to eat or take back your government; a trade that does not feed the one who practices it is not worth two beans."

The doctor was terrified when he saw how wrathful the governor was and would have made a Tirteafuera [11] of that room if at that moment the sound of a post horn had not been heard in the street. Going over to the window, the butler turned and said, "A courier from the duke, my lord; he must bring some message of importance." The courier entered, covered with sweat and very much agitated, and, drawing a paper from his bosom, he handed it to the major-domo, who read aloud the superscription, which ran as follows:

TO DON SANCHO PANZA, GOVERNOR OF THE ISLAND OF BARATARIA, TO BE DELIVERED INTO HIS HANDS OR THOSE OF HIS SECRETARY.

"Who here is my secretary?" inquired Sancho when he heard this.

"I, my lord," one of those present spoke up, "for I know how to read and write and I am a Biscayan." [12]

"With what you have just added," remarked Sancho, "you could well be secretary to the emperor himself. Open that paper and see what it says."

The newly fledged [13] secretary did so and, having perused the contents of the letter, announced that the matter was one to be discussed in private. Sancho thereupon ordered them to clear the hall, and when the doctor and all the others with the exception of the major-domo and the butler had gone, the secretary proceeded to read the communication:

It has come to my knowledge, Señor Don Sancho Panza, that certain enemies of mine and of the island are planning to launch a furious assault upon it one of these nights, and it will accordingly be necessary for you to keep a watch and be on the alert in order not to be taken unawares. I have further learned through trustworthy scouts that four persons have entered your village in disguise with the object of taking your life, for the reason that they fear your great ability. Keep your eyes open, observe closely all who come up to speak to you, and eat nothing that is offered you. I will send aid to you if I see that you are in trouble. Meanwhile, in all instances, you are to do the thing that is to be expected of your good judgment.

From this village, the 16th of August, at four o'clock in the morning. Your friend,

THE DUKE.

Sancho was astonished, and so, apparently, were the others. "The thing to be done now," said the governor, "and it must be done at once, is to throw Doctor Recio into jail; for if anybody is out to kill me, he must be the one, and he means to do it by slow starvation, which is the worst kind of death." [14]

"Moreover," said the butler, "it is my opinion that your Grace should not eat any of the food that is on this table, for it was a donation from some nuns, and, as the saying goes, behind the cross lurks the devil." [15]

"I do not deny it," replied Sancho, "and so for the present give me a slice of bread and three or four pounds of grapes; there can be no poison in that. The truth of the matter is, I cannot go on without eating. If we are to be ready for those battles that threaten us, we must be well nourished; for it is the tripes that carry the heart and not the other way around.[16] As for you, my secretary, reply to my lord, the duke, and tell him that I will carry out his orders exactly as he gives them. And say to my lady the duchess that I kiss her hands and beg her to send a special messenger with the letter and bundle for my wife, Teresa Panza, as that will be a great favor to me, and I will do all in my power to serve her in any way that I can. While you are about it, you may also put in a kiss of the hands for my master, Don Quixote de la Mancha, that he may see that I am grateful for his bread which I have eaten. As a good secretary and a good Biscayan, you may add whatever you like and is most to the point. And now take away this cloth and give me something to eat and I'll be ready for all the spies, murderers, and enchanters that may descend on me or on this island of mine."

A page now came in. "There is a farmer outside who would like a word with your Lordship on a matter of business. He says it is very important."

"It is strange about these people who come to see me on business," said Sancho. "Is it possible they are so foolish as not to see that this is no time for things of that sort? We governors, we judges, are we not flesh-and-blood beings? Are we not to be allowed the time that is necessary for taking a little rest—unless they would have us made of blocks of marble? By God and upon my conscience, if this government of mine holds out (and I have a feeling that it won't), I'll have more than one of these fellows who come on business hauled up short. For the present, show this good man in, but make sure first that he is not one of those spies or killers that are after me."

"No, sir," replied the page, "I do not think he is; for he appears to be a simple soul,[17] and either I miss my guess or he's as good as good bread." [18]

"There is nothing to be afraid of," added the major-domo, "for we are all here."

"Butler," said Sancho, "would it be possible, now that Doctor Recio is no longer with us, for me to eat something with a little body and substance to it, even if it is only a slice of bread and an onion?"

"Tonight at supper," the butler informed him, "your Lordship will be fully compensated for what was lacking at dinner."

"God grant it may be so," was Sancho's answer.

At this point the farmer appeared. He made a very favorable impression; for it could be seen from a thousand leagues away that he was a worthy man and a good soul.

"Who is the governor here?" was the first thing he asked.

"Who would it be," said the secretary, "if not the one who occupies that seat?"

"Then, I humble myself in his presence," said the man; and, dropping to his knees, he sought to kiss the governor's hand, but Sancho would not permit it. Instead, he bade him rise and state what he wanted. The petitioner did so.

"Sir," he began, "I am a farmer, a native of Miguelturra, a village two leagues distant from Ciudad Real."

"I see we have another Tirteafuera," observed Sancho. "Say what you have to say, brother; for I will say to you that I know Miguelturra very well, as it is not very far from my town."

"Well, then, sir," continued the farmer, "this is the case that I would lay before you. By the grace of God I was married, in the peace and with the blessing of the Holy Roman Catholic Church. I have two sons who are students. The younger is studying to be a bachelor and the older one to be a licentiate. I am a widower. My wife died, or, more properly speaking, a stupid doctor killed her by giving her a purge when she was pregnant. If it had pleased God to let the child be born and it had been a boy, I would have had him study to be a doctor so that he would not be jealous of his brothers, the licentiate and the bachelor."

"And in the same way," put in Sancho, "if your wife had not died or been killed, you would not now be a widower?"

"No, sir, of course not," replied the farmer.

"Well," said Sancho, "we are coming along; but hurry, brother, for it is nearer bedtime than business time."

"I will inform you," the farmer went on, "that this son of mine who is studying to be a bachelor has fallen in love with a lass in the same town by the name of Clara Perlerina, daughter of Andrés Perlerino, another farmer and a very rich one. That name, I may tell you, is not one that has been handed down for generations but is due to the fact that all the members of this family are paralytics, and by way of improving on it they call them Perlerines.[19]

"If the truth be told, this lass is like an oriental pearl or a flower of the field only when you look at her from the right-hand side; from the left-hand, not so much so, for on that side one eye is missing which she lost when she had the smallpox. The pockmarks on her face are many and large, but those who are fond of her will assert that those are not scars at all but graves where the hearts of her lovers lie buried. She is so neat that, in order not to dirty her face, she carries her nose turned up, as they say, so that it looks as if it were running away from her mouth. But, with all this, she is very good-looking. Her mouth is wide, and if it were not that ten or a dozen front teeth and grinders are missing, she might pass as one of the comeliest of maidens.

"Of her lips I shall say nothing, for they are so thin and delicate that, if it were the custom to use lips for such a purpose, one might wind them in a skein. Their color is different from that which is commonly seen, and the effect is marvelous: they are speckled with blue, green, and an eggplant hue— But pardon me, Sir Governor, for painting in such detail one who, when all is said, is destined to be my daughter. I love her and to me she is not bad-looking." [20]

"Do all the painting you like," said Sancho. "I'm enjoying it, and if I had only had my dinner, I wouldn't ask for a better dessert than this portrait of yours."

"That," replied the farmer, "is something which I have yet to serve,[21] but we will get to it in due time. I can only assure you, sir, that if I could but paint for you her tall figure and her bodily charms, you would find cause for astonishment; but this cannot be, for the reason that she is so bent and stooped that her knees touch her mouth, yet it is plain to be seen that if she could draw herself erect her head would scrape the roof. She would long since have given her hand to my bachelor son if she had been able to stretch it out, but it happens to be shrunken; nevertheless, you can tell from her broad, furrowed nails how elegant and shapely it is."

"That will do, brother," said Sancho. "You may consider that you have painted her from head to foot. What is it you want now? Come to the point without all this beating around the bush and all these odds and ends that you are tagging on to the story."

"What I desire, sir," the farmer went on, "is for your Grace to give me a letter of recommendation to her father, asking him to be so good as to let this marriage take place. We are not badly matched in the matter of worldly fortune or gifts of nature; for, to tell you the truth, Sir Governor, my son is bewitched, and there is not a day that the evil spirits do not torment him three or four times. Once he fell into the fire, and as a result his face is as shriveled as a bit of parchment. His eyes, too, are somewhat watery. But he has the disposition of an angel, and if it wasn't for his always flaying and punching himself with his fist, he'd be a saint."

"Is there anything else you would like, my good man?" Sancho inquired.

"There is," replied the farmer, "though I hesitate to mention it. But come, come, in any case I cannot let it go on rotting in my bosom. Sir, I would have your Grace give me from three to six hundred ducats to help make up my bachelor son's dowry, by which I mean, to help him set up housekeeping; for, after all, they must live by themselves, without being subjected to the meddling of their families."

"Think it over well," said Sancho, "and see if there is anything else. Don't be bashful but speak right out."

"No, I am quite sure there isn't."

No sooner did the man say this than the governor rose to his feet and picked up the chair in which he had been sitting.

"I swear, Don Country Bumpkin!" he cried, "if you don't get out of my sight at once, you unmannerly lout, and go hide yourself somewhere, I'll take this chair and lay your head wide open! Son of a whore, rascal, devil's painter! Is this any time to come asking me for six hundred ducats? Where would I get them, you stinking cur? And if I did have them, why should I give them to a crafty dunce like you? What is Miguelturra or the whole Perlerines family to me? Away with you, or by the life of the duke, my lord, I'll do what I said! I don't think you are from Miguelturra at all; you are some scoundrel that Hell has sent here to tempt me! Tell me, you wretch: I've not had the government a day and a half yet, and where do you expect me to lay hands on six hundred ducats?"

The butler motioned to the farmer to leave the room, which he did, hanging his head, for the fellow was obviously afraid that the governor would carry out his angry threat. (The rogue knew how to play his part very well.) But let us leave Sancho with his anger, and peace to them all, while we return to Don Quixote, who, when we last saw him, had his face treated and bandaged as a result of the cat wounds, from which he was not cured in a week's time. Meanwhile, during that week, something happened to him one day which Cid Hamete promises to relate with that truth and exactitude that mark every detail, however small, of this great history.

CHAPTER XLVIII. *Of what happened to Don Quixote and Doña Rodríguez, duenna to the duchess, with other events worthy of record and of eternal remembrance.*

THE badly wounded Don Quixote was exceedingly melancholy and dejected, with his bandaged face which bore the marks not of God's hand [1] but of the claws of a cat, this being one of the misfortunes that are the accompaniment of knight-errantry. For six days he did not go out in public; and one night as he lay wide awake, thinking of all his troubles and of how Altisidora was pursuing him, he heard the door of his room being opened with a key, and at once he leaped to the conclusion that the enamored maiden must be coming to make an assault upon his virtue and cause him to waver in that fidelity that he owed to his lady, Dulcinea del Toboso.

"No!" he cried aloud, convinced of the truth of his imaginings, "for the sake of the greatest beauty on earth I shall not cease to adore the one who is stamped and engraved upon my heart of hearts, who is hidden away in the depths of my bowels! O lady mine, thou may'st be transformed now into an ungainly [2] peasant lass and now into a nymph of the gilded Tagus, weaving tapestries of gold and silk. [3] Merlin or Montesinos may hold thee captive where they will; but wherever it may be, thou art mine; and wherever I may be, I am thine."

Even as he finished saying this the door opened, and he immediately stood up in the bed, wrapped from head to foot in a yellow satin coverlet, with a nightcap on his head and with his face and mustaches swathed in bandages—his face by reason of the scratches and his mustaches to keep them from drooping and falling down—all of which gave him the most extraordinary and fantastic appearance that could possibly be conceived. Watchfully he kept his eyes fastened on the door, expecting to see Altisidora enter, in tears and ready to yield herself; but, instead, he beheld a most dignified duenna in a long, white-bordered veil, so long that it enveloped her entire body like a cloak all the way down to her feet. In her left hand she carried a half-burned candle, while with her right hand she shaded it to keep the light out of her eyes, which were concealed behind a pair of huge spectacles. She came treading softly and cautiously.

Don Quixote gazed upon her from his watchtower and, noting her garb and the silence which she was careful to maintain, decided that it must be some witch or sorceress who had come in this guise to do him harm, and he began crossing himself with great fervor. The apparition, meanwhile, was drawing nearer, and when it reached the middle of the room it raised its eyes and let them rest upon the knight as he stood there furiously making the sign of the cross. If he was terrified at the sight of such a figure as this, the specter in turn was equally frightened by the tall yellow form in the coverlet with a face muffled in bandages.

"Jesus!" screamed the visitor. "What is this I see?" And she gave such a start that the candle fell from her hands, leaving the room in darkness. With this, she turned her back and made for the door, but in her terror tripped over her skirt and came down to the floor with a tremendous thud.

Don Quixote was very much alarmed. "O phantom," he said, "or whatever thou art, I conjure thee to tell me who thou art and what it is that thou desirest of me. If thou beest a soul in torment, speak out, and I will do for thee all that lies within my power; for I am a Catholic Christian and like to do good to everyone. It was with this purpose in view that I took up the profession of knight-errantry, a calling that extends even to the helping of souls in purgatory."

The bewildered duenna, upon hearing herself conjured in this manner, was able to judge of Don Quixote's fear from the fright which she herself felt.

"Señor Don Quixote," she said, "if that, perchance, is who you are, I am no ghost nor apparition nor soul out of purgatory as your Grace must have thought. I am Doña Rodríguez, maid of honor to my lady the duchess, and I come to you with one of those wrongs that your Grace is in the habit of redressing."

"Tell me one thing, Señora Doña Rodríguez," said the knight, "has your Grace perhaps come here as a go-between? For I would have you know that I am not at the disposal of anyone, thanks to the peerless beauty of my lady Dulcinea del Toboso. In short, if you but put aside all love messages, you may go back to light your candle and return, and we will then discuss whatever it is that you would have me do, with the exception, as I have said, of any kind of amorous dalliance."

"*I* carry love messages, my good sir?" replied the duenna. "Little does your Grace know me. I am not so old as to indulge in such child's play as that. What's more, praise God, my soul is still in the flesh and I have all my teeth and grinders in my mouth, save for a few which I lost owing to the colds that are so common in this land of Aragon. If your Grace will wait a moment, I will go light my candle and will be back in an instant to relate my woes to the one who is capable of remedying those of all the world."

And without giving him time to answer she went out the door, leaving Don Quixote in a thoughtful mood as he quietly waited for her to return. Then, of a sudden, a thousand suspicions assailed him regarding this new adventure, which impressed him as being ill fashioned and worse conceived, since it placed him in danger of having to break his plighted troth to his lady.

"Who knows," he said to himself, "but that the devil, who is subtle and cunning, may be trying to deceive me now with a duenna, which is something he has not been able to accomplish with empresses, queens, marchionesses, or countesses? I have often heard it said by the wise that, if he has his way, he will give you a flat-nosed female rather than one with a Roman nose any time.[4] May it not be that this solitude, this silence, and the opportunity that is afforded me, will awaken my sleeping desires and lead me, at the end of my life's span, to fall where I never before have stumbled? In such cases it is better to flee than to stand one's ground and give battle.

"But surely," he went on, "I cannot be in my right mind to be saying and thinking such nonsense as this! It is impossible that a tall, lank, white-hooded duenna in spectacles should arouse a lascivious thought in the bosom of the most graceless wretch in this world. Is there a duenna on this earth who is fair of body? Is there a duenna in the world who is not meddlesome, wrinkled, and prudish? Away with you, then, the whole duenna crew, seeing that ye serve no human pleasure! Oh, how right that lady was of whom it is said that she kept two stuffed duennas, with their spectacles and cushions, at the far end of her reception hall, just as if they were sitting there at work on their embroidery, and those figurines conferred as much respectability upon the room as if they had been real flesh-and-blood matrons!"

Saying this, he flung himself out of bed with the intention of bolting the door and not permitting Señora Rodríguez to enter again; but, just as he was about to do so, that lady returned with a lighted white wax candle, and when she saw Don Quixote at close hand, wrapped in the coverlet, with his bandages, nightcap, and all, she was once more afraid.

"Am I safe, Sir Knight?" she asked, falling back a step or two. "For I do not look upon it as very decent on your part to have left your bed."

"Lady," replied Don Quixote, "that is a question which I well might ask of you. In fact, I do ask you if I am safe from being attacked and raped."

"Of whom do you demand this assurance, Sir Knight, and of whom are you thinking when you ask it?"

"I ask it of you," said Don Quixote, "and it is you that I have in mind; for I am not made of marble nor you of brass. This is not ten o'clock in the morning but midnight, or a little later than that, I fancy, and we are in a room that is more closed in and secret than that cave must have been where the bold and faithless Aeneas enjoyed the beauty of tender-hearted Dido. But give me your hand, lady, for I ask no greater security than my own modesty and continence and such as is afforded me by that most venerable headdress." [5]

With this, he kissed his own right hand and took hold of hers, which she extended to him with the same degree of ceremony.

(Here, Cid Hamete inserts a parenthesis in which he swears by Mohammed that to have seen the two walking hand and hand like this from the door to the bed he would have given the better of the two cloaks that he had.)

Finally Don Quixote went back to bed while Doña Rodríguez remained seated in a chair some distance away. She was still holding her candle and wearing her spectacles. He then huddled down and covered himself until only his face was visible; and when they both were settled, he broke the silence.

"Now, my lady Doña Rodríguez," he said, "your Grace may unburden herself. Tell me everything that is in your anguished heart and grieving bowels. You shall be heard with chaste ears and succored with deeds of compassion."

"That I can well believe," replied the duenna, "for so Christian a response as the one you have given me was the only thing to be expected of your kind and charming self. I will tell you, then, Señor Don Quixote, that although your Grace sees me here seated in this chair, in the heart of the kingdom of Aragon, wearing the attire of an old worn-out duenna, I am in reality a native of Asturias on the Oviedo side,[6] and I come of a family that is related to many of the best in that province. But owing to my own ill luck and the negligence of my parents, who somehow or other lost their fortune at an early date, I was brought to the

court of Madrid, where, for the sake of security and in order to prevent greater misfortunes, I was placed as a seamstress with a lady of
rank—and I may inform your Grace that when it comes to any kind of
needlework, no one in all my life has ever surpassed me. My parents left
me there in service and returned to their own country; and a few years
later they went to Heaven, in all probability, for they were very good
Catholic Christians. I thus became an orphan dependent upon the miserable wage and paltry favors which servant girls in a palace customarily
receive.

"Then it was, without my having given him any occasion for doing
so, that a squire in that household fell in love with me. He was a man
well along in years, bearded and personable, and, above all, he was as
much a gentleman as the king himself, for he was a highlander.[7] We were
not able to keep our love so secret but that it came to the notice of
my mistress, who without more ado had us married in the peace and
with the blessing of the Holy Roman Catholic Church. Of that marriage
a daughter was born, to put an end to my good fortune if I ever had
any. True, I did not succumb in childbed, which I passed through safely
and in season; but my husband died shortly afterward of a shock that he
had—if there were time to tell you of it, I am sure your Grace would
marvel at it."

At this point she began weeping bitterly. "Pardon me, Señor Don
Quixote," she said, "if I am unable to control myself; every time that I
think of my poor unfortunate husband, my eyes brim with tears. God
bless me, how dignified he used to look as he rode along carrying my
mistress behind him on the crupper of a jet-black mule! For in those
days they did not have coaches and chairs [8] as they tell me they do now,
but ladies rode behind their squires in the manner I have mentioned.

"This much at least I must tell you, in order that you may see how
well bred and punctilious my worthy husband was. As he was entering the Calle de Santiago in Madrid, which is a rather narrow street, a
judge of the court with two constables in front of him was coming
out of it. As soon as my good squire saw the judge, he turned the mule
and made as if to accompany the magistrate, but my lady, who was on
the crupper, whispered to him, 'What are you doing, you wretch?
Don't you know that I am here?' The judge, being a courteous gentleman, reined in his horse and said, 'Continue on your way, sir; it is I
who should accompany my lady, Doña Casilda'—for that was my mistress's name. My husband, however, cap in hand, insisted on going
with the judge; and when she saw this, my mistress, vexed and angry,

drew out a big pin—a bodkin, I think it was—from her needlecase and stuck it into my husband's back so forcefully that he gave a loud scream and fell writhing to the ground, bringing my lady with him.

"Her two lackeys came running to lift her up and the judge and his bailiffs did the same. The Guadalajara Gate [9] was in a hubbub—I am referring to the idlers there. My mistress returned home on foot while my husband hurried to the barber's,[10] saying that his intestines had been pierced. His courtesy became the talk of the town, to such an extent that small boys ran after him in the street. For this reason and because he was somewhat shortsighted my lady dismissed him, and this in my opinion was what brought on his death.[11] I was left a widow with no one to protect me and with a daughter to care for who was growing in beauty like the foam of the sea.

"At last, as a result of my reputation as a seamstress, my lady the duchess, who had recently been married to my lord the duke, offered to bring me with her to this kingdom of Aragon, and my daughter as well, who, as time went by, grew up to be one of the most accomplished young ladies to be found anywhere: she sings like a lark; she is like fancy itself as she goes through the stately movements of the court dances, while in the dances of the people she trips it like a mad woman; [12] she reads and writes like a schoolmaster and does sums like a miser. Of the neatness of her person I say nothing: running water is not cleaner than she. She must be now, if I remember rightly, sixteen years, five months, and three days old—a day more or less.

"But to get on with my story: The son of a very rich farmer, in a village not far from here that belongs to my lord the duke, fell in love with her. How it happened I do not know, but they came together and, under promise of marrying her, he made a fool of my daughter and now is unwilling to keep his word. My lord the duke is aware of this, for I have complained to him not one but many times, imploring him to order that farmer's son to marry her, but he turns a deaf ear [13] and scarcely listens to me. The reason is that the young deceiver's father is so rich; he lends the duke money and goes security for his debts from time to time, and so my lord does not wish to offend him or give him trouble of any sort.

"What I would ask of you, then, my good sir, is that you take it upon yourself to undo this wrong, either by entreaties or by force of arms; for everyone says that you were born into the world for that purpose: to redress grievances and protect the wretched. Let your Grace bear in mind that my daughter is an orphan; think of her youth, her charm, and all those accomplishments of which I have told you. For I swear to God and upon my conscience that of all the damsels that my lady has in attendance upon her, there is not one that comes up to the sole of my daughter's shoe. Take that one whom they call Altisidora and who is regarded as the sprightliest and gayest of the lot: in comparison with my daughter she is two leagues and more away. For, my dear sir, I may remind you that all is not gold that glitters. In this girl Altisidora there is more of presumption than of beauty and more of sprightliness than of modesty. What is more, she is none too healthy. Her breath is so bad that one cannot bear to be near her for a moment, and even my lady the duchess—but I must be silent, for as the saying goes, walls have ears."

"Upon my life, Señora Doña Rodríguez," said Don Quixote, "what ails my lady the duchess?"

"Seeing that you adjure me in this manner," replied the duenna, "I can do no more than answer you in all truthfulness. You are aware, Señor Don Quixote, of my lady's beauty: that complexion of hers which is like a smooth-polished sword; those cheeks of milk and carmine, one of which is like the sun while the other resembles the moon; [14] that lightsome step with which she barely skims the ground. From all of this would it not seem that she radiates health wherever she goes? But I would have your Grace know, she may first of all thank God for it, and in the second place she may be grateful for two issues that she has, one in each leg, through which are discharged all the evil humors of which the doctors say she is full." [15]

"Holy Mary!" exclaimed Don Quixote, "and is it possible that my lady the duchess has drains of that sort? I should not have believed it if the barefoot friars had told me, but seeing that it is Señora Doña Rodríguez who so informs me, then it must be so. But such issues and in such places ought not to drain off humors, but, rather, liquid amber. Truly, now, I am beginning to be convinced that this matter of opening issues is important for the health."

No sooner had Don Quixote said this than the door of the room was thrown open with a loud bang. Doña Rodríguez was so startled that she again let the candle fall, and the room became as dark as a wolf's mouth, as the saying has it. Then the poor duenna felt a pair of hands closing about her throat so tightly that she could not even croak, while another person without saying a word, lifted her petticoats and, with what appeared to be a slipper, began giving her such a spanking that it was piteous to behold. Don Quixote, indeed, felt pity for her, but for all of that he did not stir from his bed. Not knowing what the meaning of it was, he lay there quietly, fearful lest his turn should come next. His fears were justified. Having given the duenna (who did not dare cry out) a thorough drubbing, the silent executioners fell upon the knight. Stripping the sheet and coverlet from him, they pinched him so hard and fast that there was nothing for him to do but defend himself with his fists; all of which took place in a silence that was truly astonishing.

The battle lasted for something like half an hour, at the end of which time the phantom figures departed. Pulling down her skirts and bemoaning her ill fortune, Doña Rodríguez went out the door without a word to Don Quixote. Here we shall leave him to his solitude, sorely pinched, bewildered, and downcast, wondering who the perverse enchanter could be who had placed him in such a predicament. All this, however, will be told in due time. Sancho Panza is calling us now, and the proper arrangement of this history demands that we give him our attention.

CHAPTER XLIX . *Of what happened to Sancho Panza as he made the rounds of his island.*

WE LEFT the great governor angry and out of sorts with the roguish farmer-painter, who, put up to it by the major-domo and the major-domo in turn by the duke, had been making sport of him. Sancho, nonetheless, though he may have been but a simpleton, a stupid boor, contrived to hold his own against them all. He now addressed himself to those present, including Doctor Recio, who had returned to the room as soon as the business of the duke's confidential letter was out of the way.

"By this time," he said, "I see plainly that judges and governors ought to be made of brass so that they might not have to listen to those who come to petition them and who insist that they be heard and their business disposed of, no matter what the time or season. And if the poor judge does not hear them and attend to their requests, either because he is unable to do so or because it is not the time set aside for audiences, then they at once begin to curse and slander him, gnawing at his bones and even assailing his family tree. O silly petitioner, foolish petitioner, do not be in such haste as that, but wait for the proper occasion and opportunity. Come neither at mealtime nor at bedtime, for judges are of flesh and blood and must satisfy the needs of nature. All except me, that is to say; for thanks to the Señor Doctor Pedro Recio Tirteafuera, who stands before me here, I cannot satisfy my natural need of eating. He would have me die of hunger, and to this form of death he gives the name of life—may God give him and all his stripe that kind of life, say I, and the same goes for all bad doctors, while the good one merits palms and laurels."

All those who were acquainted with Sancho Panza were astonished at hearing him use such elegant language and did not know to what to attribute it unless it was that offices carrying grave responsibilities sharpened the wits of some men while in the case of others the effect was merely stupefying. Doctor Pedro Recio Agüero of Tirteafuera finally promised that the governor should have his supper that night even though it might be in violation of all the aphorisms of Hippocrates,[1] and with this Sancho was content. He waited eagerly for night and the supper hour to come, and although it seemed to him that time was standing still, the hour so longed for arrived at last. They then served him a dish of beef and onions with a few boiled calves' feet that were rather stale. He fell to, however, more heartily than if they had set before him francolins from Milan, Roman pheasants, veal of Sorrento, partridges from Moron, or geese from Lavajos.

"See here, Señor Doctor," he said in the course of the meal, "from now on you needn't bother to give me dainty dishes or anything special as it would only unhinge my stomach, which is used to goat's meat, beef, bacon, hung beef, turnips, and onions. If I am given other victuals of the kind they serve in palaces, my stomach will turn squeamish and I'll sometimes be sick. What the butler may do is this: he may serve me what are known as ollas-podridas (for the more rotten they are, the better they smell).[2] He may put whatever he likes into them, so long as it is something good to eat, and I will thank him for it, and pay him for it, too, someday. But don't let anyone try to play any jokes on me, for either we are or we are not, and so let us all live together and eat our food in peace and good fellowship. When God sends the dawn, it is daylight for all.[3] I mean to govern this island without giving up a right or taking a bribe.[4] Let everyone keep his eyes open and look out for the arrow.[5] For I would have you know that the devil's in Cantillana,[6] and if they give me cause for it, they're going to see marvels. Make yourself into honey and the flies will eat you!" [7]

"Señor Governor," replied the butler, "there is certainly much truth in what you have said, and I promise you in the name of all the inhabitants of this island that they will serve your Grace faithfully, willingly, and affectionately; for the mild way in which you have begun to govern affords them no excuse for doing or thinking anything that would be a disservice to your Grace."

"That I can believe," said Sancho, "since they would be fools to think or do anything of the sort. Once more I say to you: see to feeding me and my gray; that is the important thing and most to the point. When the time comes, we will make the rounds. It is my intention to rid this island of all kinds of trash, of all good-for-nothing loafers and vagabonds; for I would have you know, my friends, that the lazy and idle are to a state what drones are to a hive, which eat the honey that the worker bees have made. I propose to aid the farmer, to preserve the privileges of gentlemen, to reward the virtuous, and, above all, to respect religion and to honor those in holy orders.[8] What do you think of that, my friends? Is there something in what I say or not?"

"There is so much in what your Grace says," the major-domo assured him, "that I am indeed astonished to hear a man wholly unlettered, as I believe your Grace to be, uttering so many wise maxims and observations, all of which is quite contrary to what was expected of your Grace's intelligence by those who sent us and by us who came here with you. Each day new things are seen in this world, jests are turned into earnest and the jesters are mocked."

Night came, and the governor had his supper with permission of the Señor Doctor Recio.[9] They then prepared to make the rounds, and Sancho set out accompanied by the major-domo, the secretary, the butler, a chronicler whose duty it was to record his deeds, and a number of bailiffs and notaries, enough to form a fair-sized squadron. In the midst of them all walked Sancho with his staff of office in hand, as fine a sight as one could wish to see. They had traversed but a few streets of the town when they heard the noise of clashing swords. Upon hastening to the spot, they found only two men, who, when they saw the authorities approaching, at once ceased fighting.

"Help, in God's name and the King's!" cried one of the swordsmen.

"Does one here have to put up with being openly robbed and set upon in the middle of the street?"

"Be quiet, my good fellow," said Sancho, "and tell me what is the cause of this quarrel; for I am the governor."

The other man now spoke up. "Señor Governor," he said, "I will tell you, very briefly. Your Grace should know that in that gambling house directly across the way this man has just won, God knows how, more than a thousand reales. I was present at the time and judged more than one doubtful point in his favor, very much against the dictates of my conscience, after which he made off with what he had won. I had expected him to give me a crown or so out of his winnings,[10] such being the custom where gentlemen of my rank look on to see whether the play is fair or foul and to support those who are actually losers and thus prevent brawls. He, however, pocketed his money and left the house, and, angered at this, I followed him.

"Very civilly and courteously I asked him to let me have at least eight reales, as he knows me to be a respectable individual and one without employment or income, my parents having given me no profession and left me no property. But Cacus is not a bigger thief nor Andradilla[11] a worse sharper than this rogue. He would not part with more than four reales, from which, Señor Governor, you may see how little shame and conscience he has! But, in faith, if your Grace had not arrived when you did, I would have made him disgorge those winnings of his and he'd have learned how to balance the scales."[12]

"What have you to say to that?" Sancho inquired of the first swordsman.

The other replied that all his antagonist had said was true, adding that he had felt that four reales was enough, since he very often gave the man money, and those who expect gratuities[13] from players ought to be polite and accept with a cheerful countenance whatever is offered them, without making any demands on the winners unless they know for a certainty that the latter's gains are ill gotten. There was, he pointed out, no better proof that he was an honest man, and not a thief as his accuser had stated, than the fact that he had at first refused to give anything; for sharpers always have to pay tribute to the onlookers who are acquainted with them.

"That is true," observed the major-domo; "and now, my Lord Governor, it is for your Grace to decide what is to be done with these men."

"What is to be done with them," said Sancho, "is this: you, the winner, whether you won by fair, foul, or indifferent means, will immediately pay this bully a hundred reales, and you will disburse thirty more for the poor prisoners. As for you who have neither occupation nor source of income but roam about with nothing to do, you will take those hundred reales and before tomorrow night will leave this island under sentence of banishment for ten years. If you violate that sentence, you will serve the remainder of it in the life to come, for I will hang you on a gibbet, or the public executioner, at any rate, will do it for me. And not a word from either of you or I will let you feel the weight of my hand."

The one man thereupon paid over the money and went on home, and the other, who received it, promptly left the island.

"Either I am not good for much," remarked Sancho when it was all over, "or I will do away with these gambling houses, for it seems to me that much harm comes from them."

"This one, at least," said one of the notaries, "your Grace will not be able to do away with, for it is kept by a very important personage, and what he loses in the course of the year is beyond all comparison more than what he makes by the cards. Against other houses, of less importance, your Grace may take action, and they are the ones that do the most harm and conceal the most flagrant abuses. In the houses of gentlemen of rank and of noblemen, notorious sharpers do not dare to play their tricks; and, seeing that gambling has now become a common vice, it is better that it be done there than in the home of some artisan,[14] where they catch a poor fellow in the small hours of the morning and skin him alive."

"I can see, notary," replied Sancho, "that there is much to be said as to that."

A constable now came up, grasping a youth by the arm. "My Lord Governor," he said, "this young man was coming toward us, and as soon as he caught sight of the officers of the law he started running like a deer, a sign that he must be an evildoer of some sort. I set out after him, and if it had not been that he stumbled and fell, I'd never have overtaken him."

"Why were you running away, my man?" asked Sancho.

"Sir," replied the youth, "it was to avoid answering all the questions that the officers put to you."

"What is your trade?"

"A weaver."

"And what do you weave?"

"Lance points, with your Grace's kind permission."

"So, you are being funny with me, are you? You pride yourself on being a great joker, I suppose? Very well. And where were you bound for just now?"

"To take the air."

"And where do you take the air in this island?"

"Where it blows."

"Good enough; you answer very much to the point; you're a clever young man. But please note that I am the air, and I am blowing on your poop right now and sending you to jail. Ho, there, take him away; I'll see that he sleeps without any air tonight."

"By God!" exclaimed the youth, "your Grace can no more make me sleep in jail than you can make me a king!"

"And why can't I?" Sancho demanded. "Do you mean to tell me it is not in my power to have you arrested or set free whenever I like?"

"However much power your Grace may have," said the youth, "it is not enough to make me sleep in jail."

"You think not?" said Sancho. "Take him away at once that he may see with his own eyes how mistaken he is; and it will do no good for the jailer to be generous with him, for a consideration, for I will fine him two thousand ducats if he lets this fellow stir a step out of prison tonight."

"All that is laughable," said the youth. "The fact of the matter is, there are not enough people in this world to make me sleep there."

"Tell me, you devil," said Sancho, "do you have some angel who is going to get you out, who will take off the irons that I am going to order them to put on you?"

"Ah, now, Señor Governor," replied the youth with great vivacity, "let us talk sense and come to the point. Let us suppose that your Grace orders me taken off to jail and that they put me in irons and chains and throw me into a dungeon, and let us further suppose that you threaten the jailer with a heavy fine if he does not carry out his orders but lets me out—in spite of all this, if I do not wish to sleep but choose to remain awake all night without closing an eyelid, will your Grace be able, with all your power, to make me do so?"

"No, certainly not," said the secretary. "The fellow is right."

"That is all very well," said Sancho, "so long as you stay awake merely because it is your pleasure to do so and not in opposition to my will."

"Oh," replied the youth, "nothing like that, sir. Not for one moment."

"Well, then," said Sancho, "God be with you. Go to your house and may He give you a good sleep, for I would not deprive you of it. But I would advise you from now on not to make light of those in authority or you may fall in with someone who will bring the joke down on your skull."

The youth went away, and the governor continued on his rounds and a short while later two more constables came up with a man in custody.

"Señor Governor," one of them said, "this person who appears to be a man is in reality a woman, and not an ugly one at that, who goes dressed in men's clothing."

Two or three lanterns were lifted, and by their light was revealed the face of a girl who appeared to be about sixteen years old or a little more. Her hair, lovely as a thousand pearls, was caught up in a small net of gold and green silk. Surveying her from head to foot, they perceived that she had on red silk stockings and white taffeta garters with a border of gold and seed pearls; her breeches were of green-colored cloth of gold and her jacket [15] was of the same material, beneath which she wore a doublet of the finest gold-and-white texture, while her shoes, which were those of a man, were white. She carried no sword at her side, but, instead, an extremely ornate dagger, and on her fingers were many rings of good quality. In short, the young woman made a very favorable impression upon all of them, but none of those who beheld her were acquainted with her, and the natives of the town said they could not imagine who she could be. Most astonished of all were the ones who were supposed to be playing the joke upon Sancho, or who knew about it, as this incident and encounter had not been arranged by them, and they were, accordingly, left in some perplexity and waited to see what the outcome would be.

Sancho, taken aback by the girl's beauty, inquired of her who she was, where she was going, and what had induced her to assume that costume.

"Sir," she replied, keeping her eyes fixed upon the ground and exhibiting an embarrassment that bespoke a high degree of modesty, "I cannot tell you in public of something which it is important to me to have kept secret. But there is one thing I should like you to understand: I am not a thief nor criminal of any sort, but an unfortunate maiden who by force of jealousy has been led to violate that decorum that is modesty's due."

"My Lord Governor," said the major-domo when he heard this, "have the people stand back in order that this lady may say what she has to say with less embarrassment."

The governor gave the order, and they all fell back with the exception of the major-domo, the butler, and the secretary. Seeing that they were alone, the girl then went on with her story.

"I, gentlemen, am the daughter of Pedro Pérez Mazorca, a wool farmer of this town who comes very often to my father's house."

"That will not do, Señora," said the major-domo, "for I know Pedro Pérez very well and he has no child, either son or daughter. What is more, you say that he is your father and then you add that he is in the habit of coming to see your father."

"I had noticed that," remarked Sancho.

"I am so confused just now, gentlemen, that I do not know what I am saying," was the young woman's answer. "The truth is that I am the daughter of Don Diego de la Llana, whom you all must know."

"That is better," said the major-domo. "I am acquainted with Diego de la Llana and know him to be a wealthy gentleman of some prominence. I also know that he has a son and a daughter, and that since he became a widower no one in this town can boast of having seen the daughter's face; he keeps her so shut away that not even the sun can behold her, and yet, for all of that, report has it that she is exceedingly beautiful."

"That is the truth," replied the maiden, "and I am that daughter. As to whether the report of my beauty is true or not, gentlemen, you may judge for yourselves."

She now began weeping bitterly, and, seeing this, the secretary turned to the butler and whispered in his ear, "Without a doubt, something serious must have happened to this poor maid or one of her station would not leave her home and go wandering about the streets at such an hour and in such a costume."

"True enough," replied the butler; "your suspicion is confirmed by her tears."

Sancho consoled her as best he could, begging her to have no hesitancy about telling them what the trouble was, as they would all most earnestly endeavor to help her in every possible way.

"Gentlemen," she said, "the fact of the matter is that my father has kept me shut up for ten years now, ever since they laid my mother in the earth. In our house, mass is said in a sumptuous chapel; and in all that time I have seen but the sun in the heavens by day and the moon and stars by night. I do not know what streets, public squares, or churches are, nor even what men are like, outside of my father and a brother of mine and Pedro Pérez, the wool farmer, who frequently comes to visit us—it was for that reason that I took it into my head to say that he was my father, in order to avoid having to name my real one. This confinement—I am not allowed to leave the house even to go to church—has made me very unhappy for many days and months. I wanted to see the world, or at least the town where I was born, for it seemed to me that this wish did not run counter to that decorum that wellborn maidens ought to observe.

"When I heard them talking of bullfights, jousting with reeds,[16] and play-acting, I asked my brother, who is a year older than I, to tell me what these things were, together with many others which I had not seen, and he explained them to me as well as he could, and all this only kindled my desire to see for myself. But, to cut short the story of my downfall, I may tell you that I begged and entreated my brother— oh, that I had never done so!" And once again she began weeping.

"Continue, Señora," the major-domo said to her. "Go ahead and tell us what happened; for we are all in suspense at hearing what you have to say and seeing your tears."

"There is not much left to tell, though I have many tears that remain to be shed, for that is the payment one must always make for such misplaced desires as mine."

The butler's heart was deeply touched by the maiden's beauty, and he now lifted his lantern for another look at her. It appeared to him that those were not tears, but, rather, seed pearls or meadow dew, and he even went so far as to compare them to the pearls of the Orient. He could only hope that her misfortunes were not as great as her weeping and her sighs would seem to indicate. The governor for his part was becoming impatient over the way in which the girl dragged out her story and urged her not to keep them any longer in suspense as it was growing late and they had yet to cover a good deal of the town.

With broken sobs and half-sighs, she went on, "My misfortune is that I asked my brother to dress me up like a man in one of his suits and to take me out some night to see the town while our father was asleep. I insisted so strongly that he finally agreed to humor me, and so I put on his clothes and he dressed in mine—for he has no hair on his face and looks like a very pretty girl—and tonight, about an hour ago, we left the house and, led on by a youthful and foolish impulse, roamed the entire town. Just as we had made up our minds to return home, we saw coming toward us a large group of people, and my brother said to me, 'Sister, that must be the watch; pick up your feet and put wings on them and follow me as fast as you can, for if they should recognize us, it would be a bad business.' Saying this, he turned his back and started to fly rather than run; but I was so frightened that I had not gone more than six paces when I fell, and then the officer of justice who has brought me before you came, and I find myself put to shame before all these people as a bad and willful girl."

"So, then, young lady," said Sancho, "no other misfortune than this has befallen you, and it was not jealousy, after all, that drove you from your home, as you told us at the beginning of your story."

"No, nothing has happened to me, and it was not jealousy that drove me away, but only a desire to see the world, which did not go any further than seeing the streets of this town."

The truth of what she had said was now confirmed by the arrival of constables with her brother, one of them having overtaken the lad as he ran away from his sister. He had on nothing but a skirt of rich material and a short blue damask cloak with a fine-gold border; he had no bonnet on his head nor adornment of any kind other than his blond curly hair, which resembled golden ringlets. The governor, major-domo, and butler then took the youth to one side and, being out of earshot of his sister, asked him why he had donned that disguise. He was no less ashamed and embarrassed than the young woman had been and told the same story they had heard from her, much to the delight of the enamored butler.

"Young lady and gentleman," the governor said to them, "this was certainly a very childish thing to do, and there was no occasion for all those tears and sighs in telling us of so rash an escapade. All you needed to say was, 'We are So-and-So and So-and-So, and we wandered away from our parents' home merely out of curiosity and with no other purpose in view.' Your story could have ended then and there, without all this weeping and wailing and carrying-on."

"That is so," replied the maiden, "but your Worships must realize that I was so excited I was unable to control myself."

"There is no harm done," said Sancho. "Come, we will take you back to your father's house, and it may be that he will not have noticed your absence. After this, do not be such children or so anxious to see the world; for the respected damsel has a broken leg and stays at home,[17] a woman and a hen by gadding about are soon lost,[18] and she who is eager to see is also anxious to be seen.[19] I say no more."

The young man thanked the governor for the favor of escorting them to their home, which was not far away, and they all set out. When they arrived there the lad threw a pebble against a grating, and in a moment a woman servant who was waiting for them came down and let the pair in. All the members of the governor's party were astonished at the grace and beauty of the two young people and marveled at their desire to see the world by night without, however, going beyond the confines of the town. All this they attributed to their extreme youth.

As for the butler, his heart was transfixed, and he at once resolved that he would ask the girl's father for her hand in marriage the very next day, feeling certain that he would not meet with a refusal, in view of the fact that he was a servant of the duke. And Sancho for his part began forming plans for marrying the young man to his daughter, Sanchica, and determined to carry out his scheme in due season, since, he reflected, no prospective husband would decline a governor's daughter.

With this, their rounds for that night came to an end, and two days later the government as well, all the governor's plans being overthrown and swept away, as will be seen further on.

CHAPTER L. *Wherein is set forth who the enchanters and executioners were who spanked the duenna and pinched and scratched Don Quixote, together with what happened to the page who carried the letter to Teresa Panza,[1] Sancho Panza's wife.*

CID HAMETE, that most painstaking investigator of the minute details of this true history, tells us that as Doña Rodríguez left her own apartment to go to Don Quixote's, another matron who was her roommate observed her movements; and inasmuch as all duennas are eager to know, hear, and smell out things, this one proceeded to follow her so quietly that the worthy Rodríguez was unaware of the fact. As soon as the second duenna saw the first one enter the guest's chamber, true to the tattling character of her kind she at once hastened to inform my lady the duchess that Doña Rodríguez and the knight were closeted together, and the duchess in turn told the duke, begging his permission to go with Altisidora and find out what it was her serving woman wanted of Don Quixote.

The duke gave his consent, and the two women then tiptoed along very cautiously to the door of the knight's room and took up a position near by where they could hear all that was said. As the duchess listened to Doña Rodríguez making public property of her mistress's ailments,[2] she was unable to bear it, and Altisidora felt the same way about it, and so, filled with rage and thirsting for vengeance, they burst into the chamber, where they spanked the duenna and punished Don Quixote in the manner that has already been described; for insults offered to the beauty and pretensions of women invariably arouse in them a mighty wrath and kindle a passion for revenge. The duchess gave an account of the affair to the duke, who was very much amused by it; and then by way of continuing the jest and having still further sport with the knight, she summoned the page who had impersonated Dulcinea in the little comedy having to do with that lady's disenchantment—a matter which Sancho had entirely forgotten, being so busy with his government. The page was now dispatched to Teresa Panza, Sancho's wife, with her husband's letter and another which the duchess had written, and with a large string of valuable coral beads as a present.[3]

The history goes on to say that the page was very keen-witted and anxious to be of service to his lord and lady, and that he set out right willingly for Sancho's village. Just before entering it he saw a number of women washing clothes in a brook,[4] and, going up to them, he inquired if they could tell him whether or not a woman by the name of Teresa Panza lived there, wife of one Sancho Panza, squire to a knight known as Don Quixote de la Mancha. In response to this question, a young lass stood up.

"Teresa Panza is my mother," she said, "the Sancho you speak of is my father, and that knight is our master."

"Come, then, young lady," said the page, "and take me to your mother; for I bring a letter and a present from your father."

"That I will gladly do, my good sir," replied the girl, who appeared to be around fourteen years of age. Leaving the clothes that she was washing with one of her companions and without putting anything on her head or feet, for she was barelegged and her hair was hanging down, she leaped in front of the page's mount and said, "Come with me, your Grace. Our house is on the edge of the village and my mother is there, very much worried because she has had no news of my father for a long time."

"Well," said the page, "I am bringing her some, and such good news that she may well thank God for it."

With the girl leaping, running, and skipping, they reached the village, but before going into the house she called from the doorway, "Come out, Mother Teresa, come out, come out; here is a gentleman with letters and other things from my father."

At these words Teresa Panza appeared, spinning a bundle of flax. She was clad in a gray skirt so short that it seemed they had "cut it to her shame," [5] with a bodice of the same color and a chemise. She was not so very old, although she was obviously past forty; but she was strong of body, robust and vigorous, with a nutbrown complexion.

"What is it, daughter? Who is this gentleman?" she asked as she saw the page on horseback.

"A servant of my lady Doña Teresa Panza," replied the page. With this, he dismounted and went to kneel before Teresa with great humility. "Give me your hands, my lady Doña Teresa," he said, "as the lawful wedded wife of Señor Don Sancho Panza, rightful governor of the island of Barataria."

"Ah, my good sir," she said, "be off with you. Don't do that; for I am no palace lady but a poor peasant woman, daughter of a clodhopper and wife of a squire-errant and not of any governor."

"Your Grace," the page insisted, "is the most worthy wife of an archworthy governor, as proof of which I hand your Grace this letter and this present." And he forthwith took out of his pocket a string of coral beads with golden clasps.

"This letter," he said, placing the beads about her neck, "is from my Lord Governor and the other one and the necklace are from my lady the duchess, who has sent me to you."

Teresa was quite overcome by it all, and her daughter as well. "May they slay me," said the lass, "if our master Don Quixote is not at the bottom of this; he must have given father that government or earldom that he promised him so many times."

"That is right," said the page. "Thanks to Señor Don Quixote, Señor Sancho is now governor of the island of Barataria, as you will see from this letter."

"Read it for me, noble sir," said Teresa, "for although I know how to spin, I cannot read a mite."

"Nor I," added Sanchica; "but wait here a moment and I will go call someone who will read it for us, even though it be the curate himself or the bachelor, Sansón Carrasco. They will be very glad to come and hear news of my father."

"There is no need to call anyone," said the page. "I may not know how to spin, but I can read, and I will tell you what it says." He proceeded to do so, reading Sancho's letter in its entirety, which, since it has already been given in these pages, need not be set down here again. Then he took out the other one, from the duchess, the contents of which were as follows:

Friend Teresa: Your husband Sancho's sterling qualities, his upright character, and his ability have made me feel impelled to ask my own husband, the duke, to give him an island out of the many in my lord's possession. I have received word that he, Sancho, is governing like a gerfalcon,[6] a thing which I am very glad to hear, and my lord, the duke, also. I thank Heaven most heartily that I made no mistake in choosing him for such a post; for I would have my lady Teresa know that it is extremely hard to find a good governor in this world, but God grant that I do as well as Sancho is doing now.

I send you herewith, my dear, a string of coral beads with gold clasps, and could only wish that they were oriental pearls. However, he who gives you a bone would not see you dead.[7] The time will come when we shall meet and become acquainted, but God only knows what is to be. Remember me to Sanchica, your daughter, and tell her for me that she should hold herself in readiness, for I mean to make a good match for her when she least expects it.

They tell me that in your village you have some large acorns. Send me a couple of dozen or so of them and I shall prize them greatly as coming from you. Write me at length, telling me of your health and how you are doing; and if you stand in need of anything, you have but to open your mouth and you shall have your wish.[8]

From this place. Your loving friend,

THE DUCHESS.

"Ah!" exclaimed Teresa when she had heard the letter, "and what a kind lady it is, how plain and humble! Let me be buried with[9] such ladies as that and not with the *hidalgas* you find in this town, who think that because they are ladies the wind should not touch them, who when they go to church put on as many airs as if they were queens, and who think that they are disgraced if they so much as look at a countrywoman. You can see how goodhearted she is. For all that she's a duchess, she calls me her friend and treats me like an equal—and may I see her equal to the tallest belfry in La Mancha!

"As for the acorns, my good sir, I will send her ladyship a peck [10] of them, and such big ones that people well may come to see them as a show and wonder at them. And now, for the present, Sanchica, entertain this gentleman, look after his horse, get some eggs from the stable, slice plenty of bacon, and give him a meal fit for a prince; [11] for the good news he brings and the good face on him deserve the best there is. In the meanwhile, I'll run out and tell the neighbor women about our good luck, and the father curate and Master Nicholas the barber, for they always have been such good friends of your father's."

"I will do as you say, mother," said Sanchica, "but you must give me half of that string of beads; for I don't think my lady the duchess would have been so stupid as to send them all to you."

"They are all for you, daughter," replied Teresa, "but let me wear them around my neck for a few days, for it seems as if they really gladdened my heart."

"You will be glad, too," said the page, "when you see the bundle that is in this portmanteau; for it contains a suit of the finest cloth, which the governor wore only one day to the hunt and which he now sends to Señora Sanchica."

"May he live a thousand years," said Sanchica, "and the one who brings it no less, and even two thousand if needs be."

Teresa then left the house with the letters and with the beads about her neck, strumming upon the former with her fingers as if they had been a tambourine. Falling in by chance with the curate and Sansón Carrasco, she began doing a dance as she cried, "Faith, and we are no poor relations now! We've got a little government! Let the finest lady there is meddle with me and I'll set her down as an upstart!"

"What's all this, Teresa Panza? Why are you acting like mad, and what papers are those you have there?"

"Those are letters from duchesses and governors, if you call that madness, and these beads that I have about my neck are of finest coral, with Ave Marias and Pater Nosters of beaten gold, and I am a governor's wife!"

"God help us, Teresa, but we don't understand you. We can't make out what you are talking about."

"There, see for yourselves," she said, and handed them the letters.

The curate read them aloud as Sansón Carrasco listened, and the two of them then gazed at each other as if dumfounded. The bachelor asked who had brought the letters, and she replied by saying that they should come home with her and meet the messenger, a young man fine as gold [12] who had brought her another present worth even more than this one. The curate took the beads from her neck and looked at them again and again, and, having made sure that they were really valuable, he was more astonished than ever.

"By the habit that I wear," he declared, "I do not know what to say or think about these letters and presents. On the one hand, I can perceive by touching them the fineness of these coral beads, and, on the other hand, I read here that a duchess is sending to ask for two dozen acorns."

"Make sense out of that for me if you can," said Carrasco. "But come along, let's go see the one who brought this letter; he may be able to throw some light upon the mystery."

They did so, and Teresa returned with them. They found the page sifting a little barley for his horse and Sanchica cutting a slice of bacon to be fried with the eggs for the page's dinner. Both of them were pleased by the young man's bearing and fine apparel, and after a courteous exchange of greetings Sansón requested him to give them what news he had of Don Quixote, and of Sancho Panza as well. He added that they had read the letters from Sancho and my lady the duchess but were still puzzled, being unable to make out what was meant by Sancho's government, especially the reference to an island, seeing that all or most of the islands in the Mediterranean belonged to his Majesty.

"As to Señor Sancho Panza's being a governor," replied the page, "there can be no doubt. As to whether his government consists of an island or not, is no concern of mine. It is sufficient to state that it is a town of more than a thousand inhabitants. With regard to the acorns, I may say that my lady the duchess is so modest and unassuming that she not only would ask a peasant woman for such a gift as that, but has even been known to send to a neighbor of hers to ask for the loan of a comb. For I would have your Worships know that the ladies of Aragon, however highborn they may be, are not so haughty and punctilious as are those of Castile, and are in the habit of treating people with greater informality."

In the midst of their conversation Sanchica came out, her skirt filled with eggs.

"Tell me, sir," she asked of the page, "does my father by any chance wear trunk-hose since he became a governor?"

"I never noticed, but I imagine so."

"Oh, my God! What a sight it must be, my father in tights! Isn't it strange, ever since I was born I have wanted to see him dressed like that?"

"As things are going now," replied the page, "you will see it if you live long enough. By God, if his government lasts him two more months, he'll be going about in a traveler's hood." [13]

It was plain to the curate and the bachelor that the page was speaking in jest, but the fine quality of the beads and of the hunting suit that Sancho had sent (Teresa had already shown them the garment) seemed to contradict this impression. Meanwhile, they had a good laugh over the wish that Sanchica had expressed, and they laughed still more as Teresa went on to say, "Señor Curate, I wish you would find out if there is anyone going to Madrid or Toledo who could buy me a hoop skirt, the best there is and in the latest fashion; for I certainly mean to be as much of an honor as I can to my husband in his government, that I do, and if I get my pride up I intend to go to court and set up a coach like all the other ladies, for she who is the wife of a governor may very well keep one."

"And why shouldn't you, mother!" cried Sanchica. "Would to God it was today instead of tomorrow, even though they said, when they saw me seated in the coach with my mother, 'Just look at that little nobody, that garlic-eater's daughter, how she rides around at her ease as if she were a female pope!' But let them tramp in the mud and let me go in my carriage, with my feet off the ground. Bad luck[14] to all the gossips in the world. So long as I go warm, let the people laugh! [15] Am I right, mother?"

"Indeed you are, my daughter," replied Teresa. "My good Sancho prophesied all this luck and even better, and you'll see, my child, I'll not stop until I've become a countess. For luck is all in the way you begin; as I've heard your father say many times—and he's the father of proverbs as well—when they offer you a heifer, run with the halter,[16] and when they offer you a government, take it; when they give you an earldom, grab it, and when they say *tus, tus*[17] to you with some nice present, snap at it. It would be just as if you were to go on sleeping and not answer when fortune and good luck stand knocking at the door of your house!"

"And what do I care," added Sanchica, "if somebody or other says, when they see me holding my head up like a fine lady, 'The dog saw himself in hempen breeches,'[18] and so forth?"

Listening to this, the curate was led to remark, "I cannot help believing that every member of the Panza family was born with a bagful of proverbs inside him; I never saw one that did not spill them at all hours and on every occasion."

"That is the truth," said the page, "for the Lord Governor Sancho goes around quoting them at every turn, and even though they may not be to the point, they are very amusing, and my lady the duchess and the duke praise them highly."

"Then, my dear sir," said the bachelor, "you still maintain, do you, that all this about Sancho's government is the truth, and that there really is a duchess in this world who sends him presents and writes to him? As for us, we have handled the presents and read the letters, but still are not convinced and are inclined to think, rather, that this is something that has to do with our fellow townsman Don Quixote. He believes that everything is done by enchantment; and I might say that I should like to touch and feel your Grace to see if you are a ghostly ambassador or a flesh-and-blood being."

"Gentlemen," replied the page, "with regard to myself I only know that I am a real messenger and that Señor Sancho Panza is indeed a governor; I know that my lord and lady, the duke and duchess, are in a position to give, and have given him this government, and I have heard that the same Sancho Panza is deporting himself in it most valiantly. As to whether or not there is any enchantment in it, that is something for your Worships to argue. I swear by my parents, who are still living and whom I dearly love, that this is all I know about it."

"It may very well be," said the bachelor, "but *dubitat Augustinus.*" [19]

"Let him doubt who will," said the page. "The truth is as I have told it to you, and truth always rises above a lie as oil above water.[20] *Operibus credite, et non verbis;* [21] let one of you come with me, and he shall see with his own eyes what he will not believe with his ears."

"I am the one who should make that journey," said Sanchica. "Take me with you, sir, on the crupper of your hack; I'll be very glad to go see my father."

"Governors' daughters," replied the page, "do not travel the highways alone, but only when escorted by carriages and litters and a large number of servants."

"In God's name," said Sanchica, "I can go just as well mounted on a she-ass as in a coach! What a dainty creature you must think I am!"

"Be quiet, girl," said Teresa, "you don't know what you are saying. This gentleman is quite right. Different times, different manners.[22] When my husband was Sancho, I was Sancha; and now that he's a governor, I am Señora—I don't know if there is anything in what I am saying or not."

"Señora Teresa is saying more than she realizes," remarked the page; "but give me something to eat and let me be on my way, for I intend to return this evening."

"Your Grace," said the curate, "will partake of my frugal fare; [23] for Señora Teresa is more willing than able when it comes to serving such a guest as you."

The page at first declined, but finally had to yield for the sake of his own well-being; and the curate then gladly bore him off in order that he might question him at length regarding Don Quixote and his exploits. The bachelor offered to write the replies for Teresa to the letters she had received, but she would not have him meddling in her affairs, since she looked upon him as being something of a practical joker. Instead, she gave a cake and a couple of eggs to a young acolyte, who copied out two epistles for her, one addressed to her husband and the other to the duchess, which she herself had composed and which are not the worst to be met with in this great history, as will be seen further on.

CHAPTER LI. *Of the course of Sancho Panza's government, with other entertaining matters of a similar nature.*

DAY dawned following the night on which the governor had made his rounds. That night had been a sleepless one for the butler, his mind being occupied with the beautiful face and general attractiveness of the disguised maiden. As for the major-domo, he had spent the remaining hours until daylight in writing to his lord and lady, giving them an account of all that Sancho had done and said, for he was equally astonished by the governor's actions and by his speech, finding in both an admixture of wisdom and simple-mindedness.

The lord governor finally arose and, on orders of Doctor Pedro Recio, made a breakfast on a bit of preserves and four draughts of cold water, though he would rather have had a slice of bread and a cluster of grapes. However, seeing there was no help for it, he made the best of things, with sorrowing heart and a weary stomach, Pedro Recio having given him to understand that a light diet of dainty food was the one best suited to individuals in positions of command and in offices entailing grave responsibility where one had need not so much of bodily strength as of mental faculties. As a result of this sophistry, Sancho suffered hunger to such an extent that in his heart he was led to curse the government and the one who had bestowed it upon him.

Nevertheless, in spite of his hunger and fortified only by the preserves he had eaten, he undertook to sit in judgment that day; and the first matter that came before him was a problem [1] propounded by a foreigner in the presence of the major-domo and the other attendants.

"My lord," he began, "there was a large river that separated two districts of one and the same seignorial domain—and let your Grace pay attention, for the matter is an important one and somewhat difficult of solution. To continue then: Over this river there was a bridge, and at one end of it stood a gallows with what resembled a court of justice, where four judges commonly sat to see to the enforcement of a law decreed by the lord of the river, of the bridge, and of the seignory. That law was the following: 'Anyone who crosses this river shall first take oath as to whither he is bound and why. If he swears to the truth, he shall be permitted to pass; but if he tells a falsehood, he shall die without hope of pardon on the gallows that has been set up there.' Once this law and the rigorous conditions it laid down had been promulgated, there were many who told the truth and whom the judges permitted to pass freely enough. And then it happened that one day, when they came to administer the oath to a certain man, he swore and affirmed that his destination was to die upon the gallows which they had erected and that he had no other purpose in view.

"The judges held a consultation. 'If,' they said, 'we let this man pass, without hindrance, then he has perjured himself and according to the law should be put to death; but he swore that he came to die upon that scaffold, and if we hang him that will have been the truth, and in accordance with the same law he should go free.' [2] And now, my Lord Governor, we should like to have your Grace's opinion as to what the judges should do with the man; for up to now they have been very doubtful and perplexed, and, having heard of your Grace's keen understanding and great intellect, they have sent me to beseech your Grace on their behalf to tell them what you think regarding this intricate and puzzling question."

"Certainly," said Sancho, "those judges who sent you to me might have spared themselves the trouble, for I am a fellow who has in him more of the dull than of the sharp; but, nevertheless, let me hear the case once more and it may be that I'll hit upon something."

The one who had propounded the question then repeated it over and over again.

"It seems to me," said Sancho at last, "that I can settle the matter very shortly. This man swore that he was going to die upon the gallows, and if he does, he swore to the truth and the law says he should be freed and permitted to cross the bridge; but if they do not hang him, he swore falsely and according to the same law ought to be hanged."

"My Lord Governor has stated it correctly," said the messenger; "so far as a complete understanding of the case is concerned, there is no room for any further doubt or questioning."

"Well, then," said Sancho, "my opinion is this: that part of the man that swore to the truth should be permitted to pass and that part of him that lied should be hanged, and thus the letter of the law will be carried out."

"But, my Lord Governor," replied the one who had put the question, "it would be necessary to divide the man into two halves, the lying half and the truthful half, and if he were so divided it would kill him and the law would in no wise be fulfilled, whereas it is essential that its express provisions be carried out."

"See here, my good sir," said Sancho, "either I am a blockhead or this man you speak of deserves to die as much as he deserves to live and cross the bridge; for if the truth saves him, the lie equally condemns him. And this being the case, as indeed it is, it is my opinion that you should go back and tell those gentlemen who sent you to me that, since there is as much reason for acquitting as for condemning him, they ought to let him go free, as it is always more praiseworthy to do good than to do harm. I would give you this decision over my signature if I knew how to sign my name;[3] and in saying what I do I am not speaking on my own account but am remembering one of the many pieces of advice which my master Don Quixote gave me the night before I came here to be governor of this island. When justice was in doubt, he said, I was to lean to the side of mercy; and I thank God that I happened to recollect it just now, for it fits this case as if made for it."

"So it does," agreed the major-domo, "and it is my belief that Lycurgus himself, who gave laws to the Lacedaemonians, could not have handed down a better decision than that which our great Panza has rendered us. Court is now over for this morning," he added, "and I will give orders that my Lord Governor be served a meal that is very much to his taste."

"That is all I ask," said Sancho, "that you be fair with me. See to it that I eat, and then let it rain cases and problems and I'll make quick work of them." [4]

The major-domo kept his word, it being against his conscience to starve to death so wise a governor as this; and, in any event, he expected to have done with him that night by playing the final joke upon him in accordance with the instructions of his lord and lady. Accordingly, after Sancho had eaten for once in violation of all the rules and aphorisms of the Doctor Tirteafuera, as soon as the cloth had been removed a messenger entered with a letter from Don Quixote addressed to the governor. Sancho ordered the secretary to cast an eye over it and, if it contained nothing that should be kept secret, to read it aloud.

The secretary obeyed. "It may very well be read aloud," he said after he had glanced at it, "for what Señor Don Quixote has here written to your Grace deserves to be engraved in letters of gold. You shall hear for yourself:

LETTER OF DON QUIXOTE DE LA MANCHA TO SANCHO PANZA, GOVERNOR OF THE ISLAND OF BARATARIA

Whereas, friend Sancho, I had expected to hear news of your indolence and follies, I hear, instead, of the wisdom you have displayed, and for this I give special thanks to Heaven, which raises the poor up from the dungheap [5] and makes wise men out of fools. They tell me that you govern like a man, but that as a man you are as humble as any beast of the field. In this connection, I would have you note, Sancho, that it very often behooves those in positions of authority to resist the natural humility of their hearts, and it is indeed necessary for them to do so; for the attire of one who is in a post of grave responsibility should be conformable to his station and not limited by his own humble tastes. Dress well; a stick properly clothed no longer has the appearance of a stick. [6] By this I do not mean that you should deck yourself out with trinkets and showy raiment, or that, being a judge, you should dress like a soldier; rather, the garb should be suited to the office, provided always that it is neat and well made.

In order to win the good will of the people that you govern, there are two things, among others, that you must do: one is to act in a well-bred manner toward every one (this I have told you before); and the other is to see that there is an abundance of food, since nothing weighs more heavily upon the hearts of the poor than hunger and want.

Do not issue many decrees, and when you do, see to it that they are good ones and, above all, that they are observed and fulfilled, for decrees that are not observed are as none at all but, rather, convey the impression that the prince who had the wisdom and authority requisite for issuing them has not had the power to enforce them, and laws that merely hold a threat without being put into execution are like the log that was king of the frogs: at first he frightened them, but in time they came to despise him and mounted upon him.[7]

Be a father to virtue and a stepfather to vice. Be not always strict nor always lenient but observe a middle course between these two extremes, for therein lies wisdom. Visit the prisons, slaughter houses, and public squares, for the presence of the governor in such places is a matter of great importance: it comforts the prisoners, who hope to be speedily released; it is a bugbear to the butchers, who for once give fair weight; and it terrifies the market women for the same reason. Do not show yourself, even though perchance you may be (and I do not think you are) either covetous, a woman-chaser, or a glutton; for when the people and those with whom you have to deal come to know your weakness, they will train their batteries upon you at that point until they have brought you down to the depths of perdition.

Go over time and again, consider and reconsider, the advice and instructions that I gave you in writing before you set out from here for your government; if you follow these counsels you will find in them a ready aid in those labors and difficulties that governors encounter at every turn. Write to your lord and lady by way of showing them that you are grateful; for ingratitude is the daughter of pride and one of the greatest of known sins, and the person who is ungrateful to his benefactors shows clearly that he would be ungrateful to God as well, who has conferred and continues to confer so many blessings upon him.

My lady the duchess sent a special messenger with your suit and another present to your wife, Teresa Panza, and we are expecting an answer at any moment. I have been a trifle indisposed as the result of a certain scratching that was of no great benefit to my nose, but it was in reality nothing at all. If there are enchanters who mistreat me, there are also those that defend me. Let me know as to whether the major-domo who is with you had anything to do with the business of La Trifaldi as you suspected. Keep me informed of everything that happens to you, since the distance is so short and, moreover, I am thinking of giving up very soon this idle life that I lead here, as I was not born for it. I have been asked to undertake a certain business that may bring me into disfavor with my lord and lady; but although this gives me no little concern, it really means nothing to me, for, when all is said and done, I must fulfill the duties of my profession rather than think of their pleasure, in accordance with the saying, "*Amicus Plato, sed magis amica veritas.*" [8] If I quote Latin to you, it is because I assume that since becoming a governor you will have learned it. I commend you to God, and may He keep you from becoming an object of pity to anyone.

Your friend,

DON QUIXOTE DE LA MANCHA.

Sancho listened to the letter very attentively, and it was praised by all who heard it for the wisdom it contained. The governor then rose from the table and, summoning his secretary, shut himself up in his room, for he wished to answer his master Don Quixote without delay. He instructed the secretary to write down what was dictated to him, without adding anything to it or leaving out anything, and the following is the letter that he composed:

I have been so very busy that I have not had time to scratch my head or even trim my nails, which is the reason why I wear them so long, God help me. I tell you this, my dear master, so that your Grace may not be surprised that I have not let you know sooner how well or ill I am making out in this government, where I am suffering more hunger than the two of us did when we roamed the forests and desert places together.

My lord the duke wrote to me the other day, advising me that certain spies had come to my island to assassinate me, but up to now the only one I have discovered is a doctor in this town who is hired to kill all the governors that come here. He is Doctor Pedro Recio, a native of Tirteafuera, and from his name [9] your Grace may judge as to whether or not I have reason to fear dying at his hands. This doctor that I am telling you about says that he himself does not cure diseases when they come but aims to prevent them from coming, and the medicine that he gives you is diet and more diet until he has you down to your bare bones—just as if leanness wasn't worse than fever. The short of it is, he is starving me to death and I'm dying of disappointment; for when I came here as governor, I expected to have my meals hot and my drinks cool and to sleep in comfort between sheets of Holland linen, on feather beds, and instead I find that I have to do penance like a hermit. I do not like it at all, and in the end I imagine the devil will take me.

So far, I have not laid hands on any dues or accepted any bribes,[10] and I do not know what to think of it; for they tell me that the governors who come to this island usually have plenty of money which has been given them or lent them by the people of the town, and I understand that this is the custom not only here but with governors in general.

Last night, in making the rounds, I fell in with a very pretty girl dressed like a boy, in the company of her brother who was in woman's clothes. My butler has fallen in love with the lass and has his mind set on having her for his wife, or so he says, and I have picked the lad for my son-in-law. Today we are going to take the matter up with the father of the pair, who is a certain Diego de la Llana, an old Christian and as fine a gentleman as anyone could wish.

I am in the habit of visiting the market places as your Grace recommends, and yesterday I came upon a hucksteress selling hazelnuts and found that she had mixed with a fanega[11] of fresh ones an equal measure of empty, rotten nuts. I confiscated them all for the charity school children, who know well enough how to tell one kind from the other, and sentenced her to stay away from the market place for a couple of weeks. My action was heartily approved; for I may tell your Grace that there is no one in this town with a worse reputation than these market women; they are all said to be bold and shameless creatures without a conscience, and I can well believe it from what I have seen of them in other places.[12]

I am very glad to hear that my lady the duchess has written to my wife, Teresa Panza, and has sent her the present, and I will try to show my gratitude at the proper time. I would have your Grace kiss her hands for me and tell her that she has not thrown me into any sack with a hole in it, as she will see from the outcome. I hope your Grace will not have any quarrel with my lord and lady, for if you fall out with them, it is plain to be seen that it will do me harm. And it would be contrary to the advice you yourself have given me for you to be ungrateful to those who have shown you so many favors and have treated you so royally in their castle.

That business of the scratching I do not understand, but I imagine
it must be the work of those wicked enchanters that are always tormenting your Grace, and I'll hear all about it when we meet again. I'd
like to send your Grace some present or other, but I don't know
what it would be unless it was some of those very curious clyster
pipes to be worked with bladders that they make in this island. However, if my office holds out, I'll try to send you something, one way
or another.[13] If my wife, Teresa Panza, should write to me, please
pay the postage and send the letter on to me, as I am very anxious to
hear how my wife and young ones are doing at home. And so, may
God free your Grace from those evil-minded enchanters and see
me through with my government, safe and sound—though this I am
inclined to doubt, for I think I'll rather leave it and my life behind me
at one and the same time, the way Doctor Pedro Recio is treating me.

Your Grace's servant,

SANCHO PANZA, THE GOVERNOR.

The secretary sealed the letter and dispatched it by courier at once;
and then the practical jokers put their heads together and began planning how they would dispatch Sancho from his governorship. That
afternoon was spent by him in drawing up a number of ordinances
for the proper administration of what he took to be his island. He
decreed that there were to be no peddlers of provisions in the state,
and that wine might be imported from any region whatever so long
as its place of origin was declared in order that a price might be put
upon it according to its reputation for quality and the esteem in which
it was held, while anyone who watered wine or put a false name on
it was to pay for it with his life. He reduced the cost of all shoes and
stockings, but especially of shoes, as it seemed to him that the prices
being charged for them were exorbitant. He put a tax on servants' wages,
which were out of all proportion to the service rendered.[14] He pre-
scribed an extremely heavy fine for those who sang lewd and lascivious
songs, either by night or by day, and ordained that no blind man should
go about singing verses [15] having to do with miracles unless he could
produce trustworthy evidence that the miracles had actually occurred;
for it was his opinion that most of the events that formed the burden
of their lays were trumped up, to the detriment of the truly miraculous
ones.[16]

He created and appointed a bailiff for the poor, not for the purpose
of harassing them but to make an investigation of their real status, since

many a thief or drunkard of sound body goes about as a make-believe cripple or displaying false sores. In brief, he ordered things so wisely that to this day his decrees are preserved in that town, under the title of *The Constitutions of the Great Governor, Sancho Panza.*

CHAPTER LII. *Wherein is related the adventure of the second distressed, or afflicted, duenna, otherwise known as Doña Rodríguez.*

CID HAMETE tells us that, being now healed of his scratches, Don Quixote came to the conclusion that the life he was leading in that castle was wholly contrary to the order of chivalry that he professed; and he accordingly resolved to ask permission of the duke and duchess to set out for Saragossa, where the festival was near at hand in which he hoped to win the suit of armor that was the prize in such tournaments. He was sitting at table with the ducal pair one day and was just about to carry out his intention and beg their leave when all of a sudden there came through the doorway two women (as they afterward turned out to be), clad in mourning from head to foot. Going over to Don Quixote, one of them threw herself full-length at his feet, pressing her lips to them and uttering moans so deep, so sad, and so heart-rending as to throw all those who heard and beheld her into a state of confusion.

Although the duke and duchess thought that this must be some joke which their servants were playing on the knight, they nonetheless were puzzled and uncertain as they saw how earnestly the woman sighed, moaned, and wept. Finally, taking pity upon her, Don Quixote raised her up and made her remove the veil and mantle that covered her weeping face. As she did so, she revealed—something they had never expected to see!—the countenance of Doña Rodríguez, the duenna of the household, while the other lady in mourning proved to be her daughter, the one who had been deceived by the rich farmer's son. All who knew the duenna were astonished, and my lord and lady more than any, for, although they looked upon her as a weak and pliant creature, they had not thought her capable of acts of madness. At length she turned to her master and mistress and addressed them.

"Will your Excellencies," she said, "be so kind as to permit me a word with this knight, seeing that it is necessary if I am to get myself well out of a predicament in which the impudence of an evil-intentioned boor has placed me?"

The duke gave her the permission she sought, telling her that she might say whatever she liked; and she then fastened her gaze upon Don Quixote.

"Some time ago, O valiant knight," she said, "I gave you an account of the unjust and treacherous manner in which a certain heartless peasant had treated my dearly beloved daughter, the unfortunate maid who stands here before you now, and you promised me at that time that you would espouse her cause and right the wrong that had been done her. But now word has reached me that you are planning to leave this castle in search of such adventures as God may fittingly provide, and ere you take to the road I would beg of you to challenge this impudent yokel and compel him to marry my daughter, for before they first came together he promised her that he would make her his wife. To expect my lord the duke to see justice done is to ask pears of the elm tree,[1] due to reasons which I have already set forth to your Grace in private. And now, may God grant you health, and as for us, may He not forsake us."

To this speech Don Quixote replied with a grave and solemn demeanor. "Worthy duenna," he said, "moderate your tears, or better, dry them up and spare those sighs as well; for I am taking it upon myself to redress the wrong that has been done your daughter, who would have been better off if she had not been so ready to believe the promises of lovers, promises that are lightly made but extremely burdensome when it comes to fulfilling them. With the permission of my lord the duke, I will set out at once in search of this unfeeling youth; I will find and challenge him, and, if he refuses to keep his word, I will surely slay him. The principal object of my calling is to spare the humble and chastise the haughty, to succor the wretched and destroy the oppressor."

"Your Grace," said the duke, "need not go to the trouble of seeking out this rustic of whom the worthy duenna is complaining, nor need you ask my permission to challenge him; I accept the challenge in his behalf and will see that he is duly informed of the fact and that he comes here, to this my castle, to answer and accept in person. I will afford you both

fair play, observing all the customary and rightful conditions and seeing that justice is done to each as is the duty of all those princes who
offer an open field to combatants who come to fight within the bounds
of their dominions."

"Very well," replied Don Quixote, "with this assurance and with
your Highness's kind permission, I declare that from now on I renounce my status as a gentleman in order to put myself upon a level with
the lowborn culprit and make it possible for him as my equal to do
battle with me. And even though he be absent, I hereby challenge
and defy him by reason of the wrong that he has done in deceiving
this poor maiden, who was a virgin and now, through his fault, no
longer is. I maintain that he has either to keep the promise that he gave
her or die on the field of combat."

With this, he drew off one of his gloves and threw it down in the
middle of the room. The duke at once picked it up, saying again that
he accepted the challenge in the name of his vassal. He then fixed the
time for the duel at six days hence, the place to be the courtyard of
the castle and the weapons those customarily employed by knights:
the lance and buckler and coat of mail and all the other accessories,
without any trickery, cheating, or charms of any sort,[2] the said weapons and armor to be viewed and passed upon by the judges of the
contest.

"But first of all," he added, "it is necessary that this worthy duenna
and this unfortunate maiden place their cause entirely in the hands of
Don Quixote, for otherwise there is nothing to be done and the challenge cannot be put into effect."

"I hereby do so," said the duenna.

"I, too," said the daughter, who was all in tears and very much ashamed
of her sorry plight.

These arrangements having been made and the duke having determined what was to be done in the matter, the pair in mourning took
their leave; and the duchess gave orders that from then on they were
to be treated not as her servants but as ladies in trouble who had come
to her house to seek justice. They were, accordingly, given a room
apart and were waited upon as if they had been strangers, to the considerable astonishment of the other servants, who wondered where the
folly and impudence of Doña Rodríguez and her ill-errant daughter [3]
would stop.

At this point, by way of adding the finishing touch to the meal and
bringing it to a pleasant close, lo and behold, that same page who had

carried the letters and presents to Teresa Panza, wife of Sancho Panza, the governor, now entered the room. The duke and duchess were very glad to see him, being anxious to hear what had happened to him in the course of his journey; but in response to a question from them he replied that he could not make his report in the presence of so many people or in a few words, and so he suggested that they leave it for another time, when they would be alone, and in the meanwhile amuse themselves by listening to the letters that he had brought back with him. With this, he took out the two letters and handed them to the duchess. One of them bore the superscription: "Letter for My Lady the Duchess So-and-So, of I Don't Know Where," while the other was directed "To My Husband, Sancho Panza, Governor of the Island of Barataria, and May God Prosper Him Longer Than He Does Me."

The duchess's bread would not bake, as the saying goes, until she had read the one that was addressed to her. She opened it and glanced at its contents, and then, seeing that it was proper to do so, she read it aloud for the duke and the others to hear:

TERESA PANZA'S LETTER TO THE DUCHESS

The letter that your Highness wrote me, my lady, gave me great pleasure and was very welcome indeed.[4] The string of coral beads is very fine, and I can say the same of my husband's hunting suit. This whole village is happy to know that you have made my husband, Sancho, a governor, although nobody believes it, especially the curate, and Master Nicholas the barber, and Sansón Carrasco the bachelor; but that makes no difference to me, for so long as it is true, and I am sure that it is, they may all say what they like—to tell the truth, I would not have believed it myself if it had not been for the beads and the suit. In this town everybody thinks my husband is a numskull, fit only for governing a flock of goats, and cannot imagine what other kind of government he would be good for. May the Lord's will be done, and may God direct him in the right path for the best interests of his children.

I, my dear lady, with your Grace's permission, have made up my mind to take advantage of this fine day [5] by coming to court where I may stretch out in a coach and cause a thousand who are already jealous of me to burst their eyeballs. And so I beg your Excellency to order my husband to send me a little money, and let it be quite a little, for expenses are heavy at court, with a loaf of bread costing a real and meat thirty maravedis a pound,[6] which is really frightful. If he does not want me to come, have him let me know at once, for my feet are itching to be off. My women friends and neighbors tell me that if I and my daughter cut a figure and make a fine show at court, my husband will come to be better known on account of me than I will be on account of him. For, of course, there will be many who will ask, 'Who are those ladies in that coach yonder?' And one of my servants will answer, 'The wife and daughter of Sancho Panza, governor of the island of Barataria.' And that way, people will learn who Sancho is, I'll be well thought of, and to Rome for everything.[7]

I am sorry as sorry can be that this year they have gathered no acorns here, but for all of that I am sending your Highness about half a peck; I myself went to the woods to gather them, one by one, but I couldn't find any that were bigger than these—I only wish they were as big as ostrich eggs.

Don't forget to write to me, your Mightiness,[8] and I will be sure to answer, letting you know how I am and whatever news there is in this village, where I remain, praying Our Lord to keep your Highness and not be unmindful of me. My daughter Sancha and my son [9] kiss your Grace's hands.

She who would rather see your Ladyship than write to you,

Your servant,

TERESA PANZA.

They were all very much pleased with this letter, especially the ducal pair; and the duchess then asked Don Quixote if he thought it would be right to open the one addressed to the governor, as she fancied it must be a very good one. The knight replied that she might do so if it gave her pleasure, and they found that it read as follows:

TERESA PANZA'S LETTER TO SANCHO PANZA,
HER HUSBAND

I received your letter, my dear Sancho, and I swear as a Catholic Christian that I was within two fingers' breadth of going mad with joy. Listen, brother, when I heard you were a governor, I was so happy I thought I would drop dead; for you know what they say: that sudden joy can kill you just as well as a great sorrow. As for your daughter, Sanchica, she let her water go from pure delight. There before me was the suit that you sent me and the beads from my lady the duchess, for my neck, and there in my hand were the letters with the messenger standing beside me; and yet, in spite of all that, I fancied that what I saw and touched must be a dream, since who would ever think that a goatherd would come to be governor of islands?

But you know, my dear, what my mother used to say: that you had to live a long time to see a lot. I tell you this because I expect to see more if I live longer. I don't mean to stop until I see you a farmer of revenues or tax collector; for while the devil carries off those that abuse such offices,[10] still they always hold and handle money. My lady the duchess will tell you how anxious I am to come to court; think it over and let me know how you feel about it. I will try to be an honor to you by going in a coach.

The curate, the barber, the bachelor, and even the sacristan cannot believe that you are a governor and say it is all some kind of humbug or enchantment like everything that concerns your master, Don Quixote; and Sansón says they are coming to look for you as they mean to get that government out of your head and the madness out of Don Quixote's noddle, but I only laugh and look at my string of beads and go on planning the dress that I am going to make for our daughter out of your suit. I sent some acorns to my lady the duchess and wish they had been of gold. Send me a few strings of pearls if they have any in that island.

The news of this village is that Berrueca has married off her daughter to a good-for-nothing painter who came here looking for anything that offered. The council gave him an order to paint his Majesty's arms over the door of the town hall. His price was two ducats, which they paid him in advance; he worked for a week and at the end of that time had done nothing, saying that he could not bring himself to paint trifling things of that sort. He paid them back the money but got himself a wife by passing himself off as a good workman. The truth is, he has now laid down the brush and taken up the spade and goes to the field like a gentleman.

Pedro de Lobo's son has taken orders and the tonsure, with the intention of becoming a priest. Minguilla, Mingo Silvato's granddaughter found it out and is suing him for promise to marry her, and the evil tongues will have it that she is pregnant by him, although he stoutly denies it.

There are no olives this year, nor is there a drop of vinegar to be had in all the town. A company of soldiers passed this way, taking with them three village girls; I would rather not tell you who they are, for it may be they will come back and will not fail to find those who will marry them with all their faults, for better or for worse. Sanchica is making bone-lace [11] and earns eight maravedis [12] a day, clear, which she puts into a money box toward household furnishings; but now that you are a governor, you will give her a dowry without her having to work. The fountain in the public square dried up and lightning struck the pillory (it would suit me if that was where it always hit).

I am waiting for an answer to this letter that I may know what you think about my coming to court. And so, may God give you a longer life than He does me, or at least as long a one since I would not want to leave you without me in this world.

Your wife,
TERESA PANZA.

These letters were praised, laughed over, relished, and admired; and then, as if to put the seal on everything, the courier arrived with the one that Sancho had written to Don Quixote. This also was read aloud and led them to doubt that the squire was as simple-minded as they had taken him to be. The duchess then retired that she might hear from the page what had happened in Sancho's village. He gave her a full account, leaving out no slightest detail, and delivered to her the acorns together with a cheese which Teresa assured him was very good, being better than those of Tronchón.[13] The duchess received it with great pleasure; and we shall leave her there as we go on to relate how the rule of the great Sancho Panza, flower and mirror of all island governors, came to an end.

CHAPTER LIII. *Of the troublous end and con-clusion of Sancho Panza's government.*

TO IMAGINE that things in this life are always to remain as they are is to indulge in an idle dream. It would appear, rather, that everything moves in a circle, that is to say, around and around: [1] spring follows summer, summer the harvest season, harvest autumn, autumn winter, and winter spring; [2] and thus does time continue to turn like a never-ceasing wheel. Human life alone hastens onward to its end, swifter than time's self [3] and without hope of renewal, unless it be in that other life that has no bounds. So sayeth Cid Hamete, the Mohammedan philosopher; for many who have lacked the light of faith, being guided solely by the illumination that nature affords them, have yet attained to a comprehension of the swiftness and instability of this present existence and the eternal duration of the one we hope for. Our author, however, is here thinking of the speed with which Sancho's government was overthrown and brought to a close, and, so to speak, sent up in smoke and shadow.

On the night of the seventh day after assuming his governorship Sancho was lying in bed, sated not with bread or with wine but with sitting in judgment, giving opinions, enacting statutes, and issuing decrees. In spite of his hunger, sleep was beginning to close his eyelids when of a sudden he heard a great noise of bells and shouting as if the whole island were sinking. He sat up in bed and strained his ears to see if he could make out what the cause of such an uproar could be, but in vain, for the sound of countless drums and trumpets was now added to the din and he was more bewildered than ever and was filled with fear and trembling. Getting to his feet, he put on a pair of slippers on account of the dampness of the floor but did not stop for a dressing gown or anything of the sort. As he dashed out the door of his room, he saw coming toward him down the corridor more than a score of persons carrying lighted torches and unsheathed swords.

"To arms! To arms, Lord Governor!" they cried. "An enemy host has invaded the island and we are lost unless your wit and valor can save us." And, keeping up the furious din all the while, they came to where Sancho stood, dazed and terrified by what he saw and heard.

"Arm at once, your Lordship," one of them said to him, "unless you choose to be lost, and the whole island with you."

"What have I to do with arming?" replied Sancho. "Or what do I know about fighting? [4] Better leave such things as that to my master Don Quixote, who will settle everything in the blink of an eye and save us all. Sinner that I am, God help me, I understand nothing about these squabbles."

"Ah! my Lord Governor," said another, "what kind of faintheartedness is this? Arm, your Grace; we bring you arms, both offensive and defensive. Arm, and go out into the public square; be our leader and our captain as is your duty, seeing that you are the governor."

"Arm me, then, for Heaven's sake," said Sancho.

They at once produced two large shields which they had brought with them and put them on him over his shirt, one in front and the other behind, permitting him to don no other garment. Through holes that they had made for the purpose they drew his arms and then proceeded to bind him very firmly with pieces of rope in such a manner as to leave him walled in and boarded up straight as a spindle so that he could not bend his knees or stir a single step. They then handed him a lance, on which he leaned to keep from falling, and when they had him in this condition they bade him lead them on and inspire them all with courage, assuring him that he was their north pole, their lantern,[5] and their morning star who would bring this business to a successful conclusion.

"And how am I going to lead on, unlucky creature that I am," said Sancho, "when these boards that cut into my flesh are bound so tight I can't even move my kneecaps? What you are going to have to do is, pick me up in your arms and set me down, crosswise or on my feet, in some passageway, and I'll guarantee to hold it either with this lance or with my body."

"Come, my Lord Governor," said one of them, "it is fear rather than the boards that keeps you from moving. Have done with it and bestir yourself, for it is late and the enemy's numbers are increasing, the shouting grows louder, and the danger is pressing."

As a result of these exhortations and reproaches the poor governor did his best to move, whereupon he fell down to the floor with such a thud that they thought surely he must have broken himself to pieces. He lay there like a tortoise in its shell, or a side of bacon between two troughs, or a boat lying bottom upward on the beach; nor did the jokers feel any compassion for him as they saw him in that plight, but extinguishing their torches they began shouting louder than ever, renewing the cry "To arms! To arms!" with great vigor as they trampled over poor Sancho, slashing so furiously at the shields that covered him that, if he had not drawn his head in, the luckless governor would have been in a very bad way indeed. As it was, huddled into that narrow space, he sweat and sweat again as he prayed God with all his heart to deliver him from this peril. Some stumbled over him, others fell upon him, and one of them stood upon him for a good while, as if he had been in a watchtower issuing orders to an army.

"Over this way, our men!" he cried in a stentorian voice. "Here's where the enemy is charging in full force! Hold that breach! Close that gate! Block those ladders! [6] Bring on the pitch and resin and the boiling oil! Barricade the streets with feather beds!" In brief, he shouted most ardently for every variety of engine, implement, or contrivance that is used in war and in defending a city against an assault.

As he heard and suffered all this, Sancho, thoroughly mauled and trampled, said to himself, "Oh, if it would only please the Lord to let them go ahead and take this island and let me die or else free me from this torment!" Heaven granted his prayer, and when he least expected it there came a cry, "Victory! Victory! The enemy is beaten and is falling back! Ho, my Lord Governor, rise! Come and rejoice with us and divide the spoils won by the might of that invincible arm."

"Lift me up," said the sorely battered Sancho in a sickly voice. And when they had helped him to his feet, he went on, "The enemy that I have conquered you can nail to my forehead. I don't want to divide any spoils. All I ask is that some friend of mine, if I have any, give me a drink of wine, for I am parched; and let him wipe the sweat from me, as I am dripping wet." [7]

They wiped him off and brought him some wine, unbound the shields, and seated him upon the bed, and then he promptly fainted away as a result of all the fear and excitement and the harsh treatment he had undergone. Those who had perpetrated the joke were now sorry that they had carried it so far and they were relieved when Sancho came to himself again. He asked what time it was and was informed that it was already daylight; and then, without saying another word, he started dressing himself amid a profound silence as they all watched and waited to see why he should be in such a hurry to put his clothes on. At length, when he was fully clad, he little by little (for he was too stiff and sore to walk fast) made his way out to the stable, followed by all those present; and there he went up to the gray, embraced it, and gave it a kiss on the forehead, not without tears in his eyes.

"Come, comrade and friend," he said, "partner in all my troubles and hardships. When I was with you, I had no other care than that of mending your harness and feeding that little carcass of yours. Those for me were the happy hours, days, and years; but since leaving you and mounting the towers of ambition and pride, a thousand troubles, a thousand torments, and four thousand worries have entered my soul."

Even as he said this he was adjusting the packsaddle, without a word from any of the bystanders. He then with great pain and difficulty climbed up onto the gray's back and, addressing the major-domo, the secretary, the butler, Doctor Pedro Recio, and all the others, he spoke as follows:

"Clear the way, gentlemen, and let me go back to my old freedom. Let me go look for my past life so that I may be resurrected from this present death. I was not born to be a governor or to defend islands and cities from enemies that would attack them. I know more about plowing and digging and pruning vines than I do about laws or the protection of islands and kingdoms. St. Peter is well enough off in Rome;[8] by which I mean that each one should follow the trade to which he was born. In my hand a sickle is better than a governor's scepter. I'd rather have my fill of *gazpacho*[9] than have to put up with a miserable, meddling doctor who kills me with hunger. I'd rather stretch out in the shade of an oak in summer and in winter wrap myself in a double sheepskin jacket and enjoy my freedom than go to bed between sheets of Holland linen and dress myself in sables and be no freer than a governor is.

"And so, your Worships, God be with you. Tell my lord the duke that naked was I born and naked I find myself, and so I neither win nor lose.[10] By this I mean that I came into this government without a penny and I leave it without one, which is just the opposite of what generally happens with the governors of other islands. Fall back, then, and let me pass; I must get myself poulticed, for I think that all my ribs are smashed, thanks to the enemies that trampled me last night."

"You must not do that, my Lord Governor," said Doctor Recio. "I will give your Grace a potion that will soon make you as sound and vigorous as ever; and as for your meals, I promise your Grace to do better, by permitting you to eat abundantly of anything you desire."

"You speak too late," said Sancho. "I'd as soon turn Turk as stay here. These jokes won't do a second time. By God, I would no more keep this government or take another, even though they handed it to me between two platters, than I would fly to Heaven without wings. I come of Panza stock, and they are a stubborn lot; if they say odds, then odds it must be even though it may be evens, and this in spite of all the world. In this stable I leave behind me the ant's wings[11] that lifted me in the air so that the swifts and other birds might eat me; let's come back to earth and walk with our feet once more, and if they're not shod in pinked Cordovan leather, they'll not lack coarse hempen sandals. Every ewe to her mate,[12] and let no one stretch his leg beyond the sheet.[13] And so, once again, let me pass, for it is growing late."

To this the major-domo replied, "My Lord Governor, we will gladly permit your Grace to leave, even though it grieves us very much to lose you, as your wit and Christian conduct have endeared you to us. But it is a well-known fact that every governor, before he departs from the place where he has been governing, must first render an accounting, and your Grace should do the same for the ten days[14] that you have been in office, and then you may go and the peace of God go with you."

"No one," said Sancho, "can demand that of me, unless it is someone that my lord the duke has appointed, and I am on my way now to see the duke and will give him an exact account. And, in any case, seeing that I leave here naked, there is no other proof needed to show that I have governed like an angel."

"By God, if the great Sancho isn't right!" exclaimed Doctor Recio. "I am of the opinion that we should let him go, for the duke will be delighted to see him."

They all agreed to this and allowed Sancho to depart, having first offered to provide him with company and anything that he needed in the way of comfort or conveniences for the journey. He replied that all he wanted was a little barley for his gray and half a cheese and half a loaf of bread for himself, adding that since the distance was so short there was no necessity for him to carry any more or better provisions than that. They all embraced him then, and he, weeping, embraced them all in turn after which he rode away, leaving them filled with admiration at the words he had spoken and at the firmness and wisdom of his resolve.

CHAPTER LIV. *Which treats of matters having to do with this history and none other.*

THE duke and duchess resolved to go ahead with the challenge which Don Quixote, for reasons already set forth, had given their vassal; and inasmuch as the young man was in Flanders, whither he had fled to escape having Doña Rodríguez for a mother-in-law, they decided to substitute for him a Gascon lackey by the name of Tosilos, whom they first instructed very carefully in all that he had to do.

A couple of days later the duke informed his guest that in four days' time the opponent would come to present himself on the field of combat, armed as a knight, and would there maintain that the damsel had lied by half a beard, and even by a beard,[1] if she asserted that he had promised to marry her. Don Quixote was very much pleased with the news and promised himself that he would do wonders in this instance; for he looked upon it as a great good fortune that he should have an opportunity to show his hosts how valiant and mighty an arm was his. He accordingly waited cheerfully and happily for the four days to pass, although they seemed like four centuries to him, so impatient was he for the fray.

But let them pass as we do other things, and let us, rather, accompany Sancho, who, half joyful and half sad, was riding along on his gray to rejoin his master, whose company afforded him more pleasure than the governorship of all the islands in this world.

He had not gone far from the island where his government was situated (he was never able to determine whether it was in reality an island, a city, a town, or a village) when, as it happened, he saw coming toward him down the highway half a dozen pilgrims with their staffs, some of those foreigners who go about singing and begging alms.[2] As they approached him they formed in line and, raising their voices in unison, began a song in some language of which Sancho could understand but a single word: "alms." He knew, therefore, what it was they sought, and being naturally extremely charitable, as Cid Hamete tells us, he took out from his saddlebags the half loaf and half cheese with which he had come provided and gave them to the pilgrims, indicating by signs that he had nothing else to offer them. They accepted the gift willingly enough, but kept saying *"Geld! Geld!"* [3]

"I do not understand what you are asking for, good folks," said Sancho.

One of them then took out a purse from his bosom and displayed it, from which Sancho knew that it was money they wanted. Putting a thumb to his throat and extending his hand upward, he gave them to understand that he had not a coin of any kind on him; and then, spurring the gray, he broke through them. As he passed, however, one of them who had been studying him very attentively flung his arms about him and, in excellent Castilian, cried out, "God bless me! What is this I see? Is it possible that I hold in my arms my dear friend and good neighbor Sancho Panza? Yes, there can be no doubt about it, for I'm not asleep nor am I drunk just now."

Sancho was quite taken aback at hearing himself thus called by name and at being embraced by this foreign pilgrim. He stared hard at the fellow for a good long while, without saying a word, but was still unable to recognize him.

Seeing his perplexity, the pilgrim said to him, "How can it be, Sancho Panza, my brother, that you do not recognize your neighbor Ricote, the Moorish shopkeeper of your village?"

Sancho continued to gaze at him harder than ever, and little by little he began to place him. Then, slipping down off the ass, he threw his arms about his townsman's neck.

"Who the devil would ever have known you, Ricote," he said, "in that clown suit you are wearing? Tell me, who has made a Frenchman out of you,[4] and how do you dare come back to Spain, where, if they catch and recognize you, it will go hard with you?"

"Since you did not know who I was, Sancho," replied the pilgrim, "I am safe. No one would recognize me dressed as I am. But let us leave the road and go into that poplar grove over there, where my companions are going to eat and rest. You shall eat with them, for they are very good folk. That will give me a chance to tell you what has happened to me since I left our village in obedience to his Majesty's command that threatened the unfortunate people of my nation with such severe treatment, as you have heard."[5]

Sancho consented, and after Ricote had spoken to the others they went over to the poplar grove, which was at some distance from the highway. There the mendicants cast aside their staffs and threw off their capes or pilgrims' cloaks, being clad now only in their undergarments.[6] They were all fine young fellows, with the exception of Ricote, who was well along in years, and they all carried saddlebags that appeared to be well stocked, at least with those things that are capable of exciting thirst and summoning it from two leagues away. They stretched out on the ground and, making a tablecloth of the grass, set out upon it bread, salt, knives, nuts, bits of cheese, and clean-picked ham-bones which, if they could not be gnawed any longer, could still be sucked. There was also a black substance called caviar, which is made of fish eggs and is a great awakener of thirst.[7] There was no lack of olives, and although they were dried and without seasoning, they were very palatable.

But what made the best showing of all at that feast was half a dozen flasks of wine, each of the pilgrims having produced one from his saddlebags. Even the worthy Ricote, now transformed from a Moor into a German, or Dutchman, brought out one that in size compared favorably with the other five. They all fell to with right hearty appetites, but they ate very slowly, taking up small morsels of food on the end of their knives and savoring every mouthful; and then, at one and the same time, they raised their arms and flasks aloft, with the mouths of the wine bags[8] tight pressed against their own mouths and their eyes fastened upon the heavens as if they were taking aim at the sky. They sat like this for a good while, wagging their heads from side to side as if to indicate the pleasure they found in emptying the contents [9] of the flasks into their stomachs.

Sancho took it all in and was not displeased at what he saw.[10] Indeed, by way of putting into effect the proverb that he knew so well—"When in Rome, do as you see" [11]—he asked Ricote for his flask and took aim along with the others. Four times the skins were hoisted, but the fifth time it was useless, for they were drier than matweed, a circumstance that diminished the mirth which the company thus far had shown. Every now and then someone would take Sancho's right hand and say, "Spaniard and German, all the same, good fellow," [12] and Sancho would reply, "Good fellow, by God," [13] and would burst into a laugh that lasted for an hour, during which time he remembered nothing of what had happened to him in his government; for cares have little jurisdiction while we are eating and drinking.

Finally, when the wine was exhausted, they began to feel drowsy and ended by falling asleep over their table and tablecloth. Ricote and Sancho alone remained awake, for they had eaten more and drunk less, and the Morisco thereupon took his companion to one side, where they seated themselves at the foot of a beech tree, leaving the others buried in sweet slumber. Then it was Ricote began speaking, in purest Castilian, without once falling into his own Moorish tongue.

"Sancho Panza, my friend and neighbor, you know very well how terrified and dismayed all the people of my nation were by his Majesty's edict and proclamation directed against us. To me, at any rate, it seemed as if, even before the time that was granted us for getting out of Spain had expired, I had already suffered the rigor of the law upon my own person and those of my children. And so I decided—and wisely, I think, like one who knows that on a certain date the house in which he lives will be taken from him and who looks for another into which he may move—I decided, as I was about to say, to leave town alone, without my family, and to seek out a place to which I might take them in comfort so that we would not have to depart in last-minute haste like the others.

"For I saw clearly, as did all our elders, that those proclamations were no mere threats as some maintained, but actual laws that were to be put into effect at a specified time. I was compelled to believe this because I knew of the evil and foolish designs of our people,[14] and for this reason it appeared to me to be a divine inspiration that led his Majesty to carry out so bold a resolution. Not that they were all to blame, for some were true Christians, but these latter were so few in number that they were unable to hold out against those that were not. In short, and with good reason, the penalty of banishment was inflicted upon us, a mild and lenient one as some saw it, but for us it was the most terrible one to which we could have been subjected.

"Wherever we may be, it is for Spain that we weep; for, when all is said, we were born here and it is our native land. Nowhere have we met with the reception that we hoped for. In Barbary and other parts of Africa we expected to be received and welcomed with open arms, but that is where we are insulted and treated the worst. We did not know our good fortune until we had lost it; [15] and almost all of us are so anxious to return that most of those, and they are many, who know the language as I do are now coming back here, leaving their wives and young ones behind and without protection, so great is their love for this land.[16] As for me, I can say that I now know and feel what is meant by the saying, 'Sweet is the love of one's country.'

"Well, then, as I have said, I left our town and made my way to France; but although they gave us a very good reception, I wanted to see all there was to be seen and so I went on to Italy and finally reached Germany. There, it seemed to me, we might enjoy a freer life, as the inhabitants are not overly concerned with fine points but each one does very much as he likes, since for the most part there is full liberty of conscience.[17] I took a house in Augsburg, after which I joined these pilgrims, many of whom are in the habit of coming to Spain every year to visit the sanctuaries, which are for them, like the Indies, an unfailing source of profit. They go all over the country, and there is not a town that they do not leave with their stomachs full of food and wine and at least a real in cash, while at the end of their ramblings they have more than a hundred crowns saved. Changing their money into gold, they hide it in the hollow of their staffs or among the patches of their pilgrims' cloaks, or they employ some other device for getting it out of the realm and back to the country where they reside, and this in spite of the guards that are stationed at the posts and passes.

"And now, Sancho, it is my intention to go back and get the treasure that I left buried in the ground. As it is outside the village, I'll be able to do this without danger, and then I will write to my wife and daughter, whom I know to be in Algiers, or will cross over in person from Valencia, and make arrangements to bring them to some French port and from there to Germany, where we will await what God may have in store for us. For I am certain, Sancho, that my daughter, Ricota, and

Francisca Ricota, my wife, are Catholic Christians; and although I am not as strong in the faith as they, I still am more of a Christian than a Morisco and I pray God constantly to open the eyes of my understanding and reveal to me the way in which I may serve Him. What surprises me is that my wife and daughter should have gone to Barbary rather than to France, where they might have lived like Christians."

"You must remember, Ricote," said Sancho, "that it was not for them to decide. It was Juan Tiopieyo, your wife's brother, who took them away, and, being a shrewd Moor,[18] he knew what he was doing. And I can tell you something else: I don't think it is any use for you to go looking for that buried treasure, for we heard that they had taken from your brother-in-law and your wife many pearls and much money in gold that they wanted to carry out of the country."[19]

"That may well be," replied Ricote, "but I am sure, Sancho, that they did not lay hands on my hoard, for, being afraid that something would happen, I told no one where it was. And so, if you want to come with me and help me get it and hide it, I will give you two hundred crowns, for which I know you can find good use, and you know that I know it."

"I would do it," said Sancho, "but I am not at all covetous. To show you that I am not, only this morning I gave up an office in which, before six months had gone by, I might have lined the walls of my house with gold and been eating off silver plates. For this reason, and because, as I see it, I would be betraying my king by showing favor to his enemies, I would not go with you even though you offered me four hundred crowns, cash down."

"And what office was it that you left, Sancho?" asked Ricote.

"I quit being governor of an island," replied Sancho, "and such an island that, I give you my word, you'd have hard work finding its like."

"Where is this island?" Ricote wanted to know.

"Where is it? Why, two leagues from here; it's called the island of Barataria."

"Be off with you, Sancho," said Ricote. "Islands are out there, in the sea; there are none on the mainland."

"What do you mean?" said Sancho. "I am telling you, friend Ricote, that I left there this morning and that yesterday I governed it at my pleasure, like a sagittarius;[20] but, for all of that, I gave it up, for it seemed to me a dangerous trade, that of governor."

"And what did you get out of your government?" Ricote asked.

"I got the knowledge that I am not fit to govern anything, unless it be a herd of cattle. I also learned that the riches to be had from such governments are only to be gained at the loss of rest and sleep and even nourishment; for on islands the governors eat little, especially where they have doctors to look after their health."

"I don't know what you are talking about, Sancho," said Ricote, "but it sounds like nonsense to me. Who would be giving you islands to govern, anyway? Are there no men in the world more capable of governing than you? Stop such prattle, come back to your senses, and make up your mind whether or not you wish to come with me and help me get the buried treasure that I left behind me. As I told you, I will see that you have enough to live on out of it."

"And I have already told *you*, Ricote," said Sancho, "that I will not. Be satisfied with my promise not to betray you. Go your way in Heaven's name and let me go mine; for well-gotten gain may be lost, but ill-gotten gain is bound to be, and its owner with it." [21]

"I don't want to insist, Sancho," said Ricote. "But tell me, were you in our village when my wife, my daughter, and my brother-in-law left?"

"That I was," Sancho assured him, "and I can tell you that your daughter looked so lovely that everybody in the town came out to see her off, and they all said that she was the most beautiful creature in the world. She wept and embraced all her women friends and acquaintances and all the others who were there to bid her farewell, and begged them all to remember her in their prayers to God and to Our Lady, His mother. I was so touched by it that, though I am not much given to tears, I had to shed a few myself. And faith, there were many there who felt like hiding her or going out and snatching her from the arm of the law along the highway, but they were afraid to disobey the king's command. Most concerned of all was Pedro Gregorio, the rich young heir that you know, who, they say, was very fond of your daughter. Since she left he has not been seen in our village, and we all think that he went after her to rescue her, but up to now we have had no word of any kind."

"I suspected all along," said Ricote, "that the young gentleman was in love with her, but I was not disturbed by it. You have doubtless heard, Sancho, that the Morisco women almost never have anything to do in an amorous way with old Christians; and since I believed that my daughter thought more of being a Christian than she did of falling in love, I was not worried by the attentions of this heir."

"God grant it may be so," said Sancho, "for otherwise it would be bad for both of them. And now, friend Ricote, I must leave you, for I wish to reach the place where my master is by nightfall."

"God go with you, brother Sancho. My comrades are stirring, and it is time for us to be on our way."

With this, the two of them embraced, Sancho mounted his gray, Ricote leaned on his staff once more, and thus they parted.

CHAPTER LV. *Of the things that happened to Sancho along the way, with other unsurpassable events.*

AS A RESULT of having spent so much time with Ricote, Sancho was unable to reach the duke's castle that day, although he was within half a league of it when night fell, a night that was dark and overcast. However, as it was summer, he was not greatly concerned and merely drew up at some distance from the road with the intention of waiting until morning; but luck and fate as usual were against him, and so it happened that, just as he was seeking a spot where he would be more comfortable, both he and the gray tumbled into a deep and very dark pit between some old buildings that stood there. Even as he was falling, he prayed to God with all his heart, thinking that surely he would keep on going down and down until he had come to the depths of the abyss; but this was not the case, for at a little more than three fathoms [1] the ass struck bottom and Sancho found himself still seated upon his mount, unharmed in any way.

He felt his body all over and held his breath to make sure that he really was sound of limb with no holes in him anywhere; and then, upon discovering that he was quite all right, with no bones broken and in perfectly good health, he gave no end of thanks to God Our Lord for the mercy that had been shown him, for he had thought that he undoubtedly would be broken into a thousand pieces. He next ran his hands over the walls of the pit to see if it would be possible to get out of it without help from anyone, but all he encountered was a smooth surface without foothold of any kind. He was very much distressed at this, especially when he heard the ass groaning with pain—and no wonder the poor beast did so, nor could he be blamed for it, for the truth is, he was in a very bad way.

"Ah," exclaimed Sancho Panza then, "how many unforeseen things happen at every step to those that live in this wretched world! Who would ever have said that he who yesterday was enthroned as the governor of an island, ordering his servants and vassals about, would today find himself buried in a pit with no one to help him or come to his rescue, no servant or vassal of any sort? My donkey and I are going to have to die here of hunger, unless he dies first of his jolts and bruises and I of sorrow. One thing is certain, I'll not be as lucky as was my master, Señor Don Quixote de la Mancha, when he went down into the cave of that enchanted Montesinos, where he came upon people who entertained him better than if he had been in his own house. Why, it seems as if they had the table already laid for him and the bed made; he saw beautiful and pleasant visions there, but all that I'll see here will be toads and snakes.

"What an unlucky fellow I am! Where have my follies and my fancies brought me? They'll take my bones out of here, whenever it pleases Heaven to have them found, gnawed clean, white, and smooth. And the bones of my good gray along with mine—that way, perhaps, they will be able to make out who we are, at least those who have heard how Sancho Panza and his ass were never parted one from the other. Once again I say: what unlucky wretches we are, seeing that fate would not let us die in our own country, among our own people! There, even if nothing could be done to remedy our misfortune, we'd at least have had someone to grieve for us and close our eyes at the end as we passed away!

"O friend and comrade," he went on, addressing the donkey,[2] "how ill have I repaid your services! Forgive me, and beg fortune as hard as you can to get us out of this miserable plight in which the two of us now find ourselves. I promise you, I'll put a laurel wreath on your head so that you'll look like a poet laureate,[3] and I'll also give you double rations."

Such was the manner in which Sancho Panza voiced his laments, and the ass listened to him but answered not a word,[4] so great was the poor creature's anguish and suffering. Finally the night, filled with moans and wails, came to an end, and by the light of day Sancho perceived that it was absolutely impossible for him to get out of the pit unaided, whereupon he once more began calling out piteously to see if anyone heard him; but it was like crying aloud in the desert, for in all that region there was not a human ear to pay heed, and then it was that he gave himself up for dead. The gray was lying on his back and his master now managed to get him on his feet, although the animal was barely able to stand. Taking out a crust [5] from his saddlebags—for they had shared the misfortune of man and beast—Sancho fed it to his mount, which seemed to appreciate it. As he did so, he remarked as if the gray could understand him, "With bread, all sorrows are good." [6]

Looking about him, he discovered a hole on one side of the pit big enough for a person to squeeze through, and promptly made for it. Creeping along, he found that on the inside the hole was wide and roomy and that it was light enough for him to see, thanks to a ray of sunlight that came in through what might be called the roof, illuminating everything; and he then observed that it expanded at the far end into a spacious cavity. As soon as he saw this, he came back to where the donkey was and, picking up a stone, began knocking the earth away until he had enlarged the opening sufficiently for the beast to be able to pass through without difficulty. Having accomplished this, he took the gray by the halter and led him across the cavern beyond by way of ascertaining if there was any outlet on the other side. He went in darkness a part of the time and at other times without light,[7] but never without fear.

"God Almighty help me!" he said to himself. "This may be hard luck for me, but it would make a good adventure for my master Don Quixote. He would take these depths and dungeons for flowery gardens and Galiana's palace [8] and would expect to come out of this dark narrow place into some meadow all in bloom; but I, poor hopeless wretch, with no one to lend me encouragement, am thinking at every step I take that another hole deeper than the first one is suddenly going to open up under my feet and swallow me. Welcome, evil, if you come alone." [9]

With such thoughts as these in mind he went on until it seemed to him that he had gone a little more than half a league, and then he descried a dim light that came from somewhere and appeared to be daylight, showing that this road which for him was one leading to the other world ended there in an aperture of some kind.

At this point Cid Hamete leaves him and goes back to Don Quixote, who with great elation was waiting for the appointed battle that he was to wage with the one who had robbed Doña Rodríguez' daughter of her honor, a shameful wrong and grievance which he intended to avenge. Having sallied forth one morning to practice his skill at what he had to do in the encounter set for the following day, he was engaged in putting Rocinante through a short gallop or mock charge when the hoofs of his mount came so near the edge of a pit that, had he not reined in sharply, he would never have been able to avoid falling into it. As it was, he stopped just in time and did not fall. Coming up a little nearer to the cavern, but without dismounting, he gazed down into its depths and, as he did so, heard loud cries from somewhere inside it. He listened closely and succeeded in making out what was said.

"Ho, up there! Is there any Christian who hears me, or any charitable knight who will take pity on a sinner buried alive, a poor unfortunate governor without a government?"

It sounded to Don Quixote like Sancho Panza's voice, at which he was greatly astonished. "Who is it down below?" he shouted as loudly as he could. "Who is it that is lamenting in that manner?"

"Who should it be," came the answer, "or who should be lamenting, if not the wretched Sancho Panza, who as a punishment for his sins has the misfortune to be governor of the island of Barataria, and who was formerly squire to the famous knight Don Quixote de la Mancha?"

Upon hearing this Don Quixote was doubly astonished, and his amazement grew as the thought came to him that Sancho Panza must be dead and his soul in torment down there. Carried away by this idea, he called out once more, "I conjure you by all that, as a Catholic Christian, I well may conjure you by, tell me who you are and whether or not you are a soul in torment. Tell me, also, what it is that you would have me do for you; for it is my calling to aid and succor those who are in trouble in this world, and those in the other world as well who are not able to help themselves."

"From what you say," was the reply, "your Grace who is talking to me now must be my master Don Quixote de la Mancha; there is no doubt about it: the very tone of voice tells me it cannot be anybody else."

"I am indeed Don Quixote," said the knight, "he who professes to aid and succor all those in need, both the living and the dead. And so, tell me who you are and do not keep me any longer in suspense. If you are my squire, Sancho Panza, and have died, and if the devils have not carried you off and you by God's mercy are in purgatory, then our holy mother, the Roman Catholic Church, has the means of releasing you from the torments that you are suffering, and I for my part will intercede with her in your behalf in so far as my worldly substance will permit. Therefore declare yourself and tell me who you are."

"By all that's holy!" [10] the voice answered, "and by the birth of anyone your Grace wishes, I swear, Señor Don Quixote de la Mancha, that

I am your squire, Sancho Panza, and that I never have died in all the days of my life. Having left my government owing to circumstances and reasons which it would take too long to explain, I fell last night into this pit where I am now, and the gray with me—he will not let me lie, seeing that, by way of further proof, he is right here beside me."

Nor was this all; it was as if the ass had understood what Sancho said, for he at once began braying so lustily that the whole cavern echoed with the sound.

"A famous witness," observed Don Quixote. "I know that bray as a mother does her child,[11] and I can hear your voice too, my Sancho. Wait for me and I will go to the duke's castle, which is near by, and bring someone to get you out of that pit into which you must have fallen on account of your sins."

"Go, your Grace," said Sancho, "and, for God's sake, come back soon, as I can't stand it here, being buried alive and dying of fear."

Don Quixote thereupon went to the castle to tell the duke and duchess what had happened to his squire. They were not a little surprised, although they could understand Sancho's having fallen, since the cavern had been there from time immemorial. What they could not understand was why he had left his government without notifying them of his coming. Finally, as the saying is,[12] they brought ropes and tackle and by dint of many people and much labor contrived to rescue Sancho Panza and the ass from that darkness and draw them up to the light of day.

Seeing Sancho emerge in such a manner, a student remarked, "That is the way all bad governors ought to leave their governments: like this sinner who comes forth from the depths of the abyss, dead of hunger, pale-faced, and, I'll wager, without a penny to his name."

Sancho overheard him and replied, "It was eight or ten days ago, brother backbiter, that I came to govern the island which they had given me, and not for one hour of that time did I have my fill of bread; the doctors persecuted me and enemies broke my bones and I had no chance to take bribes or collect my dues;[13] and this being so, as indeed it is, I can't see that I deserve to come out in this fashion; but man proposes and God disposes,[14] and different times different manners;[15] let no one say 'I won't drink of this water,'[16] for where you think there is bacon there are no pegs;[17] God knows what I mean and I say no more, though I could if I wanted to."

"Do not be angry at what you hear, Sancho, and do not let it trouble you," said Don Quixote, "for if you do, there will be no end of it. See that your conscience is clear and let them say what they like, since to endeavor to bind the tongues of slanderers is like trying to put doors to the open country. If a governor leaves his office a rich man, they say that he has been a thief; and if he comes out a poor man, they brand him as worthless and a fool."

"Well, this time," replied Sancho, "they'll surely have to set me down as a fool rather than a thief."

Conversing in this manner and surrounded by a crowd of small boys and other people, they reached the castle, where the duke and duchess were waiting for them. Sancho, however, was unwilling to go up and meet the duke until he first had stabled his gray, which, as he remarked, had spent a very bad night. When this had been attended to, he mounted the stairs and knelt before my lord and lady.

"Because," he said, "it was your Highnesses' pleasure and not on account of any merits of my own, I went to govern your island of Barataria. I was naked when I entered upon my government and naked I find myself now, and so I neither lose nor gain. As to whether I governed well or ill, I had witnesses who will say what they will. I answered questions, solved problems, and decided cases at law, and all the while I was dying of hunger to please Doctor Pedro Recio, native of Tirteafuera, doctor to the island and its governor. Enemies fell upon us by night and we were very hard pressed, but the islanders say that it was due to the might of my arm that they came out of it free and victorious, and may God give them health to the extent that they are telling the truth.

"The short of it is that during this time I had a chance to try out the burdens and responsibilities of governing and I find that, by my reckoning, my shoulders cannot bear the weight; it is no load for these ribs of mine, and these are no arrows for my quiver. And so, before the government threw me over, I decided to throw over the government; and yesterday morning I left the island as I found it, with the same streets, houses, and roofs that it had when I came. I asked no one for a loan nor did I try to make any money out of my office; and although I had it in mind to make a few laws, I made none,[18] since I was afraid they would not be kept and then it would be all the same whether I made them or not.

"I left the island, as I have said, with only my gray for company. I fell into a pit but kept on going until, this morning, by the light of the sun, I saw an outlet. It was not so easy to get out of it though, and if Heaven had not sent my master Don Quixote to me, I'd have been there until the end of the world. And so, my lord and lady, the Duke and Duchess, your governor, Sancho Panza, who stands before you here, in the ten days, no more, that he has held the governorship, has come to learn that he would not give anything whatever to rule, not alone an island, but the entire world. Now that I've made this clear, I kiss your Highnesses' feet; and like the small lads who say 'Leap and let me have it,' [19] I give a leap out of my government and pass over to the service of my master Don Quixote; for with him, even though I eat my bread with fear and trembling, at least I get my fill, and in that case it's all the same to me whether it be of carrots or of partridges."

With this, Sancho brought his long speech to a close. Don Quixote had feared that his squire would utter all kinds of nonsense, and when he heard him finish as sensibly as this he gave thanks to Heaven from the bottom of his heart. The duke then embraced Sancho, expressing his regret that the governor had quitted his post so soon and adding that he would provide him with another, there on his estate, that carried with it less responsibility and would prove more profitable. The duchess did the same and gave orders that he be looked after, as he appeared to be suffering from the bruises he had received.

CHAPTER LVI. *Of the tremendous battle such as never before was seen that took place between Don Quixote de la Mancha and the lackey Tosilos in defense of the duenna Doña Rodríguez' daughter.*

THE duke and duchess were not sorry for the joke they had played on Sancho Panza in connection with the government they had given him, especially when, that same day, the major-domo arrived to give them a detailed account of practically everything that Sancho had said and done during the time, ending with a vivid description of the attack upon the island and the governor's fear and departure, all of which provided them with considerable amusement.

After that, as the history goes on to relate, the day of battle came.

Having repeatedly instructed the lackey Tosilos as to how he was to conduct himself so that he would be able to vanquish Don Quixote without killing or wounding him, the duke ordered that the steel tips be removed from the lances; for, as he remarked to his guest, he prided himself upon being a Christian and so could not permit this combat to be waged at such risk and peril to the lives of the participants. The knight, he added, would have to be content with the free field that was offered him upon his host's estate, though even that was against the decree of the holy Council [1] prohibiting such challenges, for which reason it was too dangerous in the present instance to observe to the full all the rigorous provisions governing such encounters.

The knight replied that his Excellency might arrange all matters having to do with this affair in the way that best suited him, and he, Don Quixote, would obey him in everything. The dread day having arrived, then, the duke ordered them to erect a spacious platform facing the courtyard of the castle for the judges of the field and the two duennas, mother and daughter, who were the suppliants in the case; and from all the towns and villages round about a huge throng of people gathered, attracted by the novel character of the combat, for neither the living nor the dead in all that region had ever seen or heard tell of such a one.

The first to enter the field and lists was the master of ceremonies, who surveyed and paced the entire ground very carefully to make sure there was no chance of foul play, no hidden trap that might cause one of the contestants to stumble and fall. Then the duennas came in and took their seats. Wrapped in mantles that covered even their eyes and bosoms, they displayed no little emotion as Don Quixote made his appearance. Shortly afterward, accompanied by many trumpets, the big lackey Tosilos hove in sight at one side of the square. He was mounted upon a powerful steed that shook the whole place and was clad in a suit of stoutly wrought and gleaming armor. His horse looked like one of those that come from Friesland, being broad-backed and of a grayish color, with an arroba [2] of wool hanging from each of his fetlocks.

This brave fighter had been well schooled by his master the duke as to how he was to behave toward Don Quixote de la Mancha, and he had been warned that under no circumstances was he to slay the knight; [3] rather, he was to endeavor to shun the first clash in order to avoid killing him, as he certainly would do if he met him full tilt. He now rode slowly across the square to where the duennas were and remained there for some little while gazing at the one who was asking that he take her as his bride. Meanwhile, the master of ceremonies had called to Don Quixote, who was already present in the lists, and, going over to stand at Tosilos's side, he proceeded to address the duennas, inquiring if they would consent to have Don Quixote de la Mancha represent their cause. They agreed to this, with the understanding that whatever the knight did in their behalf should be looked upon as well done, valid, and binding.

By this time the duke and duchess had taken their places in a gallery overlooking the enclosure, which was filled with a vast multitude waiting to witness this most extraordinary conflict. In accordance with the conditions that had been laid down, if Don Quixote won, his opponent was to have to marry Doña Rodríguez' daughter; and if he was vanquished, the other was to be free of the promise that was claimed of him, without having to give any further satisfaction. The master of ceremonies now apportioned the sun [4] and placed each of them where he was supposed to stand. There was a roll of drums, the air was filled with the sound of trumpets, and the earth trembled underfoot as the crowd looked on anxiously, some hoping for a fortunate outcome while others feared the worst. Commending himself with all his heart to God and to his lady Dulcinea del Toboso, Don Quixote awaited the signal for the charge.

But our lackey had other thoughts in mind; he was thinking only of what I am now about to tell you. It seems that, as he gazed upon his fair enemy, she had impressed him as being the most beautiful woman he had seen in all his life,[5] and the little blind boy who in our street is commonly called Cupid had been unwilling to let slip the opportunity of triumphing over a lackey's heart and had wished to add it to his list of trophies. And so, stealing up very softly, without anyone's seeing him, he discharged an arrow two yards long through the poor fellow's left side, piercing his heart through and through. This he was able to do in perfect safety, for Love is invisible and comes and goes as he likes with no one to call him to account for what he does.

Accordingly, when they came to give the signal for the charge, our lackey was rapt in ecstasy. Thinking of the beauty of her whom he had made the mistress of his liberty, he paid no attention to the sound of the trumpet, but Don Quixote, the moment he heard it, was off on the run, bearing down on his enemy at Rocinante's top speed.

Seeing this, Sancho, good squire that he was, cried out, "May God guide you, O cream and flower of knights-errant! May God give you the victory, since you have the right on your side!"

Although Tosilos saw Don Quixote charging at him, he did not stir a step, but instead called in a loud voice to the master of ceremonies; and when the latter came up to see what was wanted, he said to him, "Sir, is not this battle being fought to decide whether or not I shall marry that young lady?"

"It is," was the answer.

"Well, then," said the lackey, "I would have you know that my conscience hurts me, and I'd be laying a heavy burden on it if I went through with this battle. I therefore yield myself as vanquished and am willing to marry the lady at once."

The marshal of the field was astonished by this speech, and, being one of those who were familiar with the affair as it had been plotted, he did not know what reply to make. Seeing that his adversary was not charging him in turn, Don Quixote had stopped midway in his course. As for the duke, he was unable to make out what was happening until the marshal came to tell him what Tosilos had said, upon hearing which he was amazed and very angry.

While this was going on Tosilos rode over to where Doña Rodríguez sat. "Lady," he called to her, "I am willing to marry your daughter, and I have no desire to obtain by strife and fighting what I can get peacefully, without any danger of death."

"Since that is so," said the valiant Don Quixote when he heard this, "I am free and absolved of my promise. Let them marry, in Heaven's name; and seeing that God has bestowed her, may St. Peter bless the match."

Having come down to the castle courtyard, the duke went up to Tosilos. "Is it true, knight," he asked, "that you yield yourself as vanquished and that, pricked by your uneasy conscience, you wish to marry this maiden?"

"Yes, my lord," replied Tosilos.

"And right he is," put in Sancho Panza, "for what you have to give to the mouse, give to the cat and spare yourself the trouble." [6]

Tosilos, meanwhile, was endeavoring to unlace his helmet and begged them to hurry and help him as it was all he could do to get his breath and he could not stay shut up in that narrow space for so long a time. They removed it for him in great haste, and then his lackey countenance was revealed for all to see.

"It's a trick! A trick!" screamed Doña Rodríguez and her daughter. "They've put Tosilos, lackey to my lord the duke, in the place of the true husband! Justice from God and the King against such cunning as this, not to say villainy!"

"Do not distress yourselves, ladies," said Don Quixote. "This is neither cunning nor villainy, or if it is, it is not the duke who is to blame but those wicked enchanters that persecute me. Enviously fearful that I might win a glorious victory, they have converted your husband's face into that of one who, so you say, is the duke's lackey. Take my advice and, despite the malice of my enemies, go ahead and marry this man, for undoubtedly he is the one you wanted to marry all the time."

As he heard this the duke came near losing his anger and bursting into a fit of laughter. "The things that happen to Señor Don Quixote," he said, "are so extraordinary that I am ready to believe this is not my lackey. But supposing we employ the following stratagem: let us post-pone the wedding for, say, a couple of weeks, and in the meantime let us keep this person, concerning whom we are in doubt, in close con-finement; it may be that he will then return to his former shape, for the grudge the enchanters hold against Don Quixote cannot last as long as that, especially when they see that these tricks and transformations are doing them so little good."

"Oh, sir," said Sancho, "those scoundrels are used to changing one thing into another where my master is concerned. A knight that he vanquished some time ago, the one called the Knight of the Mirrors, was turned into the bachelor Sansón Carrasco, a native of our village and a great friend of ours; and they changed my lady Dulcinea del Toboso into a peasant lass; and so, I fancy, this lackey is going to have to live and die a lackey all the days of his life."

"Let him be who he may who asks me for my hand," said Rodríguez' daughter, "I thank him for it; for I would rather be a lackey's lawfully wedded wife than the cast-off mistress of a gentleman—although he who deceived me is no gentleman either."

The short of the matter is, as a result of all this talk and all that had happened Tosilos was placed in confinement until they could see what the upshot of his transformation would be. They all acclaimed Don Quixote's victory, although most of them were sadly disappointed at not having seen the combatants pound each other to bits, after they had waited for them so eagerly. In this respect they were like boys who are grieved when the man to be hanged fails to appear, having won a pardon either from the one he has wronged or from the court. The crowd now dispersed, and the ducal pair with Don Quixote returned to the castle, where Tosilos was put under lock and key. As for Doña Rodríguez and her daughter, they were very well pleased, since one way or the other the affair would end in marriage, and that was what Tosilos wanted also.

CHAPTER LVII. *Which treats of how Don Quixote took leave of the duke and of what happened to him in connection with the witty and impudent Altisidora.*

BY NOW Don Quixote had come to feel that it would be well for him to quit a life of idleness such as he was leading in the castle; for he believed he was doing a great wrong in depriving the outside world of his presence, by keeping himself shut up like this and leisurely enjoying all the innumerable comforts and luxuries with which my lord and lady surrounded him as a knight-errant. It seemed to him that he would have to give an accounting to Heaven for this sloth and seclusion; and so it was that one day he begged permission of the ducal pair to take his leave. They granted his request, at the same time showing how very sorry they were to have him go. The duchess then gave Sancho Panza the letters from his wife, at which he burst into tears.

"Who would have thought," he said, "that such great hopes as the news of my government aroused in the bosom of my wife, Teresa Panza, would end with my going back, as I am doing now, to the long-drawn-out adventures of my master Don Quixote de la Mancha? But, for all of that, I am glad to see that my Teresa behaved like herself in sending the acorns to the duchess; for if she had not sent them, I'd have been sorry and she would have been ungrateful. What comforts me is the fact that they can't call that present a bribe, for I already had the governorship when she sent it, and it stands to reason that those who receive a favor should show their gratitude, even if it's only with trifles. The truth is: naked I went into the government and naked I leave it; and that, I may say in all conscience, is no small matter. 'Naked was I born, naked I find myself, and so, I neither win nor lose.'"

Such were Sancho's reflections on the day of his departure. Don Quixote had said farewell to his hosts the night before, and bright and early in the morning he appeared fully armed in the courtyard of the castle. The entire household watched him from the balconies, and even the duke and duchess came out to see him off. Sancho was mounted on his gray, with his saddlebags, his valise, and his store of provisions, and was very happy because the duke's major-domo (the one who had played the part of La Trifaldi) had presented him with a little purse containing two hundred gold crowns. The money was intended for their needs upon the road, but Don Quixote knew nothing of it as yet.

As they all stood looking on in this manner, the witty and impudent Altisidora, from her place among the duchess's other damsels and duennas, suddenly lifted up her voice and began to sing in a mournful tone:

> *Lend ear, wicked knight,*
> *Rein in thy steed;*
> *To punish his flanks*
> *There's surely no need.*
> * Whom fleest, false one?*
> *I am no dragon bold*
> *But a gentle spring lamb*
> *That is far from the fold.*
> * Ah, thou hast made mock*
> *Of the fairest of maids*
> *Diana or Venus*
> *E'er glimps'd in their glades.*
> * O cruel Bireno,[1] Aeneas untrue,*
> *May Barabbas go with thee, bring thee heart's rue.*
>
> *In thy pitiless claws,*
> *Ruthless bird of prey,*
> *A lovelorn heart*
> *Thou bearest away.*
> * Three kerchiefs hast stolen,*
> *Of garters a pair*
> *From legs pure as marble,*
> *So white and so fair.*
> * Two thousand sad sighs*
> *Thou takest with thee,*
> *If they were but flame,*
> *What Troys there would be!*

> *O cruel Bireno, Aeneas untrue,*
> *May Barabbas go with thee, bring thee heart's rue.*
>
> *As for Sancho, thy squire,*
> *May his heart be so fell*
> *Dulcinea will never*
> *Be freed of her spell.*
> *For the fault that is thine*
> *May she bear the pain,*
> *Since the just pay for sinners,[2]*
> *So goes the refrain.*
> *May your greatest adventures*
> *Betray each fond hope;*
> *Forgetting your loved one,*
> *In dreams may you grope.*
> *O cruel Bireno, Aeneas untrue,*
> *May Barabbas go with thee, bring thee heart's rue.*
>
> *May they take thee for false*
> *From Cadiz to Seville,[3]*
> *From London to England,*
> *And bear thee ill will.*
> *When thou playest at cards,*
> *May thou never hold kings*
> *Nor aces nor sevens,*
> *But lose at all things.*
> *If thy corns thou shouldst trim,*
> *Let it be till they bleed;*
> *If thy molars are pulled,*
> *May the roots all recede.*
> *O cruel Bireno, Aeneas untrue,*
> *May Barabbas go with thee, bring thee heart's rue.*

All the while the woebegone Altisidora was singing this song, in the manner that has been described, Don Quixote was gazing at her; and then, without a word in reply, he turned to Sancho.

"By the souls of your ancestors, friend Sancho," he said, "I conjure you to speak the truth. Tell me: do you by any chance have upon your person the three kerchiefs and the garters that this love-sick maid is talking about?"

"The three kerchiefs I have," said Sancho, "but as for the garters, it's over the hills of Ubeda." [4]

The duchess was astonished at Altisidora's brazenness. She had taken her for a bold, sprightly, impudent girl but had never thought that she would carry her impudence to such an extreme as this; and not having been forewarned of the joke, my lady was more amazed than ever. The duke for his part was of a mind to carry on the jest.

"It does not seem fitting to me, Sir Knight," he said, "in view of the hospitality you have been accorded here in my castle, that you should be so bold as to make off with three kerchiefs if nothing more—not to speak of my damsel's garters—an act which indicates an evil disposition on your part and is not in keeping with your reputation. Return the garters, or otherwise I challenge you to mortal combat; and I have no fear, either, that those scoundrelly enchanters will change or transform my features as they did those of Tosilos, my lackey, when he joined battle with you."

"God forbid," replied Don Quixote, "that I should unsheath my sword against your most illustrious person, seeing that I have received so many favors from you. The kerchiefs I will return, for Sancho says that he has them; but it is impossible to return the garters, for the reason that neither I nor he have had them in our possession. If this damsel of yours will look in her hiding places, I am sure she will come upon them. I, my lord the Duke, have never been a thief, nor do I expect to be so long as I live if God does not let me out of His keeping. This maiden speaks as one who is lovelorn, as she herself admits, but, since I am not to blame for that, there is no occasion for me to beg her pardon or your Excellency's. I would merely entreat you to have a better opinion of me and once again grant me permission to continue my journey."

"And God give you a fortunate one, Señor Don Quixote," said the duchess, "so that we may always hear good news of your exploits. Go, then, and God go with you; for the longer you tarry the more you add to the flame in the hearts of these damsels who look upon you. As for this girl of mine, I will so chastise her that she will henceforth offend no more either by look or words."

"O valiant Don Quixote!" exclaimed Altisidora at this point, "there is one word, no more, that I have to say to you and I would have you listen to it: I wish to beg your pardon about the theft of my garters, for, by God and upon my soul, I have them on at this moment; I made the same mistake as the man on the ass who went looking for it."

"What did I tell you?" said Sancho. "I'm a fine one when it comes to concealing stolen property! If I had wanted to do anything like that, I had plenty of chances in my government."

Don Quixote then bowed his head in a farewell to the duke and duchess and all the bystanders, and, turning Rocinante about, followed by Sancho on the ass, he left the castle and took the highroad for Saragossa.

CHAPTER LVIII. *Which tells how adventures came crowding thick and fast on Don Quixote.*

As soon as Don Quixote found himself in the open country, free to roam at will and without being annoyed by Altisidora's advances, his spirits rose and he felt at peace, ready to take up once more the pursuit of his ideals of chivalry.

"Freedom," he said, turning to Sancho, "is one of the most precious gifts that the heavens have bestowed on men; [1] with it the treasures locked in the earth or hidden in the depths of the sea are not to be compared; for the sake of freedom, as for the sake of honor, one may and should risk one's life, and captivity, on the other hand, is the greatest evil that can befall a human being. [2] You have seen, Sancho, the abundance and luxury in that castle we have just left; yet I assure you that in the midst of those delicious banquets and snow-cooled beverages it seemed to me as though I were in the straits of hunger, since I did not enjoy them with the same freedom as if they had been my own. The obligation to return benefits and favors received is a shackle on the liberty-loving spirit of man. Happy he to whom Heaven gives a slice of bread without his being obliged to thank any other person but only Heaven itself!" [3]

"For all that your Grace says," remarked Sancho, "we ought to be duly grateful for the two hundred gold crowns which the duke's majordomo handed to me in a little purse and which I now carry next my heart as a kind of soothing plaster against a time of need; for we are not always going to find castles where they will entertain us, and some-times we are likely to come upon inns where they will give us a beat-ing."

Talking of this and other subjects, the knight and his squire had gone a little more than a league when they caught sight of a dozen men dressed like workmen and lying upon their cloaks which they had spread out on the green grass of a little meadow. They were engaged in eating, and beside them were a number of white sheets, or such they appeared to be, covering something underneath, objects that were either stand-ing upright or lying flat, with small spaces in between. Coming up to them as they made their meal, Don Quixote greeted them at first very courteously and then inquired what was beneath the cloths.

"Sir," one of the men answered him, "those are images carved in relief to be used in an altar piece [4] that we are putting up in our village. We keep them covered like that to prevent them from becoming soiled, and we carry them on our shoulders so that they will not be broken." [5]

"If you would be so good," said Don Quixote, "I should like to see them, for images that are transported with such care must surely be fine ones."

"I should think they are!" said another of the men. "You can tell from what they cost; for the truth is, there is not a one of them that is not worth more than fifty ducats; but if you will wait a moment, your Grace, you may see with your own eyes."

Leaving his dinner and rising to his feet, the workman went over and took the cover off the first image, which proved to be one of St. George on horseback, with a dragon coiled at his feet and a lance thrust down its throat, a scene marked by all the ferocity with which it is cus-tomarily depicted. The entire image appeared to be one blaze of gold, as the saying is; and, as he gazed upon it, Don Quixote observed, "This was one of the best knights-errant that the heavenly militia ever had. His name was Don St. George [6] and he was, moreover, a protector of damsels. [7] Let us see this other one."

The man uncovered it, and it was seen to be an image of St. Martin, likewise mounted, and sharing his cloak with the beggar. No sooner had he laid eyes upon it than Don Quixote had a comment to make.

"This knight, also," he said, "was one of the Christian adventurers, and it is my opinion, Sancho, that he was even more liberal than he was valiant, [8] as you may see from the fact that he is here dividing his cloak and giving the beggar half of it; and it undoubtedly must have been winter at the time or otherwise he would have given him all of it, he was so charitable."

"I don't think it was that," said Sancho. "He most likely believed in the proverb that says, 'Brains are required for giving and keeping.' " [9]

Don Quixote laughed at this and then asked them to remove another cloth, beneath which was revealed a likeness of Spain's patron. He too was on horseback and bore a bloodstained sword as he trampled over Moors and human heads.

"Ah!" exclaimed Don Quixote, "this is a real knight and one of Christ's own cohorts. He is Don San Diego Matamoros,[10] the Moor-slayer, one of the most valiant saints and men of arms that this world ever had or Heaven has now."

The next cloth that they lifted covered a figure representing the fall of St. Paul from his horse, along with all the circumstances attendant upon his conversion such as are commonly to be seen upon altar pieces and which were here portrayed so vividly that one would have said that Christ was speaking and Paul answering.

"This man in his day," said Don Quixote, "was the greatest enemy that the Church of Our Lord God had to combat, and he became the greatest champion it will ever have, a knight-errant in life, and in death a steadfast saint, a tireless worker in the Lord's vineyard, teacher of the Gentiles with Heaven for a school [11] and Jesus Christ as instructor and schoolmaster."

There being no more to see, Don Quixote directed them to cover the images once more. "I take it as a good omen, my brothers," he said to the workmen, "to have seen what I have today; for these saints and knights followed the same profession that I do, which is that of arms. The only difference between them and me is that they, being saints, waged a holy warfare, while I fight after the manner of men. They conquered Heaven by force of arms, for Heaven suffereth violence; [12] but, up to now, I do not know what I have won with all the hardships I have endured. However, if my lady Dulcinea were but free of those that she is suffering, it may be that my fortunes would improve, and with a sounder mind [13] I should be able to tread a better path than the one I follow at present."

"May God hear and sin be deaf," said Sancho.[14]

The men were equally astonished by Don Quixote's figure and by his conversation, for they did not understand the half of what he said. Having finished their dinner, they took up the images and, bidding the knight farewell, resumed their journey.

Once again, Sancho was amazed at his master's erudition; it was as if he had never known him before. There surely was not a story in the world, he thought to himself, not a single event that the knight did not have at his fingertips and firmly fixed in his memory. "Truly, sir," he said, "if what happened to us today can be called an adventure, it has been one of the sweetest and pleasantest that we have had in all our wanderings. We have come out of it without any fright or beating, nor have we laid hand to sword or flayed the earth with our bodies or gone hungry. Praise God for having let me see such a one with my own eyes!"

"You are right, Sancho," said Don Quixote, "but you must remember that all times are not alike and do not always take the same course; and what the vulgar commonly call omens (for which there is no rational basis) are to be looked upon by the wise man as being no more than happy accidents. One of these believers in omens will rise in the morning, leave his house, and fall in with a friar of the order of the blessed St. Francis; whereupon, as though he had encountered a griffin, he will turn around and go home. If a Mendoza chances to spill salt on the table, he spills gloom over his heart at the same time,[15] just as if nature were under any obligation to give notice of coming misfortunes through things of such little moment as those mentioned. The man who is at once wise and a Christian ought not to trifle with the will of Heaven. When Scipio came to Africa he stumbled as he leaped ashore, and his soldiers took it for an ill omen, but as he embraced the earth he cried out, 'You will not escape me, Africa, for I hold you tightly in my arms.'[16] And similarly, Sancho, our meeting with these images has been for me simply [17] a very happy occurrence."

"I believe it," said Sancho, "and now I wish your Grace would tell me why it is the Spaniards as they go into battle call upon San Diego Matamoros; crying, 'Santiago, and close, Spain!'[18] Does it mean by any chance that Spain is open and has to be closed, or what kind of talk is this?"[19]

"You are very simple-minded, Sancho," replied Don Quixote. "Look you, God gave Spain that great knight of the Red Cross as her patron and protector, especially in those arduous struggles that the Spaniards had with the Moors; and so it is they call upon him as their defender in all the battles that they join; and very often, in those battles, they have plainly seen him overthrowing, trampling under foot, destroying, and killing the Hagarene [20] cohorts. Many examples of the truth of this will be found recorded in the veracious Spanish histories."

Sancho now changed the subject. "I marvel, sir," he said, "at the impudence of Altisidora, the duchess's damsel. She must have been pierced and sorely wounded by the one they call Cupid, who, they say, is a little blind boy; but though he may be blear-eyed, or, more properly speaking, sightless, if he takes aim at a heart, however small it may be, he is sure to hit it and run it through with his arrows. I have heard it said, on the other hand, that the darts of love are blunted by the modesty and reserve of maidens, but in Altisidora's case it would seem they had been sharpened rather than dulled."

"You must bear in mind, Sancho," said Don Quixote, "that love is no respecter of the conventions nor in its actions does it keep within the bounds of reason, but rather resembles death which without discrimination assails the lofty palaces of kings and the humble shepherd's hut.[21] When love takes complete possession of a heart, the first thing it does is to banish all fear and shame; and thus it was that Altisidora shamelessly declared her passion, awakening thereby no pity in my bosom but only a feeling of embarrassment."

"What cruelty!" exclaimed Sancho. "What unheard-of ingratitude! For myself I can say that at the slightest word of love from her I'd have surrendered and become her slave. Son of a whore! what a heart of marble, what bowels of brass, what a soul of mortar! But I can't imagine what it was that girl saw in your Grace that made her turn slave and offer herself to you. Where was the bold and dashing appearance, the grace of manner, the handsome face—any of these things singly or all of them together—that led her to fall in love with you? To tell the honest truth, I have many times stopped to look your Grace over from the topmost hair of your head down to the soles of your feet and when I do so I see more things to frighten a person than to cause one to love you. I have heard it said that beauty is the first and principal thing where falling in love is concerned, and since your Grace has none at all, I'm sure I don't know why the poor girl did it."

"Do not forget, Sancho," replied Don Quixote, "that there are two kinds of beauty, one being of the soul and the other of the body. That of the soul is revealed through intelligence, modesty, right conduct, generosity, and good breeding, all of which qualities may exist in an ugly man; and when one's gaze is fixed upon beauty of this sort and not upon that of the body, love is usually born suddenly and violently. I, Sancho, can see very well that I am not handsome, but I am also aware that I am not misshapen; and it is enough for a man not to be a monster in order to be well loved, so long as he possesses those other endowments of which I have told you."

Conversing in this manner, they entered a wood alongside the road, when suddenly, without his expecting it, Don Quixote found himself entangled in some nets of green cord that had been strung between the trees; and being unable to imagine what the meaning of it was, he said to Sancho, "It is my opinion that this is going to be one of the rarest adventures that could be conceived. May they slay me if the enchanters who persecute me are not trying to enmesh me, by way of delaying my journey and in revenge for my stern treatment of Altisidora. But let me inform them that even though these nets were made of hardest diamonds in place of green cord, and even though they were stronger than the one in which the jealous god of the forge snared Venus and Mars, I still would break them as if they were fashioned of rushes or cotton thread."

He was about to ride on and burst through them all when without warning there appeared before him from among the trees two most beautiful shepherd lasses—or, at least, they were dressed like shepherd-esses, save for the fact that their jackets and peasant skirts [22] were of fine brocade (that is to say, they wore hoop skirts made of tabby and richly embroidered in gold).[23] Their hair, which fell down loose over their shoulders, might well compete with the rays of the sun in brightness and was crowned with garlands of laurel interwoven with red amaranth. They appeared to be between fifteen and eighteen years of age, and the sight of them was such as to fill Sancho with astonishment and Don Quixote with admiration and cause the sun to halt in its course.[24] An uncanny silence held them all, and then, finally, one of the lasses spoke.

"Stop, Sir Knight," she said, "and do not break those nets; for they have been stretched not to do you harm but for our amusement. And since you are bound to ask us why they were put there and who we are, I will answer you in a few words. In a village some two leagues away, where there are many rich gentlefolk and important personages, a number of friends and relatives decided among themselves that they would come here with their sons, wives, daughters, neighbors, acquaintances, and kinsmen to seek diversion in this spot, which is one of the most pleasing to be found in all these parts. It is our intention to set up here a new pastoral Arcadia, with the maidens dressing as shepherdesses and the lads as shepherds. We have been studying two eclogues, one by the famous poet Garcilaso, and the other by the most excellent Camões in his own Portuguese tongue, but we have not as yet acted them.

"We came only yesterday, and we have erected some field tents, as they are called, among the trees on the edge of a brook whose abundant waters fertilize all these meadows. Last night we stretched the nets you see here to snare the foolish little birds that, startled by our clamor, fall into them. If you, sir, would like to be our guest, you will receive a most courteous and hospitable welcome, since for the present all care and melancholy are banished from this place."

"Assuredly, fairest lady," replied Don Quixote, "Actaeon [25] when he surprised Diana at the bath could not have been more amazed and charmed than I at beholding your beauty. I approve the way you have found of amusing yourselves and thank you for your invitation, and if I can serve you in any way, you have but to command with the certainty that you will be obeyed; for my calling is none other than that of showing gratitude and doing good to people of every sort, especially those of high station, as you quite evidently are. If these nets that probably occupy but a small space were spread out over the whole round earth, I still should seek new worlds through which I might pass in order to avoid breaking them. What I say may sound exaggerated, but in order that you may believe it let me tell you that he who gives you this assurance is Don Quixote de la Mancha himself, if by chance that name has reached your ears."

"Ah, my dear," said the other maid, "what great good fortune has befallen us! Do you see this gentleman here before us? I would have you know that he is the bravest, the most lovelorn, and the most courteous of any in this world, if one is to believe the story of his deeds which has been put into print and which I have read. And I will wager that this good man with him is a certain Sancho Panza, his squire, whose drolleries are quite incomparable."

"That is the truth," said Sancho. "I am that droll squire that your Grace is speaking of, and this gentleman is my master, the same Don Quixote de la Mancha that is in the story."

"Oh!" exclaimed the first maiden, "let us beg him to stay, my dear; our fathers and brothers would be delighted to have him, and I too have heard of his valor and his squire's amusing ways. [26] But, above all, they tell me he is the most steadfast and loyal lover that ever was and that his lady is a certain Dulcinea del Toboso to whom all Spain awards the palm of beauty."

"And rightly so," said Don Quixote, "unless it be that your own unrivaled beauty puts hers in doubt. But do not trouble yourselves, ladies, by urging me to stay, for the imperative duties of my profession do not suffer me to rest under any circumstances."

At that moment a brother of one of the maidens came up, dressed like them in gay and costly shepherd attire. They informed him that the gentleman with them was the valiant Don Quixote de la Mancha, and that the other was Sancho, his squire, with whom the young man was already familiar through the history, which he had read. The dashing shepherd then begged the knight to come to their tents, and Don Quixote was compelled to yield.

The beaters now began starting the game, and the nets were soon filled with small birds of various species that, deceived by the color, had fallen into the danger from which they were fleeing. As many as thirty persons gathered there, all of them festively garbed as shepherds and shepherdesses, and within a very short while they all knew who Don Quixote and his squire were, which pleased them greatly, for they too had heard of the knight through the history of his exploits. Making their way to the tents, they found the tables neatly laid with an abundance of choice food, and they honored their guest by according him first place among them as all looked on and marveled at the sight of him.

When the cloth had at last been removed, Don Quixote raised his voice and spoke.

"There are those who will tell you that one of the greatest sins men can commit is pride, but I maintain that ingratitude is worse; and in making this assertion, I am mindful of the common saying to the effect that Hell is full of ingrates. This sin, insofar as possible, I have endeavored to avoid ever since I had the use of my reasoning powers. If I find myself unable to repay the good deeds that have been done me with others in kind, I substitute the desire for the performance; and when this is not enough, I make public the favors I have received, since he who publishes abroad the benefits conferred upon him would surely repay them if it were possible for him to do so. Those that receive are for the most part the inferiors of those that give. Thus God, being the supreme giver, is over all; the gifts of man fall short by an infinite distance of those that He bestows, but gratitude to a certain extent makes up for this shortcoming and deficiency.

"And so, being grateful for the kindness that has been shown me here and being unable to return it in full measure, owing to the limited means at my disposal, I do hereby offer you what lies within my power. I accordingly declare that for two whole days, in the middle of this highway that leads to Saragossa, I will maintain that these ladies disguised as shepherd lasses are the most beautiful and courteous damsels of any in the world, excepting only the peerless Dulcinea del Toboso, sole mistress of my affections, if I may say so without offense to any of the ladies and gentlemen who hear my words."

Sancho had been listening most attentively to everything Don Quixote said, and he now cried out in a loud voice, "Is it possible there are any in the world who would dare to say and swear that this master of mine is a madman? Tell me, you gentlemen shepherds, is there any village curate, however wise and however much of a scholar he may be, who could make the speech you have just heard? Is there any knight-errant, however famous for his bravery, who could make the offer my master has made you?"

Exceedingly angry and red in the face, the knight now turned upon his squire. "Is it possible, Sancho," he said, "that there is anyone in this world who would say that you are not a fool—a fool lined with folly, with I know not what trimmings of cunning and roguery? Who told you to meddle in my affairs and decide whether I am a wise man or a blockhead? Be quiet and do not answer me, but go and saddle Rocinante at once if he is unsaddled, for we are going to put my offer into effect, and, with the right that I have on my side, you may reckon as vanquished all who would contradict me."

He rose from his seat in a rage, his anger plainly visible to the others present, who were amazed by it, being unable to make up their minds as to whether he was mad or sane. They did their best to dissuade him from the proposed challenge, telling him that they were assured of his gratitude and there was no need for him to give fresh proof of his courage as the instances of it contained in the history were quite sufficient. Nevertheless, Don Quixote insisted upon carrying out his intention, and, having mounted Rocinante, grasped his lance, and braced his buckler on his arm, he took his stand in the middle of a highway not far distant from the verdant meadow. Sancho followed on his donkey, with the throng of pastoral revelers hard at his heels, for they were anxious to see what would be the outcome of this vainglorious, unheard-of undertaking.

Having posted himself, then, in the middle of the highway as has been stated, Don Quixote rent the air with such words as these:

"O ye travelers and wayfarers, knights and squires, those on foot and those on horseback, who pass along this road within the next two days, know that Don Quixote de la Mancha, knight-errant, stands here to maintain that the nymphs who inhabit these groves and meadows excel in beauty and in courtesy all others in the world, leaving aside the lady of my heart, Dulcinea del Toboso. And so, let anyone who holds the contrary come on, for I await him on this spot."

Twice he repeated these same words and twice there was no adventurer to hear them. But fate, which was guiding his affairs from better to better, ordained that shortly afterward he should descry down the road a large number of men on horseback, many of them with lances in their hands and all riding hard, in close formation. No sooner did those who were with Don Quixote catch sight of the horsemen than they turned and withdrew some distance from the road; for they knew very well that if they stayed they might incur some danger. Don Quixote alone stood his ground, while Sancho shielded himself behind Rocinante's crupper.

The troop of lancers came on, and one of them who rode ahead of the others cried out to the knight, "Out of the way, devil take you, or these bulls will trample you to pieces!"

"Ha, rabble!" replied Don Quixote, "bulls mean nothing to me, even though they be the fiercest that Jarama breeds upon its banks.[27] Confess at once, ye scoundrels, that it is the truth I have here proclaimed or be prepared to do battle with me!"

The herdsman had no time to reply and the knight did not have time to get out of the way if he had wished to do so, and as a result the wild bulls and the tame leading-oxen [28] and all the many drovers and others who were taking the animals to be penned in a village where the bulls were to be baited [29] the following day—the entire troop, in short, both man and beast, passed over Don Quixote and over Sancho, Rocinante, and the gray as well, knocking them all down and sending them rolling. Sancho was badly mauled, his master was frightened, the ass was battered, and Rocinante was far from sound; but they all finally got to their feet, and, stumbling here and falling there, Don Quixote ran after the herd as fast as he could.

"Stop, scoundrelly rabble!" he shouted. "It is a single knight who awaits you, and he is not one who agrees with those that say 'When the enemy flees, build him a bridge of silver.' " [30]

But the drovers in their haste did not stop for this; indeed, they paid no more attention to his threats than to the clouds of yesteryear. It was weariness that stopped Don Quixote as, filled with rage at being balked of his revenge, he sat down to wait for Sancho, Rocinante, and the ass to reach his side. Then master and man mounted once again, and without turning to bid farewell to the imitation Arcadia they continued on their way with more of shame than pleasure in their mien.

CHAPTER LIX. *Wherein is related an extraordinary experience of Don Quixote's, which may be looked upon as an adventure.*[1]

IT WAS the bright clear water of a spring which they had come upon within the cool shade of a grove that afforded Don Quixote and Sancho their first relief from the dust that covered them and the weariness they felt as a result of the incivility of the bulls; and, having turned both the gray and Rocinante loose, without headstall or bridle, the long-suffering pair, master and man, now sat down beside it. Not, however, before Sancho had hastened over to his saddlebag-pantry and taken out what he was in the habit of calling the "grub,"[2] while Don Quixote rinsed his mouth and bathed his face, a proceeding which cooled him off and revived somewhat his sagging spirits. Out of pure disgust he would not eat anything, nor did Sancho out of pure politeness venture to touch any of the victuals before him until his master had acted as taster.[3] But when the latter saw that the knight, lost in thought, had forgotten to lift the food to his mouth, he proceeded to trample under foot any kind of good breeding and, without opening his mouth to say a word,[4] began stowing away in his stomach the bread and cheese that were at hand.

"Eat, friend Sancho," said Don Quixote, "and sustain life, since that is of more importance to you than it is to me. Leave me to die of my thoughts and my misfortunes; for you may know, Sancho, that I was born to live dying and you to die eating. That you may see how true this is, look at me now. Here I am with my name in the history books, a famous man of arms, courteous in my conduct, respected by princes, sought after by damsels, and just when I was expecting palms, triumphs, and crowns, I find myself this morning, as a climax to it all, trodden underfoot, battered, and kicked by a herd of filthy animals. When I think of this, my teeth are blunted, my jaws are numbed, my hands are paralyzed, and I lose all appetite to such an extent that I've a mind to die of hunger, which is the cruelest death there is."

"In that case," observed Sancho, who did not leave off munching all the while, "I take it your Grace does not agree with the proverb that says, 'Let Marta die, but let her die with her belly full.' [5] As for me, I have no intention of killing myself. Rather, I mean to do like the shoemaker, who stretches the leather with his teeth to make it reach as far as he likes. I intend to stretch my life out by eating until I come to the end that Heaven has fixed for it; and let me tell you, sir, there is no greater madness than to despair as your Grace is doing. Take my word for it; after you have had a bite to eat, stretch out for a little nap on this green grass-mattress and you will see how much better you feel when you wake up again."

Finding that Sancho's reasoning was that of a philosopher rather than a fool, Don Quixote decided to take his advice. But first he said to him, "If you will do what I am going to tell you, Sancho, I am certain that I shall feel better and less heavyhearted. What I ask is that while I am sleeping as you have urged me to do, you go off to one side some distance away, lay bare your flesh, and with Rocinante's reins give yourself three or four hundred lashes as a substantial payment on account of the three thousand and some that you have yet to give yourself in order to accomplish Dulcinea's disenchantment. It is no small sorrow to me that the poor lady has to remain bewitched as a result of your carelessness and neglect."

"There is much to be said as to that," replied Sancho. "Let us both sleep for the present, and afterward what is to be is in God's hands. Your Grace should know that this business of a man's flogging himself in cold blood is a hard thing to do, especially when the lashes fall on a body that is as badly nourished and underfed as mine. Let my lady Dulcinea be patient, for when she's least expecting it I'll be whipping myself until I'm as full of holes as a sieve. Until death it's all life; [6] by which I mean to say, there's life in me yet, along with the desire to accomplish what I promised."

Thanking him for this, Don Quixote ate a little and Sancho a good deal, and then they both lay down to sleep, leaving those two constant friends and companions, Rocinante and the gray, to roam at will without restraint of any kind and feed upon the grass in which the meadow abounded. Waking somewhat tardily, they mounted once more and resumed their journey, being in haste to reach an inn which they could see, about a league from where they were, as it appeared. I say inn, for the reason that this was what Don Quixote called it, contrary to his usual custom of calling all inns castles. Drawing up in front of it, they inquired of the landlord if he had a lodging for them and were informed that he did have, one with all the comforts and conveniences that were to be found in Saragossa. When they had dismounted, Sancho carried their store of provisions into a room to which the innkeeper gave him a key; then he took the animals out to the stable, fed them their rations, and returned to see what further orders Don Quixote had for him. The knight was seated upon a stone bench against the wall, and his squire was especially grateful to Heaven that this particular inn had not appeared to him to be a castle.

When the supper hour came they retired to their room, and Sancho then asked the landlord what he had in the way of fare and was told that his mouth should be the measure and he might order anything that pleased him, as this hostelry was provided with birds of the air, fowls of the earth, and fish of the sea.

"We don't need all that," said Sancho. "A couple of roast chickens will be enough for us, for my master has a delicate stomach and eats very little and I'm not too much of a glutton myself."

The innkeeper replied that they had no chickens, the kites having made away with them.

"Well, then, Sir Landlord, have them roast a pullet for us, and be sure it's nice and tender."

"A pullet? My father!" exclaimed their host. "It's the truth I'm telling you that only yesterday I sent more than fifty of them to market in the city; but, outside of pullets, your Grace may have what you wish."

"If that is so, you must have some veal or kid."

"There is none in the house just now, for as it happens we just finished the last of it, but next week we'll have plenty and to spare."

"A lot of good that will do us!" said Sancho. "I'll bet that when we come to the end of all the things you don't have, we'll end up with plenty of bacon and eggs."

"In God's name," said the innkeeper, "my guest is not very sharp-witted! Here I have just told him that I have neither pullets nor hens and he expects me to have eggs. Talk about something else that's good to eat but don't be asking for fancy dishes." [7]

"Body of me!" cried Sancho. "Come to the point, Sir Landlord; tell me what you have and stop all this talk."

"What I really and truly have," replied their host, "is a couple of cow-heels that look like calves' feet, or a couple of calves' feet that look like cow-heels, boiled with chickpeas, onions, and bacon, and right now they're calling 'Eat me! Eat me!' "

"Put them aside for me this minute," said Sancho, "and don't let anybody touch them. I'll pay more than anyone else, for there's nothing that I like better and it makes no difference to me whether they're feet or heels."

"No one will touch them," said the innkeeper, "for I have other guests, persons of quality who bring with them their own cook, butler, and larder."

"They could not be of any better quality than my master," said Sancho, "but the calling he follows does not permit of larders or storerooms; we stretch ourselves out in the middle of a field and fill up on acorns or medlars."

Such was the conversation that Sancho had with the innkeeper, and he did not carry it any further by answering the question which the landlord put to him regarding his master's calling or profession. When the supper hour came Don Quixote withdrew into his room,[8] the landlord brought in the stew-pot just as it was, and the knight straightaway fell to eating. While he was so engaged, he heard voices from the next room, which was separated from his own by a thin partition.

"Upon your life, Señor Don Jerónimo," someone was saying, "while they are bringing our supper, let us read another chapter of the *Second Part of Don Quixote de la Mancha*."[9]

No sooner did he hear his name mentioned than Don Quixote rose to his feet and began listening intently to what they were saying about him.

"Why would your Grace have us read such nonsense as that, Señor Don Juan," came the reply, "seeing that he who has read the First Part of the history of Don Quixote de la Mancha cannot possibly find any pleasure in this second one?"

"For all of that," said Don Juan, "it would be well to read it, since no book is so bad that there is not some good to be found in it. What displeases me most about it is that it depicts Don Quixote as no longer in love with Dulcinea del Toboso."[10]

Hearing this, the knight was filled with anger and resentment; raising his voice, he called out, "Whoever says that Don Quixote has forgotten or ever can forget the peerless Dulcinea del Toboso will have to answer to me, and I will show him with evenly matched weapons how far he is from the truth. Forgetfulness is not a part of his make-up, but constancy is his motto, and his profession is to preserve it with gentle bearing and without doing it any violence whatsoever."[11]

"Who is it that answers us?" came the question from the other room.

"Who should it be," replied Sancho, "if not Don Quixote de la Mancha himself, who will make good all that he has said or may say? For he who is well able to pay doesn't mind giving pledges." [12]

He had no more than said this when two gentlemen, for such they appeared to be, entered the room, one of whom threw his arms about Don Quixote's neck.

"Your appearance," he said, "does not belie your name, nor can your name fail to suggest your appearance. You, sir, are undoubtedly the true Don Quixote de la Mancha, north pole and morning star of knight-errantry despite the one who has sought to usurp your name and obliterate your achievements, as the author of this book which I hand you here has done."

With this, he placed the book which his companion carried in Don Quixote's hands. The knight took it and, without saying a word, began leafing through it, and then after a short while he gave it back, saying, "From the little I have seen of it, I have found three things for which the author deserves to be censured. The first is certain words that I have read in the preface; [13] the second is the fact that the language is that of an Aragonese who frequently omits his articles; [14] and the third (which above all brands him as ignorant) is the mistake he makes, and the falsehood of which he is guilty in the essential part of the story, by stating that the wife of Sancho Panza, my squire, is named Mari Gutiérrez when the name should be Teresa Panza. [15] And it is greatly to be feared that one who errs in so important a matter as this will be wrong in all the other particulars throughout the history."

Sancho now spoke up. "A fine historian he is! He surely must know a lot about our business when he calls my wife, Teresa Panza, Mari Gutiérrez! Take the book again, Señor, and see if I am in it and if they've changed my name too."

"From what I have heard tell, my friend," said Don Jerónimo, "you must be Sancho Panza, Señor Don Quixote's squire."

"That I am," said Sancho, "and I'm proud of it."

"Faith, then," said the gentleman, "this new author does not treat you with that decency that your person displays. He portrays you as a glutton and a simpleton, not at all droll—in short, quite different from the Sancho described in the first part of your master's history." [16]

"May God forgive him," said Sancho. "He'd have done better if he had forgotten all about me and left me in my corner; for let him who is able play the instrument, and St. Peter is well enough off in Rome." [17]

The two gentlemen then invited Don Quixote to come into their room and have supper with them, for they well knew that the inn had nothing suitable for him to eat. The knight, always extremely courteous, yielded to this request, but Sancho remained with the stew-pot and, invested with delegated plenary authority,[18] seated himself at the head of the table, with the landlord sharing the meal, for the latter was no less fond of feet and heels than was the squire.

In the course of the supper Don Juan asked Don Quixote what news he had of the lady Dulcinea del Toboso. Was she married or not, had she given birth or was she with child, or was she still a virgin, preserving her modesty and good name and cherishing amorous thoughts of Señor Don Quixote?

"Dulcinea," replied the knight, "is yet a maid, and my passion for her is more unwavering than ever. Our relations are as unsatisfactory as they were before, and as for her beauty, it has been transformed into that of an unclean peasant lass."

He then went on to tell them, point by point, all about the spell that had been laid upon the lady Dulcinea and what had occurred in the Cave of Montesinos, together with the instructions which the magician Merlin had given for her disenchantment and the lashes that Sancho was to give himself. The two gentlemen were delighted as they listened to Don Quixote's account of these strange events in his history and were at once astonished at the nonsense he talked and the polished manner in which he told the story. At times they would take him for a man of intelligence and at other times for a fool, without being able to make up their minds as to just where they were to place him in the vague realm between sound sense and madness.

Having finished his supper, Sancho left the landlord with his legs wobbling [19] and went to the room where his master was.

"May they slay me, good sirs," he said, "if the author of that book that your Worships have is any friend of mine.[20] He calls me a glutton, if what your Worships say is true, and I only hope he doesn't call me a drunkard as well."

"He does call you something of the sort," said Don Jerónimo, "though I cannot remember just how he puts it. I only know that his language is offensive and, moreover, that he lies, as I can tell by looking at the face of our worthy Sancho, here present."

"Believe me, your Worships," said the squire, "the Sancho and the Don Quixote of that story cannot be the same as those in the history composed by Cid Hamete Benengeli, that is to say, they cannot be ourselves: my master, who is valiant, wise, and in love; and I, who am simple-minded, droll, and neither a glutton nor a drunkard."

"I believe you," said Don Juan; "and if it were possible an order should be issued to the effect that no one is to dare to treat of the affairs of the great Don Quixote unless it be Cid Hamete, the original author— just as Alexander ordered that none but Apelles was to dare paint his portrait."

"Let him who will portray me," said Don Quixote, "but let him not mistreat me; for one very often loses patience when insult is heaped on injury."

"No one," said Don Juan, "can insult Señor Don Quixote without his being able to avenge himself, unless he chooses to ward off the blow with the shield of his patience, which appears to me to be great and strong."

Speaking of these and other things, they spent a good part of the night together, and although Don Juan wanted Don Quixote to read more of the book to see what it contained, he could not persuade him to do so; for the knight stated that he regarded it as read and took it to be altogether silly, adding that if by any chance the author should hear that he had had it in his hands, he did not wish to give him the pleasure of thinking that he, Don Quixote, had perused these pages, for we should keep our thoughts and above all, our eyes away from that which is lewd and obscene. They then asked him what his destination was, and he replied that he was bound for Saragossa, where he proposed to take part in the armored tourney that was customarily held there every year; whereupon Don Juan informed him that this new history told how Don Quixote, whoever he might be, in that same tournament had participated in a tilting at the ring but that the description given had shown a sorry lack of inventiveness, especially with regard to the mottoes of the knights and their liveries, in which regard it was impoverished in the extreme though rich in foolishness.[21]

"For that very reason," said Don Quixote, "I will not set foot in Saragossa but will let the world see how this new historian lies, by showing people that I am not the Don Quixote of whom he is speaking."

"You are quite right in doing so," said Don Jerónimo, "for there are other joustings in Barcelona where Don Quixote can display his valor."

"That is what I have in mind," said the knight; "and now, if your Worships will excuse me, it is time to go to bed, and so I will take my leave, trusting that you will number me among your best friends and faithful servants."

"And me too," said Sancho. "It may be I'll be good for something."

With this, they bade one another farewell and Don Quixote and Sancho retired to their own room, leaving Don Juan and Don Jerónimo marveling still at the strange admixture of good sense and madness they had observed; for the two gentlemen were convinced that these were the true Don Quixote and Sancho, while those the Aragonese author had portrayed were not. The knight was up at an early hour the next morning and took leave of his hosts of the evening before by knocking on the partition. As for Sancho, he paid the landlord handsomely, advising him after this not to praise so highly the accommodations of his hostelry or else to lay in a better stock of provisions.

CHAPTER LX. *Of what happened to Don Quixote on his way to Barcelona.*

THE morning was cool and gave promise of the same kind of day to follow as Don Quixote sallied forth from the inn, having made inquiries as to which was the most direct route to Barcelona without passing through Saragossa; for he was determined to give the lie to that new historian, who, so they told him, had heaped so much abuse upon him.

For the first six days nothing happened to him worthy of being set down in writing; but at the end of that time, having left the highway, he found himself at nightfall in a dense grove of oak or cork trees (on this point Cid Hamete is not as precise as he usually is). Master and man thereupon dismounted and made themselves as comfortable as they could at the foot of the trees, and Sancho, who had had a good noonday meal, lost no time in entering the gates of sleep. Don Quixote, on the other hand, kept awake by his thoughts rather than by hunger, was unable to close his eyes as his mind wandered here and there through a thousand different places. Now it seemed that he was in the Cave of Montesinos and was beholding Dulcinea, transformed into a peasant maid, skipping about and mounting her she-ass; and again the words of Merlin the sage were ringing in his ears, setting forth the conditions to be observed and what was to be done in order to accomplish the lady's disenchantment. He fell into a mood of despair as he thought of the laxness and want of charity displayed by his squire Sancho, who, to his master's knowledge, had given himself but five lashes in all, a very small proportion indeed of the countless number that remained to be administered. This made him feel so sad and vexed that he was led to indulge in the following soliloquy:

"If Alexander the Great cut the Gordian knot, saying, 'To cut comes to the same thing as untying,' and for all of that did not cease to be the universal lord of all Asia, this should apply neither more nor less to the present case, if by way of disenchanting Dulcinea I were to flog Sancho whether he likes it or not. If the remedy lies in his receiving three thousand-odd lashes, what difference does it make to me whether he or someone else inflicts them, seeing that the heart of the matter lies in his receiving them, regardless of where they come from?" [1]

With this idea in mind he went over to his squire, having first taken Rocinante's reins and adjusted them in such a manner that they might be used as a lash. He then began undoing Sancho's points [2] (it is the general belief that there was only the one in front to hold up the breeches), but no sooner had he approached him than Sancho was wide awake.

"What is this? Who is laying hands on me and undressing me?"

"It is I," replied Don Quixote. "I have come to make up for your negligence and relieve my own sufferings. I am going to give you a flogging, Sancho, and so discharge a part of the debt you owe. Dulcinea is pining away, you lead a carefree life, and I die of longing. Untruss yourself, then, of your own free will, for it is my will to give you, here in this out-of-the-way place, not less than a thousand strokes."

"You will do nothing of the sort," said Sancho. "Be quiet, your Grace, or by the living God the deaf shall hear us. The lashes that I owe are to be voluntary, not forced, and just now I don't feel like giving myself any. Your Grace has my word that I will whip and swat myself whenever the notion takes me and that should be enough."

"No, Sancho," said Don Quixote, "I cannot leave it to your courtesy, for you are hardhearted and, for a countryman, have very tender flesh."

He accordingly kept on struggling to undo his squire's trousers; seeing which, Sancho leaped to his feet and charged at him. Grappling with him man to man,[3] he tripped him up and brought him down flat on his back, and then placing his right knee on the knight's chest, he grasped his master's hands and held them in such a way that the poor fellow could neither stir nor breathe.

"How now, traitor?" cried Don Quixote. "So you would rebel against your lord and master, would you, and dare to raise your hand against the one who feeds you?"

"I neither unmake nor make a king," [4] replied Sancho, "but am simply standing up for myself, for I am my own lord. If your Grace will promise me to be quiet and not undertake to flog me for the present, I will let you go free as you like; otherwise not, but

> Here shalt thou die, traitor,
> Doña Sancha's enemy." [5]

Don Quixote gave the promise and swore by the one who was his life and the object of his affections [6] that he would not touch a hair of his squire's garments but would leave the matter of flogging himself entirely to Sancho's own free choice. Sancho then rose and walked away for some little distance. Just as he was about to lean back against another tree, he felt something touching his head, and, raising his hands, he found that it was a pair of feet with shoes and stockings on them. Trembling with fright, he ran over to another tree, and the same thing happened, whereupon he began shouting at the top of his voice, calling upon Don Quixote to come and help him. The knight did so, and when he asked Sancho what had occurred to frighten him, the latter replied that all the trees were full of human feet and legs. His master in turn felt them and at once realized what they were.

"There is no reason to be afraid," he said, "for these feet and legs that you feel but do not see are undoubtedly those of some outlaws and highwaymen who have been strung up here, for it is the custom of the officers of justice to hang them in this manner, twenty or thirty at a time, when they capture them; all of which leads me to believe that we must be near Barcelona." [7]

And he was right. It was daylight now, and, lifting their eyes, they saw that these were indeed the bodies of bandits; but if the sight of the dead was terrifying, they were no less dismayed by the appearance of more than forty living robbers who of a sudden surrounded them, telling them in the Catalan tongue that they should keep quiet and wait until the captain of the band came up. Don Quixote was on foot, his horse unbridled, his lance reposing against a tree; he was, in short, utterly defenseless, and so there was nothing for him to do but fold his arms, bow his head, and conserve his energies for a more favorable time and circumstance. The bandits, meanwhile, went over and searched the donkey, leaving nothing in the saddlebags or the valise, and a lucky thing it was for Sancho that he carried in his girdle the crowns that the duke had given him and those that he had brought from home. As it was, those fine fellows would have stripped him and looked to see what he had hidden between his hide and his flesh if at that moment their captain had not arrived on the scene.

He was a stockily built, swarthy-complexioned man of a little more than average height, apparently about thirty-four years of age and with a stern-looking face. He was mounted on a powerful horse and was clad in a coat of mail, and at his side he carried four pistols of the sort which in that country are known as petronels.[8] Perceiving that his squires (for such is the name given to those that follow this calling) were about to despoil Sancho, he ordered them to desist and was at once obeyed; and thus it was the girdle escaped. He was astonished to observe a lance leaning against a tree and a shield on the ground while the sight of Don Quixote in a suit of armor, standing there in deep dejection, filled him with amazement; it seemed to him that this was the most mournful and melancholy countenance that sorrow's own self could have fashioned.

"Do not be so sad, my good man," he said, going up to him. "You have not fallen into the hands of any cruel Busiris,[9] but into those of Roque Guinart,[10] who is inclined to be merciful rather than stern."

"I am not sad to have fallen into your hands, O valiant Roque," replied Don Quixote, "for your fame on this earth is boundless. What grieves me, rather, is the fact that your soldiers have found me without a bridle on my steed, whereas in accordance with that order of knight-errantry that I profess I am required to be constantly on the alert, serving as my own sentinel at all hours. I would have you know, O great Roque, that had they found me upon my horse, armed with lance and shield, it would not have been so easy for them to subdue me; for I am Don Quixote de la Mancha, with whose exploits the whole world is filled."

Then it was that Roque Guinart came to realize the nature of Don Quixote's infirmity, which had more to do with madness than with boastfulness. Although he had heard the knight's name mentioned a number of times, he had never regarded his deeds as true, since he could not bring himself to believe that such a whim could so take possession of the human heart. For this reason he was very glad indeed to have fallen in with him and to have the opportunity of seeing for himself at close range what he had heard so much about from a distance.

"Valiant knight," he said, "do not be downcast nor look upon this situation in which you find yourself as an unfortunate one; for it may

be that through such mischances your crooked fortunes will be straightened out, seeing that Heaven, by strange and unheard-of roundabout
ways that men never dreamed of, is accustomed to lift up the fallen and
enrich the poor."

Don Quixote was about to thank him when they heard behind them
what sounded like a troop of horses. It was, however, but a single horse
upon which a young man came riding furiously. He looked to be
about twenty, and his attire consisted of a gold-trimmed suit of green
damask with breeches and a loose jacket; [11] he wore a cocked hat of the
Walloon variety, tight-fitting waxed boots, and gilded spurs, sword,
and dagger; in his hands he carried a fowling piece, and at his side was
a brace of pistols. Hearing the sound, Roque turned his head to behold
the handsome figure, and, riding up to him, the youth addressed him as
follows:

"O valiant Roque, I come to seek you out and to find in you if not a
cure, at least some relief, for my misfortune. Not to keep you in suspense, for I am aware that you do not recognize me, I will tell you who
I am. I am Claudia Jerónima, daughter of Simón Forte, your very good
friend and the special enemy of Clauquel Torrellas, who is also your
enemy since he is of the rival band. As you know, this Torrellas has a
son, Don Vicente Torrellas, or, at any rate, that is what he was called
less than a couple of hours ago. But to cut short the story of my misadventure, I will tell you in a few words what he has done to me. He
saw me and took a fancy to me, and I listened to and fell in love with
him without my father's knowledge; for there is not a woman, however retiring and secluded she may be, who will not find more than
enough opportunities for carrying out her reckless desires.

"The short of it is, he promised to be my husband and I gave him
my word that I would be his wife, and the matter went no further.
Yesterday I learned that, forgetful of what he owed me, he was about
to marry another and that the nuptials were to be held this morning, a
piece of news that upset me greatly and put an end to my patience. As
my father was not in the village at the time, I donned this costume in
which you see me and, riding this horse as hard as I could, I caught up
with Don Vicente about a league or so from here. Without pausing
to indulge in any reproaches or listen to any excuses, I fired this fowling piece at him and these two pistols besides, and to the best of my belief I must have lodged more than two bullets in his body, opening in
it doors through which my honor might emerge bathed in his blood. I
left him there with his servants, who did not dare undertake to defend

him, and came to look for you that you might help me get to France, where I have relatives with whom I can live. And I would also ask you to protect my father lest Don Vicente's kinsmen [12] wreak some monstrous vengeance."

Admiring the beautiful Claudia's dash and spirit and her charming figure, and admiring her as well for what she had done, Roque now spoke to her.

"Come, Señora," he said, "let us go see if your enemy is dead, and afterward we will consider what is best for you."

Don Quixote had been listening attentively to Claudia's words and Roque Guinart's reply. "There is no need," he observed, "for anyone to go to the trouble of defending this lady, as I will take that responsibility upon myself. Give me my horse and my arms and await me here. I will go look for the knight and, living or dead, compel him to keep the promise he made to so beautiful a creature."

"And let no one think that he won't," said Sancho, "for my master is a good hand when it comes to matchmaking. Why, it's not many days ago that he forced another to marry who also wanted to break his word to a certain damsel, and if it had not been for the enchanters who persecuted the fellow and changed his true shape into that of a lackey, the maiden I am telling you about would not be a maid at this minute."

Roque, more concerned with thinking of the beauteous Claudia and her plight than he was with listening to the conversation of master and man, did not hear these remarks. He now ordered his squires to return to Sancho all that they had taken from the gray and to withdraw to that spot where they had spent the night; and, accompanied by the young woman, he then set out at full speed in search of the dead or wounded Don Vicente. When they reached the place where she had come upon her betrothed, they found nothing more than recently spilled blood; but, looking around in all directions, they sighted a number of people on the slope of a hill, which led them to believe, as was the case, that this must be the one they sought and that his servants were carrying him away either to care for his wounds or to bury him. Quickening their pace, Roque and his companion had no difficulty in overtaking the others, who were proceeding very slowly.

They found Don Vicente in the arms of his servants. In a voice that was faint from exhaustion he was calling upon them to let him die, inasmuch as the pain from his wounds would not permit of his going any farther. Flinging themselves from their horses, the pair went over to him. The servants were frightened at Roque's appearance, and Claudia was deeply moved at sight of Don Vicente as, half tenderly half sternly, she knelt beside him and took his hand in hers.

"Had you given me this," she said, "in accordance with our understanding, you would never have found yourself brought to such a pass."

Opening his eyes, the wounded gentleman recognized her. "I perceive plainly enough, O beautiful and deceived lady," he said, "that it is you who have slain me, a punishment that, by reason of the affection I bear you, I did not deserve; for never in thought or deed have I ever wished to offend you, nor would such a thing have been possible."

"Then," said Claudia, "it is not true that you were on your way this morning to wed Leonora, daughter of the rich Balvastro?"

"Most certainly not," replied Don Vicente. "It must have been my evil fortune that brought you such tidings, so that, in your jealous rage, you might be led to take my life; but seeing that I now leave that life in your hands and arms, I look upon my lot as a fortunate one after all.[13] By way of assurance that I speak the truth, press my hand and take me for your husband if you will, since there is no better way in which I may atone for the wrong you fancy I have done you."

Claudia did so, and her own heart was so oppressed that she fell in a faint on Don Vicente's bloodstained bosom even as the death spasm seized him. Roque was perplexed by it all, not knowing what to do. The servants ran for water and with it bathed the faces of the couple, whereupon the young woman recovered from her swoon, but not her bridegroom from his paroxysm, for his life had come to an end. When Claudia saw this and was certain that her beloved husband was no more, she rent the air with her sighs, made the heavens ring with her laments, tore her hair and cast it on the breeze, clawed her face with her hands, and gave all the signs of grief and feeling that could conceivably come from an afflicted bosom.

"O cruel and thoughtless woman," she cried, "how readily did you let yourself be moved to carry out so evil a design! O mad force of jealousy, to what desperate straits do you bring those who accord you a place in their hearts! O my husband, whose misfortune in being mine has taken you from the marriage bed to the grave!"

Claudia's laments were so heart-rending as to bring tears to Roque's eyes, unaccustomed as he was to shedding tears on any occasion whatsoever. The servants wept, Claudia swooned away at every step, and all the region round about appeared to be one vast field of sorrow and misfortune. Roque Guinart ordered the servants to take Don Vicente's body to the village where his father lived, which was not far away, in order that it might be given burial. Claudia informed him that she wished to go to a certain convent where an aunt of hers was the abbess, as she intended to spend the rest of her life there with another and eternal bridegroom, and Roque praised this worthy resolution and offered to escort her to her destination, promising further that he would protect her father against Don Vicente's relatives or anyone else who might seek to attack him.

Claudia, however, would not consent to his accompanying her but thanked him heartily for his kindness and took leave of him in tears. The servants bore the body away and Roque returned to his followers, and thus did the love affair of Claudia Jerónima come to an end. Was such an end to be wondered at, seeing that it was the cruel and invincible power of jealousy that wove the web of her lamentable history?

Roque Guinart found his squires in the place to which he had ordered them to retire, and in the midst of them, mounted on Rocinante, was Don Quixote. The Knight was engaged in making a speech to them in which he sought to persuade them to give up this mode of life which was so dangerous to body and soul; but inasmuch as most of them were Gascons, a rude lot with no respect for law and order,[14] his words had little effect upon them. Roque as he drew up inquired of Sancho if they had returned to him the valuables which they had stripped from the ass, and the squire replied that they had, but that three kerchiefs worth as much as three whole cities, still were missing.

"What are you talking about, man?" said one of the band. "I have them myself, and they are not worth three reales."

"That is true," said Don Quixote, "but my squire values them at the price he has mentioned by reason of the one who gave them to me."

Roque ordered the fellow to give them back at once, after which he lined his men up and had them produce all the clothing, jewels, money, and other objects that they had stolen since the last time they had divided the spoils. Having made a hasty appraisal and reduced to terms of money those items that could not be divided, he split the whole into shares with such equity and exactitude that in not a single instance did he go beyond or fall short of a strict distributive justice. They were all well satisfied with the payment received, indeed they were quite well pleased; and Roque then turned to Don Quixote.

"If I did not observe an absolute impartiality with these fellows," he said, "there would be no living with them."

"From what I have seen here," remarked Sancho, "justice is so good a thing that even robbers find it necessary."

Hearing this, one of the band raised the butt end of an harquebus [15] and would undoubtedly have come down with it on Sancho's head if Roque Guinart had not shouted to him to refrain. Sancho was terrified and made up his mind that from then on he would keep a tightly sewn lip as long as he was in the present company.

At this point one of those squires who had been stationed as sentinels along the highway to see who came and went and report to their chief on what happened, came riding up.

"Sir," he said, "not far from here, along the road to Barcelona, there is a great crowd of people approaching."

"Were you able to make out," Roque asked him, "whether they are the kind that are looking for us or the kind we are looking for?"

"The kind we are looking for," replied the squire.

"Well, then," said Roque, "be on your way, all of you; bring them to me here at once and see that not a one escapes."

The men did as they had been commanded to do, leaving Don Quixote, Sancho, and Roque alone together; and as the three of them waited to see what the squires would bring back, the leader of the band addressed the knight.

"The life we lead," he said, "must appear a strange one to Señor Don Quixote, one filled with strange happenings and adventures and all of them dangerous. I am not at all surprised that it should seem so, for I really must confess that there is no mode of existence that is more restless and laden with anxiety than ours. What led me to adopt such a life was a certain desire for vengeance, which has the power to disturb the quietest of hearts. I am by nature merciful and well meaning, but, as I say, the will to avenge a wrong that was done me so overcomes my virtuous inclinations that I continue in this calling in spite of what my better judgment tells me; and even as one depth calls to another and one sin to another sin, so have the objects of my vengeance come to be linked together in such a manner that I have taken upon myself not merely my own wrongs but those of others as well. But, please God, though I find myself in this bewildering labyrinth, I still have not given up hope of reaching a secure haven in the end."

Don Quixote was amazed to hear Roque express such praiseworthy and well-reasoned sentiments; for among those who follow the highwayman's trade of robbing and killing he had not believed it possible there could be anyone so right-thinking as this.

"Señor Roque," he now replied to him, "the beginning of health lies in a knowledge of one's infirmity, and in the sick man's being willing to take the medicines that the physician prescribes. Your Grace is sick, you know what the disease is from which you are suffering, and Heaven, or, better, God, who is our physician, will provide the remedies to cure you—but not all of a sudden or through any miracle, for they usually do their healing work little by little. Moreover, intelligent sinners are nearer redemption than simple-minded ones, and by what your Grace has said you have shown that you are a man of sense. There is nothing to do, then, but to be of good courage and wait for your sickly conscience to improve. And if your Grace is of a mind to take a short cut and obtain your salvation with ease, then come with me and I will teach you to be a knight-errant. In that life you will meet with so many hardships and misadventures that, if they were to be taken as a penance, they would land you in Heaven in the twinkling of an eye."

Roque laughed at Don Quixote's advice, and then, changing the subject, went on to tell him of the outcome of Claudia Jerónima's affair, which made Sancho feel very sad, for he had been struck by the young woman's beauty, courage, and self-assurance. By this time the squires were back with their prize, consisting of two gentlemen on horseback, two pilgrims on foot, and a coach full of women accompanied by about half a dozen servants, some of whom were mounted while others were not. The squires had them surrounded, and both victors and vanquished preserved a deep silence as they waited for the great Roque Guinart to speak. He now inquired of the gentlemen who they were and whence they came and what money they had on them.

"Sir," one of them answered, "we are two captains of Spanish infantry; our companies are in Naples and we are to embark in four galleys that are said to be in Barcelona with orders for Sicily. We have with us three or four hundred crowns, which is enough to make us feel rich and happy, as it is truly a fortune in view of that poverty to which soldiers are accustomed."

Roque put the same question to the pilgrims as to the captains and was told that they were on their way to take ship for Rome and that they had about sixty reales between them. He also wanted to know who the women in the coach were, whither they were bound, and how much money they had on their persons.

"Those in the coach," one of the men on horseback replied, "are my lady Doña Guiomar de Quiñones, wife of the president of the vicarial court of Naples, her small daughter, a young waiting woman, and a duenna; we six servants are accompanying them, and their money amounts to six hundred pounds."

"That means," said Roque Guinart, "that we have here altogether nine hundred crowns and sixty reales; my soldiers should have about sixty; see how much is coming to each one of them, for I am a poor hand at reckoning."

Upon hearing this, the highwaymen raised a shout: "Long live Roque Guinart, in spite of the thieving rascals [16] that seek his ruin!"

The captains were obviously grieved, the president's lady was downcast, and the pilgrims were by no means happy as they thought of their funds being confiscated. Roque kept them in suspense like this for a short while and then, their distress being visible at the distance of a crossbow shot, he put an end to it by saying to the captains, "Will you be so courteous, your Worships, as kindly to lend me sixty pounds, and will my lady, the president's wife, let me have eighty, to satisfy the members of my band, since the abbot must dine on what he gets by singing? [17] You may then go your way free and unhindered with a safe-conduct which I will give you in order that, should you fall in with other bands of mine that I have scattered around these parts, they may not do you any harm; for it is not my intention to do wrong to soldiers or to any woman, especially persons of quality."

The captains were most eloquent and profuse in thanking Roque for his courtesy and generosity, for such was the way they felt about his leaving them their own money. The lady, Doña Guiomar de Quiñones, wanted to fling herself out of the coach that she might kiss the great man's hands and feet, but he would by no means consent to this; rather, he begged her pardon for the wrong he had done her, explaining that he was forced to comply with the unavoidable exigencies of his unpleasant calling. She thereupon ordered one of her servants to pay over at once the eighty crowns that constituted her share, for the captains had already disbursed their sixty.

The pilgrims were about to give up the pitiably small sum of money that they had on them, but Roque told them to keep quiet, and, turning to his followers he said, "Of these crowns, two go to each one of you, which leaves twenty over; let ten be given to the pilgrims and ten to this worthy squire that he may speak well of the present adventure."

He then had them bring him pen and ink and paper, with which he always went provided, and proceeded to write out a safe-conduct addressed to the leaders of his bands, after which he bade them good-by, leaving the travelers free to go their way as they marveled at his magnanimity, generosity, and unusual conduct, for they regarded him as more like Alexander the Great than a notorious bandit.

"This captain of ours," said one of his men, speaking in a mixture of Gascon and Catalan, "is better suited to be a friar [18] than a highwayman; after this, if he wants to be so liberal, let it be with his own property, not with ours."

The poor wretch did not speak so low but that Roque overheard him, and, drawing his sword, the latter laid the fellow's head open, dividing it almost in two.

"That," he said, "is the way I punish those who are impudent and too free with their tongues."

All his men were stunned by this and did not utter a word, such was the respect they had for him. Then, going off to one side, he wrote a letter to a friend of his in Barcelona, stating that the famous knight, Don Quixote de la Mancha, of whom there was so much talk, was with him at the moment and that he found him to be the most entertaining and sensible man in all the world. He added that, four days from then, which would be on St. John the Baptist's Day,[19] he meant to set him down in the middle of the beach of that city, clad in full armor, mounted on Rocinante his horse, and accompanied by his squire Sancho on an ass, and he wished his correspondent to notify his friends, the Niarros, of this fact so that they might have some diversion with the knight. He would have liked, he said, to deprive his enemies, the Cadells,[20] of this pleasure, but that was impossible since Don Quixote's mad actions and shrewd observations and Sancho Panza's drolleries could not fail to amuse them all. This letter he dispatched by one of his followers, who, exchanging his highwayman's costume for peasant garb, made his way into Barcelona and delivered it to the individual to whom it was addressed.

CHAPTER LXI. *Of what happened to Don Quixote upon his entrance into Barcelona, with other matters that contain more truth than wit.*

THREE days and three nights Don Quixote spent with Roque, and if it had been three hundred years the former would still have found plenty to observe and wonder at in the bandit's mode of life. Daybreak would find them in one place, dinnertime in another; they would now flee, not knowing from whom, and now would lie in wait, not knowing what to expect. They slept standing up, interrupting their slumbers to move from one place to another. And all the while they were sending out spies, posting sentinels, and blowing on the matchlocks of their harquebuses, though they had but few of these weapons as all of them [1] carried petronels.

Roque passed the night apart from his followers, keeping them in ignorance of his whereabouts; for the many proclamations which the viceroy of Barcelona had issued against him, putting a price upon his head,[2] made him fearful and uneasy and he did not dare trust anyone, being in dread even of his own men lest they slay him or hand him over to the authorities. It was truly a wretched and a wearying life that he led.

At length, following untraveled roads, short cuts, and secret paths, Roque, Don Quixote, Sancho, and six squires set out for Barcelona, arriving at the beach during the night of St. John's Eve. There the bandit chief embraced his guests and, giving Sancho the ten crowns which he had promised him but which had not as yet been paid, bade them farewell and departed, leaving Don Quixote to sit in the saddle just as he was and wait for the coming of day.

It was not long before the fair Aurora began to show herself on the balconies of the east, bringing joy to the grass and flowers; and if there was nothing about her coming to please the ear, that deficiency was instantly remedied by the sound of many flageolets and drums, and the "Look out, there! Make way! Make way!" of runners who appeared to sally forth from the city. Aurora, meanwhile, was making way for the sun, which was gradually lifting above the horizon's lowest rim a face larger than a shield.

Looking about them in all directions, Don Quixote and Sancho now had their first view of the sea, which impressed them as being very broad and spacious, much larger than the Lakes of Ruidera in La Mancha. They saw the galleys on the beach with their lowered awnings, decked out with streamers and pennants that fluttered in the breeze and swept and kissed the surface of the water, while from aboard the vessels, near and far, bugles, trumpets, and clarions filled the air with a martial melody. The boats now began to move about and engage in a sort of skirmish in the quiet water, and at the same moment a large number of horsemen on handsome mounts with showy liveries came riding from the city and began executing a similar maneuver. The soldiers on the galleys discharged a countless number of rounds of artillery, and their fire was returned by those on the walls and in the forts, the deafening roar of the heavy cannon being answered in turn by the guns amidship. The sea was bright, the earth rejoicing, the air clear save now and then for the smoke from the artillery—in short, everything was such as to infuse all the people gathered there with an unlooked-for sense of pleasure.

As for Sancho, he was unable to make out how those bulky objects moving over the water could have so many feet. But at this point the liveried horsemen with cheers, cries, and Moorish war whoops [3] came galloping up to where Don Quixote waited in astonishment and some alarm.

And then one of them—the one to whom Roque had sent word—raised his voice and cried out to the knight, "Welcome to our city, O mirror, beacon, and north star of all knight-errantry, in the full sense of the word.[4] You are, I repeat, very welcome indeed, O valiant Don Quixote de la Mancha—not the false, not the fictitious, not the apocryphal one that we read of in mendacious histories that have appeared of late, but the true and legitimate one, the real one that Cid Hamete Benengeli, flower of historians, has portrayed for us."

Don Quixote did not utter a word in reply, nor did the horsemen give him a chance to do so. Wheeling their steeds again and again, they and their followers began performing a complicated caracole around him; and he then turned to Sancho and said, "These gentlemen plainly recognized us. I will wager you that they have read our history and that of the Aragonese as well, which was printed not so long ago."

The horseman who had previously addressed the knight now spoke to him once more. "Come with us, Señor Don Quixote," he said, "for we are all at your service, being great friends of Roque Guinart."

"If courtesy begets courtesy," replied Don Quixote, "then that which you display is the daughter or very near relative of the courtesy manifested by the great Roque. Take me wherever you see fit, for I have no other will than yours, especially if you choose to employ it in your service."

The gentleman replied with words equally polite; and then, closing in around him, they all set out for the city to the sound of drums and flageolets. But as they were about to enter the town, the Evil One, who ordains all things evil, and small boys, who are more mischievous than mischief itself, took a hand in the matter. Forcing their way through the crowd, a pair of impudent and prankish urchins lifted up the tails of Rocinante and the gray and inserted a bunch of furze under each of them. When they felt these unaccustomed spurs, the poor animals pressed their tails tightly against their bodies, thereby increasing the pain, and as a result they began leaping and rearing in such a manner that they tossed their riders to the ground. Very much embarrassed by what had happened, Don Quixote ran up to relieve the nag of his plume, and Sancho did the same for his donkey. Those who were serving as the knight's escort would have liked to punish the lads for their impudence, but this was impossible, for the pair were soon lost among the thousands in the crowd.

Master and man then mounted again and, accompanied still by music and cheers, reached the home of their guide, which was very large and imposing, in short, the house of a wealthy gentleman. And here we shall leave them for the present, seeing that Cid Hamete would have it so.

CHAPTER LXII. *Which deals with the adventure of the enchanted head, together with other trifling things that cannot be left untold.*

DON ANTONIO MORENO was the name of Don Quixote's host, a gentleman of wealth and discernment who was fond of amusing himself in an innocent and kindly way. Having taken the knight into his house, he began casting about for some harmless means of bringing out his mad traits; for jests that give pain are no jests at all,[1] and those pastimes that result in hurting another person are not worth while.

The first thing he did, accordingly, was to have Don Quixote remove his armor, which left him clad only in that tight-fitting chamois-skin suit that we have already described and portrayed a number of times; after which, he led him out onto a balcony overlooking one of the principal thoroughfares of the city, in order that the people gathered there, including the small boys, might have a look at him. The crowd stared as if he had been a monkey, while the liveried horsemen once more rode up and down in front of him, as if it was for his special benefit and not to celebrate some festive occasion that they had donned that garb. Sancho, meanwhile, was happy as could be; for it seemed to him that, without his knowing the why or wherefore of it all, he had come upon another Camacho's wedding, another house like that of Don Diego de Miranda's, or another castle like the duke's.

Some of Don Antonio's friends dined with him that day, and they all treated Don Quixote with the utmost respect, showing him the honors due a knight-errant, at which he became so puffed up and self-satisfied that he could not contain himself. As for Sancho's witticisms, they were such that the household servants and all the others present hung upon his every word. When they were seated at the table, their host turned to Sancho.

"We have received word here, my good Sancho," he said, "that you are very fond of *manjar blanco*[2] and forced-meat balls, so fond, indeed, that if there is any left over, you put it away in your bosom for another day."[3]

914

"No, sir, that is not so," replied Sancho, "for I am more cleanly than greedy, and my master Don Quixote, here present, can very well tell you that the two of us are used to going for a week at a time with nothing to eat but a handful of nuts or acorns. The truth of the matter is that if they happen to give me a heifer, I run with the halter,[4] by which I mean to say, I eat what is set before me and take things as they come; and if anyone says that I eat more than my share or am unclean, you may take my word for it, he's wide of the mark, and I'd put it in a different way if it wasn't for the honorable beards at this table."[5]

"I can assure you," said Don Quixote at this point, "that the sparingness and cleanliness with which Sancho eats might be inscribed and engraved on tablets of bronze, to be preserved as a lasting memorial for future ages. I grant you that when he is hungry he appears to be a bit of a glutton, for then he eats with great haste and chews his food with both cheeks bulging. But he is always scrupulously clean, and during the time that he was governor he became so dainty in his habits that he even used a fork for eating grapes or pomegranate seeds."

"What?" said Don Antonio. "Has Sancho been a governor?"

"Yes," replied Sancho, "governor of an island named Barataria. For ten days I governed it as I saw fit, and during that time I lost my rest and learned to scorn all the governments in the world. I finally ran away from it and fell into a pit, where I gave myself up for dead, but by a miracle I came out alive."

Don Quixote then gave them a detailed account of everything that had happened in connection with Sancho's government, and they all enjoyed it very much. When the cloth had been removed, Don Antonio took his guest by the hand and led him into another room of the house, where the only article of furniture was a table that appeared to be made of jasper, resting upon a pedestal of the same material, while upon it was a head resembling the busts of the Roman emperors and seemingly carved out of bronze. After they had walked around the table many times, Don Antonio spoke.

"Now that I am certain, Señor Don Quixote, that the door is shut and no one can overhear us, I wish," he said, "to tell your Grace of one of the rarest adventures, or, more properly speaking, one of the strangest things, that could be imagined, but upon condition that your Grace keeps it hidden away in the most remote and secret closet of your mind."

"That I swear to do," said Don Quixote, "and by way of further security, I will place a flagstone over it; for I would have your Grace know, Señor Don Antonio"—he had learned his host's name by this time—"that you are talking to one who, though he has ears for hearing, has no tongue for speaking. Hence your Grace may feel safe in transferring to my bosom what you have in yours, knowing full well that I have consigned it to the depths of silence."

"Relying on that promise," said Don Antonio, "I shall astonish your Grace with what you will see and hear, and at the same time relieve myself of the pain I feel at having no one to whom I may confide my secrets, which are not to be entrusted to everybody."

Don Quixote was puzzled as he waited to see what would come of all these precautions. Taking the knight's hand, Don Antonio now passed it over the bronze head and over the entire table, all the way down to the jasper base.

"This head, Señor Don Quixote," he remarked, "was made and fashioned by one of the greatest enchanters and sorcerers in all the world.[6] He was a Pole by birth, a disciple of the famous Escotillo [7] of whom so many marvels are related. He was here in my house, and for the price of a thousand crowns which I gave him he carved the head, which has the property and the virtue of being able to answer all questions that are asked of its ear. By setting up geometrical figures,[8] observing the stars, casting horoscopes, and noting the hour and season, he brought his work to that perfection that we shall see tomorrow; for on Fridays it is mute, and since today is Friday we must wait. In the meantime, your Grace may be deciding what questions you wish to put to it, and I know from experience that it will answer you truly."

Amazed to think that the head should possess such qualities, Don Quixote was inclined to disbelieve his host; but in view of the fact that he would shortly be able to put the matter to a test, he merely thanked Don Antonio for having revealed to him so great a secret. They then left the room, the master of the house locking the door behind him, and went down to the great hall where the other gentlemen were and where Sancho all the while had been telling them of many of the adventures and accidents that had befallen his master.

That afternoon they took Don Quixote out for a ride,[9] not in his armor but dressed for the street, being attired in a greatcoat of tawny-colored cloth which at that season of the year would have made ice itself sweat, while the servants had orders to keep Sancho entertained and not to permit him to leave the house. Don Quixote went mounted, not upon Rocinante, but upon a large even-paced mule with very fine trappings. Having put his greatcoat on him, they sewed a piece of parchment on the back of it with an inscription in large letters: "THIS IS

DON QUIXOTE DE LA MANCHA." From the moment they set out, the placard attracted the attention of all those who had come to behold the spectacle, and the knight for his part was astonished to find so many people gazing at him and calling him by name.

Turning to Don Antonio, who rode alongside him, he said, "Great are the prerogatives of knight-errantry, seeing that it makes the one who follows that calling known and famous in all parts of the earth. If you do not believe me, Señor Don Antonio, your Grace has but to observe the lads of this city, who, though they have never seen me, nevertheless recognize me."

"That is true, Señor Don Quixote," replied Don Antonio; "for just as fire cannot remain hidden or shut away from view, so virtue cannot fail to be recognized for what it is, and that virtue which is attained through the profession of arms shines forth above all others."

It happened, then, that as Don Quixote was riding along in the manner described, to the applause of the multitude, a certain Castilian [10] who had read the placard on the knight's back raised his voice and cried out, "May the devil take you, Don Quixote de la Mancha! What! and aren't you dead from all the clubbings that your ribs have had? You are a madman, but if you kept your madness to yourself it would not be so bad. As it is, you have the faculty of turning into madmen and fools all that have anything to do with you. As proof of this, just look at those gentlemen that are accompanying you. Go back to your home, you crackbrain, attend to your own affairs, see to your wife and children, and leave off these absurdities that eat your brain away and skim off your wits."

"Brother," Don Antonio said to him, "go about your business and do not be giving advice to those that do not ask for it. Señor Don Quixote de la Mancha is quite sane, and we who are with him are not fools. Virtue is to be honored wherever it is met with; so go, and bad luck go with you, and do not be meddling in what does not concern you."

"By God, but your Grace is right," replied the Castilian, "for to give advice to this good man is to kick against the prick; but, for all of that, it is a very great pity to see the good sense they say the fool displays on all other subjects [11] drained off like this through the channel of his knight-errantry. And may the bad luck your Grace wished me really follow me and my descendants if from this day forth, though I live to be older than Methuselah, I give advice to anyone whether he asks for it or not."

With this, the advice-giver went his way, and they resumed their ride; [12] but so great was the eagerness of the small boys and all the rest of the crowd to see what was on the placard that Don Antonio was compelled to take it off under pretense of removing something else. At nightfall they returned home, to find an evening party in progress there; for Don Antonio's wife, a beautiful lady of high station and endowed with wit and gaiety, had invited some of her women friends to come and show honor to her house guest and enjoy his unheard-of variety of madness. A number of them accepted the invitation, a splendid supper was served, and the dancing began about ten o'clock.

Among the ladies were two that, being of a mischievous disposition, were fond of a practical joke, and although they were perfectly respectable they were somewhat free and easy in their ways when it came to playing pranks for the sake of innocent diversion. This pair insisted on Don Quixote's dancing with them so often that they wore him out, not only in body but in spirit as well. He was a sight to see: long, lean, lank, and yellow-looking, clad in his tight-fitting suit, awkward, and, above all, not very light on his feet. The frolicsome ladies made furtive love to him and he, likewise by stealth, rejected their advances; but, finding himself hard pressed by these attentions, he finally raised his voice and cried out, "*Fugite, partes adversae!* [13] Leave me in peace, unwelcome temptations! Away with your passion, ladies; for she who is queen of my heart, the peerless Dulcinea del Toboso, will consent to none other assailing it and laying it low!"

Saying this, he sat down in the middle of the ballroom floor, battered and broken from his exertions as a dancer, and Don Antonio then had them pick him up and carry him off to bed. The first to lay hold to him was Sancho.

"It was an evil hour, my master," he said, "when you tried to dance! Do you think that all brave men and knights-errant can do that? [14] If so, I can tell you that you are mistaken. There are those that would rather slay a giant than cut a caper. Now, if it had been a clog dance [15] I'd have taken your place, for I can tap my heels like a gerfalcon,[16] but when it comes to your fancy steps [17] I'm no good at it."

With these and other remarks Sancho set the company to laughing, and then he went off to put his master to bed, taking care to cover him well that he might sweat out any cold caught by dancing.

The next day Don Antonio decided that it would be well to try out the enchanted head at once, and so, with Don Quixote, Sancho, and a couple of friends, together with the ladies who had worn Don Quixote out with dancing the evening before and who had spent the night there, he shut himself up in the room where the head was. Explaining to them its peculiar properties, which he was to put to the test for the first time that day, he bound them all to secrecy; for, with the exception of Don Antonio's two friends, there was no one who understood the mystery behind the enchantment, and if these two had not been informed of it by the master of the house, they of necessity would have been quite as amazed as the others, so skillfully and artfully was the mechanism contrived.

The first who came up to whisper in the ear of the magic head was Don Antonio himself, who in a low voice, yet not so low but that the rest of them could hear him, said, "Tell me, O head, by the virtue that is in you,[18] what am I thinking of at this moment?"

And without moving its lips the head replied, in a tone so clear and distinct that all were able to make it out, "I am no judge of thoughts."

The entire company was astonished at hearing it speak, in view of the fact that neither around the table nor in all the room was there any human being who could have given the answer.

"How many of us are there here?" was Don Antonio's next question; and the reply, uttered in the same tone of voice, was, "There are you and your wife, two friends of yours, two women friends of hers, a famous knight named Don Quixote de la Mancha, and his squire whose name is Sancho Panza."

This created fresh astonishment, and everyone's hair was standing on end from sheer fright. "I am now convinced," remarked Don Antonio as he turned aside, "that the one who sold you to me did not cheat me, O wise head, talking head, answering and admirable head! Let someone else come up and ask any question that he likes."

Since women ordinarily are extremely curious, the first to do so was one of the friends of Don Antonio's wife. "Tell me, O head," she inquired, "what must I do to be very beautiful?" And the answer was, "Be very modest."

"I ask no more," said the one who had put the question.

She was followed by her companion. "I should like to know, O head, whether my husband loves me or not."

"Observe the way he treats you," came the response, "and judge for yourself."

"There was no need of my asking to learn that," said the married lady as she walked away; "for it goes without saying that the way a person treats you shows the way he feels toward you."[19]

One of Don Antonio's friends was the next questioner. "Who am I?"

"You know who you are."

"That is not what I asked you," said the gentleman. "I wanted you to tell me if you recognized me."

"Yes, I recognize you; you are Don Pedro Noriz."

"That is all I seek to know, as it is enough to assure me, O head, that you know everything."

It was the other friend's turn now. "Tell me, O head, what does my son and heir desire?"

"I have already told you that I am no judge of such things, but, nevertheless, I may inform you that what your son desires is to bury you."

"That is to say," the gentleman replied, " 'What I see with my eyes I point out with my finger.' [20] I have no further questions."

Don Antonio's wife came next. "I do not know, O head, what to ask you. I should merely like to have you tell me if I am to enjoy my good husband for many years to come."

"Yes, you will," was the answer, "for his good health and temperate mode of living promise him a long life-span, which many by their intemperance cut short."

Don Quixote now came forward. "Tell me," he said, "you who do the answering, with regard to my story of what happened to me in the Cave of Montesinos, did it really happen or was it a dream? Will my squire Sancho be sure to receive the lashes that are his due? And will Dulcinea finally be disenchanted?"

"With respect to the cave," the head replied, "there is much to be said on both sides; Sancho's lashes will proceed apace; and the disenchantment of Dulcinea will ultimately be accomplished."

"That is enough," said Don Quixote. "Let me but see Dulcinea freed of the magic spell and it will seem to me that all the good fortune I could wish for has come to me at once."

Sancho was the last, and his question was, "Head, shall I have another government? Shall I ever be through with this poverty-stricken life of a squire? Shall I see my wife and children again?"

"You will govern in your house," the head assured him; "if you return to it, you will see your wife and young ones; and if you leave off serving, you will cease to be a squire."

"That's fine, by God!" exclaimed Sancho. "I could have told myself as much as that. The prophet Perogrullo [21] could not have done better."

"Stupid creature," said Don Quixote, "what answer did you expect? Is it not enough that the replies which this head gives have a bearing on the questions put to it?"

"Yes," said Sancho, "it will do; but I'd have liked it better if it had spoken longer and told me more."

This ended the questions and answers, but it did not end the astonishment they all felt, with the exception of Don Antonio and his friends, who knew the secret of the thing. That secret Cid Hamete Benengeli chose to reveal at once, not wishing to keep the world in suspense or under the impression that there was anything strange and magical about it. He accordingly goes on to state that Don Antonio, in imitation of another head which he had seen in Madrid, the work of an artisan of that city, had had this one made in his own house in order to provide entertainment and astonish the ignorant.

The mechanism was constructed in the following manner. The table was made of wood painted and varnished like jasper, and the pedestal upon which it rested was of the same material, with four projecting eagles' claws to give it greater firmness. The bronze-colored head, which resembled the bust of a Roman emperor, of the kind seen on coins and medals, was entirely hollow, and so was the table on which it stood, into which it fitted so exactly that there was no sign of any juncture. The foot of the table was also hollow, forming a continuation of the throat and chest of the head above, and the whole was connected with another room immediately below. Through the hollow foot, table, throat, and chest there was inserted a tin-plate tube very nicely adjusted and out of sight, while in the lower room was stationed the one who did the answering; he would place his mouth to the tube and voices would then travel up and down it as through an ear trumpet, the words being articulated very clearly and everything being arranged so cleverly that it was impossible to discover the trick.

A nephew of Don Antonio's, an intelligent, sharp-witted student, was the one who gave the responses, and having been previously advised by his uncle as to who were to be present in the room with the head, he had found no difficulty in answering the first question promptly and accurately but had been compelled to resort to guesses in replying to the others. However, being a clever fellow, he acquitted himself in a clever manner. Cid Hamete further tells us that this marvelous contrivance lasted for ten or a dozen days, but as the news spread through the city that Don Antonio had in his house an enchanted head that answered all queries put to it, he, fearing lest word of this should reach the alert ears of those reverend gentlemen, the sentinels of our faith, had explained the matter to the Inquisitors, who had ordered him to smash the mechanism and carry the jest no further, in order that the ignorant rabble might not be scandalized. But in Don Quixote's opinion and that of Sancho, the head remained an enchanted one with the virtues ascribed to it, though the knight was better satisfied than his squire with the answers that it gave.

By way of humoring Don Antonio and keeping Don Quixote entertained, while affording the latter, at the same time, an opportunity to display his absurdities, the gentlemen of the city arranged for a tilting at the ring six days from then, but, owing to circumstances that will be related further on, this event did not take place. In the meantime, Don Quixote wished to go out for a quiet stroll, for he feared that if he went on horseback the small boys would follow him, and so, accompanied only by Sancho and a couple of servants that Don Antonio had furnished him, he set out with this object in view.

As he was going down a certain street he glanced up and saw a sign in large letters over a doorway, reading: "BOOKS PRINTED HERE." This pleased him very much, as he had never seen a printing shop up to that time and had a desire to find out what it was like. Going inside with all his retinue, he saw them drawing proofs here, correcting them there, setting type in one place and making revisions in another—in short, he beheld everything that goes to make up a large establishment of this sort. Going up to one of the cases, he inquired what was being done there, the workmen explained things for him, and, wondering at what he had observed, he passed on. He put the same question to another printer, and the man replied, "Sir, this gentleman here"—and he pointed to an impressive individual with a rather grave look on his face— "has translated a Tuscan book into our Castilian tongue, and I am now engaged in setting the type for it."

"What is the title of the book?" asked Don Quixote.

It was the author [22] who answered. "Sir," he said, "this work in Tuscan is called *Le Bagatelle*." [23]

"And what does *Le Bagatelle* mean in Castilian?"

"*Le Bagatelle*," replied the author, "is equivalent to *los juguetes* [24] in Spanish; and although the title is a humble-sounding one, this book contains much meat and substance."

"I," said Don Quixote, "am somewhat acquainted with Tuscan and pride myself on being able to recite certain stanzas of Ariosto. [25] But tell me, my dear sir, and I ask this not to test your Grace's ability but merely out of curiosity, in the course of your labors have you come upon such a word as *pignatta*?" [26]

"Yes, many times," was the answer.

"And how does your Grace render it into Castilian?"

"How should I render it except by *olla?*" [27]

"Body of me!" exclaimed Don Quixote, "how far advanced your Grace is in the Italian language! I will lay you a good wager that you translate *piace* as *place*, *più* as *más*, *su* as *arriba*, and *giù* as *abajo.*" [28]

"I do indeed," said the author, "for those are the proper equivalents."

"And I would venture to take an oath," Don Quixote went on, "that your Grace is not known to the world at large, which always is chary of rewarding men of exceptional ability and works deserving of praise. How many talents have been lost in that way, how many geniuses have been tossed into the corner, how much of real worth has gone unappreciated! But, for all of that, it appears to me that translating from one language into another, unless it be from one of those two queenly tongues, Greek and Latin, is like gazing at a Flemish tapestry with the wrong side out: even though the figures are visible, they are full of threads that obscure the view and are not bright and smooth as when seen from the other side. [29] Moreover, translating from easy languages does not call for either wit or eloquence, any more than does the mere transcription or copying of a document.

"By this," the knight continued, "I do not mean to imply that the task of translating is not a laudable occupation, for a man might employ his time less worthily and with less profit to himself. I make an exception here of those two famous translators: Doctor Cristóbal de Figueroa in his *Pastor Fido* and Don Juan de Jáuregui in his *Aminta*,[30] where happily one may doubt as to which is the translation and which the original. But, your Grace, I should like to know, is this book being printed at your own expense or have you already disposed of the rights to some bookseller?"

"I pay for the printing," said the author, "and I expect to clear at least a thousand ducats on this first edition of two thousand copies, which at two reales apiece ought to sell in no time at all." [31]

"That," said Don Quixote, "is a fine bit of calculation on your Grace's part, but it is plain to be seen that you are not familiar with the ins and outs of the printers and the way in which they all work together.[32] I can promise you that when you find yourself weighted down with two thousand copies, you will be astonished how your body will ache all over, especially if the book happens to be a little out of the ordinary and does not make spicy reading." [33]

"But what would your Grace have me do? Give it to a bookseller who will pay me three maravedis for the rights and think that he is doing me a favor? I do not have books printed to win fame in this world, for I am already well known through my works; it is money that I seek, for without it a fine reputation is not worth a cent." [34]

"Well, good luck and God help you," said Don Quixote; and with this he moved on to another case, where he perceived that they were correcting the proofs of a book entitled *Light of the Soul*.[35]

"These," he said, "are the books that ought to be printed, even though there are many of the sort, for many are the sinners these days,[36] and an infinite number of lights are required for all those that are in darkness."

Going up to another case, he saw that here, too, they were correcting a book, and when he asked the title he was told that it was the *Second Part of the Ingenious Gentleman, Don Quixote de la Mancha*, composed by a certain native of Tordesillas.[37]

"I have heard of this work," he said, "and, in all truth and upon my conscience, I think it ought to be burned to ashes as a piece of impertinence; but Martinmas will come for it as it does for every pig.[38] Fictional tales are better and more enjoyable the nearer they approach the truth or the semblance of the truth, and as for true stories, the best are those that are most true." [39]

Saying this, he stalked out of the printing shop with signs of considerable displeasure.

That same day Don Antonio made arrangements to take him to see the galleys on the beach, and Sancho was delighted at this as he never in his life had beheld such a sight.[40] Their host thereupon notified the commander [41] that he was bringing with him his guest, the famous Don Quixote de la Mancha, of whom that officer and everyone in the city had heard. As for what happened to them aboard the vessels, that will be related in the following chapter.

CHAPTER LXIII. *Of the misfortune that befell Sancho Panza upon his visit to the galleys, and the strange adventure of the beautiful Moorish maiden.*

DON QUIXOTE pondered deeply the reply which the enchanted head had given him. No matter how much he thought about it, he was unable to hit upon the method by which the trick was worked but always came back to the one thing he accepted as being unquestionably true: the promise that Dulcinea would be disenchanted. He turned this over and over in his mind and was very happy in the thought that he would soon be witnessing its fulfillment. As for Sancho, while he hated being a governor, as has been stated, he nonetheless had a desire to give orders once more and be obeyed, such is the misfortune that a position of authority, even if only held in jest, brings with it.

But to come back to our story: That afternoon their host, Don Antonio Moreno, and his two friends with Don Quixote and Sancho repaired to the galleys. The commander had been advised of his good luck in being able to lay eyes upon so famous a pair, and no sooner had they reached the waterfront than all the vessels struck their awnings and the flageolets began to resound. A small boat covered with costly rugs and cushions of crimson velvet was lowered, and the moment Don Quixote set foot in the skiff the commander's galley fired its cannon amidship and all the others did the same. As the knight mounted the starboard ladder, the entire crew saluted him, as is the custom when an important personage comes aboard, crying *"Hu, hu, hu"* three times.

The general—for such we shall call him, seeing that he was a Valencian gentleman of high rank—then gave Don Quixote his hand and embraced him, saying, "This day I shall mark with a white stone [1] as being one of the best I ever expect to enjoy as long as I live, since it has afforded me a sight of Señor Don Quixote de la Mancha—a monument in memory of the occasion [2] when I met the one who, as we can plainly see, contains within himself the sum and substance of all that is worth while in knight-errantry."

Overjoyed at finding himself received in so lordly a manner, Don

Quixote made an equally courteous speech in reply, and they all retired to the poop, which was very well fitted out, and sat down upon the benches there. The boatswain then went to the gangway and with his whistle gave the signal for the crew to strip,[3] which was done in a moment's time. Sancho was astonished to see so many naked men, and he marveled still more as he saw them rig the awning with such speed that it seemed to him as if all the devils in Hell must be working there. This, however, was but gingerbread and cakes [4] compared to what I am about to tell you now.

The squire was seated on the captain's platform next to the foremost rower on the right; and this fellow, having been instructed as to what he was to do, now seized him and, raising him in his arms, started passing him down the line on that side. All the members of the crew were standing ready, and they proceeded to send him flying from one pair of arms to another and from bench to bench so fast that poor Sancho lost the sight of his eyes and undoubtedly must have fancied that it was the demons themselves that were carrying him off; and this did not stop until he had been returned on the left-hand side and set down once more in the poop, bruised and breathless, and sweating all over and unable to imagine what it was that had happened to him.

Upon witnessing this flight without wings on Sancho's part, Don Quixote inquired of the general if it was a customary ceremony in the case of those who came aboard for the first time; for if by any chance it was, he did not intend to follow this calling, as he had no desire to engage in any such exercises; and he further vowed to God that if anyone should lay hands on him for that purpose, he would kick the life out of him. With this, he rose to his feet and grasped his sword.

At that instant they struck the awning and brought down the lateen yard with so tremendous a clatter that Sancho thought the heavens were becoming unhinged and were about to fall upon him, and full of fear he stuck his head between his legs. Don Quixote's own legs, for that matter, were none too steady as he sat huddled and trembling with all the color gone from his face. The crew thereupon hoisted the yard as speedily and noisily as they had lowered it, preserving all the while a dead silence, as though they had neither voice nor breath; following which, the boatswain piped them to weigh anchor, and, leaping upon the middle of the gangway, he began flaying the backs of the rowers as they little by little put out to sea. When Sancho perceived all those ruddy-colored feet in motion—for such he took the oars to be—he started speaking to himself.

"This," he said, "is really magic, and not the kind my master talks about. What have these poor wretches done that they should be whipped like that, and how comes it that this one man who goes along whistling there dares to punish so many of them? I declare, this is Hell or at the very least purgatory."

Don Quixote, meanwhile, had noticed how attentively his squire was taking it all in. "Ah, friend Sancho," he remarked, "how quickly you could finish with the disenchantment of Dulcinea if you would only strip down to the waist and take your place among these gentlemen! For amid the pain and misery of so many you would not feel your own to any great extent; and it might be that the wise Merlin would count each one of these lashes, lustily laid on, as equivalent to ten of those which you must give yourself anyway, sooner or later."

The general was about to ask what was the meaning of this talk of lashes and Dulcinea's disenchantment when a sailor exclaimed, "Monjuich [5] signals that there is a vessel with oars standing offshore to westward."

Hearing this, the general leaped to the gangway and shouted, "Ho, there, my lads, don't let her get away from us! It must be some corsair brigantine from Algiers that the watchtower has signaled."

With this, the three other galleys came up alongside the commander's craft to find out what his orders were. The general commanded two of them to put out to sea while he and the other one would hug the land, and that way the brigantine would not escape them. The crew then began rowing so furiously that the boats appeared to be flying over the water. When the two that had put out from shore had gone a couple of miles or so, they sighted a vessel which they took to be one of fourteen or fifteen banks of oars, as proved to be the case. As soon as it made out the galleys, it took to flight, hoping and expecting to escape by sheer speed; but in this it was mistaken, for the commander's galley was one of the swiftest that sailed the sea and bore down so hard upon the brigantine that those aboard clearly realized there was no chance of their getting away.

The captain, accordingly, was of a mind to stop rowing and surrender, in order not to anger our commander, but fate ordained otherwise; and just as the galley came up near enough for those on the vessel to be able to hear the call to surrender, two drunken *Toraquis*, that is to say Turks, who with a dozen more of their countrymen were on board, discharged their muskets, killing two of our soldiers lined up on the wales. When he saw what had happened, the general swore that he would not leave a man of them alive and immediately attacked with great fury, but the enemy slipped away beneath our oars. The galley darted on past for a considerable distance, and while it was engaged in turning about those aboard the brigantine, seeing their lot was hopeless, hoisted sail and, trusting to the breeze and their oars, once again endeavored to flee. Their exertions, however, did not do them as much good as their rashness did them harm; for our chief galley having overtaken them after a pursuit of a little more than half a mile, we threw our oars over them and captured them all.

The other two galleys now came up and all four with their prize returned to the beach, where a huge crowd was awaiting them to see what they brought with them. The general cast anchor close to shore and, perceiving that the viceroy of the city was there, he ordered the small boat to be lowered to bring him aboard. At the same time he commanded his men to let down the yardarm that he might promptly hang the captain and all the rest of the prisoners, about thirty-six in number, strapping fellows all, and most of them Turkish musketeers. When the general asked who the ship's master was, one of the captives spoke up and answered him in the Castilian tongue, for, as was afterward learned, he was a renegade Spaniard.

"Sir," he said, "this young man that you see here is our captain." And he pointed to one of the most handsome and gallant-looking youths that the human imagination could conceive, a lad who, to all appearances, was under twenty years of age.

"Tell me, foolish dog," the general said to the youth, "what led you to kill two of my soldiers when you saw it was impossible for you to escape? Is this the respect you show to commanders' galleys? Do you not know that valor does not consist in rashness and that faint hopes should make men brave but not foolhardy?"

The captain was about to reply, but the general could not listen to him as the viceroy was already boarding the galley, accompanied by a number of attendants and townspeople.

"So, the hunting was good, Señor General?" said the viceroy.

"How good it was your Excellency will see as soon as I've strung up the game on this yardarm."

"How does it come you are doing that?" the viceroy wished to know.

"Because," said the general, "against all law and reason and military custom they have killed two of my best soldiers, and I have sworn to hang every man of them, especially this youth who is their captain."

As he said this he pointed to the young fellow who stood there, his hands already bound and the rope about his neck, waiting for death.

The viceroy looked the prisoner over and saw how handsome he was, how gallant and modest his bearing, and, the young man's comeliness being his letter of recommendation,[6] he at once felt a desire to spare his life.

"Tell me, Captain," he asked, "are you a Turk by nationality, a Moor, or a renegade?"

To this the youth replied, also in Spanish, "I am neither a Turk, nor a Moor, nor a renegade."

"Then what are you?"

"A Christian woman."

"A woman and a Christian, in such a costume and in such a plight? Why, it is astonishing—scarcely to be believed."

"If you gentlemen," replied the youth, "will suspend my execution while I tell you the story of my life, you will not have to wait too long for your revenge."

Who could have had so hard a heart that it would not have been softened by these words, at least to the extent of listening to what the poor unfortunate lad wished to say? The general told him that he might feel free to speak but that he was not to hope for pardon inasmuch as his guilt was plainly established. Having been granted this permission, the youth began his story.

"I," he said, "am of that race whose misfortunes exceed their prudence, for over it of late has rolled a sea of troubles. I was born of Morisco parents, and in the course of our wanderings I was taken to Barbary by an uncle and aunt[7] of mine. It was of no use my telling them that I was a Christian, which, as a matter of fact, I am—and not one of those pretended or seeming converts but a true believer of the Catholic faith. It did me no good to state this fact to those charged with enforcing our wretched banishment, nor would my kinsfolk believe me; they looked upon it as a lying invention on my part to enable me to remain in the land of my birth, and so it was by force rather than of my own free will that they took me with them.

"I had a Christian mother and a father who was a sensible man and a Christian as well. I imbibed the Catholic faith with my mother's milk. I had a good upbringing, and never in word or deed, to the best of my knowledge, did I give any sign of being a Morisco. And keeping pace with these virtues (for such is the way in which I regard the habits I had formed), my beauty, if I may claim any, grew with the years. Although I lived a very retiring and secluded life, I was not so shut off from the world but that a young gentleman, named Don Gaspar Gregorio,[8] had an opportunity of seeing me. He is the son and heir of one who is the lord of a village next to ours; but it would take too long to tell you how we met and talked and how he fell hopelessly in love with me while I was not wholly indifferent to him—especially since I am fearful every moment that this cruel rope that threatens me will tighten between my tongue and throat.

"And so I will merely say that it was Don Gregorio's desire to accompany me into exile. Knowing our language very well, he mingled with the Moors that came from other villages, and on the way he made friends with my uncle and aunt; for my father, being a prudent and far-sighted man, as soon as he heard of the decree of banishment, had left our village and gone to look for some place in a foreign land that would serve us as a refuge, leaving behind him, concealed and buried in a spot with which I alone am acquainted, many pearls and precious stones, together with a certain sum of money in gold, in the form of cruzados [9] and doubloons. His instructions were that under no circumstances was I to touch this treasure if by any chance they expelled us before he returned. I obeyed his orders, and with my uncle and aunt, as I have said, and other friends and relatives I went to Barbary. It was in Algiers that we settled, but it might as well have been in Hell itself.

"The king of the country heard of my beauty and of the rumor regarding my wealth, and this in a way was fortunate for me. Summoning me before him, he asked what part of Spain I was from and what money and jewels I had brought with me. I told him the name of my village and informed him that the jewels and the money were still buried there, but that I could very easily recover them if I myself were to return for them. Even as I said this I was in dread lest he should be blinded by my beauty rather than by his own covetousness, and while we were conversing in this manner word reached him that I was accompanied by one of the most handsome and gallant youths that could be imagined, whereupon I knew at once that they were speaking of Don Gaspar Gregorio, whose comeliness is beyond all praise. I was greatly disturbed, knowing the danger that Don Gregorio ran; for among those barbarous Turks a handsome boy or youth is more highly esteemed than the most beautiful of women.[10]

"The king ordered them to bring the young man before him that he might have a sight of him, and in the meantime he inquired of me if all that he had heard was true. As if forewarned by Heaven, I assured him that it was, but that I wished to inform him that the youth in question was not a man but a woman like myself, and I begged him to allow me to go and clothe her in the garments proper to her sex in order that he might behold her in all her beauty and that she might be less embarrassed at appearing in his presence. He readily consented to my doing so, adding that some other time we would discuss the means by which I could return to Spain to get the hidden treasure.

"I spoke to Don Gaspar and reminded him of the danger that lay in his appearing as a man. I then dressed him as a Moorish woman and that same afternoon conducted him before the king, who was struck with admiration upon seeing him and announced his intention of keeping the 'girl' as a present for the Grand Seignior.[11] Being afraid of leaving her among the women of his harem as well as distrustful of himself, he commanded that she be taken to the house where some of the leading Moorish ladies dwelt, which was done at once. As to the feelings of both of us (for I cannot deny that I care for him deeply), that is something that may be left to the imagination of any pair of lovers who are separated.

"The king then arranged that I should return to Spain in this brigantine, accompanied by two Turks, who were the ones that killed your soldiers. This Spanish renegade"—and she pointed to the one who had been the first to speak—"also came with me, and I can tell you that I know well that he is a Christian at heart and that he would much rather remain in Spain than go back to Barbary. The other members of the brigantine's crew are Moors and Turks who serve only to man the oars. As for this greedy and insolent pair, they chose to disregard the orders they had to set me and this renegade ashore the moment we reached Spanish soil. We were to be landed in Christian garb, with which we came provided; but they insisted upon first skirting the coast to see if they could capture some prize, for they feared that if they obeyed orders and some accident happened to us we might reveal the fact that there was a brigantine at sea, in which case, if there chanced to be any galleys around, they would be taken.

"Last night we sighted this beach and, knowing nothing of these four vessels, we were discovered, with the result that you have seen. To make a long story short, Don Gregorio, dressed as a woman, still lives among women, and his life is clearly in danger, while I stand here with my hands tied, waiting, or rather, dreading to lose the life of which I already am weary. That, sirs, is the end of my sad tale, as true as it is unfortunate. What I would ask of you is that you let me die like a Christian woman, for, as I have said, I am in no wise guilty of the offense that my people have committed." [12]

As she fell silent her eyes filled with tears, and those of many of the bystanders did so as well. Moved to compassion, the viceroy went up to her and with his own hands undid the rope that bound those of the beautiful Moorish Christian. In the meantime, as she related her story, an aged pilgrim who had come aboard with the viceroy watched her most intently, and she had no sooner finished speaking than he cast himself down at her feet and embraced them.

"O Ana Felix, my unhappy daughter!" he cried in a voice that was broken by innumerable sobs and sighs. "I am your father, Ricote, who has returned to seek you, being unable to live without you, since you are my very soul."

At these words Sancho opened his eyes and looked up, for he had been sitting all the while with his head bowed, brooding over the unpleasant treatment he had experienced; and as he gazed at Ricote he recognized him as the same pilgrim whom he had met the day he left his government, and felt quite sure that this was indeed the old man's daughter.

Freed now of her bonds, the girl embraced her father, mingling her tears with his, as he turned to the general and the viceroy and said, "This, gentlemen, is my daughter, more unfortunate in life than her name would imply. Ana Felix she is called, her surname being Ricote, and she is famed as much for her beauty as for my wealth. I left my native country to go seek in foreign lands someone who would take us in and shelter us, and, having found such a person in Germany, I returned in this pilgrim's guise and in the company of certain other pilgrims of that nation to hunt for my daughter and dig up the treasure hoard which I had left buried here. I found the treasure, which I carry with me, but not my daughter; and now, by this strange turn of events which you have witnessed, I have come upon the most valuable thing I possess, in this my beloved child. If the small amount of blame that attaches to us, and her tears as well as mine, without impairing the integrity of justice, can open the door to mercy, then I beseech you to be merciful to us, since we have never had any thought of offending you, nor do we in any way sympathize with the plottings of our people, who have justly been sent into banishment."

At this point Sancho spoke up. "I know Ricote well," he said, "and I know that what he says about Ana Felix's being his daughter is the truth;

but as to all the other things he has to say about his comings and goings and his good or evil intentions, I do not propose to meddle in that."

All those present were amazed at the strange case. "One by one," said the general, "your tears have prevented me from carrying out my oath. May you live as many years as Heaven has allotted you, beauteous Ana Felix, but these two rash and insolent fellows must pay the penalty for the crime they have committed." And with this he ordered the Turks who had slain his men to be hanged from the yardarm. The viceroy, however, pleaded with him earnestly to spare them, pointing out that their actions savored more of madness than of defiance. The general acceded to his wishes, for deeds of vengeance are seldom executed in cold blood.

They then began laying plans for rescuing Don Gaspar Gregorio from his perilous situation, Ricote offering to put up more than two thousand ducats in the form of pearls and other jewels that were in his possession. Many plans were suggested, but none of them as good as that proposed by the above-mentioned Spanish renegade, who volunteered to go to Algiers in some small craft with about six banks of oars manned by Christian rowers; for he knew where, how, and when he could and should land, and he was also acquainted with the house where Don Gaspar was kept. The general and the viceroy were at first inclined to be doubtful of the renegade and were hesitant about entrusting to his charge the Christians who were to do the rowing, but Ana Felix vouched for him and her father, Ricote, promised that he would come forward with the ransom money in case anything happened to them.

This decision having been reached, the viceroy went ashore and Don Antonio Moreno took the Morisco maid and her father home with him, the viceroy charging him to show them all the hospitality in his power, while for his own part he offered them anything his house contained that might serve for their entertainment, such was the good will and benevolence that Ana Felix's beauty had inspired in his bosom.

CHAPTER LXIV . *Which treats of the adventure that caused Don Quixote the most sorrow of all those that have thus far befallen him.*

DON ANTONIO MORENO'S wife, the history tells us, was very happy to take Ana Felix into her home and she gave the young Moorish woman a most cordial reception, being charmed by her wit and beauty alike, for in both respects the girl was more than ordinarily gifted—indeed, so attractive was she that all the townspeople came to have a look at her, as if they had been summoned by the ringing of a bell.

Don Quixote, meanwhile, remarked to his host that the decision reached with regard to freeing Don Gregorio was not a good one inasmuch as the dangers inherent in the plan outweighed the advantages. It would be better, he said, if he himself were to be set down in Barbary with his arms and steed, as he would surely effect a rescue in spite of all the Moors in the world, just as Don Gaiferos had done in the case of his wife, Melisendra.[1]

"Your Grace," Sancho reminded him, "should remember that it was on the mainland that Don Gaiferos rescued his lady and it was by land that he took her to France; but with us, even supposing that we did rescue Don Gregorio, we'd have no way of getting him back to Spain, since there is an ocean in between."

"There is a remedy for everything except death,"[2] said Don Quixote. "Let them but bring the boat to the strand and we shall be able to embark though all the world try to prevent us."

"It sounds easy to hear your Grace tell it," replied Sancho, "but it's a long way from saying to doing.[3] I'm for leaving it to the renegade; he seems to me to be an honest fellow with plenty of guts."[4]

Don Antonio settled the matter by stating that in case the renegade did not succeed they would resort to the expedient of sending the great Don Quixote. And so, a couple of days later, the rescue party put out in a light craft with six oars on each side, manned by a most valiant crew; and two days after that the galleys set sail for the east, the general having asked the viceroy to be so good as to let him know what happened in connection with Ana Felix and the freeing of Don Gregorio, which that gentleman readily consented to do.

And then, one morning, as Don Quixote went for a ride along the beach, clad in full armor—for, as he was fond of saying, that was his only ornament, his only rest the fight,[5] and, accordingly, he was never without it for a moment [6]—he saw approaching him a horseman similarly arrayed from head to foot and with a brightly shining moon blazoned upon his shield.

As soon as he had come within earshot the stranger cried out to Don Quixote in a loud voice, "O illustrious knight, the never to be sufficiently praised Don Quixote de la Mancha, I am the Knight of the White Moon, whose incomparable exploits you will perhaps recall. I come to contend with you and try the might of my arm, with the purpose of having you acknowledge and confess that my lady, whoever she may be, is beyond comparison more beautiful than your own Dulcinea del Toboso. If you will admit the truth of this fully and freely, you will escape death and I shall be spared the trouble of inflicting it upon you. On the other hand, if you choose to fight and I should overcome you, I ask no other satisfaction than that, laying down your arms and seeking no further adventures, you retire to your own village for the space of a year, during which time you are not to lay hand to sword but are to dwell peacefully and tranquilly, enjoying a beneficial rest that shall redound to the betterment of your worldly fortunes and the salvation of your soul. But if you are the victor, then my head shall be at your disposal, my arms and steed shall be the spoils, and the fame of my exploits shall go to increase your own renown. Consider well which is the better course and let me have your answer at once, for today is all the time I have for the dispatching of this business."

Don Quixote was amazed at the knight's arrogance as well as at the nature of the challenge, but it was with a calm and stern demeanor that he replied to him.

"Knight of the White Moon," he said, "of whose exploits up to now I have never heard, I will venture to take an oath that you have not once laid eyes upon the illustrious Dulcinea; for I am quite certain that if you had beheld her you would not be staking your all upon such an issue, since the sight of her would have convinced you that there never has been, and never can be, any beauty to compare with hers. I do not say that you lie, I simply say that you are mistaken; and so I accept your challenge with the conditions you have laid down, and at once, before this day you have fixed upon shall have ended. The only exception I make is with regard to the fame of your deeds being added to my renown, since I do not know what the character of your exploits has been and am quite content with my own, such as they are. Take, then, whichever side of the field you like, and I will take up my position, and may St. Peter bless what God may give." [7]

Now, as it happened, the Knight of the White Moon was seen by some of the townspeople, who informed the viceroy that he was there, talking to Don Quixote de la Mancha. Believing this to be a new adventure arranged by Don Antonio Moreno or some other gentleman of the place, the viceroy at once hastened down to the beach, accompanied by a large retinue, including Don Antonio, and they arrived just as Don Quixote was wheeling Rocinante to measure off the necessary stretch of field. When the viceroy perceived that they were about to engage in combat, he at once interposed and inquired of them what it was that impelled them thus to do battle all of a sudden.

The Knight of the White Moon replied that it was a matter of beauty and precedence and briefly repeated what he had said to Don Quixote, explaining the terms to which both parties had agreed. The viceroy then went up to Don Antonio and asked him if he knew any such knight as this or if it was some joke that they were playing, but the answer that he received left him more puzzled than ever; for Don Antonio did not know who the knight was, nor could he say as to whether this was a real encounter or not. The viceroy, accordingly, was doubtful about letting them proceed, but inasmuch as he could not bring himself to believe that it was anything more than a jest, he withdrew to one side, saying, "Sir Knights, if there is nothing for it but to confess [8] or die, and if Señor Don Quixote's mind is made up and your Grace, the Knight of the White Moon, is even more firmly resolved, then fall to it in the name of God and may He bestow the victory."

The Knight of the White Moon thanked the viceroy most courteously and in well-chosen words for the permission which had been granted them, and Don Quixote did the same, whereupon the latter, commending himself with all his heart to Heaven and to his lady Dulcinea, as was his custom at the beginning of a fray, fell back a little farther down the field as he saw his adversary doing the same. And then, without blare of trumpet or other warlike instrument to give them the signal for the attack, both at the same instant wheeled their steeds about and returned for the charge. Being mounted upon the swifter horse, the Knight of the White Moon met Don Quixote two-thirds of the way and with such tremendous force that, without touching his opponent with his lance (which, it seemed, he deliberately held aloft) he brought both Rocinante and his rider to the ground in an exceedingly perilous fall. At once the victor leaped down and placed his lance at Don Quixote's visor.

"You are vanquished, O knight! Nay, more, you are dead unless you make confession in accordance with the conditions governing our encounter."

Stunned and battered, Don Quixote did not so much as raise his visor but in a faint, wan voice, as if speaking from the grave, he said, "Dulcinea del Toboso is the most beautiful woman in the world and I the most unhappy knight upon the face of this earth. It is not right that my weakness should serve to defraud the truth. Drive home your lance, O knight, and take my life since you already have deprived me of my honor."

"That I most certainly shall not do," said the one of the White Moon. "Let the fame of my lady Dulcinea del Toboso's beauty live on undiminished. As for me, I shall be content if the great Don Quixote will retire to his village for a year or until such a time as I may specify, as was agreed upon between us before joining battle."

The viceroy, Don Antonio, and all the many others who were present heard this, and they also heard Don Quixote's response, which was to the effect that, seeing nothing was asked of him that was prejudicial to Dulcinea, he would fulfill all the other conditions like a true and punctilious knight. The one of the White Moon thereupon turned and with a bow to the viceroy rode back to the city at a mild canter. The viceroy promptly dispatched Don Antonio to follow him and make every effort to find out who he was; and, in the meanwhile, they lifted Don Quixote up and uncovered his face, which held no sign of color and was bathed in perspiration. Rocinante, however, was in so sorry a state that he was unable to stir for the present.

Brokenhearted over the turn that events had taken, Sancho did not know what to say or do. It seemed to him that all this was something that was happening in a dream and that everything was the result of magic. He saw his master surrender, heard him consent not to take up arms again for a year to come as the light of his glorious exploits faded into darkness. At the same time his own hopes, based upon the fresh promises that had been made him, were whirled away like smoke before the wind. He feared that Rocinante was maimed for life, his master's bones permanently dislocated—it would have been a bit of luck if his madness also had been jolted out of him.[9]

Finally, in a hand litter which the viceroy had them bring, they bore the knight back to town. The viceroy himself then returned, for he was very anxious to ascertain who the Knight of the White Moon was who had left Don Quixote in so lamentable a condition.

CHAPTER LXV. *Wherein is revealed who the Knight of the White Moon was, with the freeing of Don Gregorio and other events.*

THE Knight of the White Moon was followed not only by Don Antonio Moreno, but by a throng of small boys as well, who kept after him until the doors of one of the city's hostelries had closed behind him. A squire came out to meet him and remove his armor, for which purpose the victor proceeded to shut himself up in a lower room, in the company of Don Antonio, who had also entered the inn and whose bread would not bake until he had learned the knight's identity. Perceiving that the gentleman had no intention of leaving him, he of the White Moon then spoke.

"Sir," he said, "I am well aware that you have come to find out who I am; and, seeing that there is no denying you the information that you seek, while my servant here is removing my armor I will tell you the exact truth of the matter. I would have you know, sir, that I am the bachelor Sansón Carrasco from the same village as Don Quixote de la Mancha, whose madness and absurdities inspire pity in all of us who know him and in none more than me. And so, being convinced that his salvation lay in his returning home for a period of rest in his own house, I formed a plan for bringing him back.

"It was three months ago [1] that I took to the road as a knight-errant, calling myself the Knight of the Mirrors, with the object of fighting and overcoming him without doing him any harm, intending first to lay down the condition that the vanquished was to yield to the victor's will. What I meant to ask of him—for I looked upon him as conquered from the start—was that he should return to his village and not leave it for a whole year, in the course of which time he might be cured. Fate, however, ordained things otherwise; for he was the one who conquered me and overthrew me from my horse, and thus my plan came to naught. He continued on his wanderings, and I went home, defeated, humiliated, and bruised from my fall, which was quite a dangerous one. But I did not for this reason give up the idea of hunting him up once more and vanquishing him as you have seen me do today.

"Since he is the soul of honor when it comes to observing the ordinances of knight-errantry, there is not the slightest doubt that he will keep the promise he has given me and fulfill his obligations. And that, sir, is all that I need to tell you concerning what has happened. I beg you not to disclose my secret or reveal my identity to Don Quixote, in order that my well-intentioned scheme may be carried out and a man of excellent judgment be brought back to his senses—for a sensible man he would be, once rid of the follies of chivalry."

"My dear sir," exclaimed Don Antonio, "may God forgive you for the wrong you have done the world by seeking to deprive it of its most charming madman! Do you not see that the benefit accomplished by restoring Don Quixote to his senses can never equal the pleasure which others derive from his vagaries? But it is my opinion that all the trouble to which the Señor Bachelor has put himself will not suffice to cure a man who is so hopelessly insane; and if it were not uncharitable, I would say let Don Quixote never be cured, since with his return to health we lose not only his own drolleries but also those of his squire, Sancho Panza, for either of the two is capable of turning melancholy itself into joy and merriment. Nevertheless, I will keep silent and tell him nothing, that I may see whether or not I am right in my suspicion that Señor Carrasco's efforts will prove to have been of no avail."

The bachelor replied that, all in all, things looked very favorable and he hoped for a fortunate outcome. With this, he took his leave of Don Antonio, after offering to render him any service that he could; and, having had his armor tied up and placed upon a mule's back, he rode out of the city that same day on the same horse on which he had gone into battle, returning to his native province without anything happening to him that is worthy of being set down in this veracious chronicle.

Don Antonio informed the viceroy of what Carrasco had told him, and that official was none too well pleased to hear it, since with Don Quixote's retirement all those who had heard of his mad exploits would lose a great deal of enjoyment.

For six days Don Quixote remained in bed, sad and dejected, moody and ill-tempered, as he went over again and again in his mind the unfortunate defeat he had experienced.

Sancho sought to console him, and among other things he said to him, "Raise your head, master, and cheer up a bit if you can. You ought to thank Heaven that, even though you were thrown to earth, you came out of it without a single broken rib. You know that those that give must take,[2] and there is not always bacon where there are stakes.[3] A fig for the doctor; we don't need him to cure this sickness. Let's return home and give up going around looking for adventures in strange lands and places. If you stop to consider, I am the one who stands to lose the most, though your Grace may have more bruises to show. For while I lost all desire to be a governor when I left my government, I still shouldn't mind being a count; but that can never be if your Grace quits the calling of chivalry and gives up the idea of becoming a king. And so it is my hopes go up in smoke."

"Be quiet, Sancho," said his master, "for you know very well that my retirement and seclusion is not to exceed a year, after which time I shall return to my honorable profession, and I cannot fail to win a kingdom, along with some county to bestow on you."

"May God hear you and sin be deaf," [4] said Sancho. "I have always heard tell that a good hope is better than a bad holding." [5]

At this point Don Antonio entered the room with a great show of satisfaction. "Pay me for good news,[6] Señor Don Quixote," he said. "Don Gregorio and the renegade who went for him are now on the beach! What am I saying? They are already at the viceroy's house and will be here any moment."

Don Quixote was somewhat cheered by this report. "To tell the truth," he said, "I should have been glad, almost, if it had turned out differently, as that would have obliged me to go to Barbary, where by the might of my arm I should have freed not Don Gregorio alone, but all the Christian captives that are there. But what am I thinking of, wretch that I am? Am I not the vanquished one? Am I not the one who was overthrown? Am I not he who cannot take up arms for an entire year? What, then, am I promising, of what do I boast, seeing that I am better fitted to handle the distaff than the sword?"

"Stop talking like that, master," said Sancho. "Let the hen live even though she may have the pip; [7] it's today for thee and tomorrow for me; [8] as to this matter of encounters and blows, you should pay no heed to them, since he who falls today may be on his feet again tomorrow [9] —that is to say, unless he prefers to stay in bed and lose heart instead of plucking up fresh courage for battles to come. So, get up this minute, your Grace, and prepare to receive Don Gregorio; for I think I hear people stirring about, and that means he must already be in the house."

This was the truth. Don Gregorio and the renegade having given the viceroy an account of their crossing, the youth was anxious to see Ana Felix, and so the two men came on to Don Antonio's home. Although he had been clad in a woman's garments when they took him out of Algiers, Gregorio had exchanged them on the boat for those of another captive who had come with them; but whatever the garb he wore, he was plainly a person to be loved, served, and esteemed, for he was extraordinarily handsome and about seventeen or eighteen years of age. Ricote and his daughter went out to meet him, the father with tears and the maiden with becoming modesty. The young couple did not embrace, for where there is much love there should not be too great a freedom of manners. All those present were filled with admiration at Don Gregorio's comeliness and Ana Felix's beauty, but it was silence that spoke for the lovers and their eyes were the tongues that revealed the joy they felt and the purity of their affection.

The renegade then described the means which he had adopted in rescuing Don Gregorio, while the latter told of the perils and straits in which he had found himself during his sojourn among the womenfolk. He did not make a long speech, his words in fact were few, and in this he displayed a wisdom beyond his years. Ricote then paid both the renegade and the rowers very liberally for their services. As for the one who had abjured the Faith, he was soon reunited with the Church through penance and a contrite heart, and from a rotten limb became a sound and clean one. A couple of days later the viceroy and Don Antonio had a discussion as to what should be done to enable Ana Felix and her father to remain in Spain; for it seemed to them there could be no harm in permitting a daughter who was so good a Christian and a father who was seemingly so right-minded to continue residing in the country. Don Antonio even offered to go to the capital and arrange matters, since in any case he had other pressing business that required his presence there, and he dropped a hint to the effect that many difficulties could be overcome by means of favor and bribery.

"No," said Ricote, who was present at this conference, "neither favor nor bribes will be of any avail, for the great Don Bernardino de Velasco, Count of Salazar,[10] whom his Majesty has charged with seeing to our banishment, is not to be moved by entreaties, promises, gifts, or appeals to his sympathy. While it is true that he tempers mercy with justice,

942 DON QUIXOTE PART TWO

nevertheless, perceiving as he does that the entire body of our nation is rotting and corrupt, he would rather make use of the cautery that sears than of the ointment that soothes; and, accordingly, by means of prudence, sagacity, diligence, and the fear that he inspires, he has been able to carry upon his sturdy shoulders the weight of this great undertaking. As a result, all the plottings and schemings, the importunities and wiles, of our people have not succeeded in blinding his Argus-eyes, which are ever on the alert lest some one of us should remain behind in concealment and, like a hidden root, in the course of time come to bear poisonous fruit in a Spain that is now cleansed and freed of that terror that our excessive numbers inspired in it. A heroic resolve, this, on the part of the great Philip III, and what unheard-of wisdom, his entrusting the task to such a one as Don Bernardino de Velasco!"

"At any rate," said Don Antonio, "once I am there I will exert every effort, and let Heaven do as it may see fit. Don Gregorio shall come with me that he may relieve the anxiety his parents must feel on account of his absence, Ana Felix may stay here with my wife or in a convent, and I know that the Señor Viceroy will be pleased to have the worthy Ricote as his guest until we see how I make out with the negotiations."

The viceroy gave his consent to everything, but Don Gregorio, upon hearing what had been suggested, declared that he neither could nor would leave Doña Ana Felix under any circumstances; however, as he had intended in any event to go visit his parents and arrange to return for her, he ended by falling in with the plan that had been agreed upon. And so Ana Felix remained with Don Antonio's wife and Ricote stayed in the viceroy's house.

Two days after Don Antonio's departure Don Quixote and Sancho prepared to leave, the injuries which the knight had sustained in his fall having prevented his taking the road any sooner. There were tears, sighs, sobs, and swoonings as Don Gregorio said good-by to Ana Felix. Ricote offered the former a thousand crowns if he needed them, but all the money the young man would accept was five crowns, which Don Antonio lent him and which he promised to pay back when they reached the capital. The two of them then set out, followed shortly afterward by Don Quixote and Sancho, as we have said. The knight wore no fighting gear now but was dressed for the road, while Sancho went along on foot, the armor being piled upon the ass's back.

CHAPTER LXVI. *Which treats of that which he who reads will see and that which he will hear who listens to a reading of it.*

UPON leaving Barcelona, Don Quixote turned to gaze back at the spot where he had met with his downfall.

"Here," he said, "was Troy; here my ill luck and not my cowardice robbed me of the glory I had won; here it was that fortune practiced upon me her whims and caprices; here my exploits were dimmed; and here, finally, my star set never to rise again."

"Master," said Sancho when he heard this, "brave hearts should be patient in adversity just as they are joyous in prosperity. I am judging by the way I feel about it myself, for when I was a governor I was glad, but now that I am a squire and go on foot I am not sad. For I have heard it said that what they call luck is a drunken wench who does not know her own mind; above all, she is blind and so cannot see what she is doing, nor does she know who it is she is overthrowing or exalting."

"You are quite a philosopher, Sancho," said Don Quixote, "and you speak words of wisdom; I am sure I do not know who has been your teacher. But I can tell you one thing: that there is no such thing as luck in this world, and whatever happens, whether it be good or bad, does not occur by chance but through a special providence of Heaven; hence the saying that each man is the architect of his own fortune.[1] I was the architect of mine, but I did not observe the necessary prudence, and as a result my presumptuousness has brought me to a sorry end. I should have reflected that Rocinante, weak as he is, could not withstand the Knight of the White Moon's powerful steed. In short, I was too daring; I did my best but I was overthrown. However, although I sacrificed my honor, I cannot be accused of failing to keep my word. When I was a knight-errant, valiant and bold, my deeds and the might of my arm supported my reputation, and now that I am an ordinary squire I will back up my word by keeping the promise I have given. Proceed, then, friend Sancho, and let us go to fulfill the year of our novitiate in our native province, for during that period of retirement we shall obtain fresh strength, which will enable us to return to the profession of arms, one that I never can forget."

"Sir," replied Sancho, "it is not so pleasant traveling on foot, and I do not feel equal to any long marches. Suppose that we leave this armor on a tree, in place of some hanged man, and then with me on the gray's back and my feet off the ground, we will go as far at a stretch as your Grace chooses; but there's no use expecting me to do it if I have to walk."

"That is a good idea, Sancho," said Don Quixote. "Let my arms be hung up as a trophy, and round about them on the trees we will carve the inscription that was placed over those that Orlando had borne:

> *These let none move*
> *Who dares not with Orlando his valor prove.*" [2]

"All that," said Sancho, "strikes me as sound sense; and if it wasn't that we'll be needing Rocinante along the road, it might be well to string him up, too."

"But come to think of it," said Don Quixote, "I have no desire to hang either him or the armor, lest it be said, 'For good service an ill reward.' " [3]

"Your Grace is quite right," Sancho agreed, "for, according to the opinion of the wise the fault of the ass is not to be attributed to the pack-saddle. [4] Since it is your Grace that is to blame for what has happened, punish yourself and do not be letting your anger out on that battered and bloody suit of armor, nor on poor, meek Rocinante, nor on my tender feet by trying to make them travel more than is right and proper."

In this and similar conversation they spent the whole of that day and the four succeeding ones without anything happening to interrupt their journey. On the fifth day, as they entered a village, they encountered a great crowd of merrymakers at the door of an inn, for it was a feast day. As Don Quixote approached them a peasant raised his voice and called out, "One of those two gentlemen coming there, who do not know the parties concerned, will tell us what is to be done with regard to our wager."

"That I will gladly do," said Don Quixote, "and in all fairness, if I can understand the matter."

"Well, then, good sir," said the peasant, "it is like this. One of the natives of this village who is so fat that he weighs eleven arrobas [5] has challenged a neighbor of his, who does not weigh more than five, to run a race. The understanding was that they were to run a hundred paces, their weights being equalized, and when the challenger was asked how this was to be done, he replied that the other should put six arrobas of iron on his back, which would even things between the fat man and the lean one."

Before Don Quixote could reply, Sancho spoke up. "No," he said, "that won't do. It is only a few days now since I quit being a governor and a judge, as everybody knows, and so I am used to settling such doubtful points and giving a verdict in all sorts of cases."

"Answer them, then, friend Sancho, by all means," said Don Quixote, "since I am in no mood to give crumbs to a cat,[6] my mind is so excited and upset."

Having thus been granted permission, Sancho addressed himself to the peasants, who were standing around open-mouthed, waiting to hear his opinion.

"Brothers," he began, "what the fat man asks is unreasonable and altogether unjust; for if it is true that the one who is challenged has a right to choose the weapons, it is not proper for him to accept those that will make it impossible for him to come out the winner. Accordingly, it is my opinion that the fat challenger ought to trim, prune, cull, peel off, and tidy up his flesh until he has taken off six arrobas here and there on his body wherever he may think best, and in that manner, being left with five arrobas, he will be on an equal footing with his opponent and the race may be run with the odds even."[7]

"Well, now, I swear," declared one of the peasants who had heard what Sancho said, "this gentleman has spoken like a saint and given judgment like a canon. But you can be sure that the fat one will not be willing to part with a single ounce of flesh, much less six arrobas."

"The best thing would be for them not to run at all," said another. "That way, the lean man will not be battered down under the load, and the fat one will not have to part with his flesh. Let's spend half the wager on wine and take these gentlemen to the tavern where they sell the good stuff,[8] and upon my head be—the cloak when it rains."[9]

"I thank you, gentlemen," replied Don Quixote, "but I cannot pause for a moment; it is sad thoughts and unfortunate circumstances that compel me to appear discourteous and be on my way with all possible speed." Saying which, he gave Rocinante the spur and rode on, leaving the crowd to marvel equally at the knight's strange figure and the wisdom of his servant, for such they took Sancho to be.

"If the man," said one of the peasants, "is as wise as that, what must the master be! I'll lay you a bet that if they're going to Salamanca to study, they will become court judges in no time at all; for it's a joke—all you have to do is to study and study some more, have someone to back you, and a little luck, and before you know it you find yourself with a rod of justice in your hand or a miter on your head."

That night master and man spent in the fields, under the open sky, and the next day, upon continuing their journey, they saw coming toward them a man on foot with saddlebags about his neck and in his hand a javelin or pike. In short, he was the very picture of a foot-courier, and as he approached Don Quixote he quickened his pace and, coming up to him half on the run, embraced his right thigh, for that was as far as he could reach.

"O Señor Don Quixote de la Mancha," he exclaimed with a show of great joy, "how happy at heart my lord the duke will be when he hears that your Grace is returning to the castle! For he and the duchess are still there."

"I do not recognize you, my friend," said Don Quixote, "unless you see fit to tell me who you are."

"I," replied the courier, "am Tosilos, lackey to my lord the duke, the one who refused to fight with your Grace over the marriage of Doña Rodríguez' daughter."

"Why, God bless me!" said Don Quixote, "is it possible you are the one whom my enemies the enchanters transformed into this lackey that you say you are, in order to cheat me of the honor of winning that battle?"

"No more of that talk, my good sir," said the courier. "There was no enchantment about it, nor any change of appearance whatsoever. It was as Tosilos the lackey that I entered and came out of the lists. I liked the girl and thought that I could win her without fighting; but things did not turn out that way, for just as soon as your Grace had left our castle my lord the duke had them give me a hundred blows with a club for having disobeyed his orders about the combat. The upshot of it all is: the girl has become a nun, Doña Rodríguez has gone back to Castile, and I am now on my way to Barcelona with a packet of letters from my master to the viceroy. If your Grace would like a wee drop, I have here a gourd full of the best; [10] it's not very cold but it's good wine, and I also have a few slices of Tronchón cheese, which will serve as the summoner and awakener of thirst if by any chance it is asleep." [11]

"That suits me," said Sancho. "Let's not stand on ceremony, but let the good Tosilos pour in spite of all the enchanters in the Indies."

"I must say, Sancho," remarked Don Quixote, "that you are the biggest glutton on the face of the earth, and the biggest dunce besides not to be able to see that this courier is enchanted and this Tosilos a false one. Stay with him and drink your fill, and I will ride on very slowly and wait for you to catch up with me."

With a laugh the lackey unsheathed [12] his gourd and brought out the cheese and a small loaf of bread from the saddlebags, whereupon he and Sancho seated themselves upon the greensward and most peaceably and companionably proceeded to do away with the entire store of provisions, exhibiting so hearty an appetite that they even licked the package of letters because it smelled of cheese.

"Undoubtedly, Sancho my friend," said Tosilos, "this master of yours must be a madman."

"He owes no one anything," [13] replied Sancho, "especially when it comes to the coin of madness. I can see it plainly enough, and I've told him as much, but what good does it do? Above all, now that he's done for; for he has been conquered by the Knight of the White Moon."

Tosilos then begged him to relate what had happened, but Sancho replied that it would be discourteous to keep his master waiting, and there would be time for that another day if they chanced to meet. And shaking out his jacket and brushing the crumbs from his beard, he gave Tosilos an *adiós* and drove the gray forward until he came to where the knight was sitting in the shade of a tree.

CHAPTER LXVII. *How Don Quixote resolved to turn shepherd and lead a rustic life during the year for which he had given his promise, with other events that are truly diverting and that make good reading.*

IF Don Quixote had had a great deal on his mind before his downfall, it was even worse afterward. There he sat in the shade of a tree, as has been said, and thither like flies to honey thoughts came swarming to sting and annoy him. Some of them had to do with Dulcinea's disenchantment, while others were concerned with his forced retirement.

As Sancho reached his master's side, he began praising the generosity of the lackey Tosilos, whereupon Don Quixote said to him, "Is it possible, Sancho, that you still believe him to be a real lackey? You do not seem to remember having seen Dulcinea converted and transformed into a peasant lass and the Knight of the Mirrors into the bachelor Sansón Carrasco, all of which was the work of those enchanters that persecute me. But come now, tell me: did you ask this Tosilos as you call him what, through God's will, has become of Altisidora, whether or not she has wept over my absence or has already consigned to oblivion the love thoughts that tortured her when I was present?"

"The things on my mind," replied Sancho, "had nothing to do with asking foolish questions like that. Body of me! master, is your Grace in any position to be inquiring into the thoughts of others, and especially love thoughts?"

"Look, Sancho," said Don Quixote, "there is a great deal of difference between those actions that are performed out of love and those that are motivated by gratitude. A knight may well withhold his affections, but he cannot be ungrateful. Altisidora, it would seem, cared for me deeply; she gave me those three kerchiefs, as you know; [1] she wept when I departed; she heaped maledictions on my head and, casting modesty aside, bewailed her fate in public; all of which is a sign that she adores me, since lovers when angry usually end by cursing each other. There was no hope I could give her, no treasure I could offer her, for all that I have belongs to Dulcinea, and the treasure of knights-errant is like that of the fairy folk: seeming but unreal. [2] All that I can give her is a place in my memory, without prejudice to that which I reserve for Dulcinea—the Dulcinea to whom you do so grievous a wrong by your remissness in lashing yourself and punishing that flesh of yours (would that I saw it eaten by wolves), which you would keep for the worms rather than devote to the relief of that poor lady."

"Sir," Sancho answered him, "I cannot see what lashing my backside has to do with the disenchanting of the enchanted; it's like saying 'If you have a headache, rub ointment on your knees.' At any rate, I'll venture to swear that in all the histories your Grace has read on the subject of knight-errantry you have never heard of a spell being removed by such means. But however that may be, I'll see to whipping myself whenever I happen to feel like it and when I have an opportunity to do it with some comfort."

"God grant it may be so," said Don Quixote, "and may Heaven give you the grace to remember the obligation you are under to aid my lady, who is at the same time your lady, seeing that you belong to me."

With talk of this sort they jogged along until they came to the place where they had been trampled by the bulls. Don Quixote recognized it at once.

"This," he observed, "is the meadow where we fell in with those gallant and gaily bedecked shepherds and shepherdesses who were endeavoring to imitate and restore the Arcadia of old, a novel idea and an inspired one; and if you approve, Sancho, I would suggest that, at least for the time that I have to live in retirement, we likewise turn shepherds. I will purchase some sheep and all the other things that are necessary to the pastoral life, taking for myself the name of 'the shepherd Quixotiz,' while you will be 'the shepherd Pancino.' Together we will roam the hills, the woods, and the meadows, now singing songs and now composing elegies, drinking the crystal water of the springs or that of the clear running brooks or mighty rivers. The oaks will provide us with an abundance of their delicious fruit,[3] the hardwood trunks of the cork trees will furnish us a seat, the willows will give us shade, the roses will lend their perfume, and the spacious meadows will spread a myriad-colored carpet for our feet; we shall breathe the clean, pure air, and despite the darkness of the night the moon and stars will afford us illumination; song will be our joy, and we shall be happy even in our laments, for Apollo will supply the inspiration for our verses and love will endow us with conceits and we shall be everlastingly famous—not only in this age but for all time to come."

"By God," exclaimed Sancho, "that kind of life squares and corners with me.[4] And what's more, the moment they hear of it the bachelor Sansón Carrasco and Master Nicholas the barber will want to do the same thing and turn shepherds with us. I only hope to God the curate also doesn't take it into his head to enter the fold, seeing that he's so jolly and fond of amusing himself."

"You are quite right," said Don Quixote, "and the bachelor Sansón Carrasco if he joins the flock, as I have no doubt he will, can call himself 'the shepherd Sansonino,' or, it may be, 'the shepherd Carrascón'; barber Nicholas can be 'Niculoso,'[5] just as old Boscán was known as 'Nemoroso.'[6] As for the curate, I do not know what we can call him unless it is something derived from his title, such as 'the shepherd Curiambro.' As for the shepherdesses whose lovers we shall be, we can pick their names as we would pears, and since my lady has one that befits a shepherdess as well as it does a princess, I need not trouble myself with looking for anything better; but you, Sancho, may call yours whatever you choose."

"I will simply call her 'Teresona,'" [7] said Sancho, "seeing that her real name is Teresa and she is big and fat. And, moreover, when I come to sing her praises in my verses, I'll show how chaste my love is, as I don't propose to go looking for fancy bread in other men's houses.[8] It will not be proper for the curate to have a shepherdess, since he must set a good example, but as for the bachelor, his soul is in the palm of his hand."

"God bless me!" cried Don Quixote, "what a life we are going to lead, Sancho my friend! What music we shall hear—the strains of reed flutes,[9] Zamora bagpipes, tabors, timbrels, rebecs! And if amid all these different varieties of music the *albogues* [10] also resound, then practically all the pastoral instruments will be there."

"What are *albogues?*" inquired Sancho. "I never heard tell of them, nor have I ever seen one in all my life."

"*Albogues,*" replied Don Quixote, "are plates resembling brass candlesticks, which, when struck together on the empty or hollow side, make a noise that, if not very agreeable or harmonious, is still not displeasing to the ear and goes well with the rustic character of the bagpipe and tabor. The name is a Moorish one, as are all those in our Castilian tongue that begin with *al,* such as *almohaza, almorzar, alfombra, alguacil, alhucema, almacén, alcancía,*[11] and a few other similar ones. Our language has only three such nouns that end in *i,* and they are *borcegui zaquizamí,* and *maravedí.*[12] As for *alhelí* and *alfaquí,*[13] both the initial *al* and the final *i* show them at once to be Arabic.

"If I speak of this, it is because I was reminded of it by the mention of the word *albogues.* The fact that I myself, as you know, am something of a poet will be of great assistance to us in perfecting ourselves in this way of life,[14] and the bachelor Sansón Carrasco is a very fine one. As for the curate I cannot say, but I will wager you that he must have a bit of the poet in him, and Master Nicholas as well, no doubt, since all barbers, or most of them at any rate, like to strum the guitar and improvise verses. In my songs I shall lament my separation from my loved one, while you may sing your own praises as the constant lover; the shepherd Carrascón will be the rejected swain, and the curate Curiambro may choose whatever theme may suit him best. That way everything will go very well with nothing left to be desired."

"Ah, master," said Sancho, "I am so unlucky I fear the day will never come when I can lead such a life as that. Oh, what neat spoons I'll turn out when I'm a shepherd! [15] What tidbits, creams, garlands, and pastoral odds and ends! [16] If they don't look upon me as a wise man, I'll at least get a reputation for being ingenious! My daughter Sanchica will bring us our dinner to the sheepfold—but wait a minute! She's good-looking and the shepherds are not so simple-minded after all; they have plenty of mischief in them, and I would not have her go for wool and come back shorn.[17] You will find love-making and evil passions in the fields as in the cities, in shepherds' huts as well as in royal palaces. Do away with the cause, you do away with the sin;[18] if the eyes don't see, the heart will not break;[19] and escape from the slaughter is worth more than good men's prayers."[20]

"That will be enough of your proverbs, Sancho," said Don Quixote, "since any one of those you have quoted is sufficient to express your thought. Many times have I advised you not to be so prodigal in your use of them and to observe some degree of moderation, but it appears to be like preaching in the desert: 'My mother whips me and I keep right on.' "[21]

"Your Grace," remarked Sancho, "puts me in mind of the proverb: 'Said the frying pan to the kettle, get away, black-eyes.'[22] You scold me for doing it, and you start stringing them yourself."

"Mark you, Sancho," replied Don Quixote, "when I bring them in they are to the purpose and fit the subject like a ring on the finger; whereas you, in place of introducing them, drag them in by the hair of the head. If I remember rightly, I have told you once before[23] that proverbs are concise maxims drawn from the wisdom and experience of our elders, and the saying that is not appropriate is simply nonsensical. However, no more of this, for darkness is coming on. Let us retire some little distance from the highway to a place where we may spend the night. God knows what tomorrow will bring."

They did so, and had a late supper and a bad one, at which Sancho was greatly put out. He could not help thinking of the hardships of knight-errantry as experienced in the woods and wilds, even though one occasionally met with abundance in homes and castles, as in the houses of Don Diego de Miranda and Don Antonio Moreno and at the wedding of the rich Camacho. But, he reflected, it could not be always day or always night, and so he spent that particular night in sleeping, while his master kept vigil.

CHAPTER LXVIII. *Of the bristly adventure that befell Don Quixote.*

THE night was rather dark. The moon, true enough, was in the sky but not anywhere to be seen; for my lady Diana upon occasion goes for a little stroll in the antipodes, leaving the hills in blackness and the valleys devoid of light. Don Quixote complied with the demands of nature by yielding to his first sleep but not to his second, in which respect he differed from his squire, who never had a second sleep since his first one lasted from night until morning, showing what a good constitution he had and how few cares. Don Quixote's anxieties, on the other hand, kept him awake, to such an extent that he aroused Sancho.

"It amazes me, Sancho," he said, "to see how unconcerned you are. I think you must be made of marble or solid brass without any trace of feeling whatsoever. Here I keep vigil while you sleep, I weep while you sing, I am faint from hunger while you are sluggish and exhausted from pure gluttony. Good servants ought to share the sufferings of their masters and feel for them, if only for the sake of appearances. Behold the calmness of the night and this solitude round about us which invites us to break our sleep by a vigil of some sort. And so, as you live, bestir yourself, go off some little distance from here, and with right good will and courage cheerfully lay on three or four hundred lashes of those that you owe toward Dulcinea's disenchantment.

"I put this in the form of a request, having no desire to come to grips with you as I did the other time, for I know what strength you have in your arms. And then, after you have done this, we will spend the rest of the night singing as I lament my separation and you praise your lover's constancy. In this manner we may at once begin that pastoral life we mean to follow when we reach our own village."

"Master," replied Sancho, "I am no monk to be getting up in the middle of my sleep and disciplining myself, nor do I think I would feel much like singing after the pain I would suffer from the whipping —you can't go from one extreme to another like that. So, let me sleep, your Grace, and do not trouble me about the lashes, or you'll make me swear never to touch a hair of my smock, much less my flesh."

"O hardhearted one!" cried Don Quixote. "O pitiless squire! O what ingratitude for the ill-bestowed bread of mine you have eaten and the favors I have shown and expected to show you! It was through me that you became a governor, and it is owing to me that you may hope soon to become a count or to obtain some title of equal worth; for the fulfillment of that promise will not be long delayed once this year has passed,[1] since I—*post tenebras spero lucem.*" [2]

"I don't know anything about that," said Sancho. "All I know is that while I am asleep I have neither fear nor hope nor troubles nor any concern about glory. Blessings on the one who invented sleep, the cloak that covers all human thoughts, the food that relieves hunger, the water that quenches thirst, the fire that keeps the cold away, the cold that tempers heat—in short, the common currency with which all things are bought, the weight and balance that makes the shepherd equal to the king and that puts the fool on an equal footing with the wise man. There is only one fault to be found with sleep, according to what I've heard, and that is the fact that it resembles death; for between a sleeping man and a dead one there is very little difference." [3]

"Never, Sancho," said Don Quixote, "have I heard you use such polished language as now, which leads me to recognize the truth of the proverb you sometimes quote: 'Not with whom you are bred, but with whom you are fed.' " [4]

"Ha! master," exclaimed Sancho, "upon my word, I'm not the one who's stringing proverbs now; they also drop from your Grace's mouth in pairs and faster than they do from mine. The only thing is that between my sayings and yours there is this difference: yours are always timely and my own are not; but they are all proverbs just the same."

At this point they heard a kind of subdued roar, a harsh and grating sound that spread through all the valleys. Don Quixote at once stood up and laid his hand upon his sword, while Sancho crouched beneath the gray, placing the bundle of armor on one side of him and the packsaddle on the other; for he was quite as alarmed as his master was excited, and was trembling all over. The noise grew in volume as it came near the terrified pair—at least one of them was terrified; as for the other, his valor is well known.

The truth of the matter was, some men were driving to the fair more than six hundred pigs and were continuing their journey even at that hour; and so great was the din the animals created with their grunting and snorting that it deafened the ears of Don Quixote and Sancho, who could not make out what it was. Meanwhile, the grunting herd rushed onward, fanning out far and wide, and without any respect for Don Quixote's person or that of Sancho, either, it passed over both of them, knocking down Sancho's intrenchments, unseating the knight, and sweeping Rocinante off his feet. The trampling, the grunting, and the speed with which the filthy beasts came on threw everybody and everything into confusion and on the ground: the packsaddle, the armor, the ass, Rocinante, Sancho, Don Quixote, and all the rest. Picking himself up as best he could, Sancho asked his master for the sword, saying he wished to slaughter half a dozen of these gentry, these impolite pigs (for by this time he had realized what they were).

"Let them be, my friend," said Don Quixote, "seeing this is but the penalty for my sin; for Heaven justly decrees as punishment for a vanquished knight-errant that he shall be eaten by jackals, stung by wasps, and trampled by swine."

"In that case," said Sancho, "Heaven's way of punishing the squires of vanquished knights must be to have them bitten by flies, eaten up with lice, and attacked by hunger. If we were the sons of those we serve or very near relatives, it would not be so strange if we were to suffer the punishment for their misdeeds even to the fourth generation; but what, after all, have the Panzas to do with the Quixotes? Oh, well, let's settle ourselves again and get what little sleep is left us this night, for God will send the dawn and we will make out somehow."

"Go ahead and sleep, Sancho," said Don Quixote, "since you were born for that purpose. As for me, I was born to keep vigil; and in the time that remains between now and morning I propose to give rein to my longings and find outlet for them in a little madrigal which, without your knowing anything about it, I composed last night."

"If you ask me," replied Sancho, "longings that lead one to make verses can't amount to very much. So, versify all you like, your Grace, and I will get what sleep I can." Saying this, he took what space he required and, huddling down, fell into a dreamless slumber undisturbed by bond or debt or trouble of any kind.

Whereupon, leaning against the trunk of a beech—or it may have been a cork tree, for Cid Hamete Benengeli is not definite on the point —Don Quixote began singing the following air to the accompaniment of his own sighs:

> Love, when I pause to think
> Of the terrible wound that thou hast dealt to me,
> To the haven of death I'd flee
> And let my troubles in oblivion sink.

But as the port I near,
Sailing a sea of woe to my anodyne,
Such wondrous joy is mine
That life once more doth live and finds me here.

Life, then, it is that slays
And death restores to me the one I hate—
O strange, unheard-of fate
That juggles life and death and with me plays! [5]

Each of these verses was accompanied by many sighs and not a few tears, as if the singer's heart were transfixed with grief over his downfall and his separation from Dulcinea.

Day finally came, and as the rays of the sun fell on Sancho's eyes he awoke, roused and shook himself, and stretched his sluggish limbs. Beholding the damage which the pigs had done to his pantry, he cursed the drove in no uncertain terms. Then the two of them took to the road again, and along toward sunset they saw coming toward them about ten men on horseback and four or five on foot. Don Quixote's heart gave a leap and Sancho once more was frightened, for the men who were approaching carried lances and bucklers and appeared to be warriors.

"If it were permitted me, Sancho," said Don Quixote, "to make use of my weapons, if my promise did not keep my arms tied, that crew coming there would be but cakes and gingerbread for me.[6] But it may be something other than what we fear."

By this time those on horseback were upon them, and without saying a word they surrounded Don Quixote, pointing their upraised spears at his back and bosom and threatening him with death. Putting a finger to his mouth by way of signifying that silence was called for, one of the men on foot then seized Rocinante's bridle and led him out of the road, while his companions drove Sancho and the gray before them, preserving an astonishing silence all the while, as they followed in the tracks of Don Quixote and his guide. Two or three times the knight started to inquire where they were taking him and what they wanted of him, but no sooner had he begun to move his lips than his abductors threatened to close them with their lance points. The same thing happened with Sancho: the moment he showed signs of talking, one of the foot attendants would prick him with a goad, and the gray as well, just as if he too were about to speak.

As night closed in upon them they quickened their pace, and the two prisoners were more afraid than ever, especially when they heard the men saying to them every now and then, "Get on with you, you troglodytes! Be quiet, barbarians! Pay the price, you cannibals! No complaints, you Scythians! Keep your eyes shut, you murderous Polyphemuses, you flesh-eating lions!"

These and other similar epithets tortured the ears of the wretched master and man and caused Sancho to mutter to himself, "So, we are tortolites, are we? So, we are barbers and clouts, bitches that you say 'come, come' to?[7] I don't like those names at all; it's a bad wind for thrashing our corn; [8] misfortune comes upon us all at once like blows on a dog's back,[9] and I only hope this unlucky adventure that threatens us will lead to nothing worse than blows."

As for Don Quixote, he was dumfounded by it all, being at his wits' end to make out what the purpose of this vicious name-calling could be. The only thing of which he was certain was that no good could come of it and there was much to be feared. And then, about an hour past midnight, they arrived at a castle which was quite familiar to him, for it was that of the duke where he had stayed not long before.

"God bless me!" he cried as soon as he recognized the edifice, "and what is the meaning of this? Here is a house in which all is courtesy and graciousness, but for the vanquished good turns into evil and evil into something worse."

Upon entering the principal courtyard of the castle, they found it fitted out in such a manner as to add to their astonishment and increase their fears twofold, as will be seen in the following chapter.

CHAPTER LXIX. Of the strangest and most extraordinary adventure that has befallen Don Quixote in the entire course of this great history.

THE horsemen dismounted and together with those on foot at once and in great haste picked up Sancho and Don Quixote bodily and carried them into the courtyard. There nearly a hundred torches, fixed in their sockets, were flaring, while the adjoining galleries were illuminated by more than five hundred lamps, as a result of which, despite the fact that the night was somewhat overcast, the absence of daylight was not noticed. In the middle of the courtyard a funeral mound about two yards high had been reared, completely covered by an enormous black velvet canopy, and on the steps leading up to it more than a hundred white wax tapers in silver candlesticks were shedding their glow. Upon this catafalque lay the lifeless body of a maiden, so lovely as to make even death itself seem beautiful. Her head rested upon a brocade pillow and was crowned with a plaited garland of sweet-smelling flowers of various sorts; her hands were folded over her bosom and between them was a bough of the yellow palm of victory.[1]

At one side of the patio was a stage with two chairs on which were seated two personages who, from the crowns upon their heads and the scepters in their hands, appeared to be kings, whether real ones or not. This stage also was reached by steps, and beside it were two other seats, where those who were carrying the prisoners now deposited Don Quixote and Sancho, preserving a dead silence as they did so and giving the knight and his squire to understand by means of signs that they too were to say nothing. The captives, however, would have been silent even without this admonition, for the astonishment they felt at all the things they beheld was more than sufficient to render them tongue-tied.

Two persons of obvious importance accompanied by a large retinue then mounted the stage, and Don Quixote at once recognized them as his hosts, the duke and duchess. They seated themselves upon two richly adorned chairs alongside the two individuals who looked the part of kings, all of which was cause enough for amazement, not to mention the fact that the knight had discovered the dead woman upon the catafalque to be none other than the beauteous Altisidora. Who would not have been amazed?

As the duke and duchess mounted the stage, Don Quixote and Sancho rose and made a profound obeisance, the ducal pair replying with a slight inclination of their heads. An officer thereupon crossed the courtyard and, going up to Sancho, threw over him a black buckram robe with flames painted on it, and removing the squire's cap he replaced it with a miter of the kind that those under sentence from the Holy Office wear, at the same time whispering in his ear that he was not to open his lips or they would gag him or possibly put him to death. Surveying himself from head to foot, Sancho saw that he was all aflame, but inasmuch as the flames did not burn him he did not give a rap for them. He took off his miter, and when he saw there were devils painted on it he put it back on again.

"So far so good," he muttered. "Those haven't scorched me yet and these haven't carried me off."

Don Quixote also looked him over, and although he was frightened out of his wits he could not help laughing at the figure that Sancho cut. Then, seemingly from beneath the catafalque, there came the low and pleasing sound of flutes, which, unaccompanied by any human voice (for here silence's self kept silent), produced an effect that was at once gentle and amorous; and suddenly, beside the pillow where the head of the "corpse" reclined, there appeared a handsome youth clad like an ancient Roman who, to the sound of a harp which he himself played, began singing in a very sweet, clear voice the two stanzas that follow:

> *While in this court where magic doth hold sway*
> *The fair Altisidora seeks the light*
> *('Twas Don Quixote's cruelty did slay*
> *The hapless maid); while ladies all bedight*
> *In goat-hair garments* [2] *celebrate the day,*
> *With dour duennas dressing for the rite*
> *In robes of baize and wool, my harp I'll play*
> *Better than Thracian bard,* [3] *to hymn her plight.*
>
>   *And not in life alone be this my theme,*
> *But when my tongue in death is cold and still,*
> *I mean to raise my voice and thus redeem*
> *The debt I owe thee, with a right good will.*

Free of its prison cell, on Stygian stream
My constant soul shall try its singing skill
In odes to thee, and in that hour supreme
Roll back oblivion's waters, dark and chill.[4]

"That will do," said one of the "kings" at this point; "proceed no further, divine singer, as it would be an endless task to portray for us now the death and all the graces of the peerless Altisidora. For she is not dead as the ignorant ones think, but lives on by the tongue of fame and through the penance which Sancho Panza here present must endure in order to restore her to the light of this world. And so, O Rhadamanthus, thou who dost sit in judgment with me in Pluto's murky pit,[5] seeing thou dost know all that the inscrutable Fates have decreed in regard to the manner in which this damsel is to be revived, do thou tell us at once in order that the hoped-for boon be no longer deferred."

No sooner had Minos, his fellow judge, said this than Rhadamanthus rose to his feet. "Ho!" he cried, "you officers of this household, great and small, of high and low degree, come one and all and imprint on Sancho's face twenty-four smacks,[6] and give him besides a dozen pinches and half a dozen pinpricks in his back and arms; for upon this ceremony Altisidora's salvation is dependent."

Hearing this, Sancho broke his silence at last. "I swear," he said, "I'd just as soon turn Moor as let this face of mine be slapped or mistreated! Body of me! What has that to do with the resurrection of this damsel? The old woman was fond of blites . . . [7] They enchant Dulcinea and flog me to disenchant her. Altisidora dies of the sickness God sends her, and to bring her back to life they have to give me a couple of dozen smacks, make a sieve of my body with pinpricks, and raise welts on my arms with their pinches. Try those jokes on your brother-in-law;[8] I'm an old dog and it's no use saying *tus, tus* to me." [9]

"Thou shalt die!" shouted Rhadamanthus at the top of his voice. "Relent, thou tiger! Humble thyself, haughty Nimrod! Suffer and be silent, seeing that nothing impossible is asked of thee, and complain not of the hardships involved in this matter. Smacked thou shalt be, pricked full of holes, and pinched until thou dost groan with pain. What, ho, officers! Carry out my behest or ye shall see for what it was ye were born."

At this moment a procession of as many as six duennas was to be seen crossing the courtyard. Four of them wore spectacles and all had their right hands raised with four inches of wrist showing, by way of making them seem longer as is the present fashion.[10] As soon as he caught sight of them Sancho began bellowing like a bull.

"I might allow myself to be manhandled by anybody else," he said, "but to think that I am going to let duennas touch me—nothing of the sort! Cat-claw my face as they did my master's in this very castle, run my body through with burnished dagger points, nip my arms with red-hot pincers—I'll bear it all patiently to please these gentlefolk; but the devil take me if I let duennas lay hands on me!"

It was Don Quixote's turn to break silence now. "Be patient, my son," he said. "Comply with the wishes of these gentlemen, and thank Heaven there is lodged in your person such virtue that through the martyrdom of your flesh you are able to disenchant the enchanted and resurrect the dead."

As the duennas approached him Sancho became more quiet and tractable, and, settling himself comfortably in his chair, he held up his face and beard to the first comer, who gave him a resounding smack, followed by a low bow.

"Less bowing and scraping, Señora Duenna," he said, "and less paint and lotions [11] for, by God, your hands smell of vinegar water." [12]

To make a long story short, all the duennas slapped him and many other members of the household pinched him, but the thing he could not stand was the pinpricks. When it came to that, he rose from his chair with a show of anger and, seizing a lighted torch that stood near by, began laying about him among the duennas and all his other tormentors, crying, "Away with you, ministers of Hell! I am not made of brass so that I do not feel such unusual torture as this!"

Then it was that Altisidora, who must have been tired of lying on her back for so long a time, turned over on her side, beholding which, all the bystanders shouted, with one voice as it were, "Altisidora is alive! Altisidora lives!" And Rhadamanthus commanded Sancho to forego his wrath, seeing that their purpose had now been achieved.

When Don Quixote saw Altisidora stirring, he fell on his knees before Sancho.

"O son of my loins," he said, "for I will not call you squire, now is the time for you to give yourself a few of those lashes that you owe toward Dulcinea's disenchantment. Now, I repeat, is the time, when the virtue that is in you is ripe and may efficaciously accomplish the good that is expected of you."

"That," said Sancho, "to my mind, is trick upon trick and not honey on pancakes. It would be a fine thing to have lashes on top of pinches, slaps, and prickings! You might as well take a big stone, tie it around my neck, and throw me into a well; it doesn't make much difference to me if in order to cure other people's ills I have to be the cow at the wedding.[13] Leave me alone or by God I'll throw everything over, no matter what happens." [14]

Altisidora by now had risen to a sitting posture upon the bier, and at that very instant there was a blare of flutes and flageolets, and all those present cried out, "Long live Altisidora! Long live Altisidora!"

The duke and duchess and the kings Minos and Rhadamanthus then rose, and all of them together, with Don Quixote and Sancho, advanced to receive the maiden and take her down from the catafalque. Acting like one who had just recovered from a swoon, she bowed to the ducal pair and to the kings, and then, with a sidewise glance at Don Quixote, she said, "May God forgive you, heartless knight, for thanks to your cruelty I have been in the other world more than a thousand years as it seems to me. As for you, O most compassionate of all the squires in this world, I thank you for the life I now possess! From this day forth, friend Sancho, you may look upon as yours six chemises of mine which I am presenting to you that you may make yourself as many shirts; and if some of them are a little ragged, at least all of them are clean."

Doffing his miter, Sancho knelt and kissed her hand in return for this favor, and the duke then ordered them to relieve him of that head-piece, and his flame-covered robe as well, and to restore his cap and jacket. Sancho, however, begged to be allowed to keep the accouter-ments, saying he wished to take them back to his own country as a memento of this most extraordinary event, and the duchess replied that he might do so, adding that she already had reason to know what a great friend of his she was. And, finally, the duke directed that the courtyard be cleared and all should retire to their rooms, with Don Quixote and Sancho being conducted to the ones they had formerly occupied.

CHAPTER LXX. *Which follows the sixty-ninth and treats of matters that cannot be omitted if this history is to be clearly understood.*

SANCHO slept that night on a truckle bed [1] in Don Quixote's chamber. This he would gladly have avoided if he could have, for he knew very well that his master would keep him awake answering questions and he was in no mood for an extended conversation; the pain that he still felt from his recent martyrdom interfered with the free exercise of his tongue, and as a result he would rather have slept alone in a hovel than in this sumptuous room with company of any sort. His apprehensions proved to be justified, for his master began talking the moment they were in bed.

"What do you think, Sancho, of what happened this evening? Great and mighty is the power wielded by one who is scornful in love; for you with your own eyes have seen Altisidora lying there dead, slain not by arrows, or sword, or any warlike weapon, and not by any deadly poison, but solely by thought of the unrelenting disdain that I have always shown her."

"She's welcome to die any time she likes," replied Sancho, "for I didn't make her fall in love and I never in all my life disdained her. As I have said once before, I fail to see what the saving of Altisidora, a maid more whimsical than she is sensible, has to do with the tormenting of Sancho Panza. Now I begin to perceive, clearly and distinctly, that there are such things as enchanters and enchantments in this world, and God deliver me from them since I cannot free myself. But no more of that. I beg your Grace to let me sleep and not ask me any more questions, unless you want me to throw myself out the window."

"Sleep, friend Sancho," said Don Quixote, "providing the pinpricks and pinches you received and the slaps they gave you will let you do so."

"There is no pain," said Sancho, "that can equal those insulting smacks, if for no other reason than that they were given me by those confounded duennas. But again I beg you: let me sleep; for sleep is relief from misery to those who are miserable when they are awake."

"So be it," said Don Quixote, "and God keep you company."

The two of them then dropped off; and Cid Hamete, the author of this great history, takes the opportunity thus afforded him to explain how it was the duke and duchess came to devise the elaborate plot that has been described. It appears that the bachelor Sansón Carrasco had not forgotten how the Knight of the Mirrors had been conquered and overthrown by Don Quixote, an event that had upset all his plans, and he had, accordingly, wished to try his hand again, hoping for better luck the next time. From the page who brought the letter and gift to Teresa Panza, Sancho's wife, he had learned where the knight was and had then once more provided himself with weapons and a horse, taking care to have a white moon painted on his shield. He had transported the armor upon the back of a mule, led by a peasant and not by Tomé Cecial, his former squire, who might be recognized by Sancho or his master.

Upon reaching the duke's castle, he was informed of the road that Don Quixote had taken with the object of participating in the tournament at Saragossa. He also learned of the jokes that had been played upon the knight in connection with Dulcinea's disenchantment, which was to be accomplished at the expense of Sancho's backside. Finally, the duke told him of the trick the squire had played in making his master believe that Dulcinea was under a magic spell and had been transformed into a peasant lass, and how the duchess had ended by convincing Sancho that he was the one that was deceived since Dulcinea really was enchanted. The bachelor marveled at all this and laughed over it no little as he thought of Sancho's shrewdness combined with his simple-mindedness and the extremes to which Don Quixote's madness was capable of carrying him.

The duke requested him, if he found the knight, and whether he succeeded in overcoming him or not, to return and let them know how things turned out. Promising to do so, the bachelor took his departure. Not encountering Don Quixote in Saragossa, he went on, with the result that has already been set forth. Going back to the castle, he gave the duke a full account of the combat, with the conditions that had been laid down, adding that, being a good knight-errant and bent upon keeping his word, the vanquished one was already on his way back to his native village, where he was to remain for a year, in which time it might be that he would be cured of his madness; for this, after all, said the bachelor, was what had led to the assuming of these disguises on his part, since he looked upon it as a pity that so well-intentioned a gentleman should be so insane. With this, he took his leave once more and went on to the village to wait there for Don Quixote, who was coming along the road behind him.

It was then that the duke took occasion to play this joke, so great was the pleasure he derived from everything that had to do with the pair. Sending out a host of retainers on foot and on horseback along all the roads far and near and in every direction from which he thought Don Quixote might be approaching, he gave them orders in case they found the knight to bring him to the castle, either of his own free will or by force. When they came upon him, the servants advised their master of the fact, and, having already decided on all that was to be done, as soon as he received this message the duke ordered that the torches and lamps in the courtyard be lighted and that Altisidora be placed upon the funeral mound with all the pomp and ceremony previously mentioned, all of which was done so skillfully and in so lifelike a manner that it was the next thing to reality itself.

Here, Cid Hamete remarks, it is his personal opinion that the jesters were as crazy as their victims and that the duke and duchess were not two fingers' breadth removed from being fools when they went to so much trouble to make sport of the foolish.

As for these latter, one of them was sleeping soundly and the other was still keeping vigil with his aimless thoughts when daylight came upon them, bringing with it the desire to rise; for whether he was the victor or the vanquished Don Quixote was not slothful and never took a delight in wallowing in the feathers. No sooner was he awake than Altisidora, upon the bidding of her master and mistress, entered the room. To him she was as one returned from the dead, for she wore the same garland as when she lay upon the bier, being clad in a robe of white taffeta with gold flowers; with hair loose-flowing over her shoulders, she leaned upon a cane of very fine black ebony.

Greatly embarrassed by her presence in his chamber, Don Quixote huddled down in the bed, covering himself almost entirely with the sheets and counterpane. Too tongue-tied to speak, he was unable to show her any courtesy whatever. She sat down upon a chair at the head of his bed and, heaving a deep sigh, addressed him in a faint voice but one filled with emotion.

"When women of high station," she said, "and modest, retiring damsels trample on their honor and give free rein to their tongues, breaking through all obstacles to publish abroad the inmost secrets of their hearts, they are indeed in dire straits. I, Señor Don Quixote, am one of these, hard pressed and overcome by love but, for all of that, so long-suffering and modest that silence broke my heart and I died. Slain by thought of the stern manner in which you have treated me, stonyhearted knight—

Oh, harder far than marble to my plaint! [2]—

I lay dead for two whole days, judging from what I was told by those that looked upon me. And had it not been that love took pity on me, finding a remedy for me in the tortures laid on this worthy squire, I should still be in the other world."

"Love," said Sancho, "might very well have laid them on my donkey instead, and I'd have thanked him for it. But tell me, my lady—and may Heaven provide you with a softer-hearted lover than my master—what did you see in that other world? What is there in Hell, anyway? For, of course, that is where you have to go when you die in despair."

"To tell you the truth," replied Altisidora, "I do not think that I died completely since I did not enter Hell, for once I had done so I should never have been able to leave no matter how much I wished to. The fact is, I only went as far as the gate, where I saw about a dozen devils playing a game of tennis. They were dressed in breeches and doublets and wore Walloon collars trimmed with Flemish bone-lace, with ruffles of the same material that served them as cuffs and with four inches of their arms sticking out in order to make their hands, which carried blazing rackets, appear longer than they were. [3] But what amazed me more than this was the fact that, in place of tennis balls, they made use of what appeared to be books filled with wind and rubbish, which was something strange and marvelous to behold. And I was still further astonished to note that, whereas it is natural for the winners in a game to be glad and the losers sorry, in this case all those that took part were growling, snarling, and cursing all the time."

"That is not to be wondered at," said Sancho, "for, whether they play games or not and whether they win or lose, devils are never satisfied."

"That must be the way it is," agreed Altisidora, "but there is another thing that surprises me, or surprised me then, and that is the fact that no ball was of any use a second time, and it was wonderful to see the constant succession of books, new and old. To one of the brand-new volumes, which was very well bound, they gave such a whack that they knocked the insides out of it and sent the leaves flying in all directions. 'Just see what book that is,' said a devil to his companion, and the other devil replied, 'This is the *Second Part of the History of Don Quixote de la Mancha,* written not by Cid Hamete, the original author, but by an

Aragonese who, according to his own account, is a native of Tordesillas.'

" 'Take it away,' said the other. 'Throw it into the bottomless pit so I shan't have to see it.'

" 'Is it as bad as all that?'

" 'It is so bad,' said the first devil, 'that if I had deliberately set myself to write a worse one, I shouldn't have been able to achieve it.'

"They then went on with their game, batting about other books, but, for my part, on hearing the name of Don Quixote whom I so adore, I made up my mind then and there to remember this vision I had seen."

"It must undoubtedly have been a vision," said Don Quixote, "seeing there is no other in the world who bears that name. The history you speak of has been going from hand to hand for some time but does not stay long anywhere, for everybody gives it a kick and has done with it. I am not disturbed to hear that I am wandering about in fantastic garb in the infernal regions just as I do in the light above, for I am not the one of whom that history treats. If it by chance is a true, faithful, and worthy account, then it will live for ages, but if it is bad, it will not be a far step for it from the cradle to the grave."

Altisidora was about to go on with her reproaches addressed to Don Quixote when he interrupted her. "Lady," he said, "I have told you many times how it grieves me that you should have fastened your affections upon me, since I am not in a position to give you anything but gratitude in return. I was born to belong to Dulcinea del Toboso, and the Fates, if Fates there be, have set me aside for her. Accordingly, to think that the beauty of another can make any impression upon my heart is vain indeed. This frankness on my part should be sufficient to induce you to retire within the bounds of your modesty, as no one is under any obligation to do that which is impossible."

Hearing this, Altisidora became angry and excited. "By the living God, Don Codfish!" she cried. "Soul of a brass mortar, date-stone harder and more obdurate than an ignorant rustic when you ask him to do you a favor and he has made up his mind to the contrary! Just let me throw myself on you and I'll scratch your eyes out! Do you perhaps think, Don Vanquished, Don Cudgeled, that it was for you I died? All that you saw last night was pretense. I am not the woman to let the black of my nail suffer for such a camel as you, not to speak of dying for you!"

"That I can well believe," said Sancho, "for this business of people dying from love is something to laugh at. They may talk about it, but when it comes to doing it—tell that to Judas!" [4]

While they were conversing, the musician, singer, and poet who had rendered the verses given above came in. "Sir Knight," he said with a profound obeisance to Don Quixote, "will your Grace be so good as to count me among your most faithful servants? For I have long been a great admirer of yours and of your famous exploits."

"Will your Grace kindly tell me who you are," said the knight, "that I may show you the courtesy that is your due?"

The youth thereupon informed him that he was the panegyrist of the night before.

"I must say," replied Don Quixote, "that your Grace has an excellent voice, although what you sang did not appear to me to be very much to the purpose; for what have Garcilaso's stanzas to do with this lady's death?" [5]

"Your Grace need not wonder at that," said the musician. "Among the unshorn poets [6] of our day it is customary for each one to write as he pleases and steal from anyone he chooses, whether his borrowings be to the point or not,[7] and there is no absurdity that may not be attributed to poetic license."

Don Quixote was about to make a reply but was interrupted by the entrance of the duke and duchess, who had come to pay him a visit. They had a long and agreeable conversation, in the course of which Sancho made so many droll remarks, and mischievous ones as well, as to leave the lord and lady of the house wondering alike at his sharp-wittedness and his simplicity. Don Quixote begged them to grant him permission to depart that same day, as it was more becoming for vanquished knights like him to dwell in pigsties than in royal palaces. His hosts very amiably acceded to this request, and the duchess then inquired if Altisidora was in his good graces.

"My lady," he replied, "I can assure you that this damsel's affliction is solely due to idleness, the remedy for which is constant and honorable employment. She has just informed me that they wear lace in Hell, and inasmuch as she is skilled at making it, she should keep her hands occupied; for when she is busy moving the bobbins back and forth, images of that which she desires will not go flitting across her mind. It is the truth I speak, or such is my opinion and my advice." [8]

"And mine too," put in Sancho, "for in all my life I never knew a lacemaker that died for love. Young ladies who are busy have their minds on their work and not on their lovers. I speak from experience, for when I'm busy with the spade I never think of my old woman—I mean my Teresa Panza—although I love her better than I do my own eyelashes."

"You are quite right, Sancho," said the duchess, "and I will see that my

Altisidora is kept occupied from now on at some kind of needlework, for she is exceedingly clever at it."

"There is no need, my lady," said Altisidora, "of your resorting to that remedy, for the thought of the cruel way in which this scoundrelly vagabond has treated me will efface him from my memory without having recourse to any other means. With your Highnesses' permission, I should like to leave this room in order that my eyes may not have to behold his mournful countenance, his ugly and abominable features."

"That," observed the duke, "reminds me of the saying:

> *For he who doth rave, and insults shout,*
> *Is very near forgiving.*" [9]

Dabbing at her eyes with a handkerchief as if to wipe the tears away, Altisidora then rose and, with a curtsy to her master and mistress, went out the door.

"Bad luck go with you, poor damsel," said Sancho, "bad luck, I say; for you've fallen in with a soul of matweed and a heart of oak. Now, if it had been me, faith, and another cock would have crowed for you."

This brought an end to the conversation, and Don Quixote proceeded to dress himself, had dinner with his hosts, and took his leave that afternoon.

CHAPTER LXXI. *Of what befell* [1] *Don Quixote and his squire Sancho on the way to their village.*

AS THE vanquished and deeply afflicted Don Quixote went his way, he was, on the one hand, overly sad, and, on the other, very happy. His sadness was due to his defeat, while his happiness lay in thinking of the virtue his squire had shown he possessed by resurrecting Altisidora, although it must be admitted he had some difficulty in persuading himself that the lovelorn maiden had really been dead. As for Sancho, he found no cause for rejoicing but was downcast because the damsel had failed to keep her word and give him the chemises.

As he kept going over this in his mind, he turned to his master and said, "Really, sir, I am the most unlucky doctor in all the world. There's many a one that kills the patient he treats, yet insists on being paid even though all he does is write out a prescription for certain medicines which the apothecary—not he—makes up, and in this way he wheedles the sick man out of it.[2] With me, the health of another costs me drops of blood, slaps, pinches, pinpricks, and lashes, and I don't get a penny for it. But I swear, if they bring me any more, they'll have to grease my palm before I cure them; for it is by singing that the abbot gets his dinner,[3] and I can't believe that Heaven has bestowed this power on me in order that I should pass it on to others for nothing."

"You are right, friend Sancho," replied Don Quixote. "It was very wrong of Altisidora not to have given you the chemises she promised you. It is true, the virtue that is in you is *gratis data*, having cost you no effort other than that involved in receiving the torments inflicted on your person; but, nevertheless, I can tell you that, so far as I am concerned, if you want pay for those lashes with which Dulcinea is to be disenchanted, I would gladly compensate you. The only thing is: I am not certain that the cure would be effective if it were paid for, and I would not have the reward interfere with the medicine. But, for all of that, I do not see that there would be any harm in trying; so, think it over, Sancho, and decide upon your price; then administer the flogging and pay yourself off with your own hand, since you are the one who holds my money."

Sancho opened his eyes wide at this offer and pricked up his ears until they stood out a palm's breadth from his head. In his heart he was now quite willing to take a whipping.

"Very well, then, master," he said, "I will hold myself at your Grace's disposition; for I shall be only too glad to gratify your desires so long as I profit by it. If I appear grasping, you must blame it on the love I have for my wife and young ones. Tell me, your Grace, how much is each lash worth to you?"

"Sancho," said Don Quixote, "if I had to pay you in accordance with the great value of the remedy, all the treasure of Venice and the mines of Potosí would not suffice.[4] So, see what you have of mine and put a price on each stroke."

"The strokes," said Sancho, "amount to three thousand three hundred-odd, of which I have already given myself five—that leaves the rest to come. But let the five go for the odd ones; three thousand three hundred at a cuartillo[5] each—and I wouldn't take less if all the world insisted on it—that makes three thousand three hundred cuartillos, or fifteen hundred half-reales, and the three hundred strokes amount to seventy-five reales, which added to the seven hundred and fifty come to eight hundred and twenty-five reales altogether.⁶ Deducting these from your Grace's money which I am holding, I'll return home rich and well satisfied even though well flogged; for you don't catch trout ⁷—I need say no more."

"O blessed Sancho!" cried Don Quixote, "O kind Sancho! Dulcinea and I will be under obligations to serve you all the days of our life that Heaven may allot us! If she resumes her lost shape—and it is not possible that she should fail to do so—her misfortune will have been her good luck and my downfall a most happy triumph. But tell me, Sancho; when do you propose to begin your discipline? For if you speed it, I will give you an additional hundred reales."

"When?" said Sancho. "Tonight without fail. Let your Grace see to it that we spend the night in the fields, under the open sky, and I will lay my flesh open at the same time."

The night so anxiously awaited by Don Quixote was long in coming; indeed, it seemed to him that the wheels of Apollo's chariot must have broken down and the day was being unduly prolonged, as is always the case with lovers who can never adjust their desires to the course of time.⁸ At last they entered a pleasant grove a short distance off the highway, and here, leaving Rocinante's saddle and the ass's packsaddle unused, they stretched themselves out on the green grass and had their supper from Sancho's supply of provisions. Then, having made a powerful and flexible whip out of the donkey's halter, the squire retired for a distance of some twenty paces among a clump of beech trees.

Seeing him set about it so energetically and courageously, his master called after him, "Take care, my friend, that you do not cut yourself to pieces; let there be a space between the lashes, and do not be in such haste that your breath will give out by the time you are half done; by which I mean to say, do not lay on so stoutly that life will fail you before you have attained the desired number. And in order that you may not lose by a card too many or too few,⁹ I will stand to one side and keep count on my rosary. May Heaven favor you as your good intentions deserve."

"He who is well able to pay doesn't worry about pledges," ¹⁰ was Sancho's answer. "I intend to lay them on in such a way that I will feel them and yet not kill myself; for that, I take it, is where the miracle comes in."

Saying this, he stripped to the waist, snatched up the whip, and began, with Don Quixote counting the strokes. He had given himself six or eight lashes when he began to think that the jest was a somewhat heavy one and the price very cheap. Pausing for a moment, he informed his master that he had made a mistake in his estimate and that each stroke ought to be paid for at the rate of half a real and not a cuartillo.

"Continue, friend Sancho," said Don Quixote, "and don't lose courage, for I am doubling your pay."

"In that case," said the squire, "God be with me and let the lashes rain down."

Rascal that he was, however, he stopped laying them on his shoulders and let them fall on the trees instead, uttering such moans every now and then that it seemed as if each one was tearing his heart out. Don Quixote became alarmed at this, fearing that Sancho by his imprudence would do away with himself before the purpose of the thing had been achieved.

"Upon your life, my friend," he called to him, "let the matter rest there, for this impresses me as being a very harsh remedy and we shall have to be patient: Zamora was not won in an hour.[11] Unless I missed my count, you have already given yourself more than a thousand lashes, and that will do for the present; for, to employ a homespun phrase, the ass will bear the load but not the overload."[12]

"No, no, master," Sancho protested, "I will not have it said of me, 'The money paid, the arm broken.'[13] Stand back a little farther, your Grace, and let me give myself a thousand or so more. A couple of flourishes[14] like this and we'll have done with it, and there'll be cloth to spare."

"Well, then," said Don Quixote, "seeing that you are so well disposed, may Heaven help you. Lay on, for I am going away."

Sancho then returned to his task so intrepidly that before long he had stripped the bark off any number of trees, such was the severity with which he whipped himself. As he dealt a tremendous stroke to one of the beeches he raised his voice and cried, "Here shalt thou die, Samson, and all those that are with you!"[15]

At the sound of this agonized wail and the thud of the cruel lash, Don Quixote came running up and snatched from Sancho's hand the twisted halter that served as a whip. "Fate, my dear Sancho," he said, "will not have you lose your life to please me, for you need it to support your wife and children. Let Dulcinea wait for a better occasion. As for me, content with a hope that is soon to be realized, I will bide my time until you have recovered your strength so that this business may be finished to the satisfaction of all concerned."

"Since your Grace will have it so," said Sancho, "so be it. Throw your cloak [16] over my shoulders if you will, for I am all a-sweat and don't want to catch cold—that is a risk that novices run, you know, when they discipline themselves."

Don Quixote did as requested; stripping to his undergarments, he covered Sancho, who slept until the sun awakened him. They then resumed their journey, which for the time being ended in a village three leagues from there. Dismounting at a hostelry, the knight recognized it for what it was and did not take it to be a castle with a deep moat, turrets, portcullis, and a drawbridge; for ever since he had been overcome in combat he had talked more rationally on all subjects, as will presently be seen.

They were given lodging in a lower room, the walls of which were covered with some old bits of painted serge of the kind found in villages in place of leather hangings.[17] On one of these was depicted, by a very crude hand, the abduction of Helen, when the bold guest bore her off from Menelaus, and on the other was represented the story of Dido and Aeneas, with the queen standing on a high tower and signaling with half a sheet to the fugitive, who was now at sea on a frigate or brigantine. Helen did not appear very reluctant about going, for she was laughing slyly and roguishly, but the beauteous Dido was shedding tears the size of walnuts.

"These two ladies," observed Don Quixote as he surveyed the paintings, "were most fortunate not to have been born in this age, and I, above all men, am unlucky not to have lived in their time. Had I encountered those gentlemen, Troy would not have been burned nor Carthage destroyed, for all I should have had to do would have been to slay Paris, and all the ensuing misfortunes would have been avoided."

"I will wager you," said Sancho, "that before long there will not be an alehouse, inn, tavern, or barbershop where the history of our exploits will not be painted on the walls,[18] but I'd like it done by a better hand than the one that did these."

"Right you are, Sancho," said Don Quixote, "for this painter is like Orbaneja who lived in Ubeda and who, when asked what he was painting, used to reply, 'Whatever it turns out to be'; and if it happened to be a cock, he would write beneath it, 'This is a rooster,' so that it would not be taken for a fox.[19] And it is my opinion, Sancho, that the painter or writer (it is all the same) who brought to light the history of this new Don Quixote that was recently published must be one of this sort: that is to say, he painted or wrote *whatever came out*. Or one might compare him to a poet by the name of Mauleón who was at court some years ago and who was in the habit of answering offhand any and all questions put to him. When someone asked him what *Deum de Deo* meant, he replied, '*Dé donde diere.*' [20]

"But, leaving all this aside, tell me, Sancho, whether or not you mean to have another turn at flogging yourself tonight and whether you prefer that it be indoors or out."

"Upon my word, master," said Sancho, "considering what I mean to do to myself, it makes no difference to me whether it's in a house or in the fields; but, for all of that, I'd prefer that it be among trees, for they seem to keep me company and are a wonderful help in bearing the pain."

"But after all, friend Sancho," said Don Quixote, "you have to recover your strength, and so I think we had best wait until we get back to our village, which will be day after tomorrow at the latest."

Sancho replied that his master should do as he saw fit, but that he himself preferred to get the business over with while his blood was warm and while he had an appetite for it,[21] for there was often danger in delay, pray to God and wield the hammer,[22] one "take" was better than two "I'll give you's,"[23] and a bird in the hand was better than a vulture on the wing.[24]

"No more proverbs, Sancho, for God's sake," said Don Quixote. "It would seem that you are back to the *sicut erat* [25] again. Speak plainly, simply, and in a straightforward manner, as I have so often told you, and you will see how much better it will be." [26]

"I don't know what bad luck it is of mine," said Sancho, "but I can't talk without proverbs, and for me they all make sense;[27] but I'll mend my ways if I can."

And with this their conversation ended.

CHAPTER LXXII. *Wherein is related how Don Quixote and Sancho reached their village.*

DON QUIXOTE and Sancho spent the entire day at the village inn, waiting for night to come in order that the one might go out into the fields and finish the task of disciplining himself, while the other witnessed this action, which for him meant the fulfillment of his desires.

Meanwhile, there came riding up to the hostelry a gentleman with three or four servants.

"Here, Señor Don Alvaro Tarfe," said one of the attendants, addressing the person who appeared to be their master, "your Grace may take your siesta, for the lodgings appear to be clean and cool."

"Listen, Sancho," said Don Quixote when he heard this, "it seems to me that when I was leafing through that book containing the second part of my history I came upon the name Don Alvaro Tarfe."

"That may well be," replied Sancho, "but let him dismount and we can ask him about it afterward."

The landlady gave the gentleman a room on the ground floor opposite Don Quixote's and similarly adorned with painted serge. The new arrival then put on a summer coat and, coming out into the portico of the inn, which was wide and airy, he encountered the knight, who was pacing up and down there.[1]

"In which direction is your Grace traveling, gentle sir?" the newcomer inquired.

"I am bound for a near-by village of which I am a native," was the answer. "And your Grace?"

"I, sir," said the gentleman, "am on my way to Granada, which is my own country."

"And a good country it is," said Don Quixote. "But will your Grace please be so good as to inform me of your name, since it is more important than I can tell you that I should know it."

"My name," replied the other guest, "is Don Alvaro Tarfe."

"Well, then," said Don Quixote, "I think your Grace must undoubtedly be the Don Alvaro Tarfe who is spoken of in the *Second Part of the History of Don Quixote de la Mancha* that was recently printed and published by a new author."

"I am the same one," the gentleman assured him, "and the Don Quixote you mention, who is the chief subject of that history, was a very great friend of mine. It was I who took him away from his native heath, or, at least, I induced him to come and attend a tournament that was being held in Saragossa, whither I was bound. The truth of the matter is, I did him many favors and kept him from a flogging at the hands of the executioner as a result of his rash conduct." [2]

"Tell me, Señor Don Alvaro, do I in any way resemble the Don Quixote of whom you are speaking?"

"No, certainly not; in no way whatever."

"And this Don Quixote of yours—did he have with him a squire by the name of Sancho Panza?"

"Yes, he did; and although the fellow had the reputation of being very droll, I never once heard him say anything amusing."

"That I can believe," said Sancho at this point, "for it is not given to everyone to say droll things. The fellow your Grace is talking about, gentle sir, must have been some very great scoundrel, blockhead, and thief all in one; for I am the real Sancho Panza, and my drolleries come faster than rain. If your Grace would put it to the test, you have but to follow me around for at least a year and you will see how they drop from me at every turn—so many of them and of such a sort that, without realizing most of the time what it is I am saying, I bring a laugh to all who hear me. And the real Don Quixote, the famous, the valiant, the wise, the lovelorn, the undoer of wrongs, the guardian of minors and orphans, the protector of widows, the slayer of damsels,[3] he who has for his one and only lady the peerless Dulcinea del Toboso, is this gentleman here present, my master. All other Don Quixotes and all other Sancho Panzas are a mockery and a dream."

"By Heaven if I don't believe you," said Don Alvaro, "for in the course of these few words you have uttered, my friend, you have said more amusing things than are to be found in all the talk I heard from the other Sancho, and I heard a great deal of it. He was more of a glutton than a talker and more stupid than droll. I have no doubt that those enchanters that persecute the good Don Quixote have wished to persecute me through my association with the bad one. But what am I saying? I will venture to take an oath that I left him locked up in a madhouse in Toledo [4] so that they might treat him, and now another Don Quixote appears upon the scene, though quite different from mine."

"I do not know," said our Don Quixote, "whether I am good or not, but I can assure you that I am not 'the bad one'; in proof of which, Señor Don Alvaro Tarfe, I would have your Grace know that I have never been in Saragossa in all the days of my life. When I heard that the imaginary Don Quixote had taken part in the tournament in that city, I resolved not to go there so that I might show all the world it was a lie. I accordingly went straight on to Barcelona, that storehouse of courtesy, haven of wayfarers, fatherland of the brave, avenger of the wronged, home of loyal friendships freely bestowed, and, moreover, in point of beauty and situation, a city without a peer. And while the things that happened to me there were none too pleasant and, indeed, caused me much sorrow, I still have no regrets but am glad that I have seen that town.

"In short, Señor Don Alvaro Tarfe, I am Don Quixote de la Mancha, the one who is known to fame and not the wretch who has sought to usurp my name and do himself honor by thinking my thoughts. And so, I implore your Grace—for I know you must be a gentleman—to make a declaration before the local magistrate [5] to the effect that you have never in all your life laid eyes on me up to now, that I am not the Don Quixote referred to in the Second Part, and that Sancho Panza my squire is not the one that your Grace knew."

"That I will gladly do," said Don Alvaro, "although I must say I am amazed to find that there are two Don Quixotes and two Sanchos so alike in names and so unlike in the way they deport themselves. I will state and affirm, then, that I have not seen what I did see and that what happened to me could not have occurred."

"Your Grace," said Sancho, "is undoubtedly enchanted like my lady Dulcinea del Toboso, and I would to Heaven that your disenchantment depended upon my giving myself another three thousand-odd lashes as I am doing for her sake. I would lay them on without looking for any reward whatever."

"I do not undertsand this matter of lashes," said Don Alvaro; to which Sancho replied that it was a long story but he would be glad to explain if the gentleman by any chance was going their way.

When the dinner hour came Don Quixote and Don Alvaro sat down at table together, and, as chance would have it, the village magistrate accompanied by a notary entered the inn, whereupon the knight laid a petition before him, setting forth that it was necessary for the protection of his, Don Quixote's, rights that the other gentleman there present should make an affidavit. This was to be to the effect that the gentleman in question was not personally acquainted with Don Quixote de la Mancha, also present, and it was to be further stated that this latter person was not the individual referred to in a history entitled *Second Part of Don Quixote de la Mancha*,[6] composed by a certain Avellaneda, native of Tordesillas.

The short of the matter is, the magistrate drew up the document and the affidavit was made with all the legal formalities customary in such cases. Don Quixote and Sancho were very happy over this, just as if it were a matter of great importance to them, and as if their own words and deeds did not reveal clearly enough the difference between the true knight and his squire and the pair of pretenders. There followed then an elaborate exchange of courtesies between Don Alvaro and Don Quixote, with the great Manchegan displaying such good sense and moderation as completely to disabuse the other gentleman of the mistake under which he had been laboring, causing him to feel that he must have been enchanted, now that he had come into contact with a person who was the direct opposite of the one of the same name he had previously known.[7]

As evening came on they all set out from the village, and at a distance of something like half a league their paths separated, Don Quixote taking the road that led to his home and Don Alvaro the other one. In this brief space of time the knight related to his companion how he had been overcome in combat and told him of Dulcinea's enchantment and how it was to be remedied. Don Alvaro was more astonished than ever at all this, and, embracing the two of them, he went his way. Don Quixote and Sancho likewise continued their journey, spending the night in a grove in order to give the squire an opportunity of fulfilling his penance, with the strokes for the most part falling on the bark of the beech trees instead of on his shoulders; for he took care to see to it that the lashes he gave himself were such as would not have disturbed a fly had there been one on him.

Don Quixote, however, was under the same illusion as before and did not miss counting a single stroke, finding that with those of the previous night the total now amounted to three thousand twenty-nine. It seemed as if the sun that morning rose earlier than usual to witness the sacrifice, and with the coming of day they took to the road again, talking all the while of the mistake Don Alvaro had made and congratulating themselves on having secured his affidavit in the presence of a magistrate and in so binding a form.

They traveled all that day and night with nothing occurring worthy of note save for the fact that Sancho completed his task, which made Don Quixote so exceedingly happy that he could scarcely wait for daylight to see if he would meet with his by now disenchanted lady along the highway; and each time that he encountered a woman he would go up to her in the hope of recognizing Dulcinea del Toboso, for he believed that Merlin could not lie and that his promises were infallible. Occupied with such thoughts and anxieties as these, they mounted a slope from the top of which they had a view of their village, at the sight of which Sancho fell on his knees.

"Open your eyes, O beloved homeland," he cried, "and behold your son, Sancho Panza, returning to you. If he does not come back very rich, he comes well flogged. Open your arms and receive also your other son, Don Quixote, who returns vanquished by the arm of another but a victor over himself; and this, so I have been told, is the greatest victory that could be desired. I bring money with me, too; for while they gave me many good lashes, I went mounted like a fine gentleman." [8]

"Leave off that nonsense," said Don Quixote, "and let us go straight on to our village, where we may give our fancies free rein as we plan the pastoral life that we intend to lead."

With this, they descended the other side of the slope and came to the town.

CHAPTER LXXIII. *Of the omens that Don Quixote encountered upon entering his village, with other incidents that embellish and lend credence to this great history.*

As THEY entered the village, Cid Hamete informs us, Don Quixote caught sight of two lads on the communal threshing floor who were engaged in a dispute.

"Don't let it worry you, Periquillo," one of them was saying to the other; "you'll never lay eyes on it again as long as you live."

Hearing this, Don Quixote turned to Sancho. "Did you mark what that boy said, my friend?" he asked. " 'You'll never lay eyes on it [1] again . . .' "

"Well," replied Sancho, "what difference does it make what he said?"

"What difference?" said Don Quixote. "Don't you see that, applied to the one I love, it means I shall never again see Dulcinea."

Sancho was about to answer him when his attention was distracted by a hare that came flying across the fields pursued by a large number of hunters with their greyhounds. The frightened animal took refuge by huddling down beneath the donkey, whereupon Sancho reached out his hand and caught it and presented it to his master.

"*Malum signum, malum signum,*" [2] the knight was muttering to himself. "A hare flees, the hounds pursue it, Dulcinea appears not."

"It is very strange to hear your Grace talk like that," said Sancho. "Let us suppose that this hare *is* Dulcinea del Toboso and the hounds pursuing it are those wicked enchanters that transformed her into a peasant lass; she flees, I catch her and turn her over to your Grace, you hold her in your arms and caress her. Is that a bad sign? What ill omen can you find in it?" [3]

The two lads who had been quarreling now came up to have a look at the hare, and Sancho asked them what their dispute was about. To this the one who had uttered the words "You'll never lay eyes on it again as long as you live," replied that he had taken a cricket cage from the other boy and had no intention of returning it ever. Sancho then brought out from his pocket four cuartos [4] and gave them to the lad in exchange for the cage, which he placed in Don Quixote's hands.

"There, master," he said, "these omens are broken and destroyed, and to my way of thinking, even though I may be a dunce, they have no more to do with what is going to happen to us than the clouds of yesteryear. If I am not mistaken, I have heard our curate say that sensible persons of the Christian faith should pay no heed to such foolish things, and you yourself in the past have given me to understand that all those Christians who are guided by omens are fools.[5] But there is no need to waste a lot of words on the subject; come, let us go on and enter our village."

The hunters at this point came up and asked for the hare, and Don Quixote gave it to them. Continuing on their way, the returning pair encountered the curate and the bachelor Carrasco, who were strolling in a small meadow on the outskirts of the town as they read their breviaries. And here it should be mentioned that Sancho Panza, by way of sumpter cloth,[6] had thrown over his gray and the bundle of armor it bore the flame-covered buckram robe in which they had dressed the squire at the duke's castle, on the night that witnessed Altisidora's resurrection; and he had also fitted the miter over the donkey's head, the result being the weirdest transformation and the most bizarrely appareled ass that ever were seen in this world. The curate and the bachelor recognized the pair at once and came forward to receive them with open arms. Don Quixote dismounted and gave them both a warm embrace; meanwhile, the small boys (boys are like lynxes in that nothing escapes them [7]), having spied the ass's miter, ran up for a closer view.

"Come, lads," they cried, "and see Sancho Panza's ass trigged out finer than Mingo,[8] and Don Quixote's beast is skinnier than ever!"

Finally, surrounded by the urchins and accompanied by the curate and the bachelor, they entered the village and made their way to Don Quixote's house, where they found the housekeeper and the niece standing in the doorway, for the news of their return had preceded them. Teresa Panza, Sancho's wife, had also heard of it, and, half naked and disheveled, dragging her daughter Sanchica by the hand, she hastened to greet her husband and was disappointed when she saw him, for he did not look to her as well fitted out as a governor ought to be.

"How does it come, my husband," she said, "that you return like this, tramping and footsore? You look more like a vagabond than you do like a governor." [9]

"Be quiet, Teresa," Sancho admonished her, "for very often there are stakes where there is no bacon.[10] Come on home with me and you will hear marvels. I am bringing money with me, which is the thing that matters, money earned by my own efforts and without harm to anyone."

"You just bring along the money, my good husband," said Teresa, "and whether you got it here or there, or by whatever means, you will not be introducing any new custom into the world."

Sanchica then embraced her father and asked him if he had brought her anything, for she had been looking forward to his coming as to the showers in May. And so, with his wife holding him by the hand while his daughter kept one arm about his waist and at the same time led the gray, Sancho went home, leaving Don Quixote under his own roof in the company of niece and housekeeper, the curate and the barber.

Without regard to time or season, the knight at once drew his guests to one side and in a few words informed them of how he had been overcome in battle and had given his promise not to leave his village for a year, a promise that he meant to observe most scrupulously, without violating it in the slightest degree, as every knight-errant was obliged to do by the laws of chivalry. He accordingly meant to spend that year as a shepherd, he said, amid the solitude of the fields, where he might give free rein to his amorous fancies as he practiced the virtues of the pastoral life; and he further begged them, if they were not too greatly occupied and more urgent matters did not prevent their doing so, to consent to be his companions. He would purchase a flock sufficiently large to justify their calling themselves shepherds; and, moreover, he would have them know, the most important thing of all had been taken care of, for he had hit upon names that would suit them marvelously well. When the curate asked him what these names were, Don Quixote replied that he himself would be known as "the shepherd Quixotiz," the bachelor as "the shepherd Carrascón," the curate as "the shepherd Curiambro," [11] and Sancho Panza as "the shepherd Pancino."

Both his listeners were dismayed at the new form which his madness had assumed. However, in order that he might not go faring forth from the village on another of his expeditions (for they hoped that in the course of the year he would be cured), they decided to fall in with his new plan and approve it as being a wise one, and they even agreed to be his companions in the calling he proposed to adopt.

"What's more," remarked Sansón Carrasco, "I am a very famous poet, as everyone knows, and at every turn I will be composing pastoral or courtly verses or whatever may come to mind, by way of a diversion for us as we wander in those lonely places; but what is most necessary of all, my dear sirs, is that each one of us should choose the name of the shepherd lass to whom he means to dedicate his songs, so that we may not leave a tree, however hard its bark may be, where their names are not inscribed and engraved as is the custom with lovelorn shepherds."

"That is exactly what we should do," replied Don Quixote, "although, for my part, I am relieved of the necessity of looking for an imaginary shepherdess, seeing that I have the peerless Dulcinea del Toboso, glory of these brookside regions, adornment of these meadows, beauty's mainstay, cream of the Graces—in short, one to whom all praise is well becoming however hyperbolical it may be."

"That is right," said the curate, "but we will seek out some shepherd maids that are easily handled,[12] who if they do not square with us will fit in the corners." [13]

"And," added Sansón Carrasco, "if we run out of names we will give them those that we find printed in books the world over: such as Fílida, Amarilis, Diana, Flérida, Galatea, and Belisarda; [14] for since these are for sale in the market place, we can buy them and make them our own. If my lady, or, rather, my shepherdess, should by chance be called Ana, I will celebrate her charms under the name of Anarda; if she is Francisca, she will become Francenia; if Lucía, Luscinda; for it all amounts to the same thing. And Sancho Panza, if he enters this confraternity, may compose verses to his wife, Teresa Panza, under the name of Teresaina."

Don Quixote had to laugh at this, and the curate then went on to heap extravagant praise upon him for his noble resolution which did him so much credit, and once again he offered to keep the knight company whenever he could spare the time from the duties of his office. With this, they took their leave of him, advising and beseeching him to take care of his health and to eat plentifully of the proper food.

As fate would have it, the niece and the housekeeper had overheard the conversation of the three men, and as soon as the visitors had left they both descended upon Don Quixote.

"What is the meaning of this, my uncle? Here we were thinking your Grace had come home to lead a quiet and respectable life, and do you mean to tell us you are going to get yourself involved in fresh complications—

> Young shepherd, thou who comest here,
> Young shepherd, thou who goest there . . .[15]

For, to tell the truth, the barley is too hard now to make shepherds' pipes of it." [16]

"And how," said the housekeeper, "is your Grace going to stand the midday heat in summer, the winter cold, the howling of the wolves out there in the fields? You certainly cannot endure it. That is an occupation for robust men, cut out and bred for such a calling almost from their swaddling clothes. Setting one evil over against another, it is better to be a knight-errant than a shepherd. Look, sir, take my advice, for I am not stuffed with bread and wine when I give it to you but am fasting and am going on fifty years of age: stay at home, attend to your affairs, go often to confession, be charitable to the poor, and let it be upon my soul if any harm comes to you as a result of it."

"Be quiet, daughters," said Don Quixote. "I know very well what I must do. Take me up to bed, for I do not feel very well; and you may be sure of one thing: whether I am a knight-errant now or a shepherd to be, I never will fail to look after your needs as you will see when the time comes."

And good daughters that they unquestionably were, the housekeeper and the niece helped him up to bed, where they gave him something to eat and made him as comfortable as they could.

CHAPTER LXXIV. *Of how Don Quixote fell sick, of the will that he made, and of the manner of his death.*

INASMUCH as nothing that is human is eternal but is ever declining from its beginning to its close, this being especially true of the lives of men, and since Don Quixote was not endowed by Heaven with the privilege of staying the downward course of things, his own end came when he was least expecting it. Whether it was owing to melancholy occasioned by the defeat he had suffered, or was, simply, the will of Heaven which had so ordained it, he was taken with a fever that kept him in bed for a week, during which time his friends, the curate, the bachelor, and the barber, visited him frequently, while Sancho Panza, his faithful squire, never left his bedside.

Believing that the knight's condition was due to sorrow over his downfall and disappointment at not having been able to accomplish the disenchantment and liberation of Dulcinea, Sancho and the others endeavored to cheer him up in every possible way. The bachelor urged him to take heart and get up from bed that he might begin his pastoral life, adding that he himself had already composed an eclogue that would cast in the shade all that Sannazaro [1] had ever written, and had purchased with his own money from a herdsman of Quintanar two fine dogs to guard the flock, one of them named Barcino and the other Butrón. All this, however, did not serve to relieve Don Quixote's sadness; whereupon his friends called in the doctor, who took his pulse and was not very well satisfied with it. In any case, the physician told them, they should attend to the health of his soul as that of his body was in grave danger.

Don Quixote received this news calmly enough, but not so his housekeeper, niece, and squire, who began weeping bitterly, as if he were already lying dead in front of them. It was the doctor's opinion that melancholy and depression were putting an end to his patient's life. The knight then requested them to leave him alone as he wished to sleep a little, and they complied. He slept for more than six hours at a stretch, as the saying is, and so soundly that the housekeeper and niece thought he would never wake.

At last he did, however, and at once cried out in a loud voice, "Blessed be Almighty God who has given me so many blessings! Truly His mercy is boundless and is not limited or restrained by the sins of men."

The niece listened carefully to what her uncle said, and it seemed to her that he was speaking more rationally than was his wont, at least during his illness.

"Sir," she said to him, "what does your Grace mean? Has something occurred that we know nothing about? What is this talk of mercy and sins?"

"The mercy that I speak of," replied Don Quixote, "is that which God is showing me at this moment—in spite of my sins, as I have said. My mind now is clear, unencumbered by those misty shadows of ignorance that were cast over it by my bitter and continual reading of those hateful books of chivalry. I see through all the nonsense and fraud contained in them, and my only regret is that my disillusionment has come so late, leaving me no time to make any sort of amends by reading those that are the light of the soul. I find myself, niece, at the point of death, and I would die in such a way as not to leave the impression of a life so bad that I shall be remembered as a madman; for even though I have been one, I do not wish to confirm it on my deathbed. And so, my dear, call in my good friends: the curate, the bachelor Sansón Carrasco, and Master Nicholas the barber; for I want to confess my sins and make my last will and testament."

The niece, however, was relieved of this errand, for the three of them came in just then.

"I have good news for you,[2] kind sirs," said Don Quixote the moment he saw them. "I am no longer Don Quixote de la Mancha but Alonso Quijano,[3] whose mode of life won for him the name of 'Good.' I am the enemy of Amadis of Gaul and all his innumerable progeny; for those profane stories dealing with knight-errantry are odious to me, and I realize how foolish I was and the danger I courted in reading them; but I am in my right senses now and I abominate them."

Hearing this, they all three were convinced that some new kind of madness must have laid hold of him.

"Why, Señor Don Quixote!" exclaimed Sansón. "What makes you talk like that, just when we have received news that my lady Dulcinea is disenchanted? And just when we are on the verge of becoming shepherds so that we may spend the rest of our lives in singing like a lot of princes, why does your Grace choose to turn hermit? Say no more, in Heaven's name, but be sensible and forget these idle tales."

"Tales of that kind," said Don Quixote, "have been the truth for me in the past, and to my detriment, but with Heaven's aid I trust to turn them to my profit now that I am dying. For I feel, gentlemen, that death is very near; so, leave all jesting aside and bring me a confessor for my sins and a notary to draw up my will. In such straits as these a man cannot trifle with his soul. Accordingly, while the Señor Curate is hearing my confession, let the notary be summoned."

Amazed at his words, they gazed at one another in some perplexity, yet they could not but believe him. One of the signs that led them to think he was dying was this quick return from madness to sanity and all the additional things he had to say, so well reasoned and well put and so becoming in a Christian that none of them could any longer doubt that he was in full possession of his faculties. Sending the others out of the room, the curate stayed behind to confess him, and before long the bachelor returned with the notary and Sancho Panza, who had been informed of his master's condition, and who, finding the housekeeper and the niece in tears, began weeping with them. When the confession was over, the curate came out.

"It is true enough," he said, "that Alonso Quijano the Good is dying, and it is also true that he is a sane man. It would be well for us to go in now while he makes his will."

At this news the housekeeper, niece, and the good squire Sancho Panza were so overcome with emotion that the tears burst forth from their eyes and their bosoms heaved with sobs; for, as has been stated more than once, whether Don Quixote was plain Alonso Quijano the Good or Don Quixote de la Mancha, he was always of a kindly and pleasant disposition and for this reason was beloved not only by the members of his household but by all who knew him.

The notary had entered along with the others, and as soon as the preamble had been attended to and the dying man had commended his soul to his Maker with all those Christian formalities that are called for in such a case, they came to the matter of bequests, with Don Quixote dictating as follows:

"ITEM. With regard to Sancho Panza, whom, in my madness, I appointed to be my squire, and who has in his possession a certain sum of money belonging to me: inasmuch as there has been a standing account between us, of debits and credits, it is my will that he shall not be asked to give any accounting whatsoever of this sum, but if any be left over after he has had payment for what I owe him, the balance, which will amount to very little, shall be his, and much good may it do him. If when

I was mad I was responsible for his being given the governorship of an island, now that I am of sound mind I would present him with a kingdom if it were in my power, for his simplicity of mind and loyal conduct merit no less."

At this point he turned to Sancho. "Forgive me, my friend," he said, "for having caused you to appear as mad as I by leading you to fall into the same error, that of believing that there are still knights-errant in the world."

"Ah, master," cried Sancho through his tears, "don't die, your Grace, but take my advice and go on living for many years to come; for the greatest madness that a man can be guilty of in this life is to die without good reason, without anyone's killing him, slain only by the hands of melancholy. Look you, don't be lazy but get up from this bed and let us go out into the fields clad as shepherds as we agreed to do. Who knows but behind some bush we may come upon the lady Dulcinea, as disenchanted as you could wish. If it is because of worry over your defeat that you are dying, put the blame on me by saying that the reason for your being overthrown was that I had not properly fastened Rocinante's girth. For the matter of that, your Grace knows from reading your books of chivalry that it is a common thing for certain knights to overthrow others, and he who is vanquished today will be the victor tomorrow."

"That is right," said Sansón, "the worthy Sancho speaks the truth."

"Not so fast, gentlemen," said Don Quixote. "In last year's nests there are no birds this year.[4] I was mad and now I am sane; I was Don Quixote de la Mancha, and now I am, as I have said, Alonso Quijano the Good. May my repentance and the truth I now speak restore to me the place I once held in your esteem. And now, let the notary proceed:

"ITEM. I bequeath my entire estate, without reservation,[5] to my niece Antonia Quijana,[6] here present, after the necessary deductions shall have been made from the most available portion of it to satisfy the bequests that I have stipulated. The first payment shall be to my housekeeper for the wages due her, with twenty ducats over to buy her a dress. And I hereby appoint the Señor Curate and the Señor Bachelor Sansón Carrasco to be my executors.

"ITEM. It is my will that if my niece Antonia Quijana should see fit to marry, it shall be to a man who does not know what books of chivalry are; and if it shall be established that he is acquainted with such books and my niece still insists on marrying him, then she shall lose all that I have bequeathed her and my executors shall apply her portion to works of charity as they may see fit.

"ITEM. I entreat the aforementioned gentlemen, my executors, if by good fortune they should come to know the author who is said to have composed a history now going the rounds under the title of *Second Part of the Exploits of Don Quixote de la Mancha*, to beg his forgiveness in my behalf, as earnestly as they can, since it was I who unthinkingly led him to set down so many and such great absurdities as are to be found in it; for I leave this life with a feeling of remorse at having provided him with the occasion for putting them into writing."

The will ended here, and Don Quixote, stretching himself at length in the bed, fainted away. They all were alarmed at this and hastened to aid him. The same thing happened very frequently in the course of the three days of life that remained to him after he had made his will. The household was in a state of excitement, but with it all the niece continued to eat her meals, the housekeeper had her drink, and Sancho Panza was in good spirits; for this business of inheriting property effaces or mitigates the sorrow which the heir ought to feel and causes him to forget.[7]

Death came at last for Don Quixote, after he had received all the sacraments[8] and once more, with many forceful arguments, had expressed his abomination of books of chivalry. The notary who was present remarked that in none of those books had he read of any knight-errant dying in his own bed so peacefully and in so Christian a manner. And thus, amid the tears and lamentations of those present, he gave up the ghost; that is to say, he died. Perceiving that their friend was no more, the curate asked the notary to be a witness to the fact that Alonso Quijano the Good, commonly known as Don Quixote, was truly dead,[9] this being necessary in order that some author other than Cid Hamete Benengeli might not have the opportunity of falsely resurrecting him and writing endless histories of his exploits.

Such was the end of the Ingenious Gentleman of La Mancha,[10] whose birthplace Cid Hamete was unwilling to designate exactly[11] in order that all the towns and villages of La Mancha might contend among themselves for the right to adopt him and claim him as their own, just as the seven cities of Greece did in the case of Homer. The lamentations of Sancho and those of Don Quixote's niece and his housekeeper, as well as the original epitaphs that were composed for his tomb, will not be recorded here, but mention may be made of the verses by Sansón Carrasco:

> *Here lies a gentleman bold*
> *Who was so very brave*
> *He went to lengths untold,*

And on the brink of the grave
Death had on him no hold.
By the world he set small store—
He frightened it to the core—
Yet somehow, by Fate's plan,
Though he'd lived a crazy man,
When he died he was sane once more.[12]

As for that most wise chronicler, Cid Hamete, he has left us the following address to his pen: [13]

"Here shalt thou remain, hung upon this rack by this brass wire. I know not if thou beest well cut or not, O pen of mine, but here thou shalt live for long ages to come, unless some presumptuous and scoundrelly historians should take thee down to profane thee. But ere they do this thou may'st warn them and say to them as best thou canst:

Hands off, o'erweening ones!
Let it by none attempted be;
For this emprise, my lord the King,
Hath been reserved for me.[14]

"For me alone Don Quixote was born and I for him; it was for him to act, for me to write, and we two are one in spite of that Tordesillesque [15] pretender who had, and may have, the audacity to write with a coarse and ill-trimmed ostrich quill of the deeds of my valiant knight. This is no burden for his shoulders, no subject for his congealed talent; and if perchance thou shouldst come to know him, advise him that he should let Don Quixote's tired and moldering bones rest in their sepulcher and not try to bear him off, contrary to all the laws of death, to Old Castile [16] by raising him from that grave where he really and truly lies stretched out, being quite unable now to sally forth once again on a third expedition. For the two sallies that he did make to the delight and approval of all who heard of them, in foreign countries as well as our own, are sufficient to cast ridicule upon all the ridings forth of knights-errant in times past.

"Doing this, thou shalt fulfill thine obligations as a Christian by giving good counsel to one who wished thee ill, and I shall be the first one to enjoy the fruit of his own writings as fully as he desired, since I have had no other purpose than to arouse the abhorrence of mankind toward those false and nonsensical stories to be met with in the books of chivalry, which, thanks to this tale of the genuine Don Quixote, are already tottering and without a doubt are doomed to fall.[17] *Vale.*"

NOTES

Part Two

APPROBATIONS

1. Pausanias alludes to a number of statues of Dionysus that he saw in the course of his travels and also refers to various folk festivals in honor of Bacchus. Schevill states that he has not encountered the work by Bosio mentioned here.

2. In referring to Cicero's *De Legibus*, the writer possibly has in mind Book I, Chapter 8: "*Opus est et cura vacare et negotio.*" The Latin verse quoted is from a well-known work, the *Disticha de Moribus, nomine Catonis inscripta, cum Latina & Hispanica interpretatione* (Schevill cites the edition of London, 1543). The complete distich reads:

> *Interpone tuis interdum gaudia curis,*
> *Ut possis animo quemvis sufferre laborem.*

3. On the Cervantes influence abroad, see *Cervantes, A Tentative Bibliography of His Works*, by Ford and Lansing; *The Influence of Cervantes in France in the Seventeenth Century* by Esther J. Crooks (Baltimore: Johns Hopkins University Press, 1931); and *Cervantes in England* by James Fitzmaurice-Kelly (London, 1905). The reader with German at his command may be referred to *Cervantes und seine Werke nach deutschen Urtheilen* by Edmund Dorer (Leipzig, 1881). Benedetto Croce has dealt with Cervantes in Italy in *Saggi sulla letteratura del Seicento* (Bari, 1911 and 1924), pp. 125 ff.

4. For this incident, see *The Life and Misadventures of Miguel de Cervantes* by Mariano Tomás, pp. 239-40.

5. Schevill believes it possible that Cervantes may have met Márquez Torrez in the palace of the cardinal whom the latter served. Under date of March 26, 1616, the author of *Don Quixote* writes to the Cardinal Archbishop of Toledo, signing himself "your humble servant."

PROLOGUE

1. In the original Spanish editions the Prologue to Part II precedes the Dedication; and inasmuch as the same order is observed in the *Novels* (1613) and the *Comedies and Interludes* (1614), it seems likely that this was also the order followed in the manuscript. (Schevill)

2. The allusion here is to the spurious Second Part of the *Don Quixote*, published in the autumn of 1614 and attributed on the title-page to Alonso Fernández de Avellaneda of Tordesillas. This work was licensed and printed at Tarragona. For a lively account of the Avellaneda episode, the reader may be referred to Tomás's *The Life and Misadventures of Miguel de Cervantes*, pp. 226 ff.

3. A proverb.

4. Reference to the battle of Lepanto (1571) in which Cervantes was wounded.

5. One variety of envy is a mortal sin; the other consists in emulating the good example of another.

6. Cervantes is referring to Lope de Vega, who received holy orders in the spring of 1614, the title of "familiar of the Holy Office," or Inquisition, having probably been bestowed upon him in 1608, or after the First Part of the *Don Quixote* had appeared. The author's argument thus would not hold for Part I. Avellaneda had accused him of attacking Lope from motives of envy.

7. Avellaneda had described the *Exemplary Novels* as "*más satíricas que exemplares, si bien no poco ingeniosas.*"

8. The word in Spanish is "*podenco*" —"a small greyhound." Ormsby renders this by the British term "lurcher." Motteux wrongly has "spaniel."

9. Avellaneda: "Let him complain of my work because of the profits of which I deprive him."

10. No *entremés*, or interlude, bearing this title is known to have been printed, though it may have existed in manuscript form. (Schevill)

11. The *Veintecuatros*, the Twenty-four, was the title given to the municipal authorities, twenty-four in number, of Seville, Granada, and Cordova. (In Lisbon, the *Casa dos Vinte e quatro* was the Court of Aldermen.)

12. A verse satire on the reign of Henry IV.

DEDICATION

1. Don Pedro Fernández Ruiz de Castro y Osorio, seventh Count of Lemos, was known as the patron of Cervantes, Lope de Vega, and other celebrated writers of the period. In 1610 he was appointed Viceroy and Captain-General of Naples and did not return to Spain until July 1616, about three months after Cervantes' death. The interested reader may be referred to an article by Otis H. Green, "The Literary Court of the Conde de Lemos at Naples, 1610–1616," in the *Hispanic Review*, October 1933, pp. 290 ff. Despite the fact that he lived until 1619, the Duke of Béjar to whom Part I is dedicated is not mentioned again by Cervantes. Both patrons, as a matter of fact, disappointed the hopes of the poverty-ridden author of *Don Quixote*.

2. It is possible that the author's whimsy is based upon a historical incident reported to have occurred in the year 1612, when the Chinese monarch is said to have sent a letter to the Spanish crown, employing as messenger a returning barefoot friar. (Fernández Guerra, cited by Schevill.)

CHAPTER I

1. According to Clemencín, this popular phrase is derived from the game of chess.

2. An antique coin worth around ten pesetas; as previously pointed out, the dobla is not to be confused with the gold doblón, or doubloon, worth twenty pesetas.

3. This ballad has not been identified.

4. Ormsby: "*Andar estaciones* prop-

erly means to visit certain churches, for the purpose of offering up the prayers required to obtain indulgences."

5. The knights mentioned here are prominent in the Spanish romances of chivalry or in the pages of Ariosto and Boiardo. Turpin's *Cosmography* is a fictitious work. (On Turpin, see Part I, Chapter vi and note 8.) It is Ariosto who traces the descent of the Dukes of Ferrara from Ruggiero.

6. I follow the reading of the first edition, "*no quiero quedar en mi casa.*" Some editions have the reading "*me quiero,*" which has been followed by earlier translators. Ormsby: "And so I will stay where I am." Motteux: "I do design to stay where I am." The "*pues*" which introduces the following clause ("*pues no me saca el capellán*") probably should be "*puesto,*" which would make the meaning clear. (That is, "even though" in place of "since.")

7. The original has "*descubrir*"—"discover." I adopt Schevill's emendation, "*describir.*"

8. In I Samuel 17:4, we read: ". . . Goliath of Gath, whose height was six cubits and a span," that is, six and a half, not seven and a half, cubits, or about nine feet, nine inches.

9. An account of the Sicilian bones is given in Antonio de Torquemada's *Jardín de Flores Raras o Curiosas.* They are also mentioned in Haedo's *Topografía de Argel.*

10. Cervantes is referring to the Spanish version of Pulci's *Morgante Maggiore*, published at Valencia in 1533 under the title of *Libro del Esforzado Gigante Morgante.*

11. Reference to Medoro's devotion to his master, Dardinel. As he knelt beside Dardinel's body, he received a wound of which Angelica cured him.

12. The author here misquotes a couplet from Ariosto: *Orlando Furioso*, xxx, 16.

13. The Andalusian poet is Luis Barahona de Soto, the Castilian is Lope de Vega. The former was the author of a work known as *La Primera Parte de la Angélica*, copies of which will be found in the library of the Hispanic Society of New York and in the British Museum. (See Part I, Chapter vi and note 26.) Copies of Lope's *La Hermosura de An-*

gélica are preserved in the National Library at Madrid and in the British Museum. This work formed the first part of the poet's *Rimas*, printed at Madrid in 1602.

14. The text at this point is very confused and a number of emendations have been suggested. I have followed Pellicer's reading: *"fingidas, o [no] fingidas."* Schevill suggests that in the manuscript there may possibly have been some other verb in place of the second *"fingidas."*

15. As a matter of fact, the famous poet Góngora did write some satiric verses on this theme, and Quevedo touches on the subject in a heroic poem on Orlando's love and madness.

CHAPTER II

1. The word *"ciudad"* (city) is here employed in the sense of municipal government or council (*ayuntamiento* or *cabildo*). Schevill cites the *Dictionary of the Academy*.

2. *". . . insulas ni insulos."* For "island" Don Quixote always says *"insula,"* which is the form that occurs in the *Amadis;* but this highbrow term is too much for the housekeeper and the niece, who are used to saying *"isla."*

3. The *hidalgos* (originally, "sons of somebody") were gentlemen by birth, the *caballeros* by station in life.

4. "Don" today is a universal form of address where Spanish is spoken, but in Cervantes' time its use was restricted.

5. Literally, "two yokes" (*yugadas*), the yoke being the amount of land a team of oxen could plow in a day.

6. There was a proverb: *"Hidalgo honrado antes roto que remendado"*— "An honored gentleman goes ragged rather than patched."

7. Proverbial expression.

8. Proverbial expression.

9. In Spanish, *"berenjenas."*

CHAPTER III

1. Only one month is supposed to have elapsed since Don Quixote's return from his wanderings, yet the story of his adventures has already been written and printed and, as we are soon to be told, has been distributed to the extent of some twelve thousand copies. Cervantes, however, is never concerned with discrepancies of this sort, and on the present occasion explains the matter away by having resort to the magician's art.

2. Compare what is said on this subject in Part I, Chapter IX.

3. That is to say, the bachelor was dressed in the garb of the secular clergy. *"Por el hábito de San Pedro"* was a proverbial exclamation. In the Catholic Church the four minor orders of the clergy are *Ostiarius, Lector, Exorcista,* and *Acolytus.*

4. There was no edition of the *Don Quixote* at Antwerp until 1673 and none at Barcelona before 1617. Cervantes may have heard of the edition of Brussels of 1607. (Schevill)

5. Here and in the balance of the chapter Cervantes repeats the various criticisms that were made of Part I.

6. That is, "the day is not yet over," or "life is yet young."

7. The play in the original is on *"grama-"* and *"-tica."*

8. *"Mezclar berzas con capochos"* was a proverbial expression.

9. Compare Chapter LXXI following (note 19).

10. The Motteux version, as usual, substitutes "orthodox" for "Catholic."

11. The expression as it occurs in other Spanish authors is *"De pajo o de heno mi vientre lleno"*—"With straw or hay I fill my belly."

12. "El Tostado" was Alfonso [Tostado Ribera] de Madrigal, Bishop of Avila, who died in 1450. He is said to have left over sixty thousand written pages, but his works have now been completely forgotten.

13. See the *Epistles* of Pliny the Younger, Book III; he attributes the saying to his uncle, Pliny the Elder. This saying is again cited in Chapter LIX following.

14. "Worthy Homer sometimes nods." See Horace, *Ars Poetica*, 359: *"Indignor quandoque bonus dormitat Homerus."*

15. "The number of fools is infinite." See the Vulgate, Ecclesiasticus 1:15.

16. See Part I, Chapter XXIII and note 2.

17. *". . . me pondra en la espina de Santa Lucia"*—an expression meaning to feel the pangs of hunger.

18. Literally, "do penance with him" —"*hazer penitencia con él.*"

CHAPTER IV

1. See Ariosto's *Orlando Furioso,* XXVII, 84, and Boiardo's *Orlando Innamorato,* II, 40.

2. Literally, "raise it a good span higher than what it is."

3. The word employed here is "*ripio,*" a mixture of mortar and gravel for filling the spaces between large stones.

4. It was St. George who aided Pedro I of Aragon to defeat the Moors, at the battle of Alcoraz in 1096. The festival was in celebration of this event.

5. These oaths, "Body of me," "Body of the world," etc., are all milder forms of swearing by the Sacrament (body of Christ). Compare the English expression " 'od's body."

6. The historic battle cry: "*¡Santiago, y cierra España!*"

7. A proverb: "*Quando viene el bien, metelo en casa.*"

8. A proverb.

9. That is, "in the ditch."

10. Cervantes is, of course, being satirical here, but it is likely that he did not have any particular poets in mind.

11. The *décima* was, properly, a ten-line stanza; the *redondilla* was a four-line stanza, the last line rhyming with the first. Poetic acrostics were popular in Cervantes' day.

CHAPTER V

1. A proverb.

2. A proverb.

3. That is, it is better to take someone you know, with all his faults.

4. See Matthew 27:17, 21; Mark 15:11; Luke 23:18.

5. Molière has made use of this scene in Act III of *Le Bourgeois Gentilhomme.* See "Notes on the Spanish Sources of Molière," by Sylvanus Griswold Morley, in *Publications of the Modern Language Association of America,* XIX, 1904, pp. 270–89.

6. An inversion of the proverb "Laws go as kings like." See Part I, Chapter XLV and note 2.

7. This would seem to be the sense of the word "*pazpuerca,*" not "slut." (Schevill)

8. In the original the proverb rhymes: "*La muger honrada, la pierna quebrada y en casa; y la donzella honesta, el hazer algo es su fiesta.*"

9. The Infanta Uracca was the daughter of Ferdinand I of Castile. Upon being left out of her father's will, she threatened to enter upon a life of ill fame.

10. In Spanish, "*almohadas.*"

11. Literally, "I will dress him up as fine as a palm branch"—"*como un palmito.*"

CHAPTER VI

1. It was necessary to see that neither of the combatants had the sun in his eyes.

2. The *sambenito* was the garment worn by those who, having been tried by the Inquisition, had confessed and repented. It was a yellow linen garment painted over with devils and flames and was worn by the condemned as they went to the stake.

3. The word "*caballero*" has a double meaning: knight and gentleman. In this passage it apparently has the sense of gentleman.

4. The *hidalgos.*

5. These verses are from an elegy by the well-known poet Garcilaso de la Vega, written on the death of the Duke of Alva's brother, Don Bernardino de Toledo. (*Elegía primera,* verses 202–204.)

CHAPTER VII

1. A play on the double meaning of "*ventura*"—"good fortune" and a "venture" or "risk."

2. St. Apollonia, according to tradition, prayed to the Virgin for relief from the toothache and her prayer was granted.

3. "*No hay más que bachillear*"—the noun "*bachiller*" means either a bachelor of arts or a babbler or loquacious person.

4. "*Hablen cartas y callen barbas*"— that is, where there is a written agreement, words are unnecessary. Sancho here indulges, as he not infrequently does, in a string of proverbs.

5. "*Quien destaja no baraja*": prior to Ormsby, English translators had rendered this proverb as "He who cuts does not shuffle." This is due to the fact that both verbs have twofold meanings:

"*destajar*" signifying, at once, "to contract to do a job" and "to cut a deck of cards"; while "*barajar*" means "to shuffle the cards" and, in old Spanish, "to wrangle."

6. Compare our saying "A bird in the hand . . ."

7. In the Spanish this is a rhyming couplet: "*El consejo de la muger es poco,/Y el que no le toma es loco.*"

8. Literally, "you speak pearls today" —"*que hablays oy de perlas.*"

9. "*Tan presto se va el cordero como el carnero*"—that is to say, "goes to the butcher's."

10. These are all popular sayings.

11. More proverbs.

12. This is the reverse of the "bird in hand."

13. Ormsby observes that the truth of this saying "has always been recognized by politicians, diplomatists, and agitators."

14. The original text mentions only the niece as entering at this point—obviously an oversight on the part of author or printer.

15. Popular proverb.

CHAPTER VIII

1. The reference is to Garcilaso's Third Eclogue, verses 53 ff.

2. The Spanish text reads: ". . . *deve de andar mi honra a coche acá, cinchado, y, como dicen, al estricote, aquí y allí, barriendo las calles.*" The phrase "*a coche acá, cinchado*" has been extensively discussed by the commentators. "Literally, 'pig, hog there!' A cry still used by the Manchegan swineherds." (Fitzmaurice-Kelly, note in his edition of Ormsby's translation.) Schevill states that "*coche acá*" is the call used by the swineherd to drive away the hog, while "*cinchado*" seems to apply rather to the ass, but that the meaning is, simply, that Sancho's honor was being mishandled and dragged in the mud ("*maltratada, enlodada*").

3. Schevill suggests that the work alluded to here may have been Vicente Espinel's *Satira contra las Damas de Sevilla.*

4. This is the Pantheon, today known not as All Saints' but as the Tempio di Santa Maria della Rotonda.

5. There is a word play in the Spanish: "*cortesissimo Cortés.*"

6. Don Quixote appears to be speaking of the seven deadly sins.

7. "*Julio*" in Spanish means both "July" and "Julius."

8. According to Ormsby, the allusion is to San Diego de Alcalá, canonized in 1588, and San Salvador de Orta, or San Pedro de Alcántara, canonized in 1562.

9. "*Sucedió cosas que a cosas llegan.*"

CHAPTER IX

1. It is with these words that the old ballad of *Conde Claros* begins: "*Media noche era por filo.*" "*Por filo*" is, literally, "on the line."

2. Not "descended from a hill," as in Motteux, where the word "*monte*" is incorrectly rendered. The allusion is to the grove of oak trees mentioned at the end of the preceding chapter.

3. ". . . *a pierna tendida.*"

4. A proverb.

5. A proverb.

6. Beginning of a popular ballad of the Carolingian cycle which John Gibson Lockhart has translated. The quotation is given here in Lockhart's words. For his version, see the Bohn Popular Library edition of the Motteux *Don Quixote*, Vol. II, pp. 239–42.

7. For an English version of this ballad, "The Moor Calainos," see Lockhart, loc. cit., pp. 543–46.

CHAPTER X

1. These are two well-known proverbs. The first one, in Spanish, commonly reads: "*La verdad adelgaza y no quiebra*"—"The truth runs thin [or fine] but does not break." The Italians say: "*La verità può languire ma non perire*"—"Truth may languish but not perish." The second one occurs in two forms: "*La verdad siempre anda sobre la mentira como el aceite sobre el agua*" —"The truth always rises above a lie as oil above water"; and: "*La verdad como el olio siempre anda en somo*"—"Truth like oil always floats on the top." The Portuguese have the same saying: "*A verdade e o aceite andão de cima*"— "Truth and oil rise to the top." (See Ormsby's list of proverbs.)

The sentences contained in this opening paragraph are transferred by Hartzenbusch to the beginning of Chapter XVII following, as he believes they more properly belong there. Ormsby follows

Hartzenbusch in this. "It would be absurd," he says, "to call Don Quixote's simplicity in the matter of Sancho's mystification about the village girls, mad doings [*locuras*] that go beyond the maddest that can be conceived; while the lion adventure described in Chapter XVII is all through treated as his very maddest freak; one compared with which, as Sancho says, all the rest were 'cakes and fancy bread.'" However, it has seemed best to follow the first edition.

2. Three more proverbs. The one about the bacon and the pegs is misquoted by Sancho; it runs: "Many think there is bacon where there are no pegs"—"*Muchos piensan que hay tocinos donde no hay estacas*"—i.e., no pegs (in the smokehouse) on which to hang the bacon. Compare Part I, Chapter XXV (note 5), and Chapters LV (note 17), LXV (note 3), and LXXIII (note 10) following.

3. These lines are from a popular ballad. "*Con cartas y mensajeros*"—"With letters and messengers."

4. The expression "let the bolt fall" is from a rhyming couplet: "*Allá darás Rayo/En casa de Tamayo*"—"Fall there, O thunderbolt, on Tamayo's house"—the implication being, not on mine.

5. A proverb. The meaning, of course, is to look for the impossible.

6. Salamanca was full of bachelors of arts. The sense of this expression and of "trying to find Marica in Rávena" is to "look for a needle in a haystack."

7. "*No con quien naces,/Sino con quien paces.*" Compare our proverbs: "A man is known by the company he keeps" and "Birds of a feather flock together."

8. Ormsby: "i.e., the lists of bachelors qualified for degrees." Motteux: "As they do professor's chairs, that everybody may know who they belong to."

9. Ormsby: "Ordinary brocade had only a triple border." Motteux: "All cloth of gold above ten rows high." Jarvis: "All cloth of tissue above ten hands deep."

10. In Spanish, Sancho says "*cananeas*" for "*hacaneas*." I have adopted Ormsby's rendering.

11. These speeches of Sancho's may seem decidedly out of character, but this is something of which the author is by no means unaware. Cervantes in Part I was never too greatly concerned with the matter, and in Part II there can be no doubt that he definitely intends to portray a certain growth in character on the part of the squire as well as of the knight. In this connection, see Chapter XII following and note 4. It is conceivable that Sancho, who, however simple-minded he may appear at times, is not dull-witted, may have picked up from his master a good deal of the cant of chivalry and some of Don Quixote's flowery language.

12. This is addressed, not to the ass which the girl rides, but to Sancho. (Shelton and Jarvis take it as applied to the ass.) The expression "*Más jo, que te estrego, burra de mi suegro*" (note the rhyme) is a popular one.

13. An obscure oath.

14. The first edition reads "*Mucho sabeys, mucho podeys y mucho más hazeys*"—"Great is your wisdom, great is your power, and greater yet your deeds." But in place of "*mucho más hazeys*," modern editions read "*mucho mal hazeys*"—"great the harm you do," a reading which has been followed here.

15. ". . . *en agallas alcornoqueñas*.' Ormsby: "into oak galls." Motteux: "into gall nuts." Jarvis: "into cork galls."

16. The *jineta* was a saddle with high pommel and cantle and short stirrups. The expression, to ride "*a la jineta*" has previously occurred.

CHAPTER XI

1. ". . . *con voz no muy desmayada.*" Ormsby wrongly has: "in a weak and faint voice." Motteux is better: "with more spirit than one would have expected."

2. In the original, this is a question: "*quien la vido y la vee aora, ¿qual es el coraçon que no llora?*" Another version is: "*quien me vido y me ve aoras,*" etc. —"who saw me once . . ."

3. In other words, it did not resemble the type of cart or wagon that was common in central and southern Spain.

4. A Toledo dramatist and theatrical manager.

5. The interested reader may be referred to an article by Professor Crawford, "The Devil As a Dramatic Figure

in the Spanish Religious Drama before Lope de Vega," in the *Romanic Review*, September–October 1910, pp. 302 ff., 374 ff. See also Florence Whyte, *The Dance of Death in Spain and Catalonia* (Baltimore: Johns Hopkins University Press, 1931), particularly p. 145. It is thought that this passage may have been inspired by one in the *Amadis of Gaul*, II, XII.

6. ". . . *compañias reales y de titulo*." Motteux mistranslates: "especially if they be of the king's players, or some of the nobles."

7. "*Sopa de arroyo*"—slang for pebbles.

CHAPTER XII

1. Compare our proverb: "A bird in the hand is worth two in the bush." This *refrán* has previously occurred in Part I, Chapter XXXI (note 6); compare Chapters XXXI and LXXI (note 24) following.

2. Literally, "in the comedy and intercourse of this world."

3. It may be of interest to compare Omar Khayyám:

> Impotent pieces of the game he plays
> Upon this checker-board of nights and days.
> Hither and thither moves, and checks and slays,
> And one by one back in the closet lays.

4. See Chapter X preceding, note 11. We have here a clear awareness on Cervantes' part of the growth and deepening of Sancho's character. The squire like his master is a larger person than the one we encounter in Part I.

5. The friendship of Nisus and Euryalus is celebrated in Vergil's *Aeneid*. Pylades, friend and companion of Orestes, is mentioned by Pindar, Sophocles, and other Greek writers.

6. These lines are from a popular ballad included by Pérez de Hita in the *Civil Wars of Granada* (*Guerras Civiles de Granada*).

7. "*De amigo a amigo la chinche. . . .*" The phrase "to have a bug in the eye" —"*tener chinche en el ojo*"—means to keep a watchful eye out; here, the sense is that one friend is wary of the other.

8. These are folklore references on Cervantes' part.

9. We have already had this proverbial expression in Chapters IV (note 7) and XXX of Part I.

10. See Matthew 12:34, and Luke 6:45.

11. I follow the emendation of a number of editors who substitute "*atentos*" for "*atónitos*," which occurs in the first edition. It seems obvious from the context that Don Quixote and Sancho were listening attentively rather than "with astonishment."

12. Ormsby has an interesting note: "The pieces of verse introduced in the Second Part are more or less burlesques, and sometimes, as here and in Chapter XVIII, imitations of the affected poetry of the day. The verses in the First Part (except, of course, the commendatory verses, and those at the end of the last chapter) are serious efforts, and evidently regarded by Cervantes with some complacency. The difference is significant."

13. The Tartessians were the inhabitants of the old region known as Tartéside. Tartessus was an ancient maritime town under the Romans.

14. Lockhart draws attention to a similar scene in the *Amadis of Gaul*, II, LXVI.

15. Proverbial expression that has occurred before.

CHAPTER XIII

1. In the title to Chapter XII, Cervantes refers to Don Quixote's new acquaintance as the Knight of the Mirrors, but the significance of this appellation does not become clear until Chapter XIV. Meanwhile, the newcomer is referred to as the Knight of the Wood.

2. Genesis 3:19.

3. A proverb.

4. As has been seen, the fanega is equivalent to about 1.6 bushel.

5. Compare Part I, Chapter XX (note 3), and Chapter XXXVI (note 11) following.

6. A proverb.

7. There is an untranslatable play here on the adjective "*crudo*," which means both "raw" and "cruel."

8. Sancho means to say that his troubles never come singly. A proverbial expression.

9. Here again the author is deepening the motivation of Sancho's character.

10. The sense is "paltry" (Ormsby's translation), not "fresh-water squires,"

as in Motteux. The expression "*de agua y lana*" is the opposite of the one applied to nobles and courtiers: "*de gran estofa*" —"of high quality."

11. That is, large, or close together, or both.

12. Ormsby: "Anyone who has ever watched a Spanish peasant with a *bota* [flask] knows how graphic this is."

13. Ciudad Real was the chief city of La Mancha and center of a winegrowing district, the best-known vintage being Valdepeñas, to which Cervantes in his plays and novels applies the epithet "*El Católico*"—which will explain Sancho's exclamation.

14. This is a popular tale which may have been translated by the Spaniards from some other language. There are traces of it in the southeastern United States. (Schevill) See *Modern Language Notes*, June 1905, p. 183. Cervantes has used the same story in a slightly different form in one of his interludes, *The Election of the Judges of Deganzo* (*Elección de los Alcaldes de Deganzo*).

CHAPTER XIV

1. The "woman" is the enormous statue (of Faith according to some, of Victory according to others) on top of the old Moorish belfry of the Cathedral of Seville.

2. Allusion to certain stone animal figures to be found at Guisando, Avila, and elsewhere. They are said to resemble hippopotamuses rather than bulls. The "Bulls" of Guisando are supposed to mark the site of one of Caesar's victories over the younger Pompey.

3. In the Sierra de Cabra, south of Cordova. It is thought that this may be the shaft of an ancient mine.

4. These lines, incorrectly quoted, are from Alonso de Ercilla's famous poem, the *Araucana* (1569–89), celebrating the struggle of the Spaniards with the indomitable Araucanian Indians of Chile (1, 2).

5. A proverb.

6. Reference to the fine imposed in some confraternities, the wax being for use in churches.

7. According to the commentator Covarrubias, this proverbial expression is derived from rabbit-hunting with the crossbow, the sense being, "let each

hunter look out for his own bolts."

8. This proverb occurs several times. See Part II, XLIII (note 17) and LXVII (note 17).

9. The Italians have the proverb: "*Gatto rinchiuso doventa leone.*"

10. "*A esso vos respondemos*" is the form employed by a monarch in response to a petition.

11. The knobs or buttons to keep the spurs from going in too far.

12. A proverb.

13. The text of the first edition is somewhat jumbled here. At least one editor would amend to read: ". . . without any doubt the bachelor Sansón Carrasco . . . is rash and ill advised." I have followed Hartzenbusch and Rodríguez Marín, whose reading is adopted by Schevill.

CHAPTER XV

1. This is a play on the proverb "*Uno piensa el bayo, otro quien le ensilla*"— "The bay is of one mind, he who saddles him of another."

2. Proverbial expression.

CHAPTER XVI

1. Compare Chapter x preceding, where Don Quixote says: "The malign enchanter who doth persecute me hath placed clouds and cataracts upon my eyes. . . ." As Schevill points out, Cervantes evidently forgot here what he had previously written, as the two descriptions of Dulcinea do not correspond.

2. The greatcoat is the *gabán*, worn for hunting and traveling, which had a hood to cover the head. The cap is the *montera* of Central Spain, a headpiece with flaps.

3. See Chapter x preceding and note 16.

4. The first edition has "*caballo*"— "horse" which is obviously out of place in this description of Don Quixote's person. I have accordingly followed the majority of editors, who read "*cuello*"— "neck." Ormsby reads "*cabello*"—"hair" —which also seems inappropriate. Motteux: "the lankness of his horse"; Jarvis: "his lank horse."

5. These lines have previously been quoted, Part I, Chapter XLIX.

6. ". . . *treynta mil vezes de millares.*" Motteux has "thirty thousand

millions more"! Compare Chapter III preceding, where it is stated that "more than twelve thousand copies" were in existence.

7. ". . . *mi atenuada flaqueza*." Motteux: "my exhausted body."

8. For *"perdigón"*—"partridge"—Clemencín reads *"perdiguero"*—"pointer." But partridges were used as decoys in Andalusia.

9. Ormsby: "first saint in the saddle"; Motteux and Jarvis: "first saint on horseback." It seems desirable to indicate the kind of saddle as the Spanish does. A saint, for that matter, would have been more likely to ride a donkey than a horse.

10. ". . . *los modernos romancistas*" —i.e., moderns who write in Spanish. Motteux, who is even more inaccurate than usual in this chapter, has "modern romancers."

11. Reference to the *justas literarias*, which still lingered on in Cervantes' time.

12. The saying was a popular one in the Renaissance era. Schevill cites Caelius Rhodiganus (1450-1525): *"Vulgo certe iactatur nasci poetam, oratorem fieri"*—"It is commonly said that the poet is born, the orator made."

13. Ovid's beautiful line: *"Est deus in nobis: agitante calescimus illo"*— "There is a god in us, he stirs and we grow warm." (*Fasti*, VI, 5; compare the third book of the *De Arte Amandi*.)

14. Ovid was exiled to Pontus. The original reads: *"islas de Ponto"*—"isles of Pontus"; the correction of "coast" or "shores" for "isles" was made by Clemencín and Hartzenbusch.

15. The laurel tree.

CHAPTER XVII

1. With regard to the beginning of this chapter, see Chapter X preceding and note 1.

2. *"Hombre apercebido, medio combatido"*—literally, "A man who is prepared has his battle half fought." The Italian form of the proverb is nearer to the English: *"Chi è avvisato è armato."*

3. It has been remarked that lions coming from Oran would have been landed at Cartagena, and so would not have been met by Don Quixote and his party on the road to Saragossa.

4. On this knight, see Part I, Chapter XLIX, note 2.

5. The *"perrillo,"* or "little dog," was the trademark of Julian del Rei, famous armorer of Toledo and Saragossa.

6. ". . . *que sepan de tu boca esta hazaña*." Motteux has: "that they may have an account of this exploit from my own mouth," which is not only a mistranslation but does not make sense.

7. *"Antecogidos del hidalgo*." Motteux: "at the head of them"; Jarvis: "at their head."

8. The knights in the romances of chivalry frequently changed their names. Knight of the Lions was one of the titles of Amadis of Gaul.

9. Variation of the proverb *"Tanto se pierde por carta de más como por carta de menos"*—"As much is lost by a card too many as a card too few." Compare Chapters XXXIII (note 23), XXXVII (note 6), and LXXI (note 9) following.

CHAPTER XVIII

1. These are the opening lines of Garcilaso de la Vega's Tenth Sonnet.

2. *"Borceguíes"*—half-boots or buskins.

3. Shelton's rendering is: "his shoes close on each side"; he reads *"encerrados"*—"closed"—in place of *"enceradaos"*—"waxed"—a reading which Lockhart prefers.

4. The shoulder strap or baldric was easier than a belt around the waist for kidney sufferers.

5. There is a word play here which unfortunately cannot be brought over in translation: *"sus negros requesones que tan blanco pusieron a su amo"*— literally, "his *black* curds which made his master so *white*," the word *"negro"* (black) having here the sense of unlucky, accursed, damnable.

6. Literally, "and take the pulse of what he knows" (i.e., of his wit).

7. Cervantes won a first prize in such a tournament at Saragossa in 1595.

8. The allusion is to a famous and legendary fifteenth-century swimmer of Catania in Sicily, known as Pescecola, who according to the folk tale was finally drowned in the pool of Charybdis when he was tempted by the king to dive twice on the same day on the chance of bringing up a golden cup. He was also known as "Nicolao the Fish."

A work entitled *Account of How Nico-lao the Fish Reappeared in the Sea*, etc., was published at Barcelona in 1608.

9. See Horace's *Satires*, I, iii, 2-3.

> *Nunquam inducant animum can-tare rogati,*
> *Injussi nunquam desistant.*

"When asked, they never can bring themselves to sing; unasked, they never can desist."

10. The making of such glosses was a popular diversion with Spanish poets in the sixteenth and seventeenth centuries. Ticknor traces the custom to the poets of Provence, but Lope de Vega asserts that this was a Spanish invention.

11. The poet in question was Liñan de Riaza, who died in 1607. He was the author of a satirical sonnet containing the verse: "*laureado por Chipre y por Gaeta*." (Schevill)

12. This sonnet is seen as a caricature of the Góngora school.

13. Play on "*poetas consumidos*" and "*poeta consumado*." Fitzmaurice-Kelly (notes to the Ormsby translation) observes that "the joke on '*consumidos*' and '*consumado*' is not transferable," and this is doubtless true. The sense of "*consumidos*" is probably "lean" or "emaciated." Ormsby thinks the word may refer to the "*genus irritabile vatum*," and he renders it as "irritable," although a later edition has "lean poets." Fitzmaurice-Kelly: "It may be that Cervantes uses the . . . word in its second-ary sense of 'fretful.'"

14. See Chapter XXII following. The Cave of Montesinos is about six miles from the hamlet of Ruidera, which is some fifteen miles southeast of Argama-silla, amid the lakes where the waters of the Guadiana rise to flow down into the plains of La Mancha.

15. Here, as previously in this chap-ter, Cervantes in the original changes from the third person to the second (di-rect address) in the middle of a sen-tence.

16. See Vergil's *Aeneid*, VI, 853: "*par-cere subjectis et debellare superbos.*"

17. The word "castle" employed in the title of this chapter appears to hold out a promise, which is not fulfilled, of an adventure similar to those that Don Quixote met with in Part I. What we have, instead, is an episode in keeping with the more serious tone of Part II.

Don Diego de Miranda is essentially the kindly, well-meaning burgher and sub-stantial citizen brought into contact with Don Quixote the dreamer.

CHAPTER XIX

1. "*Un poco de grana blanca.*" Mot-teux mistranslates: "what seemed to be a little white grain"!

2. "*Medias de cordellate*"—grogram stockings.

3. The *zapateadores* do a kind of clog dance (the *zapateado*), in the course of which the dancer strikes the soles of his shoes with the palms of his hands. The *zapateado* (*sapateado*) is also a Portuguese dance and occurs even in the *sertões* or northeastern backlands of Brazil; it is mentioned by Euclides da Cunha.

4. A rhyming proverb: "*Cada oveja con su pareja.*" The Portuguese also have it: "*Cada ovelha com sua parelha.*"

5. In connection with this defense of the right of parents to arrange marriages for their children, compare Rabelais, Book III, Chapter XLVIII (see *The Port-able Rabelais*, pp. 507 ff.).

6. Another "rain" of proverbs. The expression, "God will do better than that"—"*Dios lo hará mejor,*" was com-monly used in predicting misfortune for oneself or for another. (Rodríguez Marín)

7. Sayago was a district near the Portuguese frontier. The Castilian of Toledo was the standard, as Tuscan was the model for Italians.

8. The old Moorish market place of Toledo.

9. The Cathedral cloisters were a fa-vorite lounging place as a refuge from the heat.

10. Majadahonda is a small village about six miles northwest of Madrid. (Cervantes has "Mahalahonda," prob-ably a printer's error.)

11. Rodríguez Marín remarks that this phrase, "*por mis pecados,*" like "*con perdón*" and "*si no lo han por enojo,*" was greatly abused, being employed in and out of season.

12. Parenthesis supplied.

13. Motteux mistranslates: "'As for turning my back,' said the artist, 'I won't be obliged to it.'"

14. "*Más espesas que hígado*": the ex-pression is not given in the *Dictionary*

of the Academy. According to Rodríguez Marín, it is a popular one, and Cejador states: *"Parece hígado, está como un hígado,* is said of thick chocolate." Schevill: "May this phrase possibly have its origin in the fact that pigs and ducks, after they have stuffed themselves with figs, have a liver that is very much enlarged and thick?" (Translated from the Spanish note.) Ormsby: "thicker than hops or hail." Motteux: "laid on like any lion."

15. The element of humorous exaggeration is not frequent in Cervantes as it is in a Renaissance writer like Rabelais, for example, but it sometimes does occur, as here. The same may be said of the pretense of exactness, likewise introduced occasionally with humorous intent.

16. *"Diestros"*—fencing experts.

17. To "fall off one's donkey"—*"caer de su burro,"* is to admit that one has been in the wrong.

18. That is, of course, all except Don Quixote and Sancho. Cervantes is never meticulous about such details.

19. The place in question is referred to sometimes as a "village"—*"aldea"* or *"lugar"*—sometimes as a "town"—*"pueblo."*

20. The one who had not gone after the sword.

CHAPTER XX

1. Rodríguez Marín raises the question as to whether the entire episode of Camacho's wedding may not be a reminiscence of an event that actually occurred at which Cervantes had been present or of which he had heard an account. The records show that there was a Don Pedro Camacho de Villavicencio who was known as "El Rico," or "the Rich," and who on August 15, 1507, drew up a will that was remarkable for the amount of property of which it disposed. (See Rodríguez Marín's edition of *Don Quixote,* Vol. VI, p. 10.)

2. The first edition has *"duerme,"* an imperative form, followed by most translators, but I have adopted Schevill's reading of *"duermes"* (indicative) as more in consonance with the text.

3. The Spanish word is *"juncos,"* which ordinarily means "rushes," but which is here equivalent to *"junquillos."* (See Rodríguez Marín.)

4. A coin worth four copper maravedis, corresponding roughly to the British farthing.

5. This expression has occurred twice before: Chapter III preceding and Part I, Chapter xxx.

6. Hero of one of the Carolingian ballads.

7. There was a popular saying: "Singing and dancing do not make up a trousseau"—*"Cantar y bailar no componen ajuar."*

8. The wine here is measured by weight, the arroba amounting to 25.4 pounds. In liquid measure, the quantity represented is between six and seven gallons.

9. The Spanish word is *"Interés,"* which Ormsby renders as "Interest," Motteux as "Wealth." "Worldly Wealth" seems a little nearer to the meaning.

10. This was the usual apparel of savages on the stage in Cervantes' time.

11. In a cockfight the winner was called *"El Rey,"* or "the Cock."

12. *"A la barba de las habilidades de Basilio!"* There has been considerable discussion as to the meaning of the phrase *"a la barba,"* but it would seem to apply to one who was "stuck" with paying for others. According to Rodríguez Marín, the expression is equivalent to *"Pierda y pague Basilio . . ."* Ormsby: "A fig for the accomplishments of Basilio!" Motteux: ". . . a fig for his abilities, say I." The French translator, Cardaillac, has: ". . . *nargue des talents de Basile!"* Tieck: *"Schade was um Basilios Geschicklichkeiten!"* (See Schevill.)

13. A proverb.

14. A proverb.

15. Literally, "people would rather take the pulse of having than of knowing." There is a Spanish popular song:

> *Más vale saber que haber*
> *Dice la común sentencia;*
> *Que el sabio puede ser rico,*
> *Y el rico no compra ciencia.*

"Knowing is worth more than having, the common saying goes; for the wise man may be rich but the rich man cannot purchase wisdom." (Rodríguez Marín) Here, as frequently, Sancho reverses the proverb.

16. The allusion, of course, is to

Horace's famous and beautiful lines (*Odes*, I, IV, 13–14).

> Pallida mors aequo pulsat pede
> pauperum tabernas
> regumque turres.

Cervantes has quoted these lines in the Prologue to Part I.

17. I have followed the majority of editors since 1738, who supply a verb here—"*tuvieras*."

CHAPTER XXI

1. The "*patena*" is a large medal, somewhat like a locket, that is worn by country women.

2. Ormsby: "The richest ordinary velvet being three-pile." With regard to the "palm-green" cloth that Quiteria wears, here as in the preceding chapter ("dresses of palm-leaf green"), in my rendering of "*palmilla*" I have followed Dr. Francisco del Rosal whose unpublished *Vocabulario* is cited by Rodríguez Marín and who states that the term was originally applied to cloth "*de color verde claro, que es el de la hoja de la palma.*" Covarrubias asserts that the *palmilla* was a pigeon-blue cloth manufactured especially at Cuenca (*palmilla* being equivalent to *palomilla*, from *paloma*, a pigeon or dove), and he notes that there were also green varieties (*palmillas verdes*) of this same cloth and that it is possible that a palm was originally woven into the border of it.

3. "*. . . que puede passar por los bancos de Flandes.*" This expression has occasioned a great deal of discussion. It has commonly been taken as referring to the shoals off the Flemish coast, a peril that was dreaded by Spanish sailors. Others have seen an allusion to the monetary banks of exchange of the Low Countries (Lope de Vega employs it in this sense). Still others believe the reference is to the *bancos* upon which beds, tables, etc., in the home were placed. See the extended notes by Rodríguez Marín and Schevill. The latter seems to sum the matter up when he states: ". . . it appears that Sancho meant to say of Quiteria that, by reason of her youth and beauty, her wealth, and other endowments (of an up-and-coming lass) the young lady was in a position to brave the perils of matrimony and the hazardous life of a married woman." (Translated from the Spanish note.)

4. But Don Quixote has never seen Dulcinea.

5. "*Tenia . . . el alma en los dientes*" —literally, "had his soul in his teeth."

6. A play on the expression "soul in his teeth" (see preceding note). Literally, "had his soul on his tongue rather than in his teeth."

7. Similar episodes occur in other works of the time.

8. Matthew 19:6; Mark 10:9.

9. Motteux slurs this passage: ". . . Basil, whose virtues, in spite of his poverty, had secured him many friends . . ."

10. This may sound like a modernism, but it is absolutely literal: "*hombre de valor y de pelo en pecho.*"

CHAPTER XXII

1. Proverbs 12:4: "A virtuous woman is a crown to her husband: but she that maketh him ashamed is a rottenness in his bones." Compare Proverbs 31:10: "Who can find a virtuous woman? for her price is far above rubies."

2. This statement may be noted in view of Don Quixote's devotion to Dulcinea. Rodríguez Marín is inclined to think it the incoherence of a madman, but it is just as likely that it is to be explained by Cervantes' usual carelessness in such matters.

3. "*A qué quieres, boca.*"

4. The obviously missing adverb has been supplied.

5. A proverb.

6. For the Giralda of Seville, see Chapter XIV preceding and note 1. The Angel of the Magdalena was a weathervane on the Church of the Magdalena at Salamanca. The Vecinguerra Conduit was the sewer draining the Potro quarter of Cordova (the quarter of the Horse Fountain; see Part I, Chapter III and note 1). On the Bulls of Guisando, see Chapter XIV preceding and note 2. With the exception of Sierra Morena, the other names are those of fountains in Madrid.

7. Virgilius Polydorus (Virgilio Polidoro) was an Italian historian, born at Urbino around 1470. He spent more than fifty years of his life in England, where he rose to a high position in the ecclesiastical hierarchy. His most im-

portant work is one on English history, *Anglicae Historiae Libri XXVI*, published at Basel in 1534 (a copy exists in the British Museum). Among his other works was one entitled *De Inventoribus Rerum (On the Inventors of Things)*. He died at Urbino in 1550.

8. Reference to syphilis and unctions of mercury.

9. In the sense of acrobat.

10. An old ballad line. Compare Cervantes' poetic address to his pen at the end of the *Don Quixote;* see also the end of Chapter XXIX (note 9), Chapter XXXIX (note 2), and the beginning of Chapter XLI following.

11. A proverb.

12. Cervantes' word here is *"sima,"* a deep cavern, an abyss, or a chasm. The possibility that this may have been an ancient mine shaft has already been noted.

13. What Sancho means is the Virgin of the Rock of France (Peña de Francia). The allusion is to a site between Salamanca and Ciudad Rodrigo where an image of the Virgin was discovered in the fifteenth century; a Dominican monastery was later erected on the spot.

14. The Trinity of Gaeta refers to a chapel dedicated to the Holy Trinity on the promontory of Gaeta, to the north of Naples.

15. Ormsby's rendering of *"valentón del mundo"* seems the best to be had.

16. Compare Psalms 102:11, 103:15, 109:23, 144:4; and Ecclesiastes 6:12. As Calderón was to put it: *"La vida es sueño -y sueño de sueño"*—"Life is a dream and a dream of a dream."

17. These are characters from the literature of chivalry. Montesinos is the protagonist of the "Ballads of Montesinos." Durandarte was his cousin and the brother of Count Dirlos (see Chapter XX preceding and note 6). Belerma was Durandarte's lady, and Guadiana was his squire, transformed by Merlin into the river of that name. The "daughters of Ruidera" are the Lakes of Ruidera (see Chapter XVIII preceding and note 14).

CHAPTER XXIII

1. Scholars have not been able to identify this personage.

2. Merlin was Welsh, though the Bretons tried to claim him. Malory in his *Morte d'Arthur* calls him "a devil's son." Compare the verses in Chapter XXXV following.

3. Covarrubias (*Tesoro de la Lengua Castellana*, under the word *"Corazón"*) makes this observation: "Timorous animals have a proportionately larger heart than others, animals such as the hare, the deer, the mouse, and similar ones mentioned by Aristotle, *lib.* 3, *De Partibus Animalium;* and so, when we say by way of praise that a man or animal has a great heart [great courage], we do not mean that his heart is great in size but in ardor . . ." (Cited by Schevill.)

4. According to Clemencín, Cervantes, copying from memory, has here mingled and altered two old ballads, one of which begins:

O Belerma! O Belerma!
Por mi mal fuiste engendrada.

"O Belerma! O Belerma! for my woe thou wert begotten." For the legend of the heart, compare the French *Roman du Châtelain de Couci* and see the account given by Gaston Paris, *Histoire Littéraire de la France* (Paris, 1890), Vol. 28, pp. 252 ff. A reminiscence of Orlando's sword, Durandal, or Durendal, has been seen in the name Durandarte. Durandarte is also said to have been the name of the sword carried by Bramante, who was slain by Charlemagne at Toledo.

5. According to this passage, the number of the lakes is ten. In Chapter XVIII preceding, Cervantes speaks of "the seven lakes that are commonly known as the Lakes of Ruidera." Clemencín says there are fifteen; other authorities say eleven.

6. The two lakes ("nieces") are in the upper portion of the valley in question where the province of Murcia and the former province of New Castile met. They were within the domain of the Order of St. John.

7. The Guadiana flows underground for a part of its course. See Part I, Chapter XVIII and note 11.

8. A proverb.

9. A proverbial saying among card players.

10. A proverb.

11. For a slightly different version of

this proverb, see Chapter x preceding and note 7.

12. In the original there is a play here on "*vino*"—"wine"—and "*vino*"—"he came." Allusion to a ballad some lines of which have been given in Part I, Chapter XIII. For Quintañona, see Chapter XIII and note 1.

13. Reference to the Fuggers of Bavaria. Founded by Johannes Fugger in the fourteenth century, the family in the course of three hundred years came to own some sixty estates. In the Renaissance era the Fuggers of Augsburg were celebrated bankers and financiers. The reader may be referred to R. Ehrenberg's *Capital and Finance in the Age of the Renaissance: A Study of the Fuggers* (London, 1928). Motteux: "if I had all the treasures which Croesus possessed."

14. See Part I, Chapter v and note 1.

15. The "seven parts of the world" was a familiar concept of the age. The Infante Pedro was the second son of John I of Portugal and brother of Prince Henry the Navigator. He traveled widely in Europe and the East between 1416 and 1428. An account of his voyages was published at Lisbon in 1554 and was popular in Spain.

CHAPTER XXIV

1. See Catherine Perry Hargrave, *A History of Playing Cards and a Bibliography of Cards* (Boston: Houghton Mifflin, 1930).

2. A tribute in passing to Cervantes' patron, the Count of Lemos.

3. The text of the first edition is confused here, although what the author wrote, or meant to write, is clear enough (Schevill thinks something may have been dropped from the manuscript by the printer). After stating that "they all three made straight for the hostelry, where they arrived a little before nightfall," the text continues: "The cousin proposed to Don Quixote that they go up to it [*que llegassen a ella*] and have a drink, and no sooner did Sancho Panza hear this than he turned his gray's head toward the hermitage [*a la hermita*]." Editors have made the obvious transposition of the pronoun "*ella*" and "*la hermita*," and Rodríguez Marín helpfully suggests that the clause "where they arrived a little before nightfall" should be regarded as parenthetical. In

addition, for purposes of translation, I have supplied "on the way" and have rendered "*dixo*" as a pluperfect—"had proposed."

4. "*Una sotahermitaño*" (in modern Spanish one would say *sotaermitaña*). Rodríguez Marín: "In this sub-hermit one may behold the brazen countenance of the anchorite's Magdalen."

5. "Little of the best"—"*de lo caro*"; literally, of the dearest. "Cheap water" —"*agua barata*." There were two classes of taverns in Cervantes' time: those that sold *de lo barato* and the ones that dispensed *de lo caro*. The former sold only *vino ordinario;* the latter, few in number (there are said to have been not more than eight at the beginning of the seventeenth century), could serve both varieties. (Rodríguez Marín)

6. A fashion said to have been introduced by the Duke of Lerma, who suffered from bunions. (Ormsby)

7. The *seguidilla* was a seven-line stanza with a special rhythm.

8. The word means "niggardliness." In the original: "*espilorceria*."

9. See Don Quixote's speech on this subject, Part I, Chapter XXXVIII.

10. It is not known where Cervantes got this, but it was not from Terence.

11. The original has "*sobrino*"—"nephew," an obvious slip on Cervantes' part.

CHAPTER XXV

1. Proverbial expression denoting impatience. Motteux: "Don Quixote was on thorns to know . . ."

2. "*Regidor*"—an officer in charge of finances.

3. "*Dadme albricias.*" The word "*albricias*" is still in use in this sense.

4. ". . . *los dexos, muchos y apresurados.*" Ormsby: "your finishing notes come thick and fast."

5. "*En bueno mano está,*" an expression used when urged to have a drink. Literally, "It [the glass] is in a good hand."

6. A proverb.

7. The reader interested in the subject may be referred to *A Book of Marionettes,* by Helen H. Joseph (New York: Viking Press, 1929). For the puppet theater in Cervantes' time, the student should consult Armando Cotarelo

y Vallador, *El teatro de Cervantes* (Madrid, 1915), pp. 574 ff.

8. Cervantes means the Monte Aragon region, in the eastern part of La Mancha, near the Cuenca Mountains, later part of the province of Cuenca.

9. Gayfer, King of Bordeaux, was one of Charlemagne's chieftains. Melisendra (properly, Melisenda) was Charlemagne's daughter who was held captive by the Moors. The story is told in the Spanish *cancioneros*, or ballad collections, from which Cervantes takes it.

10. "Gallant man" ("*hombre galante*") is the Italian "*galantuomo*." "Good companion" is "*buon compagno*," which Cervantes carries over as "*bon compaño*." The latter expression is used again in Chapter LIV following. Such foreign phrases are not as out of place as they might seem in the mouth of a provincial innkeeper, since he well may have picked them up as a soldier in the Italian wars.

11. In the original Don Quixote says this in transliterated Italian: "*qué pexe pillamo* (*che pesce pigliamo*)."

12. "*¡Voto a rus!*" The meaning of this obviously mild oath or exclamation remains a mystery to the commentators.

13. "*Señor Monissimo*."

14. Giantess in the *Amadís of Gaul*.

15. The original reads "*porque lo devo*"—literally, "because I owe it" [to him]; and Rodríguez Marín suggests this may have a meaning which becomes clear when the identity of the puppet master is later disclosed; see Chapter XXVII following.

16. There is a word play here which is impossible to carry over. Sancho mistakes Don Quixote's "*pacto*" for "*patio*" and "*espreso*" for "*espeso*," which means sometimes "thick" and sometimes "dirty" or "slovenly."

17. Reference to judicial, or divinatory, astrology. The "figures" are horoscopes.

18. John 10:38: ". . . though ye believe not me, believe the works."

CHAPTER XXVI

1. This verse is from Gregorio Hernández de Velasco's Spanish translation of Vergil's *Aeneid*, published in 1555. See the *Aeneid*, II, 1: "*Conticuere omnes, intentique ora tenebant*." On the use made by Cervantes of the *Aeneid*, see Schevill's "Studies in Cervantes, III, Vergil's Aeneid," in the *Transactions of the Connecticut Academy*, 1908.

2. In the year 1905 a puppet show based upon the story of Melisendra staged at the Ateneo in Madrid, in connection with the three-hundredth anniversary of the publication of *Don Quixote*. (Rodríguez Marín)

3. These verses are not from one of the old ballads but are the opening lines of a set of octaves of later date, discovered by Pellicer in the National Library at Madrid. As for the game mentioned here, the expression in the original is "*jugando a las tablas*"—"playing at tables," corresponding to the French "*aux tables*," found in Rabelais and other writers. The table games included chess, draughts (checkers), backgammon, and dice. See L. Sainéan: *La Langue de Rabelais* (Paris, 1922), Vol. I, p. 287. It would appear that the game that Gayfer is playing is tricktrack (*tric-trac*), or backgammon. Motteux: "draughts"; Ormsby: "playing at the tables."

4. Line from a ballad attributed to Miguel Sanchez, printed in the third part of Durán's collection, the *Romancero General*.

5. In the *Chanson de Roland*, Roland's (Orlando's) sword is named Durandal.

6. This is Marsiles of the *Chanson de Roland*, a historical personage. Sansueña is a city mentioned in the romances of chivalry and identified by Cervantes as the modern Saragossa. Later in the chapter he refers to "King Marsilio of Saragossa."

7. These verses are found in a *jácara*, or humorous ballad, of Quevedo. (Clemencín)

8. From a ballad in the Durán collection. (Schevill)

9. Góngora has a humorous ballad the theme of which is: how Melisendra must have suffered on this ride.

10. Is this, possibly, a criticism of the dramatists of the day?

11. This is literal. Motteux: "Christian lovers," which is not a bad rendering. Ormsby: "faithful lovers."

12. These lines are from one of the Rodrigo ballads.

13. A proverb.

14. *"Pillar la mona"*—"catch the she-ape"—is slang for getting drunk.

CHAPTER XXVII

1. See Part I, Chapter XXII ff.

2. See Part I, Chapter XXIII and note 2, and Part II, Chapter III.

3. See Chapter IV preceding and note 1. For the siege of Albraca, see Part I, Chapter X.

4. See Part I, Chapter XXX and note 6.

5. Cervantes seems to have been under the mistaken impression that the Mancha de Aragon region (see Chapter XXV preceding and note 8) was a part of the kingdom of Aragon. (Ormsby)

6. ". . . *como un pequeño sardesco.*" A *sardesco* is a pony or small ass; colloquially, the word means "rude" or "stubborn." Motteux: "a very Sardinian for stubbornness."

7. The terms *"regidor"* (see Chapter XXV preceding and note 2) and *"alcalde"* cannot be rendered with complete accuracy. The *regidores* were aldermen or councilmen; the *alcalde* was the mayor or a judge or justice of the peace.

8. Don Diego Ordoñez de Lara was a Castilian knight in the service of King Sancho II. Vellido (Bellido) Dolfos was an enemy spy who by a ruse slew the monarch beneath the walls of Zamora. This treacherous act was avenged by Don Diego, a near kinsman of the victim. The story is told in the *Chronicle of the Cid* and in one of the old ballads. See the Ballads of the Cid in Menéndez y Pelayo's *Antologia;* also, Durán's *Romancero General,* No. 791, and the *Cancionero de Romances* (Antwerp, 1550).

9. The original has *"panes"*—"loaves," but Ormsby adopts the reading "fishes." Lockhart, in his note on this passage in the Motteux version, renders a few lines from the *Chronicle of the Cid,* which include the imprecation "May all your harvests rot."

10. *"Pueblo de la Reloxa (Reloja)."* There has been much argument among commentators as to the identification of this "Clocktown." Rodríguez Marín, who has an extended note and an appendix on the subject, is of the opinion that there were two Clocktowns, one of which he identifies as the hamlet of Espartinas near Seville, adding that "To this day, in Espartinas, it is dangerous to ask *¿Que hora es?'*—'What time is it?' "

11. The *Cazoleros,* or "Scullions," were the inhabitants of Valladolid and derived their name from a townsman, Cazalla, who was burned as a Lutheran in 1559. The "Eggplant-growers" (*Berenjeros,* from *berenjenas,* eggplants) were the Toledans. The "Whalers" (*Balenatos*) were the residents of Madrid, so called because they were supposed to have mistaken a packsaddle floating down the flooded Manzanares for a whale. The identity of the "Soapmen" (*Jaboneros*) is uncertain.

12. Compare our Declaration of Independence: ". . . our Lives, our Fortunes, and our Sacred Honor."

13. Compare the three just conditions under which war may be waged as set forth by St. Thomas Aquinas, *Summa Theologica,* II, ii, Quaest. 40 (1), De Bello. These conditions are: the authorization of the ruler; a just cause; a right intention.

14. Matthew 5:44: "Love your enemies . . . do good to them that hate you . . ." Compare Luke 6:27 and 35.

15. Matthew 11:30.

16. *"No se me dava dos ardites."*

CHAPTER XXVIII

1. This proverb has occurred in Part I, Chapter XXV.

2. There is a confused text here in the first edition. The original reads ". . . *que yo pondré silencio en mis rebuznos; pero no en dexar de dezir,"* which is in contradiction to the obvious sense of the passage. I have followed Schevill in dropping the *"en"* and supplying *"puedo"*: ". . . *pero no puedo dexar de dezir."*

3. Both the Spaniards and the Portuguese have this proverb.

4. *"En vuestra mano esta escudillar."* Allusion to pouring broth from the *olla,* or stew-pot. (Rodríguez Marín)

5. Cervantes forgets that Sancho did not accompany Don Quixote on the first sally.

6. In Chapter II preceding the name of the bachelor's father is given as Bartolomé. Some commentators see in this an instance of Sancho's poor memory (his memory, as a matter of fact, was very good); others ascribe the discrepancy to Cervantes' carelessness; others

still see in Tomé a shortened form (based upon sound) of Bartolomé.

7. This proverb is also found in Part I, Chapter LII.

8. In the Spanish, a rhyming proverb: "*Quien yerra y se enmienda/A Dios se encomienda.*"

CHAPTER XXIX

1. Commentators have objected that Don Quixote and Sancho, traveling as they did, could not possibly have covered the distance between the Cave of Montesinos and the banks of the Ebro (something over two hundred miles) in less than ten or fifteen days, in place of the five days which the author allows them for the journey. But Rodríguez Marín observes that, with the exigencies of earning a livelihood, which prevented him even from correcting his manuscript, Cervantes had no time to spend upon geographical minutiae.

2. A proverb.

3. These malapropisms of Sancho are, it goes without saying, the despair of any translator. In such cases it is almost always impossible to render the passage literally. Here, the word play is on "*longinquos*" ("*caminos*") and Sancho's "*logicuos.*"

4. The Riphaean Mountains, a range in northernmost Scythia, are frequently mentioned by classic authors.

5. Play on "*linea*"—"line," and "*leña*" —"wood."

6. The original reads "... *según el cómputo de Ptolomeo, que fué el mayor cosmógrafo* ..." Out of this Sancho makes: "... *puto y gafo* [literally, "leprous whoreson"], *con la añadidura de meon o meo, o no sé como.*"

7. Ormsby: "In the *Theatrum orbis terrarum* of Abraham Ortelius (Antwerp, 1600), this phenomenon is said to be observable immediately after passing the Azores."

8. Don Quixote asks: "*¿ ... has topado algo?*" and Sancho replies: "*Y aun algos.*" This answer has since become proverbial and the expression has even found its way into the *Dictionary of the Academy.* (Rodríguez Marín)

9. See Chapter XXII preceding, note 10.

10. "... *dos barcadas como estas.*"

CHAPTER XXX

1. This is literal: "*con un sillón de plata.*" Ormsby: "a silver-mounted side-saddle." Jarvis: "A sidesaddle of cloth of silver."

2. Literally, "kiss the hands of her great beauty."

3. See Chapter XIV preceding and note 5.

4. Rhyming proverb: "*En casa llena/ Presto se guisa la cena.*" Portuguese: "*Na casa cheia, asinha se faz a cea.*"

5. "*A vuestra encumbrada altanería y fermosura.*" "*Altanería*" means both "haughtiness" and "hawking." Motteux: "your hawking beauty."

6. On this speech of Sancho's see Chapter X preceding, note 11.

7. The commentator Pellicer has identified Don Quixote's hosts as the Duke and Duchess of Villahermosa, who had a country place in this region. In the year 1905, in connection with the celebration of the three-hundredth anniversary of the publication of Part I of the *Don Quixote*, the Duchess of Villahermosa observed the occasion by staging an elaborate fiesta, having medals struck and paying the printing costs of a handsome Cervantes album, *Album Cervantino Aragonés* (Madrid, 1905). See Rodríguez Marín's note.

8. A proverb.

9. The text is obscure at this point. I have followed Schevill.

10. "*Escudero andado.*"

CHAPTER XXXI

1. There is a rhyme in the original:
   Quando de Bretaña vino,
   que damas curauan del,
   y dueñas del su rozino.
Compare the lines in Part I, Chapters II and XIII.

2. The Spanish word is "*juglar,*" corresponding to the French "*jongleur,*"— "a mountebank." According to the *Dictionary of the Academy*, a *juglar* in the sixteenth century was one who "for money and before the people sang, danced, or performed tricks and clownish acts."

3. The "fig" was originally a gesture of contempt made by closing the fist and inserting the thumb between the index and middle fingers. (Covarrubias)

4. Somewhat freely: "... *no per-*

derá vuessa merced la quinola de sus años por punto menos."

5. The Spanish *montera.*

6. Pellicer states that Cervantes here gives an accurate picture of the luxury maintained by Spanish grandees of the period.

7. It is believed that the author had in mind a particular cleric. Some say it was the Duke of Béjar's chaplain, who did his best to persuade that nobleman to refuse Cervantes' dedication of Part I. (See Rodríguez Marín and Ormsby.)

8. "*A buen salvo está el que repica*": the sense of this proverb is that while the bell-ringer may sound the alarm, he himself is safe in the belfry.

9. In connection with an exchange of compliments, it was a popular form of courtesy to repeat the previous speaker's words, applying them to him. (Rodríguez Marín) This particular form of word play was not uncommon in the Renaissance; compare Rabelais, Book III, Chapter IX (*The Portable Rabelais,* pp. 424–27). See also the colloquy of Erasmus entitled "Echo."

10. Tembleque is a town in La Mancha. "Hurry back from Tembleque, brother" has come to be a proverbial expression addressed to a long-winded storyteller.

11. This story may have been based upon a real-life incident. (Rodríguez Marín)

12. "*Nora tal* [en hora tal]." Euphemism for "*noramala* [en hora mala]"— "in an evil hour."

CHAPTER XXXII

1. "*Togados*"—literally, toga-wearers. Rodríguez Marín sees here the classic antithesis between *togae* and *arma*— compare Cicero: "*Cedant arma togae*" (*De Officiis,* I, xxii). Cervantes, through the mouth of Don Quixote, is fond of dwelling on the theme of arms versus letters.

2. "*Auiendose criado algunos en la estrecheza de algun pupilage.*" Previous English-language translators have taken "*estrecheza*" in the sense of its other meaning, "poverty." Ormsby: "having been brought up in all the straitness of some seminary." Motteux and Jarvis overlook the reflexive "*auiendose criado*" and as

a result get the meaning wrong. Motteux: "having trained up a few pupils straightly"; Jarvis: "a poor pedagogue, who never saw more of the world," etc. Rodríguez Marín points out that the allusion is to the hunger endured by poor students in the schools.

3. Another echo of Garcilaso, passage quoted in Chapter VI preceding.

4. "*El ancho campo de la ambición.*" Ormsby suggests emending "*ancho campo*" to read "*ancho camino*"— "broad road." "It would be absurd," he says, "to talk of the broad field of flattery or hypocrisy, and a narrow path is naturally the opposite of a broad road, not of a broad field." However, to this translator, "broad field" seems quite in keeping with the concept of ambition, and in the process of translation the difficulty may be solved by supplying "road" and "way" in the phrase and clause that follow, as has been done here.

5. Calderón (in his *Cervantes Vindicado*) is inclined to believe that Sancho threw in the verb "*perseverar*" simply for its sonorous, high-sounding effect. Hartzenbusch and Benjumea substitute "*persuadir*"—"persuade." See Rodríguez Marín's note.

6. The Portuguese also have this proverb.

7. See Chapter X preceding and note 7.

8. See "Urganda the Unknown," prefatory verses to Part I.

9. Personage in the *Orlando Innamorato* of Boiardo.

10. So-called "Neapolitan soap" (*jabón napolitano*) was manufactured in the households of princes and the nobility. There are in existence a number of curious sixteenth-century recipes for making it. Among the elements that went into its composition were wheat bran, milk of poppies, goat's milk, marrow of deer, bitter almonds, and sugar. (Rodríguez Marín)

11. The proverb ran: "*Bueno es vivir para ver,*" our "Live and learn."

12. A proverb.

13. Parrhasius, Timanthes, and Apelles were famous Greek painters of the fourth and fifth centuries B.C.; Lysippus was a fourth-century Greek sculptor.

14. Don Quixote uses the form "*demostina*" instead of the more usual "*de-*

mosteniana"—"Demosthenian." (Clemencín)

15. On the Sayago region, see Chapter XIX preceding and note 7.

16. Oriana was the lady of Amadis of Gaul. Alastrajarea, in the chivalric romances, was the wife of the prince Don Falanges of Astra. On Queen Madásima, see Part I, Chapters XXIV and XXV.

17. This proverb has occurred in Part I, Chapters IV (note 3) and XLVII (note 11).

18. Compare Chapter VI preceding.

19. Reference to nautical terminology.

20. See Part I, Chapter XXXI.

21. For the slaying of Orlando (Roland) by Bernardo del Carpio, see Part I, the beginning of Chapter XXVI. On the Twelve Peers, see Part I, Chapter XLIX.

22. Part I, Chapters XLV ff.

23. According to Clemencín, who based his information on old records, there were no noble houses in El Toboso, nor even small gentry, the population being made up of Moorish peasants. There has been some discussion, which has arrived nowhere, as to whether or not there was a real-life prototype of Dulcinea.

24. See Part I, Chapter XLI and note 9.

25. A proverbial expression, according to the *Dictionary of the Academy.*

26. Allusion to the agility of these birds, according to Rodríguez Marín. The phrase puzzled Ormsby.

27. Rhyming proverb: "*Ni hagas cohecho,/Ni pierdas derecho.*"

28. "*Con lexía mas clara*"—literally, "with clearer lye" (Ormsby). Motteux: "cleaner suds"; Jarvis's "clearer suds" is better.

29. A cosmetic water that, according to an old recipe preserved in the National Library of Madrid, consisted of a distillation of red and white roses, trefoil, red poppies, lavender root, honeysuckle, orange blossoms, white lilies, thyme, carnations, and orange rind. Directions as to the method of manufacturing it are also given. (See Rodríguez Marín.) It is of interest to compare the *eau d'ange* which Rabelais mentions in connection with the Abbey of Thélème (see Book I, end of Chapter XL or *The Portable Rabelais*, p. 210). According to M. Paul Dorveaux, *eau d'ange* was "*eau*

distillé de myrte" (see the Lefranc critical edition, *Œuvres de Rabelais* [Paris, 1913], Tome Second, p. 421, note 38).

30. In place of "*ceremonias*," I adopt the reading "*cirimonias*," to accord with the duchess's subsequent speech. It is not unlikely that this was what Cervantes wrote.

31. Don Quixote's overrefined language here is explained by Clemencín as being a parody on that of a bully of Seville.

32. The *penante*, or slender, narrow-mouthed jar, held but a small quantity of wine.

33. Commentators seem to have overlooked the fact that when Don Quixote and Sancho first caught sight of the ducal pair, it was "as they emerged from a wood at sunset" (see the beginning of Chapter XXX preceding); yet at the end of the present chapter, Don Quixote goes off to take a siesta. Apparently under the impression that the time is night, Ormsby has: "it's about as likely . . . as that it's now midnight," by way of an attempt at clarifying the sense (the original reads "*como aora es noche*"). Motteux has a gross mistranslation: "which I will put up with as it is now night."

34. "*Que me trasquilen a cruzes.*" I follow Rodríguez Marín, who interprets this expression as meaning, "to cut the hair crudely and unevenly." He cites Correas: *Vocabulario de Refranes.* This is said to have been the manner in which the hair of fools was trimmed.

35. See note 30 preceding.

CHAPTER XXXIII

1. Reference to the famous ivory seat which the Cid won by the capture of Valencia. "When the Cid returned to Castile, the king, Don Alfonso, invited him to take a seat beside him, and when the Cid out of modesty refused, his Majesty ordered him to sit upon the ivory chair." (Clemencín, quoting the old chronicle.)

2. See Part I, Chapter XXVI.

3. A proverbial expression used in connection with a speaker who wanders far afield. (Covarrubias.) Ubeda was a small town in the upper Guadalquivir valley. The region is not particularly hilly, and the origin of the expression is obscure.

4. "*Es agradecido.*" Clemencín suggests that this be emended to "*soy agradecido*"—"I am grateful," but there appears to be no good reason for the change. Ormsby (edition of 1885) has: "I'm grateful," but the edition of his translation by Fitzmaurice-Kelly reads: "he is free-handed" (*agradecido* sometimes has this meaning in old Spanish). Motteux: "he is grateful." Jarvis: "he returns my love."

5. Jarvis: "nothing in the world can part us but the sexton's spade and shovel."

6. This proverb occurs again in Chapter LIII (note 11) following.

7. "*Limiste de Segovia.*" Segovia was noted for its manufacture of fine cloth. Rabelais (Book IV, Chapter VI) has the form "*limestre,*" and Ménage (*Dictionnaire Etymologique*) states: "The serge of *Limestre* is said to derive its name from the one who first manufactured it, but there is no proof of this. It is a serge that is made today at Rouen, and at Darnetal near Rouen, and was formerly made in Spain, also, being of fine Spanish wool." (See Sainéan, *La Langue de Rabelais,* Vol. II, pp. 226–27.)

8. This paragraph consists of a string of proverbs.

9. We have this proverb in English.

10. See Part I, Chapter XXVII and note 1.

11. See Chapter VI preceding.

12. The duenna is quoting another version of a ballad, "*Despues que el rey don Rodrigo,*" that appears in the *cancioneros* (*Cancionero de Romances* of Antwerp and Durán's *Romancero General,* No. 606).

13. Commentators have seen a confused text here, finding it difficult to make sense out of the conclusion of this sentence, but the idea seems to be that Sancho will be constantly improving his lot. Both Motteux and Jarvis mistranslate; Motteux: "you will not give it up for one of triple brocade"; Jarvis: "for which he would refuse one of brocade three stories high."

14. Rhyming proverb: "*A quien cuece y amasa,/No le hurtes hogaza.*" This is something like our "Don't kill the goose that lays the golden egg."

15. Propitiatory sounds addressed to a dog ("nice doggy"). The Spanish proverb runs: "*A perro viejo no hay*

tus, tus'"—"There's no use in saying '*tus, tus*' to an old dog."

16. These are all proverbs.

17. The duchess is imitating Sancho's way of talking.

18. A proverb.

19. Reference to the *Disticha,* a well-known school text, of Dionysius Cato.

20. Miguel Verino was the author of a collection of moral couplets, the *De Puerorum Moribus Disticha,* which was in wide use in European schools and, according to Lockhart, writing in the nineteenth century, was "still used as a textbook in some of the English schools." Dying young, Verino was the subject of a Latin epitaph by Politian which began: "*Michael Verinus florentibus occidit annis.*" Commentators point out that there is nothing surprising in the duchess's being able to quote Latin, as this was by no means an uncommon accomplishment with Spanish ladies of high rank in Cervantes' time. The Duchess of Villahermosa, who may have been the prototype of Cervantes' character, was a woman of broad culture.

21. Ormsby: "The commonplace explanation is that we should not trust to appearances." The Portuguese have this proverb and its converse: "*Debaixo de bom saio está o homem máo*"—"Under a good cloak is a bad man."

22. Sancho means to say that he never gets drunk. Motteux: "though I wear breeches, I don't ill use them."

23. Compare Chapter XVII (note 9) preceding and Chapter XXXVII following.

24. "*En las cortesias jumentiles y assininas.*"

CHAPTER XXXIV

1. It was Sancho, not Don Quixote, who related the Montesinos episode.

2. Favila succeeded his father Pelayo on the throne. As Ormsby points out, however, he was hardly a "Gothic king," as that line properly ends with Rodrigo. According to an old Spanish chronicle, he was slain by a boar (not bears) that he sought to subdue by bodily strength alone, unaided by his huntsmen, in the animal's lair.

3. This comparison of war and the chase is common with Renaissance writers, particularly the Spaniards.

4. The expression "*y vereies como os*

vale vn pan por ciento" has puzzled commentators and translators. Rodríguez Marín states that the sense is "to obtain great profit from an exercise or pursuit." Ormsby gives it this meaning: "and you will find the good of it." Motteux takes it in a different sense: "you shall see how plain fare agrees with you."

5. Compare the proverb quoted in Chapter v (note 8) preceding: "The respectable woman has a broken leg and stays at home." Sancho here turns it to his own use. It occurs again in Chapter XLIX (note 17) following.

6. *Standard Dictionary:* "A game of cards, antedating and essentially like poker." Ormsby: "The game (*triunfo envidado*) seems to have been more like 'all fours.'" For some inexplicable reason Motteux has: "a game of trumps at Christmas."

7. "*Del dicho al hecho,/Hay gran trecho.*"

8. Cervantes seems especially fond of this saying. It has occurred in Chapters XIV (note 5) and XXX (note 3) preceding, and recurs in Chapters LIX (note 12) and LXXI (note 10) following.

9. Proverb with assonant rhyme: "*Mas vale á quien Dios ayuda/Que quien mucho madruga.*"

10. Jarvis: "the belly carries the legs, and not the legs the belly."

11. The *Comendador Griego* was Hernán Núñez de Guzmán, a learned Hellenist who held the chair of Greek at the University of Salamanca and who was a commander of the Order of Santiago, whence his title—not "Greek commentator," as Motteux and others have it. He left a manuscript collection of proverbs which was published after his death, the *Refranes ó Proverbios en Romance*, etc. (Salamanca, 1555).

12. The Moslem cry "*Le ilah ile alah*" —"There is no divinity but God" ("there is no god but Allah").

13. At the beginning of the chapter we are told that Sancho himself had come to believe this.

14. Ormsby: "In the carts described, wheels and axle are all in one piece. They are in use to this day in the Asturias, and their creaking may be heard on a still evening miles away. The country folk there maintain it has the effect Cervantes mentions."

15. See the prefatory verses to Part I.

CHAPTER XXXV

1. The phrase "*vn disciplinante de luz*" cannot be rendered accurately in English except by a tedious circumlocution. The literal sense is "penitents of light." There were two classes of penitents in the confraternities: the *disciplinantes de luz* and the *disciplinantes de sangre*, or "blood penitents." The former marched in processions, carrying lighted tapers; the latter were flagellants. (Rodríguez Marín)

2. "*Ni pesada ni por pesar.*"

3. Sancho says "*abernuncio*" in place of "*abrenuncio*," an expression meaning "far be it from me" or "fie on that!" The Latin form of the word is "*abrenuntio*," from "*abrenuntiare*"—"to renounce," as, for example, to renounce the devil and all his works, in baptism (it is used in this sense by the fifth-century Christian writer Salvianus). Both Motteux and Jarvis have the rather meaningless rendering: "I pronounce it."

4. "*Alma de cántaro*"—idiomatic for "fool."

5. Inmate of a school for orphan lads.

6. "*A Dios rogando/Y con el mazo dando.*" In the sense of "work and pray." In his list of proverbs in the *Don Quixote*, Ormsby cites a number of sayings corresponding to this one to be found in other European languages. Italian: "*Invoca i santi e da di piglio all' aratro*"—"Invoke the saints and lay a hand to the plough." French: "*Dieu donne fil à toile ourdie*"—"God provides thread for the web with a warp." There is also the Latin: "*Dii facientes adjuvant*."—"The gods help the doers" ("God helps him who helps himself").

7. Compare Chapter VII (note 6) preceding and LXXI (note 23) following.

8. In the sense of something fitting, a suitable accompaniment.

9. "*Que no son todos los tiempos unos*"—literally, "that all times are not the same."

10. "*Como de boluereme cazique.*" Jarvis: "as much to the thing as to turn Turk." Motteux: "I have no more stomach for it than to be among the men-eaters." Ormsby: "as little fancy for it as for turning cacique." "Cacique" is, literally, a West Indian chief.

11. See Chapter x (note 2) preceding. The Portuguese also have the proverb.

12. See Chapter II (note 7) preceding.

13. "*Si algunos . . . fueren de mosqueo.*" "*Mosqueo*" is the act of driving flies away.

CHAPTER XXXVI

1. "*La letra con sangre entra*"—proverbial with schoolmasters of the time.

2. This theological heresy was suppressed by the Inquisition in the majority of the editions of *Don Quixote* printed in Spain following the edition of Valencia in 1616.

3. This expression, which has come to be a proverb, apparently derives from someone who had been whipped through the streets mounted on an ass.

4. This is literal. Ormsby: "take care that nobody speaks evil of thee behind thy back."

5. "*Pon lo tuyo en consejo, y unos diran. . . .*" Rodríguez Marín: "*Lo tuyo, lo mio*, and *lo suyo* are vulgar euphemisms for the pudenda, abundant examples of which are to be found in our sixteenth-century writers." Previous translators appear to have been unaware of this or else have glossed it over.

6. See Chapter xxxi (note 8) preceding and Chapter xliii (note 10) following.

7. See Part I, Chapter xx (note 9).

8. ". . . *tengo de comer las manos tras él*"—literally, ". . . after it." The expression is one denoting great eagerness.

9. "*Su calongía*"—literally, "canonry." (Modern Spanish: "*calonjía.*")

10. The word in Spanish is "*orégano*" —"wild marjoram," an allusion to the proverb that has already occurred in Part I, Chapter xxi (note 2): "*Plegue á Dios que orégano sea,/Y no se nos vuelva alcaravea*—"Please God that it be marjoram and not turn out to be caraway." The connection is somewhat obscure; some would here read "*orógano*," or "*oroganoso*," from "*oro*"—"gold," and "*gana*"—"desire." At any rate, for purposes of translation, "gold-seeker" would seem to be near enough. Motteux also employs it.

11. Compare Chapter xiii (note 5) preceding and Part I, Chapter xx (note 3).

12. The name Trifaldín was formed by Cervantes after the Truffaldin of Boiardo's *Orlando Innamorato* and Ariosto's *Orlando Furioso*. "*Truffar*" in Italian, Spanish "*trufar*," means "to cheat" or "hoax." (Rodríguez Marín)

13. Commentators are not agreed as to what country is meant. Possibly a mythical one.

14. Imitation of the Latin *Dixi* with which academic orations were terminated.

CHAPTER XXXVII

1. Play on the name Trifaldi and "*tres faldas*"—"three skirts."

2. See Chapter v preceding (note 6) and Part I, Chapter xlv (note 2).

3. A proverb.

4. A number of editors, including Fitzmaurice-Kelly and Hartzenbusch, have emended "*barbero*" to "*boticario*" —"apothecary," as more in consonance with the text; but "barber" may be due to ideational attraction, suggested by clipping and scissors.

5. A proverb.

6. Compare Chapters xvii (note 9) and xxxiii (note 23) preceding, where the proverb was quoted differently: "It is better to lose by a card too many than a card too few."

7. "A word to the wise," etc. There are a number of forms of the proverb in Latin and other languages: "*Dictum* (or *verbum*) *sapienti*"; "*Intelligenti pauca*"; in French: "*A bon entendeur salut*"; Portuguese: "*A bom entendedor, poucas palavras.*"

CHAPTER XXXVIII

1. Variety of cloth worn by some religious orders and by women of the people in some provinces. (*Dictionary of the Academy*, cited by Rodríguez Marín.)

2. "*De delgado canequí*"—a cotton or calico cloth of East Indian origin. (*Dictionary of the Academy*, cited by Rodríguez Marín.)

3. Martos is a town in Andalusia, southwest of Jaen. It was noted for the size of the chickpeas produced in that region. (Rodríguez Marín)

4. "*Lobos,*" hence, Lobuna.

5. From "*zorro, zorra*"—"fox."

6. The meaning of this verbal slip becomes apparent later, when the identity of the "countess" is revealed. In Spanish the play is on the masculine and feminine forms, "*criado*" and "*criada*," and is not so obvious as in English.

7. "*Antes que salga a la plaça de vuestros oydos, por no dezir orejas*"—literally, "before it emerges into the public place of your hearing, not to say ears."

8. Play on the Latin superlative ending, "-*issimus*." Fitzmaurice-Kelly, in his notes on Ormsby, sees a satire on the "*culto*" literary style of the period.

9. The old commentators see this as originally the expression of a eunuch, who was "not so much interested in the ornamentation of his body as in that of his soul." Correas, in his dictionary of proverbs, *Vocabulario de Refranes*, goes so far as to identify "a certain gentleman, a young student, native of Avila, named Ortiz." (See Rodríguez Marín's note.)

10. See Chapter XXXVI preceding, note 13.

11. This imaginary island has been referred to in Part I, Chapter XVIII (Don Quixote's adventure with the sheep).

12. Southern point of the East Indian peninsula.

13. Lockhart (notes to Motteux) thinks it strange that Cervantes should employ as the name of his countess a term signifying a figure of speech; but the appellations of heroes and heroines in the romances of chivalry are fanciful in the extreme.

14. In connection with these accomplishments, see Chapter VI preceding.

15. This *redondilla* is translated from the Italian of Serafino Aquilano (Serafino of Aquila), whose poems were printed at Venice in 1502; there is a copy in the Bibliothèque Nationale in Paris. (Schevill) The original is itself an imitation of the Spanish verse form.

16. See *The Republic*, Books III and X.

17. Allusion to the ballad of that title.

18. It may be assumed that Cervantes is here criticizing, or satirizing, the affected character of much of the poetry of his age—which, it is to be remembered, was the age of Góngora and his followers. The "conceit" was the thing with poets of the time. Indeed, the literary manner known as "*conceptismo*" would appear to be rather deeply embedded in the Spanish temperament.

19. The author of the original form of this stanza (it is quoted a little differently here) was the Comendador Escrivá; it appeared in the *Cancionero General* of Hernando del Castillo in 1511. Edgar Allan Poe cites the stanza in his burlesque piece, "How to Write an Article for Blackwoods."

20. On this measure, see Chapter XXIV preceding, note 7.

21. Name applied to remote and uninhabited islands. Torquemada employs it in this sense in his *Jardín de Flores Curiosas*. (Rodríguez Marín) See Schevill's *Ovid and the Renaissance in Spain*, p. 176.

22. The Tibar is a river in Arabia; the phrase "*oro de tibar*" signifies super-refined gold. Panchaia, a part of Arabia Felix, is mentioned by Vergil, *Georgics*, II, 139: "*Totaque thuriferis Panchaia pinguis arenis.*" On the balsam, see Pliny's *Natural History*.

CHAPTER XXXIX

1. "Who, speaking of such things, could restrain his tears?" Vergil's *Aeneid*, II, 6–8. The passage reads, in full:

> Quis talia fando
> Myrmidonum, Dolopumve, aut
>   duri miles Ulixi
> Temperet a lacrimis?

2. The idea of a particular adventure being reserved for a particular knight is frequently stressed. See Chapter XXII preceding, note 10.

3. "Civil" is probably to be taken here in the sense of "miserable." (Rodríguez Marín)

CHAPTER XL

1. "*Responde a las tacitas.*" A word is lacking in the original. I follow Clemencín in reading "*preguntas*"—"questions."

2. "*Apostaré yo que no tienen hazienda para pagar a quien las rape.*"

3. Ladies in Cervantes' time actually removed hair in this fashion. Rodríguez Marín quotes a recipe for "removing hair from the forehead and face or any other part," found in the manuscript section of the National Library at Madrid.

4. This also is true to life. (Rodríguez Marín)

5. There is an untranslatable word play here: "*oliscan a terceras, auiendo dexado de ser primas.*" If one were to take "*terceras*" and "*primas*" in their literal signification, the rendering would be: "have a third-rate smell, having ceased to be first-rate." But "*prima*" also means "cousin," and "*terceira*" is a term for "procuress," while the verb "*oliscar,*" according to the *Dictionary of the Academy,* has the sense of "smell bad." Motteux: "their odor is somewhat third-rate." Ormsby's rendering does not seem to say anything: "most of them have a flavor of agents that have ceased to be principals."

6. "*Las caualgaduras que son de retorno.*" According to Covarrubias, "*mulas de retorno*" are "mules that come back without a load." But the phrase appears to be equivalent to "*mulas de alquiler*"—"beasts for hire." (Schevill)

7. For the story of Pierres and Magalona, see Part I, Chapter XLIX, note 6.

8. "*Clavileño,*" from "*clavo*"—"nail" or "spike" ("*clavija*" — "peg"), and "*leño*"—"log."

9. Compare the "*mediocritas aurea,*" or "golden mean," of Horace (*Odes*, II, x, 5–6). The concept is a common one with the Latin writers.

10. This proverb has occurred in Part I, Chapter XXII (note 4).

11. According to Correas (*Vocabulario de Refranes,* cited by Rodríguez Marín), the sense of this proverbial expression is "great loss," "damage," or "sorrow."

12. "*Si pensassen por ello ser reynas.*" Motteux mistranslates: "though they were to be queens thereby." In connection with the use of the pronoun *vos,* see Part I, Chapter LI.

CHAPTER XLI

1. Compare the "savages" or "wild men" at Camacho's wedding; see Chapter XX preceding, note 10.

2. Motteux is in error here: "that he will not use anything but his sword," etc.

3. It has been previously stated that the peg was in the forehead. Ormsby notes that in the case of the magic horse in the *Arabian Nights* the guiding peg

was located in the neck; he also alludes to Chaucer's "Stede of bras"—"Ye moten trill a pin stont in his ere."

4. "*Ni . . . insula, ni insulos.*" "*Insulos*" is here used jocosely for "*insulanos*" —"islanders." (Rodríguez Marín)

5. The first of these two proverbs has occurred in Part I, Chapters XXIX and XLVI; it recurs in Chapter LXXI following. The second has been quoted in Chapter IV (note 7) preceding, and appears again in Chapters L (note 16) and LXII (note 4) following.

6. This proverb recurs in Chapters LIII (note 8) and LIX (note 17) following. The Portuguese also have it.

7. See Chapter XXII preceding, note 14.

8. This is a proverb with us.

9. The word play here is untranslatable. Don Quixote says: "*eres hombre veridico,*" and Sancho, mistaking "*veridico*" for "*verdico (verdecico)*"— "greenish," replies: "*No soy verde, sino moreno*"—"I am not green but brownskinned." For once, at least, I have adopted a rendering from Motteux as the best available one: "I believe thou art trusty"—"I am not rusty but sunburnt." Ormsby: "Thou art veracious" —"I'm not voracious."

10. Don Quixote has his mythology somewhat confused. The Palladium was an image or statue of Pallas that, according to legend, fell from Heaven at Troy and during the Trojan war was borne off by Ulysses and Diomedes because the fate of the city depended on its possession.

11. "*Sendos paternostres y sendas auemarias.*" Motteux: "with two Paternosters and two Ave-Marias."

12. Clemencín notes that Pierres, Magalona's husband, was king of Naples, not of France. Hartzenbusch makes the emendation: "queen of Naples."

13. Some editors (Benjumea and Fitzmaurice-Kelly) here read "*legión*" in place of "*región.*" Rodríguez Marín thinks it may have been a slip of the tongue on Sancho's part.

14. Peralvillo was a place near Ciudad Real where the Holy Brotherhood executed its prisoners.

15. The licentiate Torralba was tried by the Inquisition in 1528 on charges of dealing in magic. His trial became famous in story and song.

16. Elsewhere (in his *Persiles y Sigismunda*) Cervantes states that the Torre di Nona is a prison, not a street. (Schevill)

17. Charles, Constable of Bourbon under Francis I, who went over to the side of the Emperor Charles V and aided in the defeat of the French monarch at Pavia in 1525. He died two years later, in the first assault on Rome by the imperial army. See the account in Benvenuto Cellini's *Autobiography*. For an account of Bourbon's treason, the reader may be referred to *Marguerite of Navarre*, by Samuel Putnam (New York: Coward-McCann, 1935).

18. "*Para cogerla, por mas que se remonte.*" Motteux is wrong: "to seize it more strongly from a height."

19. The great Portuguese navigator known to us as Magellan.

20. "*Por contento y satisfecho a toda su voluntad.*" The expression is one used by notaries, something like "for value received." Cervantes employs it in a legal document in connection with the sale of two of his comedies, under date of March 5, 1585. (Rodríguez Marín)

21. Reference is to the Pleiades.

22. The original contains a redundancy that does not go well in English: "*son como vnos alhelies y como vnas flores*—"are like so many gillyflowers and so many flowers." Rodríguez Marín points out that this double form of comparison is characteristic of the popular speech.

CHAPTER XLII

1. "*Tengo de prouar a que sabe el ser gouernador.*" Motteux misses the sense: "I wish to prove that I know how to be a governor."

2. Compare Sancho's letter to his wife in Chapter XXXVI preceding (see note 8 to that chapter).

3. The Christus was the cross preceding the alphabet in school primers, and "not to know the Christus" was an expression signifying complete ignorance.

4. Allusion to the school text, known as the *Disticha de Moribus*, etc., of Dionysius Cato (see Chapter XXXIII preceding and note 19).

5. Cervantes' phrase here, "*mar proceloso,*" has the flavor of classical Latinity. Compare St. Augustine (*De*

Civitate Dei, v, 22): "*procellossimum pelagus.*"

6. It was the custom of fathers to begin their exhortations to their sons (either by word of mouth or in writing) with this biblical maxim. (Rodríguez Marín) Compare Psalms 111:10, and Proverbs 1:7 and 9:10.

7. Allusion to the well-known fable of Aesop and Phaedrus.

8. The reference here is to the peacock's lordly tail; when it looks down at its feet, the bird is supposed to be ashamed. The image is a popular one with the Spanish mystics. (Rodríguez Marín)

9. This passage has proved confusing to editors and commentators. I have followed the reading suggested by Schevill.

10. Cervantes here alters an old saying that went: "*La sangre se hereda, y el vicio se pega*"—"Blood is inherited and vice sticks." Compare the remarks of Dorotea, in Part I, Chapter XXXVI: "true nobility consists in virtue."

11. Begging friars would refuse alms but suggest that they might be thrown into their hoods: "*No quiero, no quiero; pero echádmelo en la capilla, ó en el sombrero*"—"I do not want any, I do not want any; but throw it into my hood or into my hat." The text literally reads: ". . . or as the 'I don't want any' of your hood." Ormsby: ". . . or for the hood of thy 'won't have it.'" Motteux: ". . . as . . . a cape to cover bribery."

CHAPTER XLIII

1. This was a comparison applied to black, unclean nails rather than to long ones. That such nails were common in Cervantes' time is indicated by the frequency with which writers employ the phrase "*negro de uña*"—"black of a nail," a phrase that occurs later in this chapter. (Rodríguez Marín)

2. See Suetonius's *Life of Julius Caesar,* Chapter 45.

3. The smell of garlic was regarded as the mark of the countryman. (Rodríguez Marín)

4. This is the second time that this significant statement has occurred. In Chapter XXVI preceding, it is put into the mouth of Master Pedro of the puppets.

5. The proverb runs: "*Come poco y cena mas poco.*" Another version is: "*Come poco y cena mas,/Duerme en alto y viverás*"—"Eat little [for the midday meal], have a little more for supper, sleep at the top of the house, and you will live [long]."

6. In his *Tesoro de la lengua castellana*, published four years before the second part of *Don Quixote* appeared, Covarrubias lists the words "*regoldar*"—"to belch," and "*regveldo (regüeldo)*"—"belching," but says nothing against their use though he condemns the practice for which they stand as "a discourtesy and boorishness, especially when done in front of persons to whom respect is to be shown." (Rodríguez Marín)

7. Cervantes clearly believed that the people were the makers of language. Compare Horace, *Ars Poetica*, 71-72: ". . . *si volet usus,/quem penes arbitrium est et ius et norma loquendi.*"

8. See Chapter xxx preceding (note 4).

9. See Chapter vii preceding (note 5).

10. See Chapter xxxi (note 8) and Chapter xxxvi (note 6) preceding.

11. A proverb; compare Chapter lviii (note 9) following.

12. Proverb: "*Castigame mi madre, y yo trómpogelas.*"

13. See Chapter xxxiii preceding and note 3.

14. Don Quixote has uttered this proverb before, in conversing with the Princess Micomicona, Part I, Chapter xlvi.

15. This proverb is repeated in Chapter lxiv (note 2) following. The Italians also have it.

16. The proverb reads in full: "He whose father is a judge goes to court with assurance." The *Dictionary of the Academy* lists the phrase "*tener el padre alcalde*"—"have a judge for a father."

17. The proverb "Many go for wool and come back shorn" has been quoted in Chapter xiv (note 8) preceding, and in Part I, Chapter vii (note 4); it is repeated in Chapter lxvii (note 17) following.

18. "*A quien Dios quiere bien, la casa le sabe.*" There is some doubt as to the meaning here, whether it is "his house knows it" or "the house is sweet to him"; and Hartzenbusch in place of

"*casa*" would read "*caza*"—"the chase," with the sense: "his hunting is successful." However, if one is to follow Covarrubias, the reading given above would seem to be the preferred one. (See Rodríguez Marín.)

19. One thinks of some of the "success" maxims of the American "self-made man."

20. Compare Chapter xx (note 13) preceding.

21. "*Del hombre arraigado,/No te veras vengado.*"

22. This saying originally read "*al buen callar llaman santo*"—"To keep silent well is called holy." "*Santo,*" with the old spelling "*sancto,*" was transformed into "*Sancho*"; and Sancho Panza proceeds to apply it to himself. (See Rodríguez Marín.)

23. Rhyming proverb: "*Entre dos muelas cordales,/Nunca pongas tus pulgares.*" Ormsby cites the Italian: "*Tra l'incudine e il martello,/Man non metta chi ha cervello*"—"Between the hammer and the anvil he does not put his hand who has a head."

24. Compare Part I, Chapter xx (note 13).

25. See Matthew 7:3-4 and Luke 6: 41-42.

26. In place of "*la muerta*"—"the dead woman," an older reading of the proverb has "*la Muerte*"—"Death." (Ormsby)

27. Rodríguez Marín notes a jocular variation: "The wise man knows more in his house than the fool in the house of another."

CHAPTER XLIV

1. Ormsby: "The original, bringing a charge of misinterpretation against its translator, is a confusion of ideas that it would not be easy to match."

2. In the text: "*la del Capitán cautiuo*"—"The Story of the Captive Captain"; but in Part I (see the title of Chapter xl) the tale is referred to as "The Captive's Story"—"*La Historia del Cautiuo.*"

3. Cervantes is here alluding to those who had criticized him for the introduction of these stories in Part I, and in a manner is justifying their presence there. That he took these tales seriously is indicated by the remark concerning their craftsmanship in the next sentence.

In the introduction to his translation of *Don Quixote*, Ormsby observes: "He [Cervantes] had these stories ready written, and it seemed a good way of disposing of them; it is by no means unlikely that he mistrusted his own powers of extracting from Don Quixote and Sancho material enough to fill a book; but, above all, it is likely that he felt doubtful of his venture. It was an experiment in literature . . . he could not tell how it would be received; and it was well, therefore, to provide his readers with something of the sort they were used to, as a kind of insurance against total failure. The event did not justify his diffidence. The public . . . skimmed the tales hastily and impatiently, eager to return to the adventures of Don Quixote and Sancho; and the public has ever since done much the same."

4. In connection with these counsels that Don Quixote gives to Sancho, it has been pointed out that Cervantes is indebted to the *Galateo Español* of Gracián Dantisco, published at Barcelona in 1593. A copy of this work is preserved in the British Museum.

5. Professor Schevill thinks that the author may be indebted in this island episode to a passage in the second part of the *Amadis of Gaul*.

6. The phrase "*en justo y creyente*" —literally, "as a righteous man and a believer," has the idiomatic sense of "immediately," "at once." In English, in order to bring out the full flavor and meaning of the expression, it is necessary to give it a double translation.

7. The cap is the *montera*. "Watered camlet" (*chamelote de aguas*), according to Covarrubias, is camlet whose sheen is reminiscent of sea waves.

8. The *jineta*. The Spanish gentry had adopted this saddle from the Moors.

9. Or brand-new—"*flamantes*."

10. Two fanegas. The sense here is, of course, figurative.

11. The Spanish word "*soledad*" here has the sense of the Portuguese "*saudades*," an expression that is untranslatable in its fullness of meaning, signifying as it does a vague nostalgic longing, half pleasant, half sad. In other words, it was more than mere aloneness that Don Quixote felt. (See Rodríguez Marín's note.)

12. Motteux expands as usual: "if they come into my chamber, they must fly in at the window."

13. I follow Schevill's reading in this passage.

14. The allusion is to the poet, Juan de Mena, known as "the Spanish Ennius." He was born at Cordova in 1512. In his poem "El Laberinto," the following *copla* (No. 227) occurs:

O vida segura, la mansa pobreza,
dadiva santa desagradecida!

"O the blessed life, meek poverty, holy gift unappreciated." Ormsby: "I suspect there is a touch of malice in the words 'the great Cordovan poet.' To hear any other poet but Góngora so described would have made a Góngorist foam at the mouth."

15. See I Corinthians 7:30-31, and II Corinthians 7:10.

16. Cervantes here employs a word, "*pantalia*," the sense of which is unknown. I follow Schevill in taking it as referring to patches, since we are told in the next paragraph that "the patch on his shoe can be seen a league away."

17. There are numerous allusions to this custom in Spanish writers of the period. The toothpick was a mark of gentility. (See Rodríguez Marín.)

18. "Than a stain [*mancilla*] in the heart."

19. This is a burlesque ballad with assonant rhymes in the second and fourth verses. I have not attempted to imitate the assonance as Ormsby has.

20. Imitation of a passage in Vergil's *Aeneid*, IV, 366-67.

21. Inasmuch as these rivers meet, the effect is intended to be farcical. (Clemencín)

22. These gifts heighten the farcical tone of the piece: silver slippers, damask breeches, etc.

23. Reference to one of the crown jewels known as "La Sola," or the unmatchable one. Pellicer: "It was fished up in the Southern Sea, in 1515, and when the palace at Madrid burned, it was lost along with other most precious gems, in the year 1734."

24. This expression was too much for the editors Hartzenbusch and Benjumea, who emended "*los cabellos, como lirios*" to read "*los cabellos, como el oro*"—"golden locks."

25. *"Madama"* is a Gallicism, employed jocosely.

26. See the adventure in the inn, Part I, Chapter XXVI.

27. The expression *"cozido ó asado"* signifies "in whatever way it may be (*de cualquier manera que sea*)." (Rodríguez Marín)

CHAPTER XLV

1. *"Meneo dulce de las cantimploras."* Covarrubias defines the *"cantimplora"* as "a copper jug with a very long neck for cooling water or wine, by placing or burying the jug in the snow or moving it about in a vat containing snow." And Pellicer comments: "by the heat of the sun (which the author is here apostrophizing) thirst is excited in summer, which makes it necessary to shake the coolers." The effect is intended to be farcical.

2. Of Thymbra, or Thymbre, a city in Troas that contained a temple of Apollo; hence, Thymbraeus, "The Thymbraean," came to be one of the god's epithets.

3. Ormsby: "Hartzenbusch thinks that this outburst is a caricature of a passage in some poem of the day, and that such imitations are not uncommon in *Don Quixote*. If so, we cannot wonder at it that Cervantes was not beloved by the high-flying poets of the period."

4. See Aristotle's *Physics*, II, 2.

5. Pellicer identifies Sancho's "island" as Alcalá del Ebro, on the peninsula formed by the bend of the Ebro River. Ormsby observes: "The critics have been much exercised by the identification of Baratria, which has always been with the cervantistas a favorite hunting ground for political allusions."

6. In modern Spanish, *"barato"* is an adjective meaning "cheap," but in old Spanish it is also a noun signifying "a jest." Like Ormsby, I adopt this latter reading. Motteux: "because the government cost him so cheap."

7. Compare Teresa Panza's remarks in Chapter V preceding.

8. The abuse of the title of "Don" by those without the worldly means to live up to it was frequently commented upon in Cervantes' day.

9. It was originally the custom to beg the pardon of those present when some unclean or vile subject was mentioned.

Later, such expressions of apology came to be interjected without rhyme or reason.

10. Rodríguez Marín believes that Cervantes is alluding sarcastically to the quality of clothing (and food as well) furnished to prisoners.

11. The case of the drover's purse comes later in the chapter. The author, apparently, had originally put it first and then changed the order but neglected to elide this reference. (Rodríguez Marín) Ormsby in his translation changes the order of the incidents.

12. *"Por hazerle plazer y buena obra"* —a notary's phrase.

13. This was the procedure known in civil law as *"juramento decisorio,"* when one party agreed to abide by what the other swore. (Rodríguez Marín)

14. The rod of justice held by Sancho. It was lowered in order that the witness might place his hand upon the cross of the rod and take his oath upon it.

15. Commentators are agreed that this episode is taken from the Life of St. Nicholas of Bari as inserted in the *Golden Legend* of Jacobo de Voragine, thirteenth-century Archbishop of Genoa.

16. See note 9 above.

17. Literally, "other cats in my beard."

18. This anecdote appeared in printed form as early as 1550, in the devotional work of Francisco de Osuna, *Norte de los Estados,* published at Burgos in that year. There are other traces of the story that go back as far as 1531. (See the note by Rodríguez Marín.)

CHAPTER XLVI

1. This paragraph is omitted by Ormsby in his translation on the ground that the lines "are repeated with some trifling changes in Chapter L, which is obviously their proper place, while they come in very awkwardly here."

2. *"Vihuela"* — not "lute" as in Motteux.

3. Another burlesque ballad with assonant rhymes. See Chapter XLIV preceding, note 19.

4. The original has *región*, clearly a printer's error.

5. *"Azeyte de Aparicio"*—an ointment said to have been named after its in-

ventor, while others see *"Aparicio"* as a corruption of *"hyperico."* Hypericum, in any event, was one of the ingredients. Ormsby: "oil of John's wort."

CHAPTER XLVII

1. *"Como juego de maessecoral"*—literally, "like a trick of Master Coral." According to Covarrubias, the expression derives from the fact that charlatans and jugglers, stripping off their cloaks and jackets, were in the habit of performing in doublets of the hue of red coral.

2. Cervantes is here caricaturing a custom that actually existed in Spain: that of having physicians present at the tables of princes to advise what foods should be eaten and to see that royal appetites were restrained. This is attested by a document brought to light by the Society of Spanish Bibliophiles. (See Rodríguez Marín's note.)

3. Clemencín states that "physicians formerly applied this term to a certain subtle and balsamic humor which, so they believed, conferred vigor and elasticity upon the fibers that make up the bodily texture." Covarrubias cites Albertus Magnus: *"humidum est vitae qualitas et potentia."*

4. Doctor Recio is not quoting Hippocrates. There was a prevalent saying to the effect: *"Omnis saturatio* [or: *indigestio] mala, panis autem pessima"*— "All surfeit [indigestion] is bad, but that of bread is the worst of all." The doctor substitutes "partridges" for "bread." (Schevill)

5. *"Manjar peliagudo"*—*"peliagudo"* also means "difficult" or "dangerous."

6. The olla-podrida is a highly seasoned dish of meat and vegetables cooked in a bulging, wide-mouthed pot or jar known as an *olla.* The term has been carried over into English.

7. *"Cañutillos de suplicaciones."* This is the thin, rolled wafer known in modern Spanish as *"barquillo."*

8. This is a village in La Mancha (not an imaginary one as some have supposed) that has disappeared from the modern maps. The doctor locates it with a fair degree of accuracy. The name literally means "Be off with you." The physician's name, "Agüero," means "omen," which accounts for Sancho's

play upon it: "Mal-Agüero" — "bad omen."

9. The University of Osuna has been referred to in Chapter 1 preceding. Founded in 1549, it existed until 1820. In its prime it was an important cultural center. (Schevill)

10. Literally, "I will place them upon my head"; compare Part I, Chapter vi and note 10.

11. See note 8 above.

12. The Biscayans were prominent in the royal service under Charles V and Philip II. They were noted for their ability and loyalty and many of them held secretarial posts. (See Rodríguez Marín's note.)

13. Literally, "newborn."

14. *"De muerte adminicula y pessima, como es la de la hambre."* *"Adminicula"* is a word of Latin derivation that seems out of place in Sancho's mouth and that makes not too much sense here. Most translators, in various languages, e.g., Ormsby in English, have rendered it as "slow death." Tieck: *"ein schlimmster und schmählichster Tod."* Motteux: "evil death."

15. Compare Chapter xxxiii preceding, and Part I, Chapter vi.

16. Compare Chapter xxxiv preceding: "it's the tripes that carry the feet, not the feet the tripes."

17. *"Alma de cántaro."*

18. Compare the French peasant's expression *"bon comme le pain."* For the European peasant in general, bread, which is the staple article of his daily diet, has a significance that is almost sacramental.

19. *"Perlesía"* is "paralysis" or "palsy." *"Perlerines"* connotes *"perlas"*—"pearls."

20. Rodríguez Marín cites the popular sayings: *"Quien feo ama, hermoso le parece"*—"An ugly person whom one loves appears beautiful"; and *"El escarabajo llama á sus hijos granos de oro"*— "The black beetle calls its young ones grains of gold."

21. This passage is somewhat obscure. Like Ormsby, I have followed the reading of Professor Juan Calderón (*Cervantes Vindicado*).

CHAPTER XLVIII

1. It was customary to attribute physical defects to "the hand of God." (Rodríguez Marín)

2. *"Cebolluda labradora."* The adjective *"cebolluda"* means "bulbous," or having the characteristics of an onion ("cebolla"). Ormsby: "a clumsy country wench." Motteux: "a rank country wench."

3. A reminiscence of Garcilaso's Third Eclogue; see Chapter VIII preceding and note 1.

4. *"Antes os la dará roma que aguileña."* Motteux has the sense: "he will rather tempt a man with an ugly object than with a beautiful one." According to Rodríguez Marín, this is the tag of a popular tale of Andalusia.

5. *"La que ofrecen essas reuerendissimas tocas."* Motteux makes a bad blunder: "that which the most respectful pledges offer."

6. The distinction was a necessary one in Cervantes' time, the western part of the principality being known as Asturias de Oviedo, while the far eastern portion was called Asturias de Santillana.

7. *"Era montañés"*—that is, from the mountainous region north of Castile and León, known as the "Montaña."

8. The hand-borne litter or sedan chair.

9. Pellicer locates this gate, famous in its day, as having been at the point where the Calle de los Milaneses and the Calle de Santiago began. According to Rodríguez Marín, it was burned in 1582 and shortly afterward was completely torn down, but the name, as in the case of the well-known Puerta del Sol, remained attached to the spot.

10. That is, to the barber-surgeon.

11. Rodríguez Marín believes this episode is taken from the *Floresta Española* of Melchor de Santa Cruz.

12. *"Dança como el pensamiento, bayla como vna perdida."* In order to render this passage clearly, it is necessary to expand somewhat upon the Spanish text. As Lockhart points out in his notes to Motteux, there is a distinction (which previous translators have ignored) between the *danza,* or courtly dance, and the *baile,* or dance of the people. Ormsby: "dances quick as thought, foots it like a gypsy." Motteux: "dances like a thought, trips like a mad one."

13. Literally, a "tradesman's ear"— *"orejas de mercader."*

14. This comparison has occurred in Part I, Chapter XII. Ormsby, doubtless inadvertently, omits the clause.

15. This is the old medicine speaking, with its conception of bodily "humors," its practice of blood-letting, etc. Webster defines an issue as "a discharge, or flux, of blood"; and, "an artificial ulcer made, as by incision, to secure discharge of pus." The Spanish term is *"fuente"*—literally, "spring" or "fountain."

CHAPTER XLIX

1. In Cervantes' time there were a number of popular treatises in Spanish on Hippocrates and his aphorisms. (Schevill)

2. "Olla-podrida" literally means a "rotten pot." See Chapter XLVII preceding, note 6.

3. A proverb.

4. See Chapter XXXII (note 27) preceding and Chapter LI (note 10) following.

5. See Chapter XIV preceding, note 7.

6. The general sense of this expression is: there is disorder, or a disturbance, somewhere. (Schevill. See also the note by Rodríguez Marín.)

7. Compare Chapter XLIII preceding.

8. *"Tener respeto a la religion y a la honra de los religiosos."* Ormsby: "to respect religion and honor its ministers," rather than Motteux's evasive rendering: ". . . and honor religious men." Rodríguez Marín observes that "we have here an excellent program of government, set forth in only four lines of type." Whether or not one agrees with this, there can be little doubt that Sancho is voicing Cervantes' own view of government and society.

9. This is a slip; Sancho had already supped.

10. The Spanish word *"barato"* used here refers to a gift made to onlookers or servants out of the common fund (our modern "kitty" in a poker game) or out of the winner's gains. (Rodríguez Marín)

11. Nothing is known of this particular sharper. (Schevill) For Cacus, see Prologue to Part I, note 8.

12. *"Auia de saber con quantas entraua la romana."*

13. *"Barato"* again.

14. *"Algún oficial"*—*"oficial"* here has

the sense of *"artesano"*—"artisan" (Rodríguez Marín); not "under officers," as Motteux has it.

15. The garment here referred to is the *saltaembarca*, which appears to have been a sort of seaman's jacket open at the sides; compare the Italian *saltambarco*, a peasant's jacket. (See Rodríguez Marín's note.)

16. That is, with reeds employed as lances or javelins in a mock tournament.

17. Compare Chapter v (note 8) and Chapter xxxiv (note 5) preceding.

18. Rhyming proverb: *"La mujer y la gallina/Por andar se pierden aina."*

19. A proverb.

CHAPTER L

1. "Teresa Sancha" in the original.

2. The literal reading is "making public the Aranjuez of her issues [fountains]." The fountains of Aranjuez were famous ones. On issues, see Chapter xlviii preceding, note 15.

3. On the text at this point, see Chapter xlvi preceding, note 1.

4. Ormsby: "Argamasilla is the only village in La Mancha where such a sight could be seen; an arm of the Guadiana flows past it."

5. Tag of one of the old Cid ballads, *"A Calatrava la Vieja."* There are references in other ballads to this mode of punishment inflicted upon light women, and a number of later Spanish writers refer to it. (See Rodríguez Marín's note.)

6. For this expression, compare Chapters xxxii and xxxiv preceding.

7. A proverb.

8. Literally, "you have but to open your mouth, and your mouth will be the measure."

9. A similar expression has occurred in Chapter xlii preceding.

10. The Spanish dry measure, the "celemín," is roughly equivalent to a peck.

11. Aubrey Bell, in his *Cervantes* (pp. 12–13), cites this passage as an instance of what he elsewhere (p. 42) calls "the independent and happy poverty of the peasant."

12. *"Como vn pino de oro."* A *"pino de oro"* was a small ornament or trinket stuck in the hair. (Rodríguez Marín)

13. The Spanish word here is *"papahigo."* According to Covarrubias, the *papahigo* was a half-mask covering the face and used by travelers as a protection against the air and the cold. Duffield has: "travel with his face in a mask." Jarvis: "travel with a cape to his cap." Motteux is wrong: "go with an umbrella over his head"; and Ormsby is ambiguous: "take the road with a sunshade."

14. Literally, "a bad year and a bad month."

15. Rhyming proverb: *"Andeme yo caliente,/Y riase la gente."*

16. This proverb has occurred before; see Chapters iv (note 7) and xli (note 5) preceding, and Chapter lxii (note 4) following.

17. Sound made in coaxing a dog; see Chapter xxxiii preceding, note 15.

18. Rhyming proverb: *"Vióse el perro/En bragas de cerro,/Y no conoció su compañero"*—"The dog saw himself in hempen breeches and did not know his companion." A variation is: "The countryman [el villano] saw himself . . . and was proud as proud could be [y fiero que fiero]." Compare the Italian: *"Villano nobilitato non conosce suo parentado"*—"A rustic made a noble does not know his [own] relatives."

19. "Augustine doubts [it]." An expression employed by casuists and students discussing dogmatic questions. (Rodríguez Marín)

20. On this proverb, see Chapter x preceding, note 1.

21. Master Pedro has quoted this biblical injunction, Chapter xxv preceding (see note 18).

22. *"Cual el tiempo, tal el tiento"*—"As the time [occasion], so the behavior." Compare the proverb quoted in Chapter iv (note 8) preceding: "Manners change when honors come."

23. Literally, "do penance with me." Compare Chapter iii (note 18) preceding.

CHAPTER LI

1. Literally, "a question"; *"vna pregunta"* here has the sense of a difficult problem. These subtleties enjoyed a great vogue in the schools of the day. (Schevill)

2. This paradox is a very old one, going back to the ancient Greek logicians. (Compare the story of the King of the Crocodiles, the Epimenides Paradox,

etc.) See the discussion by Bertrand Russell and Alfred North Whitehead, *Principia Mathematica*, Vol. I, p. 61. The Theory of Logical Types invented by Russell represents the first means of circumventing all the known paradoxes within a completely formalized logical system. Other methods have been proposed, and a good deal of investigation of this subject has been made by modern mathematical logicians. (For this note I am indebted to my son, Hilary Whitehall Putnam.)

3. Clemencín and Hartzenbusch recall that Sancho on two previous occasions (Chapters xxxvi and xliii preceding) has stated that he did know how to sign his name. Hartzenbusch, always free with his emendations, accordingly would read: "*Si supiera mejor firmar*" —"If I knew how to sign my name better."

4. Motteux has the literal rendering: "I will snuff them away to air"—"*yo las despauilaré en el aire.*"

5. Compare Psalms 113:7: "He raiseth up the poor out of the dust, and lifteth the needy out of the dunghill."

6. There were a number of forms of this proverb: "Trim a bough and it will look like a young man," etc. (Rodríguez Marín.)

7. See the well-known fable by Phaedrus.

8. Schevill notes that the germ of this thought is to be found in Plato himself (*Phaedo*, xl): "If you would follow my advice, think not of Socrates but of the truth." The saying is commonly attributed to Aristotle, being a free rendering of a passage in his *Nicomachean Ethics*. Compare the Spanish proverb: "*Amigo Pedro, amigo Juan, pero más amiga la verdad*"—"Pedro is a friend, Juan is a friend, but a greater friend is the truth."

9. The name, as has been seen, means "be off with you" or "take yourself off."

10. A variation on the proverb "Take no bribe and surrender no right." See Chapters xxxii (note 27) and xlix (note 4) preceding.

11. As previously noted, the fanega (hanega) was roughly equivalent to 1.6 bushels.

12. Speaking of the dire poverty which the author of *Don Quixote* endured, Aubrey F. G. Bell (*Cervantes*, p. 43) observes: "He had suffered . . .

from the insults of market-women, whose fierce loquacity covered a falseness in their weights."

13. "*De haldas o de mangas*"—literally, "by skirts or sleeves"; the expression commonly means, in colloquial usage, "in one way or another," "by hook or crook," etc. Pellicer notes that the words have the secondary meaning of "fees and gifts." That is, the fees and gifts that Sancho would receive as governor.

14. Here we have something very like modern price-control and wage-fixing. Apparently there was a "servant problem" then, as now.

15. "*Coplas.*"

16. Lockhart (notes to Motteux) calls attention to an address to the throne by Herrera, physician to Philip III, on the state of mendicity in Madrid, with particular reference to the abuses perpetrated by the blind or false-blind.

CHAPTER LII

1. This proverb has occurred in Part I, Chapter xxii.

2. Allusion to amulets and other charms worn in the lists to bring victory. (Rodríguez Marín)

3. "*Su mal andante hija.*" Ormsby: "her unlucky daughter"; Motteux: "her forsaken daughter."

4. The expression in the original is "*bien desseada*"—"much longed for," a popular formula at the beginning of a letter, which the acolyte who serves as copyist employs even though Teresa previously had not known that the duchess existed. (Rodríguez Marín)

5. "*De meter este buen dia en mi casa*"—literally, "to take this fine day into my house." Allusion to the proverb: "When good luck comes along, open the door and let it in [take it into your house]." See Chapter iv preceding, and note 7.

6. This would mean that the loaf cost about five cents, and meat about ten cents the pound.

7. "*Y a Roma por todo*"—proverbial expression.

8. "*Vuestra pomposidad*"—used with farcical effect.

9. Professor Schevill notes that this son does not appear as a character in the story, though he is mentioned a number of times; he thinks it strange that Teresa

does not refer to the lad in her letter to his father.

10. Cervantes himself had had more than one unfortunate experience as a tax collector and was even imprisoned as a result of his muddled accounts.

11. A linen lace made with bobbins.

12. A little over three cents.

13. "A small municipality in the province of Teruel, diocese of Saragossa, now forgotten in the guidebooks and travel narratives." (Schevill, translated from the Spanish note.)

CHAPTER LIII

1. Compare the famous line of Shakespeare: "And thus the whirligig of time brings in his revenges." (*Twelfth Night*, Act V, Scene 1.)

2. The text here may not appear to make sense, but it is what Cervantes wrote: "*la primauera sigue al verano, el verano al estío, el estío al otoño, y el otoño al invierno, y el invierno a la primauera.*"

"*Verano*" and "*estío*" both mean "summer"; I have rendered the latter as "harvest season"—Ormsby has "fall." Needless to say, this passage has occasioned a lively controversy among editors and commentators. Some translators have followed the original while others have adopted the emendation of the Academy: "spring is followed by summer"—"*a la primavera sigue el verano,*" etc. Jarvis: "spring is succeeded by summer." Motteux: "spring precedes summer." Like Ormsby and Duffield, I have left the passage as it stands. Professor Schevill believes Cervantes wrote it in this manner for one of several possible reasons. I agree with Duffield that the author's intention was probably humorous, a desire to poke fun at the "Mohammedan philosopher," Cid Hamete.

3. Some editors, among them Hartzenbusch and Rodríguez Marín, emend the text to read "swifter than the wind." Schevill retains the reading found in the first edition.

4. Literally, "about reinforcements" —"*de socorros.*"

5. The term "*lanterna*" is here employed humorously for "*faro*"— "beacon." (Rodríguez Marín) The "north pole" is an allusion to the mariner's compass.

6. Scaling ladders.

7. "*Me hago agua*"—"I am turning to water."

8. This proverb has occurred in Chapter XLI (note 6) preceding, and occurs again in Chapter LIX (note 17) following.

9. The "*gazpacho*" is a kind of cold broth made with bread, olive oil, water, vinegar, garlic, onions, etc.

10. Compare Chapter VIII preceding, and Part I, Chapter XXV. The proverb occurs again in Chapters LV and LVII following.

11. Allusion to the proverb: "To her harm the ant grew wings." Compare Chapter XXXIII (note 6) preceding.

12. See Chapter XIX preceding and note 4.

13. The Portuguese also have this proverb. Motteux is wrong: "Let no one stretch his legs the more, however wide the sheet may be."

14. It was seven days, not ten, according to the statement made earlier in the chapter.

CHAPTER LIV

1. Play on the expression "*mentir por la barba*" (or, "*por mitad de la barba*") —"to lie in [by] one's beard."

2. There are many allusions to this custom by Spanish writers.

3. In the original, "*Guelte, Guelte.*"

4. The term "*franchones,*" "*franchotes,*" or "*franchutes*" was derogatorily applied to those foreigners who roamed over Spain as beggars, peddlers, knife-grinders, castrators of animals, etc. These words are not in the dictionary but are used by many good writers. "*Franchute*" (which might be rendered as "Frenchy") is still in common use. (See the note by Rodríguez Marín.)

5. Reference to the royal decrees which commanded the Moors in Spain, under penalty of death, to be ready to sail for Africa on three days' notice. The edict affecting the kingdoms of Granada, Murcia, and Andalusia and the city of Hornachos was issued on December 9, 1609; the one for Castile, Estremadura, and La Mancha was proclaimed on July 10, 1610; and others followed down through the year 1613. (Rodríguez Marín)

A standard account is given by Florencio Janer, in his *Condición Social de los Moriscos de España* (Madrid, 1857), pp. 72 ff. Cervantes further touches on the subject in his *novela*, the *Colloquy of the Dogs*. He himself appears, in general, to have been against the Moors, though this passage might be taken as indicating a certain sympathy with their sufferings. In the *novela* referred to, he is much more bitter. See the angry notes on the subject by Ormsby and by John Gibson Lockhart (notes to Motteux).

6. In modern Spanish the phrase "*en pelota*" commonly means "stark naked" (equivalent to "*en cueros*"), but here the meaning is "in nether garments"— "*ropas menores*," or "in trousers and doublet"—"*en calzas y en jubón.*" (Rodríguez Marín)

7. The stress on excitants to thirst reminds one of Rabelais.

8. "*Botas*"—small leather wine bags.

9. In the original: "the entrails."

10. Variation on a line from an old and well-known ballad, "Mira Nero de Tarpeya" (Durán's *Romancero General*, No. 571): "*Y él de nada se dolía.*"

11. "*Cuando a Roma fueres,/Haz como vieres.*" Compare our version: "When in Rome, do as the Romans do."

12. "*Espanol y tudesqui tuto vno: bon compaño*"—"a mixture of bad Italian and Spanish." On the expression "*bon compaño*," see Chapter xxv preceding and note 10.

13. "*Bon compaño, jura Di.*"

14. The excuse for the royal decrees banishing the Moriscos was the alleged discovery of a conspiracy between the Moors of the peninsula and the Barbary corsairs to restore the Moorish monarchy in Spain.

15. A proverb: "The good is not known until it is lost."

16. This is historically accurate. Many of the Moors did come back, and it was necessary to repeat the expulsion order.

17. A contrast to the Germany we have come to know in modern times!

18. "*Fino moro.*" Ormsby: "a true Moor." Motteux: "a rank Moor."

19. The Moors at first were permitted to take a certain amount of property with them.

20. As Schevill observes, this expression sounds out of place in Sancho's mouth, but he may have got it from Don Quixote, who in turn found it in the books of chivalry. In gypsy jargon a

sagittarius was one who was whipped through the streets.

21. A variation of this proverb is: "The devil takes the well-gotten gain, and takes the ill-gotten and its owner too."

CHAPTER LV

1. "*A poco mas de tres estados.*" Covarrubias defines the estado as "a certain measure, of the height of a man. . . . The depth of wells or other deep places is measured by estados." As a measure of length, the estado is 1.85 yards. "Fathom" is the nearest equivalent in English.

2. Phrase supplied by the translator.

3. This is yet another of those expressions that sound a little out of place in Sancho's mouth, but he undoubtedly got it from Don Quixote.

4. For this bit of humor, compare Part I, Chapter xxx. Cervantes is here imitating Boiardo in the *Orlando Innamorato.*

5. But Sancho was supposed to have given his bread and cheese to the pilgrims. "If Cervantes, as some critics maintain, had written the *Quixote* slowly and carefully, would he not have discovered in it such contradictions as this?" (Rodríguez Marín)

6. Compare Chapter xiii (note 3) preceding: "for troubles are less where there is bread."

7. This, of course, is humorous, but Clemencín suspects it is an error.

8. Covarrubias: "A very ancient edifice on the banks of the River Tagus, near Toledo. . . . Galiana was a Moorish princess. . . . Hence, a proverbial expression, applied to those who are not content with the quarters assigned them: *to want Galiana's palace.*"

9. Another reading of this proverb is: "Welcome, but not so if you come alone." (In the original, a matter of punctuation.)

10. "*¡Voto a tal!*"

11. Literally, "as if I had given birth to it."

12. Allusion to an old Ballad, "Doña Urraca, aquesa infanta" (Durán's *Romancero General*, No. 807).

13. See Chapter xxxii preceding, note 27.

14. A proverb with the Spaniards as with us.

15. Teresa has quoted this proverb, Chapter L (note 22) preceding.

16. The Portuguese add: "nor eat of this bread."

17. See Part I, Chapter XXV (note 5). This proverb also occurs in Part II, Chapter X (note 2) and again in Chapters LXV (note 3) and LXXIII (note 10).

18. What of Sancho's "Constitutions" (see Chapter LI preceding)?

19. Reference to a children's game. There is some uncertainty as to how it was played. Rodríguez Marín believes it is the modern game of "four corners" (*cuatro esquinas*, or *cuatro cantillos*).

CHAPTER LVI

1. Allusion to the Council of Trent (ended 1563), statute of the twenty-fifth session, canon 19, directed against knightly dueling of this sort.

2. The arroba, as has been seen, was 25.6 pounds.

3. This repetition of what has been said earlier in the chapter (such repetitions, as the reader will have noted, are by no means infrequent in Cervantes) might possibly be taken by the captious as further evidence of careless or hasty writing.

4. See Chapter VI preceding, note 1.

5. The question arises: how could the lackey have seen the young woman's face when she was so heavily veiled?

6. A proverb.

CHAPTER LVII

1. For the story of Bireno and his mistress, Olimpia, whom he deserted on a desert island, see Cantos IX and X of the *Orlando Furioso* (compare the legend of Theseus and Ariadne). It also forms the subject of a popular ballad given in Durán's *Romancero General*.

2. A proverb. Literally, "the just often pay for sinners in my country."

3. Literally, "from Seville to Marchena, from Granada to Loja, from London to England." Marchena is in the province of Seville and Loja in the province of Granada. I have here taken a hint from Ormsby, who has "from Seville to Cadiz."

4. On this expression, see Chapter XXXIII preceding, note 3.

CHAPTER LVIII

1. Compare the verse quoted in the Prologue to Part I: "*Non bene pro toto libertas venditur auro.*" As Rodríguez Marín notes, this was a favorite theme with Spanish poets of the Golden Age.

2. Having himself been a prisoner of the Moors in Algiers and in jail on a number of occasions, Cervantes could speak from experience.

3. Clemencín: "A beautiful thought eloquently expressed, and how appropriate to Cervantes' own unfortunate, poverty-stricken situation!"

4. A "*retablo*" is the carved work at the back of an altar.

5. This was the customary way of transporting images from one parish to another. (Rodríguez Marín)

6. This application of "Don" to the name of a saint was not original with Cervantes. Rodríguez Marín calls attention to a twelfth-century poem in which the expression "Don Iesuchristo" (Don Jesus Christ) occurs.

7. St. George, according to legend, slew the dragon to save the king's daughter.

8. "*Fué mas liberal que valiente*"—literally, "more liberal than valiant." I have followed Rodríguez Marín in taking this phrase as equivalent to "*aún mas liberal*"—"even more liberal." Ormsby: "generous rather than valiant." Jarvis and Motteux: "more liberal than valiant."

9. Compare Chapter XLIII (note 11) preceding.

10. San Diego, or Santiago, is St. James (San Jaime, San Jacobo), the patron saint of Spain.

11. See II Corinthians 12:2-4.

12. Quotation from Matthew 11:12.

13. "*Adobandoseme el juyzio.*" Is this a flash of insight with regard to the state of his mental faculties such as Don Quixote appears to have on several occasions?

14. A popular expression by way of wishing one success in an undertaking. (Rodríguez Marín)

15. This superstition is said to have been prevalent in the Mendoza family. Quevedo refers to it in his *Book of All Things* (*Libro de Todas las Cosas*): "If you spill the salt and . . . are (a Mendoza), rise from the table without eating . . . and that way the omen with respect to the salt will be fulfilled; for a misfortune always follows, and it is a misfortune not to eat." Such supersti-

tions, according to Covarrubias, ran in families.

16. This incident, apocryphal or not, is related in Suetonius's *Life of Julius Caesar*, which had appeared in Spanish translation in 1596. See also Livy, I, 56, and Herodotus, VI.

17. Word supplied by the translator to make the sense clearer.

18. "*¡Santiago, y cierra España!*" See Chapter IV (note 6) preceding. The sense is "close in upon them" or "attack."

19. The commentators note that Don Quixote does not really answer Sancho's question; and, indeed, it is rather strange that Sancho should ask it, seeing that he himself, in a preceding chapter (IV), has quoted this battle cry as if he understood it very well.

20. Allusion to the tradition that the Moors (Arabs) are descended from Hagar (see the Old Testament).

21. The author appears to be particularly fond of this passage from Horace (*Odes*, I, iv, 13–14), as he makes use of it a number of times, beginning with the Prologue to Part I.

22. "*Sayas.*"

23. According to Rodríguez Marín, the author means to say that the jackets were of brocade and the skirts (*sayas*) of gold-embroidered tabby. This "*tabí de oro*" was a more expensive material than plain tabby; at Seville, in 1627, a little later than when Cervantes wrote, a yard was worth forty-three reales.

24. Ormsby observes: "Hartzenbusch protests that Cervantes can never have written this; but his pen does undoubtedly sometimes indulge in a flourish of the kind." The fact is, the image of the sun halting in its course is taken from a popular love song. (Rodríguez Marín)

25. The first edition has *Anteón* (Antaeus). Authors of the time commonly confused the two names.

26. "*He oido yo dezir de su valor y de sus gracias lo mismo que tu me has dicho.*" Most translators have taken the "*gracias*" as referring to Don Quixote; but a couple of paragraphs above the author has employed the same word with reference to Sancho ("drolleries"). It would seem to be a case of lack of clarity in the writing. Ormsby makes the distinction that I do: "the valor of the one and the drolleries of the other."

27. The Jarama River and the Tagus meet at Aranjuez.

28. These tame oxen (*cabestros*) were employed in driving the bulls from pasture.

29. That is, in a bull fight. Literally, "were to be run."

30. A proverb.

CHAPTER LIX

1. The title is somewhat freely rendered.

2. "*Condumio.*" According to Covarrubias, an old word used by the peasantry to denote food (meat) prepared to be eaten with bread. Ormsby: "the prog"; Jarvis and Motteux: "his sauce."

3. "*A que su señor hiziesse la salua.*" Allusion to the custom formerly observed in the houses of the nobility and other important personages, of having the butler ("*maestresala*"—"*pregustator*") taste the food before his master and the rest of the company did. Here it is Don Quixote who is supposed to be acting as Sancho's "taster."

4. That is, he opened it only to eat, not to talk.

5. Rhyming proverb: "*Muera Marta, y muera harta.*"

6. A proverb: "*Hasta la muerte todo es vida.*"

7. The original has "*y dexesse de pedir gallinas*"—"and don't be asking for hens." Rodríguez Marín is convinced this is an erratum; I follow his emendation: "*gullurías.*"

8. Don Quixote and Sancho were supposed to have gone to their room before the conversation with the innkeeper occurred.

9. Allusion to the spurious continuation of Part I by Fernández de Avellaneda. Rodríguez Marín: "Cervantes was thinking of writing this chapter when there came to hand the *Second Volume of the Ingenious Gentleman, Don Quixote de la Mancha,* supposedly written by Alonso Fernández de Avellaneda and published at Tarragona, in 1614." See the Prologue to Part II.

10. Ormsby: "Avellaneda in chap. II of his continuation makes Aldonza Lorenzo write to Don Quixote threatening him with a beating for calling her Princess and Dulcinea, and Don Quixote, stung by her ingratitude, resolves to look out for another mistress."

11. *"Guardarla con suavidad y sin hazerse fuerça alguna."* Ormsby finds it "difficult to make sense" of this passage. He accordingly adopts Hartzenbusch's suggested emendation: *"su vida"* for *"suavidad"* and *"tuerto"* for *"fuerça."* Ormsby renders: "his profession to maintain the same with his life and never wrong it." Schevill and Rodríguez Marín make no comment, and indeed it seems that such a translation as I have given would solve the problem.

12. Compare Chapters XIV (note 5), XXX (note 3), and XXXIV (note 8) preceding, and Chapter LXXI (note 10) following.

13. See the Prologue to Part II. The author of the spurious *Don Quixote*, it will be remembered, had taunted Cervantes with being an old man, with one hand missing, etc.

14. Schevill is puzzled by this statement. "To what is Cervantes referring?" he asks. "How are we to judge the style of an author from a text that is poorly printed and, certainly, marred by the usual proportion of printer's errors?" (From the Spanish note.)

15. It was Cervantes himself who, in Part I, Chapter VII, called Sancho's wife Mari Gutiérrez; a few lines above, in the same chapter, he had referred to her as Juana Gutiérrez, and in Part I, Chapter LII, she is Juana Panza.

16. In this chapter the author clearly reveals his own conception of Sancho's character, and we can see the respect that he had for the squire and the peasant type in general. This is a point that Aubrey F. G. Bell stresses throughout in his *Cervantes.* Sancho is neither a glutton nor a drunkard nor a vulgar buffoon; he is *"gracioso"*—"droll," which is something quite different. This is one of the chief sins of Motteux and certain other English language translators who would make him out to be a cockney clown.

17. For the second of these two proverbs, see Chapters XLI (note 6) and LIII (note 8) preceding.

18. *"Con mero mixto imperio."* A juridical formula, according to Covarrubias.

19. *"Hecho equis"*—that is, with his legs forming the letter X.

20. *"El autor . . . [no] quiere que no comamos buenas migas juntos."* A free translation.

21. Ormsby: "In chapter XI Avellaneda gives an account of Don Quixote's tilting at the ring in the Coso at Saragossa, and so prolix and encumbered with details that his admirer, M. Germond de Lavigne, was forced to leave it out." The reference is to De Lavigne's French translation (Paris, 1853).

CHAPTER LX

1. Don Quixote forgets that the lashes must be voluntarily inflicted, a fact of which Sancho later reminds him.

2. A point was a tie or string with an aglet, used in the sixteenth and seventeenth centuries to join parts of the costume, such as doublet and hose.

3. *"Se abraçó con el a braço partido."* There has been some discussion as to the meaning of the expression *"a braço [brazo] partido,"* but, according to the *Dictionary of the Academy,* it has reference to a struggle "with the arms alone, without the use of weapons."

4. Reminiscence of an old historical ballad, "Los fieros cuerpos revueltos" (Durán, *Romancero General,* No. 978). The allusion is to the assassination of Peter the Cruel by his brother, Henry of Trastamara, aided by the latter's page, Bertrand du Guesclin (Beltrán Duguesclin), who as he tripped the monarch up exclaimed, *"Ni quito ni pongo rey; pero ayudo a mi senor"*—"I neither overthrow nor set up a king, but am aiding my lord."

5. Verses from another ballad, "A cazar va Don Rodrigo" (Durán, op. cit., No. 691).

6. *"Por vida de sus pensamientos."* Ormsby and Motteux render this literally: "by the life of his thoughts." Jarvis: "by the life of his best thoughts."

7. Clemencín remarks that this is a commentary on the state of law and order in the province of Catalonia in that period.

8. The "petronel" was a fifteenth-century portable firearm resembling a large-caliber carbine.

9. The first edition has "Osiris," which, Hartzenbusch notes, is an error or slip of the pen on the author's part; but, as Rodríguez Marín remarks, the slip may be Roque Guinart's and not Cervantes'. Ormsby: "The Busiris who

with Memphian chivalry and perfidious hate pursued the sojourners of Goshen." (See Milton's *Paradise Lost*, 1, 307.)

10. Roque Guinart (properly, Roca Guinarda) was a Catalan bandit who achieved considerable notoriety about the time Cervantes wrote. By 1610 he had united under his command some two hundred followers. The portrait of him given here appears to be a fairly faithful one. "Despite his evil way of life, he won the warm sympathy of all Spain." (Rodríguez Marín) For an authoritative work on the subject, the special student may be referred to *Perot Roca Guinarda, Historia d'aquest bandoler*, by Lluis Maria Soler y Terol (Manresa, 1909).

11. The "*saltaembarca*"; see Chapter XLIX preceding and note 15.

12. The first edition has "*los muchos de don Vicente*." I follow the reading of a number of editors: "*deudos*"—"kinsmen," which agrees with the reference later in the chapter to Don Vicente's "*parientes*"—"relatives."

13. The original reads "*para que, zelosa, me quitasses la vida, la qual pues la dexo en tus manos y en tus braços, tengo mi suerte por venturosa*." Clemencín and other editors have found difficulty in making sense of the passage, due, as Rodríguez Marín observes, to an error in punctuation. Ormsby omits the clause, "*la qual*," etc. Motteux has the correct translation.

14. "*Gente rústica y desbaratada*."

15. The "harquebus" was a firearm having a matchlock operated by a trigger and supported for firing by a hook.

16. "*Lladres*"—Catalan for "thieves."

17. Proverb: "*El abad de lo que canta yanta*." Portuguese: "*Abbade donde canta, dahi janta*"—"Where the abbot sings, there he dines." Compare our "sing for your supper."

18. "*Frade*."

19. Hartzenbusch points out that this ought to be the day of the beheading of John the Baptist, or August 29, since, according to the dates of the letters written at the duke's place, the feast of the saint's nativity, June 24, was already past.

20. The Niarros and the Cadells were two rival bands; Roque belonged to the former.

CHAPTER LXI

1. The first edition has "*todos*"—"all." Hartzenbusch and some other editors read "*casi todos*"—"nearly all," a reading which Rodríguez Marín feels it is necessary to adopt. Schevill retains "*todos*."

2. According to the work on Roca Guinarda by Soler y Terol (see note 10 to the preceding chapter), one of these proclamations offered a reward of a thousand pounds in the coin of Barcelona, to be paid out of the royal treasury, along with other inducements, for the capture of the bandit dead or alive.

3. "*Lililies*"—on this war cry, see Chapter XXXIV preceding, note 12.

4. "*Donde mas largamente se contiene*"—a legal phrase used in certain oaths.

CHAPTER LXII

1. A proverb.

2. Rodríguez Marín: "An appetizing dish consisting of breast of fowl, especially of hen, with rice flour, milk, and sugar, the recipe for which the reader will find in the *Libro del arte de cozina* of Diego Granado, Madrid, 1599. . . . The name was applied to this dish as far back as 1420."

3. Allusion to a passage in Chapter XII of the spurious *Don Quixote*.

4. This proverb has occurred in Chapters IV (note 7), XLI (note 5), and L (note 16) preceding.

5. A clear expression of Cervantes' attitude toward Sancho and his resentment of the manner in which Avellaneda treats the squire.

6. "There are many stories in European folklore having to do with talking heads; the eminent Roger Bacon, in the thirteenth century, who was looked upon as a necromancer, fashioned a similar one." (Schevill, from the Spanish note.) "The first *brazen head* on record is that famous one possessed by Albertus Magnus, which was broken into a thousand shivers by his disciple Thomas Aquinas, whose self-possession entirely deserted him on hearing the sayings of the head. The great Albert exclaimed on beholding the accident, '*Periit opus triginta annorum*.' Beckman, in his *History of Inventions*, says that this is all that has been recorded con-

cerning the first and most famous of all the brazen heads. Friar Bacon, in our own country, and the Marquess de Villena, in Spain, passed for having in their possession similar marvels of unholy mechanism. But I believe the *Invisible Girl*, that some years ago made the tour of all the capitals of Europe, has at last revealed all the mystery of all the brazen heads that ever existed; and Cervantes, in the text, seems to have anticipated all the capabilities of such a device." (Lockhart, notes to Motteux.)

See the play by Robert Greene: *The Honorable History of Friar Bacon and Friar Bungay* (1592). The special student will find a number of research references in Schevill.

7. "Michael Scott; it is not known where he was born nor where he died (around 1232); he studied at Paris and Oxford, learned Arabic in Toledo, and translated various texts and commentaries on Aristotle from the Arabic into the Latin; among his own books are: *De sole et luna; De chiromantia;* and *De physiognomia et de hominis procreatione;* in Dante's *Inferno*, xx, 115–17, he appears among the magicians." (Schevill, from the Spanish note.)

The lines from Dante to which Schevill refers are the following:

Quell'altro che ne' fianchi è così
    poco
Michele Scotto fu, che veramente,
Delle magiche frode, seppe il
    gioco.

The other, who looks about the flanks so slim,
Was Michael Scott; and verily he knew
The circle of magic and its frauds to limn.

(Lawrence Binyon translation.)

See J. W. Brown, *Life and Legend of Michael Scott* (Edinburgh, 1897); and C. H. Haskins, *Studies in the History of Medical Science* (Cambridge: Harvard University Press, 1924). Other commentators, however, including Bowle and Pellicer, have denied that the Escotillo mentioned by Cervantes is the thirteenth-century Michael Scott. Ormsby adopts this latter view, to the effect that the individual in question is one Michele Escoto, or Escotillo, a native of Parma, who as an astrologer and magician enjoyed a great reputation in the Low

Countries in the time of Alexander Farnese. Rodríguez Marín dismisses the subject with: "The annotators of *Don Quixote* cite various astrologers and sorcerers named *Escoto*. I shall not pause here to conjecture as to which of them Cervantes must be referring." (Clasicos Castellanos edition of the *Don Quixote*, edited by Rodríguez Marín, Vol. VIII, p. 139.)

8. "*Guardó rumbos*": "*rumbos*" here has the sense of "*rombos*," or geometrical figures, as the latter term is employed by Merlin in his poetic speech in Chapter xxxv preceding. (Rodríguez Marín) Ormsby, accordingly, is in error: "observed the points of the compass."

9. "*Sacaron a passear.*" Ormsby: "took Don Quixote out for a stroll." But one does not speak of a stroll on horseback. A little further on Ormsby renders "*passeo*" more properly as "excursion."

10. Clemencín raises the question as to why these words are put into the mouth of a Castilian, and believes that the answer is "because Don Quixote's experiences must have been better known in Castile than in other regions"; but Rodríguez Marín thinks the author means to emphasize that "it was not a Catalan but a Castilian who spoke thus to Don Quixote, a son of the people."

11. The original has "on all subjects" —"*en todas las cosas*."

12. Ormsby again has "stroll."

13. "Flee, ye adversaries!" A formula of the Church in exorcising evil spirits.

14. In the original: "Do you think that all brave men are *danzadores* and that all knights-errant are *bailarines?*" The distinction here, which cannot be brought out in English without a cumbersome circumlocution, is one that has been previously noted between the *danza*, or formal, stately dance of the nobility, and the *baile*, or dance of the people.

15. Reference to the *zapateado;* see Chapter xix preceding and note 3. Jarvis and Motteux: "shoe-jig"; Ormsby: "shoe-fling."

16. For this expression, see Chapter xxxii preceding and note 26. The sense is "agile as a gerfalcon."

17. "*En lo del dançar no doy puntada*": reference to the *danza* again.

18. This was an expression employed in folk tales.

19. Rodríguez Marín cites the proverb: "*El amor y la fe en las obras se ve*"—"Love and faith are shown by their works."

20. Proverbial expression.

21. Perogrullo was a legendary character who prophesied the obvious. Samples of his oracular(?) utterances are to be found in the collection known as *Cantos populares españoles:* "If you would have the ladies come after you, when you go walking place yourself in front of them." Another specimen: "It will be a sign, if you talk, that you have a tongue; and if you have molars, it will show you are not without them; and it is certain that if you go to the mirror you will see your face," etc. (Cited by Rodríguez Marín.)

22. Properly, the translator.

23. In the text: "*Le Bagatele.*" It is not known whether any Italian work with this title ever existed or not. Professor Schevill states that he has gone through any number of Italian and Spanish works without coming upon any trace of *Le Bagatelle.* In Cervantes' time there were numerous volumes of this sort variously labeled as collections of pleasantries, novels, tales, fables, entertaining deeds and sayings, jests, apothegms, miscellanies, etc. Schevill further draws attention to the fact that this is an imaginary printing shop and that the Barcelona editions of the spurious *Don Quixote* and of the work entitled *Light of the Soul,* referred to later on, are nonexistent ones.

24. That is, "trifles."

25. The text reads: "*me precio de cantar*"—"I pride myself on being able to sing," etc. That Cervantes owed a considerable debt to the *Orlando Furioso* as to other works that belong to the literature of chivalry, no reader of the *Don Quixote* can fail to observe; and according to Aubrey F. G. Bell (*Cervantes,* p. 19), during his five years' residence in Italy he had "learned sufficient Italian to read the poems of Ariosto and Tasso in the original." His recollections of the language, however, to employ Professor Schevill's word, are marked by a certain "nebulousness" ("*nebulosidad*") and would appear to be auditory rather than visual, as is indicated by his habit of transliterating and Hispanicizing Italian vocables: thus, "*compagno*" becomes "*compaño,*" "*pignatta*" becomes "*piñata,*" "*piace*" is rendered as "*piache,*" etc.

26. *Piñata* in the text. An earthenware cooking-pot.

27. Stew-pot.

28. "*Piace (place)*" is "pleases"; "*più (más)*" is "more"; "*su (arriba)*" is "up"; and "*giù (abajo)*" is "down."

29. This comparison had been made use of by Diego de Mendoza, author of *Lazarillo de Tormes,* and by Luis Zapata in the preface to his translation of Horace's *Ars Poetica,* published in 1591. Compare Cervantes' observations on the translation of poetry, in Part I, Chapter VI. Alexander Pope in one of his letters approves the idea.

30. The *Pastor Fido* is the work of Battista Guarini (Venice, 1590); the Spanish translation by Cristóbal Suárez de Figueroa was first published at Naples in 1602, and in a differing form was printed again at Valencia in 1609. Jáuregui's version of Torquato Tasso's *Aminta* was published at Rome in 1607; a second edition appeared at Seville in 1618.

31. Clemencín remarks that this is bad arithmetic. A thousand ducats is a sum equivalent to eleven thousand reales; at six reales the copy the returns on an edition of two thousand would amount to twelve thousand reales; but this leaves only a thousand reales—a very small sum—for the cost of paper, printing, and all other expenses.

32. Lockhart observes: "It is amusing to see, in many passages of his works, how completely Cervantes understood the tricks of the booksellers of his time." As Clemencín notes, these remarks would be out of place in the mouth of a gentleman of Argamasilla; it is obviously Cervantes himself who is speaking. The author also touches on the subject in his novels, *The Licentiate Vidriera* and *Persiles and Sigismunda.*

33. "*Si el libro es un poco abieso.*" One thinks here of the American Thoreau carrying home the unsold copies of his first book, *A Week on the Concord and Merrimack Rivers,* and remarking that he now had a library of nine hundred books, some seven hundred of which he himself had written!

34. *"No vale vn quatrín."*

35. Work by the Dominican friar, Felipe de Meneses, first published at Seville in 1555; there were a number of later editions, but none is known to have been printed at Barcelona. The title read: *Light of the Christian Soul against Blindness and Ignorance*, etc.

36. *"Son muchos los pecadores que se vsan."* Motteux mistranslates: "for sinners that use them are many."

37. *"Un tal vezino de Tordesillas"*— literally, "a certain neighbor." The title-page of Avellaneda's work identified him as *"natural de la villa de Tordesillas"*—"a native. . . ." The correct title of Avellaneda's work is *The Ingenious Gentleman, Don Quixote de la Mancha, Which contains his third sally and is the fifth part of his adventures* (Tarragona, 1614). See the English translations by Captain John Stevens (London, 1705) and William Yardley (London, 1784).

"It was hardly judicious in Cervantes," says Ormsby, "to credit his enemy with a second edition, but he seems to lose his head whenever he thinks of Avellaneda and his insults; and from this on he apparently thinks of little else. From Chapter LIX to the end, indeed, there is a decided falling off. The story is at once hurried and spun out, and in the episodes of Claudia and Ana Felix he drops into the tawdry style of the novels in the First Part. It is only when he touches earth in Sancho Panza that he recovers anything like his old vigor."

38. It was the custom to kill pigs on St. Martin's Day. The proverb ran: *"A cada puerco le llega su San Martín"*—"To every pig comes its Martinmas."

39. A statement of the basic spirit of realism that animates Cervantes' art.

40. Sancho had viewed the galleys when he and his master were first set down on the beach.

41. The *"cuatralbo"* was an officer in command of four galleys.

CHAPTER LXIII

1. Compare Chapter X preceding, where, when Sancho returns from his supposed interview with Dulcinea, Don Quixote says to him, "What is it, Sancho, my friend? Am I to be able to mark this day with a white stone or a black one?"

2. *"Tiempo y señal que nos muestra que en el se encierra,"* etc. Hartzenbusch emends to read: *"tipo y señal";* which Ormsby, who adopts his reading, renders as "pattern and image." I have followed Rodríguez Marín, who sees *"tiempo"* as referring to the day or occasion and *"señal"* to the white stone.

3. *"Que la chusma hiziesse fueraopa."* According to the *Dictionary of the Academy*, *"Ropa afuera!"*—"Clothes off!"—was an expression employed to advise the rowers to make ready. According to Covarrubias, it was used when they had to row lustily (*"con hígado"*).

4. Compare Sancho's use of this expression in Part I, Chapter XVII; it has occurred a number of times.

5. The citadel of Barcelona.

6. Rodríguez Marín points out that this concept is not Cervantes' own but Aristotle's.

7. *"Por dos tios mios."* Previous translators have rendered as "two uncles of mine"; but Rodríguez Marín, whom I have followed, states that this must refer to Juan Tiopieyo and his wife; for, as Clemencín notes, Ricote, in the story that he tells in Chapter LIV preceding, mentions only one uncle.

8. In Chapter LIV preceding, this young man is referred to as Don Pedro Gregorio; and in this present chapter, it will be noted, he is variously called Don Gaspar Gregorio, Don Gregorio, and Don Gaspar. Rodríguez Marín thinks this may possibly be a double name, like Juan José, Pedro Antonio, etc., and considers this "a fresh indication of the carelessness with which Cervantes wrote."

9. The cruzado was an old Castilian coin of gold, silver, or copper, so called because it had a cross on the obverse side. There was also a Portuguese cruzado.

10. Clemencín observes that such a remark is scarcely becoming in the mouth of a damsel of twenty. Rodríguez Marín: "And the same may be said of the words a few lines below: 'I spoke to Don Gaspar and reminded him of the danger that lay in his appearing as a man.'"

11. That is, the Sultan.

12. For the nature of this "offense," see Chapter LIV preceding, note 14.

CHAPTER LXIV

1. See Chapter XXV preceding (note 9).

2. Compare Chapter XLIII preceding (note 15).

3. See Chapter XXXIV preceding (note 7).

4. This is literal: "*de muy buenas entrañas.*"

5. Compare Part I, Chapter II (note 6).

6. Motteux is inaccurate: "without them [arms] he never felt that he was himself at all."

7. "*A quien Dios se la diere, San Pedro se la bendiga*": from the marriage ceremony.

8. That is, confess that the other is in the right.

9. In the original there is an untranslatable pun on the double sense of "*deslocado*"—"dislocated" and "cured of madness" (from "*loco*"—"mad").

CHAPTER LXV

1. Certain commentators have expended a great deal of time and energy in an attempt to establish a chronology for *Don Quixote;* but as Don Antonio Eximeno observes in his *Apologia de Miguel de Cervantes,* etc. (Madrid, 1806), cited by Menéndez y Pelayo and Rodríguez Marín: "Cervantes' geography and that of every author of works of the imagination is largely fanciful, and the time element of the fable is as imaginary as the fable itself."

2. "*Donde las dan las toman*"—literally, "where they give them, they take them." A proverb. Ormsby renders literally; Motteux: "they that give must take."

3. A variation on the proverb that has occurred a number of times: "Many think to find bacon where there are no pegs."

4. Compare Chapter LVIII preceding.

5. See Chapter VII preceding.

6. "*Albricias.*"

7. See Chapter V preceding.

8. Rhyming proverb: "*Hoy por tí y mañana por mí.*"

9. A proverb.

10. Philip III's officer charged with the expulsion of the Moriscos of La Mancha.

CHAPTER LXVI

1. This saying will be found in Sallust's *Oration on Caesar,* I, 1: "*Sed res docuit id verum esse quod in carminibus Appius ait, fabrum esse suae quemque fortunae.*"

2. From the *Orlando Furioso,* IV, 57. See Part I, Chapter XIII and note 3.

3. A proverb.

4. The Portuguese have the same proverb in a slightly different form: "*Com raiva do asno tornase á albarda*" —"With rage one turns from the ass to the packsaddle."

5. The arroba being twenty-five pounds, the fat man's weight was two hundred and seventy-five.

6. An expression used in connection with persons of small consequence. (Correas: *Vocabulario de Refranes.*)

7. This anecdote is not original with Cervantes; it will be found in the *Floresta Española* of Melchor de Santa Cruz, who, according to Bowle, took it from the Italian writer Alciato's *De singulari certamine liber* (Venice, 1544), a Spanish translation of which was published at Antwerp in 1558(?).

8. "*A la taberna de lo caro*": on this expression and the different classes of wines and taverns in the Spain of that era, see Chapter XXIV preceding and note 5.

9. This starts off as a juridical phrase, employed by someone who is going bond for another, and ends jocosely with a popular proverb.

10. "*De lo caro.*"

11. On the cheese of Tronchón, see Chapter LII preceding and note 13. These "awakeners of thirst" once more remind one of Rabelais.

12. That is, removed the cover from it ("*dessembaynó su calabaça*").

13. There is a pun in the original that is hopelessly untranslatable, based upon the double meaning of the verb "*deber*": "ought" or "must," and "to owe." Tosilos says: ". . . *deue de ser vn loco*"; and Sancho replies: "*¿Como deue? . . . no deue nada á nadie.*" By attempting to render it, other translators have succeeded only in writing bad English.

CHAPTER LXVII

1. It was Sancho who had filched the kerchiefs without his master's knowledge. See Chapter LVII preceding.

2. There was a popular saying to the effect that "fairy treasure [*los tesoros de los duendes*] is converted into a coal," and Covarrubias states that the expression refers to "all possessions that are consumed and done away with in an unaccountable manner." Ormsby notes that "the Spanish *duendes* are . . . more akin to brownies than fairies."

3. That is, acorns. Clemencín observes that "acorns do not merit such an epithet."—"Apparently," says Rodríguez Marín, "he [Clemencín] has never tasted those acorns, for there are such, that are better than the best almonds."

4. Like a cornerstone in a building. The expression is a common one in Cervantes. Rodríguez Marín thinks it was a popular saying current at the time.

5. The first edition has "*Miculoso*," which most editors have changed to "*Niculoso*."

6. The allusion is to Garcilaso de la Vega's First Eclogue. Boscán is seen as Garcilaso himself. There is a play on the Spanish "*bosque*" and the Latin "*nemus*"—a grove.

7. "Big Teresa," -*ona* being an augmentative suffix.

8. "*Buscar pan de trastrigo*"—literally, to look for better bread than that made of wheat; this was a proverbial expression signifying a quest for something out of the ordinary.

9. The "*churumbela*" was a wind instrument made of a reed and resembling a flageolet.

10. There is a difference of opinion among commentators as to what kind of instrument, properly speaking, is signified by *albogues*. According to the description given here, *albogues* were a kind of cymbals, but others say the term refers to a wind instrument. (See the note in Cejador.)

11. The reader unacquainted with Spanish may possibly be interested in the meaning of these words: *almohaza* —a currycomb; *almorzar*—to breakfast or lunch; *alfombra*—a carpet; *alguacil* —a constable; *alhucema*—lavender; *almacén*—shop; *alcancía*—bank or money-box. Schevill notes that not all these words are of Arabic origin, *almorzar*, for example, being from the Latin *admorsus* (*admordere*), that is to say, a "bite." He gives a number of philological references for those interested in the subject. As Clemencín remarks, the Arabic employs *al* as an article, "which we affix to certain Latin vocables, and this is the reason why we do not recognize them as our own."

12. *Borceguí*—a buskin or half-boot, *zaquizamí*—a garret; *maravedí*—the coin.

13. *Alhelí* — gillyflower; *alfaquí* — teacher of the Koran.

14. The text in the original is somewhat obscurely (or carelessly) worded, and this has led to a number of proposed emendations, but the sense of the passage is clear enough.

15. "*Qué polidas cuchares tengo de hazer.*" Jarvis has a suggestive rendering, though outside the text: "Oh, what neat wooden spoons shall I make when I am a shepherd!" Motteux: "Oh, how I shall make the spoons shine when I see me a shepherd!"

16. Jarvis: "What curds and cream! what garlands! what pretty knick-nacks!"

17. Variation on the proverb: "Many go for wool," etc. See Part I, Chapter VII, and Part II, Chapters XIV (note 8) and XLIII (note 17).

18. A proverb.

19. Ormsby cites the Plattdeutsch: "*Wat de oogen nich seht dat kränkt de hart ook nich.*"

20. Compare Part I, Chapter XXI (note 11).

21. Compare Chapter XLIII (note 12) preceding.

22. "*Quítate allá, ojinegra.*" The original form of the saying was "*Tirte allá, culnegra*"—"Be off with you, black-bottom." It is in this form that the proverb is preserved among Jews of Spanish origin. (Rodríguez Marín)

23. See Part I, Chapters XXI and XXXIX.

CHAPTER LXVIII

1. Ormsby, probably by oversight, omits this clause.

2. This is from the Vulgate, Job 17:12: "After darkness I hope for light." The words appear on the title page of Parts I and II of the original edition of the *Don Quixote* and certain other works put out by the same publisher, Juan de la Cuesta.

3. One cannot but recall here Shakespeare's famous lines (*Macbeth*, Act II, Scene 2):

Sleep that knits up the ravell'd
    sleave of care,
The death of each day's life, sore
    labour's bath,
Balm of hurt minds, great nature's
    second course,
Chief nourisher in life's feast.

And a little later in the same play (Act
II, Scene 3): "Shake off this downy
sleep, death's counterfeit . . ." Compare
Keats's "Endymion":

O magic sleep! O comfortable
    bird,
That broodest o'er the troubled
    sea of the mind
Till it is hush'd and smooth! O
    unconfined
Restraint! imprisoned liberty!
    great key
To golden palaces.

It may also be of interest to cite J. G.
Saxe's humorous lines from "Early
Rising":

"God bless the man who first in-
    vented sleep!"
So Sancho Panza said and so
    say I;
And bless him, also, that he
    didn't keep
His great discovery to himself,
    nor try
To make it,—as the lucky fellow
    might—
A close monopoly by patent-
    right.

4. For this proverb, see Chapter x
preceding, note 7, and Chapter xxxii
(note 7).

5. Miguel de Unamuno, in his *Life of
Don Quixote and Sancho* (see the translation by Homer P. Earle, New York,
1927), a running commentary on Cervantes' masterpiece, becomes even more
dithyrambic than usual in discussing
these lines, finding that they hold the
most deeply hidden and intimate essence
of the Quixotic spirit; but, as it happens,
Don Francisco Rodríguez Marín has
shown the verses in question to be taken
from a Spanish translation of Pietro
Bembo's *Gli Asolani*, an edition of which
was published at Venice as early as 1515,
the Spanish version appearing at Salamanca in 1551. (See the extended note
in Rodríguez Marín.)

6. Compare Chapters ii (note 8), xvii,
and lxiii (note 4) preceding.

7. Motteux is at his typical worst
here: "Trollopites, barbers, and Andrew
Hodge-podge, and bitchlings." Ormsby
slurs the passage: "We, tortolites, barbers, animals! I don't like those names
at all. . . ."

8. A proverb.

9. Proverbial expression.

CHAPTER LXIX

1. According to the *Dictionary of the
Academy*, to bury a woman with a palm
("*enterrar con palma*") was "to bury
her in a state of virginity." Rodríguez
Marín: "The old custom of placing a
palm in the hands of dead virgins has
come down to our day." He quotes a
stanza from the *Cantos Populares Españoles*, containing the line: "*Muero
moza y llevo palma*"—"I die a maid and
carry off the palm." Ormsby: "The
dried palm branch preserved from
Easter Sunday that may be seen in almost every Spanish house."

2. "*Picote*." Covarrubias: "A coarse
goatskin cloth, so rough that it pricks
you when you touch it, whence the
name *picote*." (From "*picar*"—"to
prick.") Not "sables" as in Ormsby.
With regard to the "robes of baize and
wool"—"*de vayeta y de anascote*,"
which the duennas wear, "*anascote*" is a
woolen stuff that resembles serge.
Ormsby has: "in baize and bombazine."

3. The allusion, of course, is to Or-
pheus.

4. The second of these stanzas is from
Garcilaso de la Vega's Third Eclogue.
Schevill observes that Garcilaso was a
poet whom Cervantes imitated. The
rhyme scheme in the original is ababcc.

5. Minos, Aeacus, and Rhadamanthus
were the mythical judges of the infernal
regions. The phrase "Pluto's murky pit"
—"*las cabernas lóbregas de Dite*," will
be found in Merlin's speech, Chapter
xxxv preceding.

6. "*Veynte y quatro mamonas*." "*Ma-
mona*," properly speaking, is the gesture
that consists in laying five fingers on
someone's beard as a sign of contempt
(Covarrubias); but here the word obviously implies more than that, and
"smack" would seem to be the appropriate rendering.

7. Beginning of the proverb: "The
old woman liked the blites and left

neither green nor dry." Motteux: "The old woman tickled herself with trifles."(!)

8. A proverb.

9. For this expression, see Chapter XXXIII preceding, note 15.

10. In the words of the poet Virués, "long, smooth, white, delicate hands (*blancas, largas, suaves, delicadas*)" were the fashion then as small ones were in a later era. (See the note in Rodríguez Marín.)

11. "*Menos mudas.*"

12. Vinegar water (*vinagrillo*) was a cosmetic lotion composed of vinegar, eggs, sweet limes, and honey. (Rodríguez Marín)

13. Proverbial expression signifying one who serves as the butt for the jests of others or upon whom they impose.

14. "*Que la arroje y lo eche todo á treze, aunque no se venda.*" Motteux: "Let me be, or by Heaven I will fling out, and do it all in a lump, though it be lost labour."

CHAPTER LXX

1. "*Vna carriola*"—a bed on wheels that may be pushed under another bed.

2. From Garcilaso's First Eclogue, verse 57.

3. On long hands, see the preceding chapter.

4. "*Crealo Iudas*"—literally, "let Judas believe it." Some commentators have seen here a reminiscence of Horace, *Satires*, I, v, 100–101: ". . . *credat Iudaeus Apella, non ego*"—"let the Jew Apella believe it, not I"; but Schevill thinks that such an allusion is out of the question considering that Sancho is the speaker.

5. The stanza quoted in the preceding chapter.

6. "*Los intonsos poetas*": the sense of *intonso* is "ignorant," "unpolished." Ormsby: "callow poets."

7. This habit of borrowing from another poet's work was a common one and was not looked upon as being in the least disreputable. In one of Lope de Vega's sonnets the following lines occur:

> *De Garcilaso es este verso, Juana.*
> *Todos hurtan: paciencia!*

"This verse, Juana, is from Garcilaso. Everybody filches: think nothing of it!"

8. Compare the advice which the

knight gives Altisidora in the ballad that he sings in Chapter XLVI preceding.

9. These verses are from a ballad in Durán's *Romancero General*, No. 107. They had become a proverb.

CHAPTER LXXI

1. This is literal: "*De lo que á Don Quixote sucedió.*" Ormsby: "of What Passed between Don Quixote and His Squire," etc., which perhaps more nearly reflects the contents of the chapter.

2. "*Y cátalo cantusado*": there has been much discussion as to the meaning of the verb "*cantusar*," which still, apparently, remains obscure. I have followed the majority of commentators, who take it as synonymous with "*engatusar*," signifying "to get something out of someone by wheedling" (*Dictionary of the Academy*). Clemencín takes "*cantusado*" as equivalent to "*despachado*" or "*concluído*," an interpretation adopted by Ormsby: "and, there, his labour is over." Motteux, on the other hand, has: "which they do not make up but the apothecary, and which they have got to know by cheating."

3. See Chapter LX preceding and note 17.

4. Both "the treasure of Venice" and "the mines of Potosí" were proverbial expressions denoting fabulous wealth. Potosí (now in western Bolivia) is noted for its silver mines.

5. One-quarter of a real.

6. Schevill estimates that Sancho's fee would amount to 61.1 gold crowns. Rodríguez Marín: "Sancho surely was quick at turning cuartillos into reales! And with the same speed Cervantes must have cast up his own accounts hundreds of times during the years when he was engaged in cash transactions with purveyors, finance officers, constables, muleteers, millers, etc."

7. The proverb in full reads: "Trout are not caught with dry breeches"— "*No se toman truchas/A bragas enjutas.*"

8. "*Los enamorados, que jamás ajustan la cuenta de sus desseos*": it is possible the reading here should be: "who are always unreasonable" (Rodríguez Marín suggests this). I have finally decided, however, to follow Hartzenbusch's emendation: "*que jamás ajustan con el*

tiempo la cuenta de sus desseos." Ormsby does the same: "lovers, who never make the reckoning of their desires agree with time." Motteux: "as is always the case with lovers who never make allowance for the reckoning of their desires."

9. Allusion to the proverb quoted several times before (see Chapters XVII [note 9], XXXIII [note 23], and XXXVII [note 6], preceding): "As much is lost by a card too many as a card too few."

10. Compare Chapters XIV (note 5), XXX (note 3), XXXIV (note 8), and LIX (note 12), preceding.

11. Rhyming proverb: "*No se ganó Zamora,/En una hora.*" This all but impregnable fortress held out for a very long time, and in the course of the siege King Sancho II lost his life. The Portuguese have the same saying. Compare our "Rome was not built in a day."

12. A proverb.

13. Rhyming proverb: "*A dineros pagados,/Brazos quebrados,*" the sense being: no more work to be had out of a person after he has been paid for it.

14. "*Dos levadas*": "*levada*" is a fencing term, meaning a salute or flourish with the foil.

15. Rodríguez Marín states that in his native Andalusia he has heard the saying: "Here shall die Samson with all the Philistines!"

16. The *ferreruelo* was a short cloak without a cape.

17. Rodríguez Marín: "Leather hangings (*guadamecies* or *guadameciles*) were employed as a wall covering in summer, especially in Andalusia, but during the winter their place was taken by tapestries. . . . Tapestries, however, were an expensive luxury for the poor, who in place of them and at all seasons made use of silk serges [or twill], a kind of coarse frieze adorned with painted or embroidered figures or landscapes."

18. Sancho's prophecy has been more than fulfilled. Today the image of the Ingenious Gentleman and his squire is to be found everywhere in Spain.

19. Cervantes forgets that he has already narrated this anecdote in Chapter III preceding.

20. Literally, "I gave whence I shall give."

21. "*Quando estaua picado el molino*": I have adopted the meaning given by Correas (*Vocabulario de Refranes*).

22. See Chapter XXXV preceding and note 6.

23. Compare Chapters VII (note 6) and XXXV (note 7) preceding.

24. Compare Part I, Chapter XXXI (note 6), and Part II, Chapters XII (note 1) and XXXI.

25. "As it was" (in the beginning).

26. "*Y veras como te vale vn pan por ciento*": for this expression, see Chapter XXXIV preceding, note 4.

27. Play on the double meaning of "*razón*": "a word," and "reason" or "sense."

CHAPTER LXXII

1. This is reminiscent of a scene in the first chapter of the spurious *Don Quixote*. It was Bowle who first noted a number of such references throughout the present chapter.

2. See Avellaneda, Chapter IX.

3. That is, by spurning them in love, as in the case of Altisidora.

4. The institution known as the Casa del Nuncio, an asylum for the insane founded in 1483 by Francisco Ortiz, Canon of Toledo and Apostolic Nuncio.

5. The alcalde.

6. As previously pointed out (Chapter LXII preceding, note 37), this is not the correct title of Avellaneda's work.

7. Here, as not infrequently throughout this work, a free translation, paraphrastic and sometimes slightly expanded, is rendered necessary by the impossible name-repetitions of the original.

8. See the beginning of Sancho's letter to his wife, Chapter XXXVI preceding and note 3.

CHAPTER LXXIII

1. "*No la has de ver,*" etc.: it will be noted that the pronoun "*la*" is feminine, referring to the cricket cage ("*jaula de grillos*") mentioned a little later.

2. A Latin phrase used by medical writers. Bowle cites Avicena: "*Si non videt infirmus et non audit est* SIGNUM MALUM."

3. "Meeting with a hare, even when it was not being chased by hounds, was looked upon, and still is today, as a bad omen." Meeting with a wolf, on the other hand, was a good omen. (Rodríguez Marín)

4. A small coin worth four maravedis.

5. See Don Quixote's remarks on superstitions and omens in Chapter LVIII preceding.

6. The *"repostero"* was properly a covering ornamented with a coat of arms.

7. Rodríguez Marín thinks this may be reminiscent of the proverb *"Los criados son enemigos no excusados* [or, *enemigos pagados*]"—"Servants are inescapable [or paid] enemies."

8. *"Más galán que Mingo"* was a popular saying that derived originally from the opening lines of a fifteenth-century satire, the *Mingo Revulgo*. Rodríguez Marín points out that there is a humorous play here on the double sense of the preposition *de* in certain phrases ["ass of a Sancho Panza"—"beast of a Don Quixote"].

9. Word play on *"governador"*—"governor," and *"desgovernado,"* which means either deprived of government or a lawless individual.

10. Once again an allusion to the proverb "Many think to find bacon where there are no stakes"; compare Part I, Chapter XXV (note 5), and Part II, Chapters X (note 2), LV (note 17), and LXV (note 3).

11. The first edition here has "Curambro." Compare Chapter LXVII preceding.

12. *"Pastoras mañeruelas"*: according to Covarrubias, *"mañeruelos"* was a term applied to ponies that readily allowed themselves to be handled and subdued. "The comparison of shepherd maids to horses and ponies goes well with the curate's jovial humor." (Schevill, from the Spanish note.)

13. *"Si no nos quadraren, nos esquinen."*

14. These are names from the literature of pastoral romance; compare Part I, Chapter XXV.

15. Lines from an old Christmas carol which will be found in the ballad collection of Francisco de Ocaña.

16. A proverb.

CHAPTER LXXIV

1. Jacapo Sannazaro, Neapolitan poet (1458-1530), was the author of the *Arcadia* (see the edition published at Torino in 1888).

2. Literally, "pay me for good news" —*"dadme albricias,"* an expression that has occurred a number of times before.

3. With regard to Don Quixote's real name, see Part I, Chapter I. There the name is given as Quijana (Quixana).

4. Rhyming proverb: *"En los nidos de antaño/No hay pajaros hogaño."*

5. *"A puerta cerrada"*—literally, "my entire estate from the doors inward," a popular expression still employed in Andalusia and elsewhere. (Rodríguez Marín)

6. It was a custom among the people, in the case of women, to give a feminine termination to a name with a masculine ending. (Rodríguez Marín)

7. Ormsby: "This piece of commonplace cynicism, so uncalled for and so inconsistent with what has gone before, is, I imagine, regretted by most of Cervantes' readers. The conclusion of the *Don Quixote*, it must be confessed, is not worthy of the book or of its author. After the quiet pathos and dignity of Don Quixote's death, the shrill note of the scolding once more administered to the wretched Avellaneda falls like a discord on the reader's ear, and Samson [Sansón] Carrasco's doggerel does not tend to allay the irritation." The thought expressed here is to be found in a number of Spanish proverbs and verses: "The weeping of the heir is dissimulated laughter"—*El llanto del heredero es risa disimulada*; "Dead man to the grave, the living to the loaf"—*El muerto al hoyo, y el vivo al bollo.* (See Rodríguez Marín's note.)

8. Reference to the rites of penance, communion, and extreme unction.

9. Previous translators have taken the phrase *"muerto naturalmente"* as signifying a death by natural causes in opposition to a violent one; but, as Rodríguez Marín points out, the proper sense is "actually or wholly dead," as is shown by the fact that the expression was used even of condemned persons who had been put to death by the executioner.

10. Rodríguez Marín: "Don Quixote's death is as touching and saddening as that of a person who has really existed and for whom we have felt a profound affection. 'What a worthy madman,' the reader exclaims to himself, 'in this rascally world of ours where there are so many wicked ones of sound mind!'"

11. See Part I, Chapter I and note 1. For a work in English on the geography

of the region, see August F. Jaccaci, *On the Trail of Don Quixote, Being a Record of Rambles in the Ancient Province of La Mancha* (London, 1897). The reader of Spanish may be referred to the lecture by Antonio Blazquez, *La Mancha en Tiempo de Cervantes* (Madrid, 1905).

12. Clemencín and others have objected to the introduction of these lines here. They are a doggerel imitation of the epitaphs composed by village poets.

13. Sannazaro concludes his *Arcadia* with an apostrophe to his flute.

14. The last two verses are from a ballad on the death of Alonso de Aguilar (*Guerras Civiles de Granada*, i, xvii).

The ballad in question has been translated by Lockhart.

15. Of Tordesillas.

16. At the close of the spurious *Don Quixote*, Avellaneda tells how the knight, after being released from the madhouse of Toledo, "purchased for himself another and better steed and made a tour of Old Castile, where stupendous and never-before-heard-of adventures befell him," etc.

17. This proved to be true. No new romance of chivalry appeared after *Don Quixote* and only a few of the old ones were reprinted. The last work in this category was the *Policisne de Boecia*, published at Valladolid in 1602.

BIBLIOGRAPHY

I

List of the Principal English-Language Translations of "Don Quixote"

The History of the Valorovs and Wittie Knight-Errant Don Qvixote of the Mancha. Translated out of the Spanish. London: Printed by William Stansby for Ed Blovnt and W. Barret, 1612. Pp. xii + 594. (Part I of the version by Thomas Shelton.)

The History of Don Quichote. London: Edward Blount, 1620. Vol. I: pp. xii + 572; Vol. II: pp. viii: + 504. (Parts I and II of the Shelton.)

There have been numerous reprints of this version, the latest being that of the Ashendene Press in 1927–28 (London, 2 vols.). In 1923 there appeared to be something like a Shelton revival, three editions appearing in that year: those by the Navarre Society and Macmillan & Company in London, and the one by the George H. Doran Company in New York (2 vols., 3 vols., and 1 vol., respectively). The Navarre Society edition has a preface by F. J. Harvey Darton; and the American printing, reproducing the Constable & Company London edition of the preceding year, contains a distinguished introduction by J. B. Trend and the illustrations of Jean de Bosschère. This translation, with an introduction by the noted American scholar J. D. M. Ford, was included in the Harvard Classics (New York: P. F. Collier & Son, 1909), Vol. 14. A four-volume edition, with introductions by James Fitzmaurice-Kelly, was published in the Tudor Translations (London: David Nutt, 1896), Vols. 13–16. Another four-volume edition, published at London by Gibbings & Company and at Philadelphia by the J. B. Lippincott Company in 1895 and 1901, has a preface by Justin Huntley McCarthy. A number of the eighteenth-century editions (London, 1725, 1731, 1733, and 1740) have engravings by Charles-Antoine Coypel. The four-volume edition published at London by T. Fisher Unwin in 1906 and at New York by Charles Scribner's Sons, 1906–1907, has the illustrations of Daniel Vierge and an introduction by Royal Cortissoz. It was the edition of 1725 (London: R. Knaplock) that was revised by Captain John Stevens.

The history of the most renowned Don Quixote of La Mancha and his trusty squire Sancho Panza. Now made into English according to the humour of our modern language. London: T. Hodgkin, 1687. Pp. 616.

Version by John Phillips. One printing only.

The history of the renown'd Don Quixote de la Mancha. Translated from the original Spanish by several hands, and publish'd by Peter Motteux. London: Sam Buckley, 1700. 4 vols.

The four-volume edition published at London in 1725 was the first to be revised by J. Ozell. This revision has been used as the basis for a number of modern editions (London: John Lane, 1930; London: Nonesuch Press, 1930; New York: The Modern Library, 1930). John Gibson Lockhart's notes and "Life of Cervantes" first appeared in the Edinburgh edition of 1822. They have been reprinted five or six times and may be found along with Lockhart's ballad renderings in Bohn's Popular Library (London: G. Bell and Sons, 1913, 2 vols.). A special edition of Part I of the Motteux-Ozell version with Salvador Dali's illustrations was published in New York by The Illustrated Modern Library in 1946.

The Life and Exploits of the Ingenious Gentleman Don Quixote de la Mancha. Translated from the original Spanish of Miguel de Cervantes Saavedra by Charles Jarvis. London: J. and R. Tonson and R. Dodsley, 1742. 2 vols.

As stated in the Introduction, this translation has been about the most popular of all—in England if not in America—having run through close to a hundred printings. The latest would seem to be that of Frederick Warne & Company in 1933 (London, 1 vol.). The edition put out by Dodd, Mead & Company in 1925 (New York, 1 vol.) contains the W. Heath Robinson illustrations, which first appeared in the one-volume London Bliss & Sands edition of 1897; and in 1928 the same firm brought out the Jarvis text with illustrations by Arthur Boyd Houghton. The Jarvis was edited, with notes and introduction, by James Fitz-maurice-Kelly (London and New York: H. Frowde, 1907 and 1912). It was published as Vols. 25-26 in Morley's Universal Library (London: George Routledge & Sons, 1885), with an introduction by Henry Morley. It has been something of a favorite with artists, among its illustrators being Gustave Doré, Tony Johannot, George Cruikshank, Arthur Boyd Houghton, and W. Heath Robinson.

The History of the Renowned Don Quixote de la Mancha. Translated from the original Spanish of Miguel de Cervantes Saavedra. London: J. Cooke, 1744. 2 vols.

Abridgment by Charles Henry Wilmot. There was one reprinting, in 1774(?). Ormsby mistakes this second printing for the first.

The History and Adventures of the Renowned Don Quixote. Translated from the Spanish of Miguel de Cervantes Saavedra, by Tobias George Smollett. To which is added some account of the author's life. Illustrated by 28 copper plates designed by Hayman. London: A. Millar, T. Osborne, J. Rivington, 1755. 2 vols.

Although Ormsby characterizes this version as "a mere bookseller's speculation," it has had some thirty-odd printings, though few in the last hundred years. Its popularity was due in good part, no doubt, to the reputation as a humorist possessed by the author of *Humphrey Clinker* and *Roderick Random*.

The History of the Renowned Don Quixote de la Mancha. Translated into English by George Kelly. To which are added notes on the more difficult passages. London: E. Carpenter and A. Bridgman, 1769. 4 vols.

One printing only.

Don Quixote de la Mancha. Translated from the Spanish of Miguel de Cervantes Saavedra by Mary Smirke. Engravings by Robert Smirke. London: T. Cadell and W. Davies, 1818. 4 vols.

There were two London reprintings, in 1847 and 1853. The fourth printing (New York: D. Appleton & Company, 1855) is described as "A Revised translation based on those of Motteux, Jarvis and Smollett."

The History of Don Quixote. Translated and edited by J. W. Clarke, and with a biographical notice of Cervantes by T. Teignmouth Shore. Illustrated by Gustave Doré. London: Cassell, Petter & Galpin, 1864-67. 1 vol.

There were five reprints, 1870-1906.

The Ingenious Knight Don Quixote de la Mancha. A new translation by Alexander James Duffield, with notes of John Bowle, Juan Antonio Pellicer, Diego Clemencín, and others. London: C. K. Paul & Company, 1881. 3 vols.

Compare the one-volume edition of the *Don Quixote* put out by Charles Scribner's Sons (New York, 1902; reprinted in 1909), and "Edited from the translations of Duffield and Shelton, by Mary E. Burt and Lucy L. Cable."

The Ingenious Gentleman Don Quixote of La Mancha, by Miguel de Cervantes Saavedra. Translated into English, with introduction and notes, by John Ormsby. London: Smith, Elder & Company, 1885. 4 vols.

This edition has enjoyed a deserved popularity in America. Of the sixteen reprints, 1885-1936, thirteen were by publishing houses in New York or Boston. and one of the others, the Macmillan edition of 1899, was published in London and New York. There was a Glasgow printing, edited by Fitzmaurice-Kelly, in 1901; and the Ormsby translation illustrated by Enric C. Ricart was brought out in Barcelona, in two volumes, in 1933. The latest printing is the one-volume edition by Grosset (New York, 1936). The work was published by the Limited Editions Club in two volumes in 1933; by the Thomas Y. Crowell Company in 1932 in two volumes; by Alfred A. Knopf in 1926 in two volumes; and by Dodd, Mead & Company in 1916 in four volumes. The Knopf edition has an introduction by George Edward Woodberry. The Ormsby version was a favored one for school use at the turn of the century, and there are a number of editions designed for younger readers. The Dodd, Mead & Company edition first published in 1893 has Cruikshank illustrations.

The Ingenious Gentleman Don Quixote of La Mancha. A new edition, done into English with notes, original and selected, and a new life of the author, by Henry Edward Watts. London: B. Quaritch, 1888. 5 vols.

This version was reprinted at London, in four volumes, in 1895 and was published in New York, in two volumes, in 1898, by D. Appleton & Company, with a critical and biographical introduction by Joseph O'Connor. A four-volume edition with etchings by Adolphe Lalauze was brought out at Philadelphia by G. Barrie some time in the early 1900's (date uncertain).

The Imaginative Gentleman Don Quixote de la Mancha. Translated into English by Robinson Smith. London: George Routledge & Sons; New York: E. P. Dutton; 1908(?). 1 vol.

There was a second London printing in 1910, and a third, "with a new life of Cervantes, notes and appendices," in 1914. The fourth London printing, 1914, was termed a "second edition"; and in 1932 the Hispanic Society of America brought out what is described as a "new edition," bearing the title *The Visionary Gentleman Don Quixote de la Mancha.* This last-mentioned edition is in two volumes. It has been out of print for some time.

II

Principal Spanish Editions Made Use of in the Preparation of this Translation

Don Quixote de la Mancha. Madrid: V. Suárez, Gráficas Reunidas, 1928–41. 4 vols.

This is the edition of the *Don Quixote* by Professor Rudolph Schevill in the *Obras Completas de Miguel de Cervantes Saavedra* edited by Schevill and Professor Adolfo Bonilla y San Martín of the University of Madrid. (See the Introduction and note 38.)

El ingenioso hidalgo Don Quijote de la Mancha. Nueva edición crítica con el comento refundido y mejorado y más de setecientas notas dispuestas por F. Rodríguez Marín. Madrid: Tipografía de la Revista de Archivos, 1927–28. 7 vols.

This critical edition with its vast number of notes runs to a total of more than 3500 pages.

El ingenioso hidalgo Don Quijote de la Mancha. Edición y notas de F. Rodríguez Marín. Madrid: La Lectura, 1911–13. 8 vols.

This is Rodríguez Marín's first and more popular edition, in the Clásicos Castellanos series, where it constitutes Vols. IV, VI, VIII, X, XIII, XVI, XIX, and XXII.

El ingenioso hidalgo Don Quixote de la Mancha, compuesto por Miguel de Cervantes. Edición crítica con variantes, notas y el diccionario de todas las palabras usadas en la inmortal novela, por Don Clemente Cortejón. Continuada por Juan Givanel i Mas, y Juan Suñé Benajes. Madrid: V. Suárez, 1905-13. 6 vols.

On Cortejón, see the Introduction.

III

Early Spanish Editions of "Don Quixote" Referred to in the Notes

(For other earlier Spanish editions see Section V, following.)

El Ingenioso Hidalgo Don Quixote de la Mancha. Compuesto por Miguel de Cervantes Saavedra, Dirigido al Duque de Beiar, Marques de Gibraleón, Conde de Benalcaçar, y Benares, Visconde de la Puebla de Alcozer, Señor de las villas de Capilla, Curiel, y Burgillos. Año 1605, con privilegio, en Madrid, por Juan de la Cuesta. Vendese en casa de Francisco de Robles, librero del Rey, nro Señor.

This is the first edition of Part I. A second edition with the same title (save for a couple of printer's errors and the addition of the words *"de Castilla, Aragon y Portual"* after the *Privilegio*) appeared in the same year. There are substantial variations in the body of the text to differentiate it from the other printing and establish it as the second one; but it has been mistaken for the first by such scholars as Ticknor, Bowle, and others. A third La Cuesta edition was brought out in 1608. Inasmuch as it is by Cervantes' own publisher, it is referred to in the notes to this translation as the "third edition," although the two editions of Lisbon and that of Valencia (see the Introduction and note 12) and the edition of Brussels (see the item following) had appeared in the meanwhile. In the erroneous belief that the author was responsible for the textual changes to be found in this edition, scholars for long regarded it as the definitive one.

El Ingenioso Hidalgo Don Quixote de la Mancha, etc. En Bruselas por Roger Velpius. Año 1607. (Part I.)

This is what is known as the "edition of Brussels" and is so referred to in the notes to the present translation. It was reprinted in 1611 and 1617. Attempts are made at a correction of Cervantes' text, particularly with reference to the theft of the ass.

Segunda Parte del Ingenioso Cavallero Don Quijote de la Mancha por Miguel de Cervantes Saavedra, autor de su primera parte. Dirigida a D. Pedro Fernández de Castro Conde de Lemos. . . . Año 1615. Con Privilegio en Madrid, por Juan de la Cuesta.

This is the first edition of part II. It is a quarto volume of 584 pages. Note the change in the title from *Hidalgo* to *Caballero*, probably due to inadvertency.

Segunda Parte del Ingenioso Cavallero Don Quijote de la Mancha, etc. En Bruselas por Humberto Antonio, impresor jurado. Año 1616. (The Brussels edition of Part II.)

NOTE. The complete Don Quixote in Spanish did not appear until 1637, more than twenty years after its author's death, in the form of two wretchedly printed quarto volumes from the press of Francisco Martínez at Madrid. A Brussels edition of 1662 and one at Antwerp, 1697, are much better from the typographical point of view.

IV

Continental Translations of "Don Quixote" Cited in the Notes to this Version

FRENCH

L'ingenievx Don Qvixote de la Manche. Composé par Michel de Cervantès, tradvit fidellement d'espagnole en françois, et dedié au Roy par César Ovdin. Paris: Iean Fouet, 1614. 1 vol.

Le valevrevx Don Qvixote de la Manche; ov, L'histoire de ses grands exploicts d'armes, fideles amours, et aduentures estranges. Traduit fidèlement de l'espagnole de Michel de Cervantès & dedié au Roy par César Ovdin. Paris: Iean Fouet, 1616. 1 vol. (Part I.)

Scholars have come to realize (Rodríguez Marín among them) that César Oudin, a Frenchman who was a teacher of Spanish, had a good knowledge of the Spanish of Cervantes' time. In 1618 François de Rosset published his translation of Part II, and from 1633 on the combined Oudin-Rosset rendering of the complete work became the standard one; it was brought out again as late as 1936, under the editorship of Jean Cassou (Paris: Nouvelle Revue Française); there were also editions by Flammarion in 1912 and 1926. Other French versions include a popular but unsatisfactory abridgment by Florian; one by H. Bouchon Dubournial, which Brunet condemned, and one by De l'Aulnaye, which he praised; one by the Abbé Lejeune; the well-known one by Louis Viardot (1836); and others. Ormsby in his bibliography gives the printing of 1616 as the first one.

ITALIAN

L'ingegnoso cittadino Don Chisciotte della Mancia. Tradotto di spagnuolo in italiano, da Lorenzo Franciosini Fiorentino. Venetia: Andrea Baba, 1625.

Franciosini, like Oudin, had the advantage of being a contemporary of the author. His version was reprinted at Venice and elsewhere a number of times, down to the early part of the nineteenth century. In 1832–33 it was published in an eight-volume edition at Milan, revised by L. Toccagni. There has been no subsequent printing. For some reason or other there have not been a great many translations of the *Don Quixote* in Italian.

GERMAN

Don Kichote de la Mantzscha. Juncker Harnisch auss Fleckenland, auss hispanischer Spraach in Hochteutsche versetzt, durch Pahsch Basteln von der Sohle. Cöthen, 1621.

This is only a partial translation—twenty-two chapters. It was reprinted at Frankfurt in 1648. The latest of the three editions is the one of Frankfurt, 1928, with a study by Hermann Tiemann. The first complete German version, by an anonymous hand, appeared at Basel and Frankfurt in 1682.

Leben und Thaten des scharfsinnigen Edlen Don Quixote von der Manche von Miguel de Cervantes Saavedra. Ubersetzt von Ludwig Tieck. Berlin: Johann Friedrich Unger, 1799–1801. 4 vols.

From the literary point of view this is by far the most interesting of the German versions, and it is also the most popular. The appearance of Tieck's *Don Quixote* had a considerable influence upon the Romantic movement, and in particular upon Heinrich Heine. Ormsby admits that the translation is a spirited one but adds that "the spirit is not quite the spirit of Cervantes." He also finds that Tieck is inclined to take too many liberties with the text, and, indeed, it is true that this rendering has a certain lusty and expansive quality that is often to be found in the works of the Romantics; but for all of that it remains an admirable piece of German prose. Ormsby further criticizes the use of *scharfsinnig* in the title, remarking that *sinnreich*, which had been employed by Dietrich Wilhelm Soltau in his version (Königsberg, 1800–1801) is nearer to the Spanish *ingenioso*.

NOTE. The latest German translation is the four-volume one by Ludwig Braunfels (Stuttgart, 1884), which Ormsby praises rather highly. It was reprinted at Strassburg in 1905 and at Berlin in 1923; see also the two-volume version based upon Braunfels and Florian and edited by Hermann Tiemann (Hamburg-Leipzig, 1925?).

V

A List of the Principal Commentators and Lexicographers Cited in the Notes to this Translation

(For convenient reference, this list has been arranged alphabetically.)

Academy Edition. *El ingenioso Hidalgo Don Quixote de la Mancha, etc.* Madrid: Joaquín de Ibarra, 1780.

This is the edition by the Spanish Royal Academy, in four large quarto volumes with plates. A laudable attempt is made at a definitive text, but too much reliance is placed on the third edition of 1608. Two years later (1782) the Academy brought out a less pretentious edition in four small octavo volumes. A third edition (6 vols., 16mo) appeared in 1787; there was a fourth edition (4 vols., 8vo) in 1819, reprinted in 1832; and in 1836 Little and Brown of Boston published the Academy text with emendations by Francis Sales (1 vol. 8vo, with plates.)

Bowle, Rev. John. *Historia del famoso cavallero, etc.* London and Salisbury: E. Easton, 1781.

Originally published in six quarto volumes, this edition is famous for its notes.

Calderon, Juan. *Cervantes vindicado en ciento y quince pasajes del texto del ingenioso hidalgo Don Quixote de la Mancha que no han entendido o que han entendido mal, algunos de sus comentadores y críticos.* Prólogo y notas de Luis Usoz del Rio. Madrid: J. Martín Alegría, 1854. Pp. xxiii + 256.

Cejador y Frauca, Julio. *La lengua de Cervantes. Gramática y diccionario de la lengua castellana en "El ingenioso hidalgo Don Quixote de la Mancha."* Prólogo de Rufino José Cuervo. Madrid: Tipografía de Jaime Ratés, 1905–1906. 2 vols.

On this work see the Introduction.

Clemencín, Diego. *El ingenioso hidalgo Don Quixote de la Mancha . . . comentado por D. Clemencín.* Madrid: D. E. Aguado, 1833–39.

A new and critical edition of this valuable work was brought out by Rodríguez Marín at Barcelona in 1915.

Correas, Gonzalo. *Vocabulario de refranes y frases proverbiales y otras formulas comunes de lengua castellana, en que van todos los impresos antes y otra gran copia que juntó el Maestro Gonzalo Correas.* Madrid: Tipografía de la Revista de Archivos, Bibliotecas y Museos, 1924. 3 vols.

Another modern edition of this work is that published at Madrid, by Tipografía de Jaime Ratés in 1906.

Cortejón y Lucas, Clemente. See Section II preceding.

Covarrubias, Horazio Sebastián de. *Tesoro de la lengua castellana, o española, según la impresión de 1611, con las adiciones de Benito Remigio Noydens publica-*

das en la de 1674; edición preparada por Martín de Riguer. . . . Barcelona: S. A. Horta, 1943.

First published during Cervantes' lifetime, in 1611, Covarrubias's *Tesoro* has much light to throw on the language of *Don Quixote.*

Dictionary of the Academy. Diccionario de la lengua española, compuesto por la Real Academia Española. Madrid: Talleres Espasa-Calpe, S.A., 1939. 1 vol.

This is the sixteenth edition; the first appeared in 1726 with the title *Diccionario de la lengua castellana.*

Fitzmaurice-Kelly, James. *The Complete Works of Miguel de Cervantes Saavedra.* Glasgow: Gowans & Gray, 1901–1903. 7 vols. Vols. III–VI, the *Don Quixote,* translated by John Ormsby.

See Fitzmaurice-Kelly's notes on the Ormsby version.

Hartzenbusch, Juan Eugenio. *El ingenioso hidalgo Don Quixote de la Mancha.* Edición corregida con especial estudio de la primera. Argamasilla de Alba: Rivadeneyra, 1863. 4 vols.

Jarvis, Charles. See Section I preceding.

Lockhart, John Gibson. *The History of the Ingenious Gentleman Don Quixote of La Mancha.* Translated from the Spanish by Motteux. A new edition with copious notes, and an essay on the life and writings of Cervantes, by John Gibson Lockhart. Edinburgh: A. Constable & Company; London: Hurst, Robinson & Company, 1822. 5 vols.

See the note on the Motteux version in Section I preceding and also the Introduction. A reprint of this item was brought out by J. M. Dent & Sons, London and Toronto, and E. P. Dutton & Company, New York, in 1906. Lockhart's notes and his essay on Cervantes will be found in the Everyman's Library edition (London: J. M. Dent & Sons, 1910), and in Bohn's Popular Library (London: G. Bell & Sons, 1913).

Ormsby, John. See Section I preceding and the Introduction.

Pellicer, Juan Antonio. *El ingenioso hidalgo Don Quixote de la Mancha, etc.* Corregida de nuevo, con nuevas notas, con nuevas viñetas, con nuevo análisis y con la vida del autor por J. A. Pellicer. Madrid: G. de Sancha, 1783–1802. 10 vols.

The latest edition of this work is that published at Madrid, 1905, 1 vol., pp. cxxvii + 896.

Rodríguez Marín, Francisco. See Section II preceding and the Introduction.

Schevill, Rudolph. See Section II preceding and the Introduction.

Shelton, Thomas. See Section I preceding and the Introduction.

The Best of the World's Best Books
COMPLETE LIST OF TITLES IN
THE MODERN LIBRARY

MISCELLANEOUS

MODERN LIBRARY GIANTS

A series of sturdily bound and handsomely printed, full-sized library editions of books formerly available only in expensive sets. These volumes contain from 600 to 1,400 pages each.

THE MODERN LIBRARY GIANTS REPRESENT A
SELECTION OF THE WORLD'S GREATEST BOOKS